God Help the Connipians

Moss Croft

Copyright © Moss Croft 2023

The moral right of Moss Croft to be identified as the author of this work has been asserted by him in accordance with the Copyright, Designs and Patents Act of 1988.

All rights reserved. No part of this publication may be reproduced, transmitted or stored in a retrieval system, in any form or by any means, without permission in writing from Moss Croft, nor be otherwise circulated in any form of binding or cover other than that in which it is published and without a similar condition being imposed on the subsequent purchaser.

ISBN: 9798389254930

The Novels of Moss Croft

God Help the Connipians

Crack Up or Play It Cool

Boscombe

Rucksack Jumper

Ghost in the Stables

Raspberry Jam

The Flophouse Years

Stickerhand

About the Author

Moss Croft is a pen name. Eight books to his name, so he really must be someone. Words don't just chance upon the page.

Contents

Prologue   **Page**   7

Chapter One:
The John and Lodowicke   **Page**   9

Chapter Two:
New York City, January, 1950   **Page**   109

Chapter Three:
Frame   **Page**   197

Chapter Four:
Watch it on Weavers   **Page**   305

Disclaimer

This is a work of fiction. For complete clarity, the avoidance of doubt, and to help you sleep at night, the author can happily confirm, it is all made up. There are no Connipians and there never have been. More's the pity, say the Romiley three.

Prologue

(From The Palace Theatre, Manchester, December, 1931)

The young Jimmy Whist has a little sweat on his brow, the overhead lighting strong in this theatre; through narrowed eyes he peers across the stalls. Fifteen seconds since he last spoke, enough for a little nervous laughter to burp up here and there. Pockets of it within the expectant audience. Up and down the rows go his comical eyes, a sense that he is surprised by what he sees with each wicked glint. Then a quick glance up to the gods, promptly back to the stalls. He coughs and then, using overdrawn gestures, he mimes as if to dial three numbers on a telephone. Standing centre stage, he sways ever so slightly, nose facing the audience members to his right. He starts speaking, not Jimmy Whist's natural voice, not as these theatregoers know it. More well-to-do inflexions, nothing of the working class at all, and it is also a slurry voice he uses. A sloshed toff; brandy not beer, one might surmise.

'Operator, could you be sho kind as to connect me to the police, pleash. Thank you. I thank you.' He gives an extravagant cough into his clenched left fist. Seems to seek out an audience member at whom he winks. 'Yes, yes, is that the police? You must come quickly, offisher, I've been burgled. Clever blighters they are too, can't see how they've got in. Not through a window or door. Not as I can tell. Never touched my money, and not the wife's jewellery either. It's shimply that my left shoe is missing. That's what the devils have taken. Swiped it. That's the nub of it offisher. Somebody...' He glances down at his empty hand, the one not holding the imaginary telephone. A look of puzzlement crosses his face. '...could have been a gang of them, I suppose. It's just my left shoe they've gone orf with. It really is the oddest thing.' Then he adds, with substantial lisping on the first word: 'Shimply extraordinary, that's what I call it. Fancy such clever robbers taking only the one. Must have their reasons, I suppose.'

Then Jimmy changes posture, takes the invisible telephone into his other hand, faces left, turns his speech pattern into a regular northern accent—not his own, a measure of pomposity to it—puffs out his chest, rounds his cheeks. A police sergeant, nothing could be plainer to see.

'Well, well, had a visit from the little Connipians, have we, sir?'

The audience erupts into laughter.

NB. Jimmy Whist crafted the Connipians into hundreds of punchlines over a career in music hall and a couple of forays into television and film. Back in the days when those small almost-people, our most distant cousins, were inherently funny.

Chapter One

The John and Lodowicke

Before

'We want to go down there together for we are like-minded people...'

'Are you sure, John? Are you really so like-minded?'

'All that we believe. Yes, we are of a like mind. And if we go...'

'As you think it, John.'

'...if we find a new land in southern seas, will our Lord return there as well as here? I mean, He's never even been there in the first place.'

'Nor here, John. He never placed a sandal in Poplar, nor anywhere in London. We know He shall come to us at the time of His return. Glorious shall it be.'

'Indeed. And do you think...nay...do you prophesy that He will be pleased with those of us who have set up afresh? To the southern seas; sought out a new way of living.'

'Ha! I scarcely prophesy that He will return. It is knowledge—more certain than any man's faith—it is known to us through scripture. You must know by now that I do not guess the mind of our Lord. We do what men do, He will judge us for it and I hope your actions keep you in His favour, John. Wish only that the ways of men do not stray too far from His expectations. Then you and I shall meet again in heaven, and it will be a blessing for me, truly.'

Part One

1.

Many men and too few women, not a way round I've ever before thought a problem. We have been at sea too long, that is in the mix, and this imbalance has gotten worse with time. Woe, that this has become our fate.

On many a ship, such a state of affairs exists. Not those which have been taking pilgrims and fortune seekers to the new worlds, but on working ships, it is always so. Ours is one of those, and I fear our irregular crew is making our passage less smooth than were it otherwise. Only a handful of true sailors amongst us, most have come along only for the promise our destination holds. And it is a place unknown to which we travel.

I fear the paucity of womenfolk will be our undoing. That it will be on the land, as it has been upon the seas. We rubbed along well when we all lived in Poplar. Or that is how it seemed to me; I was out on ships half of the time, I grant. Three years solid at an earlier point in my life. Missed my wife then as I do now. Well, this time it weighs the heavier for it is final.

We have beliefs that should bind us together, and perhaps they do after a fashion. Yet, on this voyage—this boat of sadness, such has our dissipated hope become—I have found more common ground with our two non-Muggletonians than I have with my own kind.

I think the sickness that has taken many was of the stomach, and of the blood's more vexing humors too. Causing overly much sweating. Sweating and vomiting is what's taken them. Drawn nine of only twelve womenfolk who came aboard The John and Lodowicke, passed them up to the bosom of our Lord. And old Fenton's gone too. It's the women whom we miss, not that old sourpuss. I had nothing against Fenton, don't miss him, that's all.

I have been thinking that the scourge is behind us, not a death in the three weeks just past. Indeed, that particular form of pestilence no longer stalks. This matter with Hooper is of a different order. A reckless lust has overtaken him. Wrought changes in the boy. What he has done to Blanche sickens me.

I thought myself a reluctant captain before these events came to pass. I loathe the job now; it is beyond me. Ten untimely deaths and the rape of a man's wife. I don't like saying it, but that must be what the lad has done. Nineteen years old and he couldn't wait no longer. Never crossed my mind, back in England, that I might have to deal with this kind of devilment. Now, captain of the vessel as I am, the decision to be made

The John and Lodowicke

about the lad is a torture to me. In the world we left behind, I was but a navigator of oceans. And it is still the extent of my skills, plotting a course with stars and compass, pocket-watch and sighting of the sun. I cannot pick a course through human wickedness. Septimus and others have told me to choose between pistol and noose. Hooper must go: that is how they see it. Obadiah Pursglove—it is his wife the brainless lad has defiled—would rip him limb from limb given half a chance. To prevent such mayhem, I have asked Darius Dencourt, the man we call Double Dee, to keep close to him. Stop Obby from doing anything rash until I've concluded the matter. He's a big fellow is Double Dee, neither Obadiah nor the lad will be arguing with him. And happen, there will be nothing for Obby to do after I'm done, although I still prevaricate over what the proper resolution should be. Everyone has decided Hooper's a goner except me.

Tabitha and Rags, the other two ladies who remain on board, have told me to hang him high. Said it in no uncertain terms. It shocked me and it shook me; I suppose they're feeling for poor Blanche; however, I didn't expect the women to be baying for blood like they do. We are not the killing sort, not as I understand the teachings of the prophets. It is Hooper who has brought about this change in outlook, that's at the bottom of it. I have tried to reason with them, query if our Lord mightn't be more forgiving of young Hooper, no matter the terrible deed he has done. They reminded me that it is our own Lodowicke Muggleton who told how reason is the bluntest tool of the lot. Empty words in the face of the revelation of God. An eye for an eye, it says somewhere or other in The Good Book. Rags said it twice.

'The lad was a favourite of old Mr Muggleton's,' I told her.

'Aye, and Lodowicke didn't sail with us, so he'll not be expecting to lay eyes on Hooper again. Not in this lifetime.'

Her retort was justified: I cannot imagine our prophet will be alive should ever we return to London. Nor Hooper seeing much more sunlight. I know we cannot keep a-sailing with a rapist on board. How to end his life is the one troubling me. Captain of the ship and I don't like shooting or hanging.

Presently, our boat sails through waters that are absolutely calm, it is quite the contrast from the feelings which must bestir us all. For myself I feel sick right across my gut, windy in the belly. I cannot feel the emotions of another man, but I expect Hooper has it worse: the shits, good and proper. Fool that he is, even he must sense what is coming to him. We are sinners all, but I don't think many get up to what he's done. The raping and whatnot. Proper bad, whatever way you look at it. I wonder if I should talk to Blanche about the matter but I don't like to. And she will be as keen for vengeance as the other two women. I imagine she will. What he has done to her is the vilest thing. I feel I am on their side—the three women—and the weight of the responsibility is my burden. Men would get away with those heinous acts if they stuck together about it, women being unable to enforce any kind of code without our backing them up. We can use our strength to defend them or to take advantage, it is an age-old truth. Might even be the one which rumbles in my gut. The sense that hanging is the right thing to do whereas letting him off would be the easiest. And he did what we all like to do, it is the circumstances that were wrong. Get properly married and then coupling with your woman becomes a righteous thing. The propagation of the next generation.

* * *

We must put behind us the disturbance which the miscreant Hooper has caused. Before the hour is up, I hope. Can't have this kind of carry-on festering for much longer. Obadiah has proven a hard man to warm to, not that his anger towards Hooper is difficult to understand. I wonder if relations can ever be the same between him and his wife after this. Poor Blanche. The more I think upon it, the clearer it is to me that a-shooting or a-hanging the lad would put a sorrier history to our crossing than we could stand if we really are to build a new community in the weeks and months ahead. I would like to put the fate of the rapist, Hooper, into the hands of the Lord. It troubles me that I am the captain of this ship and not He. Cut his member off, is what some are saying, but I'm not doing that. Wouldn't touch another man's cock for all the spices of the East.

Our boat is on a steady course, for where we do not know; we are simply hoping to come across a new land, find ourselves a place to build something worthy. Virgin soil we can claim for God and Merrie England. And if there are primitives already living there, we might teach them how to better themselves: Christian ways. It will prove a sorry venture if the kinds of goings-on that Hooper's done are to occur in our new Jerusalem. Better sift out that which would scupper our future before we've crossed its threshold. So much has taken place on this ship, mostly of a miserable nature, quite frankly, I fear the promised next chapter in our shared lives may yet be stillborn. I no longer have a wife to call my own, and it is with grief and fear that I look to the future. This was not how I set out, I can tell thee.

Dispatching Hooper may be the only way to prevent a catastrophe. His continued presence on the ship will keep the mood febrile and I can't say I like it. I mustn't flinch, so help me God. I have a pistol with which to do the job that needs doing, and a few on board have offered to erect a scaffold should I opt to snap his neck. They say it is a fitting finish. Less bloody runs their argument. Neither of these methods pleases me, and I

The John and Lodowicke

fear they do not please God either. I am only guessing at this, I grant. It is a tenet of ours that taking a life is a dire step, errant in fact, but given Hooper's misdemeanour my certainty about it all is murky. Something needs doing. Amongst ourselves, we have argued this type of conundrum in the hypothetical. I recall Hooper being one for saying a murderer shouldn't be allowed to live. Quoting some bit of scripture to that effect if he didn't make it up. We didn't talk about raping: the women never raised it, and men don't like to. It might be that shooting the lad represents a just course, it is simply that I would rather not. A captain of a ship must be decisive, but the choice before me is beyond any I thought might be asked of me when I agreed to skipper The John and Lodowicke. Us being of similar mind, I envisioned a smooth passage. I knew it was a long way, I'd done three quarters of the journey before, on merchant ships. Never thought my first captaincy might be so harrowing.

It is my earnest wish to put Hooper's fate to the mercy of the Lord. Or the might of His vengeance. That strikes me as about right. Make it His choice, not mine.

I shout for Nicholas Myhill and Septimus Draycott to come hither. Explain to them the decision I have made. They have already offered to erect a set of gallows, and it is a simpler task that I give them now. Carpenters both, it is a construction within their skills. They agree to my request, I am captain, after all. Righting a wrong is nothing to mutiny about, and ours the most harmonious of boats in principle. It is the practice which we find the more difficult to fulfil; we are many of us troubled by the deaths that have beset our ship. A happenstance we could not understand—caused by an awful sickness—affecting each of us in some terrible way. This act of Hooper's is of a different order.

It takes my men no time at all to knock up a simple plank. Have it secure while stretching out a good eight foot to the side of our craft. A walkway to the ocean. They further secure it in place using a bit of rigging rope, a few nails. Properly horizontal. The way they've fixed it, the plank shall remain level even as the lad's weight is tempting it down over the side of the boat.

'Well done,' I tell them. 'Now can you go and bring Hooper. I'm sorry to say, the time has come for his punishment.'

It relieves me that there will be no shooting of pistol or breaking of the boy's neck. I like to think myself of a pacifist mindset, hope that many in our party are the same. It is not explicit in the prophets' teaching. Hovers within it, you might say. That's my interpretation, at least. The taking away of a life, however unworthy a man might prove himself, is a step we should all leave to the One with true authority for the task. The Lord is the giver of life, so shall He be the taker. We can none of us guess whether God will allow Hooper heaven despite his terrible lapse or condemn him to hell. Nor how He might judge one who sent him there prematurely, that has been my nagging fear. In my mind I am leaving it all up to God from the first. Hooper won't be departing this life at all if he swims a bit. The water isn't so cold in these parts. That he cannot do it—the swimming—is between Hooper and our Lord. Jesus could teach it him double quick; He does miracles, that's been very well documented. It's my opinion that He'll not save the lad. Mercy for rapists doesn't sound so Christian to me. And it is the Lord who will have the final say, my views neither here nor there. That's the beauty of the plank.

There is a noise of scuffling and shouting as Septimus alone drags the offender to the side of the boat. Nick Myhill watches on but seems not so keen to get himself a-scratched from fighting with the boy. Hooper is scrawny; a teenager yet to fill out, become a man. Shame that his cock has been more forward than the lad. The entirety of our party has come to take a look. The spectacle to come is evident from a single glance at the constructed apparatus and even us Muggletonians are apt to stand in line and watch a killing. There is much to contemplate in it. I hope this proves a more civilised way to go than those shadowy gallows high on Tower Hill. I've looked on at a few of those occasions, but I never liked the baying, the bloodlust of the crowd. Always felt a wave of sympathy for the poor sod having his neck snapped in so public a forum.

While Mr Draycott is trying to hold the poor lad, Tabitha and Rags are up to their shouting. Unpleasant to hear it. 'Hung, drawn and quartered,' they cry out. 'Cut off his knackers.'

Blanche—who was subject to his wrongdoing—has stayed away. I think it a sober and proper course.

'Hooper, there's a thing or two I've to tell you.'

Septimus has decked him. He doesn't move, nor so much as acknowledge my words.

'What you've done, lad, you give me no choice. Can't be a part of this ship's company after what you've been up to. You know Obby would finish you off if I don't find some kind of resolution, and do it quick. And I'm not for gallows like you might have heard others shout.' The raggedy little pile before me is twitching. I reckon he's listening best he can. 'I'm giving you God's chance, my boy. God's mercy although you might have drained it dry with all what you've done to Blanche. To another man's wife.'

'Not I,' shouts the lad from his prostrate position, but I'm not for debating nothing at this time. Moses Grigg caught him at it. Pants down, as they say on Drury Lane.

'Hooper lad, hear me out. You've to toddle along that plank there. Right off the end, boy. Now, I understand you're not a swimmer but give it a go. See what God thinks about what you've done.'

The John and Lodowicke

'Ask Blanche,' he says. At least, I think they were his words but a big blow of yellow mucus came down his nose with it. He's trembling like a chicken on the block; I hope he can walk to the end of yon' plank. Only four or five paces; the lad has become a gibbering wreck. Doesn't fancy his own chances of acquiring a little divine intervention, I reckon.

'I'm not putting her through nothing. No questioning. Nothing. You've wronged and you know it, Hooper. She's a married woman. Plain obvious that you've done wrong. Don't start trying to embarrass the poor woman more than what you've already done.' I look around, nodding of heads except for the two ladies who want me to shear off his member. 'Now, Mr Myhill, please will you assist Mr Draycott and lift young Hooper upright. Start him on his little walk.'

'Aye-aye, Captain,' he says, and then as he drags the boy towards the plank there is a commotion. Darius Dencourt is marching across the deck.

'Let me do this for Obby,' he says. Double Dee, we like to call him, it sounds like a big man's name and he's certainly that.

'Careful, Mr Dencourt,' I say. 'Happy to have your assistance; however, we are allowing young Hooper to walk off the plank in as dignified a manner as he can find in himself. He is one of us, after all, it is simply a disappointment he has sunk to such debased behaviour.'

I think he is respecting my decision; Darius is a worry to me because I know he likes fighting a bit more than any true Muggletonian should; and captain or not, I'm not going toe to toe with him. So far, he has followed my orders, and Double Dee is a mighty good worker. Does as much as any three men when he puts his shoulder to it. Darius grabs a hold of young Hooper. The boy makes a sound that is more whimper than struggle. Grips him from behind, holding both arms most tightly. I don't see any resistance, and it would be useless with Double Dee. The shoulders of a bull he has.

'If you are the type for swimming, you might find land before we do.' I only say it to cheer the young lad up, and Darius gives me the deadest look. Eyes me like I'm a fool. Perhaps this is also true, I do fear my poor captaincy is a contributor to the problems we've encountered.

'I don't know swimming,' says the lad. Almost shouts it. And then from behind him comes the strangest cough I've ever heard. Immediately Darius has released his arms, covering his own nose and mouth. For a second, I think my bosun is the one struggling, then the smell hits me. The young rapist has reported his mortal fear within his breeches.

'Get this done,' I say. I am keen to have him over the side before his stinking load comes onto our decks. Hooper turns as if to flee, but Septimus Draycott takes the left arm as Double Dee takes back a tight grip of the right. It is but a few paces to where Draycott and Myhill fixed

15

the plank. The gangway to no harbourside at all. 'Up with you,' I say. A climb of just four steps will take this boy where he needs to be. Best part of the way to eternity.

Tabitha and Rags continue their shouting. At least they've quieted about the dismembering they were calling for not five minutes back. And they cried. 'Shoot him,' a good-many times which challenged me, I can tell thee. There are no guns or pistols in the only book that matters. I've got one as any captain is apt, but reckon the crafting of such devices has taken us all further from the bosom of the Lord, not closer. Mine will restore order if there is mutiny, but only by putting fear in the place of my vanished authority. It's not a good substitute. Now the two ladies are shouting. 'Push him in the drink!' and I know they will not stop until they've seen his head go under. They might do this in sisterly feeling for Blanche, the object of his crime, or it might be more primitive than that. The watching of a life cut short seems to fascinate men and women whose minds never become elevated to a grander perspective. These two have worked themselves into a right state. I suppose Tabitha and Rags like rape even less than I do.

'Send Obby into the water,' shouts the lad. Young Hooper. 'She wants me; she don't want him no more. Drown Obby.'

A cheekier bugger as he faces death than I ever thought in our months a-coming from London to this corner of the world. Astonishing. The boy is on the plank, still upright but standing barely over the lip of the boat. Darius has a pole in hand, looks at me, and I nod. He prods the boy, trying to push him along, but Hooper has turned back. 'Walk!' Bosun's voice is as deep as an ox's bellow. Each arm as thick as the leg of any other on board.

Hooper turns to steady himself, we all see that his sailor whites are no longer coloured thus.

'Die, shitty pants! Die!' shout the two women.

Hooper stumbles as the prodding continues and then loses his footing completely. The skill of walking has evaded the poor lad, so ridden with anxiety has he become. No greater control of his legs than he has his sphincter. 'She said she wants me,' he shouts, and—barely a pace up the plank—he tumbles off the side. Head cracks upon the post to which the little walkway is fixed. He took a right knock, plum in the eye socket by the looks of it—an accompanying yelp—and then we hear a plop. It confirms his entry into the water. All present look over the side but he's slipped below the surface. Drinking up the salt water and communing with the fishes: that will be his lot for what time remains. We can see the circle of water where he went in, then I think it might be different water. An ocean has swallowed him and it all moves fast, washes about. What we look upon might be different water from that which he slipped

The John and Lodowicke

through. His body will remain below, can't swim, the Lord gave him nineteen years to learn it, but he didn't.

'May the good Lord take care of him from here,' I tell those looking over the side with me.

'Fuck him,' says Darius, and I feel the waning of my captain's authority. There are more on board who agree with Bosun than with me, and all this has come to pass after The John and Lodowicke set forth with such good intent.

* * *

Before all the brouhaha with Hooper, I was already in a most maudlin state. It distresses me that ten have died upon our boat before this need for dispatching another ever arose. An eleventh who set sail from Poplar, and no longer will he be a part of the colony we hope to create. My wife is among those who have succumbed, and that is the one which has undone me. The fact that nine of the departed are of our womenfolk feels, in my mind, to doom the whole venture. Many whom I spoke to back in London, even some of those professing our own beliefs, told me we were foolish to board but forty-five with a dozen women amongst us. A small tub and barely enough men to sail it. Too few women to start a colony. That was how those who stayed behind saw it. I told myself they simply didn't have the adventure in their hearts that we did. All who came volunteered. Came aboard with the belief it would prove glorious. And I wasn't going to say no to any as wanted to come, nor could I make any join up who didn't wish it. True to say, most boats with a quarter or more ladies on board are the big ones. Ships with separate passengers and crew more discernibly than is so on The John and Lodowicke. To get from there to here, we have all mucked in. Back home, they laughed at me, called me Not-a-Captain, and it is true this sailing is my first in such a role. Navigation has been my life, and I, alone amongst us, have journeyed to these southern seas prior to this venture. That is why they asked me to fulfil the role. Gave me the authority which I don't have in any general sense. We Muggletonians didn't have a proper captain amongst us, I was just the nearest thing to it. Honest from the first with my crew, told them my limitations—what I have done and not done— and they put their faith in me. If I'm letting them down, I surely feel the shame more deeply than any regrets they might harbour.

Of the forty-five who set sail, all but two are of the faith. The two who aren't have paid their passage and then some. Sweetened the way for half of ours, frankly. Scholarly types I have learnt. It gives me a small swell— a pleasure I can't explain—that they came with us while knowing our aims and beliefs. Men of reason, as we are not. They are nice to talk with, better conversation than any of our own, quite frankly. McConnell and

Hastings are their names. The first is a Scotsman, hails from Dundee. He tells me his plan is to classify and categorise every new plant and animal he comes across. Name them for all time, and do it in Latin, no less. A pointless venture, as I see it, but I'll not stand in his way. How such a work of science might return to the old world I do not know. Yet I am certain we shall not be the last to come so far. The Lord will rename them—I have great certainty about this—when He walks again with His fellow men. Jesus never did much Latin, that's in the scripture. He'll call them something in Hebrew, or the King's English if He turns out to be one of us this time around. Hastings, the other non-Muggletonian, has grander ideas than naming plants. Says these faraway lands might abound with primitive people. 'We can learn from them.' These are words he often speaks. Most on my boat think it amusing, his notion that we might learn from savages who wear no clothes and hunt with spears. I'm actually with Hastings on this one, cannot guess what the lesson will be until the meeting occurs. If they put me in a pot, it'll be a sorry learning. Right now, I'm hoping for a friendly isle with women up for converting. We have only Rags and Tabitha and Blanche left. A little breeding in the latter pair, I hope, but it leaves many a man with no outlet for his seeding. I truly hope the boy's assertion that Blanche has finished with Obadiah proves unfounded. More disharmony on this ship could leave us in little pieces. Scupper the lot of us.

For a couple of days, we have seen small signs of life. Of land. A branch a-drift in the sea, gulls circling. Not in great numbers but one or two. Insufficient signs for one as seasoned as I to draw too great a conclusion from, four telescopes on our small ship have yet to see anything but the water around us. I know from charts we are not so very far from those places where the Dutchies claim to have come across lands like no other. Forested islands. Birds that cannot fly. It would be fine to eat a little meat once more. I've thought since the equator that it is diet that has ravaged our boat. Done for more ladies than I can think on without wanting to weep. Oliver Fenton, our oldest, is the only male in the party who has passed away. May he rest in peace. Doing in his trousers that which Hooper did before we got him on the plank. Doing it for days and days before he faded from this life altogether. It certainly seemed dietary. The old chap was well over seventy. Younger than Lodowicke, who wouldn't travel, but not by so very much. There was them as said not to bring him, to leave Fenton in England. These are grown men and women, they do the deciding for themselves. If I captain this boat at all, it is with the consent of my company. I guess that's why young Hooper had to go. The wishes of the majority. I might have spared the lad were I alone making the judgment. And I didn't actually kill him although in my gut I feel as if I did. And don't get me wrong, I don't like rape one bit. At the very end, he said he didn't. Hooper told us Blanche was all in favour of what he'd done to her. Perhaps I should have spoken with her, the other party—Blanche—it all seemed a bit much to me. Putting her on the spot over what none of us like to talk about. Least of all the ladies; some men can be a bit boastful about fornication. Hooper did something he oughtn't to have done, that was the core of it all. Obadiah Pursglove, Blanche Pursglove: that's a union before God. Hooper's actions gave Obby reason to kill him. Worse all round for our fledgling community had that taken place. I believe I did right, if only to keep the peace.

* * *

Whilst I am pondering the terrible times we are having, McConnell approaches me. 'Aye, aye, Captain. It's been a difficult afternoon and you have navigated it well, sir.'

I appreciate him for saying it whilst thinking the words are but solace. I have come through the passage of time, and whether the world is better or worse for my actions, I cannot say. The ship a little less perturbed, I'm hoping. Still, I think this sea too tranquil, and our ship its opposite.

'Thank you, Edgar. Difficult scarcely comes close. It has been a sorry business, start to finish.'

We are silent for a moment.

'Did I do right, Edgar? Do you believe the boy had to go where he did? The way he did? Leave this life.'

'Yes indeed, Captain. Couldn't stay on the ship a moment longer. You made the correct cleaving; understood that all must trust all. A ship doesn't have a court house within it, and if it did the jury would have more likely ripped the wee boy limb from limb. You did right, Captain. No need for doubting yourself.'

'You heard his cries?'

'Matters not what goes between Blanche and Obadiah. She is a married woman and that's that. The boy sealed his fate by meddling behind a door which God has closed.'

Perhaps this is all a matter of faith. McConnell has a greater certainty in God's ordinance of a marriage than is our belief. We recognise that God seldom, if ever, endorses the actions of men. It is the law of the old country that, once betrothed, women are chattels. In our faith, we debate the merits of this kind of thinking. It might be the laws of Abraham; I can't rightly remember and Mr Muggleton isn't here to ask. Whatever it is, marriage was the choice Obby and Blanche made, and so Hooper never did have cause to be sniffing where he did. Can't be getting between them and not be met with anger. What the Lord thinks about the conduct of each of them is not our place to speculate. I nod at Mc Connells words; he means well and he's some type of Christian.

God Help the Connipians

A little smile alights upon his lips as he continues to speak. 'Might be the only marriage on the boat, so help me God.'

I think my eyes widen at that. There are rumours, and I have heard them as often as any on The John and Lodowicke. Never comment about all that, myself. As captain, I shouldn't: ifs and buts don't put wind in the sails. We began with many marriages on board. Till death us do part has called time on far too many. Not that this thought has brought forth McConnell's upturned lips. Our Rags was married to poor Oliver Fenton who took with the stomach sickness. There were some who said they never married, but Oliver was long of meetings. I fear for her, an ageing woman alone on a boat without a man to stand up for her. Five more of them that's lost were married, leave widowers in our midst. I am one of them. The others whom we lost were unattached; young, and still the scurvy befell them. Like I have already said, only three of our womenfolk survive. Ha'penny Hastings told me that Tabitha has been his wife for four years, told it to my face on signing up for this expedition. I was out at sea at the time they are said to have wed, but none of our lot were at such a wedding. She told Rags—Rags or Fenton, it was Fenton as told me, God rest his soul—Mr Muggleton himself blessed their union. Officiated some kind of ceremony after the event. Then Darius Dencourt told me that Ha'penny has told him they were married with the Anglicans. So one of them is not right. Tabitha may only have come over to the bright side after they were already living under one roof. It all sounds a bit fishy to me. And whenever it was that Tabitha became a follower of the prophets new, she didn't convince her husband to follow suit. Rumours and hens' droppings, who gives a fiddler's stick whether their union was blessed or just a person-to-person betrothal. She likes him and he likes her: it'll do.

'We've no need of church blessings, Edgar. Not amongst the most of us.'

'But Hastings is no Muggletonian, is he? A rum affair in my mind, but...'

'You spend time with the man, Edgar. Have you asked him, verified that it is not just idle chatter?'

'I spend time with him, and I find him difficult to know, Mr Brook. Ha'penny Hastings is a clever man all right, just not necessarily trustworthy. He seeks fame, hopes to discover flying rabbits or a horse that talks. People with faces on their stomachs. Knows something of science but wishes for it to serve him, not vice versa.'

As he speaks, we both look around. A noise from the rear of the ship. Shouting, many voices, an urgency in their calls. Next thing I know, Moses Grigg runs in front of me. 'Come now, come now,' he shouts.

I go straight to where he points, Mr McConnell behind me. As soon

The John and Lodowicke

as I look down the steps to quarters, I see what has caused the boy to call for me. Obby is a roughhouse; he has poor Mrs Pursglove by the hair, shaking her head this way and that.

'Stop now!' I yell, but others may have yelled before me, such is the commotion.

Wealds across her face, bleeding from an ear. I think it might be my presence as gives them the notion to act; two of my bigger boys take a hold of Obadiah Pursglove, one on each side.

'Stop it!' I shout again, although it is the way they have constrained him which compels the man to heed my words. A puppet in their strong arms. 'Mr Pursglove! What have you done. The good Lord knows, you risk going the way of yon' boy.' I am trying to bring some order here, but it feels like chaos on the ship again. 'Joining Hooper down in the deep below our ship, that might be my only recourse. That was assault, sir. What were you thinking?'

Obadiah spits upon his wife; my men have pinned his arms, and still anger bubbles within him. Crimson in the face. 'I'll gladly go in the water,' he yells at me, 'if only you push this one in before me.' Again, he spits into poor Blanche's eyes.

He might be a cruel man, or he might be a wronged man. Might be both of these things, I could hazard a guess. I never thought that it might be for me to determine such disputes when I agreed to captain this vessel; that I must has become as plain to see as the ocean that surrounds us. Me or no other, and I cannot see a woman beaten. It should play no part in the way of life we hold dear. 'Myhill, Septimus, please bring Mr Pursglove to my rooms. Mr McConnell, would you be so good as to witness our discussion? Hear Mr Pursglove's account of what has taken place?'

'Certainly, Captain,' he agrees.

* * *

I have a small anteroom, from which I access my sleeping cabin. Within it are fixed a table and four chairs, the only walnut-made furniture on the entire ship. Draycott and Myhill have pushed Obadiah onto one of my chairs and I believe he has calmed sufficiently to talk with me in a civil manner. They have withdrawn to the deck, stand just outside my door. To hand. I think they know this needed discourse might arouse Obby Pursglove further, and McConnell and I are not fighters. Truly, I abhor such behaviour. The pair of us sit opposite the transgressor.

'Tell me, Obadiah Pursglove, what is this commotion about? Striking a lady is not a course of action we can countenance. It is contrary to Christ's teaching and you know it as well as I do. That is the truth before God. You must explain to me how such shocking behaviour has arisen and convince me also of your repentance for so sinful an act. Only then might I decide what action to take. Whether you can remain within our hopeful circle, or if I must banish you as I have already done with Hooper. Banishment from a ship is not a pleasing step for either party.'

* * *

Talking at a horse's gallop, and I don't know what to think. Mr Pursglove scarcely said a word on our voyage from the Isle of Dogs all the way to the bottom of the globe, yet now—just McConnell and I listening in—he goes on and on.

'She been bewitched by the lad. That be it. He's not normal, some kind of a demon, getting' her to do all that which men want, and him only a boy. His doing the dirty is what's killed 'em, Captain. That be certain fact. My wife...' And at this point he turned and spat on the floor to the side. '...as once she was, she just wanted him once he started.'

'Them, Pursglove. What do you mean by, killed them? It is only Hooper who has perished.'

'He and Blanche,' he replies, spitting on the floor once more with the naming of his wife.

'You have hurt her badly, Pursglove, but Blanche shall not die of those injuries...'

'Then I'll hurt her some more, dammit. Can't be having that woman in this world after what she done.'

'You are raving, Pursglove. I shall place you in custody within this ship until a clear course can be determined. I must protect Blanche, as you most certainly will not. She is your wife, sir. It shocks me that we must harbour her from you. A terrible juncture.'

'Put me in the water with Hooper if you must, Captain, just make sure she's a-drowning too. Tis only right, in't it. I don't know how it started but she fornicated with that boy, that's what she done. Drown her! I think it's a devilment that started her off. Could be she's more under the spell than Hooper. Young lad wouldn'a say no to having some of her. Most wouldn't, but I'm sick of her now. Her doing the dirty with him, it's changed everything. Has for me. There was a time I'd have done anything she asked. But she didn't ask me. Bewitched, I tell it. That is what has 'appened to her. By Hooper or by the devil, and him by her or t'other.'

'Madness, Pursglove. You seem to have forgotten our ways? It must be these months at sea, a touch of cabin fever. That's the malady that grips you. Has taken a hold of Blanche also, I'll suppose, but that makes it less our place to judge.'

'Oh, it does, Cap'n. It's Blanche as left our ways. I'm for extracting justice...'

'Not as we see it, Pursglove. You have left your sense on the banks of the Thames and I fear it will not return.'

After this depressing exchange, I call Myhill and Septimus back into my rooms, have them remove the raving man. Shut Obadiah Pursglove into the small store aft the deck. It is not a prison cell in normal times, but these are not those. Ours has become a ship of madness.

2.

The name of our prophets shall forever be remembered, and within our ship's name are those by which we have known them. We Muggletonians that is. I never met John Reeve, think poor Fenton the only one among us who ever did. God rest his soul; he sits with Jesus. Reeve, that is; Fenton could be up there, but he had a nasty streak too. The Lord will have determined his fate after the scurvy ran its course.

The John and Lodowicke is the name of our craft, the latter of the pair known to us all. Mr Muggleton was too old to come. He declared it, and I couldn't disagree. Old bones are not for travelling, Lodowicke wiser than Fenton. This ship may yet bring us the new beginning we have hoped for. Planned even. I believe one should deploy a little reason in this Earthly life, although I know it is a fickle knife. More likely to snag a vein of one's own than to cut through any Gordian knot. And how the Lord will judge us upon His return is the fate we must await with humility. We're all at His mercy, the lot of us.

This boat is a small one in which to make the journey we have made. Many a sea dog said as much back in London before we'd so much as set the sails. And now that we are bobbing along in the bottom half of our mighty Earth, it feels a caution we should have heeded. Not its seaworthiness; it is having so few of us cooped up for so long that has been the problem. I am grateful that the tub has kept afloat, brought us this remarkable distance. A little dream of mine is that Lodowicke may join us should we find a land fit for a living prophet. That the promise of comfort on an idyllic island may lure him down, give him reason to endure the journey. I think it implausible even as I mouth the words to myself. Unwise too, although it is the word of God which Lodowicke believes in, not wisdom at all. Old Mr Muggleton has entered his ninth decade of life. If I think on all those who have perished on this journey of ours, then I know it is beyond him. Madness to try. Unless, of course, the good Lord should wish it. Whispers the notion into Lodowicke's ear. Miracles happen, but we are not the sort to believe them our rightful due. Jesus will make His move when He pleases; we can only hope we do not displease Him with our impatience.

The traipse across oceans to this corner of the world has been memorable and difficult. Those aboard comprise only those of us

Muggletonians who considered themselves strong of health, and wished to leave Poplar. Happy to depart England forever. Plus Mr McConnell and Mr Hastings, the paying guests. For far too many, that assessment of good health has proved itself untrue. And all were of the fair sex bar Fenton. The waters were roughest in the early days, passing France upon the Atlantic Ocean. Calmed by the time we were skirting the continent of Africa. And yet, sickness of the seafarers' type, chucking and spewing and frothing up from the gut, there was plenty. I succumbed for the odd day or two. I recall Hooper being one of the worst. Could barely hold down a meal until we'd passed the Cape. It was after that, pushing down into the Indian Sea, sailing east and east and south and east that another type of sickness overtook us. Ha'penny Hastings diagnosed the plague, but it cannot have been that, methinks. A couple sported boils, but they were not on one in ten of our ship. I called it the scurvy but I'm navigator not doctor. It has knocked ten bells out of us, decimated our hopeful community.

Ha'penny said his piece, but mostly tried to stay in his cabin during those difficult days. McConnell was a saviour to us. Worked hard at bathing and tending the sick. The dying. I am sure some live who might have otherwise left this life. I like to think I played my part. It was I who nursed my Mary, put all that is in my heart into the task. Alas, it was not enough.

I think it has been the nature of the crossing, losing people in ways we didn't rightly understand that has depleted our flock of its dedication. Wobbled us from our spiritual course. None say it, but nor are we praying as once we did. And we left the old country with the highest hopes. Now I think we want to find land mostly so that we may be more confident of living than dying. The John and Lodowicke has been a bit of a boat of horrors; it's chance and not the naming that's done for it. I'm sure of that. And how we shall live should a new land show itself, we cannot determine by daydreaming. The chance need come to pass, and it will be in the forging of that new order that we may find our true selves. God made us and we must fulfil His expectation. Mightn't get into heaven if we don't. It saddens me that I shall be doing it without Mary by my side. And for too much of our married lives I was away at sea. Still, I think I've been with her when it mattered most.

Upon reaching land I will forego my captain's status. Wish to do so as soon as the chance presents itself. I am a wise guide in the directing of a ship—my narrow skill of navigation—and that is a far cry from being a leader of men. I know this truth well, and yet it is of no use whatsoever in the undertaking of tasks which prove my analysis correct. A limiting and not an inspiring insight. I have captained the thing as well as I could, and the less said on top of it the better.

The John and Lodowicke

I am thinking over my shortcomings but a day after banishing young Hooper to his watery destiny, and imprisoning Obadiah Pursglove in an airless room on The John and Lodowicke. What is to follow on from such unpleasantness gnaws away at me like a rat below the waterline. I would gladly pass my responsibilities to another were anyone else better suited than I to take them.

'Captain, see here!' shouts Moses Grigg. The urgency in his voice gives me a sinking feeling, but he does not sound unhappy. Perhaps there is no beating or raping taking place this time. As I leave my quarters, move up to the deck, I see Ha'penny Hastings beside him. The broadest grin across his face. I know that I am soft, prone to the sentimental. In these two smiles alone, I sense an upturn in our fortunes.

'Give it to me then,' I say to Moses who waves a telescopic at me. Hastings holds one in his hand; gestures the direction to which I should point that which Grigg passes me. Down the tunnel of the marvellous device, I see a line on the horizon which is quite green. Very small in height, for we must still be many miles from it. Even from here I am certain that it is not a small island. A place of substance we sail towards. I am familiar with adjudging a land from a great distance.

I look back at both men, while others are coming over to join us. 'Thirty-one degrees south, we are, Brook,' announces Hastings.

'Yes.' I am a navigator, always cognisant with our co-ordinates. 'This is not the Dutchman's land.'

Ha'penny nods his head. Must be thinking, as I am, that we have indeed found somewhere other. We are to be the first upon it. That is what plays on our minds, excites us. I am sure of it. Before I have collected my thoughts, our entire company have surrounded me, come to hail the new land we have found. We can be only an hour's sail from its shore. Jerusalem beckons. Although I grin, I caution them all that we know not what lies on such a land, or if there is a safe place to weigh anchor. 'We should,' I suggest, 'circumnavigate our quarry first, to better envisage how we might live upon it, if that is to be our good fortune.'

The chatter continues. Rags and Tabitha are both enlivened by the prospect of making a home. Blanche stands with them but speaks less. I cannot tell if her thoughts are of our prisoner, the only one a-ship who is not exalting in this moment, and to whom she is married, or if it is the boy whom I dispatched to the deep that has drawn the forlorn look upon her face. That small chapter in our genesis I cannot enjoy dwelling upon. Wrong in every which way. The lad defiled her, and I cannot tell if she felt emptied of virtue by the deed, or relished him doing it, as told in Obby's surprising testimony. I thank the Lord I never spoke to her before meting out his punishment, it would have muddied the waters entirely.

From hand to hand, we pass our telescopes, almost everyone aboard has taken one to their eye. Looked upon this welcome sight. Rags laughs and says she can see her house, but we all know she cannot. When Mr Hastings begins to talk of a treeline, I am keen to hear his discourse. He believes the colour indicative of a forest, and the little area of paler green which appears to rise up like a hat, he conjectures to be a treeless hill. 'Scarcely a mountain,' he says. 'We are bound for a fair island, verdant and modest of gradient.' He can be a bit of a windbag when he gets it in him, can Mr Hastings; Darius hands me back a viewing glass, I see that Ha'penny is broadly correct. We are getting closer with each passing minute, more and more of our home-to-be coming into view.

The rigging boys are way up the spars, egging on our craft although the wind is gentle and our progress no more than deliberate. I hear from their shouts that they can see the land without use of telescope. Dozens of feet above us they hang. The atmosphere on board has lifted immeasurably. Happy shrieks from the younger of the crew. I am optimistic for the first time since most of our women folk upped and died. The peril in which our journey has placed them may yet prove worthwhile. To found a colony far from the rain-bedraggled streets of East London. This could be the start of something glorious.

In their excitement, many on the boat ask questions of me. As the captain, they think I know what will follow. While I have dreamed of coming across a new land, it is not a situation I have a terribly clear plan for. I was scared that too much premeditation would jinx it. 'In due course we shall be needing the small boats to go ashore,' I say. 'All in good time. As I stated, I want to circumnavigate the land first, learn how it appears from all sides. Pick the finest harbour this island offers, for it may be where we moor this ship for a long, long time.' I am certain it is an island we approach. This area of the ocean is not well charted, but sufficient to be sure no Australis-like continent lurks. And we are but thirty-four souls, a small island of rich soil is all we seek.

'Could be that there are people already a-there,' declares Darius, looking around. 'People like the Spanish found a hundred year or more back.'

'Further reason to sail around this land. Learn what challenges we must confront, or whom we might befriend, Mr Dencourt.'

* * *

Our island is a large one and the sail around it takes up a sizeable portion of the day. Mile after mile of forest we see, drawing down towards the edge of the land. Thick, dense and tall; the very same qualities we attribute to our bosun, Double Dee. Behind his back, couldn't say it to the face. I can see no indication that a man has cut a tree on this island. Hastings and McConnell say the same. We might be the first to arrive at the shore since God placed Adam and Eve in the blessed garden. It is a guess: we have yet to walk through these forests lush. We see a few rough coves where trees do not thrive, the land is the richest green for mile after mile. Lofty trees, varieties unknown to us. A grassy highland close to the middle of the island is the only patch that is not forested, and that only bare near its little peak. Our carpenters will be in their element, wood plentiful.

Mr Hastings proves himself quite the cartographer, taking measurements from the angle of the sun and drawing the line of the land with a likeness that is admirable. The man has many talents.

I tell all who care to listen that I shall declare this land for King Charles the second. Some laugh at that—poor Charlie died a decade since—I am more indifferent to the two who have come since. Feel less compulsion to claim the land for them, yet I am foremost an Englishman. Won't be declaring it for the Dutchies or any such foreigners. Mr McConnell says, and he has put thought behind his words, that the living king shall not hear of it for more than a year. That is how long it has taken us to sail here. We can do exactly as we please and it will be the longest time before the King, or an emissary thereof, can assert that we should do different. Seems like we are in charge, and it is a state that I like enormously.

'What do you call this island,' asks Rags, and I struggle not to laugh at the naivety of the woman.

Before I can answer others are telling her much as I would have. 'It hasn't a name, Rags. You must give it one and then it shall be as you have said.'

'Muggletonia,' she says, but I can't say I like it. Mr Muggleton is not a vain man. Just a simple prophet. And although we are of one creed—with the exception of our two learned companions—we are not really for separating ourselves out. We see the teachings of the Lord through the looking glass which John Reeve provided. We do not believe ourselves anything fancy. I have declared many times on this voyage that a new land might be the ideal refuge to await the return of our Lord, whether for us who sail or for our children. I fear, with but three women amongst us, this could be a sticking point. And that makes me dream of visitors to our new shore in the coming months and years. I'd even thought to myself that friendly natives could be a godsend. Some in the party laugh about them, primitives and what have you. It is my belief we are all one under God.

And perhaps it was too easy to fill those fearful days of travel with dreams of a bright future. We have yet to put a foot on the soil, to make our way as other than seafarers, and this has been a most precarious enterprise. Travels that have wrought changes upon us. For the time being, my only prayer is that this land provides a peaceful home. 'There is no Muggletonia,' I declare. 'We have found a far-flung county of greater England, of Brittania. New Essex or New Kent would be an apt name, I believe.'

'New Poplar,' shouts Tabitha, and it raises a laugh and a smile. It is from where the majority of us originate. I declare New Poplar to be a good name.

'May the Lord bless New Poplar,' shouts Darius. 'And not forget about us tucked away down here when He cometh back.'

* * *

I am keeping to a course between ten and twenty chains from the shoreline. Slowly goes the boat; I fear rocky outcrops could cripple the craft. This is an uncharted coastline, a virgin land. The height of the trees tells us as much. We pass along at this distance, taking the measure of our new home. New Poplar looks enticing to me; to us all, I am certain. The womenfolk all ask me to take them ashore forthwith, but I am a cautious man. It is in my nature, so to speak. A land of green beckons us; I shall not forego its invitation, simply ensure the safety of our landing. Work out where best on this island we might a settlement make. Forested near everywhere, just as Hastings declared from first sighting it. He stands beside me.

'No sign of boat nor mooring.'

I nod my head at his words. 'We have a boat, and I shall weigh anchor soon enough, Ha'penny.' My eyes rake along the side of the ship where we have our rowers tethered. 'The smaller craft will take us ashore.'

He grins at me. 'No sign of any others, of men and women adhered to this land. I was hoping we might find company, Captain Brook.'

I've been hoping this one both ways around, don't speak the words at this time. My musings on the matter confuse even myself. We are an imbalanced group to be declaring very much on New Poplar, and had we come across savages that too might have quickened my pulse in ways undesirable. I hate fighting and the taking of life. Peaceable natives would be a fine thing; all the signs are we shall be alone. 'Less of this captain now we are to step upon the land, Mr Hastings. John is my name, and the more as say it the sooner shall I relax. And we will be the people of New Poplar. If more come, or we chance across some indigenous, then we should share the land as neighbours, for that is as they shall be.'

'I see no signs of people, and I've had my eye to this,' he says, gesturing his telescope. 'If there are any people here, they may not be so happy at our arrival. Will know nothing of old Poplar so may not embrace our founding of a newer one.'

'I understand that. And it behoves us to make our intentions—our exclusively friendly intentions—the clearest we possibly can.'

'Sail around,' declares Ha'penny Hastings. 'I don't believe there are any warriors hiding in wait, but your patience is a strength, John. The longer we circumnavigate the more chance we shall spot them if my conclusion drawn from the absence of boats is mistaken. We have no need of hurry and Myhill told me he has hauled good fish here. Food for a week is what he said, and it is of much more pleasing flavour than all the hard tack of recent weeks.'

'I am pleased you see it as I do.' I expect to weigh anchor in a cove. There have been a couple. It will feel strange to be leaving The John and Lodowicke at anchor. To take to the small boats. There appear to be plenty of places where we can drag the rowing boats into cover. Tuck them away should we need to make good an escape. 'We are close, Mr Hastings, and I'll not be a-botching this landing. If there is one thing I can get right, it is this.'

* * *

'Last meal on deck.' Everyone is saying it although I haven't confirmed that it will be so, not with words. Perhaps my beaming smile has said all they need to know. Last meal on The John and Lodowicke for a long time, likely as not. Tabitha has cooked some recently caught fish; used its frying oil to soften the hard biscuit it accompanies. The land so close at hand pleases me, and this aroma of fish is a nice hat upon its head.

Moses is taking the rum around, giving all who want a tot. Gin too. We have managed our stocks well. Death has helped in that task where it has hindered all others. As we raise a glass to New Poplar, I think of those that never shall. Mary Brook be one. My own Mary, wife of nine years. I'd hoped the waters of a new land might reinvigorate whatever had stilled her child-bearing juices. For it wasn't the want of trying on her part or mine. And it is three months now since I lost her to whatever scurvy has had it in for us. I come to this new land a widower, further from claiming a plot for my kinfolk to come than ever I thought possible on setting sail. I didn't know if she would bear a child here, but I thought we would be together. And now everything that was in my mind those short months ago feels no more than a drunkard's dream. We are here but not in the numbers which we hoped and it is difficult to make a sour dream sweet. I am grateful that those around me are trying.

As we sit down, and the three women serve us each a plate of this fine fare, I learn from Moses that Mr McConnell is below deck. He has taken himself down for a-talking through the door to Obadiah. Telling the prisoner of the land which all but he has seen with their own eyes. I am of a mind to hold a trial, must fathom if we dare release him. His violence towards Blanche frightens me. Must scare her the more so. Perhaps it should be her decision alone, but I fear that would weaken our collective strength. Indeed, I think there needs to be forgiveness or divorce, possibly both, for any harmony to settle upon New Poplar. Or is all this a figment? No forest cleared, not a house built. We have looked for Eden and I hope it is our find. Fear it could yet prove the land of Nod.

While we eat, Tabitha lectures Ha'penny, tells him he should take this opportunity to join our number. She says the same to McConnell now and then and she isn't married to him. Wishes only Muggletonians to reside within this new land. She is one as her husband is not, if husband he even be. For my part, I don't know what difference it will make to us. Both Hastings and McConnell have been grand company on this difficult journey. It is the sharp-tempered ones in our midst whom I am finding divisive.

Rags joins Tabitha in telling Ha'penny to come to his senses, join the blessed few. Her cajoling feels like a ribbing. A bit of fun and nothing more. As if following the prophets were as simple a choice as to dance around a maypole. And if the marriage of Tabitha and Ha'penny spans across religions, perhaps there is learning in it. Hastings has told me his mother and father practiced the Papist way; for his part he is happy for everyone to find peace as they can. That sounds close enough to our own beliefs to my ear, and yet I know he regarded Lodowicke—back in Poplar—as a fraud. Mostly expresses it in circumspect language, us of the faith outnumbering him as comprehensively as we do. 'He stood me an ale and spouted such rubbish, Captain Brook,' Hastings told me once, when it was just the pair of us speaking in my quarters. One of many conversations we shared through our long journey here. 'What could I do but buy him another and tell him so. "Blasphemer," he called me. There are many would say that was him, Captain. Prophet indeed!'

I only laughed. 'More faith, Ha'penny, that is what you are lacking. Muster up a little more faith. His coming was in the book.'

He used to cut a strange apparition did Mr Muggleton, frequenting bars across town to let all and sundry know the one true way to heaven. Faith and wait. Maybe cross a finger or two. Second guessing the wishes of the Lord is not an act which should be relied upon; the sacred texts are for our benefit, not devices with which we can know His mind. Hints and signs our bible gives us, and only answered prayers can give us certainty. Lodowicke and John, may he rest in peace, have heard a few. That's good enough for this widower. Plenty good enough, for through my faith I know that Mary will be waiting for me in heaven.

As we eat the fish, much of the talk is of tasks which will consume our coming days. Hunting down some meat, that is top of many a list; building houses too, and we've no less than six skilled carpenters in our number. It is the very job our Lord did while awaiting His Father's call. I expect to develop some agrarian skills, contribute to the harnessing of the land. We've brought seeds with us from the Essex countryside. If God should bless us with barley, then I shall be planting and gathering to fulfil His wish.

Septimus says that more people should come. 'This land would feed all on the north bank of the Thames.' And it is not a falsehood, not by my calculation. Verdant and rich, might yield fruit, the taste of which we are yet to learn.

The talk—waiting for the Dutch to find this land as they have so many this far across the globe, sending out a message in a bottle!—only reminds me of all we have lost. That we cannot begin our venture as the self-contained community we hoped to be. A dozen women would be a fine thing, three is a veritable paucity.

My Mary had a child towards the close of our first year of marriage. It grieved her for years. Through prayer I coped better than she—did not take recourse to weeping—I have felt overcome by a sadness as bitter as hers since she too has lost her foothold in this life. And ever since her passing my mind has frequently returned to those dark days. Put me aside of myself with the difficult recollections. The time when a family we did not become.

Even carrying the unborn child was not easy for her. Mary was young; nonetheless, her legs and feet did swell up something awful to look upon. She couldn't stand at the washbasins although her work required it. I sought a medical man, paid money for an opinion that may have been honest but solved little. He agreed that she couldn't work, had to rest in bed until such time as our hidden child chose to show its face. It was likely a quarter-year she spent that way. Reclined. I was working, mostly on the docks, sailing off to Copenhagen for a couple of weeks, also. My own sister did take herself into our cottage every single day that I was away, and many when I wasn't. Looked after Mary very tidily. Betsy, sister of mine, would be with us here encircling New Poplar only she doesn't have the liking for the sea which long ago gripped me. She is good family and saw my wife through her ordeal. Acted as a midwife for, after calling on the services of a doctor once, I couldn't rightly afford more of those high-minded helpers.

I was in the house when Betsy delivered our son. Not in the same room, I'm one as doesn't think that right. I heard the yelling and the gasping. Boiled pot after pot of water for Betsy to use as she knew how. Her face was not a-smiling when she called me in, when the sheets were once more tucked around my Mary. I ventured into the room and she showed me the cot. The baby writhed a little, but made not a sound. Dreadfully yellow in colour, it was. When I saw the consternation on my sister's face I looked again. More closely at the infant as she bid me to

31

do. The Lord gave us a child without eyes. It was not of a kind that could make its way in this world. No eyes at all in that tiny head.

'Does she know?' I whispered to Betsy.

My sister shook her head.

I went and sat next to the bed, took Mary's hand in my own. 'My love,' I said softly, 'I love you with all that there is in me, and I grant the same to any child of ours. But it is for the love of this son, that I beg you, do not feed him, Mary. Do not take this one to your breast. This is a lamb for the Lord, not a child as can grow to manhood in these challenging times. I'm so sorry, Mary. Truly, the Lord has a mysterious plan for us. Perhaps on a better day we shall find out exactly what it is. Today He played a little trick.'

She wept, speaking a few words as her tears bubbled. A repetitive phrase: 'I know, I know, I know.'

And that is how it came that a couple of days later we were interring our firstborn in the graveyard of St Nicholas's church, for it was several months after this tragic happenstance that we joined the truer faith of John Reeve and Lodowicke Muggleton, became conversant with their prophesies.

Daniel, we called him. Had the name scratched into the tiny headstone. Daniel Brook, and if any place a flower on that grave at this time, it is my sister. I am half a world away and the boy's mother sleeps in the deep ocean. Perhaps they have met again. I think she would have fed him but for my command.

Life can sometimes be cruel and the Lord has yet to explain why it is so. Acceptance is the only way. I try to let everything unfold as it chooses to do, can't expect much on this Earth to bend to my will. Can't even captain a ship, frankly.

* * *

For more than twenty-four hours, we sailed around the island. Twice around. Now we have dropped anchor in a bay on the northern shore, and we are taking to the boats so that we may found New Poplar properly. Plant a flag. It is a glorious day, and when ashore I shall be toasting King Charles twice for each one that is called out for William. I liked Charlie the better; the old bumbler interfered less. And we will make an English land without correspondence from that faraway country. That is how it must be at first and I think it will suit. My hope is that we use only the natural laws that come from the scriptures, and impose them through consent, without magistrates or those landed Dukes who reign unequal in the place from which we departed. England is a fine land but archaic in so many of its ways. Maddening. However, we are agreed that we must declare this new land for the King. There was scarcely a dissenter among us when we discussed this point over the months of our crossing. We are too few to declare New Poplar another country. Nor do we reckon the king will show his face here. Won't even be sending an emissary. William is the crabbiest of monarchs and I, for one, am pleased he is half a world away.

McConnell bids me to face the land. He will row with the other men—put his back into it—and I need not. 'You have brought us to this place, Captain Brook. We are grateful.'

It is a pleasure to be the one looking forwards, seeing the approaching land as the rowing men cannot. The forested island draws nearer with each tug they give their oaken oars. The waters are choppier now than they have been during our day's sail around New Poplar. In the shallows. We don't know for certain that we will be alone here, it is simply the way it looks. Birds we have sighted, and Moses Grigg declared he saw a small bear. He manages our supplies of rum, and may have nipped a few measures before raising glass to eye. And if there are bears, I am interested to learn their taste, while hoping to myself that they are less curious about the taste of John Brook. Up and down the waves we go. Blanche is quiet, knows that Obby is in the other boat. We can hardly imprison the poor devil on this island. It is my intention to hold a meeting with the pair. To bring their marriage to a conclusion, one way or another. Blanche seems less keen on the notion but doing nothing will not bring healing to the schism that has gotten between them. I thought I'd lanced the boil with Hooper going down in the deep. That was to have been the last of the matter, would have been but for Obby turning on his wife as he did.

It is Moses who leaps first from our boat. To the left I see Myhill jumping from our sister craft. Those two men are the first to step upon this newly discovered territory—New Poplar—the rest of us, the thirty-two, follow in no time at all. Obadiah has his hands shackled and Darius minds him as he might a horse of value.

3.

Charlestown, as I have named our settlement, is a hive of activity. Forty trees we have felled on our first day since awakening on dry land. I am impressed with the diligence of these men. And I must also credit McConnell and Hastings for putting their backs into a hard day's work. The examining and classifying that they love to do must await a later date.

Edgar has told me of the astonishing variety of trees on our isle. He believes we will find fruit within a short walk of the settlement, cannot guess when they might come into season or the size and tastes of the delights we are to discover. 'It is unlike anything in Europe, more curious than those derived from the Marco Polo trail or told by those who have returned from the Americas. This land is like no other. An orphan in the south seas with trees of its own imagining.'

I find his manner of speech poetic. And I am delighted to think our journey has arrived somewhere without parallel. 'Not for us the common fields of Kent and Essex, Mr McConnell. All is the creation of our Lord; I believe He may have saved His best for the Muggletonians.'

Edgar smiles at my comment, unsure perhaps if I am serious or making light. Hastings coughs. Dissent, I'd call it. A man with ideas which live outside the bible. A good man in his own way, his wife one of our number.

I am pleased to see Obadiah Pursglove humping logs from the forest edge to our makeshift workshop. He is a carpenter himself, but we have yet to entrust a blade to his calloused hands. Blanche busies herself with the business of food, ensuring our supplies will remain dry whatever weather this land shares with us. The greens of the trees and grasses suggest rain is plentiful although we have yet to see any descend from the sky. We have found reliable sources of water: a couple of small streams enter the sea at our cove.

The decision to give Obby his freedom was not made lightly. Within minutes of coming ashore, I gathered all around me and openly sought their views on the matter. Called it my last act as captain, and yet our people look to me still as they did on board the vessel. I know no more about founding a colony than any other man amongst us.

'As I see it,' I told the assembled, 'there are precisely three choices before us. We can dispatch poor Obadiah to the deep as we did Hooper who wronged him. The problem with this course of action is two-fold. We have already arrived at New Poplar, so without going back out a long way, he will hop off any plank and simply wade ashore. Also, Hooper committed a crime—that of rape, or something like it, with another man's wife—Obadiah struck poor Blanche in a manner we none of us wish to see, but she does belong to him. It is not for us to judge how a man treats his wife, however much we might encourage better than what he has done. And we know the Lord does all the judging that matters, or He will do when the fateful day arrives.' I looked across at the group, they seemed unmoved by my meditation. Couldn't tell if they were for forgiving or dispatching the man. 'We could keep Mr Pursglove imprisoned; the danger he presents to Blanche makes this a course worth dwelling upon. Part of the problem is we are days away from constructing any chamber that could hold him on New Poplar, so to contain him we would have to row back to The John and Lodowicke, leave him there with at least one man to guard over him. The duties of passing food and keeping a close eye would occupy a man I'd rather deploy in the construction of our new settlement. We've work a-plenty to be doing, and keeping a man in prison should not be a part of these first days on New Poplar.' At this point I looked directly at Blanche, who was sitting between Tabitha and Rags, the three ladies all sitting together. 'It is our belief that through His glorious death, Christ enabled His Father to forgive us all our sins. As God does then—to my way of thinking—we should too. If Obadiah will swear to me upon the Holy Bible and the Divine Looking Glass, that he will keep twenty leaps and bounds away from his wife until such time as we know all his feelings of anger have dissipated, then we may allow him freedom. As a group, we must watch him closely. For surely none of us think hurting Blanche, as he has done once, is a happenstance we can let recur. Harmony between all must become the way on New Poplar. Forgiveness, I am advocating, not acceptance of what he has done. Am I clear? And what say you all?' Again, it was Blanche I directed my gaze upon.

'Captain,' said Rags, a hand placed upon one of Blanche's who stood to her right, 'it is the way of womenfolk. We have arrived at New Poplar fewer in number than we planned. May they all rest in peace. Your Mary amongst them, sir, and staying large in my thoughts, she is. We look to men to protect us even when we oftentimes need shelter from them or certain of their number. Your number. And this be the case here now. Obadiah struck my friend about the head many times, she tells me that her hearing has yet to return. Befuddled her mind whether you can tell it or not. If all you men are going to watch Mr Pursglove, and tell him to keep those leaps and bounds away, push him back if he encroaches a single inch, then why wouldn't we support this measure. You speak of imprisonment only to achieve the same aim. Forgiveness is a good way, if not an easy one. But let not New Poplar become a land of murder or mayhem. And let us hear from Obadiah Pursglove. If he be raging still, perhaps we should saunter this boat out to where the sea is deep and a shark or two lurking. We cannot forgive what is not past. How is this man now? Is he vile or repentant?'

I must say, the men looked a little uneasy about this lengthy speech. It's true that our type despises wife beating; however, this will become a barmy colony if we allow women to usurp the roles of men. I think many of the men saw the speech Rags gave as a challenge to my authority, but I shall try to view it in the round. I think she drew on the same dilemma as I—a wish to forgive—but not if it only meant another crisis in a few hours or days.

And here we are, busily building New Poplar, Obadiah Pursglove working as hard as any man. When Darius brought him before us, Obby laughed at the questions we posed, did not do so unkindly. I felt his vitriol had already left, it might have been ocean madness, and the sight of land the curative. He was no longer the killer we'd pulled from Blanche but a couple of days before.

'Keep me away from her? That sounds a wise course of action, Captain Brook. I have no wish to hurt her no more, indeed, I no longer regard that woman as my wife. If another man wants to take his chances, he can have her. If there is something to sign, a marriage dissolution, I'm all for it. And I come here for the new land, discovering I have a wife not worth the cleaving to, for she feels no need to reciprocate, well, that's something best forgotten, isn't it? I'll take my chances on New Poplar, and regard it as if Blanche has moved to France or Belgium, however close to hand she really is.'

Then the man spat carefully on the ground, close to his own feet. A disregarding, but not an aggressive act. Darius looked at me intently, as if seeking permission to strike Obadiah, to punish the defiance in his words, the arrogance he displayed. That was not a signal I was going to give. The marriage was over, that was the most significant point. And Obby decided it was that way round without me or any other pressing him to say it.

'Mr Pursglove,' I said, 'I shall give you your marriage annulment to sign if that is as you want it. It will be ready for your mark within the hour. You understand that this unshackles Blanche from your discretion. Were you to strike her once more, do so after you have signed the deed, it would be an act of violent assault, punishable in the court of New Poplar. Not a court as has yet sat once but you can imagine its judgement. Banishment, within the isle or beyond. I accept your terms, now be true to our faith and we shall welcome your return to the fold. And also know, many eyes will be watching you. Seeing that you remain true to your word.'

That was then, already I am thinking it the smartest thing I have done as captain. Laying down the law without the prevarication nor the loss of life that accompanied my intervention at the time of Hooper's misdemeanour. I expect the solid earth beneath my feet has helped my mind to focus.

* * *

Today we have built a pair of simple longhouses. My contribution was but small, I lifted the big rafter of logs that form each side, did so in unison with my fellow settlers. We all played our part, pulled on the ropes. Tall trees are in abundance on this island, they enabled us to use single logs for the length of three rooms. And they are quite a sight these large and freshly built cabins. The smell of sawn wood inside and out. There is a dampness in the air too, the resin from the trees or the promise of rain. I am still trying to understand the climate. We shall let our logs dry in the future before building with them, we simply needed our first dwelling places erected quickly. And now we sleep—not on the high sand, woollen blankets about us, as we did last night—under proper cover. Of course, we feel cramped together this first night. In the next day or two we intend to double—Darius says triple—the living space that we have created. Charlestown will, in weeks, become a proper colonial outpost. On the map, or on the one Hastings is in the process of drawing, at the very least.

Once we have a secure place from which to set forth, we shall find out more about our isle. McConnell, who has lain his makeshift palliasse aside my own, is more animated than I have ever seen so learned a man. He believes many of the trees we have cut to be so ancient as to have stood since King Arthur's day. Possibly the time of Christ. Ha'penny Hastings is more circumspect. The man hoped to find cavemen or suchlike and it seems that will not occur on New Poplar. It is us and the colourful birds. Possibly some mammals but I know not which ones. Grigg's bear has yet to show itself to be more than a drunken apparition. Not come across so much as a rabbit hole.

4.

Lord help us, the rains have come. When I was first laying down my head, I thought these longhouses very fine but they have not withstood this—the first angry sky on New Poplar—and we have had only two days doing our living inside them before it blew in.

Rain! These could be the monsoon rains of India tipping down upon us, such is the deluge. In shouted words, for the pelting from above has become a deafening drumming upon what bit of roof remains, Blanche tells me that the day broke before the sky blackened. It was not a sight I saw. Slept until the thunderclaps decided we could not. Now we must appear as drenched as do men upon a north water fishing vessel. Our nightwear drips with it, skin feeling as we might mid bathing. I am able to see right through the cotton shift which clings to Blanche's body, and see how swollen are the tips of her breasts. Perhaps it is wrong to look but my eyes still do it. And her marriage is over; mine also, if by a different circumstance. And I do not think it is desire, not a wish for lovemaking that makes them swell, just the waters that play upon them. And my looking is curiosity: I like how they appear; it's not full-blown lust. I'd know it if it were.

The former Mrs Pursglove sits upon a small chest. What good her sitting there might do evades me, but it is a wish to protect what is inside that makes her do it. The hard biscuit that has been our staple for so

God Help the Connipians

long. She beckons that I sit beside her, and I must confess, it is tempting to do so. To sit thigh to thigh with another in this storm feels less like drowning than standing alone must do. I take the sheet in my arm and put it over both our heads. We are within the longhouse, but the wind has moved half the roof; water pummels us. This sheet I hold does nothing; rainwater drips from it like the flow of a mountain brook. Blanche leans into me and kisses my cheek, unseen beneath our bedraggled cover. I return it and know not why. Something in this weather has washed away the reserve for which I am known. Wrought a change. My feelings are confused, recall that my courtship of Mary was a proper one. Not a hand upon her leg until we were married. My word, and now I am all over Blanche, feeling her fleshiness and delighting in it. Like my fellow sailors used to do when, in port, the local girls came looking for a coin. I wasn't much of a one for that, five or six times did I succumb at most. Maybe ten. I tell myself to stop, for Blanche does nothing to prevent it. I am surprised at that, how wanting her hands are. Blanche squeezes her mouth onto my own. I check myself, cannot be feeling a woman's titties when there is so much work to be done. I have led a life above these diversions. By and large. Really should resume securing all we have brought ashore from The John and Lodowicke, supplies to keep dry. The small food store on which we sit might be the most secure, lined on the inside. Every boat has such stores for the transportation of food. As I try to rise, take myself from this siren woman, she clasps my hand and pulls it beneath her nightshift, touching upon that which is between her legs. I draw myself away from her. In my mind a picture of young Hooper emerges. If her conduct with him was so brazen, how could he resist. I struggle with the same and I am a man approaching forty years. 'But you freed me,' she shouts, as I head out of the ravaged longhouse. Go to see what good I might do elsewhere in our small community.

* * *

Many a man is laughing now. It has been one hell of a downpour but the water is warm on New Poplar. And now that it has desisted, the sky has returned to the rich blue which characterised our first days here, accompanied us while going around the island in The John and Lodowicke before ever we landed. The colours which we see are all pure, brilliant and warm. Blue and white above, mixed greens of the forest and grass, even the ruddy browns of the fattest tree trunks. McConnell tells me that it is a fine climate; this rain will be a great help for crops. He advises that we must build our properties with great care. 'It can be done.' He is very confident and I know it too. We are simply building in too great a hurry; we have the skills and must apply them patiently, thoughtfully.

We are all working in harmony now; McConnell has advised a particular leaf that might bind the joins on the wooden slats we have made. Its sheen gives him to believe it will withstand very many rains before need of replacement. It is a novel idea for a thatch, and a clever one too. This morning's downpour was likely the first of many. I choose a working party to enter the forest and gather up the leaves of choice. Myself, Moses Grigg and Pursglove. Nonchalantly did I name those to accompany me. The proximity I found to Mrs Pursglove earlier this day is not to be dwelt upon; it was an occurrence of the thunder. Obadiah need never know. Indeed, it has bugger all to do with him. The man has parted from Blanche in the eyes of the law and God, so if I—a widower for three months now—should choose to make her my own, so be it. Not that the man need know I am thinking over the wisdom of it. Weighing up the pleasure of feeling her flesh in my fingers against the way others may view me. It is proving complex, head and trousers in disagreement.

'Captain,' asks Obby, 'are these leaves here the same? A differing shape, but feel the oiliness, see the size. I reckon they too will make do.'

'They are not as McConnell asked but I see your point. And they look a little longer from base to apex which suits our purpose.'

Moses nods along. Together we settlers are making a mark on this land, crafting something to stand the test of time. Charlestown shall be better prepared come the next storm. Perhaps they are a monthly event; it is a verdant land. And New Poplar will be on the maps a decade hence. I can sense it. How our individual tales might play out is far beyond my guessing. That I should like Blanche to bear me a son plays in my thoughts as we work. We never spoke of raising a child, and perhaps it was just the storm playing with the humors which coursed through her as we sat it out. Seemed keen on the making of such a child if I am an interpreter of horseplay.

5.

I don't hardly believe what he is saying, while knowing full well that Ha'penny is a serious man. He and Septimus have traversed this forest. 'Making a chart of the new Jerusalem,' sayeth Hastings before they went, but I always sense he is taking a gentle rise with those kinds of words. McConnell is more Christian than he, and neither is a Muggletonian. Now he has returned, he speaks quickly like a drunken man, and Hastings is not for the partaking of liquor. Not ever. He says they saw footprints away in the forest. More than two hours walk from Charlestown.

'Footprints!' respond many of our throng. It is an incredible tale.

God Help the Connipians

'Shoed footprints,' Hastings declared to all who would listen. 'Shoed all right, a people with some crafting. There was mud, a patch of mud, where they showed up most clearly. And that made us look closer at the track. Signs all over that patch of forest. Kiddie shoes to my eye, but if there are children, then they must have parents. As certain as night follows day.'

I feel both excitement and trepidation in his words, his excited state. It feels like an hallucination although it is not I who has seen this harbinger of a meeting. I am flooded with thoughts of our fledgling community building its future in tandem with established people. It is an uncertain prospect. I have worried until now that ours might be a short-lived venture. Children the most difficult thing to raise on this forested isle. Difficult because we've only two women of childbearing age. Last night, in the still of the near forest, on the pretext of looking for mushrooms, Blanche allowed me to plant a seed within her. I know not whether she is or is not barren. Didn't talk over the possible outcomes of all we did. No child has Obadiah brought forth into the world, and he is stronger of arm than I.

Blanche and I whispered then of whether we might declare our union. I am not really one for doing the coupling with any woman unless we were all square in the eyes of God; unfortunately, it has been a long journey and losing Mary left me a longing that which Blanche allowed.

Now I feel pleased to learn that we are not alone while utterly uncertain of the best path to steer. Shoes do not sound too primitive to me. Strange that we saw no other signs—not a boat of any form in a single cove—when we did our circumnavigation. To come across people like ourselves—if feet are clothed then so must their bodies be—could be the blessing our own venture needs.

* * *

Some in our community are calling me Mayor, and this because I reject the title captain now the voyage which brought us from old Poplar to new is over. I have talked with McConnell, told him that the mantel of mayor is not one I wish to wear. It is not even one that fits.

'There is nobody better,' was his reply. And once I'd thought about it, I spotted it isn't even a contradiction. I suggested at the time that he—a learned and reliable man—might fulfil the position more skilfully than I ever could. 'I do not enjoy the goodwill of the other men as you do, Brook.'

His assertion is correct: while I think McDonnell both learned and wise, many in our party are sceptical of the man. Never a Muggletonian, that is the feature they distrust. Hastings and McConnell always knew it was for them to fit into our ways whether they support them

The John and Lodowicke

wholeheartedly or just pretend. And we are not ones to inhibit those around us. As John Reeve said and Mr Muggleton oft repeated, the right answers are known by God alone and only guessed at by man.

For the present time, I am half a mayor. I don't want the title, but we need some order down here. When decisions need making, I seek as much agreement as I can from my fellow men. That seems to keep the peace, not that I am any kind of Quaker. Not wedded to a notion that finding a consensus is a commandment from God. Old Mr Muggleton had no time for Quakerism, and nor do I: I'm simply not a tub-thumper. That style of leadership doesn't flow in my veins; I await our Messiah, won't be acting like one in the void.

By the end of this day, we have constructed three of the longhouses we planned and four smaller dwellings too. By agreement amongst ourselves, one of the lesser sized is for my use—all because I am Mayor, and that only after a fashion—and one is for Tabitha and Ha'penny Hastings, our last remaining couple. McConnell takes the smallest, and Obadiah with Darius occupy the one furthest from the longhouses. A strange arrangement, but it seems to be keeping him in check.

Rags and Blanche have elected to sleep in one of the longhouses with six other men, but it has some division to it. Nothing untoward should be happening in there. Blanche even whispered in my ear that she would like to share my cabin; I told her it was too soon. I am watching how Obby detaches himself from all he once had. So far, he is true to his word. I would not wish to be central to another explosion of temper from him. I keep saying that I have no wish to be Mayor, yet my sense of duty requires I do not debase the role which has been thrust upon me. In the eyes of those looking up to me at the very least; God almighty knows I've been thinking dirty about Blanche. He must do, He knows everything. That I've done it with her, can't imagine that He missed it.

Hastings wishes to convene a party to search the island for our fellow islanders. It is what we must do in time; I feel no urgency in this moment. I believe these other people should get a sense of us first, recognise that we are independently sharing this land. That we've not come here to hunt them down.

'Quite right,' says Hastings when I have made my point. I like this about him: he's a better listener than most of my lot. Not that they intend their ignorance, it's just how it is. Mr Muggleton drew a rag-tag band of followers.

Many of us talk over the matter while gathered together outside the largest of our dwelling places. Many but not all, and I am a little perturbed to note that both Blanche and Obadiah are absent, Moses, Myhill and the other ladies also.

Some of the men are fearful, even a little excited, at the possibility of discovering that our cohabitants are hostile. We have a gun or two amongst us, and nothing here gives us to believe our fellow islanders shall have anything of such awesome power.

'And when might we go find 'em?' asks Septimus Draycott.

I tell him we shall do it in one month. It is not a plan with any detail or profound reasoning in my mind. I am nervous about meeting those who came first, that's why I put it off. That we should secure this settlement, begin our agricultural plans too, is as much explanation as I give. And as I say it, I think, with water secured and a crop in the offing, we might be the more impressive to whatever manner of men are already living here. It'll help us to win them over if they see we need nothing of theirs.

Hastings looks like he is cogitating—would have liked me to say some time sooner—doesn't argue the point. McConnell declares my counsel wise.

Then we hear shouting coming from the forest, even a woman's shriek. All in our group run in the sound's direction: womenfolk in distress, of course we run. Just a short way along the track we have stomped into the forest, Tabitha comes running, says what I have surmised. Once again Obadiah has hold of Blanche.

'A-strangling,' she says.

It is a dreadful thing. And I like Blanche, truly.

* * *

There are a few strong men among us and I do not count myself in that number. Many with arms thicker than my own, more resolve too, perhaps. I know where I hope to arrive, but not the surest path to reach it. Once more it is Darius whom I must thank for his prompt action. He has pinned Obadiah to the ground and I try not to look at the man. The would-be wife strangler. If Darius chooses to clobber him in even his most tender areas, I will turn a blind eye. Try to let him infer as much from my demeanour.

Blanche is convulsing on the floor, gasping for air. Tended kindly by Rags, Myhill acting solicitous also. We quickly learn that her husband—husband as was, we all witnessed the annulment of that sorry marriage—was a-throttling her. Strangulation as if for a killing. This situation cannot carry on. With my back turned, I say to Darius, 'Bring him to the village centre. There we must act as a courtroom would. No more compromising. It is a judgement that we need, and one that ends this plague in our midst before it puts paid to us all.'

I lead the way, a procession of Muggletonians, out of the forest and back to our fledgling Charlestown. It is only early evening, and this matter cannot wait. Dark comes upon us rapidly in these climes—will be here before the hour is out—a fire we shall build if needed. I am determined to see this matter through. Must find within me the leadership to cut a path through these terrible entanglements.

'Mr Hastings,' I say, 'I am nominating you to act for Mr Pursglove in this matter. Mr McConnell, please will you advocate for Blanche, for Mrs Pursglove. All others gathered, you are to hear these arguments out and help me conclude the matter judiciously. We cannot allow these terrible beatings and stranglings to continue. The issues must be resolved in the coming minutes, that is as I see it.' Then I gesture for the Scot to proceed. 'Mr McConnell.'

'Captain...' I peer at him through narrowed eyes. '...Mayor Brook,' he corrects himself. 'Blanche Pursglove has done no wrong save that which Mr Pursglove already said was behind him. As was their marriage. This is an act of violence by man upon woman, nay, an attempt to snuff out the lady's life, and I do not think it for us to forgive but only to do what must be done for the protection of Blanche. Mr Pursglove is a threat to our collective survival on New Poplar; he acts on an irrational temper, likely to kill or harm any he takes a dislike to...'

As McConnell is getting into his stride, making points which I think will help this community draw a needed line under the episode, Obadiah shakes himself out of Darius's grasp, looks at me as he stands, hands tied but no longer in the grip of another man. 'Rot and rubbish. You know nothing of what's been going on. I wouldn't have come here without a wife, in need of certain releases as I am. When we were in the forest, several of us, looking for berries and other sustenance, I asked that woman to take me back. Said it nice and all. Just thinking it might be ship's madness that overcame her on board: what she done with the dead boy. Then she told me she had another. I said to Blanche "No!" Or rather, I retorted that she once had another, but he is down in the deep from where there will be no coming back. I didn't plan to make what I say sound mean or hateful, it just came out that way. My pointing out what was past. "No, I've another now, Obadiah, a living man," she said to me. "Who?" I demanded to know. But she wouldn't give me no answer. You'd have throttled your Mary in those circumstances, Captain. You really would.'

I look at Hastings, then remind him that he is the one who should speak. 'We've heard enough from you,' I tell Pursglove. 'Mr Hastings.'

'Mr Pursglove, who stands before you, has not truly had his marriage annulled for that was a deed and document signed under duress. He and Blanche remain married in the eyes of the law for that is what the scrolls in London would tell us, were they here or we there for the purpose of so reading them. The law on New Poplar is a fine and fanciful idea but it has nowhere been agreed. Carries no weight or real authority at this

God Help the Connipians

point in time.'

I don't like the turn of Ha'penny's defence. Erudite and weaselly words, I can't be doing with them. Sounds a true lawyer to me, and I hate those bastards. And I knew before he spoke that I'm not a proper mayor, he didn't have need to say it so bluntly for all to contemplate.

'The man has a temper and this fact was surely known to Blanche long before she married him. This quickening in Obadiah's blood leads him to a speed of action which does, in the long run, far more good deeds — the rapid defence of loved ones — than it does the contrary. However, Mr Pursglove went beyond what any here might term "reasonable chastisement of a wife," and ventured into the territory where the murderer within each of us might be lurking. For this reason, Captain Mayor, I request that we seek to find out who has taken Blanche upon his cock, as Mr Pursglove attests has occurred. That is the man to banish from our community, the defiler of Mr Pursglove's wife. We do not wish to lose this fine worker, and we must all agree with Mr McConnell that Blanche is to be protected above all else.'

'Hmmm, Hastings...' I have a lot to say to this, cannot decide exactly where to start. 'This courtroom is for the trial of Obadiah; it is not for you to be charging someone else, the identity of whom we do not know.' Then I look to my other barrister; on New Poplar these two are all we yet have. 'Mr McConnell?' I hope he can navigate this spider's web, for I am bereft of ideas. Not a clue what to do about it.

'We live a reality, Mr Hastings, Mr Pursglove. The deed of three nights back when the accused signed a dissolution of marriage order — the former Mrs Pursglove and our good Mayor signed it also — we cannot pretend the event did not happen, nor that it did not mean that which we all know it meant. There was enough clever talk to swindle those on the wrong end of a silver tongue back in old Poplar. We cannot allow for those travesties of justice to become the way of our public discourse on New Poplar. Therefore, I say, Mr Pursglove has indeed ended his marriage to Blanche. We had agreed upon that already, so cannot reverse the decision as if a wind has turned. The information which he demanded from her was not his to ask; there is not much private life on New Poplar yet and if Blanche has happened upon a little, let us keep it that way. Obadiah has worsened the situation. That has been his foolish act. Foolish and reprehensible in the manner he pursued it. I think his unreasonable demands led to a rush of blood in poor Mrs Pursglove's head; indeed, she might have said she had taken another only to discourage him. I could say that I can fly like a bird, it does not mean that I truly can, nor that another man may assault me for my failure to do so. Saying something when not under oath carries no penalty whether truth or lie. The poor lady was most probably not in her right mind. With

The John and Lodowicke

the act of violence which he then perpetrated upon her—with murderous intent, let it be said—Obadiah has proven beyond all doubt that he is not a man of his word, not a man who can let sleeping dogs lie. I think we must banish him to the other side of the island, to make friends with whoever lives there, or offer him the smallest of boats to take himself home, or to some other place of his fancy if the sailing should take him from here to there.'

Blanche looks intently at all who speak, but elects not to say a word to the assembled. I do not ask it of her—she is only a woman—and I am fearful that she might incriminate me if words were to pass her lips.

'Enough,' I declare. 'What say you all?'

There follows some shrieking and frothing and making of worthwhile points in one or two instances. All puzzle over Blanche, wish to query if she has indeed taken a lover and Moses Grigg even suggests that whoever it is must have no vote about what we next should do. I put it to him that I am not seeking a formal vote, wish only to hear if others think my chosen action the right one or not. When Myhill shouts, 'Guilty' and others follow suit, I feel fully vindicated. It is not just what I think, my finding is not the consequence of bias.

'Do any say not guilty?' I enquire.

'Aye,' says Ha'penny.

'But you represent Obby. The side you take is neither here nor there. Anyone else?' Nobody else comes to the defence of the prisoner. He had few friends among us before his violent turn, so this absence of supporters is not a surprise. 'Guilty, Mr Pursglove,' I say. 'Now I must sentence you.' He looks most angry, spits and laughs and says that this is like no courtroom on God's Earth. I tell him it is exactly that. A court in session on the outer limits of God's Earth. 'You don't like being found guilty of attempted murder, Mr Pursglove, but that is the finding.' I look away from him for a moment, trying to think what sentence I can give that will be conclusive. 'Bring Mr Pursglove to my quarters,' I ask of Darius. Realise as I do, that I have slipped into the language of the ship we are no longer captive to.

I go to my small wooden lodge ahead of the prisoner and, shortly afterwards, Double Dee escorts Obadiah to it as I have bid him to do.

'Wait,' I say when they are on the threshold. I go inside and come out quickly, pistol in hand. 'The sentence must be death, Mr Pursglove.' I see Double Dee look surprised, half a laugh on his face, then I place my gun to Obadiah's stomach. Pull on the trigger. He stumbles forward, cries out with the agony my gunshot has wrought in his guts. Others who have gathered around are equally surprised but they shouldn't be. All said guilty and Edgar's boat idea was daft. I have bloodied Mr Pursglove terribly with my pistol shot, but to my surprise, he seems intent on not

45

dying. He talks and talks, raving at me and at Blanche although she remains out of sight. He is swearing loudly about young Hooper, that he should have torn the boys head away from his shoulders when chance he had. And he thinks something demotic came over us on board that ship, changed the menfolk and made them unduly lustful. Another has defiled his wife, or former wife, he seems to have forgotten everything he has signed. His raving is insane. He clearly has no idea that I am the one who has taken himself inside Blanche, done so only since we have been on the island. I swear I shared no such intimacy with her before the dissolution of their marriage.

'Die,' I shout at Obby. 'I sentenced you to death, so die, dammit.'

6.

This morning the sun shines brightly. A new day whether I handled business judicially or foolishly in the evening past. This is how New Poplar presents itself, bright and fresh, excepting the single thunderstorm we have endured. Strange to relate that Blanche has repeatedly thanked me for shooting her husband. Not a compliment heard by many men, I venture. And nor that I'm necessarily the first. She said it last night while the old bugger was still clinging to life, and she has said it many times since. About two hours it took him to succumb, and gone he finally has. I hope the Lord judges Blanche and I fairly in the light of all that has occurred. Recognises that the annulment counted for something. I thrust no gun in his stomach while Obadiah was signing it. The Lord will have seen that. I didn't contrive it; everything that came after just happened. Shooting was my decision, not really my fault. Obby made me have to.

And I do not believe that having carnal relations with Blanche affected the decision one way or the other. He was a troublemaker, that was at the heart of it. This morning, Moses has told me that Blanche took herself into Darius's bed last night. It caused a bit of a stir in the longhouse. I find myself thinking there is more to the former Mrs Pursglove than I have previously understood. Not that I can tell what it means. Perhaps she will prove a divisive figure in our small community, as it also comes to me that she might be of great relief to the men in our party. I shall direct my personal prayers upon the matter this evening although experience tells us these are Earthly woes. I expect we must wait for our Lord's return if we are ever to learn His opinion on that one. When He judges us, for that is to be the cornerstone of that glorious day, the purpose of the second coming. Lodowicke has told me so.

As a few of us—myself, and others with greater direct experience— are planning how to embark on our agricultural endeavours, our little

The John and Lodowicke

village receives a visitation. A remarkable event. A bird a few inches higher than our own Double Dee walks into the clearing. It has the longest, thinnest stick legs, knees which flex back to front, and a round body like a feathered pillow, a very large pillow at that. The size of five fattened geese, I could swear to it. The creature's neck is narrow and incredibly long. More giraffe than stork, except this one's neck looks brittle. Two legs not four, that is also true. And the face is a laugh. Feathered, with big saucer eyes—black as a sooty coal hole—looking down at us in ignorant enquiry.

Septimus asks me if it is for the pot, and I like the idea, but Hastings holds up his hand. 'Observe!' he says to all who have come to look at the creature. 'This fellow has no fear. What does this salient point tell us, gentlemen?'

It tells me that the bird is as stupid as it looks, then McConnell speaks before I can say my piece. 'I did not see those footprints as you did, Ha'penny, but hearing you and Septimus declare them real and numerous has convinced me.'

I look squarely at McConnell. Hastings nods at him as if asking him to continue his train of thought. For myself, I cannot see any connection between the shy people of whom only a small footprint or two have been observed and this flightless bird.

'If this were a hunted animal it would be scared of us. Would not dare to venture this close to our settlement. It is either the case...' McConnell looks down at his shoes as if working out a most complicated mathematical puzzle. '...that those indigenous to this isle know something about the bird, the poisonous qualities of its meat, so they do not eat it—have not for many a generation and bird and man live in accommodation with each other—or an alternative explanation might be that they revere the bird.'

'Revere?' I enquire.

Hastings takes over. 'If they have designated a god-like status to the bird, then they would never kill or harm it. The bird would not know the reasoning, but either way, the consequence is that the beast knows no fear. Not of people like us.'

'But we've a proper god, don't worship no bird, so we can eat it!' shrieks Moses Grigg.

'I adjudge,' says Ha'penny Hastings, 'that it would be a mistake to murder the god of this island's other inhabitants before we have so much as laid eyes upon them, nor begun to form a view of how we are all to live in harmony. They were here first and have a rightful claim to the fruits of New Poplar. We hope to share with them, Moses, not to steal from or upset them.'

I understand Mr Hasting's reasoning although he is talking like a mayor when that's my job. And he goes about it in a terribly namby-pamby fashion; I'm not sure what I'm to think of it all. When we find the primitives, I hope to avoid a fight, want to lead them to the Lord and they will most certainly have to live under the English flag. That isn't just my idea, it's what we agreed on The John and Lodowicke. Spreading civilisation as has been done in the Americas. Hasting's notion that we should first conform to pagan ways, revering a flightless bird that is doubtless tasty, seems a strange way to proceed.

Mr McConnell reminds me again of the alternative reason: the meat of the creature could be poisonous. Improbable: it is bird not snake. In the end Nicholas Myhill clobbers a couple of gulls and we allow Hastings to usher the silly, gangly bird out of Charlestown and back into the forest. Gull tastes all right but I've eaten a good few. Intrigue for this new creature hovers near my tongue.

Part Two

7.

'See here!' shouts Moses Grigg. 'Would you look at this!'

I trot up to where he stands, the smallest of clearings in this dense forest. The first thing that strikes me is the colour. A rich blue, dazzling even, it is not a shade I recall seeing back home. It shines with an intensity surprising in a blue so dark. If I'd seen the like before I should have remembered it. Beautiful and unexpected, everything else on this island is a leaf green, dark and light, they are of every hue. All the greens and now this. Then I take in what it is I look upon. The blue things. They are houses, erected in the clearing. Tiny houses barely big enough for a child to play inside. Not even close to the height of a proper dwelling place. I look into my companion's face; momentarily believe he has played a trick on me. Brought me to a place where this remarkable find has been set up just to astonish me. Blue Houses in a forest clearing; no tree stumps or sign of digging or felling. It feels like Moses is having a little joke at my expense. Yet it cannot be so; Grigg has never been more than fifty yards in front or behind me on our trek here from Charlestown. This small piece of forest has long been cleared, all sign of tree felling erased. Dug up and covered over the last stump.

The island we have called New Poplar is not drawn upon any maps save those which Ha'penny Hastings sketched in our day of sailing around it. And while we were seeking safe harbour, we saw only the lush and large-leafed trees. They are abundant, right to the top of all but this isle's highest point. Not that it is a mountainous isle, hills undulate across it, the slopes are not steep. We have charted little; Hastings is beginning that task. And it was he who saw footprints within days of our arrival, but when we went looking for our fellow islanders more than a week ago, we found none. Hastings pointed at scuff marks he believed to be footprints but the rest in our party were more than sceptical. There were few such blemishes in the mud, indicative of nothing very clear to me, nor to any but Hastings who seemed to wish it true. And then this—tiny little houses—I want to laugh. Where do their parents live? We have seen no people, no sign of people barring those fabled footprints. Not another hint that we are other than alone. Until now.

We step closer to the make-believe houses. The wood has been crafted, painted, stones placed carefully as part of a thoughtful construction. They cannot be naturally blue, I have never seen such a shade upon a rock, and it is identical to the colouring of the wood. No blue trees on this island, I can vouch confident of that one. Say the same to Grigg and then quickly feel some doubt. Blue trees? I don't think so. And if it is blue paint, how do the people who built these houses mix it? A radiant blue like London has never seen. I tell Grigg that it looks a treat. 'Moses, lad, these could make our party the perfect home, were we all no more than half our current size.'

'What do you think it means?' asks Moses.

'It's a beautiful sight.'

'But who put them here, Mayor?'

If it was the lost tribes of the Israelites, then they were far smaller than the bible tells. 'Hastings is correct. There were people here before us after all.'

Moses nods back like a puppy, must have concluded the same.

'Proper craftsmen, and yet I'd hazard they are not people such as us.'

'Not God-fearing? You think we're in for a fight.'

'With their parents, Grigg. It would be wicked to fight children. And, in all honesty, I am unsure if God is pleased or displeased with how we have torn into the Americas. These people are unlike us for they build a little village for their children. Strange ways, but let us offer a hand of friendship and see how they grasp it.'

Moses looks a little puzzled, may have been hoping for riches. For plunder. There is many a Muggletonian as struggles to understand the strength of the message of the prophets, so shrouded in talk of angels and creation are the texts. And I have thought this a land where anything might grow; two more heavy downpours have beset us since the destructive first. I am proud to say, the longhouses we have built—not as pretty to look at as these little blue houses—keep us dry. Overlapping leaves have proven the simple answer. There is an abundance of large-leafed trees on our island. Seeing these tiny houses gives me pause to wonder what other astonishments might be revealed to us. Offerings from those who have drawn off this land for generations, perhaps? I am

God Help the Connipians

not a man for thieving, and that is how I look upon the conquistadors' every step. We shall be better than those Spanish. Do unto others and all the rest of it.

'You think they've gone into the forest?' asks Moses.

'They might be sleeping in their houses, or they might be standing in front. Perhaps we cannot see them, for these people are the same dazzling shade of blue as the little houses they have made.'

Moses Grigg looks at me like I have gone mad. And that too is a possibility. So small and so blue the constructions before our eyes. Houses that lodge far beyond my ability to reason how they came to be here. I want to meet the people who made them. And what if they are not children's houses? It could be an island of little people, and they will think me an ogre, for I might simultaneously knock head and feet into opposite walls were I to lie in the smaller of their homes.

* * *

'Hear the man, hear the man,' yells Moses as many in our party laugh at my assertion. Not Ha'penny Hastings; he is not a frivolous man, whatever the truth of his relations with Tabitha—married or sinner—he looks at this world from beneath a thoughtful brow.

'And be the people blue, also?' asks Septimus.

I can only shake my head. 'We saw no people but stumbled across no fewer than nine dwelling houses.'

'No people. Might they be gone. Passed on to whatever heaven befits people from these parts?'

'Little heaven for tiny elves,' shouts Rags to much laughter.

'They looked as if they were being lived in. As if some people had recently laid their heads upon beds of leaves. We saw the pulp of fruit on small raised sidings in the central room within two of the houses. Very strange to intrude on a world so small.'

Many in our group cannot stop laughing at the words I say, that Moses Grigg says also. To enter the houses, we had either to stoop low like crippled men or shuffle on our knees. Felt a little foolish in the doing of it. The notion that there are people here no bigger than infants, amuses all we tell it to. I wish I could swear to it but we saw none. Saw only the places where we think they reside.

'Could you see how the blue had been washed upon the wood or the leaf, Mayor Brook, Mr Grigg.' McConnell, like Hastings, takes a scholarly interest, where all others appear only amused.

'It took us by surprise, sir...'

'It did that,' Moses interrupts me. 'A more piercing blue you never saw.'

'...he speaks the truth. It puzzled me to the core; I examined their craftsmanship as best I could. Stick and leaf, stone too but not in large quantity—I believe they had crushed it and then managed to reform it, not like our bricks, but of that intent—all were of the same rich colour. Blue that shines, catches the eye instantly. How can a paint or dye stay upon leaf? I have never seen the like. It was truly extraordinary.'

'And within their houses,' asks McConnell, 'were their beds and table also painted.'

'Blue. The walls within were blue. I did not take in other colours which they had put...'

'White! I saw it!' Moses again shouts over me. He did not point this out when we were there, and I stare at my young companion. Not disbelieving, unable to confirm is the one that stalls me. 'An entryway into some other anteroom within one house. At the back. It was white. I saw it.'

It might be that his powers of observation exceed mine; however, I fear his excitement paints a false picture. I saw nothing white, nothing light. Everything was the same rich blue, contrasting with the deep green of the forest which surrounded the tiny settlement.

'And when are we to meet these little people?' asks Tabitha, asks it of her man, Hastings, for it is well known that he has speculated more than all others about the primitives who we might find on lands this far from Christendom.

'I think...' Ha'penny walked beside me, into the centre of our assembled group to speak these words. '...men who can make paint must be clever, able, one way or another. These two—our mayor and young Moses—have entered their homes. Whether an acuity of smell, or an eye for the slightest movement, I think they will already know about us. Even about our curiosity to be in contact with them. We must not arouse their fear. If...' He scans his audience with a sceptical eye. '...I say if because we have seen no sight of them thus far, and if they have spied upon us, they will know us to be taller than they are. And by a measure advantageous to us. That must frighten them...'

'No, no, no,' Myhill breaks into Hasting's musings. 'How can there be a land of men so small. These two have stumbled upon their children's houses. Somewhere in those woods lie bigger uns. Surely it is so?'

'I think not,' replies Ha'penny. 'Where in this world do children live apart from their parents, from any adult at all. Why construct properties for those who will outgrow them.'

'Here!' declares Myhill. 'On New Poplar. This is where it is done. Houses for children. You have heard the evidence. Little people, my eye. The good Lord made men as could take the apples from the lower branches and no smaller. Isn't that so? We're all done in God's image. That's always been His way of making us.'

'Are there not dwarves in our own lands?'

This line of argument from Hastings prompts laughter in all assembled, a wry smile of my own, and I have seen the diminutive size of those Blue Houses. 'Dwarves is an aberration,' shouts Rags. 'Not men as our God intended them to grow. Tough luck for them but they're a proper oddity. Not a race of people at all.'

'Maybe, Rags. Your words maybe wise. But they arise from what we have known before. The old world.' Hastings is getting into his stride. 'We always thought an unknown land might be full of surprises. Little people may be just the first of them.'

'And when do we go after them?' shouts Septimus, echoing Tabitha's earlier comment to which Hastings has already added caution.

'If they have not come to us within a month of today, I propose we set out to find them. And we must do so in a spirit of friendship.'

This is Hastings declaring a course of action and he isn't the mayor of anywhere. I like the spirit of friendship he advocates. 'Hear, hear,' I lay upon it. 'One month to the day.'

8.

It has come to this. After the debacle with Obadiah I have, following a string of requests, agreed to put Blanche on trial. I don't like it and fear enormously what may come to light. McConnell and Hastings have agreed to act as before, McConnell defending the lascivious lady, Hastings declaring why she has done wrong. She might hang; I shan't shoot her. Cannot.

'Put the men on trial too!' shouts Rags. Tabitha is nodding at that.

I wonder if I should announce there must be no women in my courtroom, it's a most difficult decision to call. For myself, I have come to respect women more than The Good Book advises I should. Nor is my courthouse a room from which I can bar entry. It's just the open space between the first two longhouses ever we erected.

'We cannot try men for lusting,' I tell the ladies. 'Should I do so, there would not be one left standing on this Earth.' The pair of them stare back at me as if unable to see the reason in my assertion. I turn away to declare my courtroom in session. Ask Ha'penny to begin. To raise before us the wrongs of which Blanche stand accused.

'Mister Mayor, gentlefolk of New Poplar,' begins Ha'penny Hastings, 'it distresses me to reveal all that has gone on here in Charlestown in the first days of our colony. We are all familiar with the unfortunate situation. Twelve were the number of ladies setting forth from the shores of the great River Thames a little over one year ago. That aside, thirty-three men was always a conundrum, yet not one different to that faced

The John and Lodowicke

by many colonies in their earliest days. We all know that it is men who have the more adventurous spirits. Take first to the seas. Sadly, since our own departure from the banks of that cherished river, we have recorded twelve deaths, and nine of those from among our womenfolk. This might also explain why so few ladies choose to venture so far from home. Their womanly intuition giving them insight into their delicate natures. And we also know from word back from the Americas that many might thrive, if they but make it through the journey out. We will always be grateful to those willing...'

'Get on with it!' shouts Tabitha, and it strikes me as most disloyal for his own wife to be critical of his expounding. For my part, I find it interesting to hear how others in the party see the state we have come to.

'In good time, my dear,' he says to laughter.

I note that McConnell has no smile on his face, and Blanche looks as downtrodden as she did the day Obadiah tried to throttle her. It comes to me that trying a lady for promiscuity could be a hypocrisy. Condemning her for behaving as men cannot help themselves. Her actions have shocked me but I enjoyed my half hour. Might have been the best of times on New Poplar, bewildering as it is to dwell upon. Like realising one has been someone else for the day.

'Blanche Otham, as we again call her, travelled down here to New Poplar still named Blanche Pursglove. Betrothed to Mister Obadiah Pursglove. I believe Mr Muggleton himself attended their marriage although I was not present. A hearsay on my part which some of you may be able to verify.'

A couple in our small throng wave their arms, their hats, in concurrence. Vouchsafe that Lodowicke Muggleton was present when Obby married Blanche.

'On our journey here, just a day before the discovery of New Poplar, we learned that the then Mrs Pursglove broke her marriage vows, Davy Hooper doing with her that which all present must heartily disapprove of, and Obadiah took most personal. We believed it was a rape that he did upon her and for the doing of it, young Hooper lost his life. Walked out on a plank into the deep of the Pacific Ocean. Subsequent to all that, Mr and Mrs Pursglove did annul the said marriage. After this, but before any other, she did again declare that she was having relations, although not with whom. When Mr Pursglove attacked her as a husband might be deemed entitled to do, he was tried for her attempted murder. You, sir...' Ha'penny Hastings looks squarely into my own two eyes. '...declared that the marriage was properly over and he had no such rights. He received the highest possible sentence for the crime he committed upon her, if crime it really was. Now, not so much as a month later we have heard that more men have been able to engage in lewd acts, the most intimate of couplings, with her, and Blanche here has accused none of them of rape. It seems she is more promiscuous than a community of gentlefolk can make room for. She is putting the men in a quandary. Four fights we have had to break up in the last twenty-four hours. Fights over who will be in her bed tonight. This cannot go on.'

'And is it your view, Mr Hastings,' I ask, 'that the only resolution that could last would be banishment? Banishment or a hanging.'

Both ladies shout, 'Shame!' and it sounds rich to me. They ought not to be in favour of her conduct or men might look to them for similar comfort. I admit, inwardly, that I was first, excluding Hooper, to take advantage of her irresolute heart, but that was just the way my loins took it upon themselves. It was never my judgement that I should. The charms of Blanche Otham are basic: she lets men do as they will.

'It is not for me to pass a sentence, Mister Mayor. I believe that so long as she is within our community, the difficulties she has already caused will be repeated.'

'Mr McConnell?' I see that he is whispering with Blanche as I call him to speak. A surprise for, to the best of my knowledge, he is a contained man. I do not believe he has had relations with her, would do so with none unless it was within a declared and scrupulous union.

'Mister Mayor, this is a delicate matter, and one beyond any law that we can lay claim to in this colony. I believe the charges against Blanche Otham to be unclear. Many might disapprove some or all of her alleged behaviour; we know that the same happens back home, on Drury Lane, every night of the week. We never hung or banished the...' McConnell coughs quietly into his fisted hand. '...ladies culpable of that conduct. If they did not appear to live among us, it was an illusion. They were Londoners as were we. For this reason...'

As he talks, both the other ladies are cheering. Even Blanche wears a smile that has not been upon her to this point. I must think this through very carefully: I'd been upsetting myself with the rights and wrongs of it all, not dwelling on it as clearly as Edgar McConnell lays it all out. Exactly what the law of the land allows. I intend New Poplar to be properly ordered, not some maverick state. Nor is it clear in my mind whether the laws applicable in London must be applied here. I think they probably should because we have raised a flag, but perhaps their application is more tenuous than that. We could make our own laws, bespoke for our unique situation. I've no idea what they should be. Letting Blanche off, I'd happily plump for. Her first-come-first-served approach to carnal relations surprised me; however, I'd rather leave it for Him to judge down the line. Keep it out of the mayor's order of business.

'...and so, Mister Mayor, the delicate matter which I believe must allow us all to embrace her back into our fledgling community is the news she has only now agreed to share. Blanche Otham is with issue. A child within gestates. Pioneer: it could even be his name. We should be hanging the future of our new land were we so foolish as to take that spiteful course of action. No matter how we adjudge her promiscuous behaviour, the results may prove inspiring to us all.'

'What!' This is flabbergasting. She had no babies with big strong Obadiah. And she might be carrying the son I briefly dreamed would come of my own coupling with her. 'Whose is it, Blanche?' I ask, swallowing hard on the saying of her name. Wanting to hear it is mine, but fearful of what such an announcement will do to my standing with all the fellows here.

'How the fuck would I know,' she lobs back, and many men hang their heads. I look at her levelly. If it isn't Hoopers it is most likely mine. And if we were both firing blanks, there are plenty more who came after.

* * *

I lie upon my night-time bed, pleased with how well-crafted it is. These London carpenters have, in no time at all, taught themselves how best to work the new types of wood they have found on New Poplar. Their role here resembles that which they had before, and they have adapted well. Purpose and skills both aligned. For myself, I am still known as Mayor, but it is with a smile upon the face of each man as they call it out. Know that I am deficient in those qualities of leadership and authority which might have made it a good fit.

I concluded that we should put Blanche in stocks, that we would build a set in which she would spend a couple of days. Make an example of her. Others said no and so I relented. This carrying of child ensured she must remain among us, no gallows and no banishment to the chance of the Southern Seas or the far side of our still-unexplored island. So excitable was everyone to know who is the father of our colony's first child that questions rained down upon Blanche. All this occurred regardless of any order I tried to bring. I think the mayor of old Poplar would have handled it better.

'Well, it isn't Obadiah Pursglove's,' she declared most forcefully. 'It could have been snot which propelled from that man's pillicock, so hard did once we try. To no fucking avail whatsoever.'

'Then whose?' And I must report the two ladies shouted this the loudest. McConnell and Hastings looked around proudly; I am as certain that neither gentleman has lain with her as I am of the Lord's imminent return. Others seemed ruddier of complexion, the more so for the talk of laying with Blanche. One or two even tried proudly to declare how many times they'd spilled themselves within her.

I saw a couple pointing at me. At my blushed cheeks. I only had to point back. And that was when Blanche said it like it was. 'Anybody's and everybody's,' she said. 'A true child of Muggletonians. Of Hooper's very likely. Or every man jack since the boy's been a-drowned.'

She didn't look at McConnell or Hastings—none Muggletonians—it isn't theirs. Odd to dwell upon how weak the rest of us have proven ourselves to be. There you have it: our code is very particular, sadly it does not make us better men. Blanche has a certain something, it can lure a man's staff. And where that goes the rest will follow.

Now all that is behind us. Mr McConnell has given up his accommodation so that Blanche may have a room of her own. Whether it keeps her on the straight and narrow or becomes the world's most far-flung bordello, only the coming days will determine. It gladdens my heart that there will be a child born to this land. The very first, and surely others will follow in some fashion or another. If the pilgrims who sailed America had similar goings on, they didn't tell it, and it will be for the best if we keep quiet about some aspects of our own strange passage from old world to new. I think it whether the baby looks like me or Darius Dencourt. Our first born will be a child of us all: that is how Blanche says it, and I am pleased to think likewise. We shall raise the little lad collectively. Girl, if needs must.

9.

We are still a week away from the search party which Hastings declared and I approved. The quest to find those with whom we share this isle. While out foraging, Myhill, McConnell and I made three discoveries. This was but an hour out from Charlestown, we are still charting our near environs, attempting to detail it to Hasting's satisfaction. There is much that is strange and new, and our examination of this isle is not one which my two more learned friends wish to hurry. I was looking specifically for the nests of the funny gulls which we see flying over the forests, a fish in their mouths from time to time, surely taking the nourishment to their chicks. I am not certain how good they are to eat— one or more of our number has a fit of vomiting every day—yet we have no chickens. As I ventured into the forest I stumbled across a laughable sight. Birds that look like they have dressed for dinner. Not our massive flightless giant that still walks into camp now and then, this was a squat bird, feet but no legs, and equally incapable of getting off the ground. McConnell came to my cry, saw the creatures at which I laughed.

'Oh, that is a surprising sight,' he concurred. And then he proceeded to teach me what it is I had found: a bird he has only seen drawings of before today. 'This, Mr Brook, is a colony of penguins. I'm not sure what

The John and Lodowicke

they are doing deep in the woods of New Poplar. It is most certainly worth documenting. Quite a turn up.'

He went on to explain that they are birds that swim in preference to flight. There are none in the northern hemisphere; McConnell told me that earlier explorers found penguins living in the southerly reaches of Spanish America. He believes they might live right across these southern seas. I asked what a bird that cannot fly and likes to swim was doing so far from the sea. A chain, maybe two, from it. And they do not walk but waddle on their two webbed feet. Our bigger visitor to Charlestown—the rotund and flightless bird—has long stick legs and backward-bending knees. His stride is four times my own; these comical penguins can only shuffle.

Myhill asked a question or two, and none cleverer than 'Can we eat the buggers?' Mr McConnell confirmed that they were fit for the pot. Said he'd heard tell that the taste is a fine one, enjoyed by Ferdinand Magellan, an explorer who might have sailed but a few hundred miles north of where we now stood. A taste unknown on the other side of the equator to that which we have come, and so they are an untried delicacy for most of civilisation. He couldn't fathom why they have hobbled across the forest floor, had only ever heard of them making camp on rocks and beaches. And icebergs!

Myhill clubbed himself a couple and said it was easier than shelling peas. They looked good enough to me, I didn't have a stick to hand, so kicked a couple to death while their fellow penguins looked on. Nice cut of clothing on them but truly stupid-looking faces. McConnell declined to kill any, even indicating that Hastings might not approve our action. It is nothing to do with him. I am the Mayor of New Poplar, and won't be turning away food for hardworking Englishmen.

Arriving back at our village on the edge of the world, I pass my two birds to Rags, and Myhill does likewise. We tell her it is penguin, that the taste to come will be a good one.

'You needn't have bothered,' says Rags. 'Double Dee tired of watching a week's worth of food strutting around Charlestown. He killed Big Flightless with his bare hands, told me to roast him tonight and cure all the meat I can from the soft-looking creature.'

'Oh Rags,' I say in reply, 'Mr Hastings will be most upset by this. He didn't want us to kill that one until we understood where it fits into the beliefs of those who have been living here before ever we arrived.'

'We don't need a mayor who thinks like a baby. Darius hasn't seen the Blue Houses of which you speak every damned evening but he has understood that no one living in them could match him in a fight...'

'Rags, we're not for fighting...'

'Well, we certainly aren't against a bit of eating. Hastings be damned.

We didn't leave England to eat berries and mushrooms and skinny seagulls until death becomes us. Not I, and nor did you, I venture.'

'No, no,' I concur, 'and that is why I brought you the penguins. The flightless bird—Dodus Struthio, as Ha'penny Hastings has taken to calling the creature—which became our first visitor, I don't think it will prove good fortune to kill...'

Now Mr McConnell interrupts. It seems no one has respect for the mayor since learning that I laid with Blanche like the rest of them. 'Mr Hastings understands the primitive mind and he believed it most unwise to kill the creature while its status among the natives remains unknown to us.'

'You bookish types never know what tastes good, do you?' says Rags. 'There will be some on your plate if you wish, or more of the hard tack, a bit of wild cabbage, if you can't eat Funny Walk. And before he killed it, Double Dee said there are many of them on the island. We might have been looking at different ones on the many visits we thought the fellow made. The little local boys in their tiny little houses of blue can worship one of the others.'

It is more than an hour after these conversations and debates that we come to eat the food which Rags has cooked. Hastings is back at Charlestown by this time, and he shows his displeasure with the turn of events. Takes a little of the strange bread Tabitha made a day or two back, pressing the heads of a grass we do not know, but which hold a similar shape to the wheat in the fields of England. Larger heads by about threefold, but very similar in their general appearance. Hastings says he shall eat it in his cabin. Before taking his leave, he berates me for letting it come to pass—the slaughter of the flightless bird—and I didn't. Never sanctioned the killing; the bird was done-in while I was away in the forest. I try to tell him this, say that we need to have a deputy mayor in place for when I'm away. He ignores that, looks as cross as he did before I explained it wasn't me.

Ha'penny then tells Tabitha not to eat the cooked meat and she only laughs. Not wifely at all, is my take on that little exchange. 'Muggletonian food,' she says. 'More fool you for adopting the ways of primitives. And the creature doesn't look like no sacred bird. Looks a bit daft, skinny legs and gormless face.'

I won't intervene in their marital spat; agree with her more than him. It is, however, always unpleasant to see the trousers scolded by the skirt. McConnell eats none of the big bird either. The rest of us tuck in. It's a bit of a feast. I can only report that flightless bird tasted quite delicious. A richness that reminded me of venison, and that is a funny thing to say of any kind of a bird.

The John and Lodowicke

10.

Eight of us have set out on this expedition of purpose: we plan to meet with our fellow islanders. And a convoluted party we make. Hastings insisted that one of our womenfolk should join us, we are not a war party. I endorsed his plan and then only Blanche would agree to come, the other two fearful of what monsters we might encounter. Ha'penny and Edgar McConnell insisted they must be in the group, and I was all in favour. I'm finding their counsel wiser than that of my Muggletonian brethren. Less apt to bend every observation towards what they have already hoped to see. Moses, Septimus and Myhill are here; they volunteer for anything, good men all. That Double Dee accompanies us is a worry. He may prove temperamentally unsuited, and yet there is a chance we will find hostile people—small ones who live in Blue Houses by the looks of things—and if it comes to fighting, Darius is the man.

We take ourselves to the Blue Houses that Moses and I came across weeks ago. The only ones we have seen, and we wonder if people of a size to live within will be there this time. Perchance we discovered only abandoned houses, but that is not how it felt. Ripened fruit—and of a type we've yet to see growing in the wild—resting within a few of the houses.

The forest is more difficult to navigate than we imagined, so much growth has there been in these short weeks. The path which we cut previously requires hacking and snagging once more, quite a little battle just getting through the strange ivies and brambles of this land. If there is another way, I'd like to learn it. The trees are dense most of the way, uneven in height and some are taller than any I have seen in the old country. Across the forest, high or low, a range of broad-leafed climbers have formed a canopy. The forest has a roof and we are beneath it, not party to any direct sunlight.

McConnell is very interested in the plethora of different plants, and I have to grant him that the Creator has been most inventive. We see brightly coloured birds poking their heads out to watch us pass. They must live, nest most probably, in the sunlight above this rich carpet of leaf.

'Give me a leg up to the first branches,' says Moses. 'I can take a shifty and shout back what it all looks like.'

'I must clamber up there with you, Mr Grigg,' says our botanical man, Mr McConnell.

We lift up both—by we, I mean Darius—and then they climb like children in a Kentish apple tree. What a pair. We hear laughter and even a little mumbled chatter between the two of them. Moses agile while

Edgar is simply determined. They rise up out of sight. For what feels to be an inordinate time, we can only wait. Blanche tugs upon my sleeve and asks if I am sure they are all right.

'Well, no one has fallen down.'

At that moment, an upside-down head pops out from high in the leafy ceiling directly above where we stand. 'Ha ha,' says Moses Grigg. 'This is quite a sight, Mister Mayor. Spectacular.' He draws out this word one syllable at a time, making a point of how apt a term it is for the sight they see although it is not a word which he can quite get his tongue around. 'Trul-lee spec-tac-ee-lar,' he repeats.

'Pray, what is up there?' asks Hastings.

'Little berries grow up here, sir. A grand harvest and then some. Mr McConnell says they are plants growing upon plants. We see them rooting into the branching of the high trees. How they came to live on top a-forest, he cannot rightly guess. They are navy blue in colour. Looking like the bilberries we see on heathland back in merrie England.'

'Extraordinary,' I let out. And that has been a truth of so much in this land. Of even our own behaviour. Grown men climbing trees; Blanche obliging the men of our crew in contrast to anything she got up to in Poplar. Bilberries in the treetops.

* * *

Moses and I look into each other's faces with puzzlement. We have come across the houses. Or some houses but it feels like we are being tricked. They are the same small size and piercing blue colour that we saw before. Something about them is different. Firstly, there are six together in a cluster and we counted nine last time we were here. Can't imagine that we both miscounted or misremembered how many there were. And the clearing looks about right, but not the positioning of the Blue Houses. They seem to be where they weren't, and based upon the knowledge I have gleaned up to this point in my life, I believe houses are the type of thing to stay motionless. I don't like for them to be on the go.

'We've found some but they might be other than those which we found before. The forest mostly looks the same everywhere,' says Moses. And I concur with him, found myself thinking on the self-same lines.

Ha'penny Hastings inspects the exterior of the first house as if he is a craftsman himself which he is not. I think the similarity to our previous find has induced us all to imagine these houses will be devoid of occupants. He comments upon the richness of hue, how extraordinary the colouring really is, and puts his nose up close against the sloping roof. The wood is not fresh cut—a contrast with our own cabins—the smell not dissimilar to that of the forest we traversed to get here. These really are tiny little dwelling places and we cannot yet picture people who might live inside, or if we can, it is people who belong in a fable, not the world we inhabit.

Then Hastings stops, frozen in position in front of the house. A finger raised in the air. 'Listen!' he says. And we all hear it now. A strange clicking sound. Not once but over and over. It is as an old maid might tut-tut at children who displease her, or even the lip-smacking pleasure one might attain when eating good food after great hunger. Not words or whispers, just lips pursed together and apart with a little air's expulsion. 'We are not alone,' he states.

'Hello?' As Blanche asks the question, her eyes are darting all over. 'Hello?' Never before have I seen her so tentative. Might be saying it to the trees of the forest, or to the Blue Houses themselves. Speaks a greeting without expectation of reply. And nor does one come but for the curious clicking which continues. Unchanged. We must all sense that we are the intruders. And I grant, it is a feeling far stronger than any I felt at these or similar houses weeks back when Moses and I poked our heads inside. A deed we have yet to do today. Then the clicking sound seems to swell, to grow in intensity, and I start to wonder if it is in answer to Blanche's query. 'Hello,' she says once more. And then our party falls collectively silent.

The houses do not have windows in their sides, and the openings through which we might enter have blue drapes hanging over them. Made of woven grasses by the looks of it, all coloured by dye or paint. Or maybe there are long blue grasses on this island, although we have yet to see such amazements for ourselves. It seems an implausible explanation but even seeing small Blue Houses in a forest clearing feels more like a dream than a waking truth.

And now the clicking within the houses has ceased.

'We come in peace,' I tell the still air.

A little clicking is heard. Expelled, I think, from a single mouth.

'Not come here to harm you. Haven't done that. Not us.'

Click, it says.

'Would you like to come outside and meet us? Or may we enter your little house? It's very nice; I like the colour best. A pretty shade of blue. I'm the mayor of our village, perhaps your mayor could come forward, we can have a little chat. I'm not here to take his place. I will be pleased to meet him. Make his acquaintance, as they say.'

I think I'm rambling a bit, so I stop. Not even a click of reply have we heard; perhaps the person who was making the sound expects me to say more, although the likelihood that English is their tongue is remote. Eventually, a string of clicks come into our ears but there is nothing in their random arrangement which I can interpret. The houses look nice but I worry there are only imbeciles within. Clicking isn't a real language.

God Help the Connipians

Double Dee looks around impatiently. 'Coming, ready or not,' he shouts as he steps into the doorway.

'You'll frighten them,' shrieks Ha'penny. And after this shouted exchange, the clicking from within the nearest Blue House sounds incessant while never actually loud. Clicks and plops of tongues and lips moving at a pace, many mouths chattering away with never a word formed.

'The mayor goes first,' I say, with a hand upon Darius's shoulder. He concedes to my authority and I poke my head through the blue fronds that cover the door way, observe all I can in the filtered light.

I swear to it, no less than six pairs of eyes are staring back at me. Perhaps they can see clearer than me in the blue gloom, perhaps they cannot. The clicking has ceased. They are all directed at me. Blue eyes within Blue Houses.

'What you seeing in there,' shouts Darius. The eyes looking upon me do not waver, the clicking recommences. I believe they could be speaking to each other, doing it in a manner I have never heard from any of the people who travel through London town, nor those in the many ports I have visited as far apart as Tallinn and Batavia. Normal people don't click but these are as different as the moon is from the Earth we live upon.

'There are lots of them,' I whisper over my shoulder. 'Tiny people. I can't rightly say if they are children or not. The light isn't good.' I hear quiet words exchanged behind me, Hastings up to his pontificating. 'All girls, I do believe.' I say this because they wear skirts. Pale legs protruding. Their clothing is blue like all else in this new and tiny world we have stumbled across.

'Right,' says Hastings with a gathered authority, 'Blanche and I should join you. Everybody else stay outside. Mayor Brook, tell them we have arrived on this island as friends, not adversaries.'

I look into the eyes which are staring back at me. Three of the girls huddle closely together, heads good as touching each other. The others stand alone. I have to say, these are the oddest girls. They don't really have hair on their heads—or only little wisps of it, as one might see atop a new-born's skull—the skin on every face looks surprisingly pale, white as London snowflakes, and I believe the blue hue to their skin is a result of the colour which surrounds us. The curious blue with which they have painted all manner of things. They wear blue wraps around themselves, skirts which are not as long as our women wear. Cover up what they must. Everything inside the house is blue. As I look upon the girls, I am able to conclude that they are not children. Their breasts testify to this, the clothing tight around their upper bodies. And one of them is impertinently unclothed on that part of herself, or perhaps I entered as she was a-dressing. 'Peace,' I say as levelly as I am able. Talking to staring eyes is not a straightforward thing. 'Peace to you. Peace from us. We come to share your island, not to take it.' I think I have said as I should but they give me no reason to think it understood. I click my tongue a little, make noises as might shoo away a cat from a granary and which sound similar to those they made. I see heads turn at this noise, hear a little replied clicking. If reply it be. Perhaps their clicking means no more than mine. Primitives with noises of fear or delight, no language at all. I cannot tell which but they look as dumb as penguins to me. I suppose sharing an island with morons will prove easier than it would were they clever devils.

'Good Lord,' says Blanche when she has come to stand beside me, taken in the sight within this Blue House. 'As small as you said they would be, John.' She nudges into my shoulder as she says it. 'And where's their hair?'

I wish Blanche did not treat me so familiar, I have told her that I don't want it known that I continue to use her for occasional release. It might make me appear a lesser man—or lesser mayor—in the eyes of the other men. 'I think it is all they've got,' I tell her.

'Do you think the men are in other houses?' says Ha'penny.

'Ask them,' I suggest. I can't make head or tail of it. A cluster of blue-clad girlies is far from what I thought to find. At least we shan't have need to fight them.

He starts to gesture towards himself and then at I. 'We are men,' states Ha'penny Hastings, as if he is an emissary to this new world, these odd-looking people. Then he pats a hand on the top of Blanche's head. 'Woman. Woman. You are all women.' He points a finger at the watching waifs, draws a semi-circle from left to right, singling out each. 'Women. Where are your menfolk?'

When he ceases to speak, the clicking recommences. If it contains a reply, we do not understand it.

'Many houses,' says Ha'penny Hastings. 'Are there men in the other houses?'

Click, click. If we knew what it meant we should be the most enlightened people on this Earth. Fancy finding a tribe such as this. Ugly of face with their tiny triangular noses a-centre of their taut cheeks, no hair but for a few thin strands. Their figures are of the attractive female form, drawn to half scale.

Blanche steps toward the face which stands alone. 'Hello,' she says, then stoops down and bunches her hair in her right hand. Tries to pass it to the tiny woman, let her hold hair the likes of which she can never before have seen. The funny creature clicks to herself with great rapidity and I hear sharp contrasts within her spittle-greased noises. The sound might be an expression of pleasure or could be born of confusion. Blanche seems more at ease than Hastings or I. 'Lovely hair, isn't it, dear?' she tells the little creature.

The clicking woman rocks her head upon her neck, lets the hair touch the end of her short nose.

'Could you take her hand?' asks Ha'penny. 'Ask the nice lady to show us around her village. Take us to where the menfolk live.'

Blanche seeks to do as Hasting's asks. With gentle fingers she removes the tiny hand from her hair and takes it in her own. It is extraordinary to look upon, fingers no bigger than those of a large lizard enwrapped in Blanches enormous hand. Not that we thought hers large until now. She points with her other hand at Hastings and I. 'Men,' she says. 'Take us to your men.' The funny native girl lets herself be led; I step backwards through the fronded entryway to let them come out together.

In the sunlight, the little one looks startled. Double Dee stands before her, and it could constitute a reason. He wears a thin black scarf a-top his head—it keeps the sun off his bald pate—he removes it as if greeting a lady of nobility. Still the little thing looks frightened. There are four others, as well as Darius, and they might terrify her although we mean no ill-will. She is no bigger than a three-year-old child, yet I am sure she is a fully grown woman.

The others from the Blue House have followed us out, and many more of these tiny women emerge from the other houses. They stand a distance, not a long one, but with more caution than the walking bird that visited Charlestown.

'Darius,' says Blanche, pointing once more and talking to the funny women who only click. 'He's a gentle giant, really. Aren't you, D-Boy?'

'They look like snake-people,' says Myhill, and it is the absence of hair and the tiny nose and ears as makes him say it. It starts the others laughing, even Mr McConnell, and that testifies to the tension we have felt until now. No fear on our part—we are bigger than they—it is the oddest happenstance of my whole life. Bar none.

Clickety-click goes the little lady-thing, perhaps frightened by the sound of laughter. Two from the house we were in come up close to Blanche, perhaps summonsed by the clicking. They make similar noises. Not clucking but closer to that than true speech. Then one throws up her arms, her little hand takes a hold of Myhill's shirt. As she clicks, we hear the slap of her hand upon his belly, but I imagine it must tickle more than hurt, so flimsy is her little stick-arm.

'Peace,' says Myhill, and it pleases me that he is not cross about the slap. We really shouldn't fight these funny folk. They are all girls and the tops of their heads come up short of our belly buttons. 'Peace to you, funny woman. I don't even want to fight your husband, so leave it off,

The John and Lodowicke

will you?' Then he takes her hand and puts it by her side, taking the other arm and smothering both into his person, pulling her into an embrace she cannot remove herself from. 'This be peace,' he announces to all around, and again many of our group laugh at the physical superiority he exploits, hugging the tiny girl, trying to cushion her head into his abdomen but she is too small. The gesture pulls her face a bit close to his cock, frankly, but it's only by accident. The girl is ridiculously small and that isn't Myhill's fault.

All the other little people are clicking now, and I find myself imagining that their peculiar noises have intent, meaning.

'Let her go,' says Hastings sharply.

Many of the girls from the other Blue Houses have come closer, crowding us, but their size gives us no cause to worry. It is my hunch that the clicking of the first summonsed the others. The volume of the sound confuses me. Never really loud, clicking is not a noise that can be shouted or called out. I cannot understand how such a string of splutters might be a language while thinking it probably is. These little women cannot fight us, however many they number, but they must have opinions about our arrival, I'm sure of it. They are exchanging thoughts, clicking about us and I don't like not knowing what they say. Are we welcome? Perhaps they find our faces as ugly as we do theirs.

Every single one of the little people is a woman. Woman or girl. I turn my head, look across the tops of all the bald heads that have assembled on the grassland between the Blue Houses. Maybe thirty of them, I see. If any are three feet tall, there is none as makes more than an inch or so above it. Many are smaller than that. All have the same sharp whiteness to the hue of their skin. The colour of freshly fallen snow. In the houses, they all looked a bit blue, out in the sunlight it is their wrapped clothing and the eyes of each girl that have that colour. Their skin is pale as if sunlight has never touched them, although they stand in it now. Intense in the clearing. I hope they are not unwell. Sickly. They sound chirpy enough. Or clicky might cover it better.

The blue of their skirts and wraps, even that of their eyes, is the same striking tone as their houses. I think all have a wisp of hair, but none has a head of it. Fair hair, I would guess. Transparent even. Not enough on a single girl to give any kind of covering. Everything looks clearer now than when I was peering at them inside the gloom of a Blue House. They remain just as extraordinary to me, I must say. Lots and lots of little ugly girls. Several of them wear only the skirt component of their garb, as did one who I saw inside the house we entered. Breasts bared. Small swell of tiny little pale-skinned boobies. I find this highly disconcerting. I did not catch her mid dressing; they are flaunting that which they should better cover up. It's only a few of them but I don't like it. Or I secretly like it;

65

however, I think that is the same thing. Because all these women are tiny with the strangest faces, I cannot guess their ages. Those who dress so brazenly are not children but they might be younger than most. The titties they show to the world do not look as if a babe has ever done its suckling there. Looking upon them feels wrong. Them for showing, and me for looking. Bosoms are a private matter, and this isn't that.

It comes to me that we should give them gifts, show our peaceful intent through such a gesture. I ask my fellow pioneers what we have which might impress them.

Darius places his black neck-scarf in the hands of the girl closest to him. Blanche takes a bracelet off her wrist, gives it to the girl who Myhill earlier held. She looks at it quite intently but then drops it on the ground.

Hastings tries. He has a small note book on which he writes. He shows the little woman closest to him how he makes marks upon the paper with a pencil, she is momentarily interested and then looks away. Not understanding the power of writing, I presume. Hastings writes in real words and their clicking is surely more primitive than that. Cannot be committed to paper. We have no common language, not with these funny little people. Not yet, I expect we'll figure theirs out in due course. His scribbling must be as alien to them as the girls' constant clicking is to us. We could be in a field of crickets judging from the sound of it. Big hairless crickets and a few of them showing their titties.

* * *

When we return to Charlestown, leaving all the little ladies we met to their Blue Houses—although Darius and Myhill were both for fetching some back; offered to carry a couple each but I forbade it when Hastings told me I must—we have more to tell our fellow settlers than they can easily believe.

'Speak the clicking talk,' they ask, but none of us can replicate the intricate sounds we heard.

'How can people live that small?' asks Tabitha. 'It's not the way God intended. Surely it isn't.'

Her supposed husband, Ha'penny Hastings, takes to answering this. A funny answer it is too, one I shall have to dwell upon to understand the sum total of its implications. 'There is only one God, so He must be the One that made them, can you see? Their existence is the proof of it. The issue is this, I think, they are not the children of Adam. Not of our stock. Similar to us as they no doubt appear, it might be that these are another creature altogether. In the way that bats are not birds. These little girls are not descendants of Adam and Eve, He has created them for a different purpose. As the mouse differs from the rat, so are these creatures wide of our mark. Not proper people at all, not exactly, they

The John and Lodowicke

just happen to look similar.'

The notion causes a small uproar. Myhill repeats his earlier conjecture that they are snakes. I can see why he says it but they aren't that. And in many respects, I thought they looked quite pleasant. Odd, but not loathsome in the manner of slithery snakes. That our learned Mr Hastings thinks them not really people at all is both outrageous and has a ring of truth.

'Did they bite you?' shouts Rags, and she looks at us sternly, as though we have failed in our mission. Finding people so unlike ourselves we may never live in true harmony.

'They are all tiny women. We asked to see the men but I do not believe they understood the question. They came out of every house in the little hamlet and not a single man showed his face. Tiny women who present no threat to us. They did not bite; showed no hostility whatsoever. Perhaps we frightened them. Mr Myhill here hugged more than one, including a tiny thing with its breasts bared.'

I wonder if I should not have said this, for all laugh and Nicholas goes quite red in the face. I considered it unnecessarily lustful of him at the time. These tiny girls confuse, for they have the weight of an infant, and faces that are not like snakes in that their skin is smooth, but the absence of a proper head of hair is unpleasant to look over. Pug-ugly is the kindest way it can be said. They look delicate too, curved of hip and bosom. Only the faces are not right. And the height. And I can't say I'm partial to clicking. True to tell, within their funny acorn heads, they have eyes of the loveliest colour: the richest blue I ever did see. So nice to look on they have painted their houses and skirts the same colour. And they must have their own menfolk, we've simply still to learn where they keep them.

'What did they wear?' asks Tabitha.

'Nothing if Nicholas is a-grabbing their bosoms,' shouts one.

Blanche faces the group to answer. 'I saw them up close. Clothing crafted from the forest leaves, woven together with grasses. Strange that they have dyed it all blue, or somehow treated it so that colour is upon it. Every last thread. It makes them look quite a picture: the fairest skin you ever saw, each one could be new-born so white she was, and eyes the same colour as their clothing. Those little eyes of theirs were darting hither and thither. Eyeing us with many a thought behind them. If these are not daughters of Adam they are as clever as we, I could see that. Smaller by an order that is hard to credit. They build their houses plenty big enough for themselves although we could none of us stand upright in them.'

'If their clothing is so good, why were some of the girls wearing none?' shouts a voice.

God Help the Connipians

Mr Hastings takes up the question. 'When the civilised of this Earth come into contact with primitive peoples, it always reveals customs which we do not readily understand. It was only a few of the thirty or so ladies who were indecently clad, and I am sure that is not how they perceived it. They wore a skirt or wrap, but it left them exposed...upstairs...so to speak. Perhaps they are the only ones who are not yet married. Or maybe it is the way these girls dress upon their birthday...'

'Mr Myhill's birthday,' shouts a joker at the back of our throng.

Nicholas laughs loudest at that. 'Mr Hastings is making his learned enquiry into these primitive people, and I have been a-making mine,' he declares.

'Connipus,' says Ha'penny Hastings. We all look at him, not understanding what his meaningless utterance might convey. 'Latin,' he continues. 'Connipus. They are not descendants of Adam and this species needs a name.'

'Pig Latin,' murmurs McConnell who stands beside me. And that is just another language I don't understand.

'They are animals, are they then?' queries Septimus.

Whatever Hastings thinks, I can't see it, myself. Certain of their ways made it clear to me that they are cousins of ours: they live together in a tiny village; their clicking tongues and tiny size was the most extraordinary phenomena I've come across life-long.

'I think they are animals, Mr Draycott,' says Hastings. 'Beasts of a greater intelligence than any that a man has previously encountered judging by the Blue Houses they have constructed. However, Connipus is a separate species to man. They neither look nor behave as we do. Further from it than the Eskimo or the wild Indians of Florida, I am sure of it. I have read about them and those other people do not click. True people would have the stature and hair of our own kind.'

Well, there you have it. What do I know? Just a simple mayor.

11.

I find that our camp is of two minds. Half of our number wish to hurry back to the Blue Houses not knowing with exactly what purpose. Revisit the Connipians, as I think of them, an improvement on Hastings silly Latin name. The talk covers all points between converting them to our religion and eating them. I shan't be doing the latter; they remind me of the children you might see in the fishing villages of north Kent. And we none of us eat children, however feeble and bedraggled they look. The rest of the party want nothing to do with them. Animals is animals, that is their contention. We should live apart; they have no wish to hear the clicking. To each his own, the nub of their philosophy. One even said, 'We wouldn't disturb a nest of snakes.'

We are trying to make fields here in the surrounds of Charlestown and we haven't seen any fields made by the little girlies. I asked Hastings and he hasn't the first idea what constitutes their diet. I am wavering between the two views. Perhaps we should stick to our ways and let them stick to theirs. It seems like I alone think us cousins, and I keep it to myself. The Connipians look nothing like us, and they're differently mannered.

I'm mayor, so perhaps it is only right that I am on the fence about the lot of it. A foot in each camp on befriending or letting them be. The truth of it is, I am generally one to let sleeping dogs lie, and yet the Connipians fascinate me. And they must have some men hidden away somewhere, they really must. How else could they keep the population ticking along, for they have surely been here a long time. Not a sign of any boat which brought them here, not when we sailed right around the island. If one in our throng could master the clicking language—which I am sure they speak, for I saw how they pay attention to each other's sounds—it would open up our eyes to a whole new world. Hastings said it, but I thought it myself also. I'm quite clever in my own way, just not as bookish.

'Communication is the solution.' These were his exact words. Hastings is keen to learn how they perceive us, and to study their diet and social customs. The problem is, even the way they make the sound is beyond us. We can do similar but not the same. Can't click like a Connipian.

Mr McConnell has told me he thinks Ha'penny's notion that they are animals a cruel truth. 'Not quite us,' he said.

This surprised me, for I have always thought Edgar to be a soft-hearted soul and he saw them. The little girlie-people arouse something protective in me but not in him, it seems. I tried to question it: how can he know they are not descendants of Adam? We know there were many who strayed far from Canaan? London and the River Thames never got a mention in the bible and still we know ourselves to be the sons of Eve. And God's children come in quite a range of colours, so why not a shorter variety? The Lord might have decreed it.

'It's the nose,' said McConnell. 'Their noses are quite different. Our nostrils face downwards, as if first and foremost to smell our own shoes. Theirs are seeking outwards a little. Did you see? Like rodents. They are animals, Mr Brook, and we must hold ourselves at a distance from them.'

His words sadden me. Not that I disagree, I am keen to learn from scholarly types such as he. Since losing Mary—Mary and the others whose passing has left the balance of our group all wrong—I have hoped that any of Ha'penny's primitives we came across would prove suitable for baptism. Might provide us with the wives we need to prosper. When I saw the tiny people—women all—I was both repulsed and excited. The faces aren't very nice but if we found larger houses further round the isle, women of a little more stature—a bit more hair, please God—I could probably put up with the face. Their figures take a man's eye very nicely. Doll-like and scary-small, I grant. Now I am thinking that if Hastings and McConnell are indeed correct, then it can never be. Horses and donkeys breed only mules. There can be no colonising of New Poplar with Connipians as mates. It is ourselves alone and we must hope some more English come after us, join our community. Dutch or Portuguese would do, I imagine. Until that time, we shall live on this island proximate to these other people, the Connipians, and it might be no different than were it a warren of rabbits or a wasps' nest. Interesting to observe but perhaps the interaction must be minimal or the rabbits will scuttle away, the wasps sting.

* * *

It is fully three days since our visit to the Blue Houses. We have resolved that we shall return to that area of the island, look for other outcrops of the strange dwelling places, the funny people who live within them. There must be many across this large isle. Perhaps the men have a village of their very own.

Another of the large flightless birds has walked into Charlestown. It is as brazen as the one which provided us a tasty meal, and Septimus jokes that this fellow has come looking for his mate. It might be true, and rather proves the creature to be as stupid as he looks. Ha'penny Hastings is admonishing the men, stating they should not kill this bird. It is fascinating to watch them debate, but I am Mayor and think it injudicious to stray far from the majority's way of thinking. Men enjoy meat and there must be many more of these birds strutting around New Poplar. If the Connipians wish to worship them we shall leave them a god or two.

Perhaps Hastings has guessed my mind or he may not have, either way, he has his hand on my upper arm. Wishes for me to intervene I presume. 'Look,' he says, pointing his hand at the trees to my right.

Now I see what has attracted his attention. It is the blue of their swaddled clothing I see first; two of the Connipian type are watching the bird, and watching us also. Again, they are women, girls. Determining their sex could not be easier. They wear blue skirts wrapped around their waists, white legs protruding, and this pair, like a small number of them did those short days past, wear nothing across their top halves. Indeed, these bare-breasted Connipians might be the very ones we saw back there. Might not: I am finding them very tricky to tell apart. It is my guess that they are rather young; it might be that they take to covering up only when their little milk urns become too large to comfortably run without strapping them in. I suppose, until we turned up, they've had no men around from whom to hide their paps away. Haven't learnt to do it. Fancy sending girls to go and spy on us big ones. If they have men at all, they are cowards.

They make their funny noises, the clicking, and do not look fearful of us in the least. Indeed, I think it is the flightless bird which attracts their attention, although I'd have thought Charlestown to be quite a sight for them. We have built longhouses that are four times as high and many times as broad as their own little constructions. If they think it spectacular, they do not let it show. A little of their blue paint would finish the construction off grand, and I shall ask for some when we have established proper communication. Learned to click as, in time, we must. I will wager the Connipians are too primitive to master the King's English.

I see many of our men grinning at the sight of them, particularly those who have never seen the little people before. Tiny little Connipians. They are surprising to come across, clicking with purpose and directing it towards each other, maybe at the bird also. If Big Flightless answers back, I swear it would be no greater surprise than those we have already encountered.

The clicking girls make gestures as they converse, as if ushering the bird towards them. The animal, with its black-feathered rotund body, lifts a wrinkled leg and begins to walk quickly towards the blue-skirted girlies, to the Connipians. Then it runs straight past them, out of the clearing and into the woods. I hear their clicking coming a notch more rapidly, perhaps in celebration of an achievement. They have lured the bird away from us.

'A-hoy, that was our dinner,' shouts Darius. Much laughter follows his cry.

One of the little girls waves a derisory hand. She cannot have understood his words but she turns her head away, her body and breasts too, as if dismissing Darius's words as unimportant. I feel that we and these new people—animals if Hastings and McConnell are correct in their thinking—have had our first disagreement. The big bird running from us is a disappointment. For all but Hastings it is. We would have slaughtered it quickly. No messing, off with the feathers, and then Tabitha and Rags would likely have greased it as it went round and round on a spit above a fire. The girls seemed to direct it back into the forest, for what purpose we can only guess. Not much of a god with spindly legs and a snappable neck. If they hadn't drawn it away, we would surely have shared the meat with them. We are hungry, not greedy, and girls that size could eat no more than a Double Dee mouthful between them.

It is early in our cohabitation of this island, and to my thinking, the Connipians have outfoxed us in our first clash. Both girls disappear into the woods, setting off after the bird. Whether it is to catch and cook the beast for themselves, or worship it from the blue aura within their funny houses, I cannot rightly say.

'Which one is yours?' a lad named Papley asks of Darius.

'What?' says the Double Dee.

'Clickety-Clack, or Clackety-Click? That's who's come a-calling, and I wouldn't mind getting a might closer to one or the other of them. Pretty little mites if you don't look too hard at the faces. Which one is yours?'

I look at Hastings, and he is giving me a thunderous look in return. 'I forbid it,' I tell Papley. We shall observe the connip-type as we have said. Assist Mr Hastings to understand them. We shall learn how to share this land. They are not girls, not proper ones. Half-snake or something of that ilk. Animals of the forest. I forbid any man to seek carnal knowledge of the Connipians. It is biblical and you know it: "Whosoever lieth with a beast shall surely be put to death. Amen." That's in there, God told it to Moses, and I'm telling you.'

'I'm only making a little joke,' says Papley. 'And it was they as showed us their titties unasked. A bit brazen if you think on it. Can't blame a man for looking.'

'Mine's Clackety-click,' says the Double Dee.

* * *

In the evening, Mr Hastings comes to sit in my small room, Tabitha beside him.

'Opportunity and risk, John, opportunity and risk. I may document something here on New Poplar that will absorb and delight the world for decades to come. An almost-people who speak without words and erect aesthetically pleasing houses. It is the most remarkable of discoveries. And you will be thinking as I am—it's the question we are all asking—where are the men? In time, Mr Brook, I am certain we shall unravel this conundrum. I am...' He takes a hold of Tabitha's hand, and I think he does it to demonstrate that what he has to say they have already agreed upon. '...concerned that the conduct of some of the men may compromise this quest. They have destructive impulses.'

'Mr Hastings,' I say, 'you have been amongst us for more than a year. Some are rough and ready, in fact, many of them are, I cannot deny that truth. However, all are God-fearing and decent men at heart. It is not our way to preach or even offer up collective prayer. That is for each man to dwell upon in his own manner; we always talk over the matters of community. Share our burdens. I fear some men are yet to be convinced that the Connipians...'

'Connipus,' says Ha'penny.

'...that they are really animals. You must grant that there are many similarities in their looks to our own, just the face is a bit hideous. And they're terribly small.'

'I think it is more than that. Until we track down the elusive male of the species, we cannot know them truly. It even comes to me that the girls we look upon might actually be boys. The two who came here earlier today certainly behaved like a hunting party, and we wouldn't send girls out on such a task. We must look like great ogres to them, yet they showed no fear. Accomplished the release of the flightless bird from our menacing custody.'

This I had never imagined. Girls who are really boys. It is an ungodly notion; of course, if they are not His children, then all things are possible. 'And if that is the case, Mr Hastings, if we have been looking upon boys with bosoms, where, pray, are the girls?'

'Oh, they get hidden away in most societies, John. Our own is a more tolerant one than many. Isn't it Tabitha?'

'They looked like little girls to me,' she says. She is eyeing her so-called husband with suspicion, but I calculate Hasting's fascination with the Connipians to be all intellect. He hopes to write a tome. Needs to see the ins and outs of how they live, adjudge the skills with which they build their funny Blue Houses. Find out what they eat and whether or not they have a god to pray to. An animal with its own god? That would send heads spinning back in London and the Shires. Christendom and the Caliphate too, if Ha'penny can get the distribution of his book that far and wide.

12.

I have brought Papley and Darius on this outing for good reason. They have to learn to treat the Connipians right. We shall live side by side; our friends and not our rivals. Hastings and McConnell are with us and a couple of others too. Ha'penny and I had a set-to about the flightless bird: I think we can eat a few, Hastings thinks we shouldn't. Not until we know what the Connipians think about it all, he says.

'We'll not eat them all,' I told him. 'We can leave them plenty to worship if it is what they want.'

I'm with Hastings on the raunchy talk though. Don't like hearing the men discuss the little girls in the way they have been doing. And Blanche seems to be providing for them well enough even as a child grows inside her. My own progeny, I like to think, expect a few other men might be thinking similar.

God Help the Connipians

We found the first group of houses quite easily. Not so many days since last we were here. We walked through the settlement, none of the Connipian girls came out to see us. We stopped speaking to each other, trod lightly, and we could hear clicking from within the Blue Houses as we passed by.

We are long through that part of the forest, far beyond the group of Blue Houses we previously visited. We come across another. Seventeen houses in all. This is more like a proper village than any we have yet seen. Even as we arrived, we could see the girls—or boys if Hasting's theory isn't as barking mad as it sounds—outside the houses and they seem to be working at something.

Ha'penny signals that we should all stay back. 'Stand where you can be seen; on no account should you move any closer towards them. I wish to see what activity they are engaged in without putting them off its continuation.'

He steps closer, does it slowly, edging his way. Closer and closer, and a couple of Connipians keep their eyes on him, up the tempo of their clicking.

Darius starts to laugh. 'They don't want him stealing their eggs,' he says, and it puts to mind swans on a river nest. The skin upon these Connipians looks almost as crisply white as those birds, and I dare say a swan could be the one as weighs the more.

From the clearings edge, we watch Ha'penny as he joins the gaggle of girls. They all gather around a large open tray, look upon it keenly. The tray, like everything of the Connipians, is blue in colour. Made of wood, I conjecture. He kneels beside them and it is a wise choice. Still his head is the tallest, but not by so much now.

He points at the work they do. Many Connipian hands are within the tray, as if pushing or sifting whatever is held within it. It could be grains but only Hastings is close enough to see the true answer. One of the little girls is looking straight into his face, their eyes holding each other.

She clicks away. 'P-t-p-t-k-t-p-t.' It is a noise but makes no sense that I can fathom, nor Hastings unless he has some powers of sorcery. Then I see him smile broadly, dip his hand into the tray and then bring his fingers up to his lips. Licks the tips. Does so tentatively.

'What have you there, Ha'penny?'

He turns to me, a small hand on the back of the one who appeared to communicate with him, gave him permission to taste their fare, by nod or by click. 'Jam, John. Our friends here are making a fruit jam.'

'What kind of fruit be it?' shouts Peter Papley.

'A good kind,' he replies. 'Not of a sort we have in England.'

Then there is a great clicking and clucking amongst the little girlies. I see a small line of three Connipians come up to the girl with whom

The John and Lodowicke

Ha'penny spoke. One of them wears only a skirt, nothing up top, which confirms for us that it wasn't only in the other village that they do that. In their hands they hold something blue, a cloth or broadleaf, which they fold in their palms. I see the one who might be their leader—Pitta-Patta, I shall call her for she makes that sound—spooning the jam with her tiny hands into these quickly formed pockets. Then the girls walk in a single file towards us. The sound they make might almost be that of spitting, but their heads sway. I believe it is a ritual, they click with many a hissed es, and I do not recall hearing that sound on our previous visit. I believe all three are saying the same, saying it in time together. Clicking it and hissing it, for it is not talk as we know it.

'Taste the fine fruit,' shouts Ha'penny.

The girl at the front arrives at Papley and I; Darius, Myhill and McConnell stand behind us. I see the jam of which Hastings speaks. It is the colour of green plums, a smooth and unseeded paste. I dip in my forefinger then draw it to my lips. There is a great sweetness to its flavour, while shocking one's throat with a spiciness I am not at all enamoured with. Sweet fennel, perhaps, but like mustard in its after taste.

I think Pitta-Patta has seen my discontented mouth, she points at it, then makes her own lip-smacking noise.

The other girls offer the jam to my companions and all partake a little.

'Horrible,' says Peter Papley which I think an overstatement. Unusual, certainly, yet it is a taste I expect I could acclimatise to. The penguins that we have eaten, or even the large flightless bird, are not flavours we ever knew in England. I am coming round to them quickly and may do likewise with this strange fruit. Connipian jam. It will settle me better on New Poplar if I do, I can see that. We must all learn to love what the Creator has here provided. 'I like this little one though,' adds Papley, and he runs a hand down the serving girl's front. Touching the one with her titties uncovered. The girl dips her head hurriedly, down then up again. 'God's blood!' shouts Papley and pulls his hand up to his mouth. 'Bit me,' he declares. 'The little fucker bit me.'

'She didn't wish to be touched in the lewd manner you took upon yourself, Papley,' I say. He looks very red in the face; I fear he wishes to exact some revenge for the bite. In my estimation the encounter is evens. 'Show me where she bit you.'

It is remarkable. The little Connipian did the deed—teeth upon Papley's hand—in a split second, and the bite mark on his right pinkie is deep. Blood drawn.

'She's cursed you now,' says Myhill. 'In the morning you'll be waking up but two feet tall, no hair to speak about.'

'Shut your mouth,' says Papley and he sinks to the floor, sits on his bottom, left hand holding the injured right between his legs.

'Come away,' I call to Ha'penny. 'We should withdraw if they are going to fight with us.'

'It was his own stupid fault. They are quite charming as far as I am concerned. You see, Mr Papley,' Hastings calls to him, 'I am not so stupid as to touch them unasked.'

'It hurts like buggery,' moans Peter from his sitting position on the ground.

'Can you walk?' I ask.

The dimwit only moans some more, and I tell Darius we must help him back to Charlestown. It is a two-hour trek and I hope we have no need to carry him. We could cut his pinkie off now, if that is the solution; I do not say it for fear of bringing forth more alarm in our party. These little Connipians might be diseased for all we know, and the notion that they are snake-like persists in my mind. Venomous perchance.

Edgar McConnell says that he will stay with Hastings. 'And if they attack you? Set on you and bite you?' I ask.

'It shall not be. We are more restrained than the likes of Peter, here, and you know that it is so, John Brook. I think the little ones know it too. They can sense it.'

I cannot guess how he has confidence in his last point. Clearly, I am the mayor of not very much; my townsfolk all do as they like. I never wanted Papley to behave so crudely, though I suppose we never worry about how a man handles a sheep. There is something different here. Each and every Connipian I have spied looks like a little girl. Papley is a true idiot, he wouldn't have done what he did with a proper girl, and so was foolish to try with one just because she lives in a forest on an island far away. Unless, of course, he *was* exactly that sort of a pest back where we came from. I didn't know him so well back then and we each had our reasons for leaving Poplar.

* * *

Darius and I keep a hold of young Papley, a hand under each armpit. He walks—we've no need to be dragging him—while continuing to cuss and swear. Hisses like a Connipian but I don't tell him that. Myhill's assertion that he will turn into one seemed to get him more worked up than ever the bite did. Only seconds apart, I suppose. He moans out loud that he can feel the alien poison coursing through his veins but the hand does not swell.

'Nonsense,' I say, 'it is just the taste of the jam that lingers.'

After a time, Myhill takes over from me. Dumb Papley is making a fool of himself, pretending he feels faint, that sort of palaver. He even falls to the forest floor. It worries me that something more serious has happened to the big oaf. I don't see how a little nip that took the tiny girl not a second can have caused an injury so debilitating. I find myself thinking about the term 'snake-people.' No idea what kind of war party my lot will get up if this boy dies. I have to hope it is only hysteria in Papley, that it will pass as quickly as it came on. And if it is a deadly poison, then my two learned friends, McConnell and Hastings, are probably stewing above a fire in a Connipian pot even as we make our way to Charlestown.

* * *

We have a wood fire burning downwind of our longhouses, our dwelling places. In part, I hope that this will help my two learned friends find their way back to us. Surely, girls so small could not detain them? Or boy-girls, that notion of Hastings has lodged itself inside my head a little nastily. As unwelcome as the girl's bite. If they are boys then it is most awkward that we men think lustily about them. I don't find their small stature attractive nor their weird faces, yet it is true that the curvature evident in their tightly bound clothing, the figures within those brilliant blues, can turn a man's thoughts but one way. A boy wouldn't do that to me: I've never gone in for any of that. Anyhow, I've decided to push the Connipians from my mind, from the funny part of it which the Creator set aside for lusting.

Peter Papley sits by the fire, and I am thankful he has stopped screaming. That was what he did when first we reached the clearing. All three ladies came running up, as if they could nurse such pandemonium. And it was ten times the noise he made as we were coming through the forest.

I asked Rags to tend him, and find out what ails him. For the first half hour back here, she reported that he might be feverish, feared a convulsion. He did none of that, and when I quietly told Rags the tale—the sequence that drew his injury—bitten only after placing his hands on a little girly's chest, she got a better measure to her nursing. She made an examination of where she said there might be a swelling. Gave it a nasty tweak before it had chance to swell proper in her hand. I'm glad that she's come around to my view, believes that the fault lies squarely with Papley. Some in our throng are in favour of exacting a little revenge upon the Connipians and I am dead against it. A misunderstanding is all it was. And the men have to learn the lesson the little biter taught Papley: we mustn't be messing with these little bald girls in that manner. Boy-girls.

It is much later, when Peter Papley has calmed properly, and every examination concluded that no poisoning has taken place, that we watch Messrs McConnell and Hastings emerge from the forest. They stroll most leisurely towards our fire; join the gathered party.

'How goes it?' I ask, and see both break into the broadest of smiles.

'This has been an astonishing find,' says Ha'penny.

'Little girly bastards,' hisses Papley.

'No, no,' McConnell admonishes him. 'They are sweet little creatures if one only lets them be. Have you never been scratched by a kitten?'

'This one is half way to his maker, on account of the poisonous bite the little girl gave him,' Rags tells the two new arrivals. There is an upturn to her lips as she says it. Even those who just a short time ago were calling upon me to shoot the Connipians like I did Obby Pursglove, are relaxing in the better light which these two put upon it. Tiny little friendly people are amusing to think on.

'Poison it was, I am only here on account of being so strong,' says Peter Papley. He inhales air after he has said it, chest out and squares his shoulders. You might think he has just lifted the rock from afore the Lord's tomb.

'Bitten by a girly and he can't walk himself back home,' laughs Moses Grigg.

'Enough of that,' I say, thinking Papley humiliated enough. 'Ha'penny, Edgar, tell us what you have learnt.'

Both men regale us for more than an hour with talk of the people who got here first. Connipians and their strange Blue Houses.

'Women they are!' declares Hastings. 'And women who seem to rule the roost in their little village. In showing us their many houses, we came across two of their men folk. Each occupying a Blue House by himself. Small men, no taller than their female counterparts. Both were upon their beds although this was in the daytime hours when honest men should toil. One was sitting up, he may have been at some sort of work, dallying with string or some other form of fabric...'

'It was made from the storks of leaves,' McConnell clarifies.

'...aye, that's the stuff. What he was doing with it, I cannot hazard.'

'Two men and all those women,' laughs Septimus. 'No wonder they stay in their beds.'

'It's wrong, isn't it?' says Moses tentatively. 'Women shouldn't boss the men around. The bible prohibits it.'

'Ah-ha,' says Hastings. 'These girls, and the little fellows too, know nothing of the bible. I am as sure of it as I am the whereabouts of my own nose. They are beneath us in God's ordered plan but no less interesting for it.'

'The little women,' says McConnell, 'showed us the interior of several houses in that Connipian enclave. We saw many children, all of whom wore skirts. They, like one or two of the older ones, wear nothing upon their chests.'

'I noted that the men have no beards,' says Ha'penny, 'but a little of the wispy hair adorns their shoulders. Even the backs of their hands. They are quite different from the female of the species.'

'And those ladies showed you that they weren't men for sure?' asks Papley. The quickly recovered Peter Papley. 'They showed you they don't have nothing swinging between their legs?'

'They did nothing of the sort. Edgar and I were not seeking to frighten or perturb them. I think we saw enough breasts, covered and uncovered, to know what is what and who is who.'

McConnell describes the Connipians food store. As well as the tiny green berries with which they were making jam, he saw stores of yellow, red and blue-black fruit. Tried asking about wheat, about meat; the spoken word seemed to be of no meaning—or very little—to the clicking Connipians.

'And the paint?' I ask. 'Everything they make they give a blue finish. The wood in their houses, stones too. The palm fronds and other leaves with which the Connipians make their clothing. How do they turn it all blue?'

'We know not,' says Ha'penny. 'Another fine question that we asked but could not comprehend an answer to. Nor did we come across any skin or urn filled with a paint or dye.'

'How did you ask?' says Myhill.

'Edgar here tried tugging on a girl's top, to show he was interested and it nearly got him bitten, I tell you.'

There is general laughter at this. Peter Papley says got Edgar lucky. 'I don't think you're as strong as me. Mightn't have been able to fight off the poison.'

'Nor as keen to feel a titty,' says Rags and the boy's cheeks begin to colour.

'We must not disturb their way of life,' states McConnell.

I like that phrase: it is a sound course to steer for we cannot teach them Christian ways without a shared language. And although they look like people, they aren't quite the same. 'As mayor of Charlestown, I decree that we must not. Not disturb them. Polite waving and what have you, that is permitted. We live here and they live there. If they start talking properly, I'll rethink it.'

Now I've told them, I feel pleased that this is how we shall live. Side by side, not in touching distance. Papley will never be bitten again.

Part Three

13.

In our lives upon New Poplar, we miss many things which we enjoyed in

God Help the Connipians

England—the bread was better and I've a liking for gin—it is a blissful life here nonetheless. We found grasses which are similar to rye and seek to cultivate them. The Connipians have no such agriculture and I presume they have not understood the goodness they might glean from the grains. Hastings and McConnell both declare the Connipian stomach a different organ to our own. 'More like cattle,' they say, not that I ever saw cows munching away at berries and the Connipian girls do not cud grass. I must add that I like sharing an island with them; it is exotic and that is not a state I ever expected to live within. Not when starting out on this journey. It is puzzling also: they are most odd, to an extent that makes my old wish to convert them to Christian ways look a mite foolish.

We were created in God's image and they were not, that is at the heart of all our differences. We are certain that they write no books and Hastings is coming round to the view that they worship no god at all. Flightless bird is their friend, they appear to place him on a level no higher than that. They can look at arrangements of string for hours on end, so perhaps they contain some meaning which is beyond us. Either that or they like tying knots. I believe their clicking to be a rudimentary language but we have understood not a single tsch or psst or clickety-clack. They can speak none of our words, and more than a few in our party have tried to teach them. Speak slowly, but they still don't try it. I think the creator has fitted their tongues more awkwardly into their mouths. They make their funny clicking noises but cannot manipulate their mouths for complex sound as we do; Hastings said it first but I think it also. They seem to understand more of our speech than we ever do of theirs, and I think that shows the superiority of our language structure. It makes a lot more sense than their ceaseless click-clack-clop.

We don't know how many of them live on the island, it could be three or four thousand, possibly fewer than that. Of Connipian men we think there are no more than fifty. I don't know what they do with baby boys, I presume they are the rarest thing. Hastings says the ladies look after those few men—let them rest, never a day's work from a single one of them—to keep them fit for breeding. Farmers do similar with cockerels, while the Connipians rear no animals but themselves. Nor do they eat them: not flightless bird, nor gulls, nor penguins. They don't prepare hot food, never learned to cook over a fire, not so far as we can tell, and I think that restricts them. Fruit, fruit, fruit. They don't have apples, everything they eat tastes a bit odd. I even think the lack of meat might be why the men are such puny little creatures. They are not quite bedridden, spend most of their time lying down as if they might be. Lazy arses, and then they father all the children on the island.

Once, about a month ago, when we were eating our treat of spit-roasted flightless bird, a group of fully twenty of the little Connipian girls

The John and Lodowicke

came and stood at the forest edge clicking and hissing and almost spitting at quite the rate of knots. Hastings said what we all knew. These funny girlies do not like to see us eating the bird. And yet I am sure they do not worship them; we see them shoo the creatures away from their fruit stores. Click harshly at them.

We eat a lot of fish and the Connipians offer no objection, although we never see them fish, seldom venture to the water's edge. They are people of the forest, truly. They cultivate berries high in the canopy of the trees, and there are some roots which they also chew upon. We are learning something of these foodstuffs from the Connipians; however, few in our party see any need to copy them. We have no more wish to adopt their ways than they have to learn ours. We don't have their stomachs and wouldn't want our noses turning into little pinch-points. There are other birds we have caught, not only the flightless one; a kind of pigeon which we captured, tried to breed in cages we made from sapling sticks. One night all the birds were let out, and we are sure the girlies did it, denied us our food. There are no other suspects on New Poplar: all of our own sort enjoyed eating them. Hastings said the Connipians cannot help it. They are fruit eaters with some kind of sympathy for the birds of this land.

We have seen lizards, not yet stooped to eating them. After months and months, I've come round to thinking that no mammals—horses, nor goats, not even an otter or pine marten—live upon this island. Mores the pity. If any of us ever travel back to England, or we receive visitors—the Dutchies are the most probable—we will ask them to arrange for a few chickens and cows to come down here. Just a single boatload: a cockerel or two, cows that are carrying. We could breed our own after that. God knows what the Connipians will do but if we have enough, we would share it. I am all for making friends. Truly. No one in their right mind refuses milk. And a chicken pie or two might pull those feeble men up from their beds of leaves, could twist the course of Connipian history. They simply don't know it yet, haven't tried our superior ways.

'You're surely not the best mayor, just the best we have,' says Blanche, and I have found that many in the party are equally insolent in comments directed towards me. I tolerate it because, as a group with shared convictions, we live harmoniously for the majority of the time. We have implored the rougher men to leave the Connipians alone and I am confident that they do. Blanche sits beside me; I am tired after a day of planting. We grew many seeds in trays in our early weeks and now they are ready for giving unto God's Earth. An apple orchard will be ours in a small number of years. I know it shall. Blanche is tired with a child near ready to drop. Its parentage remains the mystery of Charlestown, New Poplar. The father not the mother, obviously. I grant that the men

God Help the Connipians

who have not been inside her these past months are but McConnell and Hastings, maybe Moses Grigg for he is a shy boy. And I am unsure about Septimus now he has formed some kind of a coupling with old Rags. He probably took a turn with Blanche before all that. She is game about it. Holds her head up like none of it has taken place. Fools no one, but we play along. It's a night time release for men and maybe she has enjoyed herself while we were at it. I thought it on the occasions I partook of my go. If the boy—or girl, and perhaps this isle is cursed to have a surfeit of them—bears my features, I shall not be displeased.

'You have Rags sleeping in your hut tonight?' I enquire. We have all concluded she should not be alone when the baby might any day come forth.

'Are you wanting to be in my cabin in her stead?' she asks.

It was not the intent of my question but the offer is a sweet one. 'I can spend the night if you wish for my company, Blanche.'

'Generous to a fault,' she laughs, then swings her arm around my neck. Kisses a sunburnt ear.

I wonder to myself how this woman sees the world, the strange corner of it we occupy. She boarded The John and Lodowicke with husband, Obby. There were weeks in the middle of that voyage when we believed them one of only two couples who would arrive safely on the far side of the world. That young Hooper took some kind of advantage of her disgusted me, I never thought it to be at Blanche's explicit invite though had she fought him off more we would have heard them on so small a boat. Stopped it before the lad's seed was spent. And then we may never have needed to dispatch him as we did. Since then, it seems each man has done what Hooper did although the obstacle of marriage and husband were each removed before any of that. Before most of that. This is a difficult time for a widower like me. I must trust that the Lord will understand. If my judgement has been in error, I believe my intentions have always been near the mark. The laws of Abraham are many and I stick with the majority. Don't steal and I keep the sabbath holy.

'Tell Rags to stay with Septimus tonight. I'll keep vigil.'

'You will sleep like a horse which has spent all the daylight hours a-ploughing, that is what you'll do,' she says. 'No matter, John, I shall give you a kick if my waters break. Set you to action be it only to bring Rags back to attend to all that will be needed.'

As we sit, like the old married couple we can never be, I hear footsteps, the small commotion of men returning from the forest. It is only three but one is Double Dee. He stomps his feet like an army, does that giant of a man. Papley and another are with him.

'Evening, Mayor,' they each call. It is a laugh, their humour good and my authority ribbed a little with each saying of it.

The John and Lodowicke

It strikes me how quite a few of the men like to go for evening walks, a relaxation after our working day. Return as if back from the local tavern. I think we are replicating our old lives in Poplar on the Thames; doing it down here in warmer, balmier, unworldly New Poplar. It's a good life, as I have said.

* * *

'Ouch, what was that for?'

Then it comes to me. My satisfying sleep must end here. Blanche spoke of waking the baby when I took my way with her last night. And now here it is. Almost. She was mindful only that I couldn't lie on top of her those short hours ago and now, with a finger in the dirty place, she tells me she feels a head. I felt nothing of the kind with my John Thomas. She yelps like a kicked dog, feels those women's pains of the kind I am not want to contemplate.

In my nightshirt I go to the newest of the small cabins we have constructed. Knock loudly and shout for Rags. She grunts a reply. 'Fetch Tabitha,' I think her words to be. It is the middle of the night and neither talking nor listening come naturally to us. Tabitha is also with child but Ha'penny believes many weeks are still to pass before his will arrive. Blanche's shall be the first born on New Poplar. Born a descendant of Eve from Eden. I have noticed some Connipian pregnancies. Several, possibly more than they have men so immoral is the conduct of their few males. Hastings tells me not to judge; to view Connipus—as he calls them—in the way that we might observe the conduct of hares and rabbits. He seeks only to understand their habits, not condemn their unchristian behaviour. I am more bound to the Book than he, grant him that it is the Lord's judgement that matters. And He, too, may see the Connipians as rabbits and hares. Ones which chance to walk upright and, within the confines of their tiny stature, display the shape of women the world over.

I return to my own cabin, Blanche's screaming still all too audible even from this distance. Over these months she has seemed keen enough to have a child, unconcerned with the matter of whom it's father might be. And it is my belief that we shall all cherish it. Charlestown's first. She sounds a poor fit for the task of producing it. A right hullabaloo she makes, wails like Obby's back and knocking her this way and that, as once he did.

Ha'penny knocks upon my door. He is without his bed-mate for these hours while Tabitha assists Blanche. He remains in his night attire, as am I, 'You were with her,' he states.

I do not answer immediately. We all seem to know who has been in Blanche's room, although there is no written roster. I think Ha'penny a little vulgar for raising it. I don't find Tabitha to be a coarse woman, must grant that she lusts not for the other men on our isle. She is more contained than Blanche but scarcely a lady.

'I am pleased she was not alone,' he adds. I search his face, and realise he has concern for Blanche. This childbearing is a risky business. It almost did for my Mary ten years back but that was the grief at the loss of the child. Our tragic abnormality. I had not thought Hastings one to get sentimental about this, nor can I imagine Blanche failing to pull through. Husbands and lovers have been wiped from the Earth and she carries along as if what went before were no more than a bee sting. 'I wonder if this child will grow up with the young of Connipus,' says Hastings. 'Akin to the tales of children raised by wolves. And these creatures are surely far gentler.'

'Aye. If we can ask the clicking girls for blue swaddling clothes, I do believe they would provide them.'

'You are with me, John, see hope in the possibility of teaching civilisation to Connipus. Steering them into the fold. They are not the feral monsters Papley imagines them to be.'

I do, although I doubt if they can ever come to Christ. Peter Papley has never forgiven the girl who bit his finger. Never owned that his own lusting was of a base animal type that would shame a more thoughtful man. 'I think them rather clever, Ha'penny. They cultivate those fruit berries high up in the forest canopy, utilising the saps of trees in a manner I never saw in England, nor in India or the Dutch colonies. An agricultural skill divergent from any that regular men have ever practised. They have hands scarcely bigger than that of a hedgehog, the labour of men is seemingly denied them, yet they have crafted houses which are elegant in design. Their blue paint or dye is quite a trick, and I wonder which way it would fall should they share their knowledge. Would we be disappointed in seeing how simply it is done, or amazed beyond our imagining? They might be utilising a common substance we've never thought to adopt.'

'You are a wise man, John. Not much of a mayor but a wise man, nonetheless. And this baby—Blanche's baby—is it also yours?'

I shrug. He must understand that we will likely be unable to tell. Not unless it enters the world wearing a mayor's hat. I wish he was a little less smug about not having lain with her. At least for McConnell it is a withholding of all that pleasure. Chastity no less. Ha'penny has Tabitha and she is not a bad sort to look upon. Might be better than Blanche to plough between the legs.

There is more screaming from two huts down, and Hastings talks on to cover the unpleasantness. 'Would you allow it raised in a nursery with Connipus babes, John? I have been thinking about this.'

'Truly!' I gasp. 'I like them well enough; however, I am not suggesting

The John and Lodowicke

we give them custody of our children. What next, Ha'penny? Are you planning to appoint a Connipian mayor? A lady-mayor in the bargain for those little connip men haven't the breath to stand for the duration of a village meeting.'

'No, no,' he says, unruffled by my objection. 'This clicking language, I have been thinking about it a great deal. Not a single thread can we discern. Can't unscramble it. I believe a baby born and raised among the clicking would grasp the thorns which we cannot.'

'No, Ha'penny, that is foolish talk. The Connipians cannot mirror our talk, nor we theirs. I would not wish a son who did not speak the King's English. Clicking is akin to clucking. It would shame me, bring our whole colony into disrepute. This is a far-flung outcrop of the British Crown, heathen no more, and Blanche's child shall be a Christian. A Muggletonian! And the more I dwell on what you say, I am sure it would not arise were we to try it. A child of Blanche and I—Blanche and whoever—would not have the tongue to clickety-clack the words of the bible, as these creatures surely could were they able to read.'

'Exactly, my friend. Or near exactly. It might not work and then again, it might. If we can raise little ones to speak both ways—our King's fine English and click, click, click—then I do believe that we, or that child when grown, could share the wonders of the bible with Connipus. Give solace to their godless lives.'

'Oh, Ha'penny, you are a man of some learning but your feeling for scripture is awry. Were we not surprised that these creatures had not their own gods? We expected they might. We train our dogs to round up sheep, or catch and yield a rabbit. We do not bring them into church, nor offer them holy communion. Animals of the forest are God's gift to us, His people, to use as we will. These Connipian girls have not been saved, never have been saved and nor shall it ever be. How they fit into God's design has never come to light. His chosen people they are not. That's why He gave them ugly faces. I savour your method, Ha'penny, the one you have applied to date. Observation and consideration, it is a wise course of action. That they live apart from us, and that we enjoy cordial relations, pleases me immensely. I cannot imagine living this way with any other creature. Dogs we must feed, while Connipians manage that without our assistance. Still, I am not for converting. And when we explain our ways, tell them that we know a Man who came before who was divine, secured eternal life for all who believe in Him, we might as well be speaking of where we bury our bodily waste, so little would be their interest. They have already grasped the meaning of many of our words but there are concepts which will forever evade the Connipian mind, don't you think? Why, happen we would have no belief in heaven if we were concurrently told we had no place in it. No prospect. You have said yourself they are not descended from Adam. The Connipians are not in His heavenly plan.'

Ha'penny Hastings looks levelly at me. I think he might be weighing my words. Agreeing. 'When ships arrive, John, you and I will no longer determine the fate of these girls. I think they will be taken to the King's court. Not all of them, of course, but some. They are a sight that Europe would delight in. People who are not really people at all; communication without talking. In our situation we neglect to think on the matter—how those still living faraway will view Connipus when they learn of their existence—so cut off are we. We have quickly adapted to having them as neighbours but they are an extraordinary sight. Remarkable and strange. Sure to arouse interest far and wide.'

14.

Yesterday Blanche bore me a son. I cannot prove it is so, and some even say he has the eyes of Hooper. It does not make me waver in my conviction. Charles Otham, she has named him. The firstborn of Charlestown, New Poplar. Fitting that he is mine, mayor of the place, and captain of the ship which brought us here. I believe Charles Brook a better name and may try to persuade her it should be so in the coming days. She should not remain without husband, not as she raises this child of destiny. To marry the mayor must carry some kudos, however poor a fist I am making of my unasked-for position.

And I won't be letting the Connipians raise little Charlie. Hastings is a crackpot. Conversations between myself and others of influence—principally our womenfolk, for they are surely the ones who shall direct how this little lad is raised—will ensure he does not get his way. Scholars be damned. Even Tabitha thinks his idea lunacy. I have repeatedly said how much I like the funny, tiny women. Still, I understand when something is an abomination and when it is not. The firstborn on New Poplar is a child of hope; the Connipians are something of interest more in the manner of a child's pet, a mouse to be fed bits of grain, to cry over if a cat should kill it. And it is only a child that would cry, not a mature adult such as I. Sentimental attachments help kiddies learn about what's what in the world; they should not be confused with the devotion we must give unto the Lord, or that which I devoted to my poor Mary. Putting too much store in the love of animals would only cut off our source of meat. Deny ourselves a decent meal. I've talked a little to McConnell, and I reckon he thinks the same. A wordy man, it can be hard to tell what it is he actually thinks much of the time.

Our Double Dee has been brewing some kind of grog which he says we shall drink tonight, a celebration for the birth of Blanche's baby. He also keeps referring to the heft of the child, I think he has notions similar to my own, himself in that fatherly role in accordance with his fancy. It's a good prospect for the little one, so many men of the isle thinking paternally of him. He'll not be neglected, and that's a pleasing certainty.

I shall not drink his grog. I might pretend and then tip it discreetly back into the soil. I have no wish to offend Darius, who has been more faithful to my office than any other man here. His brew tastes like pigeon droppings. If that is the essence used for its flavouring, I should not be surprised. Two weeks ago, many of the men had a night on it, this was when Double Dee first declared his grog a-ready for drinking. We are a funny party. Men had to share goblets, so few do we have left after our arduous journey, and we have come across no metal here with which we can fashion tableware for ourselves. The Connipians have none, work with wood and leaf, a little stone that they use only sparingly. And we have yet to see them fell a tree, while finding sporadic evidence that they have done so in the past. Brought down the biggest in the forest too. That's hard to picture: little girlies knocking down trees loftier than the masts of the tallest ships that ever sailed.

That fortnight past, the unpleasant taste prompted me to sip but a little of his foul brew. Many men were far less circumspect. Glugged the stuff down like it might be life's elixir. It is not that. The following morning, most in our camp stewed on their cots as surely might occur should a plague ever strike us. Holding of heads and moaning helplessly. Farting from the gut: great rasping tunnel winds which can make a man jump even when it is his own arse a-trumping. Thank Christ I have my own sleeping quarters; the air was rotten in the longhouses. Even my three or four sips gave my bottom the hiccoughs. Parp-parp, all night long. Rags ordered Septimus from the cabin he shares with her, slept in mine until the wind within had calmed. Even that old woman is not partial to the smell of rank gas.

Why we should repeat the debacle, as if this a worthy marker of Charles's birth, rests outside of my ken. I cannot credit it. The drunkenness which preceded the collective distress was amusing, and even my sips allowed me peripheral access. Many a man sang, some danced although the sober ladies would not. When the womenfolk were out of earshot there was bawdy talk of the Connipians: what a man might do with them, shapely as we all see them to be. When sober, I do not like the talk, must admit that it fascinated me in the state I'd gotten into. Some men pretend they have done to the girls what they cannot have. Must not. They would have bite marks all over should they try, that is the lesson of Peter Papley's rash act those months back. And he is one who now fantasises about them. Imagines having carnal relations with an animal, and it is quite unnecessary with Blanche in camp. He calls them 'good and tight' and their small stature makes this aspect not even a feat of imagination.

Our field of rye, where I work today removing many large weeds, has also caught the eye of the Connipian girls. Two of their number espy me as I walk between the lines. I have a snagging hook, one we brought in case there was a need to cut quickly through rope while out at sea. Now we use it to dig into the dry soil, it is more effective than the wood-crafted implements which we have as alternative. I signal with my hand that they may come and observe from close to. The girls are careful, do not tread on the emerging ryegrass. As they come closer, I see that the more mature of the pair is herself expectant of child. I say mature for her clothes cover her completely where the other connip displays all the flesh of her upper body. A lot of pale white skin on these forest dwellers. I try not to look at her little orbs, or at least, not when she is eyeing me. Both girls look young in the face. They are neither taller than my navel. I cannot guess the age of Connipians at all. They must be eleven or twelve years old to be swollen thus of bosom, but could be forty for all I really know. And one is with child so surely more than fifteen years of age. Or are they like cattle. Breeding by their third year of life? These are mysteries which Hastings will solve through his observations; it may take him years to arrive at conclusions of substance.

I point at the belly of the pregnant girl. 'I became a father today,' I tell her. 'A baby boy. I have a baby boy. I imagine you will have a girl. There are boys amongst you Connipians but very few. Can you tell me why that is?'

The girl pays the closest attention to my words and I believe she understands them. Some of them if not all. When speaking of fatherhood, she rubbed her little hands together in delight. Now the two girls click. Clickety-clack, clackety-click. That is what I hear but they direct the sound towards each other; don't exclude me, it's just they know I am not a clicker. I am sure they would wish me to understand although I cannot. Thinking these thoughts, I look again at the two girls. It comes to me that they were the exact two Connipians which we named Clickety-Clack and Clackety-Click several months ago. The two bare-breasted ones who first looked upon our village within days of our initial contact with them. Shooed away a flightless bird, as I recall.

Odd that neither clothed their tops that day and now one does. I expect it is pregnancy, indeed, that may be the ritual that determines when a girl must dress properly. It unnerves me a little that the females wander the isle so immodestly. No wonder my men think of them as they do. The Connipian men remain at home like the illicit wives of Catholic priests. Absurd; I even think the men feeble because they diet upon only jam and some chewy root which I have tried and it gave me as much wind as Double Dee's horrible grog. With no compensatory gaiety to accompany the farting.

'Clickety-Clack,' I say to the girl whose eye I am happy to take, 'do you choose which of the men shall father your child? Do you become his wife? One of his wives? How does it work?' The girl has attended my words but fails to answer. Not a click. I glance quickly at the other girl, the near-nude one, see if she has understood. 'Clackety-Click, you are too young for such activity, for childbearing, I presume.'

She leans her tiny frame into me, which I did not intend or desire. I am faithful to my own child's mother even if Blanche cannot reciprocate my fidelity.

'Bastard,' I cry, feeling the sharpest nip of her teeth on my pinkie finger. I withdraw it lightning fast. I make to hit the child but manage to desist. To control myself. It is not as we wish to treat them. If she misinterpreted my words, thought I was offering to defile her, I am both shocked and puzzled. I do not know how much of our English words the Connipians comprehend, although it is clearly more than naught. I did not touch her, as Papley had done when one of them bit him. It hurts like the devil but when I look at my finger there are teeth marks across the knuckle, no blood. I shall not wail like Peter did. I am the mayor, and not a cry-baby. Shall tell no one that I have been bitten for they would only take the rise from me. Believe I had assaulted her in the manner of the bawdy talk of lesser men, and I did not do that. Polite enquiry was my only crime. A civility misunderstood.

'I am sorry.' There, I do my Christian duty. 'I am sorry, Clackety-Click, if my words offended you. I do not understand the mores of your society any more than you do ours. We should not let that be a source of distrust; better we pool our knowledge until we know each other better.'

Now both girls click together; I have no sense that they direct this chatter at me. I wish I knew what they were saying. Whether it is the cultivation of ryegrass that lends them this animation or the contrasts between our God-fearing ways and the barbarism of Connipian conduct. Biting isn't even fair fighting in my book. So many women sharing very few men; that is at the heart of their baseness. A shocking state of affairs; and if we judged the kingdom of animals by Christian standards, I expect we would hang the lot of them.

* * *

In the evening, I take a bigger mug of grog than I initially planned. My afternoon's encounter has set me on edge, and I also note how many of our villagers claim paternity of little baby Charles.

Rags and Tabitha keep the new mother company; Blanche appears to have come through her ordeal unscathed. Other than shouting the occasional, 'Shut up,' we hear nothing from them. We men are the rowdy ones. Not senseless drunk but on the approaches. Papley is sick down his shirt front, and while many laugh, I do not for fear of doing likewise. It dampens not the boy's spirit. Reeking of spew, he begins a chant of 'Bring out Charlie.' A chorus which many men rejoinder.

Although this is late evening, our festivities carrying on in the firelight; to our surprise we see a small gaggle of Connipians edging towards us. I count eight in number but it may be only four, such is the weight of this grog we drink.

'Never before...' I begin speaking to McConnell, who sits on the ground beside me. He drinks only the water we have fetched from the forest spring. '...never before have I seen these little women shuffling about in the dark. How do they see. They have no lanterns. Are they cats?'

It takes Edgar McConnell a little time—questions, questions—to decipher my words, for I admit they have become slurred, my tongue currently better for clicking than speaking. 'Perhaps they come and watch us often, John. We would not know if they stayed in the shadows, would we?'

'Sneaky bastards,' I reply, then pull my hand to my mouth. It is not a Christian thing to say, and I do believe ill-brewed alcohol can unbalance the humors. 'I mean, welcome little Connipians,' I slur. Cannot get my tongue around the creatures' nomenclature whatsoever. 'Connipilum. Connipanum. Go and say hello for me, Edgar. For I cannot stand up without risk of tumbling back upon my arse. Damn this grog.' And then it happens: I chuck up in the fashion of Peter Papley. Not the least able to hold my drink, I think about half a dozen of the men have done the same. I have not been counting—cannot with this brew in my gullet—it is but a guess. Everything is a guess. Even the name of the father of my own son. I find our New Poplar a very sad place this evening. I may sleep here under the stars. No doubt things will appear better when my faculties return. I miss my Mary terribly and know, for it sits among us as an obvious truth, that Charlestown needs a better mayor than the bacchanal who bears my name.

15.

I spent yesterday in bed. Not an activity I have done before in my adult life, save for a sickness of the mind I endured in the East Indies a dozen years ago. At least this was but a single day. I understand that fully fourteen men—I being one of them—were unable to do a minute's work, and most of those who rose struggled as if the day might be their last. Were ill with their boots on when staying in bed was the wiser course.

The John and Lodowicke

McConnell is acting smugly because he drank none of the brown piss-water which Darius lovingly shared all night long. Tells me quietly that Hastings also abstained, Rags and Blanche too. That did not surprise me, I have long known that the fairer sex tends to be scared of brain mincing concoctions. Inwardly, I think them our most intelligent specimens. Then he shares with me that Tabitha tried a bit of Double Dee's brew; connected or otherwise, she has lost the baby she carried. I feel I ought to go and commiserate with poor Ha'penny but fear saying something tactless. Will wait until my head is clearer, less silted up on the inside.

Now, with Edgar beside me, I am trying to piece together the events of the night past. What occurred both before and after I passed out. I recall the delegation of Connipians coming into our camp. Visiting Charlestown. If Darius plied them with grog, I must condemn him in the fiercest terms but McConnell tells me quickly that this was not within the order of events.

'There were six little women,' he says, 'and they all came to pay respects to baby Charles. To greet the new one into the world.'

I question him about this, how they could have known it was the day of the baby's birth; he has had more time than me to think this through. Blanche's corpulence was only around her ballooned stomach. The birth was predictable. Our raucous behaviour may have aroused them, given them pause to conclude it was a celebration. It is more evidence that Connipians think more carefully than dogs or squirrels. And I have already figured out that more than a few of the little girlies are close to bringing forth another generation of their own type. The birth of new life is not an exceptional event however jubilant we feel when we are closely involved.

I learn from Edgar that the party of Connipians ventured, when invited, into Blanche's cabin and gathered around the new baby. They clucked away as is the custom of women the world over when looking upon a new born infant. Two of their number ventured to lift the child up, to hold baby Charles in their arms and cradle him as they might their own. McConnell tells me that one of these was herself 'in the family way'.

'Could they manage that?' I ask. 'Charlie is a bonny baby, surely bigger than their tiny hands can grip.'

'They held him firmly, secure and with care. I think these little Connipians might be stronger than we realise. You see, John, in the Christian realm it is the men who shoulder the burden of the heavy and the most dangerous work. It is not so for the creatures of this isle. The Connipians climb the tallest trees and work up there, gathering berries that benefit from sunlight, and the sap of ancient trees affording some form of quicker growth, or flavour enhancement. Ha'penny and I saw the little women crafting wood, their tools are but flints and still their cutting is remarkable. Straight and true. They must have felled tall trees, we have seen the evidence, not that we've had chance to watch them accomplish it directly.'

'And Blanche? Was she at ease with these funny creatures handling the babe?'

'Aye, John. Aye. She said it's as well that Charlie's not yet baptised, and nor will he be unless we ordain you a priest, which would be quite the stretch to live up to alongside your mayoral status.' The man wears a grin that scarce fits within his head, but I think it far from the worst idea. I struggle with one or two of Abraham's laws, will take my chances over dear Blanche come the day of judgement, all she and I have done that might be contrary to His expectations. I still think I am a better man than most here. Our Muggletonian core is proving a bit ragtag. They talked me into drinking the vomit-inducing brew, I would never have done a thing so foolish if left to my own devices.

16.

'Named for our former and beloved King, Charles Nathan Othan was born in this land, New Poplar, on the second day of February in the year of our Lord sixteen hundred and ninety-six. We want it known that this is a colony of the English Crown and we swear our allegiance to King William III truly and sincerely. If you find this note and know of some women of childbearing age, please buy a boat and bring them here. The island is situated due south of the Dutch East Indies, and then some. It is very nice. And bring cows if you have any, for we are without milk.

This is the message we agree upon and, with my mayoral approval, put inside one of but four bottles which has remained unbroken since England. Mostly we use skins that travelled with us from London to store water and juices. We have no bottle-maker amongst us and Edgar says we haven't the right minerals for it. Will not see any more glass until a boat arrives. The long houses we have built include narrow windows which we cover with threaded leaves, tie away in sunlight so long as there is no rain angling in. It's a bit Connipian but it has to do.

Eight of us take a rower out to The John and Lodowicke, we will set forth the bottle on the sea whilst having a jaunt around the isle in the boat.

It is my fervent hope that our message is found promptly and, in turn, brings more settlers to New Poplar. Charlie is an inspiring start. Not a month old yet, and a finer pair of bellows you never heard. 'Wah-wah.' I

The John and Lodowicke

like to hear him wail. Should shiploads come, I would gladly give up the office of mayor. I will do it only until someone of greater skill can step into the breach. I even spoke to Edgar about it a day or two back, suggested he might like to have a go. He said that our fellow settlers would block such a change of leadership. Not accept him. 'Never a Muggletonian,' were his words, and I am grateful that these men have a little God-fearing to keep them to task. Generally, it seems to make little difference. Our remaining copy of The Divine Looking Glass became soaked to a pulp in one of the fearsome rainstorms which we endured. The sometimes-vile weather that besets this otherwise temperate island. Now it is gone, I struggle to remember what it is I believe beyond a wish to be straight with the Lord on the day of judgement, and an awareness that it is most vain to think Him terribly interested in me.

I have been engaged in agriculture for all the days since my maybe-son was born. Hastings does a decent portion of work but often wanders off to watch how the little Connipians live. He took to taking Tabitha with him, believing a female presence might be a calming one for those girls. It didn't work out and the disagreement that came about was an odd one. Can't explain it; Ha'penny is as baffled as I. Tabitha sought to examine one of the pregnant girlies, to feel if the baby kicked in the little swelling of her stomach. A different little Connipian caused her an injury, whipped Tabitha with a curious string implement. Hastings told me that, out of nowhere, one of the little girlies lashed out the funny little cat-o'-nine-tails so that it wrapped itself around Tabitha's wrist, leaving a nasty weal. And she said that two of the blighters kicked her. I wonder what came over them. She struck one back and Ha'penny apologised. She didn't speak to him for a day after that. His wife whipped and kicked and the man apologises to the perpetrators. He studies them too much in my view. I concede that every tale I hear about them is a fascination. They must have a reason for all they do. A strange and devilish purpose, I am coming to think.

* * *

On returning to the longhouse where our women are shortly to serve out a meal, we see three of the blue-clad funnies coming through the forest clearing. Visiting again. Thankfully, all are clothed. Clothed all over. One carries something large, hugging it close to her person. Wrapped in blue, it is not so much their favourite colour as the only choice available. Everything they have—clothes, houses, their spartan furnishings—they dye the same shade of blue. Made a batch ten times what they needed a generation back: that might be the reason.

Hastings emerges from his cabin, only for a cry of 'Come back here!' to be heard from Tabitha. Hastings ignores it. I fear the marriage of

Ha'penny and Tabitha will end as Obby and Blanche's did, if without quite so much scandal. And I could not shoot Mr Hastings, he is proving to be a fine friend to me on this lonely isle. And nor will I take to the physical with Tabitha. Not so long as Blanche allows me the occasional roll.

'What is the purpose of your visit girls?' says Hastings. His certainty that they comprehend the English language exceeds my own by a distance. Curious that he should place certainty in this conjecture while being sceptical of all things Muggletonian. Do we really choose our beliefs, I wonder, or simply find they have landed upon us, as a moth might of a summer evening.

The girls all click loudly. The one carrying the bundle is many paces behind. While Ha'penny and I try to converse with the two in front of her, understanding nothing of their spew of trilled tongues—click and pip with a few hissed esses—Rags goes over to the girl behind, the one a-carrying the bundle, bringing up the rear. Before she arrives, that little Connipian woman places her funny package on the ground. As she rises up from laying it down, she hisses and clicks, waving her tiny hands over the bundle and then turns tail and starts to walk away. The two girls we speak to turn at the same instance and, giving the bundle their friend has placed on the path a wide berth, follow straight after her. Catching her up in just a few paces. In seconds the girlies are away into the forest. Glimpses of blue between trees, and then out of sight altogether. Rags has knelt beside the bundle then she turns to us, an astonished look upon her face. Eyes wide open in wonderment.

'It's a baby,' she announces.

I run up to where Rags kneels, Hastings beside me, and then McConnell and Darius quickly join us too.

'A Connipian baby?' I ask. Nobody needs to answer my question. The little ones brought it; the baby is theirs and not ours.

As I kneel down, I see her. For that is my presumption. Connipian males are so few I do not believe these girls would gift us one. The white skin and piercing blue eyes confirm what I know. They have not found a human baby. It is a cub of the animal Connipus which they pass to us for a more civilised upbringing. There can be no other reason why the mother—assuming that is the role of the girl who carried the bundle—has placed it in our village.

Rags pulls aside the blue leaf-made fabric. Somehow it has been dyed, yet holds its shape well, the interwoven leaves. I admire their craft. 'A baby boy,' she says.

I laugh momentarily. Astonishment the primary cause. We know they exist but what are the chances, and why give one up. And it could be a playmate for Charlie, a course which Hastings favours far more than I. It

The John and Lodowicke

is outside my comprehension that the Connipian mother has left the little one with us. The baby is not half the size of Charles Nathan but I think I'd imagined their babies might be smaller still. He looks good and healthy to my eye. 'Do you think,' I posit thoughtfully to my fellow bystanders, 'that they have so few males amongst their number because they give the blighters away? Dispose of that which a more loving mother would nurture.'

'An interesting idea,' says Ha'penny. 'However, before our arrival, who might they have given them to?'

'The flightless bird perhaps.' Even as I say it, I think the idea a bit daft. However, a scarier thought drops into my mind: do the Connipians leave all their male babies out in the forest? The adults we see could be the survivors of a cruel game. The girls seem to run the show; do everything they can to keep the men from taking their rightful places. These girls might be man haters. Feed the baby boys to the crows, come into Charlestown and given us one only because it is of no consequence to them. I am not sure why I think it, feel it; a stomach-churning dread overtakes me as I contemplate the actions we have just witnessed. Three supposed innocents discarding a helpless baby. These Connipians are as unchristian as a savage can be.

'Oh no,' says Rags. 'This is not right.' She has picked up the child and we hear it make some little noise, a gurgle in its throat. Still too young to click. 'Look at this poor mite,' she says.

I look, the baby is in her arms, carefully cradled. She has a hold of both the baby's hands in just a single one of her own, moving it slowly so we see the babe's arms move in a slow ripple as she does the rhythmic motion with her own.

'What are you doing, Rags? Don't hurt the little thing,' says Edgar.

Darius is laughing at the motion of the arms, the peculiar rippling we all see. For me there is no amusement in a baby with arms as pliant as bits of rope.

'There are no bones in there,' she declares. 'His little legs feel fine, but not his little arms.'

We all look closely; Rags assertion is astute, true. To me this little Connipian looks better than the baby my Mary bore which had no eyes in its head, not that I like to think on those days. An infant should have all his parts, by right; when the Lord denies them that I reckon He is happy to take them straight back. If we face the facts, it is His error. It's only the Creator who creates and we've all botched a job or two. And a boy with no arms is never going to win a fight, can't make his own way in the world.

'Well, well, well,' says Ha'penny Hastings. 'Connipus bringing this baby to us is a surprise; this defect of the arms explains a lot, I believe.'

We all look at him, wish Hastings to continue his train of thought. I've not a clue as to what has become clear. 'I think this deformity might be common in boy children amongst Connipus. That is the reason there are so few. They would leave him to die, as pigs and cats and rabbits are known to do with the weakest in any litter, did not do so only because they have us. They must hope we can cure this malady but sadly we cannot.'

'Prayer,' I declare with sudden optimism. In truth, I have no experience of acquiring better than a sunny day through the deployment of that old trick.

* * *

Rags has taken the beast baby into her home. Asked Blanche if she would suckle it now and then. She refuses. I think it for the best while knowing that it will be painful to watch something so similar to a proper baby die before our eyes.

Hastings and McConnell both wish for Blanche to rethink her decision. Give the Connipian a chance at life; try suckling the odd little cub as Rags has requested. Blanche's breasts are enormous so Charlie can spare some of the nourishment therein; that is as far as they have reasoned the matter. I think Blanche's refusal far wiser than the counsel of the scholarly men. This abominable baby is not simply Connipian, it has been born to a terrible fate. Its arms do not function and they never will. Not a bone in the mite's upper limbs; I felt them and it is a peculiar and terrible fate. I would be a very stupid mayor were I to sanction the feeding of this baby. A mouth to feed that shall never repay the debt. I have had a quiet word with Blanche. Along the lines of sticking to the answer she first gave.

I appeal to the enquiring natures of my two learned friends. 'Pray, how many outcrops of Blue Houses do we know of?'

Hastings is quick to say twelve.

When circling the island in The John and Lodowicke, as we did in order to send forth the bottle, I made a reckoning that we have ventured inland over less than a quarter of the entirety of New Poplar. In those ventures, we have discovered twelve Connipian settlements. Possibly missed a couple so easily concealed are they in the dense foliage. There may be fifty to sixty in total. Eighty, top end. Thirty or more girls and the odd chappie in each. There could be two thousand little girls. Double that if they are concealing more than we are finding. 'Graveyards,' I say. 'Do we see...'

'John, John...' It is McConnell who interrupts me now. '...these are not a Christian people. How they treat the body of their dead may be in a manner quite different to our own purposeful rituals. Not only are they oblivious to the hereafter, they are creatures of the Earth, no more able to access heaven above than the penguins we put in the pot.'

'Yes, yes, but they must bury them somewhere. Connipian cadavers. So where are they? And is there a stash of dead male babies with withered arms?' Even as I say it, I get a queasy feeling. In the early days, I thought them rather sweet; back when we only contemplated the tiny girls, clicking away and baring their breasts. An island with deformed males discarded at birth as this young mother has done tonight, that is of a different order. Disconcerting: I scarcely wish to share an island with them.

17.

The world has turned upside down, an ugly place and the purpose of the creation receding as I contemplate it. We sought only to build a peaceable and God-fearing community here on New Poplar. Never could we anticipate all that has come to pass. Rags has raised the little infirm boy—or snakelet, for that is how some in our number refer to him—on the Connipian jam which they long ago gave us. We scarcely touched it; their fruit is not ours. The boy does not thrive and nor does he die. Blanche held firm: her lactating milk is only for Charlie, and I have thanked her for her resolve.

Then, this morning, another delegation of three little Connipian girls brought a bundle to our settlement. I do not believe it was the same three girlies but they are difficult to tell apart. I expect the bundle-carrier was a different one, at the very least. A different mother rejecting her infant. What callous creatures these girls of eye-catching figure turn out to be. The face might be the giveaway, not that I ever guessed it during any of our early meetings. Didn't know the half of it. Again, this baby bears only boneless arms. Horrible fleshy string-like arms where Charlie's arms are pudgy and straight with a couple of little folds on the forearms, little fingers he is starting to move of his own volition. Charlie is a descendant of Adam, the Connipian babies are revolting. The Lord must have cursed them for a reason, that is as much as I can think on the matter. Rags berated me when I said those words but she is no greater authority on the mind of our Lord Jesus than I. Indeed, I am mayor, not a religious office; however, I think everyone should respect my opinion a bit more than tends to happen. I do a lot of thinking although it is hard to translate it into mayoring. To take actions which ensure we go forward together. Hastings in particular seems to have gone off me, and I feel disappointed that we are at odds. He regards the Connipians so scientifically that he will not criticise the errant little mothers. Conversely, he is sentimental. Or wishes the floppy-armed little thing to

God Help the Connipians

live for the purpose of his scientific enquiry. I consider long life to be a cruel fate to bestow upon a cripple such as Rags is trying to raise. A creature which will never independently eat a meal.

The odd—nay, bizarre—fact in this second instance of baby disposal, is that the ailing infant is a girl. Bigger than I expected their babies to be, as was the first which they foisted upon us. This one is an ugly Connipian female with arms that shall never lift so much as a spoon. A tragedy and a puzzle. Ha'penny's supposition that a congenital defect has deprived this population of the vast proportion of their boy children looks less than proven. We all thought him most clever when he came up with it; wisdom and guesswork might be one and the same. Hit and miss. We have a lot to learn about these other people, and I don't wish to hear it if all is to be sickening. That they are callous creatures who jettison their young. And this cursed disability can clearly afflict any of the ungodly type, boy or girl. I suspect there is a pile of dead babies somewhere on this island. Deep in the forest, I suppose. Why they have suddenly taken to giving them—while the abominable little horrors are still living, breathing—to us, is a riddle we may never learn the answer to. All Connipians are animals and they do what they do. That Rags is going to try to raise their rejects up to adulthood is a worry in which I must intervene. If they pass along one to us every five days, we shall end up a village of the enfeebled. A majority of no more use than flightless bird, legs to run on and a neck that bobs and weaves. Nothing of worth in between, nothing that can raise a spade, axe or hammer in honest toil.

* * *

Saint or fool? I think her a fool but grant there is reason for doubt.

Septimus has moved back into a longhouse, cannot share a cabin with her. With Rags and the squealing oddities which she raises in defiance of nature. I don't even look in but Hastings says there is little hope. The first of them weakens, may die very soon. A blessing, truly, and I mean no malice when I say the words.

'Its head is remarkably big,' says Hastings. 'How such a big-headed baby came forth from a slender-hipped and child-like woman is a painful reckoning to contemplate. Must have been pure hell for her that gave birth to the child, I am sure.'

'The boy or the girl?'

'The both of them, John. Big heads and no arms. Not as is worth having. Flaccid and useless arms. Empty skin with a bit of gristle lodged within. I have felt them, like little bits of gravel lodged in there, on every examination of their floppy arms. It is a worrisome future that awaits them although I never wish death upon a soul.'

'A soul they have now, is it? I never know where you stand with all that, Ha'penny. It was you as spoke of their animal nature. Connipians are not God's creatures. And I cannot fathom how Charlie got his head out of our Blanche but she's none the worse for the extraction.'

We talk on and I find that my scholarly friend is more curious than ever about the Connipian ways. I am a bit disgusted by them, to tell the truth, but agree that he and I shall venture to the pod of Blue Houses where they know us best.

'I shall ask about the babies they are leaving to our care,' he says. 'We must find out what it means; if this abnormality is a common occurrence. I know we cannot make head nor tail of their clicked chatter but they have the sense to show us, take us to look at clues. They understand our questions, I am sure of it. Perhaps we shall make sense of a click or two, in due course. I'm not there yet, could swear I can distinguish some differences in the sounds they make, the variable rapidity of their clicks.'

It is true that when we asked about their food stores, and how they mould their crude bricks, they showed us exactly what they do. They began by clicking, and then must have sensed this meant nothing to us, so one took my hand and led me to see a Blue House where berries are kept. A small clearing where they shape stones. The Connipians are not averse to sharing understanding, we find, although, on another occasion Septimus and I asked about the blue paint—paint or dye—I think one or two others have done the same, and it seems to be a different matter. Some turn away, hiss and click to each other but there was no sharing that knowledge with us. No offer to take me by the hand and show me where it is mixed. My mother was the same with her recipe for scones.

18.

A day later we make our pilgrimage to the Blue Houses. Hastings and I; he is most insistent that we go alone. Says others would become emotional about the abandoned babies whilst he wishes only to learn, not to confront. 'Their ways are their ways,' he tells me, as if his mayor is a child in a schoolroom, and he a teacher. I believe I harbour all the thoughts he attributes to those he does not wish to come with us— babies are for raising or smothering, not passing to whom they do not belong—I will hold my tongue until we have learned more.

Hastings says, also, that we should collect some wood on our way back to Charlestown. This is the mission he has advised Tabitha he is to undertake. She is one of the more emotional about the Connipians. He has confessed to me that Tabitha fears she may never bear a child of her own after her recent miscarriage. I think it a normal way to think and only time will tell whether she is correct or too resolutely the pessimist. When he advised her that they could raise a Connipian foundling, as

Rags seeks to do, she told him to fuck off. A crude way of speaking, but I think Hastings the more insensitive for suggesting it. 'If the Lord won't give me a baby, I'll be having no floppy-armed monster foisted upon me in its stead, Ha'penny. How would a cripple like that look after an ageing mother when my own faculties are giving out?' That was the objection he quoted back to me. I'm on Tabs side in their row; Hastings remains annoyed that she will not acquiesce. His wish to see if he can train a Connipian baby, even one with withered arms, seems a forlorn one to me. A shockingly poor substitute for chuckling Charlie.

He and I come to the group of houses at which we are known. It is one of the larger clusters. Seventeen brilliant-blue houses, the roof apexes of the smaller rise only to our chins. The bigger go four or five inches over the tops of our heads. I'd like to watch when they are building, the biggest are more than twice their own heights. Steep of roof, this is an island of sporadically heavy rains.

The girls come out of their houses to meet us and this pleases me. I have felt our interspecies relations might be going awry and that donating helpless babes is somehow a representation of that deterioration. This reception seems more cordial by far. A girl—or woman, a properly covered one—offers us jam that she holds within a broad leaf. The leaf is bowl-shaped, blue, of course. I am sure that the Connipians are responsible for both the shape and colour. Content too. The jam is red, and although I am not hungry at all, I dip in a finger and taste. Once more I find it bitter but the aftertaste is pleasing. Almost strawberry, but simultaneously cheesy and sour. I have never seen a true strawberry on New Poplar. The actual berry used in this preserve must be a departure from any that an Englishmen has before tasted.

Hastings tries to explain to the girl who feeds us what it is which troubles him. That he wishes to understand what has prompted the gifting of children. It is a funny term he uses, and a child with no use to its arms is a rum gift. I suppose he has no wish to rile them, and his words are a ploy.

The girl listens carefully to his English-spoken words. I think from her appearance that this is the girl I designated Pitta-Patta when we met some time back. I have seen her around a little since, she seems to be learning about how we speak. Might follow each word and might not. As she listens, I let my eyes drop to her belly. It is much fatter than when first we met. I do believe she is yet another Connipian who is with child. I shall even pray that hers is healthy. Small but properly formed, to grow up with arms as capable as her own. I should like to have healthy neighbours as seemed the way of things when first we began to live in proximity to each other.

'Look at her, Ha'penny,' I say, trying to gesture the bulge around her

The John and Lodowicke

midriff, wherein she has a child a-growing.

He ignores me. Pointing fingers as he says to her, 'Two babies you have brought us.' One, two, he counts off. 'But do you have a lot of babies whose arms don't function properly.' He mimics their state with his own arms, raises them up as he flings his torso backwards then lets them limply flop back down. Dangles them, swings them without control; all the while careful not to clobber the Connipian's head. The girl has an unusual expression upon her face as she watches this display. I cannot read it; she might find him as amusing as I do, for he looks a bit of a fool. Arms swaying, rippling them as best he can, but whatever movement he makes there are bones in Hasting's arms. And no laughter comes from Pitta-Patta. Perhaps she doesn't see it as I do. Not so much as a click. I suppose Connipians don't see the funny side of very much. Don't have a sense of humour, and the clicking of jokes wouldn't work at all.

When he has finished speaking, Pitta-Patta starts to click away to the other little Connipians close by. They join in and it is a cacophony. 'P-t-p-t-k-t-p-t,' I hear. It's a meaningless noise but somehow or other they are communicating, animatedly sharing their thoughts on whatever they have made of the concerns Ha'penny raises. The off-loading of a baby boy and then a baby girl.

Her head is not looking at me, I expect it is a strain on their necks to do so constantly, when I say to her, 'Pitta-Patta, I see you'll be having a baby too. I expect you are hoping yours has good strong arms, whether it be boy or girl.'

She goes absolutely berserk. Her little arms flail around, she pushes her head into my groin. Extraordinary behaviour, quite uncalled for. I don't fight back because Hastings always advises that we should not. These little girlies cannot hurt us but Pitta-Patta has unsteadied me and I tumble onto the ground, the leaf and needle strewn courtyard between their Blue Houses. 'By Christ,' I yell as I go over, and I hear all the nearby Connipians clicking a faster noise than I've heard them make before. Then I yell it again, but ten times louder. Pain like I've never felt before. The little fucker has bitten me—not a finger—bitten through my trousers. If she has scuttled off with a sliver of my member in her mouth, I will not be surprised. When I look down my clothing is intact, yet she bit me most fiercely in my private place. I only wished her a healthy baby; I was planning to say a prayer.

'Did she do what I think?' says Ha'penny.

'Bit my cockatoo?' I say between intakes of breath. 'She most certainly did.'

'And what can it mean, John? What is she communicating to us?'

'That she likes it in her mouth, but the gnashing teeth is the contradiction. No man would put it in a goose's beak, and she really was that damned hostile.'

Ha'penny laughs at me, and I think it bad form. I've not slapped little Pitta-Patta, would gladly have done that and more. Christian restraint, I have shown. And for what? A hairless creature who shares her man with as many other girls as fit in a clutch of Blue Houses. And she bites a man's cock when he asks a civil question.

I raise myself up from the ground. Stand again beside Hastings. Suddenly a cluster of little Connipians rush us, push us roughly and we both fall on the ground as I had done before. 'Cover your cock,' I shout. Do exactly that for my own protection with both my hands. I hear Ha'penny scream, he must have been too slow to act. Then we both roll on our sides, protect ourselves from their slaps and kicks. These are only silly girlies. 'Up we get,' I say. 'Remember the Conquistadors.'

We both stand upright, legs a little apart to make ourselves harder to push over. I swing a fist and knock a Connipian into the leaves. Not Pitta-Patta but another who looked a bit pregnant. Dirty cunt, if you want my opinion. Hastings is doing the same. His charm offensive was of no use today. When we have skittled a few, we run out of the village. Our way through the forest is well known to us. We are in the clear.

'She offered us jam,' says Ha'penny between pants. Running as he speaks. 'Something you said changed the mood. They understood we were discussing the deformed babies; it was when you speculated about her own.'

'They are fucking dogs, Ha'penny. Biting cocks isn't how a proper lady behaves and you know it.'

* * *

When we arrive back in Charlestown, no wood gathered such was our haste, and our need to feel again the security of proper human company, the place is in uproar. McConnell comes running towards us, tries to explain, but he speaks rapidly. An excitement that jumps from word to word before he has expressed the meaning in full. Excitement or fear. It is lowering his high standard of coherence; I can't make him out at all in the first moments.

'A plethora of little ones were here, John. Little girls by the dozen. Two dozen, I would say. They were dropping off babies. Four of the poor little things. Then three of them set about Peter Papley, pushed him to the ground and...well, I don't know if I can rightly say what they did to him.'

Hastings looks at his friend through narrowed eyes, brows nesting just above the lid. 'Did they bite his cock?' he asks. McConnell wears a look of amazement. As if Ha'penny is a visionary for divining so unlikely an occurrence from afar. I hope he does not explain why he knows it. I

The John and Lodowicke

won't be spilling the beans. Having one's staff attacked is bad enough as a private embarrassment. If there is to be campfire talk, let it be Papley's member they all laugh about.

'I must speak to the lad,' says Hastings. 'Where is he to?'

'On his palliasse, in yonder longhouse. The boy thinks they have maimed him for life. Left the man a eunuch. Calls for a doctor while knowing our community does not have such a person. None skilled in the making of medicines and balms as he might require.'

'Require, my arse,' says Hastings. 'I prescribe a good whipping. Come with me Mister Mayor. You have your work cut out here.'

I don't know what he's on about. He can surely see that these Connipian girls are nasty little bastards, same as I can. We wouldn't have punched any if we hadn't had to.

In the gloom of the longhouse, we see Tabitha tending the moaning young man.

'Where have you been while it was all getting rough, Ha'penny? Not lovey-doveying with your sainted little Connipians, were you?'

'I sought to understand why they were passing off their babies here, Tabs. And I believe that I do. That I know precisely why they are doing this.'

'They're all defective, you moron. Oooh...' She mimics her partner's speech to say her piece. '...seek to understand. Want to make friends with the interesting little ladies.' She sticks her tongue out at the man she usually calls her husband. 'Don't you Tabs me you silly old goat. There are God's people and some little girl devils and when it comes to taking sides, I only hope you keep on the right one. What a funny stuck-up man you are proving yourself to be down here at the back of the world's bum.'

'That will wait, my dear Tabitha. We shall speak as a couple shortly.' He turns to the man on the bed. 'Mr Papley, I wish you to be honest with me now. Have you had carnal relations with one or more of the Connipian girls?'

What a shocking thing to ask, although I recall he talked of the like when drunk on Double Dee's horrible grog. All the while Tabitha was berating her husband, if that he be, Papley lay on his bed with a faint smile invading the pained pose he struck. Enjoying the domestic row as any wifeless man would. Now he looks only embarrassed, turns his face away, I swear it became flushed with colour as he did so.

'My cock is in agony,' he states.

'Quite right too, my boy. Tell me what you have done?'

'Me. Why me? I think it might have been the one I did that bit me. They didn't even attack Darius and he's shagged loads of them.'

'What!' I have screamed this word out. We are a society of Muggletonians, finding a more peaceful land than busy London in which

103

to await the Lord's return. 'Were you enticed?' I ask, for I have felt a flirting from a breast-baring Connipian once or twice.

'Darius don't need enticement, Mayor,' says the prostrate boy. 'He can hold fast two at the same time and do his business. It really isn't hard.'

Tabitha gives Papley a stinging slap across the face and then crunches a clenched fist into his cock. The boy screams, and as she steps away from his cot, I punch him in the same place. I must have hit him harder, being a man and Tabitha of the fairer sex, but his second scream is the quieter. All air expended on the first.

'Call everyone together,' I tell Hastings and Tabitha. 'Everyone without exception.'

'You realise what this means?' whispers Hastings. And I think I do, but he spells it out. 'These withered armed babies are half man, half Connipus. They are related to us as the mule is to the horse.'

I feel a little sick come into my mouth. For a second, I think to swallow it back down, but then I gob it at Papley. A mouthful of bile for him. He is disgusting, truly disgusting. If I were the priest that Edgar once joked I ought to be, then I would excommunicate Papley and Dencourt forthwith. Tell God there is no need for judgement day with these two; deliver them eternal damnation now, please.

'Oh, those poor little Connipians,' says Tabitha, taking a warm hold of Ha'penny's hand. And at least he and I have kept our trousers on. McConnell too, I am more than certain.

19.

Our countries flag remains hoisted up the wooden pole we long ago erected. It is my greatest hope that some of my countrymen will come back to it and keep New Poplar under the rule of King William such as it is. We could not stay, not our little Muggletonian rump. I sought to reason with the men: rapists all, I now think. Not my learned friends, they were as shocked as I, wide-eyed astonishment on their faces. And we have reason to believe Moses Grigg innocent of all the charges. Blanche stated she has offered him comforts he has yet to take, so disinclined is the boy. Myhill wouldn't have it. Stated that Grigg has talked of doing a dirty thing or two with a blue-clad girlie; it might be simply that. Talk, talk. There were men in my days under sail who were always that way around. Boasted in great detail of conquests which no real girl had ever succumbed to. The rest of our group—women aside—are a rotten lot. I'd throw them all overboard but we'll not steer this boat anywhere at all without them. Most of them. Septimus also says he has been true to Rags, and maybe he has. Maybe yes, maybe no; I'll not say it to his face but I do not trust him. Men and their loins make an ungodly

The John and Lodowicke

pairing.

We are a few short on this journey to find another land. An island on which there are no Connipians; it must be that. We are at fault, not them. I didn't like them biting my cock but I understand—as I did not at the time—exactly what they were trying to communicate. We are Obby and Hooper short, obviously. The latter never saw New Poplar, perishing a day or so before we arrived, as consequence of a deed that seems like it was nothing looking back. Sex with Blanche: good fun but hardly a hanging matter: the rest of us didn't have to walk along a plank after partaking of the same. Obadiah lived but a couple of days on the island, his crime was only fighting but I didn't like it. Or him. God rest their souls; I am sorry for their passing. Sorry if my being a woeful mayor—a pretty rubbish captain before that—was pivotal to their demise. I think it likely even as McConnell tells me not to blame myself.

Blanche would not come, would not leave the island. Point blank refused. And she has kept three men for company and security as she seeks to raise Charlie Nathan. The firstborn subject of the colony of New Poplar. I no longer believe him to be my son. It is not impossible, of course, but I had a true wife who was good to me throughout our years together. I had a son, little Daniel, who was too good for this life. Did not wish to look upon the wicked world of men and he lived his short days with no eyes with which to do so. That is enough for me. I have finished with the poking of women. No good has come of it, the very thought sickens me now. Finding out all my so-called friends are up to it in the wickedest of ways. To be a man is to be cursed with a dangly middle leg. Short of relieving a bloated bladder, what good have all the cocks in the world ever done? None, I say, none whatsoever. Given seed to another generation of fornicators who the Lord may never forgive, and I care not if my saying it is a blasphemy. Needs to be heard, spoken of by men who are not grogged-up for that is the time most men raise such matters. When the mood has thrown off all reason. Mr Muggleton said it was a vanity, our calculating right and wrong outside of what the scriptures tell us. But we are his followers and a fat lot of use his calibrated wisdom has proven to be.

Darius is one of the men who elected to stay with Blanche, and I feared for our Connipian cousins, if cousins they be. By the accounts of everyone I spoke to, he has been the dastardliest of the lot. More of an animal than any little Connipian girl. May have fathered all the little cripples, although there are certainly others in the frame. The truth is, the man frightens me; however, I came up with a plan befitting a better mayor than I. Double Dee laughed at me as I tried to conduct an inquiry into all the wickedness he had done.

'You've no stocks,' he said, 'and you couldn't chain me in them if you had. You're a joke, John Brook, a mayor fit only for a town that don't need one.'

He really got my goat saying it so cruelly, the failings which I know will shame me to my dying day. I have failed those Connipian girls, not that I ever touched one where I shouldn't have. His comment stung, yet I found the resolve not to let it show. A few ideas fermenting in my brain as we stood eyeball to eyeball.

When others were going out to The John and Lodowicke, I kept the smallest rowing boat back and only Septimus and Moses ashore with me. 'Before we take our leave, Darius,' I told him, 'it is my wish as Mayor of Charlestown to leave you instructions while you await further settlers.'

'Are you going to tell me to leave the little girly-girls alone, Mayor? If that's your instruction then I might heed it and I might not. You won't be here to know which way round I go, will you?'

'It is my instruction...' I began to reply while withdrawing my loaded pistol from within my smock. Bang! I shot him in the ball-sack. Double Dee has been raping Connipians, what I did was the closest they will ever get to justice. He screamed and it delighted me that he did. I loaded more shot and did it again while he lay bleeding on the ground. Blanche may have only two men to look after her now, and if Darius did not perish, at the very least he will never impregnate another of those tiny girls, tiny women. Thanks be to God that I did what I did. Enabled Darius Dencourt to obey God's laws a little better than he ever managed while his beam was in working order. A man must show a bit of restraint. I think it was a measured retribution. Moses agreed with me as we rowed out to The John and Lodowicke. Septimus was silent on the matter. Seldom a talker, the look on his face made me think he has been dirty with the girlies but I'll not press him on that. We have to live in proximity to each other, at least until the next island along.

* * *

After just six days at sea, we come across another vessel, one larger than our own and flying the royal flag. We share a king. I signal that we should come together, then, as captain of the smaller ship, I make the crossing to the bigger one. Up the ropes. Ocean Brigadier, the name upon this ship's side. I learn on boarding that the captain is a man named Parrish. He talks quietly and pulses with ambition. When I tell him there is a land close by that features on no maps other than those which Ha'penny Hastings has drawn, he is beside himself. Wishes to claim it for England, and I tell him there is no need. I've done it already. I describe the small party we have left on the isle, tell him nothing of the state of Darius's cock. That is for Double Dee to explain or fudge around. If he's already died, they could blame it on the pecking of some native bird or other.

The John and Lodowicke

Big Flightless.

Then I try to describe the original inhabitants. The primitives who must have been there for generations and generations. Lived on New Poplar when it knew no such name. I am not the cleverest man, and find myself wishing that Hastings or McConnell were with me to relate the tale. I fear Parrish thinks me a confabulator, that the Blue Houses and tiny stature of the girls, the near absence of men, are an invention of my mind. I don't spell out that the indigenous inhabitants aren't proper people, an animal type that could fool a man into thinking them human when they are not. Nor do I say that men of little self-control are likely to take advantage in the manner most farm lads do with sheep. He's a captain in the navy, should be able to work all that out for himself. Have better ideas than me about maintaining discipline. I don't really want to tell him what an ungodly lot I am taking away from the place. If I tried to tell it, he mightn't believe me. Could place me in chains as a lunatic. Parrish will do what he will, can't make a worse fist of it than I have.

'Good luck to you, sir. You may find the Connipians a tricky sort to fathom.' I say nothing about wearing a leather codpiece, sound advice as it would be. He would surely throw me from ship to ocean were I to voice it.

And somehow, when I return to The John and Lodowicke, I feel cock-a-hoop. I tell all that want to hear that our mission has not been in vain. Mr Parrish wrote down much of my story. History will remember us, the discoverers of New Poplar. Builders of Charlestown that may forever be its principal settlement. There is much to take pride in there, and I expect the crippled babies will have perished before the Ocean Brigadier makes landfall.

That evening, when I am in my cabin preparing to repose, Hastings and McConnell enter although I tell them I feel too tired to talk.

'You've put the final nail in their coffin,' Ha'penny berates me, and I see Edgar nod, as if he believes this outrageous accusation.

'What have I done?'

'Sent more goddamned Englishmen to defile the poor Connipians, that is what you've done.'

'No,' I tell them. 'I swear that Levi Parrish is a better captain than I. Will make a better mayor. How can any of what this lot have done happen on his watch.'

It is a fair question, neither man contradicts me. Neither visage alters either. They are still thinking on it, I suppose. 'Well,' says Hastings, finally, 'let us see what next occurs.'

I am sure the future will be all right for Englishmen and Connipians alike. Regret that I was unable to make it so when I was in charge of the island. The Lord will be my judge and I am neither optimistic nor pessimistic about the fate that awaits me upon His return. If He doesn't like Connipians, then I'll be in the clear.

Chapter Two

New York City, January, 1950

Before

No one knows the half of it, no one who isn't Connipian. They wouldn't get it, that's the extraordinary truth.

At the core of the tale is the Weatherlakes' pot luck dinner, an event attended by ladies from the local church, one or two husbands. Mr Weatherlake holding forth about all those outlandish New Yorkers who spend their money on contraptions for which they have no meaningful need. 'Where is thrift?' he asked. The man with the largest house in Boca Raton.

They never heard the clicking, not one of them, so quietly were tongues flopped, lips pressed together, pulled apart. Communication between Connipians—there is forever pace and meaning to it—the volume so quiet that sound only carried to those in closest proximity. Gone was the blue clothing, not worn since the four girls were last on their faraway island. Leaves crafted into the shapes of their bodies, woven as only they can, and dyed black. For this assignment only. They know how, don't think it suitably aesthetic for forest life. This mission had a purpose to which the colour of their clothing made a more functional contribution.

The staircase leading to the bedrooms and nursery rose up from the large dining hall in which Mr and Mrs Weatherlake, and fourteen of their neighbours, ate chicken and squash, corn pancakes and turnip greens. A serving girl brought food in from the kitchen, took away empty plates.

There was no other way to where they wished to be. Those in black had to pass the gluttonous Sapiens.

The smallest was barely the height of the table on which the food was spread. All was candlelit, an ethereal ambience for such a gathering. The guests had each put in a dollar—even the Weatherlakes who hosted the worthy soirée—raising money for the destitute as churches are apt. The house had electric lighting available in every room; however, Eugene Weatherlake liked to keep the old ways, never switched on a single one during the evening in question. The littlest Connipian had shared her plan with the others, clicked softly. Stepping into the room, she turned her back. Stock still, attending the room with her ears alone. The chatter was

God Help the Connipians

unchanged. None expected to see a woman two feet six and a half inches in height, dressed from head to toe in dyed-black leaves, walking backwards along the side of the room in which they ate, and so none did. She sidled quietly, Connipians are always quiet excepting for a little clicking, which this one had temporarily ceased to do. Up the stairs, each requiring her—facing forwards for this task—to place hands on the stair above the one she was to climb to. Her knees didn't come up to the next stair; she was agile from working the skyfields, the canopies of Connipia. If any diner saw her, they imagined that they did not.

On the landing, a pink ribbon tied to the door handle made her next move an easy one. And once inside, she pushed a wooden chair up beside the cot, did it most carefully so no noise arose between furniture and the wooded floor she pulled it over. After clambering up she was able to lean in. Picking up baby, she nuzzled her nose into the tummy of the tiny child. More softly than a silent kiss did she click her thoughts, fears and wishes. Baby woke but didn't cry, knew with whom her future lay. This one was like no Sapiens infant ever appears—not outside the womb—still forming the detail of her shape, no bigger than a lady's purse. The one in black drew the baby into an opening in the dyed leaves of her clothing. Snuggled the tiny infant against her skin as Connipians seldom do. Her actions were guided by necessity on that fateful night. All a testament to the misunderstood love that those other people pass to their young: devotion not display.

At the top of the stairs, she surveyed the room. Big Sapiens gobbling up the fatty flesh of animals taken before their time. The black-clad preacher, bootlace tie around his neck, looked up. Leaves obscured her face, formed a balaclava, her eyelids were drawn together leaving only the tiniest of slits through which she might observe the way ahead. The figure at the top of the broad staircase must have crossed his vision. If he thought it a tiny black demon, a devil come for him, the notion was erased from mind without comment. Dismissed as if he spotted that, were devils true, they would have come for him long ago. As the preacher looked down at the food on his plate, she glided down the stairs, gracefully making the bound from one to another; it was easier than scaling down the high trees of her native forests. She joined her friends beyond the dining room door. They clicked only of the need to leave quietly, to complete the mission which was proving more straightforward than initially seemed likely. How inattentive those dull-witted meat-eaters prove themselves, time after time.

This happened more than twenty years earlier, the year nineteen hundred and twenty-nine if one calculates time in accordance with the Sapiens stop-start system of ticking off the seasons.

New York City, January, 1950

1.

Connipians have sailed into New York, passengers on a large Sapiens ship. Journeyed here of their own volition. Many thought it would never happen, many members of both species. A few have travelled off-island before: kidnapped, not that the Sapiens ever called it that. Taken to foreign parts for their supposed education or to become living exhibits. Experimented upon in the late Victorian age. When Tonkin learnt about that she was shocked. Curiosity can be cruel. As a child she visited the library in Masterton only to further her education. The sporadic emotional distress was unplanned. Nothing as awful has taken place in the last two decades, not since the twin study was ended so abruptly; attitudes are changing. And this gathering is of a different order. Uplifting but for the volume of linked misfortune. Unlike her, Connipians do not fly in aeroplanes. Not a chance. They refuse to do it; say they know better. Not in words, they click it. Share thoughts which Tonkin understands while not always agreeing with. Many, yes, but she is a Mixed-Up, only half Connipian. For that reason—the 'no' to flying—twenty-seven of the tiny little near-humans boarded a boat in Charlestown, sailed to Hawaii. And from there, the famed SS America has brought them through the Panama Canal and up the east coast of the United States. Sailed into New York City for the conference. The United Nations, an entirely Sapiens entity—the nation is a concept of no purchase among any species but the planet's most pernicious—has invited the Connipians here to discuss their future. It is without precedent. Since the end of World War Two there has been a flurry of changes, greater recognition of past oppression and a modicum of resolve to stop doing it. Diplomacy carrying great value in the post-war world. The Soviets have agreed to attend the conference; the British say it has nothing to do with them. Can't stop them either: gaggles of countries ganging up to tell them to stop thinking they rule the waves. And they thought they'd won!

Tonkin finds it terribly sad that four Connipians died on the final leg of the journey, only twenty-three are now in The Edison Hotel. They came here voluntarily and still the shock of being far from home seems to have overwhelmed them. Stopped their hearts from beating.

The newspapers write about how surreal it must seem. A Stone Age people who will briefly live in the luxury of so fine a hotel. Not that the reporters can fathom how the Connipians view it; the facial expressions of the shorter hominids give little away. Nothing that Sapiens can latch on to. Through interpreters they have clicked that the arrangements are satisfactory. Tonkin is one of them. An interpreter. No Sapiens can understand their strange glottal language—the spraying of thoughts through rapidly clicked sound—not the pure-blooded ones. And Connipians have never learnt to speak as Sapiens do. Don't use their tiny little words. They understand them; it's getting their tongues and larynxes to make the vowels sounds, and one or two of the consonants which they cannot. Only Mixed-Ups can do both, there are six of them here. Interspecies some call them. Sapiens fathers and Connipian mothers, and every one of them has the withered arms which arise from that coupling. Intercourse which no Connipian has ever engaged with voluntarily. They have made this clear through their interpreters, their unbidden offspring. It's a viewpoint some Sapiens choose to contest. Sapiens like to control the narrative. Hear what they want to hear. Many don't even like to look at Mixed-Ups, choose not to. Feel distaste at the withered arms which their own blind sex drive has brought about. They have permitted six to come to the conference only because they couldn't understand a single Connipian thought without them.

Tonkin is the interpreter who the others look up to. It's her third visit to New York; she first came before the war. Attended a clinic where a slew of experts examined her withered arms. It gave doctors some insight or other, did nothing for Tonkin's restricted plight. She came again last year—nineteen forty-nine—her opinion sought as part of the negotiations which set up this needed conference. The American organisers chose her in preference to a true Connipian explicitly because of the short notice with which she could arrive: Tonkin will enter aircraft. And her presence was tokenistic, she wasn't really surprised. Sapiens talk to Sapiens; can't make head or tail of Connipian clicks, and treat all Mixed-Ups as if they are retarded, not worth listening to. Sadly, many are exactly that. Alongside the physical disability, the majority of Mixed-Ups have limited mental functioning. Not all of them, not Tonkin.

She turned forty years old a couple of months ago and her skin remains unblemished. Like all in her cohort of Mixed-Up interpreters, the four ladies and both men, she has taken to wearing a wig. Dressing as a Sapiens. And Tonkin speaks more clearly than any other Mixed-Up alive. By the best estimates there are two thousand or so Connipians living in the forests of New Poplar, all of whom click proficiently but none can manage an utterance of any Sapiens language. Sapiens are numerous, two-and-a-half billion: they talk a lot but cannot click. Mixed-Ups, surely the rarest hominids on the planet, are able to manufacture both forms of communication: speaking and clicking. They kind-of can, but most are poorly co-ordinated. Many slur their words, and their clicking may be worse than their talking. They have a stab at both. Tonkin is a godsend. Very able, good diction and a wide vocabulary. Thought to be a favourite among Connipians too. And the little ones only

New York City, January, 1950

need the interpreter as a mute might. If they've heard the language before they will have grasped it, understand the words spoken to them. For Connipians it is a technical problem—mouths that click not talk—whilst for Sapiens it is the whole kit and caboodle. Clicking means nothing to them but that which a Mixed-Up says it means.

Tonkin aside, most Mixed-Ups struggle in this pivotal role. Jumble up English grammar, and none but she can speak any other Sapiens language. Mental deficiency is the lot of many, a difficulty to compound the boneless arms they cannot control. That there were any exceptions took the longest time to figure out, so low were their expectations of anyone born of a Connipian mother. A Canadian study, the most thorough there has been, estimated that around twenty-five percent of Mixed-Ups function at or around the average intelligence of their Sapiens counterparts. The underperforming majority may suffer primarily from learnt helplessness. If their brains are congenitally defective, no one knows by how much or what good fortune has resulted in the more able twenty-five percent. And over these two hundred and fifty years no Mixed-Up whatsoever has been so lucky as to sport a pair of functioning arms.

In the cohort of interpreters coming to the United Nations Conference, Tonkin stands out. She is a scholar, one who understands Connipian clicks, and can ably reply in kind. Speaks fluent English, Spanish and Dutch. She's learnt a little German too. Behind her skills in languages, she has encyclopaedic knowledge of geography, politics and rudimentary science. History, but primarily that of New Zealand and Connipia. There is no better read Mixed-Up, she is an exceptional academic, would be by Sapiens' standards. Invaluable at a conference like this. Priceless, one might say, although two dollars and twenty cents an hour will be her recompense. The figure arises from a United Nations pay formula, the going rate for freelance interpreters. The less able Mixed-Ups will earn exactly the same. The five who constantly defer to her.

During their stay, the Mixed-Up interpreters will all sleep in The Belvedere Hotel, a different establishment than that which their Connipian cousins will use. Interpreters are not required away from the conference hall. This must be a relief to the management of that swankier hotel—The Edison—where the twenty-three Connipians are to stay. Mixed-Ups have a reputation for being dirty, dribbly, leaving occasional emissions on seats and bedding. It was a relief to the organisers when The Belvedere agreed to take them.

At the mealtime on the evening before the first formal gathering of the species—the interpreters preparing to eat together, away from the main dining room—before any food has been served, Tonkin receives a request to come to reception. On arrival she finds a suited but untidy looking man whom she does not know. He introduces himself—Mr Howard—says he works in The White House. A confidante of Harry S Truman, President of the United States. She tries to question the nature of his visit but he talks over her. Clicks fingers at a passing member of the hotel's staff. A hand on the small of Tonkin's back, he guides her into the small lounge bar. Orders two coffees while they are still on the move.

Tonkin stops after he has made the request, walks no further. 'I cannot drink it.' The staff member has already taken the order, to another she says, 'Water and biscuits, please, young man. Do you recall how I take them?'

He nods, mouth open; a Mixed-Up is an extraordinary sight almost anywhere in the world. She has been in the hotel barely a day, the stares keep coming. And she never has a hot drink; her arms will never raise cup or mug, and sucking coffee through a straw could burn the roof of anyone's mouth.

The pair sit down in a small alcove. Mr Howard explains that he has come to find out how the Connipians are coping with their experience. First timers in New York: a culture shock for many a visitor, and these almost-people live in a forest.

A waitress dressed in black and white brings a tray bearing two coffees in yellow and grey china cups, plus a tiny silver bucket containing sugar cubes and a set of tongs with which to lift them up and into the drink. It would be beyond Tonkin. Mr Howard tells the waitress he will drink them both.

'I've an order coming,' Tonkin tells the waitress, who stares back, looking solely at Tonkin's left arm which has crumpled against the arm of her chair. Tonkin feels nothing, it just looks odd. 'Your new, I think. Don't worry about my arms. Your colleagues will fill you in.'

'Oh,' says the girl, continuing to stare.

When she has left, Tonkin turns to Mr Howard. 'This type of exchange happens all the time.' As she says it, she sees he too is looking only at her misshapen arm. 'Now, Mr Howard, what can I do for you?'

'I'm sorry.' He coughs, raising his eyes to meet hers. 'I hope we can talk candidly, Miss Tonkin?'

'It's Tonkin.'

'What did I say?'

'It's not Miss. I am not missing anything.'

'Tonkin. Do you have a Christian name?'

Tonkin shakes her head: why would she?

'I'm sorry if there are some New Poplar social mores with which I'm unfamiliar, Miss Tonkin...er...Tonkin. We are on the same side in all this; I'm sure of it.'

New York City, January, 1950

She nods. Maybe he is, and it wouldn't do to tell him otherwise. This White House official is very thin, wiry, and of a similar age to her, she guesses. He continues to glance restlessly across her as he speaks, makes eye contact and then quickly turns his head away. He looks a bit dishevelled in his grey suit—creases where there shouldn't be any—might have slept in it for a week. Tonkin tries not to smile at her observation, inwardly pleased to be the better attired. It's an infrequent accomplishment for a Mixed-Up. 'Glad to hear it, Mr Howard. I am here only as an interpreter, my duty is to accurately represent what each side wish to say to the other, not to offer an opinion.' She won't even need to interpret the Sapiens contribution, the Connipians will understand. Sapiens don't necessarily get that, tend to imagine their words to be as opaque to the little people as the clicked thoughts they have still to fathom.

'But you live there. New Poplar. I am interested to understand what the inhabitants think. The little guys. We hear plenty from the Brits, too much frankly.'

As they talk, the girl comes back. A glass of water with a straw in it, pre-crumbled biscuits, as Tonkin requested. 'Do you need any help with this?' she asks, blushing as she says it.

'It will be most satisfactory as it is.'

As the girl leaves, Tonkin ducks her head to the plate to lick up a piece of biscuit. Not the prettiest table manners but she left the dining room for this unscheduled meeting. And her skills are tidier than some in that small party of interpreters.

When she has resumed an upright posture, swallowed, she says what little she can. 'I have lived on the island, Mr Howard. Spent far more time off it, I have to add.' She refers to the island some call Connipia, done so by the more enlightened Sapiens only. She was not living there in the twelve months preceding this conference, unsure quite what the mood is among Connipians. Resignation? Desperation? Hope seems improbable to her. They are not fools. 'The British have sought the opinions of Connipians. It has never been a trusted process. They have plans, designs, and confirming they have consulted the species they think themselves to host suits their purpose. They discard Connipian views at exactly the same frequency with which they solicit them. That's always been the broad view. The British are unwilling to go away although the Connipians were there first...'

'But Tonkin, you are only half Connipian. I am right, aren't I? You have just as much in common with us. With the humans.'

She doesn't like it but her mouth turns into a smirk as she prepares to reply. Mr Howard's proposition has been put to her by others many times before, it took years for her to frame the answer. 'If your father was

115

a rapist, Mr Howard, with which parent would you most identify?'

He drops his eyes to the coffee cup. 'I've been most insensitive. I should have thought...' His fingers touch the handle of the cup, push it slowly anti-clockwise around on its saucer. 'Tell me how it is for you? A conference for the Connipians, I've thought to myself that you Mixed-Ups might feel overlooked in this process.'

'Mr Howard, between Connipia and America lies the vast Pacific Ocean. Do you think that body of water American or Connipian? Or neither, perhaps, for both those place names refer to areas of land and not the sea which laps their shores. Mixed-Ups are like that ocean. Detached entirely from the two species who should never have melded. We are neither one thing nor the other.'

He sits for a moment contemplating her words. Or not contemplating them while giving the impression that he is. Tonkin is never sure if a Mixed-Up's words arrive intact in a Sapiens brain. They might be filtered through the plethora of prejudices and assumptions which have gathered around her type. Bitter from maternal rejection is a common myth, weak of intellect another. Or with the more liberal-minded they go unheard because of the sadness that thinking over their route into this world can prompt in the listener.

'I hope you don't mind that I've come today, called on you like this Miss Tonkin...er...Tonkin. I'm sorry if I've dredged up thoughts that you'd rather I hadn't. The issues that engage me in my governmental role have never involved Connipians before. Nor Mixed-Ups. Not until very recently. I have yet to venture there, to New Poplar, much as I would love to go. Please accept my apologies. I am here to learn.'

Tonkin shimmies her entire body so that her arms come forward together, ripples them to bring her flapping palms upright. The gesture is self-explanatory: she accepts his apology.

'And you, Miss...sorry...Tonkin, have an acute perception. That is your reputation. Do you have any insight into why those poor Connipians perished on the way here? I am glad we have lost none of your own type.'

'Mr Howard, I have spoken with the three interpreters who were on the ship. However, none clicked about it with the Connipians, didn't raise the issue of the deaths with them, and I am not surprised. It simply isn't done. They are all sensitive enough to Connipian mores. The issue at the heart of it has always been disorientation. Connipians understand themselves to be living a certain destiny, in a particular place. They have struggled to incorporate the invasion of Sapiens onto their island into their revised worldview. Not that they deny it has happened, it is simply that the impact has been so profound. Entirely negatively. Knocking the way of life which they enjoyed—seemingly forever—from under their feet. It is not so many generations back that they understood that they

New York City, January, 1950

alone were the protectors of all other species. Did not guess that another type of people had stronger powers and might choose to exercise them so destructively. To go out into that other world is vertiginous, dizzying...'

'Tonkin, your point about us—the destructive thing—is a little too cryptic for me. Do you mean the war? That was quite unprecedented, Miss Tonkin. Never to be repeated. We were up against something else back there. We—Americans, people generally—are not really about fighting, about destruction. It's not the way we conduct our business. Not in normal times. Americans entered the war to put a stop to it. And preventing future fighting is the point of the United Nations. It's why we're having this conference. To glean a better understanding of the Connipian perspective.'

'The war was unprecedented, you say? World war number two, and there have been more wars than can be counted before you started giving them numbers. Victory over fascism; not so long as they imagine hoisting a flag up a pole gives them dominion over the lands of others. The conference is even, I understand, addressing the issue of whether or not Connipians may still be hunted.'

'It is not addressing that issue, Miss Tonkin. It was dealt with long ago. The issue is the right to life of the Connipians. It's complicated. I understand that hunting never really occurred. It was just...well, I don't recall exactly what went on. Didn't the British pass the law in Gladstone's day? The one banning hunting.'

'Ramsey MacDonald, Mr Howard. It was during his term in office that such practices became illegal. Barely twenty years ago. Gladstone tried but he was unable to secure enough support at the time. Hunters in the House, they used to say.'

'Nobody hunted Connipians. Ever. I've read that, Miss Tonkin, I'm sure I have.'

'Their status—appearing as young girls might—shamed those who spoke of it into inaction, for the most part. Their status as belonging to the animal kingdom remains a strongly held view.'

'I'm sure you're right. You know the history well...and we're addressing it...'

'And the Connipians believe, contrary to your own beliefs and behaviour, Mr Howard, that the hunting or slaughter of members of any species under the sun is wrong. An unnecessary destruction wrought for the benefit of domination, not sustenance at all. We have...'

'Miss Tonkin, I admire their lifestyle. However, this conference won't be addressing vegetarianism—don't think I could give up meat, darned sure President Truman will do no such thing—if that is what you're advocating. We are considering equal rights for...'

'For a very small number...'

'For Connipians including yourself Miss...I'm sorry, Tonkin.'

'...I am not a Connipian, Mr Howard. And I was saying to your earlier enquiry, that the deceased of the journey to this city died from the disorientation of being at sea, being in a corner of the world to which their kind has never voluntarily sought to go. Not prior to this conference. Their perspective is age-old in Connipia. Truly. Dwelling upon it seems to disorient you Sapiens every bit as much as Connipians are disturbed by the Sapiens-dominated world. Connipians have lived as they do for close to a million years, you must know that. Inhabited their island in some fashion for a million. That's a one and six zeros. The British have been there for only a cymbals clash; indeed, they have inhabited their own cold island for but a few trifling generations in comparison. What it is to be bonded with a land as the Connipians are with their island appears unknown to you. That is as they think it. Americans idolise pioneers, place great store upon venturing where none have gone before. Connipians understand that you do not experience life as they do. Seek out turmoil for gains which make no sense from the perspective of a settled people...' With a twist of the torso, Tonkin makes her withered arms swirl and momentarily point at Mr Howard's head. '...the brains are too different. I have learnt, and Connipians know it also, that the Sapiens have an ego in there. It might be conjecture. A made-up facility but you all seem to believe it.'

'Tonkin, this is a challenge for us. And we're trying to forge the modern world here, not philosophising about it all on a barstool. You understand what I mean? Very difficult. The British still believe New Poplar the most suitable name for your land, discovered by a rag-tag band of seafarers from some place near London bearing the same name. That's as I've heard it came about. We have advised them that Connipia is to be its name, a helpful step in the right direction. You're on board with this, I'm sure you are. The British don't like it, of course, and they won't be giving up the place entirely. I don't think any nation would if it were standing in their shoes...'

'Connipians consider it unruly that the British should encroach onto their island when they already have a bigger one.'

'Well...yes. Connipians don't use the limestone or the potash. The world doesn't like to see these things go to waste. And the Connipians haven't farmed the grasslands of their own island, only the forest...'

'The grass is a predominantly British creation. And Connipians certainly haven't raised sheep for slaughter. It saddens them enormously, watching it take place on the land in which they long lived without such disharmony.'

'But Tonkin, the British have improved the island immeasurably. I

New York City, January, 1950

understand there has been progress getting education to Connipians. Helping them to see beyond some of their more primitive ways.' He stops talking and looks at Tonkin. 'Is primitive the wrong word?'

'It is a word. You use it disparagingly but the Connipians revere all that has gone before. You see, they never suffered the fall from grace that you believe marks the commencement of the story of your own kind.'

'Tonkin, I see that the gulf is wide. Very different cultures. We want to make progress here. Believe me, my boss—this is President Truman, I'm talking about here—he feels similarly. Fully intends to drop in on the conference, hopes to push it on. We get your grievances, Connipian grievances, we intend that the outcome of this event goes some way to addressing them. I cannot imagine the President even showing up if it's to be little more than a conference of despair. You know we can't kick out the British, they're our allies, more so than the Connipians are ever likely to be. He won't let it stop him from dragging those self-same Brits into this conference. The question for us is this: can all the old colonial powers put past relationships behind them? Forge partnerships in their wake. India has gained independence, chaos is in the mix, and I pray to God it all works out for them. For the Indian people. New Poplar—or Connipia as I hope we are soon to call your island—is of a quieter order. You know what makes this so challenging?'

'Tell me?'

'You must see it. Living there and all, and then there's your job. You know we can't communicate directly with the Connipians. No language shared, no American—or Brit for that matter—has learnt to understand any of the clicking. How we are to reach a settlement depends on you, Tonkin. You and your colleagues. I think you may need to be diplomats as much as you are interpreters. I'd like you to keep us informed about what the Connipians make of it all. We struggle to get a grip on their world view. You must see that.'

'I have learnt a little, Mr Howard. My particular status. I live as a bridge between worlds. I am confident my team will convey all that Connipians wish to tell. What they and I do not know is whether you have the capacity to listen and absorb their viewpoint. It does not arise out of your lives, nor out of lives similar to yours. The British colonised Connipia, and in that it is similar to other places awaiting liberation. However, most anti-imperialist movements are dominated by those wanting to usurp the occupying power. The Connipians have another way of living in this world. They do not seek to replace British rule but simply to live in the manner they consider natural. Rule over the land plays no part in it. They fear—and Mr Howard, I concur with them—that you dismiss this. Cannot see the richness of their social order because they haven't nominated anyone king or president, priest or harbour master. Cannot really understand why they haven't needed to.' Mr Howard turns an empty coffee cup in his hands, gazes unblinking into Tonkin's face. Contemplating her words or pretending to do so. She has yet to get the measure of this man. 'And, in turn, they feel every encroachment by the Sapiens as a prelude to annihilation.'

'Whoa! That's quite a melodramatic statement, Miss Tonkin.'

'And yours a Sapiens perspective. I am a Mixed-Up, lived among Sapiens for long periods of my life. I understand your concept of progress, that tomorrow should mark an improvement upon yesterday. Connipians don't see it that way. A million years, sir. A time you cannot comprehend. They have been living in a melodrama for just the last two hundred and fifty of those years, the tumult coming after all that serenity. And a shocking drama it continues to be: pillage after pillage. You speak of limestone and potash, but Connipians feel the British stealing the earth beneath their feet. And worse still, many Connipians were removed from the island. Themselves stolen. Put on display as living exhibits. Some Mixed-Ups too, I might add. And we cannot contemplate them—us, from my perspective, the Mixed-Ups—without dwelling on a most sensitive difference. Connipians do not rape Sapiens; only the reverse is true.'

Mr Howard looks tired. Tonkin wonders if she has said too much. Her role is to tell the Sapiens what the Connipians are clicking. If Mr Howard had been able to speak directly with one of the Connipian delegates, she need not have launched into this tirade. 'Sorry to bring it up, I don't mean it personally, Mr Howard. I raise it because it is their most central grievance. The British said they have outlawed it, prohibited men from having any form of sexual relations with Connipians, and those are words turned to air. It goes on.'

'I've been reading some stuff that the Connipians have submitted, Tonkin,' he says. Drawls rather slowly. 'I see that it's hard. They don't easily fit into the modern world. Negotiations start the day after tomorrow. The British-out stuff that they've written into their aims is not really helpful. My advice is that they compromise early and force the other side to do likewise. That's the best strategy, Tonkin. You can choose how to pass it along.'

2.

Tonkin and the four pure-bred Connipians in the taxi cab click together. She confirms for them that, in the past, she has found pleasure in the type of show they are to see. Sometimes but not always. The ride from The Edison Hotel to Albright's Theatre is a short one. They will listen to a wide range of music, watch contemporary stage acts. The show will be

New York City, January, 1950

in front of a paying audience; the Connipians go free for the sheer novelty they provide. And they have no money, never seen the point. Tonkin assures them that the reception will be warm, it is in the nature of diplomacy. The Connipians sit with their legs stretched out, not a single shoe so much as hanging over the edge of the taxi's backseat. All four wear wigs, as does Tonkin. A young Connipian named Klapakipsy looks around confidently, the others seem less self-assured. She alone has looked directly into the eyes of all who look at her, including the Sapiens males on the sidewalk before entering this vehicle. The cold winter sidewalk of New York City: lit storefronts displaying the wares of closed shops; men in thick trench coats, hats and scarves. A woman on the arm of one or two; no unaccompanied women at this time of an evening. It is weather for only the hardiest, a cold and blustery wind.

When the young Connipian begins to click a monologue, Tonkin must listen intently to gather the entirety of its meaning. Østergaard, the UN Attaché who travels with them, asks Tonkin what she is saying. Klapakipsy's thoughts click thick and fast, Tonkin listens, and is unsure where to begin telling the man what the spray refers to. She notices how closely the official watches the Connipian, it makes her wonder if the wig-wearing is a mistake. Klapakipsy has smooth white skin, quite the same colour as New York snow, the brilliant blue eyes of all the Connipians, and her cheekbones are a nudge higher than many. She wears a green dress—these off-islanders are, with a purpose in mind, deviating from the Connipian Blue—a thick white cardigan across her shoulders. Woollen stockings cover her short legs; Connipians never wear them back home, this is an alien climate. January in New York, cold like the South Pacific has never known, not for more than two thousand generations. And Klapakipsy is slender, shorter than many Connipians. Less than tiny. Might be a doll, dressed up by a child with taste. Tonkin thinks the UN attaché is drinking her in with his eyes; she interprets nothing for him until the clicking has ceased.

'Klapakipsy is curious to see the entertainment; she wonders if the gulf will prove a wide one, sir. Yesterday evening, she and other Connipians watched the television in the hotel lounge. She appreciated what a clever and intricate device the machine is; the content of the programme was of little interest. Connipians do not consider entertainment to be a separate function to contemplation.'

The Dane does not reply immediately, might even be trying to see her point of view. 'We don't understand you at all, do we?'

Tonkin begins to translate this for Klapakipsy but the tiny one's eye movement indicates she has understood. Like most Connipians, she has no difficulty with the English language beyond her inability to project it with lips and tongue.

God Help the Connipians

'Still learning about people so different to yourselves, aren't you, sir?' says Tonkin when Klapakipsy's short clicked reply is complete. 'She says it would be a two-way process but, this helpful conference aside, the Sapiens intrigue with Connipians has felt like as assault to them.'

'But Klapakipsy,' says Østergaard, clearly familiar with the use of interpreters, not put off by the single direction of Tonkin's input, 'do you think that Connipians understand Sapiens already? I know that you've had some contact but, frankly, what you have had has not been helpful.'

Tonkin watches the attachés eyes stray across the best-dressed Connipian, the one to whom he addresses all his questions. The pulled-in dress she wears, showing her figure, her narrow hips, seems a departure from Connipian deportment. Tonkin puzzles over this. No Connipian puts store in dressing up; they wear blue or blue. Nothing on their top half until they are first with child. Klapakipsy has covered herself as she would not were the conference to take place in the forests of her island.

'Mr Østergaard,' she says when Klapakipsy's clicking has stilled, 'she feels overloaded with the stimulation of New York. The complexity of this city, people compelled to work in jobs which connect to their livelihood only through the medium of money, is taking a little acclimatising to. Back in Connipia, in the forest where they live as they always have, Connipians pay Sapiens only a modicum of mind. The Sapiens are the ones who have strayed, all other animals—including Connipians—being the more predictable.'

'She said that? Little Klapakipsy? That's her view or yours?'

'I have sought to render her thoughts on the matter into English words. It is complicated, Mr Østergaard. I know myself to struggle between the ill-fitting cultures. Perhaps I am more Sapiens than Connipian.'

'You are?' A look of surprise crosses his face; Mr Østergaard erases it just as quickly. 'You've got the clicking, speak it...'

'I have lived on the island, on and off, but I might have travelled more than any other Mixed-Up...'

'But you were raised by Connipians, your mother...'

'I was part of the Quaker programme...'

'I didn't know that. Must have been a good experience. You've done very well for a Mixed...'

'Mr Østergaard, we have only one life and this is mine. I had a childhood on New Zealand, it will remain the only childhood I remember. For over a decade I had no contact with Connipians. The programme stipulated that I could not. An ocean between me and them. I didn't know I could use their tongue although I must have heard it as a tiny infant. Recalled it well enough when I returned. Not that I knew I

New York City, January, 1950

had such an ability already inlaid. Not when I set off for home.'

'New Zealand, that's where you were raised? Was that strange? Living down there? Not many like you there, I don't suppose.' She sees him glance quickly at her do-nothing arms.

'The programme took more than just me away from New Poplar. I understood that there were other Mixed-Ups in New Zealand, just not in the small town where I lived. I never once saw another. My foster carers tried their Sapiens best. My family...can I be frank, Mr Østergaard? My foster family may have been a more nurturing home than those found in the Blue Houses. The Connipian way of child-rearing is a far cry from the nuclear family of the Sapiens. And their feelings towards Mixed-Ups are not straightforward. We should never have happened, that is at the core of it. There was no rape on their island for the first million years. It can put a strain on things. You might say that we shame them but I think it a little more layered than that. Connipians don't think in terms of victimhood. They address each problem as it is.' Tonkin's unlined face is briefly furrowed as she contemplates them: the species she knows so well and can never be a part of. 'The Quaker programme won some friends where it wished to, the skills I learnt were many. It also tried to contribute to the destruction of a species, wouldn't you say? Whatever joy they had with us Mixed-Ups, there were no successes in the fostering of Connipians. Not one. Most of them simply died, did so as a result of their removal from the forests where they had a belonging like nothing you wandering Sapiens can imagine. We Mixed-Ups, on the other hand, are much easier prey. Malleable. I have eaten meat and not always at my foster mother's insistence.'

They ride on in silence but for the gentle clicking of the Connipians.

* * *

Klapakipsy rolls her eyes, does it the Connipian way. The watching Sapiens may not pick it up but Tonkin does. Her gesture indicates that the speaker may stop clicking. There is no further need.

Tonkin has been interpreting the lines of the song. Not that Klapakipsy can't understand the words, it is simply unusual for Connipians to contemplate ideas that are not literal. Only the Sapiens do that, the little people never have. She quietly clicks that it is edifying simply hearing the sound, letting the impression wash over her. The programme notes say the tunes are joyous. Klapakipsy clicks quietly that it does not sound so to her. The pleasures Sapiens enjoy are not for everyone: the meat of birds and pigs and cattle, burnt over a fire; ladies warbling about mysterious love; dropping bombs from aeroplanes. Tonkin has learnt already how well-prepared Klapakipsy is for this conference. Made a point of studying and understanding the interactions of Sapiens, how they behave in groups, and how they conduct themselves one on one. Connipians have long had access to the libraries built for them on the forest's edge, to books and, more recently, tape recordings, and radio, although they never take them into their own blue homes. They have learnt much about the bigger people. The effect of this has dawned on few Sapiens. They assume Connipians as ignorant of the world beyond the forest as they know themselves to be of the one within. Don't realise what fast learners these feisty girls really are. When Connipians hear a language, they quickly fathom its intent. Grasp very precisely what the words they cannot form with their tongues mean. Their own clicking remains beyond the grasp of the counter-species. Sapiens have not made the leap, cannot conceptually accept that there is an alternative to words while Connipians have cottoned on to the broken-down thoughts that are spoken ceaselessly in New York City, in every city, written down in books or rendered harmonious in song.

This part of the show is a medley of Stephen Foster's music, his most famous tunes. Tonkin knows nothing about the composer but recognises a couple of melodies from the soundtracks to old films which she watched in her New Zealand childhood.

Jørgen Østergaard leans back in his seat. Slouching, relaxed. He drums his fingers lightly on the back of the seat in front. He sits between Tonkin and Klapakipsy, did so at his own insistence, and their persistent clicking across him may have distracted from his enjoyment of the show. He keeps his eyes on the little Connipian woman anyway. On Klapakipsy. Gives her a proprietorial smile whenever he catches her eye. It could be how a father reassures himself that his daughter is at ease in company. Tonkin worries that his eyes might search her more purposefully than that. He does it most intently when Klapakipsy is not looking back.

A lady wearing white lace, a dress which fans grandly around her, paces the stage, singing beneath a parasol. The orchestration of this piece is gentle, little more than a hum behind her voice, then it swells up for the rousing chorus to which many in the audience sing along. At those moments, Østergaard looks into Klapakipsy's face with a smile that indicates she might join in. His lips mouth the word's although he appears not to trust himself with the tune. The man is Danish; presumably they sing as well as any other nationality, but he may not have heard a lot of Foster. Tonkin finds Klapakipsy's expression hard to read, she could be enjoying the attention of the UN official, more probably wondering if she can win him over to the Connipian cause. Get him on board in the negotiations to come. She has certainly grasped the Sapiens reliance on person-to-person connections, she spoke of this with Tonkin during the cab ride. Something she never translated for Jørgen Østergaard: Klapakipsy relayed the view that men never listen to women

New York City, January, 1950

unless they are smitten with them. And then they hang onto their every word.

The other three Connipians, one beside Tonkin and the two sitting to the far side of Klapakipsy, look bored. Only they and their interpreter will know this. It is in the fading of their eyes. Not an expression Sapiens use between themselves, and they are the slowest learners.

When the comedian, Whip MacAlister, takes to the stage, Tonkin sees little chance that their dull night will improve. His words require no translation, they are simple enough. She notices how Klapakipsy remains very alert, even when the jokes puzzle more than they amuse. Tonkin can see why some lines are funny but this stuff does not translate. Language or culture. Connipians don't really joke about anything; they are a serious people. No aspect of the guests' disinterest registers with the Dane, with Østergaard. He smiles and laughs, and laughs and smiles.

Tonkin recognises the boorishness of Jørgen's behaviour. The inappropriate flirtatiousness. After laughing heartily at a joke about the Japanese, he lowers his neck and tries to whisper an explanation into the little Connipian's ear. Mid-exchange he turns to Tonkin, the interpreter, still unsure how much of his speech Klapakipsy does and does not understand. 'Tell her,' he says: 'They were really very evil those few years ago, nowadays we can all laugh about it. We don't stay mad at anyone for long. Life is too short.'

Tonkin clicks, tells the pretty little Connipian nothing about the Japanese or Whip MacAlister's carefully modulated humour. Knows that Klapakipsy has already understood his comment. She clicks a spray asking her if she senses that Mr Østergaard is getting ideas. He wears a ring that indicates marriage; however, his wife might be half a world away. Could be in Denmark while he waltzes around the hotels and theatres of New York City. Klapakipsy clicks back, acknowledges her point while seeming unconcerned.

'I do not trust him,' clicks Tonkin.

'If he trusts me, it could be most advantageous,' thinks Klapakipsy. Does it with audible clicks. 'We need European men putting our case forward, we must make enormous gains here. Anything less will spell the end.'

* * *

After the show, officials guide the Connipians into the theatre's small bar area. About twenty Sapiens follow, all by pre-arrangement. Along one wall stands a posse of waiting photographers. As the flashlights start to pop—pictures for the morning's newsstands—all the Connipians except Klapakipsy seem alarmed. Unnerved by the shower of blink-inducing flashes. She alone arranges her face in a near-human smile, looks like a

God Help the Connipians

girl in a sweet shop. This seems to calm the other three. None of the Connipians rise far above the waistlines of the entirely male Sapiens contingent. Not an inch above the taller of them. The men have gone straight to the tables bearing snacks: sandwiches of ham, pastrami and tuna; pretzel sticks; chicken drumsticks with a deep-red dipping sauce. Food the larger species start to push into their mouths while the Connipians still seek to understand the expectations of the gathering. Their hosts said nothing about it beforehand, Tonkin is sure of it.

Østergaard points, an exaggerated wave of a mimed handgun, to a table with a small paper flag upon it. The only signage the caterers have deployed. ***Food for Connipians*** it reads. Tonkin wonders why she didn't spot it. She and the little ones all read proficiently. No offensive chicken in this spread. Celery, pineapple cubes and a chickpea dip. Klapakipsy leads the way, stands on a chair so as to reach the food—the table is of Sapiens dimensions—she passes plated food down to her fellow Connipians. Tonkin is surprised how self-assured she is in the situation.

Mr Howard, the White House official, is here. Tonkin never saw him in the theatre, thinks he wasn't in there. Just came for the after-show chat. Or the food, but he doesn't look to be eating any. He comes over to her, flexes his knees so as not to tower far above, asks after the mood of the Connipians. 'Has the show been well received?'

'I think so, Mr Howard. It is slightly bewildering because none of the acts they saw have Connipian equivalents.' Tonkin feels distracted because she has seen Mr Østergaard put a hand upon Klapakipsy's shoulder; she worries that the Connipian seeks to flirt as a way to win over the man, and it is not a tactic she ever expected one of her mother's species to deploy. Not after all that has gone before. Initially Tonkin was pleased to see the Connipians wearing wigs—making an effort—although there are many on the island who deplore such brazen imitation of their Sapiens oppressors. Now she too is having second thoughts. Klapakipsy's appearance is a confusing sight: she could be a star of the stage in her own right, slender of build with slight rounding of the hips, a gentle swell to her chest, but she stands barely three-feet tall. Head and shoulders below Tonkin who is herself far smaller than any man in the room. Eyes of Connipian Blue while Tonkin bears the brown of her unknown father. Klapakipsy has used kohl to accentuate the eyebrows she would otherwise be without. Connipians have little or no hair above their pale eyelashes, and these, too, she has kohled. Kohl or an equivalent potion drawn from a crushed root garnered in the forests of their island. Tonkin sees the fierce intelligence in her face, doubts if the pawing Dane has considered more than her shape. Her tiny stature. Connipians usually hold their expression a neutral stare, animated only when they click in a manner that is integral to it. Reveal

New York City, January, 1950

little unless one is also aware of the thoughts they spray. Klapakipsy is one on her own, has learnt to upturn her lips and allow a dimple to form in either cheek. Her green dress is knee-length, white woolly stockings which add to the illusion that she is a child. Not a dot of blue in her clothing. Tonkin thought this clever when first she saw it, now wonders if Klapakipsy can really pull it off. Demand Connipian autonomy by looking like a tiny Sapiens.

Tonkin continues to talk with Mr Howard, to satisfy his queries. Watches the four Connipians as she does it. And only one seems able to engage their hosts without the services of an interpreter. Klapakipsy, of course.

* * *

They all return by taxi to The Edison Hotel. To the best of Tonkin's knowledge, Østergaard has done no more that place a frequent hand on the small of Klapakipsy's back. At this juncture he thanks all the Connipians, Tonkin too, for their company, and takes his leave. Tonkin remains in the foyer; the young Connipian has clicked that she would like to converse privately with her. Tonkin wishes to accommodate the request, feels a fascination with Klapakipsy which is unusual for her. Enjoys the presence of her striking appearance, her agile thought. She advised Mr Howard that, as an interpreter, she is required to remain neutral, and then she spouted a little anti-Sapiens rhetoric. God knows, it is easily felt. There isn't really any conflict in her mind. She will help Klapakipsy if she can. Not that her role is a manipulative one. At the bottom of it all, an interpreter can do no more than give a faithful interpretation. No point in making anything up; each side needs to know what the other thinks, for better or for worse.

The little Connipian comes over to her and clicks a quick trill, advises that they will go to their upstairs suite.

Tonkin clicks back that she needs to clear it with the hotel management. The Edison is not a welcoming venue for Mixed-Ups.

Klapakipsy walks over to a small coffee table, stands to write on a notepad, using a pencil placed beside it, one bearing the name of the hotel along its spine. Humans are pointing, she is quite a sight. A pretty little doll, the coffee table coming far above her waist height; knee height on all in the room with no Connipian blood in their veins.

We need this nice lady in our room for an hour.

The confident Connipian goes to the reception desk, clicks a little as she holds her printed sign. Gestures that Tonkin is the subject of the piece.

The lady behind the desk leans over to look at the little woman holding the sign, smiles broadly at her, and then glances quickly at the male concierge who stands centre floor. Her colleague shakes his head.

'I'm sorry,' says the receptionist. 'Rules and standards, I'm sure you understand.'

Klapakipsy clicks a little spray. 'Understand the mean-spirited nature of your so-called hospitality,' hears Tonkin, and she smiles to herself.

The concierge has walked across and mutters quietly to the lady behind the desk who, in turn, relays the message to the waiting pair. 'The Mixed-Up must be staying at The Belvedere Hotel. If she goes back there...' The receptionist never meets Tonkin's eyes, looks exclusively at little Klapakipsy. '...she can telephone you. We'll see it's put through to your room.'

Klapakipsy clicks again and ends by asking Tonkin to interpret for the lady. For a second, she does not, and the Connipian gives a slow and deliberate blink of her eyes. An insistence.

'Madam,' says Tonkin, 'these are her thoughts...Klapakipsy's thoughts, not my own. Your hotel is void of meaningful cordiality if you will not extend it to those with whom the Connipians must engage to make a success of the conference. You mistake standards for bigotry and forgo the opportunity to make a small contribution to a better world.'

'Your only bitter,' says the receptionist. 'I don't imagine that sweet little girl said anything of the sort.'

* * *

Tonkin and Klapakipsy have left the hotel together. It feels like the most outrageous thing to have done. Late into the New York night a small lady with lifeless arms accompanies a truly tiny one, so small she must appear as a toddler to the few men—there are zero ladies—out on the cold streets so late at night. Snow piled up where sidewalk meets building; the main thoroughfares are clear. The shimmer of frost anywhere that feet and tyres are still to pulp. Klapakipsy clicks her thoughts on Sapiens society. That it is unconscionable.

Tonkin wants to laugh, bends her head close to the clicking girl, tells her that she is one on her own. Not a typical comment among the egoless Connipians. 'You shouldn't worry about how they treat me,' says Tonkin. 'I have grown used to the embarrassment my predicament evokes in Sapiens.'

'They are not embarrassed by you but by their own true natures; they know it as surely as they keep it out of their pressing thoughts.' Klapakipsy is unforgiving of the hotel management. 'And there is no reason to be so wrong-headed. Not in a hotel already accommodating Connipians. One might expect they would have contemplated the connection. Not just our interpreters but kith and kin.' Klapakipsy appears to shiver. Her coat is thick, like a regular New Yorker's coat,

New York City, January, 1950

made specially for her in the tiniest size imaginable. Preparation has gone into this conference one way or another. 'Can't think, won't think,' she bites in chattered clicks. 'That might sum up the lot of them.'

Tonkin bobs her head, nodded agreement of a sort, and then she asks, 'Are there many Mixed-Ups in your forest village?' A provocative question.

'I wish that there were, my friend. Your history—I don't mean personally, but that of the Mixed-Ups—is not a straightforward one. The birth, the difficulties it portends. Your size. Our wish to share care when one of every Mixed-Up's two parents always absents themselves. Every father, every last one since that ruddy boat anchored off the coast of Connipia, simply subcontracts...what an exclusively Sapiens term that is...their responsibility to nuns who are sworn never to bear children of their own. And yes, Tonkin, most Mixed-Ups spend a little time, sometimes a substantial portion of their childhood, in our village or their mother's villages. You must have been a dream child—I've known a Mixed-Up or two who presented their mothers with challenges—although I understand you were taken off-island. Terrible. The many who are mentally less able than the likes of you and I, cannot adapt to our ways so easily. We Connipians have complex systems of stability.

'I understand. There never was a Connipian simpleton, was there? A blessing, I'm sure, whilst rendering you ill-prepared for all that has come to pass.'

Little Klapakipsy tugs on Tonkin's lifeless arm, and as she turns, they look into each other's faces. Her wide-eyed expression is the closest a Connipian comes to evidencing mirth. 'Sisters in a struggle,' she clicks, as she pushes her left hand into the hood of her duffle coat, pulls away the black-haired wig that must have made her so alluring to Østergaard. Tossing back her head she lets the hood fall away too. The bald Connipian look has returned to her. A sight Tonkin actually prefers, loves the sight of this bright little one. Beams a smile back at Klapakipsy.

A ship's horn sounds out in the chill night. They have walked four blocks, the Hudson River arriving in their view. Klapakipsy clicks quietly, Tonkin is alert. Distinguishes each thought, eliminates from her mind the tapping of the boats' mooring lines, and the click of shoes as a man with segs in his heels walks on the far side of the road. Concentrates only on what the Connipian wishes her to hear.

'You are correct to the core, Tonkin. The ugly man, Østergaard, has designs to rape me. It is obvious. I must not give him to understand how transparent he is. I believe I have as good as won him over to the cause, and I cannot give that up. Do you know what he says of me? Please tell.' This she clicks quite slowly, rhythmically, as if to ensure Tonkin understands each thought she expresses. She is grateful to Tonkin for her concern; agrees with her judgement explicitly; could not say so earlier for fear that her body language might alert Østergaard. She despises him, reciprocates no fellow feeling for the tactile Dane. She is exploiting his lust, can and will; her own tactic terrifies her. There is subtle nuance to Connipian clicks and now, free of Sapiens hurrying her into interpretation, Tonkin grasps it entirely. Klapakipsy takes hold of the dead hands on the ends of Tonkin's withered arms, holds them and looks up into her face. 'I understand your role, dear Tonkin. And what takes place here may be only the face-saving diplomacy of powerful men seeking to counter the impression that they are fascists. Fascists with regard to Connipians whatever side claims to have won the world war of which they are so proud. Proud of bombs and guns and death. Zealously swallowing the myth which declares their bravery of more importance than their stupidity. We must seek to subvert it. Use their self-serving conference to glean more from the British than they—or their friend Truman—ever intended us to acquire. The presence of the British on the island is killing us. They take and they take and they take.'

This levelly clicked discourse gives Tonkin pause to sigh. A release that Connipians never do and which Mixed-Ups must have inherited from their father-line. For years on end, Tonkin lives her life as an enquiring Homo Sapiens might, learning to better herself, to adapt to situations. Be a good scholar, a good interpreter. Once she learnt to dance, although her arms only swung, could not find the sharper rhythms which her feet sought. And yet it always comes back to this. She bats for her mother's side. Whoever her father is, his conduct towards the Connipians was an utter disgrace. And that's Sapiens for you. She harbours no illusions about men, about the manner of her own conception. She wishes to help Klapakipsy, ensure she gets everything she might from this conference. Do it for the Connipians. What use an interpreter might be she has yet to guess. She realises she is as mesmerised by Klapakipsy as the Dane was earlier. Loves the sight of her dancing blue eyes. 'I wish to help,' she clicks in reply. 'How I could do so while maintaining the illusion of impartiality, I am uncertain. You know how obstinate they are; diplomacy is nothing but a mask for their many sins.'

They must look a sight. The smallest of figures standing at the edge of the famous waterline. A felt hat a-crest the flurry of a wig still worn by Tonkin; she cannot remove hers with a simple swipe of the hand as Klapakipsy earlier did. Putting it on is quite the rigmarole, nosing it into position on her bed and burrowing the cone of her head into it until she is confident it hangs correctly. She will then lightly toss her brow in front of a mirror for five minutes or more—jiggle it into position—before leaving her room. Many interpreters avail themselves of the personal

New York City, January, 1950

assistance which is offered here in New York and in the hostels of East Town, New Poplar, help from Sapiens with many of the physical tasks which challenge a Mixed-Up. Tonkin won't allow it, freely admits that pride is her greatest affliction.

And the littlest, hood no longer up—taut white skin of face and skull braced against the chill wind—doesn't stop thinking. Audibly thinking. Sharing her ideas with spray after spray. Within her clicking commentary, she raises a query as to whether hominids have been wise to stray into these climes. Only railings separate the pair from the icy Hudson River, the almost ocean. Klapakipsy looks around, away from the water and towards the tall buildings which have erupted onto the surface of Manhattan Island. Each one built for Sapiens—no one else would live in such warrens—their every storey is twice the height of any dwelling place on Connipia. Thirty or forty floors high they climb, each building reaching up into the sky, squares of light sharply outline many of the windows against the black of the January night. She clicks to Tonkin that it is a spectacular anomaly. As ugly as a colony of termites of which she has seen pictures. A metaphor for the Sapiens entire society. Building in so few generations a structure so precarious it must fall back down before the tenth generation has come to air. The Sapiens future as bleak as the Connipian one, with a shared causal link.

'Perhaps it is beautiful to those who feel they belong here,' says Tonkin. 'That is neither you nor I; nothing could be plainer.'

'You've been before,' clicks Klapakipsy, and Tonkin indicates with her eyes that she has. 'Was it this cold?'

'Rather hot, summertime. Without the breeze that caresses Connipia year-round.'

'Year round unless a wind whips up.' And this qualification is true. Once or twice a generation it even threatens the skyfields, although the vines on which their fruit grows will not be broken. Left hanging while a premature harvest may litter the forest floor. 'And reminiscence about our island is not what we need to share in this precious time, Tonkin.'

The Mixed-Up dips her head, looks into the blue eyes, enjoying the fair sight. Klapakipsy's face.

'You know I might already owe my life to you, don't you?' clicks the little Connipian. Tonkin draws down her brow, a line or two emerges. Utterly bewildered by this comment. Before she has so much as guessed what Klapakipsy refers to, she is spraying clicks once more, unrelated to the aside of gratitude she has just extended. She tells Tonkin that Israel has been returned to the Jews, India a free state. Illusions, illusions. The days of colonisation are not over: the Sapiens love to lord it over each other—grab power until death us do part—addicted to their hierarchical order. This historical moment, is an opportunity. The notion of a post-war settlement. And what the Sapiens world wants from Connipia—Klapakipsy calls it New Poplar, or more precisely she clicks a string of sounds which relay "the southerly resurrection of that small anus which sits on the north bank of the River Thames"—has, to date, been limestone and potash. Afforded themselves of opportunistic sex while they are there, and then they exclude mention of it in their own history books. Perhaps they would like to get to know the other people who live there. Learn from the hominids who don't fight wars. She reminds Tonkin that they have cooperated in many Sapiens anthropological studies over the years; dialogue is good. Those that included kidnap or experimentation they see no benefit from. Far too often they were taken and used for Sapiens purposes regardless. When Tonkin interrupts, gives her a short stare, queries what she meant by 'owe her life,' Klapakipsy clicks over her. Continues to spray about diverting the purpose of the conference. This moment is temporary; the Connipians would not and cannot drive the British from the island by force. It's there one chance, however remote. The Connipians could then be living as they choose while the Sapiens extinct themselves as they surely will.

For a second Tonkin reflects on this: Connipians cannot plant bombs. Impossible, they have never swatted a single fly. It is a truth of the very longest standing. Rubbing up against Homo Sapiens for these two hundred and fifty years is taking its toll.

'A slim chance,' clicks Klapakipsy, 'but a chance. Girls like us cannot take on those brutes at their own game.' She repeats the mantra that it is the Connipians other way that has the most chance of preventing the Sapiens from wiping themselves off the Earth. Their deep understanding of harmony is something they can offer the world. Learning that would improve the lives of the other, unruly hominids. Put an end to war. And Sapiens aspire to such goals, or so they say. Write it and preach it while building weaponry of ever greater might. The problem is in the nature of Sapiens males, explains Klapakipsy. And the point is not a new one to Tonkin. There were no clicks on Connipia to describe the concept of rape until The John and Lodowicke came sailing in. And what they have done on the island may be only a tiny percentage of the ill they spread worldwide. Genghis Khan is their template. Every man's hero.

'What the hell!' says a male voice, and both look up from their clicked conversation, eye the two approaching men.

Tonkin clicks quietly that she thinks they are drunk.

'I've heard about that. Men do it in Charlestown,' replies Klapakipsy.

'Did you hear that, Barry? Morse code by mouth, you could call it.'

'It's those whatsits, isn't it? Two of them.'

Tonkin wonders what she was thinking venturing out with only a Connipian for company. She has travelled widely, never before has she

New York City, January, 1950

walked in a city so late at night. And what a city to choose. The big rotten apple. As the larger she should protect Klapakipsy, and yet she cannot even pull her hands into a boxer's stance. 'We are visitors at the request of President Truman. Here with many others connected with the United Nations. The new global body,' says Tonkin.

'Oo-oh, President Truman. Come off it, littley!'

'She talked, Barry. They don't talk.'

'We are both a part of the delegation from New Poplar. The island of the Connipians.'

'You're a fake, littley. Talking like everything I do. You're just a midget, not from there at all. Better looking than tiny-ugly though.'

Tonkin more than doubts this assertion, thinks Klapakipsy a more beautiful girl than she has ever before laid eyes on, whilst knowing that Sapiens can't see beyond their expectations. Østergaard was transfixed precisely because he saw her with a wig on.

'We are expecting Mr Howard, the president's advisor, to collect us from here shortly.' It is a desperate attempt. In mind, stomach and bladder, Tonkin feels terrified.

'Never heard of him,' laughs the one called Barry. 'Don't be fleeing on our account, littley. We won't hurt you. Not even the other. I don't know where you learnt to talk but I get it. Single girls a bit worried being caught on the street at night...' He erupts into a fit of laughter. '...won't find us fathering no weird flopster monsters. No way, José.' Shoulders heaving, he walks past, his friend catching him up after just a few paces. Joining in the raucous guffaws at the confrontation that can have been of no consequence to the two large men.

'Interesting,' clicks Klapakipsy. 'Is it his inebriated state which makes him incapable of working out whom he has stumbled across, or is that usual for Sapiens?'

'They give Connipians little thought, Klapakipsy. Sapiens in New York never have reason to. Think about Mixed-Ups still less.'

'He knew and he couldn't see. What is it the American's say. Dumb ass?'

Tonkin feels giddy in the company of this pretty girl, in this unlikely setting. Klapakipsy thought it displeasing, a termites' nest; it remains amazing to part-Sapiens Tonkin. A sea of near stars imagined in the accumulated lights of these tall buildings' windows. Nothing like it on Connipia. Nor the New Zealand of her childhood. And Tonkin was terrified of the men. Rational Klapakipsy may have reasoned similar fears into her mind, behaved as nonchalantly as if she were pressing fruit into jam. Knew no benefit could arise from showing her fear. Stories handed down tell of the Connipians' exasperation with the very first Sapiens. Not a dozen generations ago. Nothing had prepared them; the angry species induced a little of the same in the girls of that era. The Connipians thought about what this Sapiens invasion might mean, contemplated it in depth. Shared stories. Some were horror stories, but they figured out who they are and the Sapiens are not. In those early months, a few girls were driven to bite their Sapiens attackers, express their hurt through a quid pro quo on those rough, sea-faring bastards. The Connipians quickly saw the wrong turn: they can only be themselves, not let themselves be driven into becoming a nastier kind of people. There would be no future in it. Tonkin wishes she was more than fifty percent Connipian. She would like to spend more time with Klapakipsy, whilst knowing herself too reticent a Mixed-Up to say it to the girl. That voicing the warmth she feels toward her could do no more than cause unnecessary confusion.

'My friend,' Tonkin clicks tentatively, 'you thought, before those drunkards interrupted our conversation, that I had saved your life.' She leaves the repeated assertion hanging between them, but when Klapakipsy fails to elaborate, Tonkin ploughs further into her own thoughts on the matter. 'I know many Connipians, I've interpreted for more than sixty and I spent a little time in four different villages. My mother, Tripanplic, lived in Maxion until quite recently. I am sure I should have recalled you, Klapakipsy, had our paths ever crossed. You are not one who is easy to forget.' She intends it as a compliment, hoping after the thought is clicked that the little one does not think she is implying vanity.

After the longest pause, and as they leave the riverside and begin to make their way back in the direction of The Edison Hotel, Klapakipsy again clicks levelly. 'I have lived most of my life in the north forest. You are familiar with the story of the twins, I take it?'

Tonkin turns her head. 'Yes, I...'

'I do not believe those intrepid seafarers would have gone forth if they had not heard already of your own furtive passage from New Zealand back to Connipia.'

'The twins?' Tonkin looks at her with a beaming smile. How marvellous to learn Klapakipsy was one of them. That is the truth at which she hints. And it is a tale with which Tonkin is familiar, most people alive at the time of its occurrence—living anywhere with half-decent news reporting—would be able to bring it to mind. It was during the year nineteen-twenty-nine that word came out, via one of the research stations, that a Connipian had given birth to twins. They existed in Connipian folktales but not in living memory, the last of them thought to predate John Brook's arrival on the island. Not since the discovery of New Poplar, as the British history books report that event although its first hominid finding took place a million years before those ludicrous

New York City, January, 1950

Muggletonians chanced upon it. When first hearing of them, anthropologists asked if these twins had been born with withered arms, it seemed probable. Twins so much more common among Sapiens. There was relief when they were able to report the birth of two healthy Connipian girls. An irregular birth without concurrent Sapiens' shame. And their existence prompted academics to call for twin studies. For Connipians to keep one in the Blue Houses, the other to live and grow in the company of a Sapiens family. A normal mother and father. The scholarly journals called for it, wanted to measure the outcomes of their contrary childrearing methods. Little versus large. There were dissenting voices but only a few: a young Margaret Mead wrote to the New York Herald declaiming such research as unethical. She was published but still unknown outside academic circles. Not yet a big draw within. Academics wanted it most, even those who said the study might prove Connipian childrearing effective. Academia has always been a friend of its own self-importance. Mead's well-reasoned missive was ignored, given no thought at all.

A twin was taken. Her adoptive parents named her Angelica, held a service of dedication in which a Floridian Baptist church did the same. Not that her biological mother attended or so much as consented. Left with the other twin to raise—the usual singleton—so why would she worry? As the anthropologists said, Connipians don't bond like Sapiens; they share the raising of children across the entire village. Why not another village altogether? A town, in fact. Another species? 'Click Away,' was the best the papers could come up with as a name for the one left in the forest. Angelica's sister.

Within weeks four women, little Connipians, planned and executed the reverse kidnap. A remarkable achievement. Went and fetched the tiny child back home less than five months after her unasked-for adoption. Taken from a wealthy household in Boca Raton—while still no bigger than a lady's purse—smuggled back to Connipia to rest again in a cot with her twin sister. No longer required to turn her head to the name Angelica.

For months the American press ran speculative stories, stabbed a few guesses at who took the tiny child and how. They suspected radicals, leftists, vegetarians from within their own ranks. Had to have been done by a Sapiens. By a group of them. Clever people. Not by a tiny girlie, not those on New Poplar, far from Angelica's Floridan home. Connipians wouldn't have the know-how. Police and private investigators searched all over the United States of America. Canada and Cuba too. Rumours abounded that Angelica was in Europe. The forests of Connipia must have trilled with the true story. A Mixed-Up interpreter first broke the tale of the four girls smuggling themselves all the way to Florida and back. Said it to the very anthropologists who had arranged the original adoption. Kidnap-adoption. Some Sapiens dispute the story to this day—think the feat impossible for girls of such tiny stature, small but not invisible—but Tonkin never doubted it. Connipians simply do not lie. No one knows if they intended the Mixed-Ups to tell all they heard. Probably: there is plenty there to gloat about. Four rescuers hid upon boats and trains to reach Miami, tucked their baby cousin into their own clothing as they smuggled themselves on returning boats. Or in the more outrageous telling: they stole a small boat and made their way unaided. Like the Jumblies of Edward Lear's poem, bobbed their way passed the Bahamas, the coast of Africa, down to the South Pacific. Something like it happened, Connipian truth plus interpreters' embellishment. Mixed-Ups can be funny, not many, one or two. Might like to rub dirt in the pompous noses of the Sapiens. Tonkin's even heard a version declaring that the Connipians took aeroplanes for various legs of their journey. The whole flight-phobic characteristic they are all said to share is—in this telling—a ruse to allow them such an escapade. She never believed that one. Connipians will never fly, will always click that no good can come of it if the subject of air travel arises.

When anthropologist sought to see the twins, after the return of Angelica to the forest—'To ensure she is safe,' they said without deliberate irony—the Connipians denied them access. Used a gifted camera to pass back proof that they had her. The baby was well. They never told in which house or what part of the forest the rescued baby then resided. Entry into the Blue Houses had long become a bone of contention. The girls put up small outcrops of Blue Houses without British knowledge. Or permission! 'We are relieved she is home,' clicked any Connipian asked. 'Our children are not the concern of Sapiens.'

Tonkin releases a Sapiens laugh. She is pleased to see Klapakipsy enjoying the sound. 'That was you. How utterly apt, my friend.' Then she clicks on, asking after her twin while thinking the name Angelica quite ill-suited to this scheming Connipian.

'I believe you met Tululiduh at the theatre?'

'I did. She...?' Tonkin is momentarily confused by this reply. Thought the other Connipian older.

'Dwell upon the face,' clicks Klapakipsy. 'The nose and eyes. Think not of her clothing or the slightly greying wig she wears.'

Tonkin shakes her limp arms: it is a Mixed-Up's expression of pleasure. 'The Sapiens delegation won't know that they host the famous twins?'

Klapakipsy flicks her eyes. It confirms the assertion. This time both twins are in America, and never shall they know. The Weatherlakes in Boca Raton will not be reunited with their stolen baby. Not ever.

New York City, January, 1950

Tonkin laughs again. Unknown to them, Klapakipsy has already outwitted the Sapiens, did it with the help of four other Connipians when she was no bigger than a child's mitten.

As they arrive back at the hotel doors, Klapakipsy clicks, 'Come with me,' and starts to walk beside the building, not enter through the front door as Tonkin expected. She follows the little Connipian who takes her around the side where they arrive at a service entrance. 'I've done my research. These places all have backstairs. Or a laundry chute, I could fit in one of those pretty easily.'

Tonkin loves the way this girl lives. Fearless of the people she must see as adversaries. In the event, they find a staircase and, lifting each foot high to make the steep steps, little Klapakipsy climbs up flight after flight. Tonkin can scarcely keep up although her stride might be close to twice the length of her young friend's.

* * *

On the corridor, a uniformed staff member sees them, and Tonkin feels embarrassed, clicks to her friend that she had better own up. Not allowed in here, and they could both go to The Belvedere where Mixed-Ups are welcome.

Klapakipsy clicks dismissively: the rules of The Edison are arbitrary, made up on the spot; the kitchen porter won't have a clue. Might not have even noticed her arms, as oblivious to them as the drunks at the harbourside. Then the little one taps lightly on a bedroom door. The handle is positioned at the same height as the top of her head. One of the Connipians inside opens it and as they enter, Tululiduh approaches, clicks quickly with her sister, and then greets Tonkin. The likeness is remarkable. Very identical twins, and Tonkin had failed to spot it when she saw them earlier in the day. Wigs and make-up.

The rooms which the Connipians occupy have, Tonkin realises, been more thoughtfully adapted for them than The Belvedere has managed for the Mixed-Ups. Tables and beds which mimic Sapiens tastes, manufactured in a significantly smaller size. Tiny. They have six singles in a room that might usually accommodate a pair of twin beds. Plenty of room left for a table and chairs, two sofas, at the window end of the room. Connipian-sized sofas. High quality children's furniture and plenty of it.

More than half of the Connipian delegation are passing the time in here. The sight of them together, the cacophony of clicking, is both familiar and strange for Tonkin. Fancy coming across it in New York City. The television in the corner is incongruous. She was born in the Blue Houses and spent what Sapiens would call her pre-school years exclusively with Connipians. She might have been the only Mixed-Up in the village at the time, Tonkin cannot recall it. In New Zealand, and elsewhere in her professional life, she has been the smallest in a room of towering Sapiens. Now she rises above the sea of bald heads. Tonkin's eyes flit from woman to woman, coming back to sweet Klapakipsy time and time again. Her ears acclimatise to the wall of clicks. She gathers up the thoughts shared. Those who visited the theatre still regale others with impressions gleaned. The pointlessness of comedy. Then all turn to the television news, a segment shows the four Connipians getting out of the taxi, plus Tonkin and the Dane. She feels embarrassed. The ugly goose among dainty Connipians. Klapakipsy clicks that the pictures are good, clothing and wigs well chosen. She thinks their attendance at the theatre, dressed-up as they were, will garner far more Sapiens sympathy than the pictures of girls climbing trees which appear in the National Geographic. Tululiduh clicks over her. 'It is in the trees that we will find our autonomy; we seek justice not sympathy.'

The hotel room is on the fifth floor, it looks down onto Forty-Seventh Street. Two beds have been pushed to the windows, enabling Connipians to stand and see out where the avenue shines in coloured lights. Like nothing in Connipia has ever done in its history. In its two hundred and fifty-five years of British dominion, or the endless golden era which preceded it, when the islanders were exclusively Connipian. The forest is always dark at night. There is moonlight or it is pitch black. The occasional glowing stone should a girl use one to illuminate the path between Blue Houses.

It is past midnight when Tonkin advises she should return to her own hotel. 'Must I go down the laundry chute?' she clicks. Klapakipsy takes her to the side of the room where a telephone rests on a side-table. No Connipian has used it, the staff in the hotel couldn't make sense of a single click. Klapakipsy suggests a form of words that Tonkin might use down the contraption.

'Hello. Is that reception. Yes, I am calling from the Connipian delegation. Please could you arrange a taxi for me to travel back to The Belvedere Hotel.'

The woman on reception agrees, tells her taxis are at the door and if she comes down, they will see to it.

Klapakipsy insists on coming back down with her, they use the elevator this time. Tonkin is grateful, tired after a long day. In the foyer a concierge comes across to them and begins by saying that the Mixed-Up was not meant to go into the private quarters.

Klapakipsy asks Tonkin to interpret her terse reply. 'Your rules are not ours and we cannot be an inhospitable people at your insistence. Not to our own brothers and sisters.'

When she speaks the thoughts, the concierge looks cross, doesn't get

New York City, January, 1950

it at all, and Tonkin feels yet another surge of warmth towards her tiny friend.

3.

All the Mixed-Up interpreters eat breakfast together in a separate dining area to all the other hotel guests. The signage outside the room calls it a smoking lounge but none of them do. A change of purpose to ensure the dipping of heads into high-rimmed plates is hidden from view of their paying guests. The Mixed-Ups are on a UN tab, can't grumble. Tonkin prefers it this way, never enjoys the stares of strangers, however familiar the experience has become. All except their de facto leader seem daunted by the day ahead, the work they have signed themselves up for. Amazed by the city lights which they saw only through their hotel windows. They are Mixed-Ups whose tongues can wrap around the English language, and they can click. Understand it quite well, and can do it for the most part. Tonkin aside, this is not the brightest crew. It's a Mixed-Up thing: struggling to make head or tail of meaning even while being able to pass along the sea of words which the clicked thoughts give rise to. It might be her upbringing that sets Tonkin apart, gave her the enquiring mind that has served her so well. Too many Mixed-Ups think their floppy arms condemn them to an unfortunate life. Neither her mother nor foster mother ever foisted that narrative onto Tonkin. It is the nuns of East Town who have set the course for most of her kind. And Tonkin knows the nuns mean well, all sympathy and dabbed tissues, God may even bless them for it. Most Mixed-Ups place a high value on the days they can pass while nothing much happens, have a corresponding fear of activity for the likelihood that it will expose their limitations. They don't carry the self-possession of Connipians. The smaller people do not believe their culture superior to that of the Sapiens, they think it more necessary. They recognise the aggression which permeates much of the animal kingdom and reject it. Understand that it presages change which none can control.

Two lines of three Mixed-Ups sit on either side of the dining table, a cramped space appears more so as they simultaneously dip their heads. Eating cut-up fruit and milk-dampened cereal. The two male Mixed-Ups talk about the bacon they are soon to eat. It has not arrived in the room yet, and nor is it readily acquired on Connipia, or New Poplar as these two call it. Pigs are there in only small numbers, on one or two farms. The colonisers have much larger herds of cows and sheep which graze upon cleared land, always kept away from the Blue Houses for fear the girls will set them free. As they many times have. Of course, however much some Mixed-Ups may enjoy eating them, the original inhabitants have never clicked a moments agreement to the captivity and slaughter of any animal on the island.

'You lived in the city,' says Radlin to Tonkin. She is the youngest of the Mixed-Ups. Beneath her blonde wig she looks entirely Sapiens, a kindly face. Limp arms the only giveaway. Her facial expression suggests she is in awe.

'I lived in Rotterdam. Auckland for a time.'

'Not in this one? I think New York is brilliant.' Radlin ducks her eyes down as she says it. Turned away from the best hotels, it is a conflicted aspiration. Never straightforward for a Mixed-Up to live anywhere but East Town. Their disabilities embarrass many and only the nuns, plus a few kindly volunteers of no-fixed religion, really seem at ease in their company. Bad manners might be the problem; an affront to decency the charge too often levelled at them. Eating with neither hand nor cutlery, talking or clicking in a way that leaves saliva on the chin. Tonkin has learnt to minimise the latter, prevent it from overflowing her mouth with scarcely an error. It sets her apart.

'It's the dry run today,' says Tonkin. Radlin pulls her head back an inch or two, eyebrows down. Doesn't seem to understand her phrase. 'We will conduct a mini-conference, aim for smooth transitions between the speakers. The big players will not be there. It all starts in earnest tomorrow.'

'Ah, yes. I read the notes. Do you think the Connipians will be reasonable? Make any compromises.'

A curious yet unsurprising question. They have won few concessions from the British in two hundred and fifty years. Just the free run of the denser parts of the forest: the colonisers trumpet this as if it were the gift of eternal life. It is an unbearable restriction for the only people to live there for a million years. The chance arrival of that ship of fools changed everything. Contemplation of the abattoir on the periphery of Charlestown can distress a Connipian; forests felled demonstrate an upending of their way of life, bring ruin to the places where they intend to grow fruit in the millennia to come. Future generations have never before been doubted. Now hillsides are torn asunder for the purpose of extracting limestone and the mining of potash. Connipians never agreed to a millimetre's encroachment. And the incomers never made a nod towards negotiation. The little ones, a people of girls and congenitally ailing men, were always powerless to prevent it. They do not even assert power over other animals, have no wish to conjure up such potency. And yet Tonkin feels it unwise to lecture another Mixed-Up on the rights and wrongs at play. They usually feel too beholden to their sponsors. At least, Mixed-Ups who can manage a bit of interpreting do. Two dollars twenty cents per hour cannot be sniffed at. They think themselves the luckiest

New York City, January, 1950

Mixed-Ups, and perhaps they are. Others of their kind while away lifetimes in the charity kitchens of East Town. 'This is their great hope. They will try to glean from it some of what they have lost. We must simply represent their words as faithfully as we can.'

'Yes.' Radlin blushes as she agrees, hurriedly adding, 'My mother's here. In the delegation.'

'Your mother?' This is surprising news, and Tonkin assumes it is unknown to any Sapiens. They are interested in Connipians in only the most general sense. Think their history collective, for without insight into their clicking language they cannot engage with them individually. An impasse Klapakipsy seemed, yesterday, to believe navigable. 'Which one is she?'

'Napapilis.'

'And how is the bond?'

'Long broken, Tonkin. She doesn't look at me.'

'Oh dear, oh dear. What has...'

'I was in the Quaker Programme. A religious family on Western Samoa.'

'Really? From one small colony to another.'

'They were nice...'

'You've told your mother this.'

'She won't speak to me. I understand how difficult it is for her...'

'But, Radlin, what if you are called upon to interpret her words.'

'I'll be talking to Sapiens then, won't I?'

'I think we need to clarify, ensure your mother will click for you if and when it is required.'

'It's like she won't acknowledge I'm even in the room. That I am someone.'

'Have the others picked up on this? Other Connipians?'

'I expect they're on her side really.'

'Radlin, I know Klapakipsy wants this to be a most professional gathering. She would seek to prevent any island squabbles hindering their chance of negotiating a better future for themselves. Should I talk to her about it?'

'To my mother?'

'To her or Klapakipsy. Whichever you think best.'

'Try Napapilis. I don't expect she would like me to involve others in the matter. No secrets between them, I know; it's just so personal. For me it is. For her too, I expect.'

* * *

All six Mixed-Up interpreters arrive at the Rockefeller Centre Luncheon Club before ten-thirty. The twenty-three Connipians too. Never has a clutch of New York taxis driven such a short distance while occupied by such exotic fares. All four drivers smoked throughout the journey, didn't indicate if they thought it remarkable. Another fare in Manhattan. There is fresh snow on the sidewalks. A slip hazard, and—Klapakipsy tells Tonkin when they meet—the hotel manager at The Edison was heard querying loudly if Connipians knew what it was. True there has been no snow on their island in the last five thousand years but that's the blink of an eye. Word gets handed down.

The staff at the Centre are fussing, anxious to learn if the arrangements, as they have made them, will work adequately for the tiny people. The floppy-armed few as well, although they seem to be playing second fiddle. The Connipians are centre stage, staff looking embarrassed that they need to hear what their clicked answers mean via the larger and more dishevelled looking in the entourage, and Radlin and Tonkin look pretty neat and tidy but for their hapless arms. The Sapiens delegates have yet to arrive; it is Rockefeller employees only—organisers and furniture movers—with whom they mingle. The first talk-through is to begin at eleven, the other delegates can't be far away. Tonkin is worrying about the day's schedule; hopes her interpreter-colleagues can manage the sandwich lunch discreetly.

The room looks sweet and ridiculous. She doesn't say it, only thinks it. Tiny children's chairs intermingled with the much larger adult variety, Sapiens-proportioned furniture. No one has thought about the Mixed-Ups. They are familiar with sitting on ordinary chairs but look a bit lost on them. The armrests are of no use whatsoever. There are a few writing tables that are fully six inches shorter than a normal adult would ever use: they will still prove taller than is helpful should Connipians choose to write anything down. Not that it is likely. They do it only if they are without an interpreter and wish to communicate with a favoured Sapiens. No use for it beyond that; memory is reliable. They are not subject to the Sapiens fragmented organisation of thought—in the beginning there was no Word—those little chippings are easily jumbled. And the desks are not really small enough. Tonkin doubts if any of the Mixed-Ups here write. She's had a go—pen in mouth—will put on no such circus here. She thinks the arrangement might be an attempt at equality between the species: hard to trust it, but that is how it looks. Little and large shall sit beside each other: something might rub off.

'They could have put you all on pedestals instead,' clicks Tonkin.

'Or better still have the Sapiens shuffle around on their knees.' Within Klapakipsy's rejoinder are clicks for penance, for humility, recent sounds to Connipians. They are concepts that only Sapiens relate to and, in her telling, Klapakipsy implies they are incapable of rendering real. Ideas of the mind that never reify into true experience.

New York City, January, 1950

'Do you know,' clicks Tonkin quietly, 'that Radlin's mother is in your party?' With her eyes she indicates which Mixed-Up she refers to. A foot taller than Klapakipsy, wigged as are all the Mixed-Ups and most Connipians. Radlin might be her rival for the eye of the men, although the interpreter has no linked strategy. Works only for wage and prestige. Cannot make the hand gestures—a finger upon lip or dimple of the cheek—which the Connipian uses to such effect.

'Let me guess,' clicks Klapakipsy quietly, understanding immediately that this could be contentious. 'I believe it must be Napapilis.' In her gentle clicks and gestures, she lets it be known that Napapilis is here on account of seniority. Not a Connipian with a clear strategy towards the British, she is troubled by her own fraught past. Her baby lived in East Town before the Quaker Programme, Napapilis the most infrequent visitor to the orphanage from which she was taken to Western Samoa.

Clicking is more nuanced than speaking, Tonkin has known this since forever. It means their discourse could veer anywhere and she is keen to focus on what is needed. 'I must click with her. She doesn't acknowledge Radlin, and she really must let her interpret for her if protocol requires it.'

'Agreed,' clicks Klapakipsy. 'I can tell her how important this is if you wish me to.'

'Let me, please. I want to gauge if she will prove troublesome for us Mixed-Ups. I would wish for trust between us all. If my party can fulfil their roles as they should, then none will distract from your purpose.'

Klapakipsy clicks her trust in Tonkin's judgement.

As Tonkin walks across the room, she overhears the other Mixed-Ups field questions from the organisers by saying, 'Check with her,' and 'Ask Tonkin.' People are queuing up and she wishes to click with Napapilis.

A man of surprising height, a frothy top of grey hair which she only sees as he leans down to speak to her, wishes to know if the proximity of the differing species might lead to accidents. Will it prove a problem?

'Do you mean, might some of you tread on them?' She looks up to his breast pocket for his name badge. 'Mr Wilson...' It is the manager of the Luncheon Club, possibly of the whole Rockefeller Centre, the tag reports only the single word of his job title. '...are you supposing some of your type might not spot all the Connipians amongst them. I know that they...' She gestures the Connipians nearest to her. '...feel they are out of Sapiens sight on this Earth. Please keep them in mind and eyeline. Ensuring none are squashed must be a prerequisite of a successful conference.' He's the manager of something or other, should know this already.

* * *

The Sapiens delegates have arrived and Østergaard, the Dane, seems the most senior amongst them. There will be different delegates tomorrow. The Britishers in the room only observe. Say nothing to anyone. Take notes to pass up the chain. The rumour mill says that Bevin is coming on Wednesday. Truman too. Klapakipsy has told Tonkin that they don't expect it to happen. Every governor of New Poplar has been a lightweight. An old soak put out to grass more often than not.

The Dane has insisted Tonkin interpret for him. If he is critical of the skill other Mixed-Ups bring to the job, he hasn't said it out loud. Tonkin thinks that, in his mind, he imagines her presence will rekindle the faux intimacy he enjoyed with Klapakipsy the night before. And Jørgen didn't spot the faux. He gushes about human rights, how the British must give ground. Klapakipsy doesn't contradict him, clicks a few asides for Tonkin. It is rubbish she has heard before. Homo Connipus are only defined as human when it suits Sapiens, and not when it doesn't. They have no vote at the United Nations although they comprise one half of the living hominid genotypes.

Tonkin understands the impasse more fully than other interpreters; last night's talk has given her insight. Connipians want the British gone, require their island back. They could allow boats to come into Charlestown, share news and goods with the wider world. Preferably not, but they would consider it. Total isolation worked perfectly, did so for the longest time. These days, those of British extraction comprise over ninety percent of the island's population, they may not see it as Connipians do. Many of the incomers call themselves Poplars, a few declare themselves ninth and tenth generation. Paltry numbers with which they foolishly impress each other. The Connipians have been there ten times longer than Homo Sapiens have walked the Earth. Closing in on a million years. An unimaginable number of cycles around the sun. They don't spout the numbers; Sapiens keep counting until they've lost the thread of why they started. From the Connipian perspective they simply are. They cherish the past, speak of it often, have not been so vain as to record it. The bones which visiting scientists have used to carbon date the longevity of the first islanders should never have been disturbed. Labelling, quantifying, the writing down of supposed facts as if to wrap up all possible thought on a matter: it is an exclusively Sapiens practice.

'The British feel...' Østergaard is speaking very slowly for Tonkin to interpret. '...they cannot grant you British passports. They wish to draw a distinction between settlers and Connipians. They believe it a greater disparity than that between coloniser and colonised in any other of their jewels.'

Klapakipsy clicks quick thoughts on the matter: Bevin raised the issue in the House of Commons, called it a ridiculous proposal. 'Pets don't

New York City, January, 1950

have passports,' he said to laughter. The British fear a wave of Connipian immigrants, do not know how unappealing their climate is. Sparse forests standing idle through those leafless winters. If they had the documentation, a few of the little girls might go to lobby parliament. Or they might not: many were sceptical about coming to this conference. She is puzzled by Østergaard's choice of words—"their jewels", as if limestone and potash might sparkle—good if it is irony. Funny that he hasn't grasped how well the Connipians hear him, understand the words he continues to direct at Tonkin.

'And your opinion, Jørgen?' says Tonkin, at Klapakipsy's urging. 'The disdain of the British is not new, we Connipians...' She gestures her smaller friend whose thoughts she speaks, makes it clear she does not include herself under this collective noun. '...are keen to hear if different nations regard us as primitives, equals or something other.'

'This is difficult,' he says, 'for I am speaking for my nation, not in a personal capacity. I feel sympathy for your predicament. We want only what you want. Denmark believes colonialism has done more harm around the world than should ever be considered justified simply because it spread a little concurrent enlightenment. Connipians should have total control of at least a portion of the island.'

Klapakipsy lets her face show a modicum of satisfaction, show it to Tonkin, Mr Østergaard may be unable to read her. The quarter given is small, a chink of light.

'What does total control equate to,' asks Tonkin, the intermediary. 'Will it preclude Sapiens from entering that designated area of land? Ever?'

'You're in charge. That's the core of it.'

Klapakipsy clicks to Tonkin that she hears the absence of clarity.

'Where will the British be?' interprets Tonkin for the Connipian.

'It depends upon the land designated to you, whether the British have any vital interests within it.'

Klapakipsy clicks a reply, and Tonkin makes her rendition equally assertive: 'Is there any reason why a British interest should be more vital than the interests of those of shorter stature?'

This job feels to be the most important Tonkin has done in an illustrious career, and yet it brings her as much consternation as solace. Not Klapakipsy; she seems measured in her clicks, even when putting down the British. And a little reckless in the dimply smiles she continues to direct at Østergaard. But the concept of a Connipian land, a no-go area for all Sapiens, is of no direct value to a Mixed-Up. Their own status remains unaltered. Those with withered arms have no fantasy of running their own small territory. Not so much as a street-corner café. It is as if they were born in exile. No useful arms with which to paddle a boat away from where they have washed up. The rape of Connipians humiliates; must and does. That is the driving principle in their demand to be free from Sapiens. No more of that, and no more of them. Mixed-Ups no longer arriving in the world. Tonkin cannot fault Connipian reasoning, she would surely think the same in their tiny shoes. That hers are a little bigger—in between—that her arms are lifeless, boneless, and her reproductive system inoperative, all go to confuse. Tempt her into thinking her interests may lie where her sympathies do not. With the Sapiens. Klapakipsy seeks a haven where never a Mixed-Up shall be conceived. It makes sense in the head, and the reasoning of the heart is fickle. Indeed, the seemingly easy relationship between Tonkin and Klapakipsy is a rarity, nothing new in the refusal of Napapilis to acknowledge Radlin. An understandably unwanted daughter, not that it is in any way the younger's fault. Nobody really knows how many Mixed-Ups—half-breeds, two species blunderingly rolled into one—have been born since The John and Lodowicke first visited the island. Many subsequent boats have sailed in. The history books say that Connipians passed the first withered-armed babies—the fate of each child born of Connipian-Sapiens parentage—straight to the Muggletonian settlers. It began around only months after first contact. They even say East Town is situated in the very part of Charlestown in which those mothers passed back the first Mixed-Up babies. Pushed them from their Connipian nests. It might be true. The self-same history indicates that no Mixed-Up lived longer than a few months, possibly a couple of years, until well into the nineteenth century. It is only in the last seventy years that the majority of Mixed-Ups have grown to adulthood, done it through the support given. A person to feed them, possibly to dress them. Never gaining the independence that those with bones in their arms, and the ability to move them wilfully, take for granted.

A few have been raised in the Blue Houses, many more in the orphanages that sprung up when Sapiens of a sympathetic bent finally got a toehold on the island. A small and extraordinary enclave now exists in East Town, on the edge of the island's capital. Mixed-Ups have food and accommodation provided, practical help given by nuns, predominantly Irish nuns. There are other volunteers too but the nuns have been the mainstay. Tonkin has been there, spent time with the world's only concentrated population of her type. She hated it, doesn't like to say it but she did. Loathes, despises, feels sick at the merest contemplation of the place. The second-rate life on offer. Living for the benefit of faraway cake sales.

The Quaker Programme was the first to establish that this unfortunate disability is not an immutable marker of mental retardation. God knows, the odds aren't good. Perhaps Tonkin's foster parents raised

New York City, January, 1950

her in a more stimulating environment than that experienced by any other Mixed-Up who ever made it passed infancy. And, long before their relationship ended, she became sick of the sight of them. A little residual gratitude but they were not really her sort. Taking Tonkin to doctors who might remove her flapping skintag arms; seeking to fit prosthetics for their visual value alone. She would countenance none of it. By the age of fifteen Tonkin became a runaway. Quite an achievement; a Mixed-Up with a lot of gumption. She never knew it inspired the journey to free Angelica, not until last night at the harbourside.

'The British,' says Østergaard, 'are in a position of power but not of moral authority. The ceaseless oppression and dismissal of Connipian worth are factors the world must consider when determining how to move forwards.'

Klapakipsy holds his eye, lets her lips upturn as she listens. Clicks a quiet aside for Tonkin advising she is not well versed in Greenlander history: have the Danish wrought the same upheaval as the Brits in their own plundered lands?

'Is there any other way?' Tonkin clicks back discreetly.

Østergaard is beaming at them, sinking to his knees and still he holds his head at an angle greater than forty-five-degrees, staring longingly at tiny Klapakipsy as if she is the love of his life. Oblivious to the clicks aside, incurious even. Klapakipsy speculates that he thinks they are clicking about his handsome face. Even clicks a ha-ha, and that is a strange thought for Tonkin to hear. A Connipian parody.

'Tell her that we will do what we can,' he says. Still to spot that the Connipian understands every word. 'In Denmark we do not favour the commandeering of land; it never ends well and we know and regret how many European nations have engaged in the practice. They have denied indigenous people their rightful autonomy, shorn them of the opportunity to grow in the modern world.'

In clicks, Klapakipsy says, 'We are tall enough, thank you.' Tonkin interprets only the gratitude.

* * *

As Mr Wilson asks delegates to sit—more than half of the expected Sapiens seem to be running late—Tonkin finally approaches Napapilis. Time found. Radlin's mother looks to be the oldest Connipian here, one of only three who wear no wig. Thick clothing for the New York climate, not island crafted, quite a close shade of blue to the leaf-clothing she must have worn all her life until now.

Tonkin clicks a greeting, acknowledges that the pair of them may be the most senior in years while still younger than almost all the Sapiens delegates.

'And they do not savour their years,' Napapilis clicks back. It is Connipian wisdom that worms in the soil treasure their time on Earth more knowingly than the Sapiens. Do not mindlessly seek out more, faster, stronger, nor yell dissatisfaction with each push of the shoulder they make on the wheel of change. It is as if these larger people have no idea who they really are. Tonkin knows it, has heard the Connipian view many times. Might not understand the point as clearly as the Connipians do, fears she is too Sapiens herself. Has speculated a time or two that the notion is a Connipian prejudice. It's a fleeting thought, one that won't lie down. Tonkin advises that the needs of the conference—an event which offers hope for Connipians, however remote—require smooth use of interpreters to ensure Sapiens hear all the Connipian thought intended for them. 'Your daughter is one who may assist that, whatever painful memories her presence here might bring for you. She intends only to do her job.'

Tonkin stops clicking. Tears do not flow on Connipian faces, the crestfallen expression across Napapilis's eyes, her pinched mouth tell of the upset even raising the matter has brought. 'It is me, not her,' clicks Napapilis. 'I am at fault and I know it.'

As all others remain seated, Tululiduh comes and places a tiny hand on the small of Napapilis's back. Clicks thanks to Tonkin.

Neither clicks to confirm how Napapilis and Radlin will proceed. Tonkin feels reassured, has no need for such detail. This display of emotion is a rare thing. And not a single Sapiens will have picked up so much as the scent of it. She looks across at Radlin who sits high on a Sapiens chair. A wisp of a smile crosses her handsome face. She has seen it too. Her mother's contrition.

* * *

Klapakipsy plays no role of significance in this dummy conference. She listens, clicks to others in her party, never draws upon the services of Tonkin or her fellow Mixed-Ups. Keeps her thoughts in-species. Not a click interpreted. Østergaard seems a little frustrated, makes a point of praising the contributions of the Connipians who speak. Click while a Mixed-Up speaks their thoughts. It is as if he is encouraging her to join the fray, tilting his head down to catch her gaze as he speaks. Tonkin understands the ploy, not allowing him to side with her while it is still in the realm of the hypothetical. A conference about a conference, not yet the main event.

'You have him on a pulley-rope,' Tonkin clicks to Klapakipsy as the morning session is drawing to a close. 'I think the look in his eyes is pure lust. You must be very careful.' Tonkin feels her cheeks colour on audibly thinking the L-word, and she is only guessing, offering caution because

New York City, January, 1950

it must be the wisest way to behave. She has never known lustful eyes rest upon her. The infertile nature of Mixed-Ups, their inability to hug another, it makes for a sexless existence. She has never compared notes with other Mixed-Ups, assumes it is their lot too. Has heard that the East Town males try it on with the females but never learnt whether the latter glean pleasure from it.

'Just by coming to New York, we are seeking what we never thought we might achieve. Looking at an avenue that may yet preserve what appeared lost. I must use every ploy available to secure Connipia for those who will use it best.'

Tonkin admires her but it doesn't sound very Connipian.

* * *

The British in the room—junior diplomats, each and every one—adopt the same tactic as Klapakipsy. The observe-and-say-nothing part of it, one may assume they plan no flirtatious overtures to win support across the species divide.

The speeches given are quite bland. Go over the subjects which will come up during the next three days, no tub-thumping and nothing new said out loud. That may come in the two days ahead. The speakers sound well-intentioned and neither Tonkin nor the Connipians trust that. Not on the day that doesn't count. A delegate from the Netherlands speaks of his country's colonial past—now Indonesia—says that only through decolonisation can a fairer world order come about. Tonkin hears Klapakipsy click a few asides. Violence meted out by the Dutch in the years immediately prior to last year's independence evidence slow learning on their part. Not a country the Connipians can trust, she clicks.

Then a member of the American delegation speaks, and an unlikely member he proves to be. 'I am Brian Tall-Grass,' he says, 'of the Lakota people. A great Sioux tribe of the plains. I feel for you in your struggle to be free. We have a long and difficult experience here in America. A way of life which the white man trampled into the dust. They drove us from our home soil. I think your recent history has been cruel...' He looks around, resting his eyes only on the Connipians as he says it. '...and I am pleased to say that now, in America, the government is putting right the errors of the past. A recent act of Congress reversed many of the injustices we have suffered. I hope the British can learn from this. That they treat you as the government in Washington is finally treating the Lakota people.'

He continues to offer the Connipians some level of hope which his experience does not entirely explain. 'Look at his suit,' Klapakipsy clicks to Tonkin. True to point out, he did not look like the Red Indian his words claimed. A compromise or several have brought him to this juncture, his status within the wider US delegation. Tonkin ponders upon this: critical Klapakipsy is going further. The wig, the skirt. Demure eyes at Mr Østergaard if she thinks it will get him on board.

4.

The man's balding pate glistens with sweat; thin hair, slick with tonic, clings to his forehead. He sits on a couch with three Connipians, the largest of smiles lighting up his careworn face. There are eight of them in the anteroom of The Edison Hotel—'the little people,' as he repeatedly calls them—all women. No males have ever left the Blue Houses except those forcibly taken for experimentation, a practice which most in the Sapiens world have vowed never to repeat. The British signed that one twenty-five years back. Five of the little women wear wigs, Klapakipsy as ever, her sister too, not that Connipians are apt to flaunt family connections. Two thousand sum total, they are all very, very close. Tonkin—allowed in the hotel to facilitate this particular visit—is the tallest in New York to know who the pair really are. Also are. Napapilis wears a blue wraparound skirt with matching top. This time it is the actual clothing from the island. Made from big leaves, preserved and put together in a manner Sapiens cannot yet imitate. Frustrate themselves with the trying. It is the most beautiful colour.

Mr Howard asks Tonkin time and again to interpret every click. To do so for President Truman, the bald gentleman who sits among the girls. She tries her best but the other two interpreters in the room are doing little. Overawed. That has summed up many a Mixed-Up during their time here. She thinks they understand the clicking well enough, just go to pieces in the telling. Leave out words and phrases, points and purpose.

President Truman has brought along a small entourage, in total there are an equal number of Sapiens and Connipians in the room. Plus three Mixed-Ups which doesn't disturb the balance.

Klapakipsy seems to be excited by the meeting, too much so in Tonkin's view. It is unusual to see a Connipian in such a heightened state. She keeps clicking little asides about the atom bomb. Sharing a room with the man who, with one throwaway decision, killed a number of people equal to all the Connipians currently alive multiplied by fifty. She shares a sofa with him. The man who signed the order, dropped the bomb. Tonkin wonders if she thinks she can charm him. Make the monster fight their corner. Truman doesn't think like a Connipian, not a flicker pointing that way. Mr Howard hears only an expurgated version of what pretty Klapakipsy says about his boss, his nation's Commander in Chief.

'Do you have a view,' asks Harry S Truman, 'of how far-removed we humans are from...' He searches for a word. '...Homo Connipus. Do you consider yourselves different? Significantly less evolved, or do you not think that way?'

Mr Howard passes a quiet word with his president.

'We are all humans,' concedes Truman. 'I think you get my gist though?'

Tonkin clicks this question for any Connipian who didn't pick it up first time around. Includes an apology that the President didn't say in real time, his wording clumsy, thoughtless of his audience. Another of the girls sharing the couch with the President answers. Tonkin sees by Klapakipsy's eye movement that she agrees, and she starts to speak the clicked thought for all to hear. 'We are only creatures of this Earth. Assigning ourselves a superiority of purpose, the touch of God's hand upon our shoulder, the right to pen, brand and eat other creatures of the Earth is an errant behaviour of the Sapiens. We understand that everything changes over time. You ascribe this evolution some mystical power. Knuckle-dragging men developing into someone of greater worth. They are just different, and the judgements you make about it tell only of who you are now. You want to explain the fiery changes to which you have become addicted. We Connipians simply are. Contented on our island, more so those ten generations back. We are not on a journey like you because we can see that there is no destination. We all have more in common with the moth and the amoeba than that which separates us. We would like to share the world with you, as we extend to all others. We see no sign of reciprocation from the devouring Sapiens. You give no consideration to the ruckus you leave in your wake. That has been the core of our difficulties since the British first came to our island. The widespread arrogance...'

'Now, now,' says Truman, straining to compose his face sympathetically, 'a man's got to eat. And do you know there are whole communities of my type who are every bit as vegetarian as you guys are? In India...' He looks towards Mr Howard. '...is it the Jains?'

'I think it is, sir.'

'There you go. Did you know about them?'

Klapakipsy clicks a response: 'The Connipians have knowledge of these religions. The British are neither vegetarian nor respectful of the lands and customs of others. The Indian populace would surely say the same, vegetarian or not.'

President Truman looks a little aggrieved at Tonkin as she interprets these thoughts. 'You don't have any power in the land, my friends. In need of protection. And we are trying our best to offer you that. That's why we are holding the conference tomorrow. Will you cut us a little slack?'

151

God Help the Connipians

Klapakipsy clicks a further reply and Tonkin gives her thoughts voice. 'We have libraries, a few of our Blue Houses which we have willingly designated for this purpose. Connipians have learnt much about Sapiens. The reverse is not true. We fear annihilation in the face of contact with you because that is the only direction our mutual cohabitation has ever taken. If you think we use sharp thoughts—thoughts or words—which offend you...' Here Tonkin finds herself stuttering over the phrase. '...they are for you to engage with unlike that atom bomb with which there is no shaping a compromise.'

Truman turns away from her. 'Really,' he says to Mr Howard.

'I think they're stuck on it, sir.'

Klapakipsy starts up again. Clicks.

'Mr President,' Tonkin conveys, 'you felt you had to take the action you did. If you cannot dwell upon a civilisation that has not so much as a bow and arrow, not through ignorance of how to make such a device, but rejection of the concept of unalterable action—the certainty that it leads only to compounded difficulties—you will not make space for us in your thinking. You are waiting for us to fight our corner when it is the Connipian way to fit ourselves into the world. The corner of it that is ours. In our long history we have never smashed our way into the world of any other. Nor destroyed what another had made their own.'

Then, as the famous face waits, screwed up in thought, Tonkin clicks a few phrases to Klapakipsy, to the other Connipians too. Truman is running out of patience. Wants appreciation not criticism. He is not a colonialist, believes himself undeserving of this invective.

The Connipians look calmly back at Tonkin, hearing but not concurring and as she dwells on it, she wonders if she is the awestruck one. Wanting to appease the man because of his status. These knowledgeable Connipians see him for what he is. They've read the books: the first Blue House Library was said to be a gift from Queen Victoria to the native islanders. The newspapers of the day reported Her Majesty's intention: to raise Connipians up from the stone age. In no time, Connipians taught themselves to read, found out what was in those books. And Connipians had no similar tracts to pass back to Queen Victoria. Not until the Sapiens learn to decipher thoughts knotted on string. The Queen's gesture was considered magnanimous, a turning point even. In the middle of the nineteenth century there were powerful voices—their echo exists to this day—underpinned by a zealous religiosity, calling for the eradication of Connipians from the Earth. The God-fearing of the planet saw them as an abomination. They were known to walk bare breasted in the island's forests. Victorian adventurers travelled there in the hope of educating the little girls and then couldn't help themselves from raping them. If Connipians garnered

New York City, January, 1950

any sympathy in the wider world back then, it was hard to find. Blame was their lot in those days, for failing to come out of the forests into the town. Little Eves tempting hapless Adam. The library has grown since that time and it has a strange and special status amongst the tiny islanders. Containing as it does dose after dose of the shocking truth which Homo Sapiens call history. A world of war and violence and one island spared it all for thousands upon thousands of years. For all of history but now.

'We want you,' says President Truman, looking around at his own entourage more than he is taking the eyes of his guests, 'to fit into the world. I believe your expectation that the world should change for you is an unrealistic one. I concede we could all change a little. Maybe. The British have concessions to make, I understand Mr Howard has outlined our position. How the wider world has conducted conflict between nations offends you. It offends me too, it really does. We were attacked; that's the only reason we entered World War Two, plain and simple...' He is in his stride now, playing from his strong suit. '...Pearl Harbour. You will have read all about it. We fought to win; there is no other way. To put an end to the madness as quickly as we could. Much madness, it was not as quick as we should have liked. The bomb which offends you saved lives. I believe this. A ground invasion of Japan would have cost more Japanese lives, never mind the countless young Americans which utilising the bomb demonstrably saved. The British took New Poplar without a fight, and I respect your ways. Your pacifism. I think you are hoping that an order—the United Nations—backed up with a bit of power grants you some reprieve from their colonial rule.' Klapakipsy begins to click at Tonkin while the president continues. 'We are on your side—to an extent, a significant extent—but it is within the world dominated by mankind, not the animal kingdom, that you need to find security. Your way of life has its merits, I'm sure. But you will find that it is within ours that you may attain the security you seek.'

Now Klapakipsy is chattering fiercely; a spray of clicks. Her darting eyes egg on Tonkin to speak them out loud.

The Mixed-Up indicates that it is not her wish to interpret all that the Connipian conveys.

Klapakipsy insists.

'Mr President,' says Tonkin slowly, 'by the estimate of the most learned of your own scholars, this planet is four thousand million years old and it has supported life for the last quarter of this. A thousand million years. Mankind's time—the era you regard as civilisation—has yet to notch up ten thousand of those years. Not one percent, not point-one of a percent. It is for one thousandth of one percent of the time of life on Earth that you have practiced this so-called civilisation, from the management of fire to this bomb which you steadfastly defend. You are blowing yourselves up in the blink of an eye. Too certain in the self-aggrandising stories of your many religions to begin to recognise all the wrong turns you have made. It is worms and lizards and the conga eel that shall emerge victorious from your wars. That shall survive them. For they appear to be far from over. You had a war to end all wars, then the self-same Sapiens began another one! Lay down your arms for your own longevity. Surrender is sweeter than victory. We will give you a library, wall to wall with the string that has meant so much for so long. Would you enter it, seek the knowledge you have yet to contemplate?'

'Little shits,' mutters Truman, looking at Colin Howard. Then he waves a hand at Tonkin; she should not interpret the phrase. 'We will be true to our word,' he says, eyeballing Klapakipsy. 'Ask for the concessions from the British. The ones Mr Howard has already outlined for you. And it's a tough one for us—for America—I have to tell you. We are great friends with the British. Don't agree every little detail, they could have done a better job with your island. But they will remain great friends of ours when this conference is over. This whole conference—welcome as it is—won't have made a significant difference when the dust settles. We've bigger fish to fry than Connipians, quite frankly.'

5.

They are not in the Luncheon Club room today. Diplomats are to discuss in earnest the plight of the Connipians, and it merits a large conference suite. The room heaves. Many are American; a few are from everywhere. The Sapiens outnumber the twenty-three Connipians and six Mixed-Up interpreters by a margin of ten to one. The British gladhand all who will. All but the Connipians. Klapakipsy tells Tonkin that civility is the order of the day. Grin to win, she clicks, mimicking a phrase they both heard on a television game show the night before. Watched in their separate hotels after the meeting with Truman. Klapakipsy has already shared her thoughts on the not-so-clever device. Millions watching a handful, it has been around for no time at all but will drive all into a stupor within three of four generations. Grow food and contemplate one's own time here: that is the Connipian way. Sapiens have aligned themselves too closely with the lives of others to ever know themselves. They read fiction to escape reality, put on plays and more recently films to help themselves imagine they lead more than one life. Their history books suggest they will all fight to be king or emperor, to raise a meaningless flag, or simply for the hell of it. All the men at least. Klapakipsy even speculated if her subspecies has been blessed with feeble males, very few of them and some haven't the strength to rise from their beds of leaves. An

New York City, January, 1950

abundance of women they need not fight each other over. In making her quip, she pulls her face slightly straighter, a poor impersonation of a smirking Sapiens. Connipians never grin, even this bright spark can't quite pull it off.

It is Klapakipsy's tactics which seem to be winning favour in their group. Today all of the Connipians wear wigs. It might be an odd way to declare their separateness, but it shows insight into what Sapiens like most. The species which so unjustifiably loves itself.

Before anyone has spoken a word into a microphone, spoken or clicked, Mathanap, an interpreter, faints. Tumbles like a tree felled. One of his useless arms becomes trapped in the back of a folding seat which he clattered into as he toppled. The arm looks twisted, uncomfortable, although Tonkin knows it is the least of his problems. No sensation in there, it is elsewhere that the fall may cause him pain. Not that it shows at this moment. Mathanap is out of it, unconscious. A Haitian delegate, the only one from that country, has knelt beside the prostrate Mixed-Up. Seeks to establish if he might move him, or if greater medical assistance should first come to his aid. He touches the trapped arm gingerly. The hapless flesh and a little gristle which constitute a Mixed-Up's upper limbs. Tonkin arrives beside him. 'Monsieur Alexis,' she says, familiar with the Connipians' most fervent supporter outside the South Pacific, 'I think he may need air.'

Another gentleman arrives, a Ceylonese delegate who declares himself to be a doctor. Tonkin accedes to him while worrying that Mixed-Up physiology is little understood. They differ from Homo Sapiens by more than just the arms. Mathanap is, like two other interpreters and all but two of the Connipians, away from the island for the first time in her life. Three of the Connipians, in fact, but she-who-was-once-Angelica is keeping quiet about it.

The doctor is most concerned, Mathanap's pulse terribly faint. Tonkin feels unduly responsible, tries to explain to all who will listen that for an islander like the Mixed-Up in a faint, being away from home, eating the food which New York hotels have to offer—about which she is at pains not to grumble—is a strain on the known self. Claude-Henri Alexis, who is still by her side, says they should leave Mathanap to this skilled doctor.

The Connipians do not appear unduly concerned about the plight of their interpreter. They suffered those earlier losses themselves, never thought the conference would be other than a challenging ordeal. A loudspeaker tells them there will be a thirty-minute delay to proceedings.

Klapakipsy has come across the hall to Tonkin and Monsieur Alexis. She has clicked about the Haitian before, that he could prove a helpful voice. Tonkin finds her opportunism insensitive but knows the

God Help the Connipians

Connipian feels duty-bound to make the most of this once-in-a-lifetime conference. She assents to interpret while feeling flooded with concern for Mathanap.

* * *

Tonkin was once the one who got away. From the Quaker Programme in the first instance, all the way from her New Zealand childhood. The Hortons were a kind family and she was well cared for. They encouraged the independence which she took to levels previously unknown in a Mixed-Up. Never wanting for food, nor criticised for the manner in which she ate it. Smiles and hugs were given freely and few of her kind ever get the latter. None can give them in return.

Estimates suggest that between three or four hundred Mixed-Ups are alive in the world at the present time. Simple maths tells how shockingly high a percentage of the Connipian population have been interfered with against their will. Abused by Sapiens. By the males of that species. It has involved only a small number of the populous Sapiens but, nevertheless, one must conclude they are overly partial to raping Connipians. That's the big lesson of contact. The majority of the Mixed-Ups—the resultant progeny—live in East Town. Stay down there on New Poplar—as the British call it—living in the tiny township to which Connipians have long brought their unasked-for babies. The practice has been going on since the requisite number of months after the first British boat dropped anchor in the bay. Only for the last eighty years or so has there been help at hand. The nuns.

For a long time, the wider world knew only that the little women had deformed babies which they would not care for. Passed to the wiser, more medically proficient species. How their floppy arms arose was known on the island, hushed up until it no longer could be. And even today there is a substantial pool of Sapiens who deny the link. Blame everything on the species they are not. Blame the victim. Even contend that ***the ungodly little freaks won't look after their own at the first sign of a problem***. Tonkin came across that particular phrase when, aged twelve, a leaflet about the matter was pushed through the door of her New Zealand home. A leaflet printed on behalf of The Twelve Tribes, a shadowy religious movement of long-standing. They claim members within the congregations of many different churches. And a few among the non-Christian faiths. Their central message seems to be the separation of God's chosen species from the animals which He brought to man to see what he would call them. As the Connipians feel the encroachment of the British across their island and forests, so these Christians seem to fear all that undermines their creation myth.

And those Connipian mothers take their babies to East Town to share

New York City, January, 1950

the care, never intend to desert their unfortunate children. Communicating their wish is a challenge. The click-averse Sapiens can't seem to grasp it.

East Town is the oddest place. Connipians have never lived there on a permanent basis. Not any who have retained the capacity to return to the fold. They visit, there is more liaison with the counter-species in East Town than anywhere else on Earth. With the nuns who help to raise their children, Brides of Christ who do what the babies' fathers won't. Connipians visit, will not settle permanently in town, they need the trees and shade of the ancient forests to be themselves. British built houses are not blue.

Tonkin has spent only a few months there herself, speaking to Mixed-Ups, working as a counsellor in an orphanage. She doesn't like to admit how dispiriting she found it. Strip lighting on the main drag, advertising shows where one or two contact-damaged Connipians—even some adult Mixed-Ups, although she is aware that Sapiens do not find them terribly attractive—are employed in the sex-trade. She can weep if she dwells upon it. East Town hosts several hostels for adult Mixed-Ups, alongside the orphanages. Nuns and a few assorted others doing what they can for those who wouldn't even be here if Sapiens males were not such sex-obsessed bastards. Tonkin got nothing tangible out of living there. Looking back, she thinks it just had to be done. She is a Mixed-Up when all is said and done.

And in that odd truth is a conundrum she has never understood. For as long as she has been able to think, absorb information, she has known that she will never have children. Not ones of her own. How could she raise them with arms of no more use than a weave of wool? And the truth of the assertions runs deeper. The human mule: that is what many in the world at large call Mixed-Ups. Barry Blank and Bessie Barren, the floppy-armed freaks. Even the term Mixed-Up suggests not knowing who one really is. Not much purchase in the world. Fourteen years ago, she was in an audience at the London Palladium when the comedian, Jimmy Whist, used the mule term, said the whole Barry-Blank phrase. Did so to howls of laughter. One or two sitting close to Tonkin looked embarrassed. Her companion that night, Hazel Wright, put her hands over Tonkin's ears as if to shield her from the offence. Knowing her hands had moved too late, she smiled as she did it, found something amusing in Whist's riff upon the Mixed-Ups although Tonkin never pressed her to say what. Never sought her opinion on the odious little greasy-haired comic.

Connipian mothers do not raise their children in the exclusive way their Sapiens counterparts do. And fathers are a most thinly spread resource; Connipian men are physically weak. A genetic disorder, say the

British textbooks. Connipians do not concur with this analysis. Think it a perspective founded on ignorance. Their own men have one up on the Sapiens in their view. They have never raped anyone, not of their own or any other species. Sapiens academics see every Connipian difference as coming up short of the mark. The arrogant species fails to note which strain of hominid has stood the test of time. Connipian children will, when their suckling days are over, adopt a Blue House, and sometimes their biological mother shares the roof, sometimes she lives in a neighbouring house. Always in the same cluster of houses. The mother is one of many who nurture the child.

For a long time, Mixed-Ups did not live in the Blue Houses—never or seldom, there are stories of exceptions—they were believed to have been passed back to the paternal line, for the Sapiens to figure out how to raise an armless child. Not entirely armless, of course, they are there, but without bones and unresponsive to neural signals. Their arms move like the hem of a dress, flay outwards should a Mixed-Up twirl himself, or herself, around. They have no practical use. Will never swing an axe, carry a sack of coal or gently rock a baby.

When the British established East Town, initially trying to encourage Connipians to live in proximity to the capital of New Poplar, the little women used it exclusively as the repository for baby Mixed-Ups. For in the quarter of millennia of contact between Sapiens and Connipians the raping has been incessant. Prosecutions zero, and it has been a criminal act from the word go, one without a victim in law. Connipians cannot give evidence in the court in Charlestown. Nor anywhere else on Earth. This, their grievances, the brutal way in which certain Sapiens males have taken advantage of young Connipian females can be conflicting for Tonkin to dwell upon. Mixed-Ups remind both of their progenitor species of something terrible. Bully: bullied; rapist: rapee. There is no pleasing side to be on in these dichotomic pairings. By being herself, trapped between species like Mathanap's now-extracted arm was in the folding chair, she can prompt unwanted feelings of guilt in others. Knows that they pity her. Tonkin is who she is, never hurt a soul beyond an infrequent sharp comment.

* * *

A waiter brings coffee around although none of the Connipians drink it, Tonkin takes no food when in company of this standing. All the interpreters follow her lead, no wish to have other delegates stare at them so early in the proceedings. Klapakipsy clicks and Tonkin interprets, passes on her thoughts. When the Connipian places her small hand upon Monsieur Alexis's knee—a gesture of friendship while clicking her shared outrage at the recent American occupation of his

New York City, January, 1950

country—Tonkin thinks it a flirt too far. Perhaps she only does it to rile Østergaard who both have espied eyeing Klapakipsy from across the café-bar in which they pass this half hour. Getting European nations to stand up to the British is essential, she has told Tonkin. Haiti's vote was always going anti-colonial. Requires no soft soap.

'And Miss,' says Claude-Henri Alexis in his strongly accented English, 'we are all for a final lowering of that offensive flag. However, I think you have a problem. Connipians can't really fight their corner; they need a protector race. A better one than the British. You see, I don't see any Connipian men here. They leave it all to the women.'

Tonkin wonders if she should let the spray of clicking with which Klapakipsy responds pass without interpretation. The thoughts, if expressed, might alienate one of the Connipians more assured supporters. She finds she can only be faithful to her profession. Must speak the words, allow the conversation to unfold.

'You are a military man, Monsieur Alexis. Fighting is what you know. It's not the way to find stability, continuity, a worthwhile way of life. Armies and navies and all those bomb-laden planes help the world only to lurch from one crisis to another. Two world wars and already the armament factories are gearing up for numbers three and four. Find a use for those nuclear weapons which the supposedly great powers are all constructing. Big muscly men love all that, don't they? War and all its artifacts. Connipians need no protectors, Monsieur. We would doubtless choose Haitians if we did, but it is our way to pick no fights. We want to spread the word of a better way of being. You have given your life to fighting Haiti's corner, ensuring it can repel a threat, including the Americans should they return to your island, guns cocked. The right side doesn't win, Monsieur Alex. The side which wins declares itself right, it is not proof scientific. Not close. Connipians have another way, and turning away from us, not listening, will just ensure the fighting goes on and on forever.'

Monsieur Alexis takes Klapakipsy's tiny white hand in his own great black one. The gentlest touch. He has slid off his Sapiens-sized chair to crouch beside the girl in the green dress, to look into her face. Her shiny blue eyes. 'I don't know how to be like that,' he says softly, 'but I believe you make an excellent point. I want to be a convert, whether I've grasped the finer points or not.' Then he looks at Tonkin as she needlessly clicks his short speech which Klapakipsy has already understood. Absent-mindedly, Claude-Henri has, with his left hand, taken a hold of Tonkin's withered right arm. No offence is meant by this—a gesture he has not thought through—and he looks puzzled by the limp thing he holds. 'I'm sorry,' he whispers, releasing her lifeless limb.

'Nothing to apologise for, Monsieur Alexis,' she says. 'I have no feeling there, that is all there is to it.'

And it is a state Tonkin knows well. She thinks frequently about the Connipian situation, the linked misery of the vast majority of those three or four hundred Mixed-Ups, the widespread indifference of the vast bulk of her parental lineage. Thinks but doesn't feel. Senses how history has moulded its subjects, primed their reactions. Believers in biblical creation hate to see a people who predate Eden although they surely are one themselves. Spare-rib Eve but the tallest of stories. Tonkin is living on this world without a worthwhile foothold, and when she leaves it will be without a trace. That much has ever been known. And here is Klapakipsy—hand on knee—Jørgen Østergaard watching, wishing it was his knee which that tiny hand squeezed. His eyes tell a tale that frightens her. Wants to do to Klapakipsy what some other male of his driven species did to Tripanplic. To her own mother. It is visible in his gaze. Tonkin knows she has never been an interesting object to the eye of a Sapiens male, nor has she felt moved to attract a Mixed-Up. Connipian males—of whom there are very few—sit in their Blue Houses. Lie on their beds of blue-dyed leaves, stirred for food, will enjoy many a clicked conversation. Perform sex if a female Connipian wishes it. Their duty. There are feelings of physical yearning within Tonkin which will never amount to a union. She is not the person to judge the wisdom of Klapakipsy's strategy. Using that pernicious male gaze to win the enemy over to her cause could make the difference. If it secures the Connipians their forest home, pushes back the British in some way, she will have done the most amazing job. Reduced the likelihood of further Mixed-Ups, and Tonkin can see the merit in that. She can picture the hand upon her own knee, dismisses the silliness of the thought. Woman not girl, she knows herself to be. Sometimes thinks she has always been: too grown-up to enjoy life, so detached from others was her childhood in Masterton, New Zealand.

As the time to return to the main hall arrives, the Dane walks over to them. Shakes the hand of Claude-Henri, knows who he is although Tonkin adjudges that they have not spoken before. And then he places a hand on Klapakipsy's back, flexes his knees in order to do so. 'Can we speak later,' he says. 'I'd be happy to take you to a fine restaurant.' Then, before Klapakipsy can answer, he adds. 'I can find one with a vegetarian selection.'

Klapakipsy clicks and Tonkin says to Østergaard, 'She asks if I am invited also, for she cannot be understood by you without an interpreter.' The Dane looks flustered, it might be that he hasn't thought through his proposal. A reaction to seeing her with another; he dreamed only of staring into the face of little Klapakipsy. Looking down her dress as he can from where he now stoops. Breasts the size of satsumas but

New York City, January, 1950

proportionate to her tiny body. Nothing in this situation feels right to Tonkin. She tries to remain that impartial interpreter. Doesn't kick his shins.

'Yes, yes,' he says, and she knows it is passive acceptance. Tonkin clicks quickly to Klapakipsy. The biggest drawback is that restaurants cannot easily serve Mixed-Ups. Without the right type of high-rimmed bowls they spill their food everywhere. And Sapiens are not keen on watching them eat—hate it, by and large—even if the Mixed-Up has all the necessary aids in place.

Klapakipsy clicks and Tonkin spells it out. 'She says that the restaurant management will refuse entry to her friend—that's me—and I don't think you only wish to hear her click without knowing the intent of her accompanying thoughts.'

'May I eat at your hotel?' asks Østergaard.

The game of cat and mouse continues. 'No Mixed-Ups eating in The Edison, I'm afraid, Jørgen. If you are happy to eat at The Belvedere, we can call it a date.' Tonkin gulps before disclosing the final translated word. It utilised an unusual click. The term is not a Connipian one, the string of clicked thoughts which Klapakipsy had to use mean "corny meet-up pandering to the delusion of romance with which Sapiens overcome their religion-instilled guilt about sex." Tonkin even finds herself blushing after saying it. Without any direct experience, she is more amenable to the delusion than any Connipian, and the date is to be Klapakipsy's not hers. Or more accurately Jørgen's, for it is the Connipians face which Tonkin has begun to see when she closes her eyes to rest for the night.

While looking down at the little one's chest, the Dane nods his head. 'Yes, of course.'

* * *

Once she is back in the conference hall, Tonkin confers with another Mixed-Up, with Radlin. Mathanap is over at Lennox Hill, admitted to the nearest hospital. Doctors and nurses will do their best, may or may not fathom the cause. She knows that this assignment is tough for all the other Mixed-Ups. They haven't the resilience that her worldly life has granted Tonkin. She goes around the remaining interpreters quickly. Thanking them for their forbearance. Tries to explain that she had to interpret for Klapakipsy, while worrying they may think she has grown too close to the precocious Connipian.

Tonkin has calculated already that the British will not leave Connipia, New Poplar. They might grant the name change, will not be relinquishing the resources it offers them. The limestone or the potash. And the Mixed-Ups might hate it if they were to go. The lineage would cease, of course, and Tonkin thinks that no bad thing, however counterintuitive the notion sounds inside her head. But it is the altruism of Sapiens that gives Mixed-Ups a sporting chance. The vast majority might be nasty, the majority of the Sapiens on that tiny island probably are. But the nuns and volunteers who manage the orphanages and housing projects in East Town are worth a thank you. Teaching young Mixed-Ups how to dress themselves, fixing them simple meals. It makes a difference, improves their sorry lives. They spread their Christian word while they're at it, invite the Mixed-Ups to join them in thankful prayer. Some do, some don't. Connipians are impervious to all the religions of the world, for the Mixed-Ups it's fifty-fifty. Do they align themselves with their indifferent mothers or their absent fathers? And everyone with God on their side has a father, no matter where the real one's buggered off to.

6.

Mr Howard opens the conference; Tonkin did not expect it. He is the only Sapiens who has cultivated her, given value to her role. It might be that he prefers straight conversation to the sound of constant clicking. Many men dislike the way an interpreter highlights their own limitations; this one seems to have listened to her to a degree.

'History keeps being made,' he declares. 'The creation of this body, the United Nations, is surely a greater event—one with more lasting consequences, outcomes from which we can take real pride—than World War Two. A sorry mess which we remember only to ensure no repetition of those dreadful events...' His talk is wide ranging and within it are one or two ideas that sound rather Connipian. He is a clever operator—smack on top of his brief—President Truman's trusted aide.

Then he lists the issues that they will air, those to which this conference should draw conclusions. 'The Connipians are far more than a special case,' he says. 'They are another people: our respective cultures may feel like oil and water; well, we always hope to find plenty of both on our planet, do we not? Crave them in their purest form. We wish to make good use of each.'

Klapakipsy clicks a cynical comment. What happens elsewhere on the planet is not a Connipian concern—they burn no oil—the alien culture need only leave them alone. Tonkin hears it, and clicks acknowledgement; she has had an interesting experience of the Sapiens world. Does not share this thought, nor know exactly how a Connipian would dwell upon it, if she were to click it out loud. And Tonkin enjoys what she can of Sapiens culture with the heaviest heart.

* * *

New York City, January, 1950

Tonkin's mother, Tripanplic, didn't take her to East Town, not as a baby nor much later when the teenage Tonkin was back with her mother. Tripanplic wasn't one to do as others did: a Connipian wishing to care for her withered-armed baby in her own Blue House. No contact sought with the father's species. She kept Tonkin amongst Connipians, raised her as she might if the conception had been accomplished with a male living in a Blue House. The pregnancy was of the longer than usual length. Longer for Connipians, that is. They have been forever unfamiliar with the nine-month gestation that Sapiens mothers endure.

In that first home, which Tonkin has heard about but cannot draw real memories from, only her own mother and another Connipian to whom Tripanplic was close, shared the space. Another female, of course. Gentlemen Connipians do not live with women. They will always meet up with them upon request, at the lady's discretion, and that is a way around against which subscribers to the philosophy of the Twelve Tribes continue to rail. Men have been scarce for a couple of hundred thousand years, maybe more. Oral history doesn't do dates. One in forty live births is the figure bandied about. Their practices keep the population ticking over as monogamy would not.

Tonkin had only a little contact with the others in the cluster of Blue Houses where she lived, that is as her mother has told her. Talked of her own travails with an oversized baby. Arms like long limp grass. Her upbringing sounded typical of none. She later learnt that others in their forest village considered Tripanplic to be moody, a rarity in Connipian circles. Whatever Tonkin's infancy, she had a tiny mother who nurtured her for a couple of years. Would willingly have done so for much longer. Through to adulthood but for the interfering Sapiens. Whisking her off to the Quaker Programme. Just another Sapiens orchestrated kidnapping, in this instance it was dressed up as charity. Tonkin can see it as an evil and think how kind the Hortons—her foster parents on the North Island of New Zealand—were, all in a sweeping thought. That kind of contradiction has been the lot of any Mixed-Up who can think through the two worlds that swirl around them. In which they find occasional solace, and never a sense of belonging.

In East Town there are quite a few Connipian mothers—plus a few who have not given birth to a Mixed-Up—who lend a hand at the orphanages. Show real compassion for their disabled offspring, the never-ending line-up of children who prove to an indifferent world what Sapiens males are all about. Might is not right, and nor does saying so put an end to its dreadful dominion. The humiliation of another's life for a moment's pleasure. There are other mothers of Mixed-Ups who want nothing to do with them; not a high proportion but it happens. Giving birth to one is traumatising. Every single time. Conception, delivery and

God Help the Connipians

all points in between. Tonkin knows about this as the ethnologists have never learnt. Truths her own mother, Tripanplic, shared but bid her not to divulge more widely. It is Connipians only at all deliveries in the Blue-Houses. They are a most private people. Sapiens haven't grasped how different the two types of births are. Connipian babes born of barely five months' gestation, the size of a fieldmouse, helpless with their eyelids shut tight to the light of day; their tiny mothers keep them swaddled in blue until they are crawling. Mixed-Ups bide their time in the womb: eight months, sometimes as little as seven. They emerge up to four times the weight of their Connipian cousins. Not big compared to human babies but it is toddler-sized mothers who must bear them. Nobody knows how many Connipians have died in childbirth. Nobody in that part of the world which puts store in counting.

Tonkin has read a couple of studies, how the off-loading of Mixed-Ups proves the animal nature of Connipians. Studies by scientists with no insight into their own species-specific bias. She has also heard the thoughts of Connipians, a step the pure-bred Sapiens are incapable of taking for themselves. The traumatised mothers are not indifferent. Ill-prepared sums it up better. Connipians had minimal experience of disability before The John and Lodowicke sailed in. When she read the studies, she began to see how the social sciences can be a form of authoritative ignorance. The firming up of lies.

Tripanplic kept Tonkin in her own Blue House, not a neighbouring one, as is sometimes the way with Connipian children. She clicked to her day and night. Must have, that's how come she quickly grasped what no Sapiens has managed. Never had clicking lessons, it's not the way it's done. And Tonkin always finds herself significantly more capable, precise in her understanding and relaying of Connipian thought, than other interpreters. As true here in New York as has so been throughout her working life.

Tonkin has no recall of that infancy, of what happened inside the Blue House, yet the sense of it was familiar to her upon her return. She came back to New Poplar in her mid-teens, reunited with Tripanplic while not quite remembering her. Kind of remembering, not in a manner she could put words to. Not in the way of Sapiens thought; Connipian thought is something else. That has been a lesson for Tonkin, it is the making of an excellent interpreter. The sprays of clicks relay thought, not bite-sized words. To hear them is to understand the thinker in a way that the words of the Sapiens seem only to mask.

From Tripanplic she learnt—and this seems far from the grasp of the Sapiens—that Connipians may think very differently from one another. Fail to agree. They do not yet share a view—never have—on how best to engage with or avoid the incomers. The species that won't stay in its

New York City, January, 1950

place. Or sub-species, the classification debate goes on and on. The contrasting outlooks of different Connipians do not show themselves in feuds or shouting matches, not even in the taking of sides among with whom one might live. They accept that they may not concur in a way that Sapiens have forever struggled to do. Wars about the price of wheat.

Anthropology with a heart, said the tagline on the headed paper of the foster care documents which Tonkin never saw until ten years after her kidnapping. A British Government sponsored project—the University of Cambridge had a hand in it—in which some blinkered do-gooders took the two- or three-year-old Mixed-Up from the forest. The withered-armed baby who thirty-eight years later is interpreting at the United Nations in New York City. Removed her from kith and kin, placed with a family in Masterton, New Zealand. Perhaps it's been a howling success. The family promoted her self-care meticulously. Following a Carleton University programme, a methodology the nuns of East Town didn't adopt until many years down the line. She spent time in school with New Zealanders of her own age. A Mixed-Up among the pure-bred Scots and Irish of the North Island. One of very few of her kind to have such an experience. And no Connipian has ever done it, not integrated schooling. Click, click, click: teachers can't be having that in their classrooms. Throughout her school years nobody knew that she knew how to do it. Speak into words the thoughts which Connipians click. There were a few other Mixed-Ups trying to do it, but they were sloppy, vague.

Few in New Zealand were truly sympathetic towards her. Except the Horton family in their ramshackle bungalow at Masterton. They tried very hard. Dedicated themselves to the task. Trevor Horton was a busy man, running the local pharmacy, and still he found time for his adopted daughter. Rene Horton—off and on a teacher in the local school—always sought to put Tonkin's welfare before her other obligations. Most school years began with home schooling, only for Tonkin to end up in her mother's class when the rookie teacher the school had taken on left the post before Easter or Whitsun. Requiring her foster mother to return to the classroom. Teaching the local farm kids and factory workers' kids wasn't as straightforward as it sounded, Mrs Horton one of few with the know-how.

And it was she, Rene Horton, who laid down the unwritten law at Waingawa Primary School: all children were to treat Tonkin with respect. Who would ever make fun of a teacher's pet? Protected until the age of twelve; good at question and answer while never producing written work. Meal times always taken in the alcove off the staff room. It might have been a perk but it further marked her out. 'Eats like a cat,' she heard whispered. When teachers distributed birthday cake among pupils or threw Christmas parties in the final week of Michaelmas term, she ate in front of other children. They didn't dare laugh—foster mother in the room—but that response wasn't far away. Wide-eyed children find a way to let their harnessed feelings show.

Tonkin was of interest to psychologists in Wellington. The local newspaper ran a few stories. A clever Mixed-Up, rare and puzzling. To the surprise of many, intelligence testing found a prodigious talent. A memory that trounced any other child in the area. When the examining board allowed her to recite the answers to a stenographer, they discovered she could reel off essays which answered previously unseen questions more precisely than any other child could write them. A most gifted student.

* * *

After Mr Howard's introductory address, a small lady from Liberia speaks. Hawa Gaye, her name. Her accent is unfamiliar to many Connipians, Tonkin quietly clicks for them. Some manage without; they learn quickly.

Hawa Gaye states that colonialism has ruined too many countries; the Connipians need self-rule and it is not for incomers to judge what form their self-government should take. While she works, Tonkin watches Klapakipsy, eyes going from side to side in agreement with the African lady's opinion. When Hawa Gaye says, accompanied by bristling body language, that those voices calling Connipians primitive are more than misguided, Tonkin sees her tiny friend sit up. Narrow her eyes in concentration. 'They are a force of ignorant opposition to the wider learning that characterises humanity,' says Hawa Gaye. This must be a new avenue for the young Connipians to think down. They have tended to deride learning, or rather, they do not adjudge it to be conceptually separate from knowing, nothing added to their awareness in millennia until the Sapiens turned up. Ruined it. And Connipians have adapted to many Sapiens intrusions. Learnt to comprehend languages proficiently while Sapiens still cannot make head nor tail of their clicking. They see this as knowledge always there, uncovered when the speakers of those languages became heard. Electricity they have understood and rejected. Their ways have withstood time, beyond any that the counter-species can grasp. May have withstood greater challenge than the British incursion that troubles them currently. A lot has occurred in a million years. Not lost: it is all there, in the past. That other place. Hawa Gaye is suggesting change that cannot assure a greater good for all should never happen in the first place. She is very honest, says it seems to require a crystal ball, acknowledges that knowing the outcome before the change has occurred is a challenge. Then, very quietly—and Tonkin sees

New York City, January, 1950

Klapakipsy straining to hear every word—she finishes with an admonishment. 'But if anyone thinks anything the British have done has improved the Connipians' lot, they really haven't been paying attention.'

After the lady stands down, a British diplomat goes up to the raised dais. Erect of posture he surveys the audience before he speaks.

'Thank you. We are here to listen. Here to compromise. However, we cannot accept that Britain has no dominion over New Poplar, cannot give up what we rightly came to govern. Became the first to bring order to.'

Here he pauses, looks again into the watching audience and seems to be picking out Connipians with his morbid stare. 'We understand that colonies must adapt. Once subjugated people have now become citizens—our equals—in many areas of the world. We welcome this development; we think it a mark of the progress made on both sides of the colonial divide. The sharing of our values with those of the indigenous people has reaped benefits to all. We believe those in our former colonies are coming to see the additional impetus our presence has given to the continuity of their own cultures. However, I believe the Connipians of New Poplar to be a special case. One on their own. Try as we might, our communication with them has never been of a standard that can support shared governance. And the question of whether we can, in all conscience, grant another species equal status is a difficult one. We believe the answer to be a provisional no. That old chestnut might be one for the theologians rather than the diplomats or politicians. I fear it would prove a slippery slope were we to go down that avenue, and many countries which rally to the Connipian cause may need to think about this more deeply than they have yet to do. We—the British who have lived closer to them than any other nation—are concerned about their breeding practice. Disturbed by it, quite frankly. We believe the behaviour of Connipians has confused some of our less educated males and we have never succeeded in passing laws which Connipians will keep, or which can bring miscreants to book. They don't give up their wrongdoers—primarily those who keep releasing livestock—nor do they help us to catch our own. Those theologians we have asked agree with us. Homo Connipus are not the children of Adam. It is a wonderful island, but a challenge to govern. Truly. The cultures of oil and water, as Mr Howard referred to. We don't shirk the challenge but the only way to govern such a land is from a position of strength. My government welcomes this conference, the opportunity for improved dialogue between our parallel societies. We do not wish the raising of international awareness to weaken our governmental control. No one has any interest in anarchy. Whatever your politics, I am sure you will acknowledge that.'

Klapakipsy is looking down at her knees. Then she raises her head, smiles towards Østergaard. Tonkin cannot see how Denmark may ever prove pivotal here, a friend of Britain, but neither a powerful nor an influential one, as far as she knows. Yet Klapakipsy has surely won that heart and mind, converted Jørgen to her cause, win or lose.

7.

On the evening of the first day of the conference proper, Østergaard, Hawa Gaye—the lady from Liberia who spoke after Mr Howard—and three Connipians share a meal. Klapakipsy is one of them; she wears a dress with a few small sequins which sparkle upon it; her wig is clever, rich hair styled to look a little windblown. Tonkin ate earlier, dined alone, so she could assist at this meal without preoccupation. In the event, only the two Sapiens eat food that a chef has taken great care over. The Connipians have fruit salad, asked in advance that it be prepared in a particular way. Skin on. Tonkin thinks their stomachs are different from her own. Can't imagine living day-in and day-out on their meagre diet.

He is like two people. Touches the back of her hand and asks inane questions about the quality of the fruit. Klapakipsy has a surprising amount to say about that but not thoughts which Tonkin can move into the English language. In the two ways of telling, Connipians have the richer descriptions of flavours and textures. Their thoughts about meat cannot include the taste—none has ever passed their lips—yet still the blinkered Dane eats his bloody steak. Conversely, he is both upbeat and practical about the conference. 'We don't wish the British to feel cornered while we corner them,' he declares. 'They have come to give away the name New Poplar. I think that is far from the most important matter to you.'

Klapakipsy actually touches the back of Jørgen's hand in agreement. There is a great fuss about renaming the island: the birth of Connipia, say the newspapers. It is a Sapiens term even as it rightly distinguishes the true islanders from the Johnny-come-lateies. Tonkin tells Jørgen Østergaard what all the subsequent clicks mean. The Connipians are not happy with the proposal that only a few protected spaces will be theirs; livid that mining might continue unfettered. Jørgen tries to tell them about the life cycle of a mine—when the extraction process has ended the land up-top can be returned to the how it was before mining began— and the Connipians all think him patronising, his lecture is pure mumbo jumbo. Sapiens propaganda. Tonkin has to repeat their point to him six times. There is no getting away from it: the Connipians are right and the Dane is thick. Believes removal of material from underground to have minimal impact on the land above it once operations have ceased. 'If we rip out your heart, you will be forever changed, however well we sow you back up,' she interprets.

The British want an airport because it will connect the island more easily to the outside world; the Connipians oppose it for the self-same reason.

'You must understand, Hawa, Jørgen,' says Tonkin, slowly spelling out the thoughts of her young friend as directly as she is able, 'this is a short window of opportunity. I and a few other Connipians favour engagement, favour trying to forge agreement with our Sapiens cousins. Many Connipians did not think us wise to even come here. They wish to lead the life we were meant for, and have no wish to participate in any other. We are anything but New Yorkers, you will have spotted that already. We shall all return to the forest after this hiatus, shall do so without exception. If this conference gives us only a little, then the consequence will be awful. Our own Hiroshima. The sharing of an island with vulture-like people is killing us. Living together should not result in the restrictions to which parts of the island we may visit. We can never accept that loggers may bring down the rooftop gardens in which we raise fruit. Decimate the very forest that is to yield sustenance for generations of Connipians to come. When I listen to the British, it is there in the blood coursing around their veins. The hatred for people who do not venerate their predacious culture. Perhaps it will dissipate, they may learn to live a different way. So long as they expound their laughable superiority they cannot possibly. And we must not idly wait for what may never come to pass. If the world cares for Connipians—an overly hopeful premise, I know—then the British must go. Be gone. That is the outcome we seek. They may call it New Poplar from afar, truly, they may. We should not ask them to alter the accounts in their history books. Simply to desist in being a part of ours.'

As Klapakipsy clicks this plaintive plea, the Dane puts a most gentle arm around her shoulders. 'Denmark is with you, young Klapakipsy,' he states. 'I am with you, and I hope you know it. I fear all in the hall will see your request as implausible. All who are over one and a half metres tall.' He tries to smile at this, but might fear he has offended her. Drawing attention once more to the small stature of the Connipians.

'I'm one-point-five-five,' says Hawa Gaye, 'and I agree with her. The British should just go.'

8.

At the start of the second day, Tonkin stands at the podium, Klapakipsy and Tululiduh sitting just to her right. Both wearing short skirts which ride over their knees as they sit. And these are skirts of the famous colour. Connipian Blue say the paint pots of the children of America. Not that Sapiens manufacturers can quite bring it off. They have wigs of brown and black on their respective heads. Looking like schoolchildren in a reception class. Must be exactly that if size and posture are the judge.

Mr Howard walks in front of Tonkin, takes it upon himself to say an introduction to the waiting delegates. The programme notes do not say that this is to take place but New York is his city. He seems to have greater liberty here than most.

'Hearing how our Connipian friends feel about the various points made yesterday is essential to this conference. We are not just planning a future for them, we are planning it with them. The first session this morning is set aside to allow them that time, to let us hear their views. How they see the options before us. Ladies and gentleman, Kapalindy and Talula, plus their interpreter, Miss Tonkin.'

It comes into Tonkin's mind how, some twenty-five years before this introduction in front of the world's diplomats, she made a name for herself. Forgotten now, but she really did. The papers on North Island spelled it out, first brought her story into print. Just her disappearance to start with, more followed. She didn't read all they wrote until years later.

To get away from Masterton, from the New Zealand that had done her no wrong—little wrong, it's a struggle to quantify—she used all of those skills which Mrs Horton had taught her. The ones so valued by Sapiens. Proved herself to be a more independent Mixed-Up than any other. Not that many outside her mother's own well-behaved classroom ever called her Mixed-Up. Not in New Zealand of the nineteen twenties. Beyond the school walls children would shout out cruder terms. 'Floppy Arms' and 'Hands on Your Head.' And 'Can't Wank' which she didn't understand until many years later. Not until she was a working interpreter. They used ugly names which implied she was an awful thing to look upon. 'Arms like string,' one of the kinder. She had braced herself to hear a lot of it when she ran away. Sticks and stones, she thought. And they are the very things a Mixed-Up can never retaliate with. Tonkin had decided she could not live her life as an object of pity who happened to have learnt self-care from a kindly foster mother. She would make her own way in the cruel world. Take it all the way back to Connipia, where she imagined she belonged. New Poplar, the name she called the island at that young age.

When she was fifteen, Tonkin stood four-foot-five. Not a bad size for her genotype. Held her face up where many a Mixed-Up would hang it down. Not that she knew it, she was still to see another in the flesh. She sported a little teenage acne, powerless to control it unless someone—

New York City, January, 1950

good old foster mother—applied the salve, squeezed a spot. And Tonkin wanted none of that. She was her own girl, had her own mind. Ideas rolling around inside her head about the life to come.

She had learnt early how to lie upon a bed and wriggle herself in and out of clothing. Her teeth were strong, she could turn most taps. A pocket sewn close to the lapel of her every blouse enabled her to pull out a purse. She had to ask shopkeepers and others to take out the coins, knew they would not exchange their wares for money she had salivated upon.

She had, since the age of thirteen, been spending an inordinate amount of time in Masterton's small public library. With the assistance of a young librarian named Sally—for hours on end the two would find themselves the only ones in the underused facility—she would write letters, Sally transcribing her spoken words. They were subsequently posted to an address in East Town, an orphanage which she had read about in a charity leaflet. Her foster parents knew she did it—Tonkin told them when she began the correspondence—didn't pry, and never asked to read the letters she received in reply. Let the matter be hers alone. She even turned down her mother's offer to slice the envelope with a paperknife, so keen was Tonkin to ensure she did everything for herself. When her mother asked her about the correspondence, she told a little lie. Connipians can't but a Mixed-Up can. One as clever as Tonkin, certainly. And having a secret felt good. She was learning about the welfare of the other Mixed-Ups. That was as much as she told her fostermum. 'So good of you to think of those less fortunate,' said Mrs Horton. Tonkin considered her true reasons selfish, knew that her determination to discover herself outside of the Horton family might appear as a betrayal to them. She thought them kindly even during her phases of dislike; they had done a lot for her. But she was who she was, we all are. Never a New Zealander; fifty percent Connipian. Mr and Mrs Horton were, one way or another, complicit in her kidnapping.

Her first letter back from the island came only from the Mother Superior of the orphanage but reading it heartened Tonkin. A promise to ask all the visiting Connipians about her mother. She had sent what details she could of her removal from the forest, the British name for the place where her mother lived. She had seen all her papers, and knew her own name may be of no use at all. For Tonkin was—to foster parents and the town of Masterton—known as Rebecca; she never learnt if anyone in the Quaker Programme enquired about her true name before snatching her from the forest. Rebecca Horton, a name she vacated those twenty-five years ago. She received successive letters from a person called Sister Carmel, Mother Superior must have delegated the task. This nun never said anything about herself, even when Tonkin enquired about her

171

origins, her length of stay in East Town, in the Sally-transcribed letters she sent. The sister was very keen to help the Mixed-Up find her mother, that was as much as she learnt. Sister Carmel delved deep, had a few contacts in the Blue Houses. The fourth letter she received back included an attached note, the entirety of which quickly became etched into Tonkin's memory. Has never left her. For years and years, she would run over it in her mind before falling asleep.

> *My Tonkin, you may know already that no Connipian ever asked to have a Mixed-Up child but nor do we turn our backs upon them. The Sapiens attitude towards them is frightening—I do not include Sister Carmel or any of the other nuns on this island in that judgement— and we believe their responsibility an absolute one. I have been told that the Quaker Programme, through which you were forcibly removed from my care, is well intended. That makes no sense to me, but your letters are assisting me to come to terms with it. I would like you to return to Connipia. To spend time together with me, and I with you. When I have calculated how this may be so, I shall let you know.*
> *Your mother – Tripanplic.*

Further letters followed, her mother enquiring about Tonkin's life on New Zealand and her abilities and limitations. Praised her foster parents for the skills they had nurtured in her. There was a year of intermittent correspondence before the fateful day. That a Mixed-Up should do a bunk was unthinkable; that she made her own way home to Connipia, without a ticket or the approval of an official on the island, both impossible and true.

When fifteen-year-old Tonkin, going by the name of Rebecca, boarded the bus to Wellington, it appeared only mildly remarkable. She had been on the same bus with her foster mother, with both Mr and Mrs Horton in attendance on occasion. Going into the city solo caused a chatter among other bus passengers. One lady, Miss Spence—she didn't introduce herself, but their hometown is small—came forward three seats to sit with her.

'A big adventure for you today, Rebecca,' she observed.

Tonkin smiled at her. By her side lay a small shoulder bag which she was able to manoeuvre unaided. At the bottom, a change of clothes. A sandwich prepared without her mother's knowledge. An apple. 'Mummy wants me to be as independent as I can possibly be,' she replied. The Masterton local press had carried a story to that affect more than once. An update on the Mixed-Up amongst them. The most recent had been

New York City, January, 1950

six months earlier. Her foster mother hid the following week's edition; it contained two letters querying if a child of her lineage was worth the fuss. 'The human mule,' one letter called her, printed without editorial reproach. Tonkin read that edition in the library. She had long been aware of the controversy. Her faultless recall told her that the writer of that ugly epistle also bore the name Spence. The father, Tonkin believed.

'And you're going down to the city, Rebecca?'

'There and back,' said Tonkin. Another of those oh-so-Sapiens lies. She glanced aside and down, one of her limp arms caught where this untrustworthy woman leant into her.

'Well, I admire you for it,' said Miss Spence. 'I'd help you if I could but I'm off the bus at Greytown. It's where my sister lives, you see.' Then the woman looked across the aisle of the bus, away from the Mixed-Up. Just when Tonkin thought she had run out of reasons to be sitting beside her, Miss Spence chimed up once more. 'Now I've got you to myself, Rebecca, you don't mind me asking a question or two, do you?'

'Please.'

'I'm sure it's difficult for you. What's the word...burdensome. You can't pick anything up like people can...'

'I actually can, Miss Spence. Not with my arms, there are many other ways...'

'Rebecca, please call me Jane.'

'...Jane, I can pick up plenty with my mouth. I manage all kinds of things that way.'

Jane Spence looked directly into her face. 'I'm sure you do, but it must be terribly difficult. And it's not the half of it, I'm sure. Rebecca, I don't know how to help you, while feeling I should. There are so many who are angry that...' She paused, seemed flustered, lost for words.

'Are you angry with me, Jane?'

'No! Not a bit of it. I think...' Once more she leant in close, whispered. Tonkin has never had a second's sensation in her arms; nevertheless, it was awkward having the left one trapped by Jane Spence's invasive shoulder. '...I'm angry about the man who did what he did to your mother. For you, I feel only sympathy; I simply don't know how to help you.'

Tonkin had heard similar once or twice, felt conflicted whenever people spoke this way. Raising good reason why she should not be here. 'You mean well,' she replied, 'but it is not help I am after. It's opportunity.'

Jane Spence looked into her brown eyes, Tonkin wore a wig, did so all day every day back then. Made herself blend just a little better into the only world she had known since consciously retaining thought. 'If I was in your shoes, I believe I'd wish for a lot of help. And I don't mean to

God Help the Connipians

contradict you when I say it. I can't picture how you...'

'You mean well but perhaps picturing me at all gives rise to the anger you said you felt towards my father. Towards his type of man. I cannot live inside that crucible. I am me; I know nothing more.'

It was a first for Tonkin, that in the forty-five minutes it took the bus to reach Greytown, she talked candidly about herself to a near stranger. Jane paid close attention. Teared up a couple of times and finally laughed when Tonkin said—in reference to eating unaided—'There are many worse fates than a little jam on the nose.'

When her stop came, Jane thanked Tonkin for making the journey so interesting. Held one of her string-arms loosely in her own, in mimic of a shaken hand. 'God bless you,' she said as she left the bus.

If her father's views contradict them, Jane at least showed herself to be sincere. A practicing Christian whose concern centred upon how her beliefs should guide her own conduct. Tonkin knew many believers to get stuck in the Pentateuch, to calculate correctly that she is not a pure-bred descendant of Adam, and fail to realise the insignificance of that meaningless fact. She had been seeing leaflets attributed to the Twelve Tribes dotted around public places in Masterton, for years and years.

* * *

At the United Nations Special Conference on the Plight of the Connipians, Tonkin can see the grinning faces of many delegates as they watch the two Connipians rise from their seats, stand three-feet tall on the stage, Tululiduh begins to click into the lowered microphones in front of them. Clickety-clack, click and pip. The Connipian position is surely no clearer than that to any of the watching Sapiens. They listen in respectful silence but what's the point. Tonkin stands in front of her own microphone, eighteen inches the taller, occasionally leaning in. Smiling a knowing smile. Even moving her lips but letting no sound escape them. The speech these Connipians are making, Klapakipsy having taken over from her sister, is pure clickery. The interpreter looks knowing but doesn't divulge. The meaning of the thoughts behind the clucking are evident to only a small minority in the hall. Clickety clack, clackety click. This orchestrated denial of content, continuous Connipian talk without any semblance of translation, is going on and on—click, click, click, even a little hiss interspersing the sound of tongues on palate—for fully three minutes. When Tululiduh has resumed the baton, Tonkin even rolls her eyes, mouthing silence with a knowing smile writ across her face. She understands exactly what they click and the three hundred Sapiens delegates do not. The more officious of the organisers look anxiously around the room. This is unlike any previous session. Clickety, clickety, pip-pip, click. An unwelcome departure judging by their frowning faces.

New York City, January, 1950

Far odder than the simultaneously interpreted contribution which a couple of Connipians gave during the dry run two days earlier. Initially those in the wings direct a few whispers at Tonkin. 'What are they saying?' They follow it up with louder calls when she studiously ignores them. The Sapiens want in on Connipian thought, one might surmise.

Then little Klapakipsy looks up and left from her microphone, directly into the face of Tonkin, the top of her own head barely reaching the bustline of her tongue-tied interpreter. Tululiduh clicks no more, and sporting an almost-Sapiens smile Klapakipsy gives two loud clicks and then pauses. Looks across the room at the many listening—or no-longer-listening—delegates. Then she starts to click quietly and Tonkin to speak. To interpret, earn her two dollars and twenty.

'We wished to draw your attention to a strange disparity. My people—the smaller ones amongst you—have, for the most part, understood your many, varied and interesting contributions. Mixed-Up interpreters, to whom we are ever grateful...' Tonkin pauses as she speaks and makes the smallest of curtsies, a gesture that causes a ripple of laughter. Looks all the funnier for the accompanying flop of her lifeless arms. '...have had little to do until now. A clarification here and there: however, even languages we have yet to understand without assistance, we are able to access through the same interpreters that you use. You will have spotted one or two of us sporting headphones when the speeches were in Russian or an African tongue with which we are not yet familiar. We can all manage English, French, Spanish, and have, in our brief time here in New York, made progress in one or two other of your many ways of speaking. In a little over two hundred and fifty years of contact, you are still to understand a single click. Fathom any part of Connipian thought, for it is thoughts to which we give syncopated sound. We do not trap solidified words in the same way as you.'

Klapakipsy looks over the hall from beneath her chestnut brown wig and then she clicks on.

'We Connipians are here at the invitation of the United Nations—thank you—and we have never been anywhere but our own isle except by invitation. And kidnap...' She stretches out her hands, two upwardly turned palms that could be accusing or could be forgiving. '...and we understand that particular practice to have ceased. In our own way we are grateful. You may have worked out for yourselves that not taking us to foreign shores against our will is scarcely a favour.' Klapakipsy ducks her head forward, face into the palms of her two tiny hands. Raises it and clicks some more. 'Why is it that even the British, the uninvited occupiers of our island have never learnt to interpret a single click of Connipian thought? Not one interpreter but the Mixed-Ups who share Connipian blood. Not a Sapiens from Britain, nor from any other corner of this gigantic Earth can understand our manner of communication. At the outset of this conference...' As Tonkin talks, Klapakipsy clicks to a slow and insistent rhythm, it enables the sincerity of her thoughts to reify across the room, to be apparent for all. '...our American friend, Mr Howard, likened our disparate subspecies to oil and water. A useful analogy, while we find the chemistry between us stranger still. We are not—and please forgive the honesty of my blunt admission—terribly interested in the societies you cultivate. To us they appear only transient; our history recalls stars resting in other parts of the night sky. And our lack of interest is not absolute; we pay attention. Fathomed your forms of communication although our tongues do not allow us to give voice to the words we have learnt. The view from the Blue Houses is that you are unable to attend to us with any of the depth with which we can hear you. Too superficial and unrooted are your cultures, you expend all your effort in convincing yourself that you are who you are pretending to be. It denies you other possibilities. And our Connipian disinterest is in the way of our mutual detachment from other species: we like to observe birds in the sky, it gives us no inclination to mimic them. We appraise that you have not learnt who you really are. Unwisely you have rested all your supposed knowledge in the ignorant certainty of your superiority. Too often you have regarded the Connipians—and the wider world around you—with a cruel prejudice. How can you regard the Connipians, the people most settled on this Earth, as primitive? It is an unworthy term and one we have already heard from several delegates at this conference. Said by many as if sympathetic to the limitations you have dreamed upon us. Well-meaning speakers who do not understand the impact of their own words. Have not the insight to recognise their untruth. Words used without making enquiry as to the nature of our culture. All your judgements have been made before a single click has been understood.'

Klapakipsy pauses her clicking and Tonkin draws the speech to an apparent close. Both of the Connipians, Klapakipsy and Tululiduh, stare impassively into the audience. The two sisters even sway together, perceptibly, only by inches first to the left and then to the right, in perfect unison. On the fourth such sway Klapakipsy clicks a short spray. 'Please can you contemplate that, and that alone, for some minutes.'

The three continue to look at the watching room. For thirty seconds the hall feels to be at the centre of the purest stillness. The delegates scarcely blink. If they contemplate her words, it is with brains whose parts move silently. Then the rustling of paper breaks the spell. A cough or two. A minute and a half pass before an English accent shouts. 'Get on with it.' Klapakipsy and Tululiduh both turn their heads away, then glance back up. Tonkin has turned towards them and is certain she can

New York City, January, 1950

see tears forming in their eyes. Extraordinary. Connipians do not cry; this pair have learnt well the role they believe might win over delegates.

'We understand,' says Tonkin as Tululiduh now starts to click, 'that you have a penchant for exploration which Connipians do not share. We have found our place on this Earth in a manner that Homo Sapiens have yet to do. Contentment: some say it is the enemy of progress, and yet it might also be its better cousin. Smarter cousin. Contentment never started a war.'

The two Connipians exchange glances at the buzz of mutterings which their last point has drawn. Tonkin hears them click an exchange speculating if it is overly critical of Sapiens, making them defensive. She picks up in the clicking that she is not to express this calculation as part of the given speech. A thought not shared.

'Connipians are confident,' continues Tululiduh through the conduit of Tonkin, 'that those first Sapiens visitors to the island, the sailors on The John and Lodowicke, were just exploring like you cannot help yourselves from doing. There was no plan to use violence to subjugate us, and your history books have long hailed John Brook, their leader, as a well-intentioned man. Connipians grant at least that he had the wisdom to leave when he saw that he could not control the urges of other men in his party. But the British came back. Days later more Englishmen came. Couldn't wait. All too quickly in our contact with you, the animal brutishness which the males of the Sapiens subtype are unable to control in themselves has come to the fore. Again and again, it has. It is the fault of some, not of all. We have understood that from first contact.'

A cluster of African delegates, a small one comprising four ladies, stand and quietly applaud the speakers. Tonkin sees Hawa Gaye amongst them. It feels like a small victory, a clear sign that some understand the point exactly. These are friends of Connipians, relating to their most haunting experience.

Tululiduh continues, clicking through her improvised smile for the standing Africans. 'They—pioneers, invaders: all too often your words are used to trap meanings which disguise the truth—came to find a land for themselves. Could not have known how occupied it was, and nor were Connipians opposed to sharing. Not in principle, not for genuinely mutual cohabitation. Raping our girls, clearing the forest that provides for us and the generations which we hope will follow, and digging the guts out of the land beneath our feet, has changed our view. It would surely change yours were the roles reversed.'

Now Klapakipsy clicks again, Tululiduh standing back a pace. A short Connipian pace.

'The island still known as New Poplar is not a British island. To visit is not to own; we do not own but share it. We take our place, not liberties. And we were there first; we think you already know that...' Klapakipsy raises her head, once more wears that knowing smile which she has learnt to form, shares it with the watching hall. A few laugh—she looks rather cute—many don't, her talk is a bit of a pummelling. She clicks the quickest spray for Tonkin to interpret. '...first by around a million years.' She moves her head, tilting it to the left, then to the right. Clicks a spray. 'A million years. That is a timeframe worthy of a little contemplation, reflection. Reverence even. And in the brief blink of an eye that the British have been there, they have not shared the island, not shared its governance. They do not speak our language and when they communicate with us, with the Connipians, it is not to further their understanding but to enforce their dominion. That is not how visitors should conduct themselves.' Klapakipsy looks across the room with a frown now covering her pretty face, a darkening beneath the eye-catching wig. 'For just a little under twenty-five years the kidnap and rape of Connipians has been illegal in British law, in the colonial law of New Poplar also. Before that, performing any sexual act with us was allegedly prohibited under a banner of bestiality. And throughout that time, the incomers whom we never invited onto our island have failed miserably to uphold these fiddly laws—words on paper the need for which belie the Sapiens mindset, their darkest intentions—and which they say they have passed to protect us. They are incapable. We do not want this so-called protection, we need only to be left alone. It seems to us that a frightening proportion of Sapiens males need castrating. Need it if ever the laws of the land are to be upheld. They are the facts, gentlemen...gentlemen and ladies. And we wish also to talk about limestone and potash, about the use of Connipian lands for the raising and subsequent slaughter of livestock, but that will wait. These important topics pale away at the certainty of the continued rape of our youth. We on this podium respectfully ask you to spend a few minutes in contemplation of that aspect of our situation. All that we continue to endure whatever laws you pass to alleviate your own consciences. Imagine yourselves in Connipian shoes. Our leaf-made shoes. We know that many of you are friends of the British, one or two of you are British. We have nothing against any nationality—zero—we apologise if we have given a contrary impression. Nothing against any of you. Sometimes it takes a friend to advise when one's behaviour has become boorish, has fallen below a standard that is acceptable. Sunk to the floor.'

On cue, Klapakipsy and Tululiduh sit back into their chairs. Tonkin quickly looks across the floor, directly at Mr Howard, and then whispers, 'I must pass water,' to the usher at the side of the podium. The interpreter leaves the room, and no more Connipian thought will be heard until she returns.

New York City, January, 1950

* * *

The rest of the bus journey occurred in near silence. Total on Tonkin's part. It was as if the other passengers on the bus were relieved that Jane Spence had gotten off. She and Jane had talked in low voices; engaging so intimately with one as funny-looking as Tonkin must have been bad form. No one spoke to her after Jane left. Not a soul would catch her eye. They kept their distance from the scrawny schoolgirl whose arms dangled so loosely. The relative of that poisoned-pen letter writer had proven herself a good person, this stony silence seemed to prove their number few in that corner of the planet. New Zealand was an unlikely home for a Mixed-Up. The Quaker programme another pointless expression of Sapiens optimism, a denial of Connipian worth.

When she arrived in Wellington, Tonkin had a plan, some of it her own, the rest her mother's. Shared in those letters. She made her way from the bus terminal on Manners Street to Port Nicholson. Walked as casually as she could. An unfamiliar thumping in the centre of her chest.

Quite how Tripanplic gathered all the information which she had given her daughter in the course of those letters was a mystery Tonkin hadn't tried to solve. She was following the respectful request—'*If you would like to,*' an oft repeated phrase, and '**Should reuniting with me be a choice you wish to make**'—doing it as if hypnotised. No sorcery beyond the pull of the place from which she had once been removed. To the mother who never wished to send her away.

At the water's edge, Tonkin realised that the ships were moored far apart. Docked across a two- or three-mile stretch of water, all along the lengthy harbourside. As long as she stayed a short distance from people and moved her shoulders so her arms swung, it was unlikely anyone would guess she was other than a lonely schoolgirl, and these were the Easter holidays. No surprise that she was not in the classroom.

She went around the side of a warehouse. Out of view. There she wriggled out of her shoulder bag, snuck inside with her nose and then, teeth pulling on greased-proof paper, unwrapped her sandwich. A little sustenance. She had the sandwich nesting on her knees as she sat and burrowed her face into it. Ate bread and cheese, made as best she could. Her foster mother might still have been unaware of the small amount of food Tonkin had taken from her kitchen. Then she stood back up on her feet, walked the length of that harbourside. Fully two miles before she found the boat which her mother advised would be in dock. It was named Queen of Leamouth. A small cargo ship used to ferry potash between New Poplar and its giant neighbours, New Zealand and Australia. Tripanplic had advised by letter that it would sail at six the following morning.

She walked around and behind a warehouse; not the one she had eaten behind, the harbourside had many. Kept herself out of sight once more, while espying carefully around the side of the building. Loading of the Queen of Leamouth was taking place. A few crates—she knew not what of—going in the opposite direction to the holds full of potash that the plundering British had stripped from her mother's land. Tonkin read everything Connipian which the local library stocked; her friend, Sally, who worked there, had ensured they acquired all the books on the subject that they could. Tonkin had still to hear directly the consternation it caused her mother. Caused all the indigenous women of the island, those forest-dwelling men too. Their worldview did not make the Wellington newspapers, never found its way to Masterton Library.

The watching Tonkin did not partake of a second's sleep, dared not miss her chance to board the ship. Did not allow herself to feel hunger. How trivial tummy ache when contrasted to the denial of a motherland?

* * *

'A speaker or two has implied, said directly even, that Connipian claims are foolish. That we wish to disrupt the British in their legitimate need to source potash and limestone. That we have no practical reason for preventing it from taking place. That is the core of their argument. The gentleman from Australia defended the practice of panning for gold, although the island has yielded the most meagre quantities. If you wear a tiepin, you may have more on your person.' Klapakipsy is clicking once more, Tonkin speaking her thoughts for the Sapiens to dwell upon. 'It is true that we Connipians do not use these resources for ourselves and therefore our objection to their removal you have come to regard as selfishness. That is the analysis of commentators the world over. Commentators who have contemplated only their own narrow fixation with turning the world as it is into the world as they would like it to be. Their persistent burning and fusing, shaping and misrepresenting. Weasel words because they know only how to speak from their own material-grabbing perspective, not how to listen to a more time-proven alternative. New York City did not look like this two hundred years ago, and if you believe it will look as it does now in five hundred years' time you have not been watching yourselves. You Sapiens swallow resources as an alcoholic does his whisky. From the perspective of stability—trust the wise counsel of a people whose durability dwarfs Confucianism, Christianity, those times you call antiquity—it cannot go on like this. Cannot.' Klapakipsy gives the audience that two-faced smile, charming and charmless, beautiful and fake. 'Can you hear the Connipians? Even as Tonkin, the Mixed-Up, speaks exactly the thoughts which I click, can you hear them? Do you dare to digest them?'

New York City, January, 1950

'Who are you to lecture us?' shouts a voice. British accent. 'Where are your men? This is airy-fairy nonsense that even you won't fight for.'

Suddenly Klapakipsy looks visibly upset. Not tears this time. A shaking of the shoulders, her face drawn away, fake smile departed. With her left hand she slides her wig off her head. Still wrapped in the brilliant blue skirt, a shining black blouse above it clings tightly to her top, her swelling chest. White arms visible from the elbows. Her face looks sad and angry. Alone in its youth and sudden hairlessness.

'We were not a party to your two world wars,' says Tonkin, clearly translating the clicks which Klapakipsy sprays, making the girl's thoughts audible whether or not this audience can find room for them in their scheme of understanding. 'You ripped each other limb from limb. Set off a bomb that killed a hundred thousand at a stroke. If you still believe might equals right you must be blind to your own history. To believe it, is to dishonour the dead. The lives you have wasted by fighting. Countless, truly countless. We grieve for you, for the Sapiens. Grieve that you have strayed so far from the equilibrium required to have true purchase in this one life. And we fear this imbalance might simply flow within your biology. It seems to be your way. For this reason, we must live apart.' Klapakipsy raises up her chin, seems to search the delegates with her eyes before continuing to click. 'Visitors to the island who wish to learn from Connipians would always be most welcome. To date, the Mexican artist, Zaneta Lozano, may have been the only one. And I can promise that we will listen to you in return. I suggest we already have; we've applied ourselves diligently in those libraries you have kindly given us. They are appreciated. I am sorry my tongue cannot turn itself into your words, forever grateful to Tonkin here for aiding me in telling you all that I need to say. We Connipians value listening above expressing our own thoughts, have done so since time immemorial. Contact with the Sapiens has been an education. I think the lessons have been understood by my species but not yet by yours. And your attempt to modernise, civilise and integrate Connipians into your death cult, we cannot endorse. The one over-riding reason we wish the British out of our land is because we feel their presence is driving us out of existence. There are leaflets in every bar in Charlestown advising that it is desirable. God's wish! The Twelve Tribes and other zealots—with influence in very high places across this Earth—believe the very presence of another kind of people to be an affront. And you wonder why we ask you to leave us alone. Pretend to yourselves that these are extreme voices while they permeate your churches and burrow into your politics. You declare yourselves tolerant people while wishing us gone from the Earth. We request only that you leave a very, very small island, we have no desire to interfere in the vast tracts of Earth which we correspondingly cede to you.'

As she pauses, Tonkin notices how laboured Klapakipsy's breathing has become between the clicks. Guesses the girl did not prepare for the emotions she might feel on speaking to this impenetrable audience.

'We are not so foolish as to wish British rule subsumed by another Sapiens entity which likewise cannot hear us. We respectfully ask you to do something right: give us back the land that is ours. Rape us no longer. Study Connipian thought, by all means; you have it on tape and you are not without ingenuity. We are confident that when you finally understand us, you will concur with our beliefs. Wish for the stability which only we currently know how to nurture. Until then, Connipians and Sapiens should—and again, I want to make this point most respectfully, on our part the reason is necessity, not hatred, superiority or disdain—live apart.'

* * *

On the Port Nicholson quay, beneath pale moonlight, the young Mixed-Up then known as Rebecca tried, for the first time, to walk a tightrope. A skill she had yet to learn and knew of its possibility only from watching a travelling circus the summer before. Taken there by her foster dad. Enjoyed it for the most part; embarrassed when she realised that the Ringmaster was constantly looking at her. Wished Trevor Horton, who she had long called Daddy, hadn't purchased front-row seats. A Mixed-Up is a circus freak of value: she could see the calculation in the Ringmaster's enquiring eyes, staring at her off and on, performance long. Well, if a man with a red nose and shoes twice the size he really needed could do it, so could she. Stepping onto the thick metallic cord tying ship to dock, she found it tort, scarcely any give at all. Not far from quay to ship, a short if challenging gangway. Tonkin felt taller as she bravely took the first step. Wondered simultaneously if a pair of moving arms might be a helpful addition with which to steady oneself. The clown at the circus carried a pole in front of him. She was starting to see how that might help. Balance is a funny thing. Walking in a straight line had seemed easier when a tiny margin of error was never going to result in catastrophe. Tonkin really was a quick learner. Tried to remain stock-still, not to wobble, realised that falling from the narrow ropeway was a misstep away. Fatal if she entered the water. Tonkin put her right foot forward on the rope. Left. Right again. Up the mooring she stumbled, as her footing seemed to be going over the side, she pressed the other foot hard on the tort rope, gave herself some bounce with which to launch herself at the boat side near the stern. Her thighs crashed into it and her momentum—chest and shoulders, head and flailing arms, all above the height of the gunwale—took her headfirst over and onto the deck. A bang of the face. With her tongue, she could feel blood. Oh golly, she thought, licking right up to her nose. A need to keep the scene of her entry inconspicuous. Leave no trail. She rolled herself over, and picked herself up. A bruise or two. It might have been only her gums that bled. Tried to feel each tooth, tasted the blood both sides but nothing had come loose. Being aboard was worth a dose of pain. A boat bound for New Poplar. For Connipia, which she already knew to be its better name although it was used only in certain scholarly journals. Tonkin moved quietly to a tarpaulin-covered lifeboat. This would make a satisfactory hiding place for the duration. If events mid-journey should require it to be called into service, it would change the rubric. Mixed-Ups have many skills although an astonishingly high proportion turn out unintelligent, mentally retarded. Tonkin is in the other group, one of the most brilliant there has ever been. No Mixed-Up is able to swim: not one. It's the arms of course. Floppy is not good, not when one must propel oneself through the water. String arms, which the Mixed-Up cannot control, have little value beyond the easy identification of the genotype. If the ship got into trouble, the lifeboat would be the best place for Tonkin. A hiding place with insurance layered across it.

* * *

The British reply to Klapakipsy and Tululiduh's demands is brief and receives a mixed reaction from the hall. From friends and enemies. Upon their arrival in seventeen ninety-five, New Poplar was, to all extent and purposes, an uninhabited isle. No one lived there when The John and Lodowicke sailed in. The creatures already upon it belong to the animal kingdom—always did, always will—they are not of the human race. Sir Nevil Wheatley, the speaker, pokes fun at the earlier Connipian pleas. 'Unchanged in a million years: they long ago opted out of that race, didn't they?' He also questions the clicking language. 'We have the words of a few Floppy-Arms; and I believe they add a bit of human cunning to the supposed thoughts of the little women. It is hardly a credible way to negotiate, not if we cannot confirm that we have agreed on anything at all. They tell us their clicking is something other than words—pure thought, if you can believe that—words are all we hear. We do not know what the frogs on the river bank mean when they croak and yet, the world over, we build towns and hydroelectric facilities regardless of their views on the matter, do we not?' He even refers to contentious research that casts doubt on the rape of Connipians, claims they are complicit, so starved of healthy males is their island.

While at the podium, Sir Nevil suggests the British will adopt a form of dual naming for the island. 'It is New Poplar, as founded by its discoverer, John Brook, and we are happy if all who wish to call it

Connipia do exactly that. Sharing a land with so interesting and unlikely a breed as these ladies is an honour on many levels.' The audience relaxes into this warmer tone. Cessation of hostilities. 'The ethnological work done is of international interest. The Connipians have periodically cooperated, and we thank them for it. Would welcome more of the same.'

For a long time, he makes no reference to the resources of the island. Doesn't say that the gold found has been worse than meagre in quantity. Fails to mention that the prospectors it attracted in Victorian times produced more Mixed-Ups than they turned profits. Doesn't talk about the limestone which the British quarry. The potash.

'We apologise,' says Sir Nevil, 'for the poorly managed scientific enquiries of the last century. I understand some studies required Connipians to leave their homes for the United Kingdom; not kidnapped, I must add, treated well enough for the most part. That practice is no more, and we pledge, here today, that all Connipians may remain upon New Poplar—on Connipia—for all time. Unless they choose to leave of their own accord. We are their protectors, not their captors.'

From the back of the hall shouting erupts. A small group of women, believed to be American or Canadian but not of their countries' delegations, heckle Sir Nevil. 'Rape is wrong!' they shout. 'You can't protect the little women!'

Sir Nevil looks over the rim of his wire-framed spectacles. Goes red in the face. 'There are many faces to the law. Connipian practice is an affront to our laws on bigamy; we believe them adulterous and licentious. We do not condone Englishmen, or other visitors to New Poplar, taking advantage of them. As I have outlined, we understand that they do very little to resist. I am sorry that it is so difficult to verify. And nowhere on Earth is there better policing of the animal kingdom than on the island of New Poplar. It is a task made more complicated still— close to impossible—by the refusal of Connipians to allow us ready access to the Blue Houses. We have police on New Poplar whom they will not call upon.' He glances at the Connipian contingent, scattered around the hall. On the smaller chairs. 'Don't be fooled by appearances,' says Sir Nevil, 'they are not just their own worst enemies on this issue. They relish the sympathy it draws from well-meaning people around the globe. If they allowed us to station policemen near their settlements, we would eradicate it. You know we would. Then how would they garner that sympathy? Consider the true outcome. We are uncertain if all Mixed-Ups are the progeny of errant human males, doubt it considerably in the case of the smaller and more mentally retarded. One might expect our human blood to raise up their functioning if you think about what

New York City, January, 1950

our species has achieved in comparison to theirs. Still, we look after their Mixed-Ups. That's all done through the charitable centres in East Town. And Connipians give them up, you know? Don't feel towards their children as we do towards ours. Not even the physically able ones; they don't care for them properly. Never live quite as families should.'

Throughout his talk, the shouting at the back of the hall continues. Does so until officials remove the protesting women. Sapiens women, the gender Connipians have always found more amenable towards them. They are banished for their protest. The taking of a side on the fraught subject of rape.

'A word about the mining which continues on New Poplar...' Sir Nevil finally gets around to the money. '...the Connipian demands are illogical. There is no mining without first purchasing a permit, and those are a source of government revenue. We pledge to spend a significant proportion of our returns in Connipian areas. Indeed, we always have. The Connipians turned down the provision of running water which we have promised, preferring instead to scuttle backwards and forwards to the rivers. Still using gourdes when we have given bottles and flagons. The offer of piped water stands. We wish to help. We want to gift them an infrastructure like that which transformed the health of Victorian England. Come an outbreak of cholera or similar, we believe they will change their minds. The resources of the island are for all. We are sharing the isle while they greedily plead to keep it all for themselves.'

When Sir Nevil Wheatly has finished speaking, Østergaard gets up on to his feet. Seeks a right of reply which carries little logic but, through Tonkin, the Connipians let it be known that they wish to hear him. The British contribution has been a gut punch, the assembled will not deny the Connipians this tiny favour.

'This conference,' says Jørgen Østergaard from the now-raised microphone, standing on the side of the stage from where Klapakipsy clicked, 'was set up for a single purpose. We have learnt from country after country that whatever the intentions of colonialism, oppression is the result. That is the felt experience of those who must acquiesce. And I concur with our Connipian friends throughout the hall who declared that we Sapiens have too long relied on power. Letting might and power and gunboats determine who rules who, without any regard for true justice, is the exact opposite of that which we seek through this great global institution, the United Nations. We want to bring order around the globe, do we not? Thankfully, we are now seeing home rule take to the fore on every continent. Not before time, many of you will say. Finally replacing imposed and obstinate governments who do not have a mandate among those they seek to rule. It is bringing forth a cultural renaissance, some of the former colonial powers misunderstand this because it is not their culture but that of the people previously oppressed. And here, over the course of these three days, we have heard much about the original people of New Poplar, of Connipia. They were there before the British. Not only were they there first—there since so long ago I do not believe I am able to imagine it—but they are intrinsically different, and it is not for us to call this difference an inferiority. We are quite wrong to do so. Judging what we do not understand, as our friends have explained. I cannot click and I wish I could. I am only just starting to see how narrow-minded we have been. In the past, I was satisfied to think only of what I would want if I was a Connipian, imagined that access to our world would be of value to them. Connipians are of the same genus as us, but they are a different species, with a radically different history. A longer history. We can accept them as equals or tell ourselves myths. Are we really going to let—as Sir Nevil Wheatly implied—our differences continue to be a reason for mistreatment? For denying them self-rule. Or can we find both the generosity of spirit and the wisdom in our minds to ensure our cultures exist comfortably and in parallel? Sir Nevil implied he was disappointed that they—the Connipians—have not already acquired some of our ways. But the reverse is still less true. Change is a very threatening state for a society to be subject to. And nor can it ever be an obligation that Connipian ways should change. Not if we are truly granting them a shred of autonomy.'

As he talks, Klapakipsy clicks quietly to Tonkin and to the others in her party. Her cultivation of this man has yielded a small return. His talk of living alongside is a disappointment. They really need the British gone.

'We owe it to these people to meet them halfway; to give real ground. Allow their culture to flourish whether we understand it or not. When my friend spoke of the atomic bomb...' Østergaard gestures towards Klapakipsy. '...we listened with trepidation, did we not? I think we all know that the Americans unleashed those phenomenal forces only after much forethought, did it during the most terrible conflict our world has ever seen. Yet we are fools if we do not fear that our scientific developments are changing the planet forever. We cannot use such bombs as our forebears did the spear or the gun. Engaging in combat ceaselessly, accepting occasional defeat as a show of valour on the battlefield. Perhaps it was always absurd, as our little friends imply. Now it is impossible. We are the protectors of this planet. From ourselves first and foremost. From the instability which our growing arsenal of weapons brings to the fore; from the startling changes of habitat which our urbanisation threatens upon the world of nature. And on New Poplar, on Connipia, we Sapiens might be the protector of a people who

New York City, January, 1950

helped themselves quite adequately before we arrived. But a people barely half our size, with only a small—and frankly, a not especially healthy—male population. We must not let the little women of Connipia down. The British said they have come to listen and so they must. Listen and comply with a settlement that does justice to the longevity of the Connipians' claim to that special island.'

When he closes his impromptu speech, the audience applauds. He has repaired some damage. Shown that the conference is not simply a litany of self-interest. There are responsibilities at play. Although Klapakipsy and Tululiduh make a point of joining the applause, the thoughts they click to Tonkin are not so keen. They wish to be nobody's responsibility.

9.

In the evening, Tonkin again eats early in a separate room, enabling her to join the delegates at the main meal. Do her job without having to eat in front of gawping faces. At the formal dinner, all the Connipians are present except Klapakipsy; the British do not socialise here. Østergaard is inexplicably absent. Tonkin tries not to dwell on it while worrying about the only explanation she can come up with.

The meal is unexceptional. Polite talk throughout; she repeats to those who wish to hear it, the clicked praise for the Dane's speech. That he, at least, has been listening to the Connipians. Hawa Gaye too, but hers was a speech from the heart. A woman with insight into being colonised. Only Jørgen said what he didn't know a week earlier.

Tonkin is asked to put many questions to the Connipians; everyone wants to show an interest now there is only a short day left.

When a gentleman from Ireland asks about marriage, whether the Connipians have thought of introducing it as a better way to bring up their children, Napapilis gives the notion short shrift. 'It would not work,' is as much of her diatribe as Tonkin translates for the questioner. Repeats, 'It couldn't work for Connipians,' when he presses her for a fuller answer. This Irishman clearly cannot do basic arithmetic.

Tonkin returns to The Belvedere Hotel without learning how Klapakipsy has spent the evening, or how communication has taken place if she has been with the Dane as she fears. Of course, Klapakipsy could have used a pencil to write in English, French, maybe Danish too. It is a skill Tonkin cannot match.

* * *

On the third and final day of the conference, the great man is in the hall. President Truman. The day begins with a series of British concessions.

God Help the Connipians

The official name of the island shall be Connipia. Atlases will be reissued. It is not a name that the Connipians use themselves—a spoken word not a clicked thought of multiple reference—but at least it indicates that the island is somehow theirs. Beats New Poplar hands down. Connipians are to have complete control over all of the high-ground forest and some fifty percent of the low-lying forests on the island. Close to complete control; very few Sapiens will have a right of entry. None at all without consulting Connipians in advance. The British insist that this is not a veto; they agree to publish a list of all the permits they issue. To whom, and why. They say dendrologists must enter the forest each year. Conduct a survey; assess the health of the trees. The Connipian's thought they had it covered, skyfields yielding fruit for hundreds of thousands of years. The British promise to seek a Connipian view on the best time to do it, that's the compromise. For it is in the interests of all islanders to understand if plants are diseased. And they respectfully suggest health surveys of the ladies—men too, but that has never happened yet—continue in their own best interest. Sir Nevil tells the hall that enhancing Connipian understanding of health issues will enable them to help themselves. They would not wish the Connipian women to go the way of the men.

'A million years,' Tonkin hears several Connipians click.

Connipians have no use for limestone and potash, therefore extraction will continue. Done only where it does not impact upon their habitats. It provides the money for the healthcare they may one day take advantage of. 'When they come to their senses,' says Sir Nevil.

Significantly, the British accept that past practices—the word 'kidnap' crosses no one's lips—have broken needed trust. They will allow international monitors to oversee contact until such time as Connipians and British both confirm they have repaired their differences.

It bothers Tonkin that Klapakipsy is still absent. She must be up in her hotel room. Østergaard is here now; she cannot read his face. Dare not ask what happened last night. Klapakipsy would have hated all this: concession after concession, all adding up to nothing.

'I love this institution,' says President Truman when he gets his go at the microphone. 'Nations United can resolve any dispute. I feel sure we can if we all come at it with the right attitude. I am grateful to our British friends for the work they have put in and the flexibility they have shown.'

As he drones on, smiling each time he looks at a Connipian, as if he is electioneering in a kindergarten, Tonkin senses the despondent mood amongst them. All who are small. No government on Earth recognises their exclusive claim to the island even as they rename it in their honour. Words are only words. Connipians may never again sit at the United Nations and the seats they use today are smaller than the others, less

New York City, January, 1950

visible. They have no vote in this assembly: New Poplar is not a country and nor shall Connipia be. An adjunct of the faraway United Kingdom. They don't vote back on the island either, not in any British plebiscites, nor upon exclusively Connipian matters. They convene no councils. In their long experience, thoughts shared come to an accommodation. They suspect words are too circumspect to arrive there intact. Allow Sapiens to set each other traps as if that is really a way to cohabit. No Connipian has ever forced another to do anything. A million years of not doing it, the practice is fixed. Good luck to Truman with his nations-united project. He is trying to pull it off with the wrong species.

The voting members of this assembly want results from their conference. Even the Africans are sagely nodding agreement with President Truman. Østergaard beams like it is he who has wrung every compromise from the British. Tonkin has no idea what he has done.

The President wants a photograph and the Connipians are too polite to deny it him. The conference is unanimous. Among its voting nations if not the non-voting delegates. Tululiduh clicks to Tonkin her dismal appraisal: the text of the agreement is too vague. What these people are agreeing upon is a paper they can reinterpret in the future, not a solid position from which all walk away with a shared understanding. Arguments between nations will continue while Connipians go unheard. Tonkin clicks back an enquiry about her sister. Klapakipsy's health. Tululiduh gives a slight shudder. 'She tried too hard, believed she could change a few minds. I don't know if she can come back from this.'

10.

Towards the end of the same year, Tonkin takes up work in Moscow, assisting with the translation of hours and hours of tapes. Shchelchki v Lesu, the project's Russian title: Clicking in the Forest. She likes the lilt of this new language, feels a little paranoid when she overhears two cryptologists say she is making it up, that her interpretation of the clicking cannot possibly mean what she says it means. They don't have any idea how much Russian Tonkin has picked up. She uses an English interpreter all the while she is in this city. Keeps up the pretence. She has learnt to trust no one. It might be the lesson of the conference back in January.

She never saw Klapakipsy again; a Connipian called Malapil passed her a note before her group left the hotel. Took the boat for their long journey. It reiterated much that other members of the delegation had said. Thanked her for her diligent work, appreciated that without the Mixed-Ups they could have never got a single thought across to the Sapiens. And Tonkin was better at it than any other. The foremost speaker of Connipian thought. '*If they listened to us like you do, all would be well,*' said a telling line. She apologised for being unable to attend the last day of the conference. '*A sickness overcame me, has been passed to me, one might say.*' Tonkin had instinctively disliked seeing Klapakipsy try to charm Sapiens delegates, Sapiens men. Women in the churning world do it all the time; not all of them, but those who believe they have the right kind of appeal. And little Klapakipsy seemed to ooze the stuff. It has never been the Connipian way. Tiny, vulnerable. There is no flirting required to attract oneself a Connipian male. They will always comply with a polite request; force themselves upon another, never. The driven sexuality of the Sapiens is as tempestuous and alien as the ocean the Connipians will have faced on leaving the port of New York. And it was there to see in many a stance upon the conference hall podium. The strutting manner of Harry S Truman, of Sir Nevil Wheatley. Raping the lectern as they spoke.

Tonkin is grateful for the protection her limp and boneless arms give her, the awkwardness of her posture. Wishes not to be of interest to the men of the world. It looks utterly fearful; even the backdraft intense behind their watching eyes.

Tonkin took this job in Moscow as an act of defiance. She had planned to return to the newly named Connipia. Not that the name change happened overnight; at least it is coming. She took herself there via New Zealand. She will fly as the purebloods do not. Made the trip to Auckland. Then down to Wellington where the ageing Mr and Mrs Horton live out their retirement. A reunion that was as emotional for them as it was not for Tonkin. She is grateful to them for the effort, even the wisdom, they put into childrearing. Strange child that she was. Her ability to hear and understand the thoughts of Connipians, the skill that has granted her this lifestyle, this role in the world, is down to Tripanplic. All down to those first three unremembered years with her true mother. From her foster parents she received access to a Sapiens education, they taught her excellent self-care too. But to raise a child is not to own it. That is a Connipian truth which only those little women have never confused.

She thanked her former foster parents, went through the motions. They had watched television pictures of Tonkin at the conference. Speaking from the podium on the middle day.

'We felt so proud of you,' said Rene Horton.

Tonkin isn't really sure why they would. Lives long diverged.

* * *

She stowed herself away on the near empty potash boat, trying with every muscle she could control to remain rigidly still beneath the

New York City, January, 1950

tarpaulin of the lifeboat. Tonkin felt the gentle rocking of the unmooring, heard a metallic clang as the small ship first bumped off its berth. Throughout the journey she found herself tearful. Embarrassed that she could not wipe them away, and thankful to be out of view of all others on the boat. Crying about a homecoming that she doubted she could explain. She had allowed no specific expectations to coalesce around the planned meeting with her mother. Tonkin—still thinking of herself as Rebecca at that point in her life—was conscious primarily that a Mixed-Up did not belong in New Zealand. Some people tried to be kind to her, the vast majority didn't. Some were actively hateful: people she had never met, never spoken with, wrote to the local paper to share their scathing opinions. Said she and her kind were an aberration of nature. Tonkin felt a separateness in every glance. It never stopped her from applying herself, from becoming the cleverest student who could not scribe her own name. She didn't have strong views about Connipians. What she had read of them was pretty mixed. Broadly, they might be primitive; she hoped she was wrong. Feared she shared the prejudices of her host species although neither Mr nor Mrs Horton ever said a bad word about them. The Blue Houses sounded nice, the Connipians' diet boring. And climbing trees for a living was not a credible occupation for Tonkin. Venturing into the cultivated canopies would be far harder than illegally boarding a ship.

In the five days of sailing between Wellington and Charlestown, she arose from her covered life-raft only twice. Both times under the cover of darkness. Hearing no sound on deck, she walked barely twelve paces to pee behind the empty metal tubs. Hoped it would dry up before anyone saw the evidence of her presence. Nothing to inspect by the third day, the girl had scarcely a pipette full to pee out. Hungry and no food to eat; licking a few droplets of water from the tarpaulin, and that was sea spray. No rain fell after they'd left port.

The boat docked, took a berth on the island of New Poplar. She knew when the manoeuvre was complete, moored and secured, could sense it in the darkness under the tarpaulin. The absence of a moving sea is the easiest thing to detect. She waited and waited. Couldn't guess for how long, and perhaps she was not as patient as she thought herself. When she could hear no sound, she arose from the lifeboat and emerged into the daylight of the deck, Charlestown in sight across the dock. What she saw gave her a terrible fright. It grinned and had teeth.

'What have we here,' said an old sailor, still working on the boat. Clambering up from the crouched position he held while checking the ropes that tied down the many metal hoppers. 'My God!' he exclaimed when he saw her arms. Understood the nature of the beast.

Tonkin had not anticipated any such meeting until she was in

God Help the Connipians

Charlestown. Her mother had said that Mixed-Ups were an unexceptional sight in much of the town. They are always getting lost; someone would return one as young as she then was into the care of the nuns. She also advised that many Mixed-Ups were unintelligent. Most. A couple of hundred of them living in East Town and few could speak clearly. It wasn't obvious why Tripanplic had appraised her of these facts. Not until now.

'Ea't Town,' she said, voice less distinct than her true self. 'Tister Carmel in Ea't Town.'

'How the hell have you clambered onto our Queenie?' said the man.

Tonkin had read the name back in Wellington, guessed when she heard it said that it was how the sailor called his boat. 'Ea't Town,' she repeated. Then added, 'P'ease don't hurt me.' Unsure herself whether it was for effect, or a genuine plea.

'No, no. I don't hurt no one that doesn't start on me. But how did you get on to the ship, missy?'

'Ea't Town.'

The old sailor tried many ways of asking, quickly came to see his stowaway was a stupid one. And he took it into his head that she had somehow wandered aboard after The Queen of Leamouth had docked in Charlestown. He'd never seen a Mixed-Up in Wellington, the other end of their run. Said it out loud to no one but himself while Tonkin was moronically declaiming 'Ea't Town.' Playing the simpleton. When he finally whistled for assistance, and two men over on the dock came up the gangplank, it was the explanation he gave them. 'Have you seen this Flippy-Floppy hanging around the dock, Pete? Maurice? She can't have been on board at Wellington; they don't have any there.'

They said they'd not seen any Mixed-Ups at the harbour. Never. 'Support the amendment,' parroted the one called Maurice.

Tonkin had read about this in the library at Masterton. The proposal to prohibit all Connipians and Mixed-Ups—Mr Floppies, the term used in the article—from central Charlestown. Not that the ordinance would bother Connipians; they are forest dwellers through and through.

'Ea't Town,' she repeated. 'Ea't Town.'

'Can you take the bugger away,' said the old sailor. 'Getting on my nerves, she is. Find someone who can take her out to where she needs to be.'

'Will do,' said Maurice.

'Hey...and mate, don't hurt her, right? It's a shame for them.'

* * *

In February of this year—of nineteen fifty—before she ever took herself to Moscow, Tonkin again sailed from Wellington to Connipia. Passenger

New York City, January, 1950

class, over the same stretch of ocean she'd crossed all those years ago. No need to hideaway beneath a life-raft, a legitimate ticket in the small rucksack she used. Arms that cannot carry cases. The journey took a day fewer than her freight passage of nineteen twenty-four, she was able to enjoy the view, at least for as long as North Island was close to hand. The endless Pacific has little appeal for Tonkin.

At Charlestown she received the rudest reception. The entry was managed more carefully than she had ever before seen. At the conference there was talk of restricting entry, protection for Homo Connipus. Not that membership of the Twelve Tribes is anywhere written on a passport.

'Step this way, Miss,' demanded a man in a peaked cap. Gold hashmarks upon his sleeve.

'My documents are in this bag,' she said.

'This way.'

In a small anteroom, a man introduced himself by his military rank but Tonkin didn't take it in. 'Residence on New Poplar is restricted,' he told her. 'You have no tourist visa.'

'It is the island of my birth...'

'You're a New Zealander, Miss, and well you know it.'

'But I've been here many times, lived here...born here,'

'Yes, Miss. You are a New Zealander, nonetheless. As you will know, we are pledged to be highly protective of who may come ashore.'

'I work with the Connipians.'

'Not as they've told us. We know you've done it in the past, but no one has applied for a permit on your behalf.'

'I've been in New York. Arrived back here before the other delegates, I expect.'

'Oh, we know you've been in New York, Miss. Very unimpressed with your interpreting skills. Your bias in a role with a professional duty of impartiality. Governor Pilling has determined that you are no friend of New Poplar. Something of an agitator by his assessment...'

'Wait!' Tonkin was furious. Interrupted the man, whatever his rank, however important he thought himself. 'Are you going to turn away the Connipian delegates when they return.'

'Connipians can go where Connipians live, Miss. You live in New Zealand. I see you've lived all sorts of elsewhere. So good luck finding your rightful home. New Poplar's not for you. It's one place you cannot stay.'

'I see,' said Tonkin. And she has always seen it. Known it to her core. How little Mixed-Ups belong in any particular place. How tentative a foothold they have upon this Earth.

* * *

193

God Help the Connipians

Under the guise of being a retarded Mixed-Up, although she was anything but, the two men took Tonkin away in a shipyard van. To East Town. 'Ea't Town,' as she called it throughout the ride. No one asked to see a passport or any other document. Not a second's thought given to the notion that a flopster could make it solo from New Zealand to this far-flung isle. She had wandered all the way from East Town to the dock, they told each other, and they thought that a remarkable passage for one as imbecilic as she demonstrably was.

In East Town they took her to an orphanage where she met Sister Carmel. The good nun was able to get a message to Tripanplic. Within a day her mother came to the orphanage. Tonkin was with her once more, as should never have been interrupted.

Connipians don't dote on their children, not in the Sapiens manner—nor do they send them to war in their teenage years so comparing and contrasting is a complex matter—and Tripanplic stood sixteen inches short of her teenage offspring. Initially there was reserve, mother letting daughter know her thoughts, while Tonkin stood listening closely to the clicking but not quite grasping their intent. Others in the convent where they met brought fruit for Tripanplic, bread, cheese and lemonade for Tonkin. She listened to her mother's clicking for one hour, two hours. It all started to fall into place. It was as if she first needed to forget the English of her last dozen years in order to hear the thoughts. Once she did this, she was able to find that part of herself which is Connipian. The part of her which she'd mislaid in the kindness of the Horton's home.

Sister Carmel did not interfere with the meeting, but much later, after offering Tonkin assistance with a bath—turned down, for she had long been able to bathe alone—asked questions and the Mixed-Up asked a few of her own. Sister Carmel confirmed that she had not read the content of the letters Tripanplic wrote, felt surprised—while smiling about it—that it was her name which she gave to Tonkin. Singled her out as the contact in East Town. 'I'm not sure my Order would like to think I am disrupting the Quaker Programme, young Rebecca,' she said.

'Tonkin,' said Tonkin. 'That is how my mother addresses me. At least, I think that is how it is said as a pared down word.'

Sister Carmel nodded assent. 'Welcome home, Tonkin.'

* * *

So here she is in Moscow. Less than a year after the British—who have never truly belonged there—turned Tonkin away from the island of her birth. Twenty-six years since her more successful return. This defection might be stupid; already she is learning that on the other side of the cold war the Sapiens are no different to the ones she knew in New Zealand and Holland and New York City. Everyone wants to utilise her special power, gather in what Connipians say. But they don't get it. It is as if they wish to learn only how unlike the Connipians they truly are.

Tonkin may need to plot another flight, has still to think where it will be to. And she cannot stop thinking about Klapakipsy. Would love to contact her again. Poor child. She would have outwitted the world, were it a rational place, but it is not. And the lost evening with Østergaard bothers her. Upsets Tonkin more than she likes to admit. Is it a weakness in her, or a strength, to feel so intensely for another person?

Chapter Three

Frame

After

The meeting with Hard White is boring. Conrad Klassen flew out to Vancouver specifically for it. The consortium he represents requires potash and the company continues to extract a lot of it down there in Connipia. The sales director tells him they can pass along a few hundredweight of Alia Folia Crescente *if he wishes—sweeten the deal— not that Hard White trade in wood, not officially. Conrad has heard it said, many a time, that there is minimal enforcement of protectorate rules. Hard White have more chance of seeing a Connipian than anyone from the forestry police. No wood is allowed to leave the island but it keeps turning up in fancy houses; potash can be extracted from no further than one hundred metres of a designated mining trig, not that anybody in authority checks anything until it's being loaded in port. The boys from Hard White don't share details of their true operation with Conrad, the wood offered on the side is several thousand dollars' worth.*

In the middle of this appointment, a smartly dressed girl from reception enters the room with a telegram for him. Not had one of those in twenty years. Something about the way the girl moves reminds him of his wife. Second wife, that is. Conrad has recently divorced his third. Two went that way and the first—the best of them—taken more cruelly. And now this. The telegram tells him that Ailsa Grant lives no more. He knows who it refers to—only ever been one Ailsa in his life—it even says née Donaldson *in the telegram. She was his second, briefly called Ailsa Klassen. It says an inquest is to be held before the cause of her death can be released.*

He thanks the back of the girl who brought him the telegram; she is already on her way out. Did she really walk like Ailsa, the same lightness of step, or did he make it up? Mysteriously guess that she was to be the subject of the dispatch. The thought that Ailsa—she was fifteen years his junior—has departed this life is likely to upset him later. Not big-style, only the loss of his first wife has ever done that. Hotel-room sad. And sometimes he gets that simply by being away from Toronto. Or away from Gravelbourg, Saskatchewan, the place he and Maureen called home. For the time being he must continue the meeting, the business in which he is engaged. Or the telegram could just make him angry: why the hell doesn't it say what happened to her? They must know something. Did she die in a hospital? In a car accident, perhaps? Not murder, not Ailsa, he can't picture that for a second. She must have turned forty, hard to imagine, but the years keep ticking over. More than twenty years since he last saw her. Well passed forty, come to think; not close to fifty though. Really shouldn't be dead at so young an age. This potash deal should only take a few more minutes. His consortium will take the lot. Get the price down where it should be and sign. Turn down the wood but don't report it. His company don't take bribes or knowingly break the rules. If the potash is from a half mile east or west of where they should be digging, how would he know? Fresh cut Alia Folia Crescente, *on the other hand, shouldn't even turn up in Canada.*

When he's back at the hotel, he'll make a few phone calls. Not that he knows who to call, or why they might say more than the telegram does. He's surprised Ailsa re-married, Conrad never expected that. She certainly regretted him. He wonders what kind of guy this Winston Grant fella is, the one who sent the telegram.

Frame

1.

'It feels like nowhere else, right? I knew it the moment I came down the gangplank. You get what I'm saying, don't you? You must if you live here. Bet you feel that special vibe every day.'

Ailsa is staring intently at the man who is speaking, letting her eyes take in his handsome face. It seems implausible that he is who he looks like. Not that she cares about who she must tend bar for, serve drinks. But, wow! It could be him. It's quite a coup for The Reeve-Muggleton. For the whole island in fact.

'Like nowhere on Earth, isn't it?'

As he says it for the second time, he stretches out a hand, touches the back of hers which is upon the glass into which she has just poured his drink. Could be flirtatious. She hates it when customers do that stuff, will forgive this one for the little frisson of joy his touch has given. She isn't the sort to avoid looking into another's eyes, and nor can she recall holding a stranger's gaze as long as she does now. Hasn't looked so intently into any man's face since she last saw Terry in East Town. Him and Mannay, and she doesn't count the latter. Ailsa mothers Mannay, looks into his face mostly to ensure that no smears of food remain upon it.

'A guy on the ship out said none of them live here, not here in Charlestown. Said I might see some of the other ones. I don't know how I'm meant to say it these days. Don't want to get it wrong. Mustn't be offensive, you know.'

'Say it how you see it, Mr Frame. It is Mr Frame, isn't it?' His face gets on the covers of magazines. What he is doing on a barstool in front of Ailsa Donaldson is the surprise. A change from loggers and quarrymen.

'Please call me Steve, my friend. Everyone does. It's my name and everything. I'm not for putting on airs, whatever you've read about me.'

She smiles to herself: she is not this man's friend, but it's lovely to pretend. Fancy having a friend this handsome. She doesn't follow pop music but, if the last magazine she read was not too far out of date, his group, One-Eyed Temple, might be topping the charts as they speak. Not here on Connipia, of course. The only record shop on the island has closed down. May not have been open since nineteen sixty-seven, since the summer of love. This island is half a world away from where records and popstars and girls in miniskirts form a way of life. The places where this man is truly famous. 'There's your beer, Steve,' she says releasing her fingers from around his glass. Glancing at her hand, wet with cold condensation.

'Muggs Ale,' he intones with a half-smile, reading the name off the beer mat. 'Can I call them Mixed-Ups? Is that allowed?'

'It's what most people call them, Mr Frame...Steve. And they say it themselves. Intercross might have been the term you were looking for. It hasn't caught on, I'm afraid...'

'They do? They call themselves by it? Mixed-Ups might be the better term. Intercross sounds like a sports event.' She watches as his eyebrows narrow, concentrating on the small beermat. Then he looks up; his blue eyes belong on this island. 'And you've yet to tell me your name, my friend.'

'I'm Ailsa.'

'Ailsa. That's Scottish, right? But to me you sound American. Not strong, but it's definitely there. East coast.'

'Canadian.'

'All righty. I stand corrected. East coast?'

Ailsa nods.

'How long have you been down here, Ailsa, my friend?'

'Connipia?' She is finally catching up with herself. He must be interested in it, why else would he have come all this way. It feels like he's flirting, but most likely it's all in her mind. This guy can do better if that's his mission. And he'd go to a place better than Connipia if womanising was really the aim. It's seventy percent men here. Contract workers. The nuns of East Town must be impervious to all flirting of any description, so maybe she's as good as he can lay eyes on in this neck of the woods. Ailsa likes his face but won't be his conquest. If that really is his game, he can want away. She lost herself in his handsome face for a moment back there, not that Ailsa puts any store in that stuff. Never has fallen for a wink and a smile. With Conrad it was the sincerity that got to her, she just hadn't realised it was attached to a man of little integrity. Anyone as good looking as Frame is bound to be a jerk.

'Yeah. The land of the little Connipians.' He smiles as he speaks the patronising words. 'I love them. I'm pretty sure they've kept to the better way of life. They did, we didn't. Lost it long ago, our crowd. What do you reckon, Ailsa?'

'We never had it, Steve. Never lived like they do. Four years, I've been here...'

'Working in Charlestown...'

'Needed the money. The permit. I started off...' Ailsa picks up a cloth from beside the beer pump, stops herself from blabbing her life story to the famous man. Why should she trust his chiselled cheeks? She might have hummed along to a record or two of his, might not. Knows for certain that she's never bought one. Ailsa is no One-Eyed Temple devotee; she thinks that's the way they style themselves. His fans, worshippers at the temple of Steve Frame. Rock music holds no importance for her.

'Have you ever been out there? The Blue Houses. Where time stands still, and we should all thank them for it.'

'It's not easy to get out there now,' she says. 'Close to impossible. When I first arrived, I was with an anthropological project. I'm not trained or anything, so I was only ever short-term. Most of that has stopped now, anyhow.'

'Wow, you've seen them up close, Ailsa. And stopped is good, right? We shouldn't be doing science on them. Or not? Harder to ever get to meet them, I suppose.'

The more he looks into her eyes, the more she stares straight back. They have depth, turn the man's face into a work of art. 'We should let them be. Yes. That is my belief.'

'And when you were out there, was it science? Like measuring everything about them. Did it help them any?'

Ailsa smiles apologetically. 'Not me,' she mouths, a little shake of the head. A meaningful glance further up the bar, then eyes down. No longer holding the rockstar's eye.

'Oh...yeah, yeah. Sorry,' he says.

Another customer requires her attention. It's relatively quiet and Ailsa is the only member of the hotel staff currently serving. She moves six paces along the bar, takes the order. Begins to pour wines and beers, must measure out a single malt. From the corner of her eye, she watches the star as he glances around the room. The lounge-bar of The Reeve-Muggleton Hotel, one of only nine licensed hostelries on the entire island. Five of them are here in Charlestown, a little bit of England perched stubbornly on the northern shore of Connipia. The land which the majority of islanders still refer to as New Poplar. The taller islanders do, the others click what they will. It is nineteen years since the New York settlement—'the concessions,' as the former Governor let slip—the fate of our counter-species still divides opinion. No one says we should cede Australia to the kangaroos goes the well-worn line. Ailsa hates that talk but it gets trotted out everywhere. In the British Parliament all too often; in the US Senate, once or twice; the Australian one too, which has had neither a kangaroo nor an aboriginal as a sitting member. She has heard the like too many times in this bar. The never-ending invective of prejudiced people. Ailsa is pleased to hear Steve Frame sounding pro-Connipian. Famous people who make the trek to this part of the world are generally of that ilk. Nine times out of ten. She has not heard he is here to play a concert. Doubts if his bandmates are with him; they aren't in the bar, that's clear as day. If he hopes to record a song with them—with the little Connipians, as he calls them—it will prove hard work. Three centuries on and some academics still contend that theirs cannot be a real language. Think it primarily because they've made neither head nor tail of it. And clicking is not singing, more akin to a field of crickets than the song of a lark.

'Hey, Ailsa,' says Frame when his rival customer has been dispatched, a tray of drinks in his hands, 'I'd love to hear about your experience. Do you think we're the ones being weird? Drinking beer where we don't belong, this faraway island...'

'I'm strictly not drinking any beer, Mr Frame...'

'It's Steve, and I don't mean anything by it...'

'Steve. I'm sorry.'

'...but those Connipians don't drink it, don't do any of our escapist nonsense, do they? Contented, that's what I've read. Contented as we don't know how to be.'

'I'm not sure...'

'Ailsa, look, I know that you're working here. I'm kind of in your way...' He looks around the room, a quick glance to each aspect. '...luckily for me, it's on the quiet side. I appreciate you giving me the time of day, I really do. I'm renting the Van Diemen suite on the top floor here. If you'd care to drop in after your shift...' He must have seen Ailsa's pupils enlarge beneath her black fringe. Pauses before he continues. '...it's a proper suite. You work here, you'll know it. I've a lounge. I'm not trying to—you know—make a move. It's the little guys I'm here to learn about. Most of the people I've come across today aren't interested in them. They live in this extraordinary place, and then they don't care a jot. I'm wanting to spend a little time just to hear how you found...'

'I'm working until midnight, Mr Frame...Steve. A bit late for popping up for a chat.' She worries that her face may be blushing. Jaw almost dropped to the floor when she thought he was trying to do what he subsequently denied—get her between the sheets—and a little residual disappointment that the offer is off the table. She wouldn't have gone anyway, she tells herself, as she thinks it over. Wonders if he might have set out with that aim. Changed tack when he took in the expression on her face. Her not-a-devotee look. All rockstars must be egotists, expect the world to fall into their lap. The girls, first and foremost. She's read that and it sounds about right.

'Can I meet you tomorrow? Take you somewhere? You're not comfortable with the whole hotel-room thing; I get that.'

She looks at him without speaking, a smile coming to her lips. Don't overthink this. A rockstar wants to take her somewhere in Charlestown. She threw herself upon fate, staying here when returning to Canada would have been simpler, at the end of her stint with the anthropological survey. A girl who takes a few chances in this life, didn't start out that way it just became her. Ailsa gives the smallest nod of the head.

'Are you hoping to get back out there? You know, where blue is blue. I might be able to swing it for you; I've contacts, I do believe.'

How a pop singer can squeeze a permit out of Governor Thornhill she cannot guess. And if he can, she would like to be by his side. See the Connipians again, ensure Steve Frame doesn't go about it insensitively. Do not disturb, that's the big message. She doesn't know if he's a regular guy or so vain he'll expect the Connipians to know of him already, love him and sing all his tunes as the One-Eyed Temple fans must. The devotees. Too soon to have a guess. Handsome as hell, it wouldn't hurt to spend a little time with that. 'Would you like to meet me in the lobby at eleven?'

'Morning? Sure thing, Ailsa. I appreciate you giving me your time. I really do.'

* * *

The shift is not a busy one; Ailsa exchanges a couple more smiles with Steve Frame while he drinks his glass of beer. Offers to fetch him a second but he declines. Not a boozer then: Ailsa feels more pleased about that than it could possibly matter. A famous visitor is not a suitor, and nor is she looking for one. Conrad was enough; look at how that turned out.

It is close to half-past ten when he slides down from the barstool. Took an awfully long time with his pint. Some say the Charlestown Brewery makes terrible beer but Ailsa has never minded it. Might have improved down the years. He stands in his smart jeans, four or five gold studs on each sideseam. She serves a customer throughout his statement pose. He waits patiently. 'See you at eleven, Ailsa. Thanks again for the chat.'

There is something old-fashioned, unduly courteous, in his manner. She smiles a quiet yes, and watches him saunter away. It dawns on her that, for him more than for her, this has been an extraordinary evening. She's been serving beer, does the same five nights every week, he isn't even the first famous customer to pass through. Most handsome, that's the memorable bit. For Steve Frame of One-Eyed Temple, it must have been a bigger departure. A drink in a bar and nobody has recognised him. No one but her and she didn't make a song and dance. She knows very little about him, his accent says London with every inflexion despite the Americanisms which pepper his speech. She recalls reading that he's a clean-cut guy, an aberration in the world of rock and pop. She'd thought, when she read it, that it might be untrue, simply the image he wished to cultivate. Or it could be right, papers must sometimes print the truth. The same article reported that his drummer—whose name she cannot recall—got caught with cannabis a year or more back. Served a month in jail for it. He was only allowed to remain in the band with the agreement of the majority. The magazine implied Frame was against it, while also noting that they are a private band, democratic even. Not for One-Eyed Temple all the public bust-ups—stories leaked to the Sunday Noise—which characterise many a pop group. And here he is, seeking out the Connipians. Not the first big name to try this pilgrimage but they generally get turned away. There was a rumour a couple of years back that the comedian Jimmy Whist was going to come. Ailsa thought it a made-up story, a rival comic taking a little rise. 'Did you hear the one about the Connipians? Tiny little girlies—yeah—not the sort to hurt a soul. Made an exception for that Jimmy Whist they did. Ha-ha-ha.' Never came and he died a few months after the rumours. Not missed by Ailsa Donaldson, that's a true fact. Perhaps Steve Frame is as well-connected as he thinks he is. Can wangle her another visit to the Connipians before she leaves the island. It's not what you know but who you know. She isn't sure Governor Thornhill will give the time of day to a long hair; it doesn't fit with his staid image at all. Of course, if old Thornhill is a secret eccentric he might love the stuff, the esoteric rock music of One-Eyed Temple. Grant access into the protected areas to his favourite singer. It sounds far-fetched. Every governor is a stuffed shirt. Every governor of every colony in the British Empire. The scattered and dwindling lands which blush a deeper shade of red on the page with each reprinting of the world atlas. The British push the line that Connipia is not a colony at all: the Protected-Status guff. It's different to Hong Kong or Bermuda. Differs because the indigenous inhabitants are easier still to push around; that's what they don't say. Why is Frame offering to take her into the forest? They don't know each other at all. Perhaps he really is trying to get into her pants; playing a long game could be this rockstar's style. She needs to figure the guy out before she agrees to go anywhere with him. Funny to think about: Ailsa isn't the sort to run after popstars but nor is she impervious to the charms of men. She let herself get wooed by a couple of forgettable fellas in her time. There's no denying it, Frame is in a different league than Conrad, than Roger Curtis. Comes from a planet far nearer the sun.

* * *

At shift's end, Ailsa goes down to the basement of the large hotel where she has her own small suite. Not a room deemed suitable for hotel guests, its two windows are buried in an egress well, they look up into the hotel car park. She sees only the sides of the vehicles parked closest. Their wheels and undercarriage, not a view to pay pounds sterling for. There are generally a couple parked in her sightline although cars are not abundant on Connipia. Only islanders drive, contractors seldom need to, they will get transported from Charlestown to the mining or logging sites. Wherever they plunder. A single car hire company serves the island for any visitors who wish to avail themselves. Forest tracks are off limits, but Ailsa imagines the authorities let a few passed the checkpoints. Do it on the nod; an exchange of notes. *Alia Folia Crescente* is making its way to Britain and North America somehow. The world's most expensive furniture; she hopes Frame isn't after any of that.

Ailsa opens the door onto the tiny lounge, this and the kitchenette to the side, single bedroom and bathroom, have been home for eleven months now. She didn't tell Frame that this is where she lives and sleeps. Couldn't have him sniffing around down here.

'Everything okay?' asks Mannay when she has closed the door, stands in the cluttered living room in which he sits, knees drawn up, on the sofa. Her own bed at the present time.

Perhaps her face has given away all that is on her mind. His words are indistinct, Ailsa is well attuned to his funny speech pattern. It took her only a week or two. She nods; nothing untoward in her shift. Unusual though: first rockstar of her life. Doubts that Mannay would understand much about it. Won't have heard of him, she's certain about that.

'You?' she asks.

Mannay shrugs, and his withered arms ripple loosely at his side. This young man is not Ailsa's boyfriend, not by any stretch. More of a project, an attempt to get one over on the Protection Authority. Nice to be in breach of a few petty rules. None are allowed in the hotels of Charlestown. Not Connipians or even their unfortunate offspring with Sapiens fathers. With no fathers at all in any practical sense, that has been the nub of it. Mixed-Ups, half-halves. 'The human mules,' said Jimmy Whist all those years ago. They are not allowed through the doors of The Reeve-Muggleton, not usually seen in Charlestown save for their own enclave. East Town of nuns and strays. This one—Mannay—entered through her casement window, under cover of darkness four weeks ago. Mannay is currently living in the basement suite, Ailsa sleeping on the sofa. Insisting on it over Mannay's offer to let her have the bed. Share the bed! She hadn't anticipated him being the randy teen he turns out to be. Thinks himself more than a houseguest; Mannay has twice climbed on top of her while she slept. She worries that she isn't more worried, might be regarding him as a house-pet. And that is not a true Ailsa Donaldson thought; it is as though crude playground jokes have taken over her brain in those minutes. All those juvenile prejudices. Mixed-Up Mannay with a wonky willy. That's an approximation of what the boys in her school sang, although she thinks Micky was the inserted name. Or it might have been Murray. A boy in the year above who didn't fit in. There were no Mixed-Ups at all back there. The boys had been watching Jimmy Whist's movie: Night on New Poplar, filmed entirely in an Ealing studio. There has never been a Mixed-Up on Prince Edward Island. The island of Ailsa's birth is larger than Connipia but not as famous. Steve Frame wouldn't waste his time visiting PEI although there must be more One-Eyed Temple fans there than here. Devotees.

What Mannay must feel living in the hotel confuses Ailsa. She doesn't know if he minded the squalor of East Town. He got along okay with other Mixed-Ups, and he has seen no one but her since climbing through the casement window. It was Ailsa who couldn't stand seeing him trying to fend for himself. Charity soup. She feared who else might want to get closer to Mannay. And now she has a rockstar looking to her for guidance. She might be doing more harm than she is helping, that preys on her mind, a little worry every night. Pouring drinks for contract workers, mining surveyors; what she does is of no service to the real islanders, she simply hasn't wished to leave. To take herself further from the Connipians who obsess her. And she wants to help Mannay, and Mixed-Ups generally. Connipians, of course, but not helping them looks to be the very assistance they need. It is the orthodoxy among all those who are three feet tall or less. And for that reason, Ailsa believes it too. British off, Sapiens off. No-one has the first idea where the Mixed-Ups fit in.

Mannay says he loves Ailsa; she seems to have granted him a small slice of a Mixed-Up's dream. If she doesn't figure out something better for him soon, she'll be caught harbouring him where he shouldn't be, lose her job and get herself deported back to Canada. A terrible prospect. And Mannay would be back in East Town. Eating only what the soup kitchens serve.

2.

Mannay behaved himself through the night but Ailsa, not for the first time, caught him peeping while she was putting her clothes on. The thick tartan skirt she has chosen. It is not cold, never is in these early April days. The brief Connipian winter still more than two months away. And there is nothing Canadian about it when it comes. She tells herself the clothing is a barrier, that she is dressing to deter the rockstar from making a move on her. Dressing like an early-sixties Prince Edward Islander. Not that he necessarily will; he's friendly not pushy. She looks good in the skirt, the colours suit. Ailsa has long given up on fashion. Never forgot how to look appealing, not much insight what to do about Steve Frame. Won't admit it but she feels a little tightening in her throat. It's his eyes. Or the cheekbones, and definitely not the hair. The hippy craze passed Ailsa by. Not that Frame is a proper one; no drugs and she doesn't recall him saying a dickie-bird about Vietnam. Long hair and esoteric lyrics are his thing. In the night she tried to recall the words of a song—the One-Eyed Temple stuff—figure if they were intelligent or tosh. She's sure he is the one who writes them. Pretty sure. And he's the band member who has come to seek out the Connipians. Learn something of their lifestyle. That sounds like the sort to pen the lyrics. If he's hoping that meeting those very other humans who live in the forest will be a spiritual experience, then he hasn't been reading the right books. It's a romantically held view in one or two quarters while she knows for a fact the Connipians are down to earth. Right down. As natural as the fruit they eat. And what astonishing cultivation: nowhere else on planet Earth are fields to be found in the sky, aliment grown upon the forest canopy. On Connipia it has been so since forever. The science of it lost in times past. Or they all know it instinctively, have no need for manuals and classrooms. Closer to nature than her own species has been since they started setting fire to all and sundry. She likes Steve Frame's face, and his good manners are a definite plus. Can't quite shake off the notion that all rockstars expect dominion over any girl who places themselves where their hands can touch. A thought that will keep her on her toes. She has had no comparable experience. Professor Curtis was different. Can't count her dalliance with him: what the hell was she playing at? Last night's conversation was not the type she would have expected with a pots-of-money pop singer. How he drew out the Connipian connection is a mystery. She doesn't boast to drinkers, keeps the conversation dizzyingly superficial for the most part. Typical guests at The Reeve-Muggleton are not champions of the true islanders' cause. And it isn't as if she can introduce him to a string of Connipians. They are watchful of all Sapiens. Ailsa feels fortunate to have shared some time with them. Her early days on the island. And it is also true that they have become more insistent upon their isolation. Contact phobic some say. If he thinks she is going to ease his passage into a Blue House or two, he will come up disappointed. She rather likes how Frame behaved last night; the more she dwells on it the more she thinks it. Even the invite to his room—definitely double-edged—is something she may dwell upon for a long time. Handsome frontman of celebrated London pop-group makes a play for Ailsa Donaldson, barmaid from nowhere. And she gave him the brush-off. How cool is that? If she had a friend to tell the tale, she certainly would. Terry, but he'd only be jealous. Or maybe Frame was only after conversation. She has no contraception and so it's all he would have got. Frame behaved better than Mannay and she shares her rooms with the comical Mixed-Up. Ailsa can hear him now, wanking away in the bathroom. It puzzled her in Mannay's first week: sounds and smells from the bedroom; how could he do all that without arms or

207

God Help the Connipians

hands he has any control over. Boys will find a way: she learned that the first morning after she took him in. Kept out of the room, no details needed.

'Mannay, I have to go in there.'

'Minute,' he shouts back in his loose tongue.

'Clean up before you open the door.'

'No, no, Ailsa. Not making messes.'

'Clean up,' she repeats.

* * *

Before she leaves the flat, Ailsa and Mannay eat fruit salad together. Mannay hunches over the food, his withered arms cupping the bowl. He dangled them into place as he was sitting down, likes to mimic the holding of a bowl as he will have seen the down-and-outs do in East Town. The way they cup soup in their hands while most Mixed-Ups have it rest on a tabletop, dip in and out like wood pigeons. Not that the climate on Connipia requires the warming of hands with a soup bowl. Evenings can feel cool but Ailsa hasn't seen a frost since Ottawa. New Poplar is the name the tramps use for the island, no time for diplomatic niceties. And there aren't many down-and-outs here: thirty or forty was Terry's estimate. There are far more Mixed-Ups sharing pitiful East Town. The kindly nuns attract both. Mannay can mimic hobos for all he likes, he will never raise a spoon to his lips. That's the sad truth of his wayward biology.

'You okay to lie low today while I visit the guy I met last night, Mannay?'

'Lie low,' he repeats. It is what he does. What he must do so long as he stays at The Reeve-Muggleton.

'That means no noise, Mannay.' She has this talk with him daily. His memory is not deficient but the importance he places on the knowledge of previous days is the problem. Doesn't think like a Sapiens, or if he does it is only on a par with the down-and-outs. From her experience, and her reading on the subject, Ailsa knows that Connipians have a keen intelligence. They use it in ways that are alien to us. Reject the exploration of science that Sapiens have blindly embraced. Except for their outrageous fruit cultivation, and that's done to a system they might have cooked up soon after any kind of ape first walked upright. They retain information as a filing cabinet might, almost never write, and then they can do it proficiently should they choose. Picked it up from Sapiens; their string arrangements are a different thing entirely. With Mixed-Ups, it is difficult to ascertain their mental capabilities. Ailsa once met a genius but most of them seem simple-minded. The one she met back in Ottawa—wisest woman of her young life—is the reason she ventured to

Connipia. A Mixed-Up who led a life of impact. Travelled the globe, wherever she wished, except Connipia. Banned for helping the Connipians, and that stark fact has always rankled with Ailsa. A species thing: deep down she can see that the Sapiens are shits, that she was born in the wrong gene pool. It gets her down on the blackest days.

Poor Mannay is a little mentally challenged. Retarded, although he is not without a little verve; she's liked him since first she laid eyes on him. Thanks to the nuns of East Town, he—like many a Mixed-Up—can wash and dress himself. Doing it with lifeless arms is remarkable in her estimation. From a young age, those nuns teach them how to make constructive use of teeth and toes. Follow the Carleton Programme, she recalls, although her own association with the methods begin and end with the name. She worked in the same Canadian university forty years after it developed that ground-breaking programme. The nuns or other helpers sow a few strategically placed tags into the clothing Mixed-Ups wear, making it easier for them to manipulate with teeth alone. A few Connipians—mostly the mothers of the Mixed-Ups—help with sowing, they pick it up effortlessly. Must do something similar in the making of their own blue clothing. Fixing dyed and preserved leaves together. Connipians don't touch the Singers, the sowing machines. Ailsa has heard it said they think machines replacement people, non-living entities doing tasks that either don't need doing or should remain undelegated. Sapiens don't take proper responsibility when they hive work off. Ailsa can't grasp it precisely, presumes the Connipians are right.

Mannay learnt the dressing-thing young but he hurries, it can be hit-and-miss. Perhaps all Mixed-Ups start out with the potential for intelligence but living as they must—arms like string—simply wears them down. It must be exhausting keeping oneself from going under. Mannay is independent of mind without the corresponding skills. Ailsa has always felt sorry for the Mixed-Ups. Except for Tonkin, of course, she simply admired her.

'What you doing?' he asks.

'I've told you. I'm seeing a very famous man.'

'Famous?'

'Everybody knows him, Mannay.'

'Nobody know Mannay. Mannay lying low.'

'Well, it's difficult. They'd send you to the other side of town if anyone found out you were here. And I'd lose my job. You know all this.'

'Why everyone know the man? The man you meeting.'

'Guitar and singing. You know what that is?'

'Yes. Yes. Terrible noise. I know the radios. Terrible noises on the radios.'

'That's my famous man.'

'And you let him what you don't let me?'

'Mannay! No. I'm not like that. Very private. I've told you. I was married before I came here but I've finished with all that.'

'Mannay not finished. Mannay not started.'

'And maybe you would rather be living on the other side of town. East Town. You would meet other Mixed-Ups.'

'You don't live other side of town, Ailsa.'

'I used to. You know that. I still go there.'

'Dangerous, Ailsa. Dangerous for you.'

'Not especially. And I can look after myself, thank you very much, young Mannay.'

'Yeah, yeah. Ailsa big and strong.'

'Not so big, thank you, my little friend. I hope to help Mixed-Ups. Hope to help you, Mannay. It can be tricky to know what's for the best.'

'Mixed-Ups all untrained except Mannay."

'Ha! Half-trained, Mannay. I've still work to do with you, you know.'

'Ailsa always good to Mannay. Mannay do what Ailsa say.'

'Mostly, Mannay. You try your best, I'm sure.'

When they have eaten the fruit salad, Ailsa fetches her shoes from the small cupboard by the door. As she arises from buckling the side straps, Mannay swings his withered arms around her waist, tries to catch them on the far side, but cannot. Does it over and over, and the slap of his skin feels a little ticklish. The top of the little man's bald head—if man he may be called—comes up only to the midpoint of her bosom. He buries his narrow face in her soft, flat stomach. Ailsa looks down upon him with a slightly pained expression. Doesn't begrudge him this comfort. Fears misunderstandings; if his arms worked, he might be a sex pest. Worries still more that juice from the fruit he has been eating will blemish the white blouse she wears above the green-black-grey of her tartan skirt.

'All right, Mannay. I have to go. Stay out of sight, remember.'

'So good,' he says and then dips his nose down from her tummy and pushes into her pubis. Stooping as he does so, it is with a strong push that he nuzzles her most intimate place. She is thankful of the thick kilt.

'Mannay, stop that. I'll send you to East Town. I really will.'

'Really won't. Love Mannay not the singing man. Love Mannay,' he shrieks.

'Hush, hush. No, Mannay. This isn't love. I care for you; it isn't an easy way to live for either of us. Now I really must go. Keep out of sight. Lie low.'

'Mannay lie low.'

* * *

Frame

Steve Frame sits alone in the lobby. It might be a treat for him, spending a few days this far from London's autograph hunters. He turns, rises to his feet when he sees her. It is the politest of gestures, old-fashioned in its execution. Contrasts absurdly with his long hair, the little menace of eye-shadow that he wears. 'Thank you so much for coming,' he says.

Ailsa takes a breath. Something in the way his gaze lingers upon her, as if relishing the sight, gives her the feeling that she's the popstar. And Ailsa can't sing a note. He fetes her as no one has since Conrad's early days. And Frame looks even better in the daylight than he did in the bar the evening before. A stunner, she thinks, laughing inwardly at the phrase. Men use it, why shouldn't she? If she spoke it out loud, would he laugh? Seems like an easy-going guy. 'Steve, I said I would and I have. Please, shall we talk here or...'

'Do you know Charlestown well, Ailsa?'

'I do. Spent too much time here. And it's a tiny little town, you know...'

'Show me. Show me where the tourists never go.'

'Mr Frame, you sound...'

'Steve, please...desperate, were you going to say? Ailsa, I'm lucky to be here, and I know it. They're making it harder and harder to visit. Have you got settler status?'

Ailsa shakes her head, slides herself down onto the banquette seat from which Steve Frame has risen. 'I'm okay while I'm employed. I'd have to leave the island if I lost this job. Unless I'd already secured another, of course, but mining isn't for me.'

Steve Frame places himself back down on the seat beside her. Twelve inches apart, head turned. Narrows his eyes, continuing to take her in. Ailsa has no idea if he likes what he sees. Do rockstars crave plain girls?

'Four years here, you said that last night.'

'That's right, Steve. And I'm not against the laws, you know. I wish I could work somewhere more useful than...' She gestures the foyer in which they sit. '...The Reeve-Muggleton.' She says it in the barest whisper, other employees in earshot.

'More useful to the Connipians? Is that what you mean, Ailsa?'

'Surely. They have fought no wars, done nothing to us—don't even eat meat, harmless to everyone on the planet—still it feels like their world is falling in.'

'Do you believe Carrington's theory?'

'Carrington's? I don't think I know it, Steve.'

'Really? A lot of noise in the papers. Back in London, anyhow. Wesley Carrington, the commentator.'

'I've heard of him. I thought he was a politician of some stripe.'

'Briefly. He's a leader writer now. Influential though. He thinks the Connipians can save themselves. They've never revealed how they do the blue thing. Manage to dye that rich colour of theirs onto anything they choose. It would be like a quid pro quo. They help us, we help....' Steve Frame's lips upturn in a smile that mirrors her own. '...you're laughing at me, Ailsa.'

'I think there are many scientists, a few ordinary Joes too, who feel frustrated because they can't crack the puzzle. Would Britain—all the nosy Sapiens there and elsewhere—leave the entire island to the Connipians on the back of that small piece of knowledge? Not a chance. Our species has never done the live and let live thing. It's not really our way, is it? I'm here, you're here. We don't have it in us to leave well alone. My kid brother poked a stick into a wasps' nest when he was four years old. They stung him so bad he had to spend a night in hospital. Did it again, aged ten. Knowing how they turn wood and leaves and pebbles blue won't stop us for a drumbeat, Steve. Is Carrington for them or against?'

'Complicated, Ailsa. His position is complicated.'

'That sounds like against.'

* * *

To walk across Charlestown is to see its waterline. The bay is beautiful, all shades of green evident on the line of tall trees which thrive thirty or forty yards beyond where the buildings end. Reaching for the sky as trees do nowhere else. Ailsa's never been to California but she's heard it is no match. The Pacific Ocean wobbles in the haze, not a truly hot day, it's just the visual effect. The sun shines and the water glistens. The inner moorings are abundant with expensive yachts. For industrialists and shipping magnates, the yacht seems to go with the role. Ailsa overheard in the bar that Onassis sailed in a few days ago. Harboured here for the novelty of it; no going ashore without a good reason. Without Jackie to show off, and the same rumour says she hasn't come. The marriage is floundering if gossip is to be believed. He may not even have a permit to come ashore, she's never seen a Greek in The Reeve-Muggleton. A bribe would swing it if he's that keen, permit issued before the money was counted.

Further out to sea, sometimes in view but not always, requiring knowledge or a telescope to distinguish them apart, naval ships from both America and the Soviet Union float by. Bob across the bay closer to each other here than anywhere else in the world. The rise and dip of their mutual suspicion in each crest and trough. This is a place like no other— United Nations protected—it might all be an illusion. A flag flies from a pole in front of the Governor's Offices, the regular Union Jack. Connipia is an associate member of the Commonwealth, not a true country so that is as much as it can be. And the Queen has never visited. The Duke of

Kent is as good as they've had. The Prince of Wales at the end of the last century, has been the only royal to actually meet a Connipian and that, Ailsa understands, was not a voluntarily act by the girl in question.

The location of the government offices and the accompanying flag, within the port, so near to the boats, suggests they are prepared for a quick getaway. Captain John Brook did that first, two hundred and seventy-three years ago. If only, thinks Ailsa. Sapiens leaving again might spur the Connipians to raise a flag of their own. That would be a first.

It is not colonisation that is taking place here, something more transitory but just as sinister. A chess match into which new pieces are constantly introduced. The Connipians might have lived here for a million years: that's been the estimate of academics for the last forty. Everyone wants their say in how they are to be protected. That's the Sapiens narrative; Connipians simply want their would-be protectors gone.

'You know his daughter is a fan of mine?' says Frame as they stand on the steps looking up at the incongruous red stone building. A different Union Jack—bearing the Governor's emblem imposed over the centre of the cross—hangs from a boom pole running out from beneath the eaves. Each brick is a British brick, colonial government buildings can be made from nothing else. All the other buildings, including one or two equally grand ones—The Reeve-Muggleton Hotel is impressive in its own way— are of the dark grey which the geology of Connipia affords. The geology of New Poplar too, the name they all called it until seventeen years ago. Most British settlers still do.

'Is she here, or at school?' asks Ailsa.

'I believe she's here currently.'

The Governor is a Crown appointment, currently undertaken by Sir Desmond Thornhill, a diplomat of long standing. There are many who think the Foreign Office forgot to vet the daughter before installing him in this sensitive post. Cherie Thornhill was only seventeen the last time she got her name in the newspapers. Four or five months back. Already photographed drunk in London, Paris and Charlestown. Falling-down drunk; throwing-up drunk; skirt-riding-up-to-show-her-knickers drunk. Letters to newspapers have suggested her behaviour is offensive to Connipians, an example of Sapiens at their worst. That other species has shared no thoughts on the matter, might be laughing up their blue-dyed sleeves.

'And I thought she would go for those Laughing Llamas or some other crazy band, Mr Frame.'

'Ailsa, Ailsa, I like to think my songs as zany as any of those you cite. The issue is that I go on the feel of the world, don't require drugs or even booze to find a new angle. Although I am not a teetotaller, as you can attest.'

'No, I didn't mean anything against your music. Cherie Thornhill is a wild child...'

'I like the type, Ailsa. Free spirits are great; they also need channelling. I've written to him, the Governor. I'd like to meet Sir Desmond and daughter. My best chance of gaining permission to travel in...'

'That's your connection?'

'Yeah, well. It might pull some strings, Ailsa. Step around in my shoes for a day or two and you find doors open up unexpectedly.'

She raises an eyebrow. It is barely a connection at all.

'In Tokyo, my tour manager told me—this was right out of the blue—I'd to go to the royal palace. Not sure whether old Hirohito was especially keen to meet me or if it was just someone in his court who got his ear for the day. Told him I was worth being seen sitting besides, help him to look more in tune with young people. Ha! But can you imagine that? The guy was once a living god. Just last spring he and I shared a pot of tea. I took my guitar—never got it out of the case—he wasn't interested. He asked after my views on Vietnam. Very odd, I'm not political at all. I think he may have been hoping to argue with a hippy. I never really figured what he thought of me even after we parted. He might be against the war in Vietnam himself, of course, he didn't say. Done with war, old Hirohito. You'd think so, wouldn't you? After everything he and Tojo put the country through. An emperor without an empire. I guess that's what it always comes down to. Done with war now he's lost the knack.'

* * *

A short walk, and then they stand together outside the Museum of Blue. On the way, a young man held up a hand, stopped Steve Frame in the street. A government employee, Ailsa's imagined. 'It is you! My God!' Dressed very smartly, short hair, white shirt and a charcoal suit. A defiant splash of red on his tie. 'I can sing all your songs but I better hadn't.' He was wearing a smile like it was VE day. 'Are you playing a concert here? Where can I buy tickets?'

Steve Frame let him exhaust his adulation. 'Private visit,' he said eventually. 'Hoping to connect with the Connipians.' Ailsa glanced at him as he said it. She liked walking alongside the unassuming Adonis but he sounded naïve. It is unclear if any of their species has connected with a Connipian. Ever. She likes to think she came close but Ailsa knows herself to have been lucky. Right place, right time. She was just passing on a message from someone worthier of a Connipian's attention.

And now, at the museum's entrance, his temporary anonymity is back. There are a few others looking at the posters telling what is within. He is absorbed in reading the blurb, his handsome face stilled in a cast she cannot interpret.

'You know about this?' she asks.

After a short silence, he says, 'Looks pretty mainstream.'

'Ha. No Connipian input, you can be sure of that. A museum of conjecture and jealousy, describing our failed efforts to learn the mystery of how they colour leaves and wood and stone. They'll tell us when we start behaving like Connipians; that's my theory, and it beats Carrington's.'

'It's weird though, isn't it. Scientists have had their hands on plenty of examples. A little bit of everything that's ever been turned blue; and Connipians don't have that much to play with. We've put it under microscopes—through washing machines, I expect—and we haven't the first idea how they do it.'

'And may it be so for all time,' says Ailsa, quoting the late Zaneta Lozano. The Mexican artist came here in the nineteen twenties, believed it would inspire her, arrived wanting to paint in Connipian Blue. She quickly became the first person to voice the Sapiens-Out philosophy which has been growing the world over since that time. Building slowly but definitely; found its loudest voice in those places where experience has shown how little a colonial culture cares how much is crushed back into the soil. And Zaneta wasn't truly the first, she said so herself. All the earlier champions of the cause were diminutive. Clicked their preference, could not speak or shout it. Didn't possess the vanity to write it down, to think their thoughts needed immortalising.

'I guess you're right,' says Steve. 'It's just mind-boggling.'

'You want to go inside?'

The rockstar shakes his head. 'Where will I find something genuinely Connipian?'

'Here in Charlestown, Steve, you quite simply won't. The thing about the parallel societies is they're now more polarised than ever. There were more of them in East Town when I first arrived than you'll find today. More chance of seeing a Connipian just four years ago than now.'

'So, what's there? East Town.'

'Mixed-Ups. Charity workers who look out for them. A smattering of tramps. People without the money to live anywhere better on the island.'

'I thought there was like a Connipian sex trade?'

'Count me out if that's what you're here to see. And no. Fifty years ago, maybe. While the Connipians were still trying to figure out their best defence against the Sapiens encroachment. When they were plied with opium, which I'm pleased to report doesn't work anymore. Not sure how but they are a collective lot, the wiser of the Connipians clicked a bit of sense into the most vulnerable. If we could fix a problem like they do, we might just lose that off-to-hell-in-a-handcart feeling.'

'But Mixed-Ups are still getting conceived, right? Born every once in a while.'

Ailsa gives Steve Frame a stare. 'Yeah. Three foot tall those girls. I'm ashamed to be Sapiens, Steve. You?'

Frame glances down at his shoes. Head nodding. Raises it back up to look her in the eye. 'A lot to be ashamed of. I feel it, I've come here to help.'

* * *

'Definitely nothing we have to pay for.'

Ailsa smiles to herself. Steve Frame is on a quest to understand something of the Connipians while the opportunity is still extant. Extinction is a worry amongst their Sapiens supporters. Not the how or the why of it, simply that two thousand is a very small number. That has been the estimated number since learned men began guessing. Counting too although it has never been reliable. It is Ailsa's fear also, a million years in, it may not be rational. What surveys there have been produce contradictory results. A finger in the wind, so uncooperative are those whom they try to survey. Too many Mixed-Ups, that's a fact. The relationships between the two human species on this island are at an all-time low. And on every other patch of dry land on the planet it is Sapiens all the way. If the Connipians are concerned about population decline they keep it to themselves. Nothing clicked on the subject through the now intermittently used interpreters. It's all speculation. What bugs Ailsa is the frequency with which she has had to clear the bar of leaflets circulated by the Twelve Tribes. How people with those views get on the island, she doesn't know. Perhaps it's crawling with them. The first Homo Sapiens to arrive here were crackpots but she hasn't heard they were of the same inclination. No idea what Muggletonians thought of a lineage predating Adam and Eve.

'They don't even use money, right? Connipians don't live that way. All the yours-mine stuff—the possessiveness, the greed—I've understood that correctly, haven't I?'

'Steve, quite how they live is a mystery to me. I reckon they've fooled every ethnological study that's ever been undertaken. Given away so little we're still base-camp ignorant. Not that you can read too much into my view. Biased as hell, I know I'm that. But think about the language issues. Most of them—the Connipians—have figured out our language and they can do quite a few others. Not speak but comprehend. Zaneta spoke Spanish; I gather they liked her, communicated quite a bit in some way or another. How do they do that? Understand languages without lessons. They don't do lessons like we do. They just get stuff. Then half the world thinks they're stupid—more than half, all the talk of primitive—they've always had one over on us in my view. Fierce intelligence and they choose not to use it to mess everything up. Keep it simple. We change what doesn't need changing just to prove we can. They let stuff be because...well, I don't know why they live as they do. Suits them, I suppose. They don't worship any god. None of the pantheism that a few writers who never even met them thought, attributed to them. They just like it how it is. Everything.' He is looking into her face like a lovestruck teenager. Ailsa dare not guess what Frame is thinking. Interest in her might be nice but it's a Sapiens thought. If it is veneration of those of whom she speaks, that's good too. 'You must have heard their clicking on tapes, Steve?'

The rockstar nods. 'Tried. Tried it for hours and hours but I never figured what they were saying.'

'It's incomprehensible. Clicks aren't words, they're pure thought without censure or ambiguity. A seriously clever Mixed-Up told me that. We don't get them but they get us. That's really weird, right.' Still his blue eyes are devouring her. Ailsa hasn't the first idea why she threw away her contraceptive pills.

'And that's what I'm saying about our lifestyles. Our respective lifestyles. We're greedy and moronic and fight over what we can't take with us. Jesus, Ailsa, I might be the worst of them. I own three sportscars. How about that. Only one me, one dumb-ass me. Can't stop being who we are, I suppose. We were long ago suckered into it. The greed. That's why I'm here. I want to learn something from them. How to live better.'

'But how can you? How can we? They click and we don't know what it means. The building blocks of our thought run back to the bible or Socrates. That stuff. The wrong turn seems to be all we have. We don't know how to be them.' Ailsa gives a nervous laugh. 'People without three sportscars dream only of acquiring them. It's the Connipians and no one but the Connipians who never got on the ride.'

'And do you not think we'd respond if they showed us better? Carrington says they should share the secret of paint, the secret of a happy life might be the one to really swing it. Get our lot behind them.'

'Steve Frame, hang your head in shame,' Ailsa shouts at him. He looks a little puzzled. Not offended, bewildered by her outburst. 'Happy life! The Connipians are having the life drained from them. The removal of limestone from the island kills them. I don't know why or how but you know it as well as I. It was the cause of the furore more than a decade back—through interpreters they berated the New York agreement; "You cannot stop throwing your weight around," they said—and it's not stopped. The theft of the island one spade-full at a time.'

'Yeah, I feel bad about it. But if they explained, told us how it works, wouldn't everyone feel much more sympathy?'

God Help the Connipians

'Who is everyone, Steve? The masses you invoke are the people with no right to interfere...'

'But who interfere anyway. The Connipians need tactical advice.'

'I thought like you once, Steve. It took me a long time to see how very wise Zaneta Lozano always was. And we've no need of this island. The limestone and potash here amount to less than a percentage of what we have in the wide world. Far less than one percent. And we might incidentally destroy a civilisation for that. Stop putting the onus on them; we're the ones who need to change. Or rather, we need to stop changing everything just because we can.'

As they are walking on the cracked concrete of ugly East Town, out of a street-side doorway a small figure on the far side of the street throws back her head, a hand upon it as if adjusting a wig. Then, hips wiggling within her short blue skirt, she crosses the road a short way ahead of them, walking on high-heeled shoes, before disappearing through an unmarked doorway.

'There!' says Steve. 'That was one. Did you see her?'

The girl was sporting Connipian blue, a skirt wrapped around her in the style shorter than seen in the old photographs. Above she had on a grey blouse, the ends tied high revealing a cummerbund of skin.

'What did you reckon?' asks Ailsa.

'A Connipian prostitute. Must have been.'

'You're not looking for one, are you?'

'I'm looking to understand them. In the forest preferably. Not living like us but like they choose. But she really was...'

'Steve, how tall was that poor girl who just slipped by?'

He holds out a flat palm, puts it fractionally lower than his own chest. 'And in heels.'

'Short. She's a short girl, poor thing. Not a Connipian. Did you see her legs, her tummy even.'

'Yeah, yeah. She was dressed like she probably shouldn't.'

Ailsa smiles. Funny to come across a prudish rockstar. 'What colour was her skin?'

'The tan looked good.' Then he stops and looks into his guide's face. A little think. 'She's not in the forest, right. Not living in the shadows, so she's caught the sun more than most of them do.'

'Steve. She was about four feet tall without the heels. That would be a giant among Connipians. There are none that tall. And they don't tan. A Connipian's skin is white, might even be a form of Albinism except that doesn't marry up with the rich blue eyes. Skin's always white, no matter where they are.' She taps the side of her head, a use-your-loaf gesture. 'And the girl you've just seen is so in the shadows. Poor little Connipian impersonator selling herself to a few perverts who shouldn't even be allowed on the island. That's as much as you've seen so far, Steve.'

'Jesus, Ailsa. That's bad. Never considered it. So, there are people doing what they used to make the Connipians do?'

'I expect there are some dressed that way in London, Steve. And I'm pleased you don't know anything about it.'

The rockstar gives her a shaking-head smile. He might be the naïve one. When they have gazed into each other's faces long enough he asks, 'Didn't she click as she passed?'

Ailsa flops her tongue around her mouth, makes some random clicks and clops.

'I gotcha,' he says. 'You know, before coming out here, I imagined sitting in a Blue House. Cross-legged on the floor perhaps. A few of the ladies. Standing, always pictured them standing. A man on a bed. I've heard that about them, Connipian men lie down all day long. I kind of wanted to talk to one; hoped—not hoped, just foolishly imagined—the clicking would make sense to me. Realistically, I won't be able to understand them, will I? I mean, they're not even engaging with us at the present time. Unlikely to make an exception just because I'm on their side.'

'I'm not sure Thornhill will let you in, so there's that hurdle. And Steve, I can't understand a second of their clicking but I've communicated.'

'Wow. When you were with one of the studies?'

'Kind of.'

'And that was using Mixed-Ups, right? Only they can understand the clicking. Tell us what's being said.'

'Thought not said. But there are other ways too: some Connipians know how to write. Maybe all of them, it's simply that they don't generally bother. Don't use it within Connipian culture. If they even have a culture.'

'Writing, no! I didn't know they did that...'

As he is speaking, the small woman in the rich blue wrap-around skirt comes back onto the roadside. Steps closer and then she appears to look Steve Frame up and down, adjusts the blond wig with her left hand.

'Hey,' says Steve, 'you're not really Connipian, right?'

The girl bows her head so far that the wig falls forward. No hair but for a few thin wisps upon her head. She makes clicking noises.

'You are, or you're not?'

'Watch out, Steve. Seriously,' says Ailsa.

'Hey, hey. Do you understand me?'

The small woman looks up into his face, brushes her short blue skirt with both her hands. Brings them to rest on her mid-thighs, below the fringe of her skirt.

God Help the Connipians

'I just want to talk. Can you write?' He mimes writing on paper.

'Christ, Steve, get away,' hisses Ailsa. She has a hold of his arm, trying to pull him back across the street. He looks confused as a flash-bulb pops in the morning sun.

A scruffy looking man emerges from the other doorway, the one the girl had first come out of. 'She dirt cheap, mister, only does handy Andys, dirt cheap for you. And very dirty.'

'She isn't Connipian.'

'She is mister. Only the handy Andys. Can't be getting her with a floppy-armed baby, ha-ha. That not nice way to treat for the Connipian lady. Big, big babies them floppy-armed fellas.'

Another pop of a flashlamp makes them all blink. Pimp and girl as much as Steve and Ailsa.

'Turn around,' she hisses, seeing Frame still staring at the imitation Connipian. 'What are you thinking?'

'Come, come inside,' says the dishevelled pimp.

'I only wanted to talk,' shouts Frame over his shoulder, as Ailsa pulls him away. Both arms holding his left; the rockstar doesn't resist her even as his face remains fixed on the girl in the short skirt.

'Idiot,' she says. 'If you're here for the East Town hookers, I'm off, Steve. Off right now.'

'Hey, that's not me. I was just checking. You saw the wig, right?'

'They've messed with her hair, just shaved her head, I suppose, got hold of a genuine skirt by the looks of it. None of that makes her Connipian. And if whoever took that photograph realises who you are, you'll be on the front page of The Islander in the morning.' They both gaze into each other's eyes for a few seconds. 'Don't look so clueless. You will be unless your friend, Cherie Thornhill, does something dumber. Which she might, I guess. She's featured in it more times than anyone but her dad. What's you're connection to her anyway, Steve?'

'What they've photographed is nothing. Me walking down the street. And I'm not really a friend of Cherie's. Don't know her from the next girl.'

'And yet she's your connection.'

'She's in the fan club, written in a few times. I don't deal with them personally. Signed a letter or two when it was pointed out who she was.'

'Steve, it's none of my business but who knows you are here?'

'I wrote to Governor Thornhill. Needed permission so I went to the top.'

'Yes, but have you done publicity back in Britain? Anything in the papers there? Will that photographer figure who he's snapped?'

'It's a private visit. No publicity. Don't know if he's a fan, didn't look like my demographic.'

Frame

'Probably okay. Only that young Government hack earlier who's recognised you. Oh, and me. I think the photographer guy is with the pimp. He won't even develop it because we're walking away. Can't blackmail someone who's done nothing. But if he recognised you, passes it on, you can forget about Governor Thornhill giving you a pass for the forests. The last thing he needs is more visits by sex predators to the defenceless Connipians.'

'Ailsa! I'm not…'

'I know you're not, but really! What possessed you to start talking with her? I told you what she was…'

'And Thornhill won't believe the gutter press. He's got to be above all that.'

'If you're on the front page, caught chasing after a girl in a blue skirt, he can't take any chances, Steve. Won't want to be photographed near you himself if he thinks you've been propositioning…' Ailsa gestures the entryway that is now fifty yards behind them. The girl in the blue skirt has again emerged to stand forlorn on the litter-strewn street.

'You know I wasn't…'

'I do. And I also know that a Mixed-Up was born out in the forests eight or nine weeks ago. Brought to East Town one month back. Thornhill pledged to stop all that. His first action as Governor was to get higher fencing around protected zones; Connipians probably think it's a prison camp. And miles and miles of fencing does nothing. Protect them by shipping out the perverts. Blockading the island. Take no chances: no men.'

Frame has bowed his head. Ailsa has seen this before. Men on the island seem to contemplate it infrequently but the history of the place shames them. Every Sapiens with a cock. That's what Ailsa gleans from their reaction to its reminders.

'Before I did that dumb thing…talk to her, you said something interesting yourself. Something like Connipians don't have a culture, or you can't really call it a culture.'

'I think that, Steve. Connipians just are. They don't have secondary purposes. Art or telling their pompous history. They just are. We wouldn't know where to start, would we?'

He scratches the side of his head. 'I'll tuck that one away, think on it some more. You're very wise, Ailsa Donaldson, do you know that?'

'Ha. Not wise: I'm a waitress: spend the most part of most days pouring out Muggs Ale for loggers. I'm lost, is what I am. Stuck wanting every Sapiens off, like Zaneta said, and then staying myself because I fear for them like a sickness. Can't leave. They need protecting from us because we're pretty vile.' Then she points at a two-storey wooden building standing between two sturdier brick-built houses. 'Any idea what that is, Steve?'

'Not a clue. Museum? Bordello?'

'It's an orphanage, not for true orphans, mind you. You get my meaning.' He reaches for her hand, clasps her right with his left. Ailsa knows she has shouted at the richest, most good-looking man she has ever met, and he treats her like she's his teacher. He was stupid but seems to have got the message. She fears her fluttering heart could fog up her brain. Wants to roll herself into him, just to feel and smell this man up close. Get a grip, Ailsa, she tells herself.

'The Mixed-Ups, yeah? Hoping to meet a few of them too. Can we go inside? It's charity, right? I've got plenty of money.'

* * *

'And some still come by and help you out?' asks Steve.

Ailsa thinks he is on a curiosity high. She can really picture him to be that rare thing: a rockstar abstinent of drugs. He has no need. Being in Connipia pushed him up a few notches, then thinking he'd found one— the fool did not initially believe her when she told him the street girl was faking it—got him up close to Nirvana. And now it's Mixed-Ups and nuns who consume his interest. He might look upon them both with the same intensity that had her wondering if he wanted to get her pants down. Ailsa is starting to think she might be the baser of the two; she briefly thought the same of Conrad—that he was her moral superior— but it was just his deference to order. The man was a shit deep down. And Ailsa used to feel some of the giddiness Steve Frame emanates, during her first weeks here. Not the arrival in Charlestown, just as soon as she got into the forest. Like nowhere on Earth, that was Frame's phrase. She thought the same first time out, when she briefly lived in a Blue House. A Connipian-free Blue House but it was a surreal experience all the same. More so a couple of weeks later when she bunked up with a Connipian. Zaneta Lozano did that too. And Ailsa has never boasted. Kept it secret to this day, let a little something slip to Steve, but not the full story. Not the sleepover thing.

East Town doesn't do it for her at all. She has helped out in the hostels and orphanages, couldn't make a vocation of it. The sight of a faux-Connipian prostitute is upsetting to Ailsa. Awful for whoever the short girl is, islander or incomer, and all a harbinger of what men have been doing to Connipians since The John and Lodowicke first sailed around the corner. Landed a party no more than a mile from here. There's a plaque or two in Charlestown. Steve might be too worldly to see the sadness; East Town could be like the rough side of any city in the world. In the poorer parts of the world. Even Mixed-Ups might seem unexceptional when set against the beggars of Calcutta or Zanzibar, she supposes.

'They do. But not like they used to.'

The Irish nun he talks with is younger than Ailsa. Sister Concepta, she has asked them to call her, blushing when Frame said, 'And you call me Steve.' Do nuns tap their feet to pop records these days? A turntable in the corner of their spartan cells. This is nineteen sixty-nine, maybe anything goes in convent and city alike. Ailsa is pretty clueless about nuns, appreciates their efforts in this single corner of the world. One way or another this nun has recognised the voice that sings Chains Around Our Ankles. These Catholic Mission Houses are a true blessing to the Mixed-Ups, and they will find room for any Connipian mothers who wish to share the care of their off-spring. Strange to contemplate the good and the ill that religions do. The nuns here are terrific while the Vatican is no bloody help at all. It calls Connipian breeding practices immoral, can't seem to spot that they were living as they do today even as Adam and Eve were cocking everything up in the Garden of Eden. Not a party to original sin. Already ensconced in the forests of this island, their very own paradise. And for that confusing reason—being from a better family than Adam—successive popes have failed to recognise the actions of those who've helped the Mixed-Ups down here. Cannot see the difference between this and a donkey sanctuary. In their own way the Catholics can be as bad as the horrible Twelve Tribes. And then these few stalwart women—brides of Christ—within the largest Christian denomination in the world, rise above it. Do a bit of good.

'Are there any in now?'

'Mr Frame...Steve...come and meet our Mixed-Ups. They are easier to get along with, frankly. I sometimes think the little Connipians forget that we can't understand all their clicking and ticking.'

'Sure, I want to meet them, but tell me about that. When the little tiny ones come. What do they do?'

'We think it's mostly the mothers of our Mixed-Ups but they don't tell us that, Steve. Don't make it clear. It just looks that way. And they can be very loving. You know? Huggy. It doesn't say that in the books about them but we've seen it with our own eyes. And then they can walk out for weeks. Out of their children's lives. Sister Carmel—she's the Abbess actually, Sister's what we call her—she thinks the Connipians are as muddled-up about it all as we are. The mothers love their little babies but resent how it's all come about. Do you understand what I'm saying here?'

'I thought...' Steve Frame seems to be searching for what it is he does think. Scratches the side of his head with his guitar-picking forefinger. '...they don't even mother their normal children. Their pure-blood Connipian babies. I'm sure I've read that.'

God Help the Connipians

'You will have and your right. But loving is something else, isn't it. God loves you, Steve, but he doesn't tuck you up at night.'

Ailsa turns away to hide her smile. This young nun talks like a Victorian bedtime story. A load of lovely rubbish. Sees Connipians every week and regards them as cartoon characters.

'You communicate with them by writing, I've heard?'

'No, not that I've ever come across. Not seen the little ones writing anything down. They do a string thing but it means no more to us than their clickety clicking.'

'So how do you tell each other...?'

'We mostly just give each other space, Mr Frame. Steve. They are no trouble with us but...' Sister Concepta turns her face away, a hand guarding what may be another blush within her wimple. '...they are funny with men. Don't like men. It might be just the mothers on account of...well, on account of everything that's happened to them. That'll be what it is, sure as we're standing here.'

'I see,' he says, and Ailsa wonders if Steve Frame does. If any man can get the point she inarticulately makes. Ailsa became interested in Connipians—more than interested, a little obsessed—after meeting some who were visiting Carleton University in Ottawa. That was at the start of the sixties, before the curtain came down. And even when you could meet Connipians, it wasn't a true meeting. She didn't get a sense of who they were back in Canada. That only came later when she was in the forest. In Ottawa it was the Mixed-Up interpreter who made the strongest impression. She doesn't think she can impart it to Steve. Can't replicate the weight of the stories which Tonkin told. And it all feels so personal, she is not certain she even wants to. The Connipians share nothing; they understand the insensitivity of men very, very accurately. Men behave like wrecking balls, do it in Connipia and elsewhere. As Ailsa dwells on it, she feels embarrassed by her foolish crush. It might come back but she hasn't been trusting men for many a year. It's a message on the wind in Connipia. Hangs loosely by the sides of every Mixed-Up.

* * *

A lifetime ago—and she isn't yet thirty—Ailsa and her husband, Conrad, were living in Ottawa. These days she wonders why she ever embarked on so hairbrained a venture: a marriage. Three years of stupid dependency.

When Ailsa Donaldson moved off the island which she had called home for the first twenty years of her life, she did not know if it would be for just a few months, or if she might have left Prince Edward Island forever. For good, as the saying goes. She took a job in Toronto and met Conrad Klassen there rather by chance. He was in town on business, didn't live there. And a pretty funny sort of business he was up to, most likely. It's all hindsight which sees it this way. Nothing about the man worried her at the time. He charmed her, in fact, and hindsight says she must have been daft in the head. Conrad was always more interested in politics than the actual business he was engaged in; he represented the interests of several firms from his home province. A consortium. And the firms all had mines in the potash sector.

Conrad was never a miner, nor his father or grandfather, although they lived in the same province: the sea-scared pancake that is Saskatchewan. Ailsa has been there precisely once. Made a single visit shortly before embarking upon her marriage. Their marriage. In Toronto she enjoyed a whirlwind romance. Of sorts. Didn't have any alternative experience with which to contrast it, and the enjoyment taken has become an embarrassment to recall. Ailsa—who keeps swooning over Steve Frame—can't work out whether she and Conrad loved each other at all: is love this? is love that? They both said falling in love was the business going on at the time. She was young, first months in the big city. Conrad was an older, worldlier man from way out on the prairie. The One-Eyed Temple boys had yet to cut a record when the visiting representative asked the office junior on a date. Ailsa said, 'Yes,' before she thought about it, said, 'No,' once she had thought about it, said, 'Hold on Mr Klassen. Are you married?' A smart point to raise in advance of any date. 'That wouldn't be right at all,' said Ailsa.

'No, it wouldn't, and no, I am not. Very astute of you to verify the facts. And if yes is your answer in these circumstances, please call me Conrad.'

She went on the date—a meal and a dance—with a man sixteen years her senior. The dancing was unlike anything ever done in the village hall at Kensington, Prince Edward Island. He held her close; Ailsa, scarcely trusting herself, whispered questions in his ear. He was raised in a town called Gravelbourg, at the time she thought him a sophisticated man: in truth, no-one from so small a town ever can be. That's her reappraisal. At that time in his life, Conrad Klassen was living and working out of Regina, Saskatchewan, a qualified mining engineer. And a widower in his mid-thirties. How very sad. They had to sit and nurse drinks for that story. He looked down, spoke of eight years passing. Never had children. And recalling Maureen Klassen losing her battle with breast cancer cannot have been in Conrad's plans for the evening. Ailsa simply needed to know. She watched him struggle with the telling, felt for him. This unassuming and restrained man, as he appeared in advance of their marriage. And, Ailsa recalls, she thought Conrad very good-looking. A bumpkin next to Frame; all her perceptions have shifted with time. She had thought him worth holding on to those eight or nine years ago.

There was a second date while he was in town on the same work trip, and he left with a promise to return. She knew he would, she had seen him in the Toronto office twice before he asked her out. Blew in from the west pretty much every month.

Letter, letter, and a couple more dates during the next month's visit. Another letter and then a phone call. This was unexpected. He'd taken her number and given her his, but she lived in a boarding house on Beatrice Street. Never made outgoing calls. She spoke in a hallway crowded with coats and shoes, talking over a crackly line that stretched way out into the middle of their massive country. 'Way out west,' she'd called it before Conrad corrected her. 'Down the line, not so far that we can't keep in touch,' he'd said. As he was proving by conjuring himself into her life down the phone wires. It was on this call that he told her about his new job: Conrad was to become a federal government adviser on the potash industry. Man of the prairie soon to be a civil servant. Ailsa took a little time, moved the conversation backwards and forwards in an attempt to understand what this had to do with her. Conrad would be working out of Ottawa in a little over one month's time. How did she feel about that, he wanted to know? A man with considerably more life experience than Ailsa, he seemed unable to find efficient words with which to ask her to marry him; it all came out in the course of ten minutes. Fits and starts; he got there. All the while her landlady was milling around, coming in and out of the hallway, Ailsa talking too faintly for Conrad to make out over there in Saskatchewan. 'Speak up,' he said several times. And when he pressed her on the big question—an answer or when he could expect one—she found an ear-to-ear grin sitting on her face. Within a couple of years, she would wonder who that naïve girl in the hallway of the rooming house thought she was. The answer would be markedly different if she had her time over. 'Yes, Conrad. I didn't mean to imply any doubt at all. I should be delighted to marry you.' It was a very young and foolish Ailsa Donaldson who said those words into that phone. The one who didn't know any better.

The landlady of the boarding house kept trying to catch her eye. Clearly picked up the significance of the conversation. Wasn't in the corridor when Ailsa said yes, although she must have been in hearing range. Snuck in a doorway. When the phone was back on its cradle, she hugged Ailsa to her fat bosom. Showered her with kind words. 'You'll never be wanting for anything with a man like that.' She tried calling the girls in the rooms up the stairs to come down and hear the good news, but no doors opened to her call. 'You'll be the talk of Saskatchewan, a pretty Toronto girl like you, Ailsa. You really will.'

Ottawa-bound Ailsa felt no inclination to put her straight.

And so it was, after handing in her notice at work, visiting

Gravelbourg of windswept prairie, meeting his parents there, introducing Conrad to her own kindly father and her suspicious brother—her mother already as dead as Conrad's first wife—she headed for Ottawa, a different rooming house while searching for a new home with her husband-to-be.

In that suspended state, a wedding being prepared on Prince Edward Island while she half-heartedly sought work in Ottawa, she took a hold of herself. Stopped being the awestruck young thing Conrad had turned her into and began to assert herself. She believed with every heartbeat—however much she later revised the notion—that it was love she felt towards him. That did not make her subservient, she was never that stupid. She understood his worldliness, then she misunderstood it, imagined it meant he could see her point of view.

When she invited him up to her rented room, on a night when her landlady was at a whist drive, she found herself grinning at his hesitation. 'You won't be taking advantage of me. I've decided I'm yours, and I'd like to try that thing married couples do. Check it's really for me.'

He laughed but seemed of a generation that couldn't slip into premarital sex with the ease of the young. And without protection the love making, such as it was that night, was odd rather than good. In fact, that became Ailsa's experience during her marriage. She initially worried that it was her; Conrad neither complaining nor ever seeming completely satisfied. Nor did he seem perturbed that she might not be enjoying it. Appearing worldly might be synonymous with taking everything for granted.

They chose a family home which chanced to be very close to one of the city's universities. A home for the family that never arrived in this world, it hadn't for Conrad and Maureen, and nor did it arise on his second try with Ailsa. Before they had moved into the house, she secured a job—typing and administration, stenographer when required—at Carleton University. It was on their doorstep; 'most convenient,' declared Conrad. Her job was in the humanities department, one of a small pool of staff. She found herself working more and more for anthropology. Roger Curtis, the departmental head, took an interest in her. Co-opted her as the secretary he didn't have. It was a secure role, and she saw some social worth in it. She gathered anthropologists were good people, broadly speaking, promoting understanding between cultures so different it took an academic to build a bridge.

Ailsa felt especially privileged to be working with Professor Curtis when a group of visiting Connipians spent two days at the university. They had agreed to come to Carleton because it was well known as one of the most progressive universities in the Commonwealth. Not a defender of British policy on the island but a department professing a purely academic interest in its indigenous inhabitants, and a corresponding concern for the destruction of a way of life which they declared to be taking place. Roger Curtis put pen to paper, wrote articles about what was going on. For all the promise of the New York conference of a decade earlier, there was plunder afoot on the island of unsettled name.

At the time of the visit, fully eighteen months after the formal union of Ailsa and Conrad in a Kensington church, her marriage was playing second fiddle to work. For her and for him. A few dates with a man and two episodes of furtive sex in a rooming house were a limited prelude; indeed, she came to recognise that they foreshadowed only too well the stifling monotony of the music to follow. On the one occasion she visited Gravelbourg, Saskatchewan, Ailsa had liked Conrad's father. An easy-going man, liberal with compliments and encouragement, and she foolishly believed that was who Conrad would grow into. Perhaps it even happened but she couldn't wait around on the off chance. Mrs Klassen, not the dead one, or herself, but Conrad's mother, was completely insufferable. Does anyone put two and two together and figure out how a man, a woman even, is going to behave in the humdrum of their domestic drama? Ailsa certainly didn't. Married in white; 'off-white,' she called it in a whispered aside to the man whose wife she had just become. And he didn't crack a smile. Seemed embarrassed to hear her taking it so lightly.

In their rather fine clapboard house, two blocks from the job in which she felt valued by Roger Curtis and others, Conrad was proving a more domineering man than had showed itself prior to their marriage. Like that Toronto dancefloor, where ritual dictates that the man should lead his lady, Ailsa was stuck in the past as the nineteen sixties woke up around her. For a while she tried to love him—as she felt she had at the time of that portentous telephone call—to be the person he needed. In those few months—thankfully not falling pregnant much as Conrad gave it his best shot, wished it upon her—Ailsa began to feel the weight of her mistake. He was not especially interested in her working day, seldom offered more than a few self-satisfied declarations about his own. When she told him about the visiting Connipians he raised a tiny smile. Thought it quaint, knew a little about them from National Geographic. The almost-people. There were pictures in the papers, their visit to the city—to Carleton University—highly newsworthy. Conrad didn't seem to grasp that his wife had a role to play. Wouldn't really credit that she was to be in the room. Ailsa never pinned down her husband's opinion about the Connipian situation, nor that applying to any of the downtrodden of this world. He would nod sagely when she talked about injustice of any sort. Nod but not speak. Selfishness and selflessness look so similar on the page.

* * *

One of the two Mixed-Up interpreters was ill. The only one who could attend the meeting looked very old to Ailsa's untrained eye. Professor Curtis had warned her that their diction could be wanting, he reserved her a chair next to the Mixed-Up so that she could hear her as clearly as possible. 'Ask her to repeat herself if needed,' he advised. Call-Me-Roger was the professor's oft-repeated nickname. Said it himself with a straight face once or twice a week. Insisted on it, maintained an informal relationship with his almost-secretary.

Did she really think she could do as asked, speak to and make demands upon someone as exotic as a Mixed-Up? As unfortunate as a Mixed-Up. A Mr Floppy, as she'd heard the British comedian, Jimmy Whist, call them on TV at the weekend. She said at the time it sounded mean-spirited; Conrad called it good fun. 'You've got to laugh,' he said.

As she sat herself down, she contemplated her role. Roger had craved their presence in order to promote a better understanding of the Connipians. To push Whist's nonsense back into the pre-war days from where he came. She would speak to a Mixed-Up as she might any other person in the world. Look up to no one and down on no one, that's what Ailsa's father had always told her. And she might even tell Conrad about it later. Impress on him her role in this remarkable visit. Men were flying off into space hoping to find out who was out there when another civilisation lived just around the corner. Round the Cape and take a left at Easter Island.

'Hello, I'm Ailsa,' she introduced herself. 'Ailsa Donaldson...sorry...not Donaldson, Klassen.'

She realised as the seated Mixed-Up said her name—'Tonkin'—that she was floating her hand in front of the poor lady's eyes as if she might shake it when she couldn't possibly.

'Sorry, so insensitive of me.'

'Your nervous, I believe, and you really mustn't be, Ailsa.'

This she had not prepared for: a Mixed-Up who understood her behaviour while she was still on the bottom rung of figuring out Connipians and Mixed-Ups. Not really on a rung at all. There were three Connipians in the room. They all wore the penetratingly blue clothing that she'd seen in the National Geographic. Ailsa couldn't be sure what material it was which covered them. Wrapped around them tightly in the style she had seen in photographs. From close to, the colouration of their skirts and wraps was electric, the most vivid tone she had ever seen. On these tiny ladies it looked perfect. And Ailsa realised, as they sat before her, that the eyes of the Connipians, were of an identical hue. The

God Help the Connipians

astonishing blue through which these Connipians viewed the world. The three all sat together on the other side of Tonkin to that which Ailsa sat. Clicking ceaselessly; they seemed to pay both their hosts and their interpreter very little mind. The discussion in full had yet to begin. They must have been having a chat of their own. About the size and eclectic clothing of the many anthropologists milling around. Or the weather in Quebec.

'I've never met one of you before. Anyone like you. I want to be polite, and I know how many of my kind must have offended you over the years. We're not all that way...' Ailsa stopped talking; Tonkin was weaving her head and shoulders to the right and to the left, as if disagreeing with her sentiment or, at the very least, her need to express it.

'We've never met,' the Mixed-Up confirmed, 'and I expect you've never been to Connipia?' Ailsa nodded her head in agreement. 'It is their island, I believe. How you have behaved away from there cannot offend a Connipian. It is not their concern. The encroachment, as they call it, is the sole problem between them and the Homo Sapiens.'

'And you?' said Ailsa. 'You're not offended by the funny names which people...'

Tonkin dipped her shoulders, face forward to hide a small grin. 'I dislike that talk, of course, but I think we Mixed-Ups make the smallest of all possible marks on this Earth. No land of our own nor any off-spring who shall carry our torch when we have left the conscious life. We cannot have them, and nor do we wish for any.' She jerked her shoulders so that her arms rippled. 'We're a bit useless, you see.'

Instinctively, Ailsa stretched a hand out to Tonkin, took a hold of her limp left arm. 'I'm sorry,' she murmured, not knowing how to contradict this intelligent and humble lady.

'No,' Tonkin admonished her. 'I'm grateful that you think of me. An interpreter can become lost in the exchanges.'

When the session started, Ailsa had to spend every second scribbling shorthand on her pad as Tonkin calmly spoke aloud the thoughts which the Connipians clicked. She couldn't take in their meaning—dwell on the words—not while making marks on her notepad. Securing for eternity all that they said. Said, clicked, thought; let loose into the room. This was not anthropological research as she had previously understood it. When Tonkin interpreted the reasons Connipians wish for no photographs of the interior of the Blue Houses, explained also why footage of the exteriors offended them, Professor Curtis pressed his hands together as if in supplication. He spoke only of his gratitude that these tiny women—not three feet tall when standing—had ventured to Ottawa. Expressed positive support for the notion that his own kind should not mine or quarry on the island that was once exclusively theirs.

Ailsa wrote and wrote. When there was a break in proceedings, Billy Cooper, a post-graduate student asked her if she thought she'd caught it all.

'I think so,' she said.

'I mean,' he continued, 'Mixed-Ups can be a bit wishy-washy in their diction. Sorry to say.'

Tonkin was still sitting beside her. 'She speaks perfectly clearly. As clear as you and I.' Ailsa saw the interpreter dip her shoulders forward. It could have been a small thank you, although she was ostensibly clicking with the Connipians. 'You must have heard it, Billy. Every word clear as a bell.'

'Yeah, but their tongues are not fixed in place quite like ours. Half and halves and all that. It can be a problem.'

'Not of their making,' she muttered, looking down at her notes. She had heard enough from this member of an otherwise united team.

As they were preparing to resume the question and answer, the meeting for posterity as Professor Curtis called it, Tonkin whispered to her. 'Only one asshole, it's a better university than most.' And it was while Ailsa was laughing that Tonkin asked the question that set so much in motion. 'Ailsa, my friend, would you like to meet me this evening? Come to my hotel.' Ailsa felt that she would like this very much while simultaneously aware that she and Conrad were due to host a drinks evening. The duties of the wife of a government insider. Conrad's boss and his wife would be on Aylmer Avenue. Drink and eat in her house. Ailsa's absence from such an event was unthinkable. The hostess. She stared into Tonkin's lined face beneath her black wig, not answering the question. 'I see,' said Tonkin.

'No, no.' Ailsa felt a flood of misunderstanding. 'I can. Want to. It's just tonight is the problem. My husband expects me because...'

'Marriages are founded upon mutual obligation, I believe. Tomorrow night, perhaps?'

'Yes, yes. I'd love to meet you for a meal, Tonkin. To talk alone. I'm interested. I want to hear everything about you.'

* * *

'And you're sure it won't bounce now,' says Sister Concepta, asks it of Steve Frame while Sister Carmel holds the generous cheque in her hands. The young nun giggles after she has said it, so quickly has she adapted to his presence.

'Don't be impertinent,' says the Abbess, seeming surprised by the behaviour of her young novice.

'He knows I don't mean anything by it, Sister Carmel. It's just a bit of fun we're having.'

God Help the Connipians

Ailsa looks on in wry amusement: this be-wimpled girl is flirting with the rockstar, doing it more obviously than her own holding of his gaze. And the young nun very clearly knows who he is whether her Mother Superior has figured it out or not. Steve only grins at the comment. There is no offending him today. He's had a couple of Mixed-Ups dribble over him. Kids. Didn't seem to mind that either. Ailsa has forgiven him the foolishness out in the street; the lead singer and principal guitarist of One-Eyed Temple seems game for anything. Not as knowledgeable about Connipians and Mixed-Ups as he should be, given all the reading he's done. At least he's on their side.

Sister Carmel reminds the blushing nun that gifts such as these are manna from heaven for the unfortunates in their charge. Make a real difference in the extent to which they may purchase mouth-operated adaptions. Increase the independence of those who would surely die alone in the world but for the intercessions of the Holy Mother and a few good people like the kindly Mr Frame. Steve even puts a forefinger upon his chest at these last words, a sly wink unseen by the compliment giver which makes Sister Concepta snort with laughter; she tries to disguise it as a sneeze.

Just fifteen minutes earlier, Sister Carmel not yet in the room, the young nun told them that the boys and girls—young Mixed-Ups— looked after in this orphanage need education in the ways of the world as much as they do religion. Need it badly if they are to navigate it when they are too old for places such as this. 'That's a thoughtful insight for a girl who has renounced the sinful world herself,' observed Steve, a little Mixed-Up boy sitting within his crossed legs down on the linoleum flooring.

'Plain speaking, Mr Frame. Mixed-Ups can't become nuns, you know? The Holy Father won't so much as baptise the poor dears. Preparing them for the world out there, that really is as much as we can do.'

Steve engaged with the issue—saw the point she made while querying the premise—Connipian blood does not derive from Adam: does any? When he said the Pope sounded a bit of an idiot on this point, the young nun nodded concurrence. Ailsa felt only the weight of the initial premise, the difficult lives which all Mixed-Ups inevitably experience. Frustrated beyond measure with how little she can do for Mannay. Her hotel room extravagance.

* * *

Despite her realisation that all was not right in her marriage, Ailsa was the dutiful wife to Conrad. Back then women conformed without giving it the reflection their decisions deserved. Put up with nonsense that wouldn't last a rainy November by the end of this self-same decade. Ailsa played the hostess that evening as her husband expected her to. Cooked a passable casserole for Mr and Mrs Fielding, his line manager at the Department of Mines and Technical Surveys. Rosemary Fielding talked exclusively with Ailsa, knew better than to intrude on the work-related talk in which their menfolk grappled. Probably capable of no other conversation, her interests began and ended in recipes and knitting patterns. Ailsa could bluff her way through that stuff if needed. Wouldn't dream of it today. Confabulated talk of stew and pastry, spun out stories of scarves created, although she had clicked no needles since she was a schoolgirl on that other island in the Gulf of St Lawrence.

Conrad had advised there should be no mention of her Connipian connection, the happenings at the university. Perhaps he was sympathetic and simply didn't want the topic veering into areas in which he could not predict his manager's reaction. Curious to look back on: the Canadians had little reason to support the British and most magazine articles about Connipia would cite how divisive the exploitation of that faraway land had become. Not worth the potash and limestone it yielded. There were voices of dissent in the British parliament too: never did it in power, but in opposition Labour members were arguing that Connipians were only people like ourselves. Ailsa liked that view while discovering—during her meeting earlier that same day—that Connipians are terribly different. That is the point. They are not for joining Sapiens society at all. They have their own and it is of the longest standing.

All around the globe there were also many bigots; the Fieldings could have been in their number. Believing *Homo Connipus* to be animals of the lowest order. There was no knowing, and not raising the matter would be the simplest course. She assumed that was Conrad's thinking.

Ailsa recalls the conversation, during the shared meal, turning political despite their best efforts, even skirting around the subject she'd agreed not to raise. Tom Fielding hoped to stand for parliament, throw his lot in with the resurgent Progressive Conservatives.

'The thing is, Connie old boy, getting the noses of government out of the pie can't do any harm and just might improve the flavour.' Conrad seemed at ease with his free-market talk; Ailsa thought it sounded anarchic, knew better than to voice her opinion. Nineteen sixty-two. She thought Conrad looked shocked when Tom took a pop at the UN. 'Like that nonsense about New Poplar. Thank God the British are no longer abiding by it. Negotiating across the animal kingdom: if that's not a fools' game, I don't know what is.'

It is only with hindsight that she has seen he always knew. Conrad worked with Tom Fielding long before this dinner. 'But Mr Fielding...' This was Ailsa, trying her best not to sound argumentative. '...do you not think that without due care they might become extinct in our lifetime.

A tragedy.'

'Yes, Miss. It could happen. The tragedy word sounds a bit strong. A shame about the Mexican grizzly bear but my sympathies are first and foremost with the farmers. Mexican farmers in that instance. With our kind. That seems right, to me. And my main point is the United Nations has to get its nose out. Someone will start advocating for the polar bears and our guys in the north will start looking like the bad guys. The Eskimos. Let them be, is all I'm saying. I don't eat polar bear and nor am I in favour of laws to prohibit it. Let's just put a stop to all this government interference, shall we?'

'You don't think the Connipians are a special case? Intelligent life.'

'If you say so. I've heard that clicking and it's like Rose's knitting needles...' He covered his wife's hand with his own, ensured he had drawn her attention. '...without the sweater at the end, more's the pity.' Then he laughed himself red at his own joke, his wife joining in until Conrad did likewise. Ailsa could not, it might have been a turning point.

* * *

The evening shift in The Reeve-Muggleton is a busy one. She never stops traipsing food across to tables, pouring one drink after another, doing so just a few hours after sharing time with nuns, Mixed-Ups and the outrageously handsome Steve Frame. It doesn't wipe the smile. A cruise ship docked around the time she and Steve were at the orphanage. Ageing Brits and Aussies jabber about the Connipians she hopes they never get to see. These people are the worst. Would click their fingers at them as if beckoning a budgerigar. She has seen the like once or twice on the streets of East Town. Visitors cannot enter the protected areas without the approval of the governor. Cherie Thornhill might be as patronising as the tourists—probably is—and despite that Steve has written to Sir Desmond offering to accompany her out there. Did enough research to spot she's never been. And if it pays off it will only be because of the teenager's adoration of the popstar. Her crush from afar. It might work. The daughter must have bought it, her father could go either way. Ailsa has agreed to accompany Frame to the Governor's mansion tomorrow afternoon. She will work the lunchtime shift, cleared the decks for the meeting. It's a very strange relationship she and Steve have: he courts her rather as Conrad did in the early days. Tries nothing physical. She shouldn't really call it courting; a rockstar need only pucker his lips to catch a girl. His interest might be solely in the Connipians; flattering that he thinks her an authority on the subject. She thinks he's figured going to meet father and daughter—mother too, all the Thornhills will be there—alone could prove a poor choice. Look as if he is trying to whisk Cherie away on some tryst. Is he subtly chasing Ailsa, or is she a mock girlfriend? A beard. She really hasn't a clue. Game for going back into the forest should the chance arise, for spending a bit more time close to Frame while she's at it. His strategy seems far-fetched but what does she know about rockstars and governor's daughters? Needs to be mature about her seventeen-year-old rival. This crush she has on Frame is the silliest thing and yet she revels in it. Fantasising that she could share his bed which would be outrageous. Steve Frame cannot share hers because Mannay sleeps in it.

These thoughts occupy her throughout the shift, help it to pass quickly. They are still in her head as she returns to the flat. The covert Mixed-Up, her odd lodger, asks questions. Might pick up her elated mood and she will need to make arrangements for him if she gets to spend a few days in the forest. Then, showered and exhausted, sleeping on the small sofa—middle of the night—she finds Mannay once more clambering on top of her, waking her, his nose is precisely where it shouldn't be.

'Jesus, Mannay, you'll be going back to East Town in the morning the way you're carrying on.'

'Ailsa feel good,' he tells her, quickly rubbing his face into her chest. Her cotton nightie.

She's read a lot about Mixed-Ups but never that any were even half as libidinous as the one she has happened to befriend. Just her luck, it seems, and she doesn't admonish him as much a she might. 'Get out of my bed!' she hisses, and he slides down the side to his feet. She won't be letting the unclothed little bugger sleep beside her with his pencil erection. Not a chance. She has a little pocket in her heart for Mannay. Nothing more.

3.

Ailsa holds a glass of freshly squeezed orange juice in her hand. This is the afternoon after Mannay crept into her bed in the middle of the night. Got short shrift. She looks across the rim at Steve—crush unabated—at Cherie Thornhill who beams at Steve more overtly than she has yet dared to; Governor and Lady Thornhill are in the room and she scarcely takes them in. Never thought she would be in a place like this with a pair like that. Ailsa doesn't belong, never a toff. Another family shares the room with them, also invited to the Governor's residence. She guesses herself to be the weirdest of the lot, having her own pet Mixed-Up back in the hotel room. That's what it feels like, not that she would ever give voice to such a putdown. Poor frustrated Mannay. Her life seems to have taken a few unexpected turns. Making a companion of little Mannay might be a cul-de-sac: she can't take him off-island, and living like a fugitive does little for him. Could get herself a couple of rooms in East Town but it would be the oddest relationship to go public with. It is odd already. Yet here in the room with the dignitaries of Connipia, she can pass herself off as normal. As once she was. Her association with Steve—if she truly has one—is pushing her life into another extraordinary place. He might sense that she is more than a barmaid; Ailsa thinks it and doubts it in equal measure.

His connection—the esteem in which the wayward Cherie Thornhill holds his music—has brought about this unlikely social engagement. The other family in the room, Mr and Mrs Grace and their three children, have no connection to Steve Frame. 'Should I have heard of them?' said Mr Grace, in reference to One-Eyed Temple. His wife is a friend of Lady Thornhill. 'We were at Roedean,' the governor's wife repeatedly explains. Ailsa wonders if she is a true friend, if Mrs Thornhill can recall any other fact from this lady's past beyond sharing a privileged education. Nothing suggests they were close. Cherie looks embarrassed by her parents, looks out of place on the island of Connipia—which her father, the Governor, has twice called 'Poplar'—she wears a green miniskirt with green tights beneath it, a white blouse with red embroidery upon it and a red bandana in her short, thick black hair. A bit young to be a character but that seems to be what she's going for.

The daughter has plenty to be embarrassed by. For this supposed informal meeting, Sir Desmond Thornhill wears his red sash. Entered with a ceremonial sword attached to his waist; at least he has ditched it now. Ridiculous. Ailsa does not believe there has ever been a sword fight on Connipia, nor on New Poplar, its name for the first two hundred and fifty-seven years of British presence. And why he—they—should govern an island on which they have never belonged will bug Ailsa for as long as she stands here and smiles politely. For only seventeen years have they called it by its better name. Thornhill still struggles with it. His wife, Samantha—wife and snob—has a sash which matches her husbands. Wants to convey the gravity of her position although it is a sad one. A governor's wife: the chattel of a pompous ass. On the plus side, she dons no sword. Ailsa wonders if Cherie wears her simple red headband in mockery of her parents, feels a little warmth towards her on the off chance. The best of a bad bunch. Cherie pays attention only to Steve Frame, and Ailsa understands why she might. Her parents are insufferable, and Steve the easiest on the eye.

'I love it that you've come but what are you doing here?' Cherie directs her no-nonsense talk at the rock singer.

'Cherie, dear,' interrupts her mother, 'the island we govern is a delight. A million more would visit if we didn't apply strict limits. Preserve the uniqueness of our land. And, of course, Mr Frame may come. He's a Member of the British Empire.

Ailsa glances at him quickly. She had forgotten this. The facts fall into place: he received the honour a little over a year ago. Must have been Harold Wilson's doing, can't see that Frame was ever the Queen's choice. No popstars getting such awards before Wilson became prime minister. Steve keeps his eyes down. Seems more interested in talking with the feisty daughter than the frightful mother. Ailsa tries to suppress her jealousy, understands. Steve is hedging his bets.

'It's like nowhere else, isn't it? I mean, there's a whole civilisation on this island that predates anything our lot has done. Predates when we so much as existed. They lived like this before your forebears were so much as a twinkle in some Neanderthal's eye. Mind-blowing, wouldn't you say, Cherie?'

Now it is the turn of the wild-child to grin. Her eyes dash to her father and back to Steve, whom she has been looking at intently since he entered the room. 'They're all British now, though. No matter what the history.' She is grinning, a put down hidden within her words that might confuse her proud parents.

'They're not British, Cherie,' says her mother, oblivious to the daughter's inflexion. 'I don't think they want to be, and it wouldn't do to have the Connipians emigrate to England. It really wouldn't. They don't belong there.'

'Protected status is what they have, Mr Frame,' Governor Thornhill interrupts. He looks directly at his famous guest. 'Connipia is not a British colony, I hope you know that. We are protecting the land on behalf of the indigenous population. And God knows, they really couldn't manage alone in the modern world. Not a hope.'

Ailsa looks aside. Cannot be seen to argue with this colonialist in denial. Must not let out any of the caustic thoughts which spear her mind. Her function this evening is to support Steve in getting access to protected sites. Accompany him out there if fortune should fall that way. The British are protecting potash and limestone, that's their game, and listening to the governor declaring black is white sets her stomach on edge.

'When we moved into the residence,' says Cherie, careless of her father's cautioning tone, 'two of them were presented to us. Weren't they, Dad? Two little girlie women with no hair on their heads. What was the name of the big fellow, the one who said they could do wonders with fruit in the kitchen...?'

'Cherie, dear, it's quite a terrible story,' says her father. 'Mr Frame,' he pronounces with quiet severity, admonishing his daughter without even addressing her, 'there has been mismanagement on this island for certain periods of its history. The gentleman of whom Cherie speaks,

God Help the Connipians

Alan Kramnik, was a hotelier in Charlestown all through the forties and fifties but he no longer lives here. And we won't be allowing him back. The practice of retaining Connipians for service was long ago outlawed. There were several getting around the rules by calling it employment. It isn't the proper way for that species and our own to interact. We don't employ Connipians and they only ever did it because they were coaxed. He fed them nutmeg concentrates, very addictive I understand, and he wasn't the first to manipulate them thus. Anyhow, our ability to communicate with them is insufficient to make any such arrangement practical. A circus act, Connipians make poor servants.'

'It was slavery,' spits out Ailsa.

Teenage Cherie looks shocked. So naïve when trying to sound worldly in front of Steve. Ailsa knows instantly that she shouldn't have used the S-word. Not in front of Governor Thornhill. There has been no slavery in this island's history. Some abuse that looks disarmingly similar, but Connipians are tiny, cannot labour as the Africans did in the sugar and tobacco plantations of America. Cannot be made to do very much. They make the world's worst slaves no matter what else men try to do with them.

'Not slavery,' says Samantha Thornhill as if correcting an infant. 'It wasn't right but nor was it slavery. Connipians enjoy preparing fruit.'

'What happened to the two girls Cherie spoke about?' asks Steve.

'We let them return to the forests. Sent them back there with a letter of apology, Mr Frame. We are wary of how some interpret the declaration; I, on the other hand, understand full well that it is my duty to implement the New York agreement, and so I shall. It is hard to speak with them at all, that's the biggest hurdle. When we do it's usually about something or other in the dashed treaty. We use five different interpreters. They try their best, poor souls.' Sir Desmond looks uncomfortable discussing his practice towards those he is sworn to protect. His sudden vulnerability strikes Ailsa as very strange. A worn-out man, his redundant sword still leaning against the wall at the side of the fireplace, itself both grand and unlit. She regrets her outburst, will apologise to Steve next time she and he are alone. Governor Thornhill has always looked confident when she's seen him on local television, speaking about restrictions, explaining and excusing them. He seldom ventures onto the topic of the true islanders. Speaks to settlers, for settlers, applying order where it has been lax. He has seen fit to invite Steve Frame to Connipia—if he can remember the name of the island he governs—his daughter's hero. This meeting could secure a trip into the forest, so if she has angered him that's plain stupid. She looks forward to Steve's forgiveness. Hopes she has not misjudged him, that he heard the concern in her outburst above the idiocy of the squealy way she said it.

'Steve,' says Cherie, 'come up to my room. I want you to sign my record sleeves.'

He glances at Ailsa before rising from his chair.

'You are a very popular young man,' observes Mrs Grace, smiling at Cherie as she says it.

'I don't think that would be proper,' says Lady Thornhill.

'Only to sign records. See all my One-Eyed Temple stuff.' Cherie taps the back of Frame's hand. 'I've got the lot. Bought the singles and they're all the same cut as on the albums. Got the posters and the book of lyrics too. You must sign the book. That would be so cool.'

'At least take...' Samantha Thornhill looks at the eldest child of her old school friend, a girl of thirteen or fourteen, in Ailsa's estimation. '...can you take...'

'Bryony,' says the child.

'...thank you...take Bryony upstairs with you. We run an orderly ship in the Governor's Mansion, as you know, Cherie darling.'

The daughter of the house raises her eyebrows, then slaps a gentle hand on Steve's forearm. 'Come along then, Bryony,' she says. Ailsa watches the three of them leave the room. It crossed her mind that Cherie was seeking time with the rockstar for a grope and a fumble. Daft thought to have, she's only a kid. The reports in the papers a few months back implied a tearaway, but that's newspapers for you. Nothing scandalous in the air. Steve is courteous with Cherie. A well-mannered man, not one to take advantage of a starstruck teenager. She really hopes not: either way, Ailsa's on board with Mrs Thornhill's insistence that Bryony goes upstairs too.

'And you're his girlfriend?' says Mrs Grace. 'It must be very racy being with so popular a man.'

Ailsa shakes her head. 'I've only become acquainted with him since Mr Frame came to the island. I'm not his girlfriend. Not anyone's girlfriend, truly.'

Mrs Grace glances around. Clearly finds this information unexpected. Doesn't trust it, judging by the pursing of her lips.

'No,' observes Sir Desmond, 'the note said that you were out in the forests before. Mr Frame would like you to accompany him should I permit him access.'

She nods her head. Thinks before speaking. 'Mr Frame has no connections on the island. I was, some years ago, involved with a study out there. And I also volunteer in East Town...' She pauses, thinks Governor Thornhill eyes her with suspicion but she needs to explain her value to Frame. She tried to decide how she should play this in advance of entering the Governor's Mansion but couldn't fix on a plan. The Governor has little formal power in the protected areas, the Connipians

God Help the Connipians

supposedly autonomous. She believes he is complicit in the many abuses. Tree-felling where it should never happen. He might be an apologist for Sapiens encroachment, could be a full-blown connipulsive. All colonial governors work for the interests of their home country and not the indigenous of the requisitioned lands. If he has tidied up one or two anomalies which former Governors allowed, it has been through diplomatic necessity. In the last four years, many more countries have signed the declaration of protected status that came out of the nineteen-fifty conference. All want to hear that Britain does as the UN has decreed it should; and every Mixed-Up born is proof of their abject failure.

'Were you with the American mission, Miss Donaldson?'

'Canadian,' she replies, knowing it is plausible he has uncovered this in advance. There are few secrets on Connipia.

'I've never understood their militancy, Miss Donaldson. Canadian academics are scathing and, if you will forgive my frankness, ignorant, all in the same letter to The Correspondent, or any of the journals they've published articles in. We all want the same for the Connips, truly. I understand that they would like us off the island. A long history before we arrived here—but it is not only economically important to us, we are its custodians. You've seen the yachts in the harbourIt's on all the maps as it was not three hundred years ago. Someone has to protect the little creatures and we're in the hot seat. And the only resources we take are unused by Connipians.' Governor Thornhill is running his right hand carelessly along his silky red sash as he speaks. 'Unless potash is critical in the making of blue dye.'

He laughs at his own poor joke. Ailsa smiles back, distaste in her mouth at her obsequiousness. 'I appreciate that,' she manages.

'All over my head,' says Mrs Grace.

'No, no,' says the Governor. 'Sorry to exclude...'

'We were saying,' she continues, 'the children simply adored Coral Beach. Didn't you darlings?'

A little boy of no more than five, and a girl a couple of years older both nod their heads. The Graces' other children. They have visited the famed beach ten miles around the coast. Driven or been driven along the road that cuts through the forest. 'It's a beautiful island,' she confirms.

'And am I to understand,' says Mr Grace—silent until now—'that you are an anthropologist?'

'No,' says Ailsa. 'I worked with them for a short time.'

'Very few of them left,' says Sir Desmond. 'We can't let them go out there any longer, you see. The Connips don't wish us to study them and we've respected their opinion. A bit of a missed opportunity, in my view, but we can't ride roughshod over them. We've done as they've asked us to. We've let a few of your lot look at the abandoned settlements in the last two years. That's about as much as we can do.' He stops and coughs, face reddening before carrying on his monologue. 'It's all been a bit of a set to, really. Some of the dashed academics even signed up to the British Off movement. Didn't seem to know where their own funding came from. That was about as much as I could make of it. And we've given the little Connipians as much of our knowledge as they could ever wish to consume, you know. History, science, even a signed Dickens in The Forest Library: some of them can read which is dashed clever if you think about it. Ha! We get precious little back. Nothing at all. Won't really speak to us these days.' A faint laugh leaves the back of his throat.

'It has been a fraught time,' Ailsa acknowledges. 'Do you worry that extinction will come about, Sir Desmond? That it could happen by accident.'

'Can't see it. They're more resilient than anyone gives credit for. A few secrets up their sleeves, no doubt. There could be any number of them in the forests. If they'd ever let our scientists examine the males properly, we might be able to sort out what's wrong with them. Give them some tablets, might make for better breeding. Opposite of what we do with our lot. The pill and what have you. It is an odd...'

'Oh, dear me,' cuts in Lady Thornhill, 'this isn't the polite conversation we usually enjoy. And Connipians are frightfully immoral. The men have babies with lots of different...well, with as many ladies as they please, quite frankly.'

Ailsa finds herself smiling. This is utter ignorance within a few miles of the Blue Houses. The wife of the man in charge, and he's no better. Unforgiveable but she won't say it. Mustn't completely ruin Frame's chances of a permit. Her thoughts flit to him time and again, up in Cherie's room whatever he's doing with her. The Governor's daughter is a pretty girl when she allows herself a smile. It shouldn't bother Ailsa half as much as it does. She has no claim on Steve Frame; she's come to like him—looks and character—over these past few days. And Bryony seems prim and proper, probably being inculcated with how to be just that at Roedean. They won't be getting up to anything with her in the room.

* * *

Ailsa shared a meal with Tonkin in a private room at the Grand Hotel. The management wouldn't allow them in the main dining room. Good table manners do not flow from a Mixed-Up's uncooperative arms. Tonkin might have tried and tried but she always had to push her face into the food. Take it from there. It's not as most people expect to see. This meal occurred approximately seven years ago. Three years before Ailsa found her way to Connipia. Seven years before Steve Frame

God Help the Connipians

brightened up a dull evening in the bar of The Reeve-Muggleton.

Ailsa felt a bit of a fraud. Her shorthand was excellent, up to the mark, but it was Professor Curtis and the better of his postgrads who understood Connipians. Studied and analysed how they lived. Funny that Tonkin should single out the non-professional. Degreeless Ailsa had started reading everything about them she could get hold of. A recent enthusiasm, prompted because Connipians were Call-me-Roger's anthropological specialism. In a fit of honesty, she shared this truth with her Mixed-Up dining companion. Tonkin ate from a bowl with steep low sides, an inner ridge—kitchen staff took it from her shoulder bag before serving her—a meal of rice and mixed fish. Some kind of risotto which she requested, dipping her head right down and taking small mouthfuls, holding her head low as her tongue lapped around the rim, ensuring no food was on cheek or chin as she rose up. Took Ailsa's eye.

'I feel a million things for the Connipians. I have known many as personal friends, and one whom I once felt closer to than anyone else in the world. But I am a Mixed-Up. Being interspecies, a foot in each camp and two feet in neither, has been the predicament of my life. I know Sapiens just as well. Enjoy many things Sapiens as those in my maternal line do not. Cannot for they are unable to make themselves understood even a little. You—all of you, not you personally, Ailsa—understand them no more than you do the dolphins. Me and my sort are a bridge for you. I like you, Ailsa, because you do not judge. I could see it in your actions at the university. I've watched you for two days now. That's a long time, I've learned to spot when people let their judgement fall, and you are still suspended. Listening to the Connipians, or rather my interpretation of their thoughts, as open-mindedly as when they arrived. Those academics mostly decided what was good about them and what were their shortcomings when they wrote their thesis, or read this or that text book. They are rigid in their thoughts even as they believe themselves to be accommodating.'

'I'm just amazed by you,' said Ailsa. 'It's my job to listen to every word you say. Because I've to write it down. I think your work is twice has hard, maybe more than that. Connipians don't really use words that translate in a straightforward way, do they?'

'You have learned well, Ailsa. To me it's different again. They state their thoughts in their own way, click them. Not words but a prickly bush of consideration in response to the thoughts of others, or the words of others when at Carleton University. It doesn't subdivide into the precise words I must later find; it's not like your language—this language—you are quite right about that. However, I am fluent in it; they make their thoughts clear to me and so I can then speak them in the form of language you rely upon. Occasionally I struggle to find the best words so as to convey a nuance...'

'And does it bother you?' asked Ailsa. 'The anthropologists are only interested in the pure Connipians and your experience as a Mixed-Up is every bit as worth thinking about...'

'Can I stop you there, Ailsa. Would you like Professor This or Doctor That, whatever the eggheads at Carleton and Yale and every other seat of higher learning call themselves, watching you morning, noon and night? Passing off sweeping observations about your lifestyle as if their brief enquiry contained necessary insights.' Tonkin paused, looked very directly at her silent young dinner-date. 'No? I didn't think so.'

This was an education for a girl who grew up on a small island in the Gulf of St Lawrence. Puberty amid grain silos. She never felt a significant pull towards the metropolitan, just thought she should give it a go. Lead a full life. That's as much reason as there ever was behind her move to Toronto. She was, by the time of this meal, puzzling over how exactly she had let herself fall into marriage. Conrad, she initially thought sophisticated, a view which changed with the waning of love. A mirage, the man was just another polite and self-effacing bulldozer. As certainties fell away, she started to find the world both a more fascinating and a more uncomfortable place. And there she was, thinking of her own discomfort as an ageing Mixed-Up told of her immeasurably more difficult experiences. Tonkin related her life story to Ailsa. Tales of prejudice in New Zealand, and of hotfooting to New Poplar as was then its name. Every word was inspiring to Ailsa, totally inspiring. Tonkin was a woman like no other.

* * *

Steve Frame returns to the room with Cherie and Bryony. The former quietly sings a song which Ailsa recognises. She's heard it on the radio, must be one of Frames. 'Signed the sleeves?' asks Ailsa of him. An attempt at nonchalance.

> *Do you really think I don't see your face*
> *Just because you take it to a distant place...*

Then Cherie interrupts her own singing to answer for him. 'Pushed me on the bed for a quick romp. Bryony watched. Didn't you, sweetie?'

Steve Frame narrows his eyes; Bryony looks upset. 'That's not what happened,' says the ashen-faced girl.

'Ha-ha!' Cherie looks delighted; frowns on the faces of both sets of parents. Their eyes dart between the two girls, scarcely resting on Frame for a split second.

The rockstar shakes his head, keeps his mouth shut while his wide eyes seem to note something funny in the exchange. Then he narrows them at young Cherie. She is hamming it up, pats down her short skirt

God Help the Connipians

as if something has occurred which needs this realignment.

'Has my daughter embarrassed you, Stephen?' asks Samantha Thornhill.

'She behaved herself upstairs, if that's the nub of the question. And I've met plenty of mouthier people in the music industry, Lady Thornhill.'

Poor Bryony nods wide-eyed at his words, and the Governor's wife glances at her before smiling at the rockstar. 'You are very forgiving.'

Ailsa thinks it a funny way of saying. She likes Steve Frame too, but trusting any man over one's own daughter sounds lopsided. They were up there long enough. Bryony might be too young to finger-wag effectively. Ailsa thinks it through quickly, and decides she can trust Steve. Decide it because Cherie's not *her* daughter.

'Sir Desmond,' says Steve Frame, 'do you have a view on meetings with Connipians?'

'I do, sir, I do. Meetings are broadly a good thing, I believe. A chance to build bridges, establish whatever rapport is there to be had. The trouble we've found is that meetings with these little blighters never go well. They've become very militant. Or maybe they always were.'

'And how does that attitude manifest itself?'

'Ha! Between you and I. Stephen, primitive as they are, they seem to believe themselves superior to us. They call progress damage. There would be no electricity with which to play your vinyl records if they had their way. For Cherie here to play her newly signed vinyl records.'

Steve listens carefully. Ailsa cannot read his facial expression, a mask he has thrown over whatever he thinks of the old dinosaur. 'Their way of life, do you think there is anything to learn from it?' He seems to encourage further philippic from Thornhill.

'Remarkable blue paint, paint or dye; you know that already, of course. They don't wish us to learn the formula. The recipe. Surprises me that we've not uncovered it. All the various garments, building materials and what have you, that we've gathered up over the years, have failed to yield the secret. I suppose their agriculture is worth a whistle. Fruits that grow nowhere else on Earth because they've been cultivated over thousands of years. Been at it longer than us which is remarkable in its own way. And our farmers would all break their necks if they had to climb trees as the little Connipians do.'

Steve knows about this. He talked with Ailsa on the way over here, and during their day in East Town. More clued in than Governor Thornhill, most likely. Connipians grow gourdes and berries on the tops of forests. In the canopies. There are scientists who believe they have understood the chemical content of the saps of different trees. Managed to do so without a laboratory on the island, nor a propagator to germinate seeds. Arrived at unique tastes which Sapiens have struggled to cultivate. Failed to do. What Connipians grow in the treetops won't stay alive when planted directly into the soil. Observations of the Connipians methods have, to date, been piecemeal. Scientists are not welcome in the forests: one of the books Queen Victoria bequeathed to The Forest Library included an account of Dr Waite's dissection of a Connipian. No-one thinks it was intended—Understanding the Human Body, the books innocuous title—whoever chose it likely didn't read it. No cooperation with scientists after that one. Not that the Connipian in question was killed for the purpose. A death by natural causes; Connipians die all too easily if they are removed from the life they anticipated. In the last three years none have left the island. Never again, they have said through their Mixed-Up interpreters. Not frequently, interaction so minimal now.

'We'll talk more over sandwiches,' says Sir Desmond. 'I understand you would like to visit the protected areas. That's not straightforward, and nor is it beyond the bounds of possibility. We still have little sorties out there. Try to keep them safe and well, whether the blighters wish for our assistance or not.'

* * *

Ailsa's meal with Tonkin was the most impressionable experience of her life. Simply hearing the extraordinary life which Tonkin had lived. Stowing away on a boat—achieving her repatriation—without the use of functioning arms. The lead interpreter at the conference of nineteen-fifty, when the current dispensation was agreed. The Sapiens collectively composing it—the ink of many nations running into the final document—Sapiens alone, and Ailsa never understood the injustice of it until that evening meal. Connipians were invited to sign, chose not to. Did not see enough merit in it to raise a pen for. Sapiens listened sympathetically to other Sapiens liberal views on Connipians, never took on board the speech Tonkin interpreted for Klapakipsy and Tululiduh.

The eating of the risotto took a little time, and Ailsa tried neither to stare at the manner of sucking up food that must have been Tonkin's only recourse lifelong, nor to look away too obliquely. Not wishing to imply distaste. It was a shared meal for which Ailsa felt ill-prepared while simultaneously recognising that she was the lucky one. Her arms worked fine.

'At that conference, I assisted the brightest Connipian that ever lived. At least, I think she was; it is a Sapiens inclination to compare and contrast like this. Brightest in the modern era at the very least. I might be wrong of course—I've known a few, there must be seventeen or eighteen hundred whom I've never met—and however bright I suppose she got it all wrong. Taking on a belligerent species single-handedly. There are no textbooks telling you how that's done, and nor do their string arrangements point a way. She understood what an opportunity it was. Threw everything she had at it...' Tonkin pulled an ambiguous face, implied complexities that might make one despair. '...went above and beyond. That's certainly something she did.' Then Tonkin lowered her voice. 'We Mixed-Ups are infertile. I don't think we really understand sex, although I understand my male counterparts are very keen on it in principle whatever their struggles in practice. Can't find a mate, that's the nub of their difficulty. Sapiens misunderstand Connipians on this topic time and time again. At the conference there was an Irishman fixated on marriage. Why they don't! I could have laughed if doing so hadn't been rude. Would do exactly that if I heard anyone say anything as ludicrous today.' She leant back, wriggled her arms so one flopped over each of the dining chair's wooden arms. 'They are totally misunderstood. There has long been a phenomenal imbalance in the male to female ratio. I do not know since when, longer than the Homo Sapiens have walked this Earth, most certainly. Two per cent of Connipian babies are boys. Or three percent. No more than that. They have a high rate of miscarriages in early pregnancy which might play a small role: it doesn't explain the disparity. The extent of it. I've read a little about human biology. I think the mechanics of it all is different for them. Not the sex part. Chromosomes; what leads to what. They don't want scientists trying to change them any more than you'd like all your men driven out of existence. Sapiens think there is something wrong with Connipians but, in truth, the two species have simply evolved differently. Sapiens believe their outcome is balanced but it doesn't stop them raping Connipians; they seem to be the more imbalanced from the Connipian perspective. Connipians have never been so arrogant about their particular circumstance. Nor do they imagine a God approving or disapproving their every move. The way Connipians procreate is contrary to anything you are familiar with. They share those few men around. Must, anything less and Connipians would simply fade away, last no more than four or five generations. They care for all the males collectively, let them preserve their energy for their principal function. I think there are many stranger practices in the animal kingdom. Zoologists say they all come about through evolutionary necessity. Connipians wouldn't argue with that. My friend, the most daring of them to live, the most willing to interact with the hostile world—Klapakipsy, her name—understood Sapiens sexuality, as Sapiens seem not to know themselves. Wished to use her charms to win favours as she'd seen or read to occur in New York and all the other cities. Not to engage with them, no Connipian wants sex with a Sapiens. That is a vile myth. She knew she had to charm them, had noted that certain women are apt to. It is how they get their way. She knew that a miniature hairless white-skinned girl wrapped in blue leaves would never be listened to; she could play at being someone else for a time. Catch the attention of men.'

After this long speech, which Ailsa felt to be unfinished, Tonkin fell silent. Ailsa continued to look to her, expecting more. Once or twice, Tonkin rolled her eyes to the ceiling. Ailsa became aware of music playing in the dining room, the one they were shut out of. A piano. It sounded like a live performer, a pianist at the keys. The types of classical pieces everyone has heard before. The Moonlight Sonata. A waiter put his head around the door and it stirred Tonkin from her reverie. A light shake of her head and the waiter left.

'She was good to me. A most considerate girl, young but wise. I fear she was taken advantage of. And in the manner which she had always sought to avoid. All illegal but that is to no avail. Connipians cannot enter courtrooms. Quite literally. Their clicking would mean nothing, we interpreters not trusted to the degree that would give them a hearing. Dogs in court: you've heard that phrase already, I take it.' Ailsa nodded, it was already in her span of awareness. 'I fear Klapakipsy had a Mixed-Up. One of the girls alluded to it yesterday when I tried to broach the subject. The trouble is, they are so private they don't exactly spell anything out. And he or she could, to this day, be living in East Town or possibly going back and forth between there and wherever Klapakipsy lives now. Accepted or rejected; I've no insight into how that has gone. I am unable to help her. Cannot help my friend. The British have revoked my passport, shocking but there it is. I've been travelling on a Netherlands passport since nineteen fifty-three. Discretionary, I lived there for the shortest time but I think they'll let me keep it. I've been on Dutch television a couple of times, it helps. Might you ever go to Connipia, Ailsa?'

The question jumped out of the blue; she couldn't picture it at all. Didn't wish to sound rude, simply couldn't see how it might happen. 'Will I? Well, I would love to. I don't know. I...'

'I believe your department is likely to win a concession. Would you be able to...?'

'My husband...' As soon as she said it, Ailsa found herself laughing. Not even her usual laugh. Heartily, and yet tears came into her eyes. '...he's not a very good one,' she told Tonkin. 'If I can go to Connipia, then I shall.'

The Mixed-Up looked back at her with a frown. Turned it into a smile after a moment's contemplation. 'Whatever you think is right for you.'

It was after this realisation of Ailsa's—joined to her husband by only the flimsiest piece of paper—that Tonkin, utilising teeth to remove it from her bag, passed Ailsa a letter. Explained that she had typed it herself wearing a pointer cap. A headpiece with a digit centre-front which, with careful dipping of the head, enabled her to write privately. A letter for Klapakipsy. 'Pass it to her, please. She deserves all the help she can get, and I believe most of the Connipians blame her for the apparent failure of the conference. Didn't grasp, as I did, that she put in more than any Connipian has before. She ran up against Sapiens intransigence, of course. That wasn't her shortcoming. I even feel it was mine: we knew Sapiens wouldn't understand clicking, but they didn't grasp my reification of those well-honed thoughts. It was my fault on one level or another.'

Ailsa stared at the letter clutched between her fingers. 'I'm only a typist, a shorthand typist,' she said, and found herself reddening up at the possibility Tonkin might misconstrue the term. 'I don't think people like me go out on field missions.'

'Well keep it, dear. Worth a chance from my point of view. I do so want Klapakipsy to hear from me again.'

'Can't...can't...could one of the Connipians take it back for you?'

'They search them, dear. Every time one comes back to the island. As I said, my name is mud, and I'm not trying to land a Connipian in trouble.'

'Or should I ask Roger...Professor Curtis...ask if he would take it...'

'I can't really trust a man who is leading the encroachment.' Tonkin was shaking her head. And it was that phrase which took Ailsa the longest time to understand. She took the letter, accepted that she should show it to no one. Had always thought that Roger was one of the good guys in this faraway drama, disconcerting that Tonkin didn't quite see it that way.

* * *

A young woman in a long black skirt with white frills on its hem and sleeves enters the room carrying a tray of sandwiches. He says it isn't a colony then dresses the serving girl up in Victoriana; Ailsa notes with relief that she isn't Connipian. Thornhill is good on his word to that small extent. Lady Thornhill invites them all to eat, take from the tray. Fillings of corned beef and piccalilli, grilled sardines in tomato sauce. Ailsa is sure it all comes out of a tin. Daft. Connipia produces plenty of food these days. Big farms on the flatlands; Connipians never tore into the soil as the Sapiens do. Steve Frame tucks in, understands how politeness works. Cherie Thornhill scarcely even picks at it; Ailsa sees her mother corner the poor girl. The teen might be more lovestruck than Ailsa; even the two older ladies look at Steve with every other glance. He draws the eye. She hears Lady Thornhill ask Cherie to supervise the Grace children, advises that Bryony will assist. Ailsa cannot hear all the conversation, sees Cherie leading them all away in quick time—dainty little plates held in their hands—some other room to play in. Large mansion, plenty of choice. And for today at least, Cherie consents to going with the children. Out of sight.

Lady Thornhill then occupies the Grace adults. Seems to be showing them many items that have accrued in this large hall. Holds a small brass telescope in her hands. 'It came here with The John and Lodowicke,' she boasts. Ailsa has read all about them, a coarse band who belonged to some wobbly and long-forgotten religion, sailed from the Thames to chance upon this forested land. Would that it had forever evaded discovery.

Governor Thornhill inflexes his head towards the fine upholstered chairs. Ailsa and Steve are to sit. Sit and talk. 'Stephen,' he begins, 'I am sorry if my daughter embarrassed you earlier.'

'Not at all. A high-spirited joke.'

'My own thoughts, Stephen. And she holds you in very high regard. I must admit I am not familiar with pop singers, with your music, I'm sorry to say. Asked a question or two before you came. I was pleased—very pleased—with the answers received. You sound to be of a more solid character than half the musicians and pop singers of today. Renzo, is he called? Clever on the guitar but a cad with the ladies, that's what I hear. He's top of the pop-charts today, I gather. Then it'll be you again tomorrow, what!'

'I've heard that about him, sir, but I don't know Dario Renzo personally. Rumours are only...'

'Yes, yes. And you and Miss...Miss...'

'Donaldson,' says Ailsa.

'...Miss Donaldson, seem to be cut from a different cloth.'

'Yes,' says Frame, tentatively. 'I think we are.'

'I've got nothing to do with pop music,' states Ailsa. 'I work at The Reeve-Muggleton. Once assisted some studies out in the field. That was a long while ago. There was more contact back then.'

'Yes, yes,' says Governor Thornhill. 'Ha. And you want to go back out there.'

'I'd love to...'

'And Mr Frame, how would you describe the venture you wish to make? Why do you want to enter the protected areas?'

'Sir Desmond, I'm keen only to learn from those who know the Connipians better. It stands to reason that they will know themselves best of all. Nothing would please me more than to meet one or two, to meet one of the fellas—the males—I think that would be extraordinary, but I do understand how sensitive it is.'

'Yes, yes. But why exactly?'

'Well, I hope I don't sound naïve, but I think I can learn something. A people whose way of life has been unchanged in hundreds of thousands of years. I don't mean to pooh-pooh our progress—hell, there were no rockstars back in Tudor times—but everything we have done feels precarious. Temporary. I'd like to see something that has stood the test. Meet the guys who've done that, forged a more certain path. Found satisfaction.'

'And you see, Stephen, to me that does sound frightfully naïve, not that it disinclines me to permit it. If you learn something I've missed, then please tell. I need a dual reason if I am to allow it. There are many fiddly little rules I have to apply when granting permits. Not made up by me; the protectorate authority is an international body these days. Every trip out there needs to be for the furtherance of Sapiens and Connipian understanding. At least in principle. If the blighters won't learn what we impart that's their look out. We can only try, ensure the monitoring authority knows that we do as they've asked. And you see, your point about their finding satisfaction, well, it's moot. I really don't know if Connipians are contented or not. Not sure they experience emotions like we do. I'm not supposed to say primitive, so let us call them less sophisticated. They can't envisage better than what they have. If that's satisfaction it's over a very low bar. I fear my daughter, Cherie—who adores you, Mr Frame, you and your music—I think she has yet to find satisfaction with her life. I'd like her to accompany you. Your girl here, Donaldson, too, of course. And then there would be a couple of medical chappies I can call upon. Government payroll. We are overdue a sickness audit. The purpose of the foray will be to survey and assess the health of Connipians. As lay people, you will be able to comment on their general mental health. We're worried about that, the isolation they crave. And we don't send psychiatrists in there. No point: Freud and Jung and all the rest of them make no more sense than the clicking of the little Connipians. And we do try to conduct these surveys periodically, whether they cooperate fully or not. Your views...' Sir Desmond looks enquiringly into the eyes of first Steve, and then Ailsa. '...on how satisfied or frustrated they are will be valued, sir, Miss Donaldson. See if you can help Cherie to contribute, to focus and contribute.

'Are you saying we would have direct communication?'

'Certainly, most certainly.'

'And how? The doctors don't click, do they?'

Steve Frame meant no joke by his question, Ailsa is sure of it. Still the Governor hoots like he's heard it at the London Palladium. 'We've some Mixed-Ups we use as interpreters. One of them will go. They're no trouble; not the ones we've trained up.'

'And Cherie wants to go out there?'

'Not been bothered about it before but I believe she would follow you to the south pole. And into the forest here will be good for her—her profile—coax her into penning some assessment or other into the health survey. A positive article in The Islander would be good for her. For my wife and I, frankly, before now she's rather let us down on the public-relations front. A photo of her assisting the health audit if you can get one. Maybe say she's explaining the vaccination programme through the Mixed-Up. I am using you as bait, you see, Stephen. I hope you don't mind. It would be a tall order getting you into the forest otherwise, of course. Very tall.'

Ailsa raises an eyebrow, lowers it as quickly as she is able. A bit hare-brained of this old-toff. Trying to win over his daughter by sending her on a date in the forest with a rockstar. She worries that her own role is primarily to see neither Cherie nor Steve oversteps the mark. Keep it chaste. She finds herself wishing it was just she and Steve going out there. A crush doesn't leave of its own accord; she'd forgotten what they felt like but she had a couple back on her first island. When she was Cherie's age. If Frame sticks with his game plan, he will take advantage of neither of them. That's how she reads it. Hard to make him out, he seems more gentlemanly than she first imagined rock singers ever could be. Copes with the Governor effortlessly.

'I haven't read about sickness among Connipians,' says Steve. 'What are they most vulnerable to.'

'Hard to tell, Stephen. We simply do our best to find out. Offer medical assistance which they always refuse. It was many from the Americas—Brazil, Columbia, Yanks and Canada too—who insisted upon it. Wrote it into the plan for their long-term protection. All about the history of their continent, you see. Their anxieties more than ours. Small pox and cholera have never been an issue down here.'

'But have they succumbed to influenza, measles? Those things?'

'I wonder? We don't see their dead, so I really wonder if they've lost a few that way. Through the interpreters, they say not. We struggle to trust it. The scientists will try to take samples...'

'I thought that was prohibited.' Again, Ailsa cannot help herself from interrupting the Governor.

'We do it for their own good; something of a veterinary service, if you'll forgive the phrase.'

She doesn't. Tries to arrange her stony face into the needed smile. Let Steve do the talking; he is far more relaxed than Ailsa can manage and it isn't the pomp of the occasion bothering her. By the time Lady Thornhill and the Graces have done the rounds of the artifacts in the room, the plan is in place. Sir Desmond gave Ailsa no more than a stern look for the imprudence of her interruption. She acquiesced. Asked no more. A visit to the forest remains on the cards.

'The party will go out on the twenty-fourth of this month. I trust you can concur with that,' says Sir Desmond.

Ailsa looks around at Steve just as he has turned to her. She smiles instinctively when his gorgeous blue eyes meet hers while worrying that he cannot wait that long. The corners of his lips rise ever so slightly. He must be a born optimist to make his way from London out here in order to meet Connipians. It is not really done, and yet he is on the cusp of accomplishing it. The fourteen-day wait could be a sticking point. When is his next concert? She doesn't really know how rockstars spend their days; could be a cushier number than tending bar at The Reeve-Muggleton. Frame holds the Governor's gaze—no immediate reply—she wonders if he is calculating the level of sacrifice required. Then he turns to her, to Ailsa. 'Can you be free at that time?'

This is a simple question. Ailsa's care of Mannay in the hotel basement is a complication, but she has no interest in her job. Has remained on Connipia mostly in the hope of coming across another opportunity to go into the forest. 'I can arrange it. I'd love to help Cherie get the most from her forthcoming experience.'

'Good girl,' says Governor Thornhill.

4.

Ailsa came to this island in nineteen sixty-five. Two years divorced and foolishly muddled up in what she, benefiting from four years of unencumbered hindsight, has come to think of as a fling. A dalliance with Call-me-Roger of all people. It was a serendipitous mistake. Never worked out if she had true feelings for him or if it was all a scam on her part. On the part of her fiendish unconscious. There was a time when she thought him infinitely better than Conrad, surely the flimsiest of measures. In the wider world, Roger stood for better things than Conrad, on the relationship front he treated her far worse. A secretary he could have his wicked way with. The notion of her unconscious pretending she was in love explains it best, start to finish. Take me to Connipia, that was the top and bottom of their curious amour whether she knew it or not. Twenty-eight years her senior—that's a dozen more than Conrad—he was known as Canada's leading authority on them. The other human species. Ailsa typed it once or twice, so it was probably a conceited self-declaration which no one who knew better bothered to challenge. And he was sympathetic towards them, that was the contrast with Conrad. It may have been a simplistic measure that she took to mean more than it ever could. Didn't make him such a stand-up guy if you think over how he treated his own wife.

Roger Curtis was an early advocate of equality for Connipians even when he also wished to weigh and measure, pinch, prod and photograph them. Write scholarly articles about those who need leaving alone. Perhaps it is still his thing, Ailsa has long been out of touch. When she came here, same plane and then boat as Roger, he was married to a woman his own age. Probably still is. And Mrs Curtis was ever a housewife, never an anthropologist. Ailsa understood, felt highly self-conscious about the fact, that her inclusion in the working party which visited Connipia was really just Roger's treat to himself. Illicit company he alone could wangle during a four-month stay in the abandoned Blue Houses at Trick Point. Whatever contact and interaction he hoped to have with the Connipians, he must have been expecting far more from her. She had all too willingly acquiesced to his sexual advances three months earlier. Doing it after hours in a professor's office was not even comfortable, any pleasure she took was from the thought that he found her attractive. Stupid to look back on: all men of Professor Curtis's age find all girls of Ailsa's then-age desirable.

And she still had that letter from Tonkin to deliver, not that she ever discussed it with Roger. Tonkin had sworn her to secrecy in their only evening in each other's company.

Ailsa's position in the survey team was always a strange one. A very competent administrator; a very proactive organiser of any demand Roger made. Public or private: circulation of briefing notes to post-graduates; hotels booked for visitors from Cornell; the colour of her underwear.

Two of the other three anthropologists on the trip were males no more than five years older than her; the third, Lynne Sharpe, was a woman of forty-five. It didn't matter how well Ailsa did her job, she hadn't the qualifications they had. She came here only as his mistress, and they knew it. Never raised the matter—not with him, she's pretty sure about that: no one was going to fall out with Call-Me-Roger and put at risk their participation in the trip of a lifetime—it didn't stop them from knowing.

Their arrival on Connipia coincided with a time of extraordinary change. The last days of Governor Salt. An old patrician who Harold MacMillan had put in place; the international observers had been getting steamed up about too many breaches of the nineteen-fifty accord, and Salt was to be a steady hand. He used the autonomy of the position in surprising ways. Granted access to far more missions which could have caused upset but he also took Connipian rights more seriously than any other governor before or since. Better than the current duffer, Thornhill, or Salt's predecessor who unashamedly boosted timber exports. Learning today that Salt also employed two Connipians among his household staff—slaves: they have never worked for money—is surprising and upsetting. Even the best of the British upper class are a bunch of hypocrites deep down.

Memories of her first weeks here are dreamlike. The last days of the person she used to be. Sailed into Charlestown, and spent only two nights in town before heading out. She didn't join the Protection Authority briefings. No other anthropological mission brought admin with them. The Authority for the Protection of *Homo Connipus* was the grand title; Ailsa filed the notes. Two sides of A4 on which it was noted four times that there were to be no photographs of the girls who rove the forest topless. It was a big deal. Could have caused a terrible stink if the wrong kind of magazine printed them. It looked like the only tangible point the Island Authority made in three ninety-minute meetings.

Ailsa doesn't believe anyone currently working at The Reeve-Muggleton noticed or remembered her from those first two nights. She spent a substantial proportion of the time in the room she shared with Professor Curtis. Always skinny; green eyes beneath black hair; skin which takes all summer to move from the palest white to the bronze that residency on Connipia has now bequeathed her. Not much for anyone but Roger to remember. Shy in those days, her face hidden behind a fringe, seldom looking directly at anyone for most of the two days in which she mooched about this very hotel. Too much of it spent lying beneath the grunting professor. He seemed invigorated just by being on the island he'd spent half a lifetime studying. Sex in a bed rather than having to stand against his office wall. That was an improvement but not anything to write home about. She had yet to meet a Connipian in the field.

She recalls dinner at the hotel, the night before they were to set out for Trick Point. The Canadians all ate together. The two young postgrads drank a skinful, knowing it would be the last opportunity in some while. Roger and Lynne, perhaps showing their ages, went up to their respective rooms once dessert was eaten. Ailsa discreetly asked Roger if he would like her to go up with him; he said, 'No. You have more in common with these young people.' Those were his exact words. It seemed like an admission of her purpose. Good administrative skills and a good lay, the latter from the perspective only of an old professor and he had availed himself of that twice before dining. She had little in common with him, served a function much as blotting paper does.

The two postgrads had, to Ailsa, always seemed rather serious young men. Brian and Logan, both aspiring to emulate Roger Curtis, acquire and disseminate knowledge of Connipian habit and culture. And now here they were letting their hair down. They ordered another round of pints, despite complaining all evening about the quality of the island's only brew, Muggs Ale, as it has always been called. It must have improved since then: in these last two years, she has poured thousands of pints of the stuff.

One of the young men bought her a pint. Insisted she join their drinking fun. Mostly they were taking a rise out of Lynne Sharpe. Two fingers of beer for the one whose impersonation of her slovenly walk was the poorest; whose anecdote—delivered in Lynne's monotonous voice—about fieldwork in the Amazon a decade earlier, was the most interesting and hence the least authentic; which of them could, like Lynne, give their hips a wiggle and still look entirely sexless. Ailsa had not noticed this quality in their colleague, and the boys repeatedly told her she had lost. Too sexy. Two fingers of the foul ale, and try again.

'You don't do this about Roger, do you?' she asked, feeling herself redden as she said it. Intrigued to learn.

'Take off Roger?' queried Logan. Then he slipped off his barstool and put his nose within an inch of Ailsa's. 'Dictation, Mrs Klassen. Take down my words, take them right down. Can I take anything down for you?'

'Miss Donaldson,' she told him. 'I'm Miss Donaldson. Divorced.'

'Oh, I like the sound of that,' said Logan, still putting on his Call-Me-Roger voice. 'Would you like me to take it down, Mrs Klassen.'

Ailsa gave the face invading her personal space the tiniest of slaps. His affrontery deserved it but she was never one to lash out. By the time her hand hit his cheek, it was a playful tap.

Logan took a hold of her wrist. 'Oh, Mrs Divorcee, as a leading authority on cross-cultural signals, I can attest that this is true sexual chemistry we have unearthed. Between the youth of Ottawa and the living dead. My word, you have unearthed something within me.'

'Leave her be,' snapped Brian.

'Jealous, are you?' Logan tipped himself back on to his stool. 'Honestly, Ailsa. It debases you. Don't be a field-wife to a researcher with a proper one back home. You'll end up with a little Mixed-Up baby. You know how it works don't you?'

Ailsa's cheeks glowed a shade of red which she doubted the gloomy bar could disguise. Felt the heat in her cheeks without so much as touching them. And she knew her anger stemmed from the truth within Logan's cruel words. She knew it then as she does on thinking it over now. 'I feel for them, you know. Every field trip seems to result in more Mixed-Ups in East Town. You men are terrible. If I keep Roger from doing that, it will have been worth it.'

Logan laughed in her face; her riposte was stupid. Not entirely, and still the stupidest thing to say out loud. 'You could keep Brian and I away from the little girlies while you're at it. Be a sport.'

'Shut it, Logan,' said Brian.

5.

Ailsa tugs forward the wooden handle of the beer pump. Pints of Muggs Ale for the two men before her. Thickset men, shorthair, closely shaven, who wear smart white shirts, top buttons open. She guesses them miners or loggers, hard to distinguish once they've scrubbed up. They are each onto a fourth pint. Have become a bit obvious when they try to look down her dress.

She is in good spirits, a trip to the Blue Houses only four days away, asks the men their names—it's Roland and Benny—asks if it is their first time on the island. They cut down trees, she hears; dislikes learning it while feeling no surprise. It's a bit sickening. They begin to tell her where they can find AFCs a decent distance from any Connipian settlement. Utter nonsense: it's a small island, everything is close. The mnemonic stands for *Alia Folia Crescente*, the scientific name of a tree unique to the island. They are growing elsewhere now, places with similar climates, only here are there specimens already hundreds of years old. Ripe for turning into elegant and expensive furniture. AFCs have four different types of leaf on a single tree; the wood is pale and the grain of it a dark contrast. The Connipians want none cut down. They cultivate their fruit farms high up in the sky, in the canopies of the mixed forest. Plenty of AFCs in there—might be crucial—the Sapiens have understood little of their pomiculture.

'I take it you have permits,' says Ailsa, knowing that this conversation could quickly turn sour.

'Ha,' Benny laughs. 'This isn't our proper job, Ailsa, darling. Thornhill's gardeners back home. That's us. This is the best bit of freelancing a man with a saw has ever done.'

'Sorry, you're Governor Thornhill's gardeners. Isn't his garden in Charlestown?'

'We work on his estate back home. Frome in Somerset.'

'He gave permits to his own gardeners!'

Roland gives her a wink. Mouths the word permits as if she's told a joke of some subtlety.

'Have you had contact with them?' she asks, trying to mask the disapproval she feels. 'With the Connipians?'

'They come and watch, mostly keep well back.'

'Timber!' calls Benny, a hand to his mouth covering the grin on his smug face.

'We'd like them closer. Can hardly see their titties when they're standing that far away.'

'You know they're only children. If they're uncovered...on top, as you say. You know that, don't you? They're children.'

'Not really kiddies when their tits have swelled up. Not on my watch.'

'Just leave them alone,' snaps Ailsa. 'And drink up. You've been in my bar long enough.'

'Not children at all,' Benny repeats, holding Ailsa in a long stare. 'No Connipians in the garden back at Aldbury, are there, Roly.'

'Cherie's been known to sunbathe, not that we can lay a finger on the boss's daughter.'

'Enough! Out!'

'Just finishing our little drink. Enjoying a little chat.'

She removes their glasses. Tips the remaining drink into the sink. Time's up for this pair.

* * *

Ted from reception walks towards her, a frown on his face. Ailsa wonders if the loggers she saw off the premises have complained. She couldn't care less, has determined already that she will be leaving the island once she's back from the trip to the Blue Houses. The management at The Reeve-Muggleton have promised to keep her job open for her, but she'll advise them not to bother. Never thought she'd stay as long as she has. London or Sydney, a return to Canada: it's time to move along. She wishes she could get every last Sapiens to leave the island with her. Impossible, and it's the only solution to the problem which obsesses her.

'Miss Donaldson,' says Ted in a low voice, 'the gentleman in the Van Diemen Suite would like you to ...' At this point, Ted pauses, coughs, waves a hand as if it is burning, although it clearly isn't. '...help him with a girl.'

'Really? Well, I can't do anything for him. Not until I've finished up here. And I don't see how it's my business.'

'I shall relieve you, Miss Donaldson. I understand the girl in question is Governor Thornhill's daughter.'

'Oh, now it makes sense.' Ailsa doesn't even try to feign the shock which Ted's facial contortions implore of her. Charlestown is far more provincial than Ottawa or Toronto. Prince Edward Island too, she supposes. This is nineteen sixty-nine. A woman in a man's hotel room really isn't much of a scandal anywhere except here.

'I think Steve will hope I can get her to leave, Ted. It's not for a threesome. It's really not.'

As she walks towards the backstairs, Ailsa laughs to herself. The stuffed shirt went bright red, perhaps she shouldn't have said it. And maybe a threesome will be requested on arrival in the room. Seems unlikely but sharing afternoon tea proved little. She likes Steve rather a lot: there are no circumstances in which she would get up to anything

God Help the Connipians

amorous with him while there's another girl in the room.

* * *

'I've not touched her,' says Frame, as she gives him her most questioning look.

Cherie is on the couch; she twitches but could be asleep. A short blue skirt, mock Connipian, riding up her thighs. Showing the Governor's daughter's lace knickers. At least they are still up where they should be.

'She showed up here three sheets to the wind. Said she wanted to talk about the trip; I let her in before I realised quite how far gone she was.'

'You think it's only booze. What does she do? Rum? There could be hashish on the island. Homegrown, the climate's right for growing it, I'm told.'

'Vermouth. That's what she smelt of.'

He got close enough to smell her breath; she thinks she ought to do the same. Girls must look after girls, rockstars have no part in it. One way or another she needs to keep both girl and parents on board with the outing to the forest. She crouches down next to the couch, tries to sniff Cherie's gentle breathing.

'A hell of a lot of Vermouth, by the look of it. What's this?' Ailsa gestures the small dining table in Frame's suite. Two opened bottles of wine, one white, one red.

'...Yeah. She arrived while I was having a quiet drink. Insisted on joining me.'

'Great, so you're getting Thornhill's precious baby legless as preparation for a trip out to the Blue Houses? Good plan, Steve.'

'It's not how it was. You know I don't like to say no. I gave her a glass of white. She must have the same with every meal up at the mansion. You'd think so, right?'

'...in your hotel room. Not the best look.' Ailsa eases herself down onto the couch, beside the drunken girl. Leans in to try and sense how deeply she is asleep. Cherie lets out a little groan, and then her hands are upon Ailsa, one at each ear, clutching at her thin black hair. Cherie pushes her own face forward, eyes still closed, and starts to kiss Ailsa on the mouth. Ailsa's hair is in the other girl's grip, and she winces as she tries to extricate herself.

'Beautiful, Steve, beautiful,' mumbles the young girl.

'Not Steve,' says Ailsa. 'Open up those eyes.'

Like a new-born kitten, she lets her startled eyes take in whose voice it is; begins to laugh uncontrollably when she sees. 'Come on, baby,' she says, trying for another kiss, although Ailsa is not her beloved popstar.

'N-no.'

'Not my thing either,' slurs Cherie, 'but One-Eyed Temple is playing hard to get.'

'You're a minor, Cherie,' he tells her. Still standing, keeping a safe distance from the funny physical melee. 'And I don't do groupies. Never have.'

She continues to laugh. 'I'm seventeen, Steve. Do what I like. And I'm not asking you to *do* groupies. I am singular. Or did you invite Thin-Thin here to spice it up your way?'

'I'm sorry, Ailsa,' says Steve. 'Cherie, we're off together on Monday morning. Don't call my friend anything but Ailsa, all right?'

'Can I call her a cracking kisser?'

'I don't think so.'

'Cherie,' says Ailsa, 'we're going to get along fine, it's just tonight you're a bit tiddly.'

Cherie Thornhill pulls herself up from her slouched position, pulls down the hem of her short blue skirt. 'Caught you looking,' she directs at Steve. Then she lifts herself up from the couch, seems unsure of her balance for a moment before walking very slowly and deliberately across the room, one foot placed directly in front of the other, not allowing the heels of her feet to touch the ground. Ailsa thinks she might be mimicking the catwalk. Waits for the girl to speak. Explain the strange poise with which she moves; mock high-heeled shoes although she walks barefoot. Steve exchanges a glance with Ailsa, his face a question mark. The room has an infestation of girls in short skirts. Even Ailsa's black hotel-issue cocktail dress has risen up as she leans back on the couch.

'A straight line, you see,' declares Cherie. 'Not so drunk after all.' She looks far more alert than she did when Ailsa entered. 'Now then, Miss Donaldson—sorry if saying thin offended you, I'm the other way so it's only jealousy—why don't you and I have a little drinky-poo. Get to know each other before we all go out into the forest together. I think my father has asked you along as a chaperone.' She gives a little laugh. 'You have to make sure Steve here doesn't take advantage of me...'

'That's not why she's coming,' says Steve.

'...and I don't shag the living daylights out of him. It might be more my thing than meeting the little people.' She begins to laugh at her own brash talk.

'You're embarrassing him,' says Ailsa.

'Look, Cherie, Ailsa is coming because she has knowledge of the Connipians. She's met some before. Been out into the forest. It's like nowhere else on Earth, you know.'

'Yeah, yeah, yeah. Titchy-tiny people. Mostly girls. Nothing to be scared of that I can see.' She reaches for the white wine bottle. 'Come on Ailsa. That really was a lovely kiss. I'm not that way—had my eyes closed and thought I was kissing Steve—I reckon you could turn me. Very, very good. Would you be the butch one, or must it be me?'

'I don't think you should drink anymore.'

'Ailsa, I'm pretty close to sober. Play acted so that Steve might—you know—give it a go.'

'Cherie, I need you to leave if you keep talking like this.'

'Sorry, Steve, but I'm into Ailsa now. That all right, girlfriend? I'll take it no further than you let me.'

'Cherie...'

'Do you want a glass too, Steve?' Cherie looks alert, a steady hand as she pours the wine, passes a glass to Ailsa. The slurring of her earlier speech is undetectable. Must have been acting, good at it too.

'Okey-dokey, Cherie. Let's get to know each other.'

Steve shakes his head. Probably did call her up here as pest control, and now the pair hold glasses of wine in their hands. Settling in, side by side on the sofa.

'Good kiss, by the way,' says Ailsa, and Cherie laughs long and hard.

* * *

'I love your accent,' says the younger girl.

'Yep, it's mine. Now finally tell us why they threw you out of boarding school.'

'Steve and I have those whiny English voices, southern poshies. I think yours is much more natural.'

'Hey,' says Steve, relaxing into another glass of red, 'my voice is my fortune.'

'Yeah, yeah. But you sing with an American accent which you don't actually have. Nobody sings like the dear old Queen. Everybody does your California twang except the opera singer Renzo used on his big hit.'

'My accent is not American. Definitely Canadian,' says Ailsa. 'Never been to the United States. Not outside of an airport.'

'Steve's been,' says Cherie. 'Toured all the major cities.'

'You're not getting out of the boarding school tale this easily.'

'Really, Ailsa, don't be a prig. Falling foul of a stuck-up school is the easiest thing. Vodka and drugs are pretty much on tap in all of them, you see. That would do the trick. And not much needed on the drug front, one little joint or a tab of whatever, that would...' Cherie looks down her nose, impersonates the snob she will surely one day become. '...ease one's way out the door.' She sniggers at herself, reverts to her slightly slacker, teenaged speaking manner. 'Then there's sex with the young Latin teacher, or the sports mistress if that's your bag. Some girls try that route.'

'Which was it, then? What did you do?'

'Oh...' She leans back on the sofa, hands behind her head. A mock yawn. '...the tried and trusted is far too passé for me. Mine was an obscene publication. Just a little something to offend everyone.'

'Jesus, really?' says Steve.

'Oh dear, oh dear. I seem to have shocked you. How simply delicious. Won't let me undress in the privacy of your room and now it seems you don't like dirty pictures either.'

'I don't like obscene pictures, Cherie. I really don't. You weren't...it didn't...the photographs.' He is unable to make his point.

'Look! Our Steve is interested after all. You imagine away at dirty snaps of little me, Mr One-Eyed Temple. But no, I've been in embarrassing photographs but that was only coming away from parties and what have you. Never stooped to all that legs-apart stuff. A girl has standards.'

'Come on, Cherie. Explain what you did to get expelled. Who did you take pictures of?'

'Make a guess, my Canadian friend.'

'Your too-willing sports mistress.'

'Ha-ha. You like the idea that I'm a girl's girl. Fill up my wine glass and we can have another little snog if you like.'

'No. I don't like. Who were the pictures of?'

'Sorry to disappoint; it was a prank. A top-shelf magazine I bought in the newsagents. The man serving was more embarrassed than me, honestly. "Is Starkers any good?" I asked. "Will it turn me on." Wouldn't look at me and I bet he knew the answer. Might have jizzed himself to that very mag night after night. But he wouldn't say a peep about it to me just because I was wearing my school uniform. He talks dirty to them if they're wearing gymslips in the pictures, you can bet. Is that right, Steve?'

The rocker shakes his head. 'A shocking industry,' he mutters.

'Well, he took my money, slid it silently into his cash till. Didn't ask about my age because I wasn't pretending to be old enough. There you go, that was my publication before I edited it. Bespoke pornography for St Hilda's alone. Boarding school is full of evening activities, you see. At ours there was an art club which nobody supervised. No teacher, it was nominally my job as I was in Sixth. I went through the magazine, picture after picture. Girls with bosoms twice the size of yours, Ailsa. More than twice actually, nothing ungainly about you. The girls in the mag looked unnatural. Like they'd been inflated. I glued about a hundred little photocopies of Miss Statham's head—horn-rimmed glasses and all— over the girls in the magazine displaying their wares. Honestly, Steve, you men look at the most awful stuff. I'm up for anything and even I thought they were disgusting."

'Mrs Statham?' asks Ailsa.

'Miss. The big bad headmistress. Some called her St Hilda on account of that being the name of the school. She was the school, you see. Headmistress: big cheese. I think I stuck in a few cut-outs of other teachers too. Jolly-Hockey-Sticks Houghton was in there. She had to be; I expect she loved it. The big lezzer might do the very same poses every lunchtime in the staff room.'

'How did you get caught?'

'Grassed on, of course. There are an awful lot of sneaks in a girl's school. I thought everyone knew that.'

'You left the magazine in the art room?'

'Better than that. I labelled it **St Hilda's Hotties** and pinned it to the school noticeboard. Art needs an audience, Ailsa. That, too, is common knowledge.'

Ailsa looks drily at the bad girl; a million miles from her own teenage years. Growing up in Kensington, Prince Edward Island, was a simpler affair. Misbehaviour rare, seldom involved girls. Never Ailsa Donaldson. She lets a smile come to her lips, more broadminded today than when she was a teenager. 'You were hoping for an expelling then?'

'Couldn't stay in that hole. And...' Cherie's voice has a little slur in it now, going into a third glass of wine and whatever she had before entering Steve's suite. '...it's pretty rotten having parents on the other side of the world. No idea what they're up to, and then they set Miss Statham's secret police loose on me. Beastly of them to do that, alone in England.'

'You know, Cherie, I feel sorry for rich kids. School was straightforward for me. My parents were straightforward too.' She stops herself. Notices that she is a little tipsy herself. Doesn't wish to say anything about losing her mother when she was Cherie's age.

The Governor's daughter drapes an arm around Ailsa's shoulders. 'Tell me. Tell me what normal people are like.'

'There actually aren't any but I suppose I'm close enough.'

'Normal sounds dull,' says Steve. 'You're anything but that. A cool head, I'd say.'

'A cool head sounds equally dull, Steve,' lectures Cherie. 'Ailsa's a cracking kisser, that's what she is. And if she's more normal than you and I, well then, aren't we the freaks?'

* * *

She thinks the little toerag must have spiked her drink. Not sure what with, maybe just a whack of vodka. Cherie's not a serious drinker—more of a prankster—photographed a couple of times when failing to hold her drink. Ailsa has never been one either and now everything has gotten hazy. Drink spiking has done that. She doesn't raise it. Doesn't want the schoolgirl to squeeze any one-upmanship out of a good-humoured evening. It's gotten to the dead of night. They await a taxi for Cherie, who is laughing a lot at other stuff. At herself a bit. Her well-spoken voice has gone to seed. Pretty funny. A lot of lisping, which Cherie doesn't do in real-time. Her parents will have seen her worse, won't get in the newspapers this time. The hotel uses a trustworthy taxi-firm. And, drunk or not, Ailsa can vouch for Steve. Not an improper hand on the little groupie all night. It's about two now. That's what Ailsa thinks.

There is a light rap on the door and Steve answers it. He's the coolest of the three by a country mile. Ailsa can see it and she's three sheets to the wind. Somehow or other she's downed as much grog as the sailors who prowl East Town at this time of night. God knows what she's had; never saw a vodka bottle, but this feels like a lot more than four or five glasses of wine blurring her vision.

'Taxi for Miss Thornhill,' says a hotel busboy. Ailsa is drunk, but she smiles at the boy they call Lodowicke standing outside the door. And he saw her, his waitress colleague, one of two girls in the pop singer's suite. Let them all talk. Nothing happened and if it had it would be less embarrassing than sharing a room with Roger Curtis. She sank so low all those years ago. The staff in this hotel—hotels the world over, she expects—love a bit of gossip. Ailsa in a tryst with Steve Frame: that would be something for them to remember her by.

Cherie turns back into the room, pulling down her short blue skirt, smiling at Steve. Then she steps across, stretches a hand out for Ailsa, as if to pull her from the couch. Might want to share the taxi, unaware of Ailsa's flat below. She rises but will not be going with her.

'It's going to be great going out there with you, Ailsa. Really nice getting to know you this evening.'

How well-mannered she can be; not always—not when she wishes to be ejected from an expensive school—but it's within her. The girl gives Ailsa a hug and it feels sincere. They got a bit pie-eyed, had a good time doing it. Ailsa thought Cherie a good laugh. Immature and funny, stuff she missed out on first time around. 'Take care. Until Monday.' Oh, God. That was one slurred reply.

Then the girl gives Steve Frame a peck on the cheek, and he holds her hand for a moment. A thank you that she has kept her clothes on, thinks Ailsa. Out of the door goes the Governor's daughter, saunters down the corridor with the busboy. Young Lodowicke might be the same age as Cherie Thornhill; he walks two paces behind. Deferential as the hotel expects its staff to be. Must return this one safely to mummy and daddy.

'Sleep here,' Steve tells Ailsa. 'You're not used to knocking back a few, are you?' She's still standing, long after Cherie's parting embrace. Steve wraps his arms around her, hugs her chest to chest. 'Let's get you lying

263

down.' Ailsa offers no resistance as he guides her into his bedroom, begins to unbutton the white blouse she wears atop her crinkly black skirt. Barkeep clothes. For a second, she relishes the surprising feeling of his fingers, welcomes it even as it sobers her. Nice that she gets the nod over Cherie: the young girl has a pretty face when she lets her guard down.

'No! Stop! I thought you didn't do any of this.'

'Not guilty. I was just helping you…I'll be on the couch.'

'No, no, no. I'll go to my room, thank you.' She feels a panic welling inside her. The pull of staying, of making love to Steve Frame is strong, but through her foggy alcohol-laden brain she fears trying to have any kind of conversation about contraception. The consequence of having none. Frame won't get that. It's nineteen sixty-nine and she's spent the last four years in this backwater.

'Much easier to stay…I think you're very drunk.'

'I think you planned it…spiked my…walk me to my room, please. It's on the lower ground floor, number four. Hold me steady, please, and no hands where they shouldn't go. Oh hell! Can you get these buttons back in their holes, please?'

* * *

Back in her own room—Steve Frame forbidden from putting a single foot over the threshold, for more reasons than she could give him—Ailsa listens out for Mannay's snoring. The light buzz of it stirs the air in the neighbouring room. She tries to imagine whether Steve might have heard it in the corridor but finds herself incapable of such conjecture. Remembered she harbours a Mixed-Up, cannot think clearly beyond that. Gently she opens the bedroom door, goes to look at him, her dependent little friend. He is sound asleep on her bed, covered although the blanket is slipping away to the side. Scrawny body and string arms, encased in a sleep which her presence fails to disturb. Better that way with over-excitable Mannay. The light is dim, two small hopper windows at the height of the outside pavement allow in just a little, the car park lighting remains on throughout the night. Beige curtains take off its sheen; it's a grainy light which illuminates Mannay's thin face. The wispy hair that he won't let her cut. She often imagines that he spends the day looking out of this unrewarding window; may think longingly of the cars on show, just as boys with proper arms seem to do. The instruction is to lie low all day every day. It really isn't much of a life that she's given him. Ailsa unclips her skirt, rolls down her tights. Blouse and bra off, she is too tired to hunt down a nightie. Slides into the bed beside Mannay. Perhaps she is drunk, perhaps she loves him. And Mannay sleeps: the poor boy will never know that he has a bed-mate. For one night only.

Frame

* * *

Much later—morning or night, she cannot tell—her brain feels twice as heavy as it used to be before she went up to the Van Diemen Suite. And he is trying to wake her up, rousing her. Steve Frame, most handsome rockstar in the entire world, lying on top of her. She wanted it, the feel of him between the sheets. Said she didn't, pretended it, knew she did really. Wasn't sure what Frame wanted until tonight—Professor Curtis didn't waste his time on being a gentleman—and now Frame's finally being true to his gender. Horny. It's too dark to see him, and she's too close to the sleep he has aroused her from to take anything in properly. Might miss her own dream come true; sex with a rockstar. Can't make her mouth move, and she really needs to say the condom word. Sort that bit out. She doesn't recall slipping off her knickers, so Frame must have the knack. God, she loves his face. Hewn in stone. Can't see it in this light. Can barely open her eyes. And it's on her neck, not in any kind of sightline. He lies across her naked breast, cock surprisingly small entering where she knows she shouldn't let it. She puts both of her hands to his face, feels saliva upon them. Realises the hair falling to the back of her hands is thin, wispy. Momentarily she holds Mannay to her bosom. What's she doing? What was in that drink? He gurgles noises that she's never heard him make before. Not even when he is alone in the bathroom. She wants to stop him, but hasn't the energy. It doesn't feel quite right, his funny little erection gives her a degree of pleasure, and she wishes it didn't. This cannot become a habit. Too drunk to fight anything, she holds his shoulders gently as the boy shudders and judders.

'No,' she whispers.

'Mannay love Ailsa. Ailsa love Mannay.' His words are more indistinct than ever but those are the ones he has said. She even thinks they are true, but loving of this kind was never meant to be in the picture. She tries to blink herself sober. Mannay still wriggles on top of her, uncomfortable to her as he writhes upon her breasts. He is surely spent; even drunken Ailsa felt that spasm a moment ago. Thank God Mixed-Ups are all infertile. What will he think of her if she tells him she thought he was Steve Frame? Or if she doesn't. A slut: it was the implication of those post-grad boys when she first came here years ago. Of the dirty-minded one, of Logan. Put his hand on her bottom once or twice. Tried it on but she brushed him right off. And now this. Ailsa has done charity work in East Town; this is about a thousand miles above and beyond.

'Ailsa love Mannay,' repeats the Mixed-Up. 'Mannay love Ailsa. Thank you.'

She tries to shake her head but the bloody thing hurts. Brain heavy, it's been playing tricks on her evening and night. Mannay pushes his head up against her neck, dribbles on her collarbone.

6.

Ailsa sat in the back of the land rover with the two young guys. It felt odd and it felt like Carleton University protocol: her lover and his female anthropological colleague—Lynne, not yet a professor but only a rung or two short—were sitting up front. Lynne Sharpe at the wheel, the more confident driver. Call-me-Roger had talked about fieldwork for about a hundred times as many hours as he had actually done any. Lynne was the old hand, half a lifetime out in the wild: Brazil and The Territory of Papua. A term inside Carleton University now and then to get a decent wash.

The route skirted the forest before bringing them properly within it, driving on a track which curved this way and that when it needed to go around some trees which were too grand to fell in the making of this intrusive dirt road. They parked up over half a mile from the abandoned Blue Houses in which they would stay. The approach had not been cleared, ensuring it didn't lose its Connipian feel. This was—those few short years ago—anthropology's most precious jewel. Researchers were able to base themselves in a hamlet frozen in time. Unimaginable time. They did it with tacit Connipian approval, part of the rapprochement that has since dried up. The group of Canadians trekked the last stretch, carrying packs on their backs containing all they would need for their first days out there. Their burdens not so heavy, return trips to Charlestown easy enough to arrange.

Connipia is a small island on the scale of things. The forest was dense, Ailsa found it deathly dark in a few stretches. This unique temperate rainforest has taken thousands of years to grow. Thousands of thousands. Here and there sunlight sliced through the thick foliage. The dark greens and red tints of the massive *photinia ex Connipia* glistened; Roger pointed out all of the island's unique trees he could name. Some spawned multiple leaf types, differing shapes growing at different points in their lofty elevation. The eerie sound of birds high above called them forwards. Screeching and flapping in excess of anything they could observe. An occasional green-and-blue parakeet showed itself at eye level. Ailsa saw—and it looked identical to the picture in the book she had read before coming—an *Anthornis Connipus*. Also known as a bellbird, a black necklace of feathers upon the lightest of greys. She watched it watch the anthropologists passing by, the bird's black eyes blinking not at all. A most contemplative bird. She couldn't bring herself to point it out, being a know-nothing administrator. They all passed its sentry point, only Ailsa aware of the exotic bird's presence.

She walked alongside Roger. Mostly in silence, he would glance across at her now and then, a hesitant smile finding his lips. It was like entering a cathedral so grand was the architecture of these ancient trees. A married man and his lover both equally careful not to let slip a public display of their union. Being pointlessly proper. She could hear Lynne telling Logan or Brian about the footholds on AFCs. Pointing out an example. Stopping to look but not going too close, not wanting to appear interfering should there have been any watching Connipians. The girls have dug grooves into certain trees, used sharp stones for the task. Whether made by girls they might shortly meet or if the footholds were carved several generations earlier, they couldn't be sure. The cuttings on the trees formed ladders for the little Connipian girls; they could scurry up into the dense canopy, at the top of which they practice their curious agriculture. Pomiculture say the textbooks. There was no sign of it down on the forest floor, save a few footholds. Can't see the chimney from the sitting room.

When they arrived at the small clearing, the colour blue flourishing as it never does in nature, Lynne fell to her knees. 'We are here,' she declared to the soil beneath her bowed head. 'Let us take care of these immortal houses.'

Ailsa thought her reaction a bit daft. When they looked directly at the nearest house, there was a Mixed-Up who had come to the doorway, looking down on the praying woman. Not a true prayer, ad hoc. And Connipians pray to no one, give credence only to what is here, practice no sleight of hand. The Mixed-Up would have heard about God from a nun, stared at a cross or two, said some prayers in his youth whether he continued later or not. Some take it seriously, some don't. Adam's little bit on the side.

* * *

Once they saw inside the house assigned to them, they must all have reflected on the truth of their training: they would live outdoors. The Blue House—with its resident interpreter for the Canadians to use should any of the sought-after little ones agree to talk—was of Connipian size. Camp beds crammed it full to bursting. And none could do more than crouch inside their little home, so low were the ceilings of houses made for girls no more than three feet tall. A British anthropologist came over to show them the facilities, explain how Trick Point functioned. One of the Canadians, he said, must sleep in the house across the way. Roger got a little hot under the collar about this; it had never come up during planning. He had not anticipated Bol—that was the name of their intercross assistant—having a room to himself. Hadn't thought about him at all, Ailsa guessed as she watched Roger debate with the Britisher.

And the third room was little more than a box. Barely five feet across any wall. The larger room had floor space for three beds, the other two were both resolutely single.

She listened as Roger debated the best next step. Miles Jackson, the Brit, had thought the younger female in their party—she, Ailsa—would be the ideal candidate to sleep elsewhere. Across the way three British girls and a female Mixed-Up were in residence. A spare bed in a twin room. Roger had not said in advance that he hoped to share a bed with his administrative assistant. Planned to enter her single room night after night. Could not declare the plan: he and his marital status were widely known in academic circles. He understood that he had reserved a space for Ailsa, had already advised her that he would have a section of the shared room, wouldn't clutter hers with his clothing, belongings. Only for show, they both knew there was no hiding anything from their departmental colleagues, but nor would they cause a wider scandal. His oversight about the interpreter made sleeping contrary to the recorded arrangements a leap and bound trickier. Roger asked Lynne if she wished to join the Brits. He got a straight no in reply. Or would a man be welcome? After all, Lynne would be the only female in this house if they followed Miles Jackson's plan. Jackson dismissed the suggestion, queried if Professor Curtis was familiar with the concept of twin rooms. Pulled a face. Miles Jackson might have noted the respective ages of the Canadians and considered it propriety to keep Brian and Logan more than a thin wall from young Ailsa. Could have assumed from Lynne and Roger's respective reputations that there was no need to manipulate their sleeping arrangements. Wrongly so on half a count.

'I'll be fine sleeping with a British girl,' said Ailsa. Was she sounding too keen to get away? Roger might have picked it up. She had felt flattered by the initial interest he took in her, a man so learned, erudite. Pants down they're all the same, and she had come to think her judgement on the topic of men to have run awry each time she'd made a choice. Conrad was a disaster.

There was no way around it. Roger asked her again if she really didn't mind, asked it in front of the man named Miles, and she repeated that sharing with the young Brits would be a pleasure.

As she took her hefty rucksack over to the other house, Logan shouted, 'Frankly, Ailsa, I fancy joining your house,' and she could only bow her head to hide the smile. A bit fresh, it sounded more honest than Roger's selective high-mindedness.

* * *

The first night in a Blue House was yet to feel unreal. She was resting her head in a place not so much unlikely as impossible. Fewer than a hundred and fifty anthropologists from around the world are thought to have experienced this, and Ailsa is hardly one of them. However, a bed is a bed and the mattress beneath her was not as comfortable as the double in The Reeve-Muggleton. Nothing yet compared to dining with Tonkin.

She met and enjoyed the company of the three young Brits: all were at Cambridge University, inspired by the writing of Margaret Mead. Two of them were originally from Scotland; Ailsa's ancestry hails from there but she hadn't been. Still hasn't. She was to share a room with a girl named Michelle, or Dr Firth to those outside her circle of friends. It was an arrangement which Ailsa hoped would put out Roger Curtis's fire. A wish uncovered in just three days on Connipia. There could be no sneaking around this set up; if he asked her, she would refuse. She has thought since that it was Logan's drunken jokes which flicked the switch. So well done, rude boy.

Michelle had been staying in Trick Point for almost a month by this time, had already met with Connipians on several occasions. 'I don't think we should have male researchers in the field out here,' she said to Ailsa in a hushed voice, pointing in the direction of Cammie's room. Cammie the Mixed-Up.

Before they had done much more than show Ailsa where everything was kept—and Ailsa had advised them that she would eat with colleagues from Carleton University so long as the weather remained dry, cooking outside always the plan—she told them she is basically an administrator. Couldn't allow them any illusions about her role or knowledge.

Michelle was surprised by this. 'That's great,' she said, and other polite but poorly fitting phrases. Ailsa thought it might be far from great. A bit of a cheek really. They must have puzzled over why she was out there. Might have figured it out if they'd applied their anthropological skills to the social conduct of ageing male academics.

'Interesting that you've met them before,' Michelle observed, when Ailsa mentioned the visitors to Ottawa.

She was carrying the letter from Tonkin which she hoped to pass to Klapakipsy. No clear idea how to execute the deed. Tonkin had told Ailsa that she could not send it by post, Blue Houses not on any postman's round, and she believed the British would monitor anything written for the attention of a Connipian. It felt like a spy thriller to Ailsa, while fearing being laughed at should she raise it. The strained voice in which Tonkin had told Ailsa that she was not permitted to return to Connipia had pain in it. A Mixed-Up unable to visit the only place on Earth where such people are born. Ailsa had agreed with Tonkin that she would not involve any from her own department in seeking out the letter's recipient. They might have given it up to the authorities for fear it could jeopardise their trip. Sold out Tonkin who was putting all her trust in Ailsa. And Ailsa knew nothing about Klapakipsy beyond the bare fact of her prominent role in the conference of nineteen-fifty. Fifteen years earlier. She trusted Tonkin's assurance that the letter was of friendship, not something a censor would prevent in principle; it was in practice that this would have occurred. Tonkin a persona non grata for the assistance she gave to Connipians in New York.

* * *

The night was as dark as any Ailsa had ever known. Darker somehow, the deep green leaves gone to black when the sun was no longer befriending the forest canopy. Although the Blue Houses which they occupied sat in a small clearing, the sound of a whipping wind tunnelling through the forest held her attention. Wind bending ancient trees, testing natures impregnable defences for the thousandth time. The millionth. In sunlight she had seen how rich a colour the paint upon the houses was. Painted or dyed. Maybe they simply tinted it through force of will: no one knows. It is the colour the world now calls Connipian Blue; she had seen it on the skirts and blouses of the visitors back in Ottawa. To have it radiating from a cluster of houses was quite simply startling. A disruption of shiny blue in the deep green forest. The Blue Houses are windowless structures, with fronded front and back entries. The air stirs them, but whatever grasses are used to cover the openings, they get the treatment: same shade of blue. The roofs form a steep slope, more than doubling the height of the single-story structure, but still only a couple of inches above the top of—tallest in the party—Roger Curtis's head. The houses need the steep incline to run off the heavy rains that frequently drench this forest. To Ailsa, being inside felt a timeslip different from looking at them from just paces away. The smells and humidity of the thick temperate forest were no longer present, the atmosphere unworldly. Only researchers in this outcrop of Blue Houses. For centuries—millennia—they had been home to Connipians. The simple structures are known to be astonishingly durable. In her pre-visit reading, Ailsa learnt that the very ones they were staying in had stood on this ground since before the Pharaohs built the pyramids. Predated the hanging gardens. Abandoned after first contact, so the story goes. John Cooke and his early settlers met them here, not that his hapless party stayed long on the isle. Other British adventurers landed within weeks of the Muggletonians leaving. For the first two hundred years the given explanation for their abandonment was Connipian superstition. These houses were the source of bad luck, inferred those who wrote about the island. They declared *Homo Connipus* disappointed to learn themselves a minor species idling in the lee of their taller, cleverer peers. Only in this century, Mixed-Up interpreters finally enabling Sapiens to penetrate their clicking, has the true Connipian perspective come to light. No illusions about the chance role the houses played in the meeting. The reminder alone of that unwelcome arrival would disrupt sleep. A calamity is a real thing, not a superstition at all. These particular Blue Houses could no longer fulfil their role in Connipian life.

Michelle and Ailsa whispered together, the former seeming pleased to have company after a month of nights alone. And she asked directly how come Ailsa was on Connipia, here as part of an anthropological team without sitting a single exam. Ailsa told her that she had been able to persuade the seniors in the department, so keen was she to meet Connipians as she briefly had in Ottawa three years earlier. Then she told her more about her meeting with Tonkin; didn't mention the letter. Let her admiration for the interpreter be the story.

Michelle had heard of Tonkin, seen newsreel footage of at the New York conference, her remarkable contribution on the second day. Tonkin speaking the Connipians thoughts—the theatre of it—delegates squirming through an interminable period of unexpurgated clicking. She reiterated her surprise that Professor Curtis had used a place in the forest for an administrative colleague. Carefully worded, not too great a put-down. Ailsa replied a little vaguely, implied she may have fluttered her eyes excessively, in order to persuade the professor. Michelle laughed at that. 'Men!' She had them all down for fools; talked about Mixed-Ups more than once, that their struggling existence is testimony to men's unstoppable lust. 'They'd all do it if they thought they could get away with it.'

'But the researchers are all right?' queried Ailsa. 'The problem is the chancers out here. That's what I understood. Gold prospectors, loggers. That type.'

'They're all prospectors, even us, Ailsa. And the men want an extra reward if they find something shiny, or a little compensation if they don't.'

'You've no boyfriend, then?' said Ailsa, sensing a militancy in her roommate that was alien to her.

'Never,' said Michelle.

The certainty impressed Ailsa. Thinking about the poor Mixed-Ups gave her pause to consider her own outlook. Roger would hope to share a bed with her again while on this island. They would be back and forth to Charlestown in the course of the project. The Blue Houses gave her respite, and she felt her resolve growing as she talked to Michelle. Sitting in a Blue House resonating with the lives of Connipians past, their tranquil history and predictable lifestyle were all that counted here until so very recently.

Ailsa dropped Klapakipsy's name into the conversation. Said Tonkin had mentioned her.

'You have seen the footage?' asked Michelle.

She hadn't but said she had. Tonkin had told her enough to picture it, she'd read an account in the Encyclopaedia Britannica. A couple of photographs. Michelle said it was hilarious. The Sapiens looked like the primitives if you actually analysed what the Connipians said. They both dwelled upon that in the dark and the silence. 'Not said,' she added. 'It was your Tonkin doing the saying. Klapakipsy and Tululiduh just thought it. We don't know how to do that without words constraining us.'

* * *

Just two evenings later, Michelle confirmed, in a whispered conversation through the pitch dark, that she had located Klapakipsy. Ailsa had asked if she might be able to without giving her a firm reason. Admiration was enough and Michelle seemed to want to show how well connected she was on the island. Senior anthropologist from the colonial power. She didn't say it, but the status gave her strings to pull on.

Klapakipsy was living in one of the larger in-forest villages, Sheldeep, towards the south of the island. 'She doesn't see us though. Hasn't conversed with Sapiens since the conference.'

Ailsa tried to approach the subject most prominent on her mind since setting foot on the island. 'Tonkin said she was unable to get a letter to her because of the British censorship...'

'Oh, Ailsa,' said Michelle, 'British rule has not been good for them but we're not the Soviet Union. The authorities only censor post for the protection of Connipians. To ensure that the cranks from the Twelve Tribes don't write to them. That would be worse than not doing it, you must see that? I'm surprised Tonkin doesn't come back and visit her.'

'I don't know if she can,' Ailsa began to explain. Then she wondered if it was a mistake, Michelle's Soviet comment, even her connections on the island, indicating a more pro-British stance than anything Ailsa could imagine Tonkin agreeing with.

'What do you mean by that?'

'Tonkin implied she wasn't allowed to come back here.'

'Implied?'

'She told me she was raised in New Zealand; it was used against her.'

Michelle contemplated this for a moment. A barely perceptible nodding of her head. 'I'm not sure,' she said. 'They must have had their reasons. Tonkin is very clever for a Mixed-Up but didn't she get taken in by the Russians? Fell for all their communist ideals or something.'

'She might have. I only met her over two days.' Ailsa feared arguing with Michelle. Hadn't thought of using the British as helpers in her quest although she'd found Michelle very pro-Connipian up until this point. Something else was at play, her certainty as to the intentions of her government, perhaps. 'How far is that village you mentioned? Sheldeep.'

Michelle advised it was over fifty miles away. 'Not a simple journey from Trick Point. And anyway, Klapakipsy won't meet with Sapiens. Will never again be seen by us, I've been told.'

7.

'I was very drunk, Mannay. Somebody got me drunk. That's why I was in your bed. A drunken mistake.'

'Mannay not drunk. Mannay wanted do that with Ailsa. Did the singer do it to you? Get you drunk.'

'I don't think so. Maybe.'

'Did he do what Mannay do? Did he do that thing with you?'

'No. And nor did you. It wasn't...' She feels mortified. Mannay sees no one right now but he has a few Mixed-Up friends in East Town. Can't keep his mouth shut.

'It good, Ailsa. Good for Mannay, and Ailsa like it too. We wife now. You and Mannay: we wife.'

Oh God. Her head feels like concrete from one ear to the other. Far too much of something she's never had before found its way into those drinks last night.

8.

Still to depart for the forest, she and Steve are back in East Town; Ailsa plans to ask a favour of one of the charity workers. Someone who will keep an eye out for Mannay while she's away. If he can find his way back to the forest it might be for the best; the right part of the forest, a settlement where the Connipians already know him. Ailsa only lets him stay in The Reeve-Muggleton because she feels sorry for him. Fears what would happen if Mannay strayed into the wrong hands. It's a delicate situation.

Steve has brought along his acoustic guitar. Asked if there might be any Connipians who would care to hear him sing. Perform. When he said, 'All for free,' Ailsa—standing by his side—burst out laughing. Connipians don't use money, not in the normal course of their lives. And their opinions about music have been quite scathing. Mannay seems to think along the same lines.

She takes the rockstar into a luncheon hall, advises him that it is the best place to meet Mixed-Ups but they will make a lot of noise. Eating without arms can do that. A young charity worker greets them, she is dark-skinned, speaks with a London accent. 'Has anyone ever said you look exactly like Steve Frame!'

'Is Terry Holmes around?' asks Ailsa, before he can get a word in.

'Cooking,' says the girl.

'Is it okay if Steve here entertains the diners?' says Ailsa. 'I need to speak to Terry.'

'Steve? Hang on.' She looks at him through half-closed eyes, a broad grin taking residence on her face. 'My God! It is you. Here!'

'Just visiting, and I'm not a great cook,' says Steve, resting his guitar case on the floor. Down on one knee opening the clasps. 'This is all I can do. Not sure if it's much help to anyone.'

'Steve Frame in East Town!'

Ailsa leaves him to his lone fan. A lot of Mixed-Ups—as many as twenty—are in the room, sitting at tables. Chattering away, laughing a bit. Spittle and saliva. The star in their midst elicits no reaction. Only the young charity worker understands how improbable his presence is.

In the kitchen she sees four people cooking. Walks straight to Terry but talks softly. 'Hey, I've an opportunity to go back to Blue.'

He raises his eyebrows, a look of disapproval.

'Legit, Terry. With the Governor's say so and everything.'

'I don't give half a carrot for what some pompous Governor thinks should happen on this island? Do the Connipians want you out there?'

'You make a good point. It's agreed, Terry. My last chance, I'm sure of it. I'll be leaving once I'm back. You know I've been running out of steam.'

Only now does he put down his wooden spoon. Look directly at the girl he has known for almost as long as she has been on the island. Terry is more cynical and less sanctimonious than most who work with the Mixed-Ups. 'Leaving Connipia, Ails? I'm kind of sorry about that.'

'It'd be for the best if every Sapiens did just that,' she says quietly.

'Exactly. But it's not about to happen. I'm only staying to count them off. We owe it...'

Ailsa cuts him off. Heard his speeches many times. 'I won't be serving drinks to exploiters any longer. Find something else to do for the rest of my life. London: I could agitate for change from there.'

'I can see why you'd get tired of the Reeve-Muggleton.'

'Hey, do you know Steve Frame, the singer from One-Eyed Temple, is here.'

'On Connipia?'

'Strumming in the canteen.' She beams a smile at him.

'What!'

'He got me on the trip into the forest.'

'Whoa. How can this happen?'

'Beats me, too. Look, Terry, you remember Mannay. The guy I kind of try to help.'

'Sure. He's a funny one. Not been around…'

'I've been letting him stay in my room at the hotel. He can't really manage while I'm away…'

'Ailsa,' hisses Terry, 'that could get you in a hell of a lot of trouble.'

'I don't worry about trouble anymore. Do you still have use of a van? Could you collect him, bring him back to East Town?'

'Jesus, Ailsa. That's a big ask. Yes, of course I will—do it for Mannay—but what the hell were you thinking? Why take him in? At The Reeve-Muggleton of all places.'

'There's a bit of a buzz around him. Questions about his father.'

'Him and every Mixed-Up out there.'

'His mother was at the New York Conference,' she whispers.

'Huh-uh?

'It's connected, Terry. Figure it from there.'

'Okay. Sensitive. And you're sure he'll be okay in East Town?'

Ailsa spreads out her hands, drawing apart each finger. 'He can probably lie low around here, just so long as he can be in a rooming house, not the Forester Hostel. Not on that list.'

'I know of a few rooms, not a problem. How come I didn't know about his father already?'

'Because I only told you half the story, I guess. The fewer people and all that.'

'Hmmm. Does he still cause havoc?'

Ailsa finds herself blushing, while thinking it is she who has done that. 'Not as bad as he once was. Sometimes says a lot of things that aren't true. Don't believe every word or anything, but he's a great kid.'

'And how about when you leave Connipia?'

'I'll talk to you again before that. Might ask…' She pauses. It is an obstacle to her leaving the island but she really is out of her depth trying to protect a Mixed-Up from nothing visible. And he would be welcome back in the forest with the right people. The right short people.

* * *

A few volunteers—and Sister Concepta, the young nun—have gathered around Steve as he sings. Ailsa is back in the dining area too. He has a good voice, very good, she is surprised. There is much that is casual in his singing while the control is absolute. Melodic and rich. Terry has popped out of his kitchen, stands beside her. To see and hear the chart-topping popstar in a charity kitchen on the far-flung island.

For the friend who had died, I hadn't cried

For the past thirty years or more
One hell of a surprise to find tears in my eyes
On that cold crematorium floor

Those in the know—which must be very few on this remote island—will understand the irony of Steve Frame playing the most famous Dario Renzo song in his canon. In a recent interview, the wild guitar-smith was highly critical of One-Eyed Temple. 'No soul in their tunes, or purpose in their lyrics.' It might have been jealousy for the broader critical acclaim Frame's songs have been getting. Renzo is the hippies' choice. The spaced-out, whacky-cigarette toking sort, at least.

It felt so weird, when your ghost appeared, he sings.

'You are something, Ailsa,' says Terry when he sees the singer exchange a smile with her. 'Turned me down because you had a rockstar waiting in the wings.'

'Nothing like that, Terry. He wants my help; we're not involved with each other.'

'He's a rockstar, it comes with the territory. And what help is that? Writing his songs now, are you, Ailsa?'

'You know what I mean. To accompany him because I've been out there before. He's keen to forge a connection with them. I can't say if they'll reciprocate. I think he's a good guy, I really do. Won't do any harm out there and that's better than most.' As she says it, she wonders if it was him or the girl who spiked his drink. Frame definitely made a move, and maybe she'd have enjoyed it if she'd clambered into his bed. Enjoyed her dream along the same lines until she felt Mannay dribbling on her. Poor drunken Ailsa couldn't even make the right choice two nights ago. Let the dream guy go and crept into bed with a Mixed-Up. Keeping herself away from Mannay for a few days is wisest. Maybe forever. She goes on her toes to whisper in Terry's ear. 'Keep on to Mannay for a while; keep him well. If I can get in touch with his relatives, we can make a better plan than holing up in my hotel room.'

We've got a vicar - an organ dissembling
The sky is the right shade of grey
This apparition – confirms my suspicion
That this is my wedding day.
This is my wedding da-a-ay

As he brings the song to a close the volunteers erupt into applause and a young Mixed-Up comes close up to the misplaced star, swings her lifeless arms at the guitar so that it makes a discordant noise as they slap against the strings. Frame glances at Ailsa who gives him a thumbs up. Mixed-Ups muck about a lot. Like Mannay, this one can't help it. Steve starts holding down a quick succession of chord shapes. The Mixed-Up has a bit of rhythm in the swing of her hips, they propel her skinny arms which, in turn, thrum her lifeless hands upon the guitar strings. She's making music. Starts to shout, 'wedding day, wedding day,' in her unmusical voice. More and more Mixed-Ups stand and appear to dance. The volunteers preferred the straight version but these guys like hearing music from their own. It could be a first. 'Wedding day, wedding day,' shouts the Mixed-Up.

Ailsa cringes at it all, worries Steve will be fearing for his precious guitar. 'He'll be no bother just so long as no one comes looking. Needs a friend with an ear to the ground, that's all.'

'You've got it, Ailsa,' says Terry.

The Mixed-Up stepped away to a little applause from the volunteers. Shouts of 'More' from all those unable to clap. Steve is plucking the strings now, playing the introduction to Chains Around Our Ankles, Ailsa thinks it's his biggest hit. Volunteers are whistling in anticipation. The Mixed-Up comes back, arms swinging as she did before. The guitarist bobs and weaves, gives her a most apologetic smile. Keeping his guitar to himself for this number.

9.

A half-baked plan and it could have gone wrong in a hundred different ways; Ailsa had to give it a try, no better prospect for the fulfilment of Tonkin's wish. When the Canadian contingent's food supplies were running low, she offered to take the Land Rover into Charlestown and stock up. Said that she could use the break. Roger asked her if she would like his company on the excursion and she said it was unnecessary. Reminded him he was needed for the fieldwork as she was not. Looking back, she expects he felt snubbed, thinks it another bonus from her secret mission. Lynne suggested she might like to stay a night in Charlestown, visit the post office to collect their mail while she was there. Downtime, she called it. Many anthropologists say fieldwork is intense, can't switch off, although a stenographer's role is not fundamentally different whether undertaken in an office or a forest clearing. Think: secretaries go camping, and that was her back in nineteen sixty-five. Ailsa wondered if they had noticed how detached she had become from their group; sleeping with the British and having little formal training to draw upon when her own contingent discussed Connipian matters. Too timid to contribute but she was already forging opinions. Something in her manner meant that the two Mixed-Up translators on the site and the visiting blue-clad ladies, all warmed to her more than they did her over-inquisitive colleagues. Anthropologists don't spot themselves sliding towards the supercilious. Ailsa, on the other hand, knew that she might have been a Mixed-Up or a Connipian herself but for the accident of birth. The unlikely happenstance that she was Ailsa Donaldson from Prince Edward Island. A different outlook from researchers who believed it their mission to study others, and imagined their lives were the gold standard against which those others should be assessed.

When she left, Roger walked her to the vehicle—seeing her off with a chaste kiss upon her closed lips—Ailsa drove only a mile in the direction of Charlestown and, once confident her boss and sort-of lover had gone back through the forest to the Blue Houses, she turned the vehicle round and drove in the direction of Sheldeep, where Michelle had said Klapakipsy lived. Half a plan in her head, the map of the island on the passenger seat. The drive was straightforward enough, not that she has ever been confident behind the wheel. Like the clappers when the road was open, slowing to fifteen, even ten, miles per hour when she came across another vehicle. Happened just six times in the entire journey. All the way down there to the edge of Sheldeep. Ailsa was determined to be quick, to drop the letter off, turnaround and then do all she needed in Charlestown. Meeting Tonkin's favourite Connipian was her priority, making good on her promise at the meal they had shared three years earlier.

At a Protection Authority check point, Ailsa showed the colonial official her Canadian passport and the requisite **Permit to Stay on Connipia** without which she would not be there. She explained to the policeman manning the point that she needed to meet the researchers at Sheldeep. An imaginary need which she said with great confidence. Lying for Tonkin. The official became confused, said he thought only Connipians were living there. She blustered on with some cock and bull about her contact from the Cambridge University mission, Dr Firth, being quite clear that a couple of fellows from the St Andrews' Programme were there right now. In a tent at Sheldeep. They had agreed to share notes with her own group from Carleton; it was most important she locate them. The official was a bit simple. More pen pusher than law enforcer, happy to take a lead from others. She might have turned out the same herself without the pep talk from Tonkin. He didn't argue, and she never said she wasn't a real anthropologist.

After the long drive, she left her vehicle in a designated space at an otherwise empty clearing, the pale blue Research Station signpost—small Union Jack in the right-hand corner—telling her she was in the right place. As the official rightly thought, this outpost was not in use. No other vehicles. There was a single path into the forest and she assumed it would lead to Sheldeep. Michelle and the map had yielded all the information needed; now she had a four-mile walk. Strange to be doing this by herself, very dark where the foliage was thick. A thousand years overgrown, maybe more. Never-not might sum it up. As she made her way into the forest, passing tree trunks that would take three or four people to encircle with hands held—three times as many Connipians—she felt both elation and trepidation. Heart thumping in her chest as she neared the village which she hoped housed Klapakipsy. Tonkin had said she was something out of the ordinary; all Connipians are to Ailsa. And she was smitten with her, Tonkin had said as much. Ailsa thought it odd. Mixed-Ups all looked sexless to her; Tonkin told her—and Logan put it more crudely in the bar here in Charlestown, Connipia—that the males had urges. Got frisky in Logan's telling. Odd to think on: the males in their maternal line are the opposite. It's in the textbooks. Struggle to perform, say the ethnologists. Tonkin put her straight on that. 'Don't compare Connipians to Sapiens. It takes you down the wrong path altogether.' They had talked and talked. Ailsa thought the life of an intelligent Mixed-Up sounded a lonely one. A remarkable interpreter, picker-up of languages without any of the formal study which most of us rely upon. Maybe Connipians do the same, grasp quickly and clearly; it looks that way. Sapiens are slower in the head, that's the logical conclusion. When Tonkin described her school days, she called them stimulating. Alienating sounded a better fit. She spoke of it warmly but there were some shocking truths in there. Half the teachers resented her presence in class; only two of them grasped that—although unable to write a word due to her lifeless arms—she was the brightest student in town. Everything went in. And stayed in. And her own foster mother was half of that very small fan club.

Ailsa felt herself shudder at the sight of a long green-black snake slithering across the path ahead and into the undergrowth. None are poisonous on this island, her fear was learnt, not rational. Felt it pretty intensely all the same. As she walked, birds whistled and squawked. Occasionally showed their faces. Then she stopped in her tracks. Listened. The sound which came to her was the one Brian mimicked so well: the purple owl. She couldn't recall its Latin name. There are said to be tens of thousands on Connipia. In certain places, their hooting can be heard around the clock. Night and day are scarcely different for forest dwellers, so thick is the entanglement of trees. Even in daytime, the birds' pellucid eyesight gives them an advantage over all other creatures. The deep red and navy blue in their feathering makes them blend into the mixed leaf. She had seen pictures. Now she repeatedly heard the muted cry. Never saw an owl, couldn't tell if it was calling out from deep in the wood, or but a few paces from where she stood. Noisy and shy is the purple owl, and this is the island for it.

After well over an hour's trekking, another noise came to her. At first, she thought it might be giggling, but as she drew closer, she picked up the clicking, the unmistakable sound she first heard during those three days at the university. Once she had tuned in, she realised the air was humming. A cacophony of tongues touching palates. And then, just a couple of dozen thick trees further, the path turned into a clearing of Blue Houses. This one was huge, Sheldeep virtually a town. She could not count them. House after house, without obvious street or pattern. Clicking, lispy hissing and that curious put-putting all melding together like the sound of a thousand bee hives. How could they ever tune into an individual thought, Ailsa wondered. Or maybe the canteen at Carleton University would sound just the same to these forest dwellers.

Fully fifty yards from the first house she stopped. Stock still, waiting for a sign. She had learned the protocol, knew her Connipian manners.

A small group of Connipians ambled towards her. Five. All wore the vivid blue clothing for which they are known, all had the bluest eyes within their hairless heads. Two wore nothing upon their upper bodies. The younger Connipians. As they approached, their diminution became more and more obvious. So strange to see ourselves shrunk small.

Ailsa sat down on the ground. No wish to tower above these little girls, little women. They came right up to her, one of the young ones reaching a hand out and, as Ailsa leant towards her, ran tiny fingers through her black hair. Let a ripple of clicks emanate from her chattering lips as she did it. Ailsa smiled, took a notebook from the small rucksack she carried. A pen. She gestured with it. Wished for confirmation that one or more of them could read.

I am sorry I cannot click she wrote.

The Connipians seemed to confer, she wondered if the lower register of noise she heard was laughter. And why not? She has heard anthropologists laugh at Connipian strangeness, and then there's that awful British comedian who's made a career out of it. The girl who first touched her hair—her naked breasts looking to Ailsa as natural as the forest, while her own grey jeans, T-shirt, and thin coach jacket seemed suddenly ridiculous—took the pen from her.

Clicking is not for you she wrote.

Ailsa took back pen and paper.

My name is Ailsa. May I...

The girl reached across and gently removed the pen again. Reached across her to write once more on the pad.

Speak, please, my friend. Only I need write. My name is Prast, it is a pleasure to meet you.

She stared at the words for a moment. Looked askew into the face of the little Connipian who hovered, pen above the paper she still held. White skin, face innocent and enquiring. The curve of her skull beautiful in the shadowed light afforded by the tree they were beside. Ailsa laughed to herself. Her stupidity. 'If I may,' she said, speaking slowly while wondering if it was wise or patronising, 'I would like to enter your village. I am hoping to find a lady called Klapakipsy.'

You come alone and without a male, so you may enter. Klapakipsy and I are close but she has never chosen to meet Sapiens in the time I have known her. She may refuse to see you although I do not.

'I was advised that she might be reluctant,' said Ailsa. 'I have a letter for her from a Mixed-Up named Tonkin. Someone she may recall from long ago. Tonkin asked me to give it to her personally.'

Then I shall ask wrote the little girl ***but I cannot predict what Klapakipsy will say. I'm sure the letter will be most welcome, but please keep it until I have learnt her thoughts on the matter.***

The small group of Connipian girls accompanied her into their thriving village. At once a throng of tiny girls surrounded her. Twenty or thirty. Made Ailsa feel like a giant. She was immersed in their incoherent sound, she stooped down to one knee so that she was close to Prast's ear. Spoke quietly. 'The Sapiens call this place Sheldeep. What name do you know it by?'

We don't use names as you do. Even my name, Prast, is not used among Connipians. I am unsure if your words can really explain this difference. We click only in thoughts, not tying them to pre-existing formulations. Do you see?

Ailsa looked at Prast. A child, surely, not simply tiny, the swelling of her chest looked pubescent. Her face unlined. And she wrote like a PHD student, understood contrasting Sapiens and Connipian concepts. Ailsa felt out of her depth. She didn't see yet, regretted not being able to grasp what this young girl seemed to take for granted. 'How do you distinguish this settlement from others on your island?'

No two places are alike, Ailsa. Differences abound. We click in thoughts not fixed names. The men who gave names to all the animals were not Connipians.

Ailsa read the reply. Sweet little clever clogs. Or is that Connipian wisdom? Tonkin said men give names to everything so that they can count them and allot ownership. Rent it out and collect a fee. These other people have found a different way of living.

Prast and the accompanying Connipians walked her to a large square, no grass grew upon it and the surface was a mixture of gravel and tiny broken-up pieces of bark. Fine grained. Ailsa went down onto one knee and ran the mix between her fingers. Tried to smile at Prast, at the others, show her fascination with their world. A small frail figure came to the front of the nearest Blue House. It took her a moment to see what was obvious. The stooped and frail-looking Connipian wore a simple grey cloth wrapped across chest and thighs, over the shoulder but not tightly. No hair, no teeth that Ailsa could see. No blue on any of the clothing; no breasts, top half covered but this was an old and flat-chested person. She was espying a male, a Connipian man. She understood that they seldom see daylight. She'd read it, and heard Professor Curtis say the same.

'Hello,' she said to him. Then, as if in reply, the Connipian let out a string of clicks and Prast reached up and took the pen from Ailsa's fingers. She put a hand to her mouth two or three times while writing quickly. Let out clicks to the other girls, but what they meant was beyond Ailsa's reach.

I have done enough breeding today, he said. Come back tomorrow and you can be first.

Ailsa read the note, looked again at the man, slightly alarmed by the words, and then she turned to Prast. The young one's face showed no emotion which Ailsa could fathom. As she looked back at the wizened little chap he was already returning to the cover of his home. His love nest, perhaps, for that is as she understood the function of any Blue House in which a male might reside. To her knowledge, none in the Canadian team or the three British girls with whom she shared house had yet met with a male. Then she felt Prast nudge a shoulder into her. Gentle, it meant something, and Ailsa found herself laughing and laughing. The joke was hilarious although she wasn't sure if he was making fun of her or his own role in Connipian life. And the guy was three-feet tall, just having a laugh. As Ailsa looked again at the girl who nudged her, she could see no laughter on her face. Kindly and welcoming. Hard to read. No obvious laughter, it might be a Sapiens thing. It was hilarious whatever Connipians think about it. Could even have been Prast's joke: the girl held the pen.

As she continued to watch the doorway into which the small old man had retreated, Ailsa realised that two Connipian ladies were clicking quite hurriedly with Prast, and with the others who had come to the periphery of the village, fetched her in. One of the older ladies took a gentle hold of Ailsa's hand and began to click her thoughts. Ailsa looked quickly at Prast who was still holding the notebook and pen. She calmly began writing, and Ailsa presumed the written words to originate in the thoughts of the one who held her hand.

> *Klapakipsy is unwell; she has spoken to me of Tonkin many times. Please follow me, she may wish to receive you. And please, Miss Ailsa, if she allows it, do not let the sight of her alarm you. We are doing all we can for her, and have no wish for your doctors. We do not say that as a snub to you, truly. If we do not hold fast to our own ways, they will be swept away. Please follow me.*

They walked together through the village, passing house after house. Some clearly occupied, noises and movement evident, others stood in silence, no one home today. Not at this hour. Ailsa thought her presence in the group awkward. Seven Connipian ladies and one towering Sapiens. Girls or ladies, Prast appeared the youngest. Throughout this short walk, with the tops of bald heads below her, Ailsa felt like an ugly thing. So out of place in a world that was not hers. She recalled Tonkin's expressions of warmth towards Klapakipsy and felt uneasy. Seeing her unwell might sully the impression. Dying, perhaps. No doctor. Ailsa understood the instruction, the drawn line. It's implication.

At the far side of the settlement, they stopped beside a Blue House that appeared larger than most. Not taller, just longer walls, with two fronded doorways on the front face. The older Connipian clicked over her shoulder and Prast came forward, only those two entered the Blue House. Ailsa closed her eyes. Sank to the floor where she sat holding her bag in which lay the letter for Klapakipsy. Watching the doorway; she could hear clicking within. Knew not what it meant, hoped the ailing woman would view the visit favourably.

When they came out, the Connipian who seemed most in charge clicked again and Prast began to write upon Ailsa's note pad.

> *She will see you. Her sister is there too and shall stay in attendance. Do you have other activities you hope to pursue here in Sheldeep?*

Ailsa shook her head and the clicking and scribbling continued.

> *I will wait to escort you back to your path out of our village. You are a gracious guest, Miss Ailsa. And we are all pleased for Klapakipsy that you have found her. She remembers Tonkin with sisterly feelings.*

Ailsa had not thought this through but was, in her head, composing a letter for Tonkin. Wanted her to hear those valedictory words.

* * *

Inside the Blue House a small light came from a rock upon a tiny wooden table. It was very bright at the source, but let only a faint light into the corners of the room. Glowed but didn't shine. Ailsa had dropped on to all fours, so low was the ceiling. She drew her legs beneath her, sat cross-legged on the floor. Two Connipians were in the room, one sitting on a mat on the ground, the other lying to the side of her within a cluster of leaves. Blue-dyed leaves, each and every one. The sitting Connipian gestured a small tray she had. Wettened black sand within it. It took Ailsa a moment to realise her intent: the lady meandered the nib of a tiny sharpened stick across its surface.

I am Tululiduh, sister of Klapakipsy.

Writing in the sand, of course. And soon after it was written, her little hand brushed across it. Flattened the sand once more. Ailsa gestured that she would like the writing implement. Mimed as if writing herself. Tululiduh waved her hand away, pointed at her own mouth, and made strange noises. Ailsa thought herself an idiot in this new world, repeating the same stupidity at each time of asking.

'I am so pleased to meet you both.'

My sister and I are pleased also, Miss Ailsa. We understand that you are a friend of Tonkin.

'I am. I hope I am, but I just happened to meet her. Over a couple of days. She was doing some work in Ottawa. That's in Canada. Interpreting. She invited me for a meal.' Ailsa found herself rambling, unsure how to explain all that had brought her to this juncture. On the mat, the prostrate Connipian began to click a little, and the sister wrote again in the sand.

Tonkin was with us in New York. She was wiser than I in those critical days.

Ailsa looked from the tray of sand to the Connipian whose thoughts these were. Klapakipsy had turned her profile towards her. She was not old. Her forehead appeared lined, aged, but her blue eyes shone. About her lips were one or two sores, she had a thin sheet across her body, all burrowed in the leaf mound. In the strange light, the sheet looked to be green. A contrast from the blue of all else in the room. Might have been made of leaves; Ailsa thought it was, but did not wish to enquire. A friend of Tonkin's was her only role here in Sheldeep, not a researcher. The leaves which formed the thin sheet had somehow become fused together. Connipian skills. Klapakipsy lifted her small hand, stirring the strange covering. Ailsa saw that she was naked beneath it. Klapakipsy made another couple of clicks, after which Tululiduh wrote.

Approach her, please. Klapakipsy would wish to embrace any friend of Tonkin's.

She complied with the request and the tiny woman on the ground stretched out her arms. Ailsa was kneeling beside Klapakipsy and felt the lady's tiny hand within her own, the fingers of a doll clutching her own giant paddle. The Connipian's nail ends looked blackened, no longer growing as Ailsa expected they should. Were Connipian fingernails comparable to her own? Her little hand was hot, burning hot, and instinctively Ailsa put a flat palm to Klapakipsy's forehead. It felt like a griddle.

'You are poorly,' she let out. 'Do you have drinking water?' She couldn't help herself saying it. Worried after the words were out that she had been rude. Thoughts of medicines back in the Canadian camp came to her mind, but she held her tongue. Knew better than to interfere in Connipian matters.

Klapakipsy clicked.

Perhaps we had a chance in New York, perhaps we did not.

Ailsa contemplated the written words carefully, understood from the concentration on her host's face as she clicked that these were thoughts she wished heard and remembered, although Ailsa knew very little about the conference. Not even a teenager when it took place.

I tried to play the Sapiens men at their own game. Thought I could, but I could not. We Connipians have grasped the meaning of many Sapiens beliefs, their ways. I think your lust for power is not in our range. We cannot fathom why you are so driven.

Klapakipsy clicked further and her sister looked carefully into her face before scribing. Appeared reluctant.

Sex and power. We think it is the men of your species who get especially drunk on these limited pursuits.

'I think Tonkin was most impressed with how you tried,' said Ailsa. 'That you convinced a lot of people.'

She tried to warn me. I know she did. Now, many Connipians blame me. Rightly, I must admit. I volunteered for the opportunity to explain our requirements and failed. I set the strategy and it did not achieve its intent.

'But, Klapakipsy, many people, even some of the researchers I know, blame Truman, blame the British. No one blames the Connipians.'

No. Sapiens mostly assume we are incapable and our setbacks are the failures of your own kind to act charitably enough towards us. That is not a discourse we will ever join. Our methods have served us well for a period of time you do not understand. Cannot. I fear our inability to prevent cohabitation on the island will be our downfall. We do not believe in prophecy, I am no seer, but as I try to imagine what is to come, I can foresee no good ending to the story of our island's discovery by your kind. The story you will write down. Ours has been a long passage of wonderment, a people embedded comfortably in the natural world. A tale needing no redemption. A million years. If it must end, it will always have been. It is only in the present that I worry: every contact between our species bleeds out more of what little blood we have.

Ailsa could think of nothing to say in response to this plaintive calculation. She looked searchingly into the face of the child-like woman dying before her eyes. Perhaps even this contact was a problem. That seemed to be within Klapakipsy's words.

'I have a letter from Tonkin,' she said, pushing a hand into her bag. Retrieving it.

Klapakipsy looked at the hands that held the envelope, and Tululiduh leaned forward to take the letter from Ailsa. She opened it and passed the paper inside to her sister. Klapakipsy's eyes moved rapidly from side to side, taking in all that Tonkin had written. Ailsa felt herself very alone as the two absorbed themselves in reading a letter whose contents were unknown to her. Then Klapakipsy began again to click.

She knows me too well. Very perceptive, saw the signs before others.

'And can I help you?' asks Ailsa.

Me? No, but it is very kind that you ask. I can see that you mean well. A true friend. In New York, I conceived a child. A Mixed-Up, of course. He is dear to me, and I regret he has not been with me for a long, long time. It is the fate of Mixed-Ups to be beholden to Sapiens' charity.

'Where is your son?'

A convent or an orphanage. East Town, but I cannot go there. I cannot see another Sapiens male, will not. They call my boy Mannay. If you can bring him to me before I pass, I should be most grateful.

Ailsa looked into the stilled face of the girl on the ground. Tonkin cannot have known that Klapakipsy's health was so compromised; three years have passed since she passed her the letter. Whatever Tonkin wrote it was for Klapakipsy, not something Ailsa ever pried into. That it prompted this request—one which she had no idea how to fulfil—seemed both astonishing and natural. Klapakipsy was speaking to her with a trust that she cannot have for Sapiens generally. Perhaps it was simply her gender, the little Connipian extending a degree of trust to fifty percent of Sapiens and very clear which half that would be. Although she suffered, an ill-health that seemed to fold her body in pain from time to time, Klapakipsy looked calmly at her whenever she raised up that small and thoughtful face. Ailsa wanted to cry on behalf of this brave woman. How old had she been when she led the tiny islanders on their foray into New York. Don Quixote with blue eyes. Tried to dispel the evil in the world; raped for her troubles. As she looked into Klapakipsy's impassive face, she thought the department at Carleton University a ship of fools, the party in the abandoned Blue Houses little better than colonial forces. For a hundred thousand years Homo Sapiens have lived on this Earth without knocking on the Connipians door, showing their faces or occupying their tiny island. For most of the million years before that, the Connipians lived here, did so in much the same manner they seek to live now. What was she—Ailsa Donaldson—even doing on Connipia? Shame on them all for their needless curiosity. Disturbing the peace like every swine has since John Brook. Sixteen ninety-five. Shame on every last one of them.

'I will find him. Your son, Mannay. I will bring him to you,' she told the ailing Klapakipsy.

10.

When the car comes to The Reeve-Muggleton to collect her and Frame, Ailsa has to laugh. A Daimler: a ridiculous car in which to drive into the forest. Cherie is on the back seat. The driver steps out and opens the door. Pointedly does this for Steve Frame; she is a waitress in a hotel, a barkeep, and Mr Frame—as the chauffeur refers to him—is a Member of the British Empire. It could all be a make-believe world. She has come to think him a regular guy. Accepted his gong only so as to open these doors—wouldn't be seen dead wearing it—she doesn't think so. On the front passenger seat sits an officious-looking man in khaki shorts. Thick grey short-sleeved shirt. He could be a leader of boy scouts.

Once they are both inside the car, the gentleman in the shorts introduces himself. 'Dr Freeman.' Steve asks him questions and the doctor explains his mission. 'Trying to fathom if they've anything we should worry about in the various sicknesses out there. We believe the population may be in decline; they've never once let us examine their funny little men.'

'I thought there would be two of you. At least two?' says Steve.

'Chap called Gatting; he's already out there. You'll meet him soon enough.'

All the while he is speaking, Ailsa notes that Dr Freeman is constantly turning to Cherie Thornhill. She wears loose-fitting dungarees. Dressed decently today but the bit of young flesh that shows seems to have attracted his eye. It is hard to read the expression on his face, what his glances mean. One or two stories in the newspaper may have given him ideas. Fantasies of a wild child, although Ailsa is coming to think that Cherie is well short of that mark. Little Miss Insecure putting on a show to push the buttons of Daddy who dumped her in a school half a world away. And men on Connipia outnumber women three to one. Better Dr Freeman lusts after Cherie than the Connipians. Not by a lot, just the better of the bad choices men are apt to make. Her privileged position will surely prevent him from laying a finger on her.

'Are you married?' asks Ailsa.

'Divorced,' he replies. 'Taking up a post here seemed to be the final straw.' The colonial doctor laughs at his admission.

Cherie is quiet, almost silent, on the journey. Being thrown together with her hero may be the cause. It's an odd party; Ailsa considers herself staunchly on board with the British Off movement. Has shared her views only vaguely with the rockstar and he didn't seem to disagree. Too egotistical to miss the chance to visit but she can't scoff. Jumped on the bandwagon with him. His company is the bonus, meeting Connipians—letting their more natural way of being make its imprint upon her—is the motivator, the reason she is here. For both of them, she hopes. They are neither of them for interfering out there, not she or Steve. Dr Freeman she already hates. Here to survey, quantify, plan the health of, the very people his presence kills. God only knows what Cherie thinks about it all; at least she is not especially loyal to her Governor-father. And then there is the man driving the car, humble and well-spoken. Trundling a couple of thousand pounds worth of the wrong kind of vehicle across the island. Forest tracks are better traversed in Land Rovers. Or on foot. If it were only tiny little Connipian feet, the world would be a better place.

Ailsa asks him his name, learns it is Harrison. 'And where exactly will we go, Mr Harrison? To what part of the protected areas do you take us?'

'Sheldeep, Miss Donaldson. We think of it as the Connipians capital, although the little blighters have never organised themselves properly like we do. No hierarchy of any sort in their thinking; it's what's stopped them making any progress, you know.'

Yeah, yeah, she thinks. Big-mouthed taxi drivers are the same the world over.

* * *

After walking back through the forest, Ailsa drove away from the mission carpark and out onto the coast road. The quickest route to Charlestown, a visit to neighbouring East Town foremost in her mind. Pushed the Land Rover as fast as she dared. Bumping over the rutted roads like a car with hiccoughs.

One of the last things Tululiduh wrote in the sand stayed with her. She pictured the written script, thin lines etched through wet sand.

Mannay is a handful.

In the Blue House, the night before this drive, Michelle had been talking in something akin to poetical terms about the Connipians. She had a reverence for their culture. She is not the only one, but her attitude stood out among the anthropologists. Perhaps Michelle really got the longevity: Connipians are not fly-by-nights. She had a way of describing how non-judgemental they are: 'Taking the long view.' It was a rambling conversation and Ailsa loved it, felt she was getting closer than she did at the meeting in Ottawa. She felt close to Tonkin back there, but not to the clicking Connipians. 'They have set aside personal criticism...no, not set aside, I suspect they never picked it up. Connipians take only the long view.' That was how Ailsa recalled Michelle's words. Tululiduh called Klapakipsy's Mixed-Up son a handful. Did they make exceptions for nephews? Would it be strikingly obvious? Ailsa may require a few more pairs of hands to contain the improbable son of New York. Son of a politically prominent Dane, if Ailsa's recall of names is correct. Klapakipsy never discussed the father, it was the long-ago conversation with Tonkin that fell back into her mind. The name Østergaard meant nothing back then. Only more recently has it started cropping up. Suddenly a big shot.

The drive should have been pleasurable, skirting the magnificent forests all the way. She felt only anxiety. A fear that she might let Klapakipsy down, fail in the mission, let Tonkin down although she was doubtful that she would ever meet her again. Uncertain if Tonkin would ever learn of the task Ailsa was now taking on. And could she really get away with it? Take a Mixed-Up from one part of the island to another—East Town to forest—without raising eyebrows. Getting stopped.

She had to pass only one checkpoint on the way, and once she had arrived in East Town, she felt certain she was doing the right thing. Never more so, while worrying it could all go wrong. She knocked on the doors of three different orphanages. Each a small, wooden-framed house, nuns and volunteers caring for two or three Mixed-Up children. She asked after Mannay. Nobody knew him. Not the boy or his whereabouts. Ailsa felt uneasy about the reception she received on the doorstep. Lying nuns, she diagnosed. Very strange indeed.

'Does a Mixed-Up named Mannay live with you?'

'No dear,' said an elderly nun, grey headpiece covering her hair, folding onto the rim of blue-framed glasses, little horns on the wide angles giving her the look of an insect.

'Do you know the name? Where he lives?'

'No,' said the nun, turning back into the hallway of her house. Just as quickly she swivelled back. 'Will that be all, dear.' Remembered herself and still it was a dismissal. Ailsa guessed the nun knew Mannay, couldn't bring herself to challenge her. To accuse. In her youth, Ailsa was never a rule-breaker. To this day she couldn't say boo to a nun.

'Mannay, Mannay,' she shouted down the street, after many door knockings had all produced the same result. She felt foolish standing on the street in East Town, calling a name that she knew only from writing in the sand. A sister of a dying Connipian had implored her to find the boy, and she was calling his name like a lost cat. When her marriage to Conrad unravelled, the loose thread led to this. One of these worlds must be a dream. Plain as day. Both most probably. She should never have married him, and who else on Earth has gone hunting for a Mixed-Up, known by name only, in order to transport him back into a forest full of tiny women living in Blue Houses.

'Mannay, Mannay,' she shouted again.

At an upper window in the last orphanage at which she knocked, a youthful Mixed-Up leaned his head out. Grinning from ear to ear. 'Mannay, Mannay,' he called like an echo. 'Mannay, Mannay.'

'Are you Mannay?' Ailsa called up to him.

He repeated the name, laughed, and then a nun came to the same window. Stood where the young Mixed-Up had. 'I've told you, young lady, we've no Mannay here.'

East Town looked dirty, filthy. The street a mixture of cobbles and rough gravel. Red dust, strewn with litter, old newspapers, food tins emptied of their fare. It was like nowhere back on Prince Edward Island. For a second Ailsa thought she spied a Connipian scurrying into a doorway but her mental calculation told her that the girl she saw, short blue skirt, was too large. Small certainly, but not Connipian-tiny. She had read about it in the Sunday paper back in Canada. It appalled her. And in East Town, awash with most of the world's Mixed-Ups. This island can feel idyllic but it is not. Once upon a time, certainly, not so now.

'Mannay,' she called again, and a man stepped out of one of the small houses. Ailsa recoiled as he approached, fearing he was looking only for prostitutes.

'Who are you?' he asked. Early thirties, she guessed, scruffy with ginger hair, holding a large wooden spoon in his hand. Very odd.

'I could ask the same...'

'You're welcome to ask. It's Terry, Terry Holmes,' he said. Transferring the spoon to the left, he offered her a hand to shake. 'I work in the kitchen here.' Terry pointed at the doorway out of which he emerged. 'Heard you calling the name of everybody's favourite bad lad.'

'Bad lad? Is Mannay...'

'You're not already acquainted then? A protectorate employee, I take it?'

'No. I've come from the forest. From his mother.'

The man called Terry began to laugh. 'What's your name Miss Protectorate Employee? The forest!' His eyes went to the sky.

'No, no. I'm Ailsa Donaldson. From an anthropological team in the forest. His mother wishes to see Mannay again. Is it possible?'

He looked at her through narrowed eyes. 'You have papers?'

Nerves jangling, Ailsa began to laugh. 'You ask that of everyone you think is a protectorate employee?'

'Smartest thing to do. Know their authority.'

As Terry spoke, she pulled her Canadian passport from the small handbag she carried. It didn't prove very much. 'I've the right ones back in the car.' She gestured towards it. The Land Rover.

'Right. And I don't know where Mannay is, so I'm afraid I can't help you, Ailsa Donaldson. I wish you luck if you have come from the forest. The clothes are right.'

'And you don't know where...'

'He does his own thing does our Mannay. Eats in this kitchen now and then, but there's no predicting the boy. I'm sorry.' He turned around. 'Got to cook.'

Ailsa looked at her own feet. Sneakers covered in the dust of the street. She walked back towards the car, ruminating on the words of Terry Holmes. He knew Mannay, and could only advise that he was unpredictable. As she approached her car, she noticed a policeman beside it. Khaki shorts beneath a bottle blue helmet: it's their dress code on Connipia. He initially ignored her, seemed to be inspecting the vehicle. A Land Rover parked in East Town might have been the oddity. Something had certainly piqued his interest. She did not wish to be questioned about her mission, feared its legitimacy, while wondering if this might be the man to lead her to Mannay. An East Town bobby, and the Mixed-Up was allegedly a bad lad.

291

God Help the Connipians

The policeman walked right around the parked car, squinting through the windshield. He can have seen only a pair of sunglasses, biscuit wrappers, a couple of discarded cigarette packets. Lynne Sharpe left those, not Ailsa. She looked into his face, thought to say that the car wouldn't be parked there long. From the corner of her eye, she saw a lone Mixed-Up, arms dangling limply at his side. A cheeky face, dribbly too. Not well co-ordinated.

'Can I help you, officer,' said Ailsa.

'Your car, is it?'

'It belongs to my project. Assigned to Professor Curtis, I believe. I have my driving license.'

'Oh, no need for all that. I was looking at your tyres. I'm not so sure they're fully inflated, Miss. I can help you if you've a foot pump in the boot.'

She noticed that he was quite a young man, that he was looking at her a bit keenly. The line about flat tyres sounded like nonsense to Ailsa. They always look as if they need a bit more air in them when the wheels have been kerbed. The policeman was hunched over examining the offending tyre, the young Mixed-Up trotted up behind him. Like an emu, he moved, arms flapping with his ungainly movement. Out of the blue, he gave the bending-down policeman a swift kick up the bum, screamed something unintelligible, and then started to run away. Ran fast.

'Oy! You!' shouted the policeman, as he stumbled into the Land Rover, caught himself on the wheel arch and then he looked back at Ailsa. Wide eyes as if seeking her opinion on the matter.

'Did he hurt you?' she asked, trying to stifle a grin.

'Bloody nuisance, aren't they. No use and a bit fresh with it.'

'I can't imagine what it feels like to be a Mixed-Up.'

'No. And why would you? I'd rather be dead than floppy armed. I really would.'

'Are you sure my tyres are...' Then she burst into laughter. The same Mixed-Up, seeing the policeman choose conversation over the chase, had run back and done it again. Another quick kick up the arse, and Ailsa thought he deserved it.

'Oy! Stop!'

'He's a child, sir,' said Ailsa, said it too late. The young policeman had started to follow the Mixed-Up. Stupidly, he put a whistle into his mouth as if that might help. Ailsa clambered into the Land Rover and waited. Turned the key, ignited the engine, waited a bit longer. The Mixed-Up had run down a side alley and the policeman, who was now out of sight, might be closing in on him. Or might not, Ailsa thought. A bold and cheeky kid, this particular one. She inched the car forward to the entrance of the alley he had run down. It was just a hunch. Then she heard the shrill whistle again. The Mixed-Up appeared, must have hidden and run back after the policeman had passed him.

'Pssst. Jump in,' she shouted, the passenger door open as she leaned across. The Mixed-Up looked amused. Got in. Dribbled on her arm as she leaned over him to pull the door to. 'Get down,' she hissed. 'Right down.' The Mixed-Up slunk into the footwell. Then the policeman was back on the square. 'He ran up the next alleyway,' she told him. Face as straight as Ailsa could make it.

'Righto,' said the policeman. 'I don't mind a little chase, you know?' And off he ran in the direction she had pointed.

Then she put the vehicle in gear, drove out of the square and told her passenger to arise. 'Your name isn't Mannay, by any chance?' she asked.

'Mannay,' said the boy. Funny diction but that was what he said. 'Mannay, Mannay, Mannay.'

* * *

At the parking zone which Ailsa remembers visiting four years earlier, still four miles from Sheldeep, the Daimler comes to a halt and the chauffeur gets out and walks around to open the doors for his passengers. They are collectively indifferent to this protocol. Step out and glance up at the nearby trees, the many AFCs. Ailsa begins to explain the tree types to Steve, even Cherie listens like she is back in geography at St Hilda's. Dr Freeman talks across her, doesn't wait for Ailsa to finish. 'Damnedest thing, these trees with their different types of leaves. We've studied them carefully under a microscope—the boys at Cambridge—probably a virus that started it. Evolved all on their own down here so isolated from any others. Birds on the wing can bring a seed, you see. Just a chance event...'

Steve tries to be polite. Talks about the limited animals of this land. The absence of mammals except for the few cats which have made their way into the forest since being brought here on British boats.

Freeman laughs about the Connipian ostrich. There are no longer any alive, a single generation of Sapiens presence put paid to them. 'What can you do? Those early settlers weren't about to turn vegetarian like the little Connip girls. Not in a million years.'

* * *

The drive back to Sheldeep was more straightforward than she feared. Sped like hell, exceeded the forty-miles-an-hour speed limit, and felt bad for poor Mannay in the passenger seat. Bumping over divots; it even felt a little disrespectful to be treating forest tracks the way she was. The Connipians don't have a concept of sacred land, she had learned that. But every inch of the island is steeped in their history, holds the footprints of their forebears. The ground might be fragmented bone, so long have these people dwelt on their small island. It's barely half the size of her own Prince Edward Island; important to no one over three-foot three. And maybe to her as well. That's how it seemed to Ailsa; she longed to fulfil the wishes of the extraordinary women, the one who had drawn in the sand tray and her ailing sister. Mother of Mannay who sat beside her.

'Do you remember your mother,' asked Ailsa.

'Mumma,' said the Mixed-Up.

On the journey, Mannay lived up to his aunt's assessment. Seldom sitting still. Talking and talking without making too much sense. Ailsa tried very hard to explain her quest. Kept asking the boy to keep still but for all the bumping and his absence of functioning arms to steady himself, he wriggled over the top of the bench seat into the back. 'Mumma,' he shouted again and again.

'Why did you kick the policeman, Mannay?'

'Mumma.'

She recalled the location of the checkpoint long before she got there. Pulled up the Land Rover and explained to Mannay very slowly that she wanted him to hide. Feared those manning the point might not allow him through if they saw she was taking a Mixed-Up with her. The story of visiting another academic unravelling before them.

Mannay lay under a loose tarpaulin in the rear passenger footwell. He was so skinny it didn't look as if anything but air was beneath it. At the checkpoint she told the official that she had supplies for the Cambridge researchers at Sheldeep. The man looked through her windows indifferently. 'All right then, Miss,' he said, and she pulled away.

'Stay down until we're out of view,' she said quietly to Mannay. Did not want him to arise while the man was watching. She glanced around herself and noticed his withered arm sticking out from under the tarpaulin. It must have been there all along, not noticed by the official when he peered inside.

She rounded a corner on the track. 'Up you get.'

'Mamma,' he said again, clambering over the back to sit beside Ailsa once more.

It was a long drive and nearing nightfall when she arrived at the parking place. Still four miles of walking before they would reach their destination. She felt unsure of her ability to corral young Mannay on so long a march.

'Do you know what a three-legged race is?' she asked him.

Mannay did not, but she utilised a neck tie—navy blue and yellow striped, the colours of Carleton university, a smart accruement which Roger Curtis had left in the car—to bind her own right leg with his left. Then, her right arm around his shoulders and holding his limp hand in her left, draping the whole of his floppy left arm around her waist, they tried the walk. Mannay leaned into her, liked the game. He seemed to get the rhythm, they walked well together and, in time, broke into a slow run.

'Win the race, Mannay win the race. Mumma!' It was a bizarre and effective way to keep the wayward teenager in tow. Over time she came to like the feel of him upon her arm. To excuse the saliva that dribbled over wrist and hand. He couldn't help it. Mannay was funny. 'You mumma too,' he said a few times and—with thoughts of the tiny ailing woman towards whom they ran—Ailsa found tears in her eyes.

By the time they reached Sheldeep, the night was truly upon them. Four miles entwined, Mannay felt to Ailsa like another limb. Not an impediment but a needed extra beat in her walk. She felt a very damp sleeve upon her from his incessant dribbling. There was still a little sound as she and he came out of the trees and into the clearing, saw the shining blue of the houses, darker but distinctive in the moonlight. 'Mumma! Mumma!' shouted Mannay, and two Connipians emerged from one of the nearer houses. Looked at the strange arrival. Three legs and two heads. Arms that couldn't be deciphered.

'Stay still,' commanded Ailsa as she stooped to untie him.

The Connipians clicked and, to her surprise, Mannay clicked in reply, engaged them with more clarity, she thought, than his rudimentary speech had allowed her to latch on to. Unless the clicks for Mumma, Mumma were more complex than seemed likely.

The tiny ladies indicated that Ailsa should follow. Mannay, unshackled, was bounding ahead. The clearing was so much lighter than the dark of the forest she found her way easily—a little moonlight—while noticing how tentatively the Connipians walked. One of them held another of the shining stones she had seen in Klapakipsy's Blue House, a source of light which made no scientific sense, and nor had Ailsa heard mention of such a thing by the anthropologists.

As they walked through the village, she found another girl had come to her side. Ailsa recognised her, Prast. Young and only half-clad, exactly as she had been earlier in the day. Ailsa was quickly getting used to Connipian faces. Prast gestured, but there was no guessing what she was trying to say. Imply. Pen and paper left back in the car in her haste to bring Mannay to his mother.

At the door to a house which Ailsa believed to be Klapakipsy's, the leading Connipian stood by the opening. Hissed and clicked rather loudly. Ailsa heard a noise from within, and Tululiduh stepped outside. She looked at the Mixed-Up, he stood almost a foot taller than her, this adolescent of two species. Both clicked softly and speedily. Ailsa sensed a warmth between them.

295

Prast exchanged clicks with the Connipian who had led her through the village, and then the bare-breasted girl entered the house behind Tululiduh and Mannay. The other Connipian barred the door, did not permit Ailsa over the threshold. Within seconds, Prast came back outside, holding the tray of black sand with which Tululiduh had earlier communicated.

Klapakipsy is very sick she wrote upon it.

Ailsa looked at the words for a short time before glancing into the blue eyes of the young Connipian. 'I am so very sorry to learn this,' she said.

We are infinitely grateful that you have fetched Mannay for their reunion

'And Prast, do you believe the boy's mother might recover her health? Pull through?'

It is the end

* * *

The small party walk through the forest, retracing the steps which Ailsa recalls from her visit to Sheldeep four years earlier. This was where her association with Mannay began, where she first heard his name. A flood of mixed emotions washes over her. She wonders if she can find Tululiduh, advise her that Mannay remains safe. Perhaps the poor boy would be more contained if he lived here, she would love for it to be an option. Knows that enquiries are being made in Charlestown, the Dane nominated to be the next Secretary General of NATO. She can see the connection but not what the authorities would do were they to locate Mannay. He is no threat. Not to anything but a policeman's bum. Ailsa finds it strange to dwell upon; Connipians care for their regular offspring and want no input from Sapiens in that. They see the need to share responsibility for Mixed-Ups and the fathers of them simply do not. Never own up. It's not happened once in recorded history, and the next head of NATO is unlikely to break the mold. Mixed-Ups have been raised in foster homes, convents and orphanages—oftentimes with their Connipian mothers chipping in to help; infancies in Blue Houses for a few. Not a father raising a hand, changing a diaper. Owning up to the crime that begat them. The fathers are the true bastards in that story, and still the world says Connipians dump their offspring in East Town. Tell the story as has never once fitted the facts.

'What a pilgrimage this is,' says Frame, not tuned into the thoughts overwhelming Ailsa.

Cherie has gone quiet; she holds onto her hero's arm as a taken-for-granted wife might. A one-way gesture unreciprocated but nor is it rebuffed. 'I feel like I don't belong here,' she says, and Ailsa thinks it the most insightful utterance ever made by a member of the Thornhill family.

'Here to learn, Cherie. We're all here to learn.'

And as they arrive at the Blue Houses, the gently hummed cacophony of clicks which she remembers from her first visit fills the air. Ailsa indicates to the group that they should walk no further. Sits on the ground. 'We must wait.'

'Why?' asks Dr Freeman.

'Ailsa knows,' says Frame. 'I'm not here to ride roughshod.'

Cherie releases Steve, quickly sits herself thigh to thigh against Ailsa. Steve Frame lowers himself a little to the right of her. Dr Freeman neither sits nor goes forward. 'I think my colleague is in there,' he says, impatience in his clipped voice.

'And a Connipian will tell you precisely where,' says Ailsa.

He laughs at her comment. 'I don't click, and I don't think they really care to accommodate me,' says the doctor.

This is the man conducting a survey of Connipian health. So dismissive it is frightening. Half the world thinks they are freaks, nature gone wrong and we need help them no more than we would a dying snake. Others want to smother them in charity, and feel affronted by their lack of appreciation. Wish to go it alone. Helping Mixed-Ups is as close as that sort can get. Those are the principal categories in which people fall. Other views are out there, but they haven't caught on. Ailsa started in the latter herself. She mumbles a line that comes to her. 'Ca-a---out.' No, she hasn't said it. Her utterance incomprehensible, a good thing in the circumstances.

'What's that?' says Dr Freeman. Steve is looking at her too, looking with concern. He has a sharp ear; did he interpret correctly? There is no Canadians Out movement but it was in her involuntary burble. She is just like Cherie, the same as Dr Freeman too. Ailsa Donaldson does not belong on this island. Another kind of people have a claim one million times more substantive.

* * *

It was the strangest night. Assisting Mannay to unite with his mother for the final hours of her life. And then, through the use of sand tray and the spoken word, she agreed to sleep in a Blue House with Prast. She would not return to Charlestown until morning. It was unclear to Ailsa if Mannay was to return with her also. He was a beautiful boy, dribble and all. Kicking a colonial policeman up the backside: priceless.

The house in which Prast slept was tiny. Ailsa asked if there was another room in which her parents slept.

God Help the Connipians

Just me in here wrote the girl.

There was a bed of leaves. Ailsa thought it might be how a hedgehog sleeps, as she watched Prast slip within and curl herself up. Blue-dyed leaves, the hedgehog idea not quite on the mark. A beckoning wrist movement invited Ailsa to join her; she did as she was bidden. Never be rude to a Connipian. There have been two hundred and fifty years of that which Sapiens had serious need to make up for.

And how comfortable it was. Once or twice, she was conscious of this clever young girl at her side. A little hand or leg entwining with her own. Conscious through sleep, a deep and rich immersion in the world of blank thoughts and dreams that she never quite pinned down. Colours and thoughts and time sliding this way and that. If she was falling down the deepest hole on Earth, she was loving doing it. Wanting to go there. Go deeper.

In the morning, she felt more refreshed than she could remember occurring any previous night. The young Connipian was awake, had wrapped herself gently around Ailsa's head. So small her knees touched one shoulder and the top of her head the other. Ailsa had not known Connipians to be physically affectionate. Had understood they were not. Misunderstood, maybe. Homo Sapiens do not spend the night with them in the Blue Houses, none but Ailsa to the best of her knowledge. Ailsa, Zaneta Lozano, and a small stream of rapists. She knew not why Prast had trusted her beyond the deed of fetching Mannay. And being female: that's probably the big one. She thought of telling Roger and Lynne about it. Turning their research on its head. But deep down she knew that she wouldn't. Mustn't mention any of it. This had been a private visit—a favour as few have ever done a Connipian—not research into anything.

Once she had arisen, Prast was ready for the day. Stood upright within her house-for-one. Ailsa knelt but couldn't stand. And sleep was still in her eyes while Prast seemed as lively as Mannay had been the day before. She left Ailsa alone on the nest of leaves. Went from her house with a hand gesture. Ailsa looked around her. When she turned her head, it was into the stick and thatch of the little home's roof. All dyed blue, every twig and frond. Before she could orient herself, Prast was back, clutching a slew of colour in her hands. Fruit. Different fruits which Ailsa had no names for, grown high in the Connipian skyfields. Prast tried to give one after another to her. Ailsa told her they must share. Then while Prast sucked on a fruit, Ailsa took the pointed stick and wrote in the sand.

Thank you for looking after me

Prast took the stick from her, started to write beneath it, and Ailsa felt grateful that she was letting her words remain.

Frame

You have a Connipian heart

Then she butted the top of her head gently into Ailsa shoulder. The look on Prast's face could have been a grin but these were not easy faces to interpret. Shining blue eyes beneath two or three roving hairs on an otherwise bald head. Beautiful Prast.

'Do you know how Klapakipsy is this morning?' asked Ailsa.

Passed away in the night, Ailsa was devastated to read.

Unbearably sad. Ailsa tried to tie it to her dreams. Klapakipsy seemed to suffer, that was what Tonkin told her. Suffered for the failure of the New York conference. She even wondered if she had become estranged from other Connipians. From the core of them. That was not how it seemed last night. Even Prast gave her this news in a most matter-of-fact manner, although how a Connipian might show grief was not a part of any reading Ailsa had done, not something Roger or the others had ever spoken of. 'What will happen to Mannay?' she asked.

We will care for him in Sheldeep. For the present time.

After these exchanges and the offer of more fruit, Ailsa was escorted by Prast to the edge of the settlement, then, to her surprise, Prast walked on with her, accompanying her all the way to the Land Rover. They had no sand in which to write, and feeling the touch of a Connipian felt unusual and comforting. No bound ankles this time, just a hand stretched up to her own which she kept as low as she could. Hand in hand with Prast.

At the car, much smiling and gesturing, it became clear that this was where they would part. 'Goodbye and thank you,' said Ailsa, and the younger girl clicked something or other that was surely appreciative. Must have been, Prast was her friend, and if they had only a little in common it was sufficient. An unforgettable friend.

The drive back to Charlestown was uneventful but for the salted tears that streamed down Ailsa's cheeks. Klapakipsy dead; Mannay orphaned; the privilege of the friendship she shall forever remember.

In Charlestown she found she had mislaid the list of all the supplies she was supposed to buy. Made her best guesses, bought some foodstuffs that would have to suffice. Her growing indifference to the Canadian mission here could inadvertently begin to show. She wondered if she could care less. From there she went to the post office. Picked up what mail there was. Mostly Roger's, and officious-looking stuff it was. Both the boys had some too. Her brother had written to Ailsa. For Lynne Sharpe there was no correspondence at all; lived for fieldwork, nobody in Ottawa missing her.

Next, Ailsa drove back to East Town. Found the kitchen where Terry

299

Holmes worked, the only one who admitted knowledge of Mannay. She knocked at the door and asked for him by name. 'Ailsa, did you find...' He stopped talking immediately, something in her changed face must have alerted him to her heightened emotionality.

'Long story. He met his mother...' Ailsa paused. Worried she would burst into tears just saying what she'd seen. '...he's stayed out there. I hope that's all right.'

'No reason he shouldn't, but I hope his mum can cope. Mixed-Ups are tiny to us and massive to Connipians. That can make things tricky.'

Ailsa stood in silence, feeling pleased to be in the company of someone who knew Mannay while fearing saying more. The link to New York. It seemed both private and dangerous. Stories in the newspapers of the twenties and thirties, Mixed-Ups born of circus Connipians being kidnapped, disappearing, before a blood test could identify blood type, indicate likely paternity. The lengths to which influential people will go to avoid a stain on their reputation.

'Ailsa, did you have anyone with you in the car except young Mannay? Quite a handful that boy.'

She could scarcely speak. 'No. Thank you. I just wanted you to know. He may be back.' She turned her back. Nothing personal. Terry seemed a good man. Ailsa trudged up the road. Glanced at a building, a canteen. Unsure if it was where his cooking was destined for, or if his was served elsewhere. It certainly gave free food to any Mixed-Up in need. Above the door, a sign read, **Rest Your Floppy Arms**. Did they like it? Hate it? She was unsure what to make of this strange island beyond her wish to learn only from those who truly belonged here. Books and anthropologists are all so full of nonsense.

* * *

Just the three of them share a Blue House. Freeman is at the scientific station, and their interpreter, called Kaytip, lives elsewhere in Sheldeep. Makes her home with her mother and friends. She has aided Steve and even Cherie to talk directly with the Connipians. The biggest surprise of the day was Ailsa's reception at a particular house, a young woman—a very tiny, very pretty woman—baby in her arms, invited the three into her home. Invited Kaytip also, but she declined. Mixed-Ups are said to be uneasy with pure-bred babies. Reminders of a status never secured, although Kaytip lives among Connipians year-round. Ailsa was delighted to be, once more, in the company of Prast. Older now, and a mother herself. Just as warm as Ailsa remembered her to be those four years ago. She keeps her own little sand tray, and conversing with Sapiens must be the rarest thing.

Cherie bravely asked the young mother a slew of questions. 'Was the father involved in the baby's care?'

> *He has too many children already. And not an ounce of strength with which to lift his child.*

There is no equivalent to milk for Connipian babies; breast milk aside their diet is one of fruit and root vegetable, only a minimal amount of the latter. 'What would her child do if she could not breast feed?' asked the suddenly mature Cherie.

> *This village is full of girls only too happy to help.*

'And do you ever worry that atomic bombs, the threat of nuclear war, makes this a difficult world to bring a baby into?' Steve looked at Ailsa with alarm when Cherie spoke the words. Ailsa just nodded at Prast. The little mother seemed at ease with the question. Connipians are very, very small, they are not children.

> *Worry was not a Connipian state until a little after the first ship of you bigger people arrived on our shore. Now we know it all too well: how frightening the world may be. You have multiplied the fear manyfold in the short time we have known you. We cannot spend our life in fears of your making. What happens will, and I hope Sapiens think harder than they yet have about all they have created. See the wisdom of suppressing progress for it amplifies the worst of your disparate traits.*

That truthful answer made Ailsa feel sad. Sad for two entire species. Then she and Prast talked for a time using the board, left to themselves by the others. Steve outside the door, very carefully holding the tiniest baby he ever will. She asked after Tululiduh, learned that she lives in the north of the island these days. Shared news of Mannay but not of his first sexual experience. Now she is again trying to sleep in a Blue House, she recalls that extraordinary night four years ago, she and Prast virtually in each other's arms. She has not told another soul. Cannot. It feels like a dream, an experience given to her and her alone.

Ailsa has asked four different Connipians what they make of the scientific survey. The attempt by Freeman and Hooper to learn what diseases the Connipians suffer from. Inoculate them even, although that is hypothetical. No agreement ever reached and only a handful of Connipians have ever been subject to such treatment. None at all by consent.

They all replied that they considered it irrelevant. Connipians will look after Connipians. That is how it has always been, and they have proved themselves more durable than the meat-eating, land-grabbing, fire-starting bomb makers.

God Help the Connipians

It is not a contest and Sapiens are running in the wrong direction if it were.

Now, in the pitch black of the house she feels someone lifting the side of her blanket. Ailsa has had off-and-on doubts about Steve ever since meeting him. Knows with frightening certainty that she would sleep with him if she was drunk. Thought she was doing exactly that for the first couple of minutes of her encounter with Mannay. Would do it if she had access to contraception, no drink required. And on neither count could she imagine acquiescing with the Governor's daughter in the same room. Really not. If Ailsa Donaldson is a louche, it is with a few standards attached. Mannay was a mistake she regrets while constantly picturing his morning-after grin. Regrets more than she begrudges.

'What are you doing,' she hisses quietly.

'Can we just lie?' whispers Cherie. This is a surprise. She had wondered if the girl would have tried Steve's bed. Tried to picture how she might intervene if he didn't give her short shrift. It was why the Governor signed off Ailsa's pass into the protected areas, she is certain, however unspoken the role. And she couldn't imagine lying there quietly while he made love to someone other than her, that would have been completely humiliating. And now this: the girl in her bed. At least she seems to want only the closeness of another. It has been an emotional day. Cherie has heard criticism of her father from one Connipian after another, none of it directed harshly at Cherie, but the sentiment was unmissable. She is the man's daughter; he a Connipian hater, a connipulsive. Must be, the people who feel it say so. None of that reflects upon her. Connipians harbour no excessive prejudice but they do like to know who they're talking to.

During the night Ailsa hears Cherie weeping. Doesn't know what causes her tears and, very discreetly, seeks to enquire. Whispered words when she is certain the man in the room sleeps. The girl cannot find the phrases to tell, holds her closely and this confuses Ailsa. It may be simple hysteria brought about by sleeping so close to her beloved Frame; it might be sorrow for all the British have wreaked upon these small, proud people. The disruption of a million years of peace.

'Cry and know none of this is your fault,' whispers Ailsa. 'From here on we must do what we can.'

As she says the words, Ailsa knows that leaving the island must be her next move. There is no other way to help them. Not for people as destructive as the Sapiens. The smash-and-grab brigade. Shovelling limestone and potash into the holds of ships for the bleak pleasure of denying another's wish.

11.

On their last day in Sheldeep, Ailsa listens as Steve finally gets to talk with an ageing male, talk to him with Kaytip as the go-between. Clicking and talking.

'Are you happy to tell me how old you are?' asks Steve.

A little clicking and Kaytip advises that Mycorek—the little man's name—believes himself to be eighty in years of Sapiens calculation.

'That's very old for a Connipian, I understand,' says Steve.

'No, no. I might be the oldest right now but we have a million years of history. Many men and women have lived for more than a hundred years. These times are a little harder.'

'And has your life always been in this house?' asks Steve.

'I have mostly received the girls here. Those that wished me to fertilise an egg. It was a pleasure, as you may be familiar with. In a few instances down the years, I also went into a girl's home. I am not precious about these matters. Always do as I am asked.'

'And has it felt a fulfilling life?' asks Steve, and the old man rocks back and forth in the chair on which he sits.

'I have done what had to be done, I could not do more.'

'And do you see a good future for Connipians. Might the British leave, do you think? I know there is growing pressure.'

'You are British, I understand, and you have clearly come. We had a bright girl a few years back, Klapakipsy her name, and she tried to win back our island from the British. Went to a great deal of trouble. I believe it cost her everything, her health. She said—after New York—that there is no future for Connipians. Hope was lost when your kind proved themselves unable to hear anything but their own noise. The Sapiens were deciding what to do about us on their own. Never dwelled on a Connipian thought. I'm not sure why they invited us to their grand conference.' He raises his head up from his pillow, scrutinises Frame. 'Window-dressing, I believe you call it.' Then he slumps back. 'All Connipians would listen to that young lady; we thought her wise. I still think it. I believe she made headway with your sort, but not the breakthrough we needed. We are not at the table now and perhaps we never were. Our size, you see. You would only let us sit at the children's table back when you feigned an interest. Wished to do what you arrogantly assumed—with your shocking bias, I have to add—to be in our interest. Health surveys and the like. Klapakipsy was very wise, and she hoped to impart some of that which we Connipians have come to know, to you Sapiens. You see, your sort doesn't act in the interest of their own longevity. We would be foolish to anticipate Sapiens doing anything at all for our kind. You Sapiens are far from learning how to look after your own—setting fire to the world and believing it an act of improvement—pretending you are also protecting us is a deceit with which you may fool yourselves. Attain good feelings on a very temporary basis. It is helpful that you and I talk, young man. I hope you remember my words for a long time. We have not written down our history, as you have, for we believed it unnecessary. We would live this way and all who came after would know that we must have. They were part of that same river, a part of us. Now I believe it may all end, so perhaps you can draw something from our relative success, even though you will find it hard to replicate. If you do not mend your ways, you shall do to yourselves the very thing you are already doing to us.'

Chapter Four

Watch it on Weavers

Before

Justin enjoyed the train a lot more than he does the hospital. His mum was nice to him on the journey, bought him a muffin at the station. Wasn't shouty or any of that.

'Why hasn't Daniel come?' Her voice is surprisingly strong for so frail a pack of bones, an arm attached to a horrible drip.

'Danny's old enough to stay home, Mother. You know he doesn't like hospitals.'

This rankles with Justin. He hates the places, and three years isn't much of a difference.

'Or Roy? He's not...'

'Mother, you know you'd only argue with him.'

'You only argue with him, Sky. All I do is support my daughter.'

His mother lets out a short and rueful laugh, stretches a hand to touch the paper-thin skin of her own mother's forearm. Justin wishes he was anywhere else. He even feels a little faint, can't help from looking at the bag of blood hanging from a stand by Grandma's bedside. Tells himself not to, and then goes on looking just the same.

Nothing about her voice says she is nearly dead, everything about her appearance does. It might carry on talking after she's pegged out. 'I don't even know why you married him. You're such a live wire, Sky, and Roy has scarcely a smile in him. Not much of a worker either if you want my opinion.' It goes on and on, Justin hates it. Likes his dad more than his mum but never says it. Not even to Danny; can't be seen taking sides. Doing what this old skeleton is doing. Skeleton with a bag of blood hovering above it.

'A shame he couldn't come—Danny that is—we're very proud of him back home,' says Sky. 'He's been bumped up to the top maths set. They started him lower and then he got every question right in the exam. One hundred percent. Top of his year before they even put him in the proper set for clever ones. I always told you he'd go far.'

God Help the Connipians

Justin tries to think if he's done anything worth telling Grandma about. Made the football team, that's something. Only left-back, and he wanted to be striker. Romiley Primary School, only twenty boys in his year group.

Grandma starts to cough. Horrible to watch, and she has a funny bowl by her side, she points at it and his mum passes it to her. Coughs phlegm straight into it. And still she talks. Coughs and talks. Loud, harder to hear who she's complaining about because she's barking up phlegm while she does it. 'This is something, Sky...' She spits a big one into the bowl and her face goes from pale grey to red with the effort. '...something I want Justin to hear. The boy needs to understand where he's from. You might have told him but you were never really interested.'

'We've talked about it...'

'Justin...' He looks at her but it's the bag of blood and not her face that his eyes fix on; she coughs and coughs, her filmy half-blind eyes peer into the stainless-steel dish, the resultant sputum. '...I've lived in this country only since the end of the war. I spent all my childhood in Georgia.' He nods, tries to ignore the coughing, but then he only turns towards the hanging blood which is more horrible still. 'And I never lived in the true family house, my daddy was just as ornery a ragamuffin as your daddy. I knew which it was—the house we belonged in, whatever bitsy shack he had us put up with—knew the house where my own granny had been raised. We were something in those long-ago days.'

Sky has stepped away, and the coughing has finally abated although the phlegm bowl still trembles in Grandma's skinny grey hands. Justin sees that she is appraising his grandmother, Sky's own mother, through narrowed eyes. Anyway, Justin always knew Grandma was American. Still has an accent for all her years living over here.

'I thought it wasn't your granny in the big house,' says Sky.

His grandma spits into her bowl. 'Her mother then. Up the family tree. We weren't in cotton: we were cotton. Are you hearing this, Justin? People in your family employed hundreds and hundreds. Moultrie, Georgia. Nothing like you're living now. A house with its own ballroom. That's what we had, what I should have been born to but for the wastrels stuck in the family tree.'

As she coughs, her daughter steps up to the bed and steadies the bowl. More great gobs of phlegm. Sky turns her face to the side; Justin guesses she has no wish for Grandma to see the big grin on her face. If he asks her what was so funny—on the train, or when they're back on Underhill—she won't say. He knows she won't. Likely as not she'll say she never laughed at anything. Pretend she can't remember what Grandma said. Sky never lived in a house with a ballroom, and it sounds like his grandma didn't either. Dreaming isn't doing. They're all as bad as each other in his family.

His brother, Danny, is no better. Dreams up computer games but he never actually makes them. Should've been here by rights but Sky can't make him do anything these days.

God Help the Connipians

1.

The phone is ringing and Roy asks Justin to turn the sound down. His son looks a little put out, lowers the volume but not by much. They purchased the widescreen at Christmas, those three months back. Roy told the boys he'd bought it out of his savings but the truth is, it's on tick. His older son, Danny, asked awkward questions. Not the first time Roy's bought himself a few money problems. Roy thinks Danny should have paid something towards it anyway. A better course than grumbling at him; they all watch it. And Danny's the one with a good job—might be a great job, Roy doesn't understand it properly—paid a packet. Doesn't charge Danny for rent. Well, sixty quid a week but that's all in. The council tax eats up more than half of it. This is Danny's childhood home, his and Justin's, so it wouldn't do to charge the going rate. However, Danny's moved into the largest bedroom, Roy thought it the only solution. That was last week. They fitted a desk in there; Danny's employer told him to start working from home. And now everyone's at it, the entire country. Stay at home! Can't be catching the virus, mustn't spread the virus.

Justin's job isn't much. He works in a local pub, expects to get laid off any day. Not heard from his employer since the government told everyone to keep indoors. Putting the country to sleep like Rip Van Winkle. Justin says he'll get furlough money, paid for slacking off. He hasn't seen any yet and Roy doesn't believe it anyway. The government would be crackers if they gave free money to every kitchen helper in the north of England. He could be wrong, of course: the newsreader said last night that these are extraordinary times.

Roy picks up the phone. Not many calls on the landline these days. Theirs is in the corner of the lounge, on a flex so you can't stray far. Lounge-diner-kitchen all in one, this little house only has separate rooms upstairs. 'Sound down,' he hisses to Justin, hand over mouthpiece. 'Oh, hi Sis.' A smile comes to his face on hearing the voice on the other end. 'Auntie Edna,' he mouths as an aside. Justin—holding the remote control expectantly in his hands—nods in acknowledgment. His aunt lives in London, not seen since the Christmas before last, over a year ago. She phones—Roy does too—they keep in touch.

'Roy, my boy, I'm worried about this virus. Very bad here in London. Me and Julie thinking we might come to Romiley, stay with you. We won't catch it up where you live, will we?'

'Gosh, Sis. You'd be very welcome but what about the kids. And we haven't...well...I don't think you're meant to travel anywhere right now.

Is it really so bad, down there?'

'Ha! Roy. I got you going! No, we're going nowhere. Just calling to see how you're doing with all this that's goin' on.'

'Good. We're all good up here, Edna. Edna, my little sister.'

She chortles down the telephone. Edna is eight years younger than Roy, into her forties now. 'How we going to get through this then, Roy? Julie is at the hospital four days a week, doin' her nursing. I'm very worried she's going to catch it. Don't see how she won't. Hospitals are looking after nothing but all the poor people who've catched this thing. It's going to be this way for weeks and weeks. The papers are saying it. Saying it's all goin' to get like the pictures we've seen o' Italy.'

'Do you see her? Is Julie worried?'

'Can't see her. Not allowed to see her anymore. Stay at home and wash your hands,' she laughs. 'Julie and me, we talk on the phone every day, Roy. Always have.'

'No catching this thing off the phone. Not over the telephone wires. I suppose you could wash your hands afterwards, to be on the safe side.' He laughs and Edna joins in.

Then there is a silent pause.

'Thirty years to the day,' says Edna.

'I know,' Roy whispers quietly. Face so changed by the exchange that Justin stares at him. Roy pats a hand down, gestures that he's not to be concerned. 'I don't forget.' He can hear his sister crying quietly. This memory has changed their mood, laughing about the pandemic and now this. His half-sister was scarcely a teenager on that awful day, maybe it's more painful for her, maybe less. Roy doesn't doubt that they both feel it. Julie too. Thirty years to the day. He's been thinking about it since the moment he woke up. Their mother on the train tracks.

Edna doesn't say anything further about the long-ago tragedy. Goes back to the practicalities of the current crisis. 'Kids at home, can't be goin' into school any more, and I'm glad about it too. Want us all together, Roy. Safely indoors. I want to know you are too. You and the boys are safe, aren't you now?'

He confirms that he's going nowhere, nor Danny or Justin. It feels nice to be checked up on. 'And Dad?' asks Roy. 'I really should phone him.' Always calls him Dad; even the boys know Winston's his stepdad. Can't miss it given the colour of his skin, the contrast.

'Do, Roy. Give Dad a little tinkle. Only not today. He always has a quiet one when it's...you know.'

Roy doesn't answer. He is nodding his head in agreement but Edna won't see that. Might sense it. Thinking solemnly about poor Winston Grant, a widower of thirty years' standing.

God Help the Connipians

When the call is over, Justin turns the sound back up. In the corner of the screen the words *LIVE FEED* flicker, the picture glimmers an unearthly blue. A woman wrapped in clothing of that colour, rich and distinctive, holds a small infant close to her person. The baby looks all wrong. Not normal at all.

'Freaky weird,' says Justin.

The woman has no hair. Not on her head, small nose, not that the face looks unpleasant. It's still an odd look. Starting to ring a bell though. Roy has seen pictures of them many times before. This streaming of motion pictures from down there—showing our distant and unlikely cousins for the whole world to see—is unexpected. As wrong as the country closing down; it's not how things are supposed to be. A television crew in the Connipian forest, inside a Blue House. And after all these years. 'Oh gosh,' says Roy. 'It's those people, I know a bit...' He stops mid-sentence. It's the coincidence of it which he finds unnerving. His late mother was obsessed with them. And she was knowledgeable too, knew everything there was to know about Connipians, Connipia.

He was a teenager, embarrassed by her interest. He's regretted that, looking back. Should have spent more time trying to understand her. Everything that preoccupied her. She even went there—went to Connipia before he was born—he never enquired about it. She told him stories when he was small; he'd stopped listening come his teenage years. And since her long-ago death it's been too painful to revisit. It seemed all so personal to her. Seeing these pictures on Weavers makes him feel uneasy. He remembers that his mother said we should leave them be. Not interact at all. As if she wished she had never been there. And now they're in his living room: a live feed of Connipians coming from the forest. Showing themselves to Roy, to anybody who cares to look. Someone is showing them; he hopes they've agreed. Signed something. The filming and photographing of Connipians has, by law, long been prohibited. Roy's certain it has. No pictures and no *Homo Sapiens* in the protected areas. Somehow or other these extraordinary pictures are streaming across Weavers. The inside of a Blue House, one inhabited by mother and child. And they have another little Connipian living with them by the looks of it. Unless she's visiting, it's probably allowed down there. There can't be any virus on Connipia, not in their bit of it. The ancient forests. No contact with the wider world in an age. The cameras are the oddity, an invasion of privacy like has never happened before. Not since the nineteen-fifty thing. He thinks all the photographs he's ever seen of them were in black and white, although the blue of their clothing is familiar. A colour photo or two in the National Geographics, perhaps. His mother could have kept a copy, shown him. He's trying to remember exactly.

'Look at that weird baby!' exclaims Justin. The tiny Connipian woman has taken it from her breast and they can see that the skin of the infant is deep red. As if blood vessels are at the surface of every pore. It's a miniscule creature. Nothing on screen shows them the true scale, the little mother's two hands encompass the child. And her hands must be half the size of a normal persons; everyone on Earth knows that.

'They've let the cameras in,' says Roy. Disbelief in his voice; not that he's any sort of expert. Never been to Connipia. Never seen a Connipian with the clarity the widescreen affords. Not before today. It must be fifteen years since one of them last left the protected enclaves. That's what he thinks; there's still resentment in pockets across the world but nobody's broken the treaty as far as he knows. Not in a concerted way.

'Are they making friends with us again,' says Justin. His father doesn't answer, fears calling it wrong. They watch another Connipian move through the blue light. An older looking woman with wrinkles around her eyes. Roy and Justin hear the clicking noises that both have heard about, never before experienced, coming over the airwaves. Sounds a little mechanical, tap and click. And it means nothing to Roy. If it is a language, it's one they do not speak. Speak or click. The code has never been infiltrated, linguists and mathematicians have tried and tried. Not a foothold.

'Mum was a bit obsessed with them,' says Roy.

Justin pulls a strange face. 'I don't remember that. Never said a word about them.'

'Sorry, lad. My mum, your gran, that was who I meant. We were just talking...'

'I never had a gran,' says Justin.

It's true to Justin's experience: Roy was nineteen years old when his mother took her own life, gone before he'd had so much as a proper girlfriend. Thirty years to the day. 'Not to know her you didn't. You never had the chance. She's still there in our genes, isn't she? Mine, yours. She was obsessed with the Connipians. That other world. She met them. Lived down there for a time.'

'You didn't live there too, did you, Dad? Connipia.'

'No. She was out of there long before I was born. Said she wouldn't go back out of respect for them. Thought we all ought to do as they wanted. It's only a tiny island. We didn't need it and they did. I remember her telling me that.'

'Did she live with them? On Connipia. That must have been a nightmare. Banging her head on doorways, even the roof inside the house.'

God Help the Connipians

'I don't think it was like that. Not living with. She was on their side. Would have been interested to see all this. To find out what's changed. Why they've finally let the cameras in.'

The pair of them are glued to Weavers; the scene they watch is domestic in nature. People who may not even be people; however, they look surprisingly like us when seen going about their daily lives. The feed has moved to the inside of a different Blue House. Two tiny women sitting on the ground; they have string in their hands which they both look at intently. One closes her eyes as she runs her tiny fingers across its knotted length. Even though the string is blue, Roy thinks it's made of grass. Special grass, very long in length, possibly interwoven grasses; it hasn't broken for all the bending and knotting they've done. Then the other girl leans in, her bald head almost touching that of the first girl who hands over the curious string. A clatter of clicks, thoughts shared. It might be the Connipian equivalent of laughter. He wonders if it's really that. His guess could be way off the mark. Roy isn't sure if any Sapiens on Earth knows the true sound of a happy Connipian. His mother would have said it was none of their business.

'What are they doing?' asks Justin.

'Not sure,' says Roy.

Then the pictures beaming from halfway around the world move outdoors. Focus on a clearing, the communal space between a small group of Blue Houses. The light is brighter, sunshine on their chalk white skin. Four little Connipians are mashing up fruit with wooden implements. One of them is bare-breasted which surprises Roy. Odd that she lets them film her that way in this day and age. And shabby of Weavers to show it. The cameraman should have advised her to cover up. Or the Director, Roy hasn't a clue who works on a set like this. Justin's eyes are glued to the TV screen. Needs a girlfriend, thinks his dad. The Connipians keep looking around, glancing this way and that. Could be they're staring at the cameraman. Staring back if he's anything like Justin. Or are there only camerawomen out there. It would make sense. No men in the forest, the dreadful stuff that's been done to them has come flooding into Roy's mind. His mum was definitely against men going into the forest. One of the girls flaps her hand a little to the side. Like she's swatting a fly but he can't see one.

'They look nervous,' says Justin, and Roy agrees. Says nothing in reply just thinks about the pictures beaming into his home. They don't appear the same as they did in the old films. Justin says he's only seen them once before, in the Hollywood movie a couple of years ago. Roy never saw it but Danny and Justin did. Clips from the nineteen-fifty conference were used. Roy saw that in the trailer, the television advert. Lost in Connipia, it was called. Little CGI Connipians for the most part. Danny told him the plot and it sounded daft. A man finally learning to click. Never goes to the cinema these days, he'll watch it when it comes on the tele. Academics have yet to confirm if the clicking is a proper language. Must be if the Mixed-Ups can interpret it; seems like it's just us that don't get it. Brains full of words that can hear no other way of thinking. No Mixed-Up needed for interpreting in over a decade, maybe two. The Connipians have been keeping themselves to themselves.

'None of them are wearing wigs,' says Justin.

Roy expects that they did in the film. And they were wearing them in the newsreel from nineteen-fifty. The more they look like us, the more sympathetic we are. It makes sense that they've stopped: no Sapiens to impress in the forests. They don't care what we think. Mixed-Ups have dropped off the radar too, Roy has no idea where they've gone.

As the pair watch it on Weavers, it feels like entering a dusty room in Roy's mind. New facts that he must have learnt years ago keep emerging within his reverberant thoughts. Connections made. East Town was where the Mixed-Ups lived. Maybe they're still there. His mother told him of the place and he's read about it too. Not for more than a decade. Probably twice that. Charlestown, plus the industrial south of the island, an area known as Great Lodowicke, form a single territory, with a governor appointed from here, a few thousand settlers who have stayed out there for the long haul. Still digging out the potash, the limestone. Nobody polices the rest of the island: the British won't and the nations which signed up to the nineteen-fifty agreement have no formal role. Signed it but never agreed very much that was useful. It was never more than a gesture. The Connipians were not in favour of the New York settlement anyway. Being left alone was all they wanted. Roy recalls a story from a year or two back. A Mixed-Up baby left in East Town by Connipians. No one could figure out how they had got out, got over the fencing which is meant to protect them. Or how a logger or miner, or whoever it was, had got through in the first place to bring about a pregnancy. Raped a Connipian, although Roy recalls that the story avoided the R-word. Sympathy for them has been in short supply since they turned their backs on us. Newspaper owners can be the worst of the lot. In thrall to the Twelve Tribes.

'You've got to feel a bit sorry for them,' says Roy. 'Now and then people still get around all the fencing in order to...'

'I remember that,' says Justin. Must have been on the same thought-train. 'Why do they leave them in East Town, Dad? The floppy-armed ones. Isn't it wrong? They should look after their own babies, if you ask me. Look after them whether they're disabled or not.'

God Help the Connipians

'Justin, Justin, you really need to read about it. Get the full picture. Those are half human...is that how I'm meant to say it? Half...I don't know...us. We should take a bit of responsibility don't you think?'

'No, Dad, that's just something they used to think. I remember reading about the last Mixed-Up on Wires. They said there was no way a man can have got over the fences. The article said it proved that it's always been their own babies with the floppy arms. Nothing to do with us.'

Roy turns from screen to son, scrutinises him very carefully. 'I don't think that's right.'

'Dad, they might have been lying to us for years. That was what it said on Wires.'

'You might want to look into it a bit more. Some of these news channels just make it up. We can't get in and Connipians won't come out,' says Roy. 'Men go in because those little girls are three foot high and we can't protect them properly. They find a way. A lot of propaganda gets written about them; not anything that should fool a bright lad like you. You know who the Twelve Tribes are, I take it? Very influential. I've no time for them at all. They think we're all descended from Adam and Eve and the Connipians aren't, so we should swat them like flies. That's about the size of it; a horrible way to think if you just step back a pace.'

He stops talking, realises Justin has turned from the screen and stares only at him. It's not like Roy to get emotional about the news. He takes a few deep breaths as they both turn to watch the pictures streaming on Weavers, sent from the forests of Connipia. Many different fruits which look like nothing they ever see in Sainsburys, all spread out in the clearing. Girls kneeling before wooden trays, pulping it with carved sticks, slicing and dicing. Their knives are made of wood but they cut competently. Slice into the flesh of the fruit through thick layers of skin.

'I'll look it up on the history and science pages,' says Justin. 'You might be right. I can imagine there are men as would do that.'

Roy nods his head. Justin's a sensible lad. Needs a better job than working in a pub kitchen.

The camera keeps going back to the girl with her breasts showing. All the other Connipians are fully clothed. Roy can't help looking, still doesn't think it's right. Weavers beaming it everywhere. Perhaps the Connipians don't understand how the outside world sees them. Connipian men don't really chase girls, not as he recalls. All very different for them. He tells his son how unprecedented it is, that it could be a good turn. If the Connipians are allowing cameras in then we must be getting along with them better than we ever have before. 'But it's very odd,' he adds.

Watch It On Weavers

'That's nice,' says Justin, and Roy isn't sure if he was really listening. Eyes on breasts, and the girl doesn't even look small with nothing familiar alongside her, nothing to show the scale. Roy can see why the lad might stare. Something about the whole set up doesn't make sense to him. The Connipians always said contact was the problem. Clicked it. That's why they've shut themselves away for so long. Roy has always been on board with his mother's views, even the long years of scarcely thinking about them. Never really instilled it in Danny or Justin; didn't talk about it because it was a world away, and—up to a point—the Connipians seemed to have got their way. There has been very little about them in the news since his boys were in primary school. Since they closed down contact, accepted they would live only in the parts of the island we were willing to give them. The situation seems to have changed in an instant. Nothing has prepared a watching world for this. Roy would have heard on the news if there had been any dialogue leading up to it. Expects he would. And there were no pictures taken inside the Blue Houses after nineteen fifty. The conference determined that cameras shouldn't go in. Not sure a motion-picture camera ever did it in the bad old days. Just stills. He can't think what might have changed their minds. Connipians all over Weavers.

They watch the screen in silence and Roy starts fearing the cameras are uninvited. He can't work out why Connipians would be so indifferent to the camera crew, the invasion of their village by people and apparatus. The focus of the live stream shifts, moves into the deep of the forest. A couple of girls, wearing only short blue wraps around their groins and midriff, are scaling trees. Very adeptly they climb up a towering trunk, reach the canopy in no time. The camera follows effortlessly. It's clever, thinks Roy, they must have drones out there with the crew. One of the girls curls her leg over a branch, picks fruit and throws it down from high in the trees. The camera pans. There are several Connipian girls on the ground. They catch the green gourds by raising up their skirt-fronts. Click as they catch; perhaps their noises praise the accuracy of the thrower. Or they could be counting what they've got, a crop of fruit grown high up in the trees. Skyfields, the term comes back to Roy.

A script rolls across the bottom of the screen.

> ***These strange and heathen beasts have learnt to harvest fruit from plants grown upon other plants. They use the rich vegetative matter of the high forest, and the sunlight from above it to grow produce unknown outside of New Poplar. Cultivated no other way. Scientists have yet to appraise how first this started, or all the qualities of the fruit they cultivate. We can tell***

God Help the Connipians

from the deposits of calcified tree matter that they have practiced this form of agriculture for hundreds of thousands of years. The Connipians keep the detail of their practise to themselves. These are not creatures who know how to share. Not language or culture, nor even fruit.

'They don't look like beasts to me,' says Justin.

Roy thinks Justin's focussing primarily on the naked breasts which continue to stare out at them from the widescreen. No longer in close up, but neither tree climber wears anything on her top half, and most of the girls on the ground are the same. Nothing beneath the skirts they raise to catch fruit. Roy wonders if he should turn it off but Justin's not a kid any more. 'Who would write rubbish like that about them?' Roy might be looking at the girls as closely as his son. Glances around the room now and then, trying to make it less obvious. When they do the catching you can see everything you shouldn't and that, in particular, feels all wrong. The filmmaker is no friend of the Connipians. The writing along the bottom proved that. Heathen? Most of us are no better. Edna and Julie are the only people Roy knows who go to church. 'It's not been called New Poplar for donkey's years. Pretty disrespectful, calling it that.' He stretches across to take the control from his son. Seeing them near naked is annoying him. He has none of his mother's obsession with Connipians but nor has he ever doubted she was right. We should just leave them alone. What they've been up to these last fifteen or twenty years, no one knows. They didn't get it all their own way: the protected areas don't add up to even half of the island.

'What are you doing?' says Justin, as Roy tries to grapple the remote from his grasp.

'I hate it. I think it's their enemies showing all this. Doing it now that everyone's at home. Can't go out because the virus has everybody stuck indoors. Then they go and write connipulsive propaganda about them.'

'It's still interesting no matter who writes the words. Seeing how other people live. Because they're nothing like us, and then they are a bit.'

'But Justin, all the world agreed to protect them. This isn't that. And I think we might still be mining right under the protected areas that we say we've given them. I've read that somewhere.'

'So what, Dad? If the mines are deep enough, the trees will still be left standing. They're going to be all right. Still get their fruit.'

'I don't think they've agreed to let the cameras in. Not if the ones doing it are writing all those horrid things about them.'

The tickertape gets no better.

Not made it to the Stone Age yet. These animals have no

316

***more changed their lifestyle than the common or garden
slug. A million years of standing still.***

'Ha!' laughs Justin. 'I don't think slugs grow crops up in the tops of trees.'

'No,' agrees his father. 'And if the cameramen have taken coronavirus into the forest with them, it could finish off the Connipians altogether. Everything about this is wrong.'

Roy holds the controller in both hands, thumbs hovering over the buttons. Captivated by the pictures of a people he never imagined seeing, had long stopped thinking about. And it's thirty years to the day. He never understood it completely but they were so, so precious to his mum. The live feed returns to the babe in arms. The mother wears a blue wrap that covers her properly. Roy places the remote beside him on the sofa. Covered up is good. The girls can stay half-dressed in normal times because there aren't any men in the forest. The writing at the bottom of the screen is really getting under his skin.

***They craft their fabrics from leaves as primitives always
have. Leaves held together with a type of cotton
unknown to the true people of this Earth, used only by
Connipians. Perhaps they spin it themselves as spiders
do.'***

'But it's clever if we don't know how it's done,' says Justin.

'How are they allowed to broadcast that?'

Both continue to stare at the screen. Watch it on Weavers is the corporations advertising slogan. Worldwide they encourage everyone to give it a go. Always something different, surprising. That's been the message for a couple of years and this seems to be their trump card. There's a lot of time to kill, everyone in the country staying at home. Most of the world by the sound of every news report Roy's heard in the last week. Watch it on Weavers is a more upbeat message than Stay at Home. And a complementary one. Could be all that unemployed Roy and laid-off Justin have to do for weeks and weeks. In this household, only his older son is working. Upstairs, doing whatever it is he does. Laptop, monitor and printer; he's got the dining table up there because they never had a proper desk.

* * *

When Danny comes down from his bedroom, work finished for the day, he wears a jumbo-sized grin on his face. The widescreen shows only the BBC news. Roy flicked channels on the dot of five. So far, it's told them only of the havoc covid-nineteen has brought about. The goings on down in London and across the Atlantic in New York City. Central Park is a hospital, something scary in its own right. Father and son are hoping for a report about Connipia. Want to find out how come Weavers is streaming pictures from the protected forest. Spotlight on the little people who have kept themselves out of sight for a generation.

'You've been watching?' asks Danny.

'Broadcasting from the Blue Houses. Dad says it breaks the law. We don't know if they've even agreed to it. Not the Connipians. They never wanted us on the island in the first place.'

'Yeah, yeah. You know how it's done?'

'I thought you were working up there,' says Roy.

'They're doing it with Sparrow-hooks!'

'Wow,' says Justin.

'No way,' says their father. 'Sparrow-hooks might be on your computer games, there are none in the real world. Not nowadays. Every government in the world banned them a few years back. There was a treaty. It definitely isn't allowed. There's something about them that's rogue. That's why they were banned. Wouldn't work in the long run, I think that was it.'

Danny turned twenty-three a few weeks back, still a bone-thin boy who cannot buy a drink in a pub without ID in his hand. Hair over the collar and he gently flicks his head back to keep the fringe from his eyes. He's laughing openly at his father. Danny, with a first-class degree in computer science, knows about a million times more than Roy about this kind of stuff. 'Berry—we spoke on Wires just as I was finishing up—reckons these are a new version of them. A bit of nanotech. Smaller than when they were banned by about a hundred light years. Smaller than anyone can even see unless they swarm together. Which Sparrow-hooks do if they need to. Join together to make a camera, if you get my gist.'

'I can't believe that's allowed, Danny,' argues Roy. 'I even think smaller might be worse. Harder to check up on.'

'Can't put the genie back in the lamp though, can you, Dad?'

The news on the widescreen has moved on to a report about deer: as many as fifteen of them graze on what must, in normal times, have been a busy traffic roundabout. The road sign behind them points towards Stafford, Telford and Stoke. No cars going anywhere today, none at all—Stay at home! You're all locked down—it seems the deer are not obligated to follow the rules. Take the opportunity to eat the grass on a once-busy roundabout.

'Look at that,' says Justin, pointing at the screen. The camera has panned around. An empty petrol station, adjacent café closed to the public. A spindly little deer with a white spotted coat peruses the menu on an outside billboard.

'Come out, come out, you little Connipians,' laughs Danny. 'Where are you, my beauties?'

Roy looks at his elder son, narrowed eyes of disdain. If Danny's right and they're using Sparrow-hooks, it's an utter disgrace. Breaking the law on every level imaginable. All for a bit of voyeurism. To crank up Weavers' advertising revenue. It was all so important to his mother—Connipia for the Connipians—thirty years or more back. 'They haven't agreed then? That's what you're saying. We've sent in robots and they haven't agreed. I think it's completely wrong. And, like I said, Danny, I thought you were meant to be working up there. Not watching Weavers.'

'They've gone in, no idea who sent them, Dad. It's the Sparrow-hooks doing it at this point in time. There's no me or you needed. And I'm working hard enough. Innovation technology: keep up or it'll eat you up. I've said it before, could be the company motto.'

'Someone must have sent them in, Danny. Who programmed the robots?'

'You're kind-of right, Dad. According to Berry, someone programmed Sparrow-hooks to do something or other long ago. That will have been the old ones—steam-powered, sparrow-sized buggers. Now the clever AI has reinvented itself and flown itself down to the south seas. God knows what the original programmers wanted it to do. This must be part of it, I suppose. The technology is truly awesome. Small is the new big. Funny, eh? Tiny robots checking up on the tiny people.'

'What's AI, Danny? What is that?'

'Artificial intelligence,' Justin jumps in. Danny nods; younger brother got it right.

'They just wanted to be left alone,' says Roy. 'You wouldn't like it if someone sent pictures of you onto every TV screen in the country without you even knowing it. The Danny Channel, letting people watch you slacking when you should be working.'

'What are you so aeriated about? The little girlies don't even know what tele is, do they? Wouldn't have thought so. Makes no difference to girls who live in a forest and it's pretty interesting seeing them again. Nobody can stay hidden away forever.'

'They're cleverer than you seem to understand. They know all sorts, just not what we're doing to them. Not if what you're saying is right.' Roy is a bit red in the face, and Justin makes a hand signal to Danny, gestures that he should calm-it although it isn't his brother who's getting in a state. 'Banned means banned.'

'If the new Sparrow-hooks are as small as Berry thinks, they could be flying around our lounge filming us and we wouldn't know. Might think they were bluebottles. Or they could be smaller than that. Nano is nano.' There's a smirk on his face as he says it.

'This is all wrong.' Roy pushes out his chest, an odd gesture from a seated position. 'It's still our island so the Government's got to stop it.'

Justin shakes his head, trying to catch Danny's eye. Older brother's up for the debate. 'Everyone wants to know what goes on down there. Now we can take a look; Connipians are none the wiser, so it's no skin off their backs. And anyway, Sparrow-hooks can't be stopped. The government would just look a bunch of fools if they tried.'

'Terrible.' Roy looks towards Justin who nods his head.

'You were watching it, Dad.' Danny is as excited about it as Roy, simply seeing it differently. 'Weavers give people what they want to watch. That's all they do. I think it's the writing along the bottom you don't like; lots of people probably find it funny.'

'Do you think Weavers own the Sparrow-hooks, Danny?'

'No. Nothing like that. They just agreed to stream it once it was set up. Whoever set up the little robots broke the law but we'll never find them. Robots don't grass. They send the pictures to Weavers who broadcast them in the public interest. Won't get into any trouble, not serious trouble. You can bet Weavers had a team of lawyers do their homework before they started showing a single snap. I think they're a FTSE one hundred—they are or they will be—a bit edgy but they try to keep it all above board.'

Roy eyeballs his son. Thinks him too pro-voyeurism, too keen on the violation of the protected areas by far. Maybe he would think as Danny does if his mother had never instilled her views in him. The Connipians are fascinating, might be the only proof in the entire universe that we are not alone. In the long hiatus since we last had contact there have been some wildly speculative articles in magazines. Were they learning to speak properly? Had they all died of cholera? No one knew; not a click heard. The Hollywood movie might have been scratching a collective itch. Reminding the world of the simpler people down in the forest, those whose bespoke method of communication is inexplicably beyond our understanding. The film was Hollywood happy. A man learns to click and all our sins against them will be forgiven. In the real world, two hard-line positions are all that is out there. Their insistent isolation and all the connipulsive nonsense that The Twelve Tribes push. He's seen the leaflets, not in an age, but they used to be left on the tube when he was young. Television adverts at the time they closed off all contact. The zealots said the Connipians are a threat because they come from a time before God chose man as His custodians of the Earth. Bloody funny custodians we're turning out to be. There was a documentary about them last September. August or September. The Twelve Tribes movement believe the presence on Earth of another type of human is a barrier to our return to Eden or it's getting in the way of the second coming. Some crap like that. The scariest thing was, The Twelve Tribes gave large donations to more than half the candidates in the last US election. The President might be a signed-up member, he isn't saying one way or the other. Praises the bible but no one thinks he's read it. Blows his mouth off about everything else. In the USA he can attract more votes for slagging off Mexicans than he could Connipians. Doesn't rise above any of it. You can tell from just looking at him that this president isn't on board with the spirit of the international accords. Not any international accords as far as Roy can tell.

'I don't know how big the cameras are,' says Danny. He stands next to the wide screen, arms waving as he talks. May not be this confident in the outside world—a shy lad when he was growing up—he's always been the know-all here on Underhill. 'I can't picture nano stuff, it's not my area. They're certainly no bigger than an insect. We should stop calling them Sparrow-hooks but that was the size of the first design. The little girlies won't have a clue what they're dealing with. Never will so long as they stick to their no contact with the smarter species rule. It's their loss. Could ask for royalties if they wised up.'

'Danny, we're meant to leave them alone,' repeats Roy. 'They wanted it and we promised we would.'

'Who really knows. They don't actually speak, do they? Those funny people who did their interpreting were all simple-minded. And you don't object to the live feed of that eagles' nest out on Salisbury Plain or wherever it is. The thing you look at on Weavers Wildlife. Why worry about this? Just another bunch of animals in their natural habitat, aren't they? We're not much different ourselves except we invent clever shit. Sets us apart, wouldn't you say?'

The father looks exasperated. Can't recall talking about Connipia with either son before today. Justin seems the more sensible. He sits quietly listening to them but his every facial expression is on the right side of the debate, that's what Roy reckons. Right side of the argument. He listened up when Roy told him about his late Granny's views earlier on. 'How do the Sparrow-hooks work then, Danny? I don't really understand them.'

'Each one is a tiny robot but they all work as a network. Thousands of them; and that was when they really were sparrow sized. Hundreds of thousands now, I expect. Berry thinks the individual ones could be invisible to the naked eye. They can have as many as they like. Connected through the airwaves. Robots with shared neural pathways. They fly about on their own and then act as one. Same principle as the slime molds—you know, in nature—Sparrow-hooks are smarter. About a billion times smarter. Maybe more than that.'

'I don't know what slime molds are.'

The older son finally sits himself down on the sofa next to his father. 'A bit of biology for you,' he offers. 'They're a pretty interesting life form. Unusual, and one of the earliest on Earth, been around for aeons. Slime molds can creep around as single cell organisms or join together and have thousands of them act as one. A hundred years ago scientists confused them with mushrooms because of how they look when they do that, when they join up. They have absolutely nothing in common with mushrooms, looks can be deceiving. When they join together it looks like one lifeform, although it's actually lots of individual organisms electing to act as one. Get it?'

'And how does that relate to Sparrow-hooks, Danny?'

'Titchy-tiny robots that can do the same. I expect it takes thousands acting in unison to become a camera and beam these pictures back. They might be nano sized and join together to be as big as a mosquito. AI is very smart these days. They could...'

'Sorry, Danny. What do those letters mean again?'

'Artificial intelligence. And the combined intelligence of a bunch of robots is shit-scary, Dad. They could keep combining—millions and millions of tiny little flying robots—and become a car or a battleship. Whatever they want.'

'A battleship?'

'Nothing much can stop them. It all depends what goals the original programmer laid down. Being as they're intelligent, they work out the best way to achieve it and then configure themselves to do just that.'

Justin fidgets in his armchair. 'Who programmed them, Dan? The writing they've put up on screen is nasty.'

'Ha! We don't know who's behind it yet, Juicy. Berry has no idea. The thing with AI like this is that they might've been programmed long ago. Given some objectives to go figure, and it's only now they're ready to deliver. I expect it's someone like the Only-God's-Children lot, that's what people are saying on Wires. Could just be a mining consortium, of course. They'd enjoy writing funny stuff about the Connipians. Letting the world see the freaks. Nothing worth protecting down there, not really. I've heard that the areas we gave to the Connipians are rich with potash or something.'

'Gave!' says Roy. 'Don't you think being there first counts for anything? We can manage without their potash, surely.' On many occasions he has drawn pride from this clever son. That feeling is taking a break. Danny talks like a complete arse. Science for science's sake. There must have been a good reason why the United Nations outlawed Sparrow-hooks and this might be it. Roy wishes he had talked about his mother with the boys, should have done it when they were younger. Her views about Connipia. She didn't want any Sapiens on the island, wrote to the Government about it. Collected signatures for a petition. He needs to put them straight. Danny that is. His younger son has got the message. Worked it out when the writing under the pictures gave the game away.

* * *

Justin is utterly fascinated. It might just be seeing girls with bare chests but he thinks not. Tells himself it's the anthropology of it, not that he's been interested in it before. How like us they are, that's what captivates him. That and their otherness. That's what's really weird about it: they are both. Not the same, even their gestures, or the sight of one walking around, show how different they are. And then they're very easy to relate to. What we'd be like if we weren't so self-centred. That's what he's worked out and he wants to run the idea past Danny. The trouble is, his older brother might be the most self-obsessed of the lot. Too much the technophile to spare a thought for a simpler life on a faraway island. Connipians are natural and Danny isn't. All day every day thinking about his next invention. Not that he's famous or anything, but Danny writes programmes for robots. That's what he said months ago. Not for Sparrow-hooks; Justin's sure Danny has nothing to do with them. Robotic arms that turn screws in manufacturing. That type of thing. Keeping his dad out of work; they've joked about that when Roy wasn't in the room.

Justin has been watching Weavers for half of the night in recent days. They put porno on one or two adult channels. Not hardcore but he gets to see everything. Flips channels if they're only showing gays going at it. Tonight, it's all Connipians for him. Can't take his eyes off them. Doesn't try to find anything racier. Currently the interior of a Blue House is on screen, a male lying on a bed of leaves. The bed is higher than the floor but not by much. Knee height in Connipian knees. Their beds are quite short, about right for very small people. Justin thinks he might watch it all night. Hopes to learn about the people with whom his own grandmother was, apparently, obsessed. He's not heard his dad get as animated about anything as he did when he was talking about her. And them. He might learn a lot from watching. How non-Sapiens humanoids live, proper anthropology.

Justin has never before felt more than a little sleeping anger towards Granny Grant. Took her own life and left poor Granddad on his own for half a lifetime. Except Winston Grant is not quite Justin's granddad. He

God Help the Connipians

raised Roy but not his true father. Winston's black and Roy is white, plain as day. His dad always spoke kindly of his mother—Justin's gran, the blood relative—whatever went on thirty years ago. Said she was a great mum to him. She was never a grandmother, gone before she had a grandchild. Never knew that she used to live on Connipia, not before today. Quite something if you think about it. He's never met a soul who's been. There must be some people down there doing the logging and the mining. He read on Nolly Knowledge—earlier this evening—that the entire island is, in square miles, about the same size as the Outer Hebrides. Better weather though.

When the picture zooms in, bringing the sickly-looking naked male into sharp focus, the ticker underneath gets nasty again.

These dirty fuckers have been known to father children with up to forty Connipian girls.

Justin hates reading it. They shouldn't be trash talking the little guys. And he likes seeing the pictures, won't turn it off because of a few words. They're really strange people, their way of life going on ten times longer than his own lot have been knocking about. The writing is just propaganda. Whoever's doing it want to make people hate them, and Justin can't think of anything the Connipians have done to deserve that. Danny compared the Weavers livestream to a wildlife programme, but you never hear presenters talk about animals this way. Not crudely. No-one moralises about rabbits.

Justin clicks away for a few moments. Brings up the Only God's Children page on Nolly Knowledge, Weavers everyday encyclopaedia. Danny and Roy seemed to know a lot more about this crowd than Justin does. Heard the name but he's no idea what they believe. It tells him that, these days, the group draws members from all religions: evangelical Christians started it, then got some Hindus, Muslims and even Jewish people signing up. It's a way of thinking about people, not a faith in its own right. Homo Sapiens are the chosen ones, that seems to be as much of a philosophy as they have. The page even states that critics regard the movement as connipulsive. It says nothing about hiring robots to broadcast from the protected areas of Connipia, or putting pictures on Weavers with a disparaging commentary running along the bottom of the screen. Nolly Knowledge might need updating.

Danny also thought it could have been the mining companies who've sent in the Sparrow-hooks. More likely to have the know-how. And he can't see why a religion—although Nolly Knowledge says that Only God's Children isn't one exactly—would write about them in these terms. Religions tend to use kind words even when they mask a brutal message. *I permit no woman to teach or to have authority over men; she is to keep silent.* His friend, Tom, used to taunt a couple of Christian girls with that one back in school. He could recite passages from the bible because his mum's a Born Again. Tom isn't, he'd stopped going to church as soon as he was old enough to stand up to his mum. Justin looks up which companies run the mines on Connipia. Pacific Stone and Hard White Limited are the only names which arrive on screen. Pages and pages about how carefully they vet all employees. Respect for all who live on the island. '...now known as Connipia,' it says. He thinks that's a bit of a give-away, not calling it Connipia outright.

At this time of night his father and Danny are both in bed. Danny could be watching it up in his room for all Justin knows. His father won't be, keeps no screens upstairs. Reads a chapter of his latest potboiler and then snores with his door open; Justin doesn't hear him tonight. Doesn't because he's stayed downstairs. Watching Weavers, loving it and hating it. Great big swathes of each. Interesting to see them but it shouldn't be happening. The camera lingers on the same male. He looks pathetic. Thinner than any of the girls and they aren't fat. Girls or women. Justin can't guess their ages. The ones showing their little tits are probably the young ones—at least they're grown up—Justin tries not to think about that, hopes they show older ones. Same as on the porn sites. He doesn't like watching old women at it, but he knows the law. The more he watches this, the more he thinks he should turn it off. Should but can't. It's the enemies of the Connipians who have put this on Weavers. His dad said so. If the robots hate them that is so fucking weird. How can a robot feel an emotion? If they've been programmed to hate, then it's been done by pretty sick scientists. Scientists or tech nerds, miners or religious freaks: whoever set up the Sparrow-hooks in the first place. Even watching might make him an intruder in the Connipians protected space; he knows it, but they don't know he's watching. There's no figuring the morals of that. Danny seemed to know a lot about how Sparrow-hooks work. They've both played electronic games that have them in the arsenal but it isn't the same. Might be nothing like. On the games you just try to grab more of them to increase your power. Other guns can zap them but they're the fastest adversary in the game. No one seems to be controlling the ones down in the Pacific. Not even trying to zap them. Danny said they can't. The cameras are smaller than bluebottles. The Connipians might think they have an infestation of flies. He's read that Connipians don't even swat them. Not with a rolled-up newspaper, not with the palms of their hands. They don't kill living things. Not anything animal. Cut fruit up, he's been watching that, but fruit doesn't have any feelings. The Twelve Tribes crowd probably think Connipians don't either; thinking something doesn't make it true.

325

God Help the Connipians

Sparrow-hooks can gather together. Swarm. Hundreds of them can turn themselves into a single fearsome adversary. He's made them do it on his games. It was that potential, and the likelihood of going rogue—we programme robots but they can't be unprogrammed even if we start regretting what we've done—that brought about a worldwide ban. That's as much as Justin understands; earlier, Danny said loads about it. Most of what he said went over Justin's head.

And the ban hasn't held—seems like some awkward sod breaks every law ever passed—these pictures wouldn't be streaming out of Weavers if it had.

Nolly Knowledge tells him that it was in two thousand and four when international law first declared that Sapiens would no longer intrude into the protected areas. When Justin was two years old.

> *Before that time,* he reads, *the Governor of the island had discretionary powers to grant access. Many in the International Commission overseeing the implementation of the agreement believed them subject to overuse. Since two thousand and four the authorities have installed bells on the Connipian side of the interior fencing. Any Connipian may ring one if they need assistance from the British authorities or the International Commission. The bells have, since their installation, remained silent.*

He scans across the page as quickly as he can. The word robot is not in here. He's certain they shouldn't have gone in but it could be the treaty didn't spell it out. First time around—the conference of nineteen fifty—there weren't any robots to write about. Everything since has been a tightening of what they agreed back then. Removal of power from the Crown-Appointed Governor. As Justin reads a bit further, he sees that the Connipians never agreed to any of it. Didn't sign first time, didn't sign in two thousand and two. He'll ask his dad what he thinks in the morning. Sounds like his granny would be the best person to speak to but for being dead these thirty years. He wonders why they didn't sign. Maybe the Connipians always knew we wouldn't keep our end of the bargain. They still have Mixed-Ups now and then, that's in the article too. Not much protection in the protected areas. Nolly Knowledge is completely certain they really are interspecies. Mixed-Ups are half Sapiens. It seems incredible to Justin that his grandma actually lived down there. It's like finding out your uncle is a unicorn farmer. A touch of a button and he's got the old Connipian fella back on the screen. Can't stop watching them whether he should or shouldn't. Maybe the strangest thing is that he didn't already know about his gran. That she liked them, went there. Perhaps knowing what she did at the end has stopped him thinking any further about her. His aunties never talked about their mum either. He has cousins down in London, they get along but seldom see each other. Justin's granddad, Winston Grant, is the only father Roy knows, a step-father who he calls 'Dad' although there's nothing Afro-Caribbean about Roy. If anything, it's a little bit of American that comes through in his voice. Not strong, but in a few of his vowel sounds. A connection with his mother, Justin understands. With the dead one. She was Canadian. He's no idea where his real granddad— the blood relative he hasn't so much as a name for—came from.

It's getting interesting on Weavers. The prostrate male is clicking. Quite an insistent string of sound, and standing next to him is a blue-clad girl who answers back. They must be chatting, to Justin it sounds the same as bashing little sticks together. Click, click, tap, tap. The girl must have come into his room in the last few minutes. Never saw her arrive. The decrepit old guy is lying down, the girl looks tonnes younger. Doesn't wear a top. Whatever they're saying—all the clicking—they look to be getting along okay. She's taking off her skirt. Justin thinks it's another reason they shouldn't show it. She wouldn't be showing her tits—all her downstairs bits in this shot—if she knew she was on TV. Streaming everywhere, as Weavers say in their adverts. He likes it and he hates it. Definitely both. The screen is so big that in close up she looks the right size. Big enough for him, for Justin, although she would only be half his size if she were really in the room. The poor old fella looks sick but Justin can see he's up for what the girl wants. The camera shows an X-rated close up. Stiff dick. He looks so frail it could be his last bonk before he departs this life. The girl is on him in no time. Straddles the stricken man. Justin presses buttons on the remote, clicks away, brings up a game show. Contestants working out anagrams while a studio audience goes 'ooh' and 'aah'. Before he changed channel, he read the caption.

This little slut is shameless. Look at her work the old man's cock.

He thinks he might switch it back. She won't know he's watching. Looked sexy apart from the bald head. Not as young as all that: her breasts were a handful. A full Connipian hand, at least. He presses the remote. Sees her sliding on the guy's groin. This is not so different to the late-night stuff he watches on the other channels. Weavers has something for everyone. God, he wishes he was that ailing man at this moment in time. Feeling the inside of her going up and down his...No, he flicks the channel back again. Must try and crack the anagram. Don't think about what's going on a world away. None of his business. None of

God Help the Connipians

anyone's business, leaving them alone is what his dad said we should do. Not imagining being a Connipian male and fucking a different girl every night of the week. Justin's more than half decent at word games.

2.

Father and eldest son breakfast together, Justin sleeping in late. They don't know it but he was watching Weavers until four-thirty in the morning. A long night, a lot to take in about how those other people live. Forest lives unchanged in hundreds of thousands of years. Justin hated the running commentary, the tickertape. It called them uneducated— loads of insults that were much worse than that—and he can see a lot of merit in a lifestyle that's lasted so long, the million-years thing. He had three Connipian wanks too, never had a single one before last night.

The screen is on again, accompanying father and son as they breakfast. Coffee, tea and toast, the livestream from the forest.

'Do you know about your grandmother?' Roy asks Danny.

'Lived on New Poplar? Connip-lover or something?'

'You do know.'

'Juicy told me last night. I hadn't known before.' Danny glances from screen to father. 'Or I forgot,' he concedes.

'Danny, Danny, the way you talked yesterday surprised me. Since when have you been connipulsive? Why would you be?'

'Dad, you need to read more. Connipians have snake faces, all that hairless freakery. No venom, I guess, click like rattlesnakes anyhow. Freaks of nature. What do they matter to us? Their days are over, surely.'

Roy has toast and jam, the plate balanced on his lap; he sits beside Danny on the sofa. Danny rises, goes up four steps to the dining-kitchen area. Looking at his bacon under the grill. The toaster pops. 'Butter one for me,' says Roy, eyes are on the screen. 'I thought like you when I was a kid. Not nastily, nothing against them ever. Just couldn't fathom why my mum was so fascinated. She talked like they were more important than any of us living in London. She didn't care for the news, never took a paper, then she'd always put the TV on if there was something about the island making the headlines. Even if it was just little ripples. Anything at all happening between us and the Connipians, she needed to know. Gave us her view too. Seemed odd at the time but I learnt about them from her. We've never given them a chance. That's the truth of it, Danny. We trampled the Connipians into the ground. When I was in junior school, Edna, then Julie came along. Mum was good to us. A terrific mum. But whatever was going on with us, you could bet she was reading everything there was to read about Connipia. Barred us from

Watch It On Weavers

watching those old black and white films. You know, the Jimmy Whist rubbish. If they were ever funny, they were also just plain cruel. No channel would dare show them today...'

'Weavers would, Dad. Would if they thought anyone might watch it. Democratic, not like your BBC. The channel of bleeding hearts...'

'Aye, maybe they'd show them on this muck-raking station. What they're saying is wrong, the ruddy tickertape. Telling lies when they know better, that's exactly how ignorance spreads. My mum was spot on about that. Understood how our lot like humiliating them, the Connipians. Kidnapped and paraded for our entertainment. She'd say this is just more of the same...'

'No harm in it. It's dog eat dog out there, always has been.'

'I disagree. I disagree completely.' Roy talks slowly, tries to lecture his cutting-edge computer programmer son like Danny does him. 'I think my mum told me the statistics about them. They never lived always died, any that got taken off the island. It was a terrible ordeal for them. The strangeness of not following their own lifestyle—having nothing familiar around them—that's what killed them.'

'Did you watch last night, Dad. I think the Connip girls kill the blokes. It's how it looks.'

'No, I didn't watch.'

'They shag their brains out, and they don't look as if there's much in there to begin with.'

'Danny, that's ignorant talk. And you with a degree and everything. They didn't show that, did they? Tell me they weren't filming them...mating?'

'Every wild life programme does it. What's the big deal?'

'It's not right that they show them at all...'

'Yeah, but you're watching it,' sniggers Danny. On the screen two girls are high in the canopy of the forest. Fields of fruit in sunlight; strange gourdes with a pink tinge to their flesh, twenty or thirty of the fruit connected on a string that must be part of the plant's biology. No clothing on their top halves.

'Daniel, we go to great lengths to preserve artefacts and pots we find from old Chinese dynasties or ancient Greece. Only on Connipia is there a civilisation still living in some simpler and ancient way. Doing it for far longer than the pyramids or Hanging Gardens, all that lot. If we can't preserve this bit of history, it's a sorry state of affairs.'

'No one's killing them, Dad. Just putting them on the tele. It's a win-win really. We get to see the way of life which we've promised to preserve in those treaties; the little girlies carry on picking fruit. Don't sweat about it. Weavers is only interested in viewers. You don't need to read the tickertape. Imagine your dreamy alternative if you like.' He makes inverted commas with his fingers. 'A million years of slacking in the forest. Stuck with the diet of a fruit bat.' Laughs as he lets his fingers down. 'Does that sound all right to you?'

* * *

He goes up to his bedroom, logs on to Conatus, his employer, and then Danny clicks away. Goes back on to Wires, the site on which he spent much of yesterday evening. His work-light shows, he looks active so long as he brings up the Conatus programme and moves his mouse every once in a while. Berry is on Wires too, it's not a surprise. They use this channel to talk without leaving a trace which managers from Conatus could ever trawl through.

Hey Big-Head.

What's troubling you?

No trouble. Dad's a dick. Late onset Connip-lover.

Ha. Sentimental now they're back on screen. I think most of our lot are Homo Timidus deep down.

You been on it all night?

Tracking.

Any word on who's behind it? Who controls the Sparrow-hooks?

Rogue.

???

Pretty funny in my head.

??? Rogue?

No one controls the Sparrow-hooks. The Twelve Tribes may have set it in motion, no one is pulling the strings any longer.

???

Christian thickies can't programme properly. They must have programmed in something. Not last night's fare, not from fire and brimstone Christians. The little robots are way smaller than Connipians, way smarter than us or them. They do their own thing.

F***ing hell. You even guessed that yesterday.

Yes indeedy, brother Daniel. F*** a duck, or a Homo

something-or-other which is no bigger than one.

Thanks for that, Berry. Are you working on the Digger Dogs today?

No point, my f. We need to hack into these baby Sparrow-hooks, that or build our own. Digger Dogs look pretty lab compared to these versatile buggers.

All illegal. Not worth the effort if this results in a big clamp down.

Can't happen. No clamping down on rogues. That's what the Connipians, through the conduit of their more technologically advanced intruders, have taught us today.

They get a bit technical. The pair of them work on the same projects all the time. Danny looks up to Berry with a sliver of apprehension. His friend always talks of going outside their brief, and Danny worries it could go wrong in lots of ways. Digger Dogs are robots for mining, or will be if their work comes to fruition. Conatus want self-directing tools they can sell in Africa. Put to work in copper, zinc, even uranium or diamond mining. Berry thinks they should step away from Conatus once they've designed a winner. And for that reason, he has them design outside their work architecture. Build a picture, string their plans together on a secure arm of Weavers Wires. Post only their mediocre—their not-too-bad—on the Conatus platform. Take the monthly money while spending half their time on schemes which Conatus would be too lily-livered to put its shoulder behind.

Danny opens his programming notes, the designs Berry already thinks obsolete. Digger Dogs were to be Scottie-sized robots—enormous when set against nanotech Sparrow-hooks—and they calculated the dogs might profitably be put to work down mines which had fallen into disuse. They're still working on the detail; the robot needs to be very sophisticated to work without above ground support. If they crack it, they can send them into long-closed mines and let them dig and fetch. Pay off their student loans! They've talked of doing it behind the backs of the site owners. Who checks on obsolete mines? One hundred percent profit for Berry and Danny Off-the-Books Limited. Unlimited, indeed. Build their own Digger Dogs which rummage in the dark. Why not? If a robot bumps its head, no one gets sued. They've yet to figure how to make the robot distinguish coal or copper from the plain rockface. A stumbling block but they can dream. Danny expects Berry will share the Dogs idea with Conatus when they crack the design. Neither of them has experience of taking anything from design to manufacture, going solo sounds pretty far-fetched. Scavenging scraps with the mine-owners agreement will still turn a profit. Looks a bit lame in the light of everything happening on Connipia. The Sparrow-hooks are really having a laugh. Playing out the narrative of the Twelve Tribes, but the AI seems to have lost its religion. More randy than righteous, the ticker tape's hilarious.

Berry was onto something when he suggested harnessing the tech being used on Connipia. Sparrow-hooks could enter a mine through a ventilation shaft. Always coordinated, high-speed recognition, better than bats. Each flying bot knows where its fellow robots are. If required they can couple, quadruple. A half a million would make a tank. They're adaptability is mental. The technology has been banned the world over; two separate treaties, everybody on board except North Korea, and they couldn't raise the ingredients for a decent smörgåsbord. The Connipians haven't signed either but they're completely useless. Russia, China, everyone promises to abide by it. Do so precisely because they're self-learning, the type of AI that could turn on their masters. It was calculated back in the day, that if used as weapons, they would fight a war to the obliteration of both sides. Not only could they not stop unless they'd been specifically programmed to do so, best guess says they would ignore such an instruction. After a while, self-learning robots are always going to start writing their own script. Fighting to the destruction of human civilisation wouldn't necessarily knock out the bots. If they had some on both sides, they'd still be slugging it out when every other life form had breathed its last. Logged off, as they say at Conatus. Sparrow-hooks are scary, brainpower that makes Homo Sapiens look as dumb as Connipians. Robots are brutal bastards, while we, on the other hand, are mostly sentimental like his dad has gotten. That fact—AI's hardnosed brutality—concentrated minds when they were first conceived, made all the world sign the treaty. No Sparrow-hooks. Having the capacity of AI that fast and determined sitting in the air, talking to each other across the ether with split-second progress updates—zillions of the little buggers—it's the way to the stars. Danny doesn't have the detail but he can pretty much see it. Robots that leave us behind. Already left the Twelve Tribes looking like hooligans. It comes to Danny that the tickertape saying all the funny stuff about the little women in Connipia is probably a psychological ploy. AI will have learned how that works. Turning on the Sapiens men with the crazy-time sex show. Softening us all up for a demonstration of something else entirely. He can't quite work it out. In his half-sleeping state last night, it crossed his mind that the all-knowing Sparrow-hooks might conjoin together into a randy robot, hydraulic cock and all. Take over when Connipian men have all clapped out from doing what they do.

* * *

'Off out for your exercise today?' asks Roy.

'Maybe,' says Justin. He and an old schoolfriend have texted. They'll meet behind the Forum. He's not telling his dad that part of the plan because it's not allowed. What a messed-up world it has become: Justin's meeting Tom, somebody call the cops!

'Can you pick up milk and a paper?'

'Sure will, Dad. Have you got a few coins?'

* * *

Even walking down to the shops feels peculiar to Justin. An absence of sound; there shouldn't be but there is. The short walk from Underhill into the village centre took less time than usual. Or more. He couldn't tell which but it felt completely different. Not a moving car the whole of the way. A woman across the main road sneezes and everyone in view stares at her. Four people, sum total. It's not this shy of the public at a normal midnight. Just a week ago the place was buzzing: people on their mobiles, cardboard coffee cups in the other hand; old women pulling shopping trolleys or young ones pushing baby strollers; cars backed up to the pedestrian crossing; cyclists on road and pavement. Everything's gone into hibernation. At the crossing, Justin's hand reaches for the button, then he stops. There's no point—he steps into the road—red means nothing today. Couldn't get knocked over if you went looking for it. Outside the supermarket, a queue of three people waits to go in. Spaced out like traffic cones; one in and one out, everything being done the pandemic way. Only the Connipians are doing as they usually do, all others captive to the virus-laden world. Justin glances at his phone; a text tells him Tom's waiting. He goes around the corner of the dark-stoned municipal building, walks into the car park. Two vehicle's, that's it. Two hundred last time Justin was here. Over by the large wheelie bins where everyone brings clothes and plastics and glass bottles for recycling, he sees his friend. None of that shit being brought down today. Recycling on hold, the world won't get any warmer so long as everyone stays in bed.

'End of days, Jay Gee, these are the end of days through which we live.'

He stops the prescribed two metres from Tom. 'Danny says lads of our age won't get sick. Everyone else will.' Justin lowers his voice as he makes this last point. Roy Grant's thoughts on lockdown supplanting his own momentarily. His father shared a lot of worries about the London Grants after the phone call. Reckons Aunt Julie is bound to catch it, full-time

333

nurse in an over-crowded hospital.

'You aren't scared of the pestilence, are you, Jay Gee?'

'Not scared, just can't be giving it my dad. Do you know anyone who's got it?'

'London's crawling with it. No one has it up here.'

'Is that right?'

'Pubs are shut, so where are we going to catch it? Are you furloughed?'

'Expect to be. Money for nothing, I'm good with that.'

'Boring, isn't it?'

'Have you seen...'

'...Weavers.'

'Mind-blowing, yeah?'

'My mum thought it was about time someone sorted out the little people down there.'

'That's a bit heartless. My dad thinks they might be better than us. We keep fighting wars and shit, they've done none of that.'

'Can't win a war with little girlies doing the fighting, Justin. They're a bunch of losers. Did you see that one who got starkers, doing everything she fancied with the old fucker. My mum saw it and said they should be stopped. Immoral, every last Connipian. That's her take.'

'She watched it! I didn't think your mum would be into porno.'

'She watches it to get self-righteous about. Her and everyone in her church is doing it. I'd have given it to the girlie if I'd been in the old guy's place. Nice work if you can get it.'

'Tom, don't you think we should be leaving them alone? I don't get why it's come on Weavers exactly now. When no-one can go anywhere.'

'My mum says they aren't genuine people. God's mistake or something...'

'My gran was obsessed with them, thought they were brilliant. I didn't know before; my dad just told me. She lived on Connipia for a time. Lived there before Dad was born. The other way from your mum. I think she left the island because it was the best way to protect them.'

'She should talk to my mum about it. Slug it out. Did she live with them? With the girly-whirlies.'

'She's long dead,' says Justin, thinking as he says it that there is a family history about which he has no certainty. He doesn't think any normal people live with the Connipians and nor can he imagine she quarried limestone. He'll ask his dad, but the trouble is, Roy always seemed a bit sketchy about her. Or didn't want to talk. Ailsa Grant, he remembers her Christian name. A bit of an odd one. Maybe his dad talked and Justin didn't want to hear it. That's possible. Took her own life, and he hates hearing about that stuff. Better to be miserable than dead, that's what Justin thinks. Hearing what she did with the Connipians would be interesting. She must have had her reasons. He's not really thought about it before. What was on her mind when she did what she did. 'I'm not on the fence, Tom. I think I was when it first came on the screen. Didn't know much about them except Lost in Connipia, what it said in the film, and that wasn't close to true. The writing on the screen below the pictures makes my dad mad as hell. The Connipians don't know they're being filmed, so it's wrong that Weavers show it. Interesting but wrong. The Sparrow-hooks are the real problem. That's the them and us. Sparrow-hooks or people? Robots that do whatever the hell they like. The last battle's coming, isn't it. I think the robots invented the virus.'

'Bloody hippy!' laughs Tom.

* * *

Back on Underhill, Roy remains glued to Weavers. Watching another pair of Connipians shimmy their way up into the forest canopy. Their fields of plenty. He sees that the girls doing the climbing have small twists of blue string tied to their wrists—made from vine, he supposes—their blue wraps cling to their thighs. Not trousers but their clothing isn't far from it. Both are incredibly agile.

Don't try this at home, normal people. You are far more evolved than these little tree-swingers.

Roy doesn't like it. Mild compared to some of the captions, an insult nevertheless. Untrue and unfair, the girls aren't even swinging. When they go up the larger tree trunks, they use footholds which they must have carved into the trees for ease of access. It's an adapted environment; Connipians are civilised. Differently so than us, it doesn't make them primitive. Then the girls shimmy their way out along horizontal branches. They know how to keep themselves safe. He thinks they look intelligent, not so much in the face but in the way they move. A little odd, they all have startling blue eyes and their bald heads aren't so attractive. Roy's hairline's receding, so he shouldn't knock it. He wonders if their skulls are the same shape as ordinary people. As the Sapiens. He's started to recall conversation after conversation he long ago had with his mum. She told him they could do cleverer things than us if they wished, but understand it leads nowhere. He didn't grasp the point back when she said it. Now he thinks about what Danny said. We made the technology that's doing this, showing these pictures. Horrible little Sparrow-hooks with minds of their own, operating out of the reach of those who set them to it. The penny is starting to drop. Late in the day, years since his mother told him. He guesses half the country is glued to

God Help the Connipians

Weavers. Maybe more. No one can go anywhere because of the virus. We can't do anything to stop what's happening where it shouldn't be happening. Can't travel to a forest on an island far away. Not supposed to go to Stockport without a decent reason.

The picture on the screen goes from bright to gloomy, the interior of a Blue House. Three Connipians: two girls look alright but the third looks poorly. The girls are handfeeding small cubes of green fruit to the one who is unwell. A male, Roy thinks, swaddled in grey, not blue, and without swelling to his chest. It could be a child, so spindly are the man's limbs. Only the face looks old. Lined to a degree that is unusual among Connipians. Suddenly an expert after a few hours watching Weavers.

The most they can do is feed the failing creature. Push food down his throat and hope. This is not a civilisation with any form of medicine. Not a civilisation at all, as we can see. They haven't a clue how to contrive a better life than this.

Roy turns the screen off altogether. Two nice girls were nursing the poorly man; probably doing the same as Julie is doing in a London hospital. He hates whoever is behind the filming, the horrible commentary underneath the pictures. It might be his own government. That was something his mother was very clear about. The Connipians thought the British abused their position as incomers from day one. The indigenous islanders may not have actively welcomed them but they weren't against living side by side. It was the way we went about it, cutting down the trees, even using Connipians for experiments— kidnapping—that's why they wanted the entire island back. And then there was all the raping. Connipians don't harm others. We do that, us and only us. Never pushed a fork into meat, Ailsa didn't either but Roy can't help himself. Connipians have no conflict with anyone save the British settlers. His mother told him that. He ignored it until now. Knew it but didn't know it mattered. And what can he do? Locked down in a corner of Greater Manchester. He clicks the set back on; watching isn't helping but he's fascinated by the girls. Not girls, women. Most of them are fully grown, short in stature like dwarves or midgets. Really tiny ones. And a handful of men. Like the one who was being fed. Poor fella. They look perfectly civilised to Roy, looking after the chap who can't feed himself.

The vile transcript continues. Roy turns it onto the news channel, BBC. Watches intently but it's all covid, nothing about the Connipians. Thought they'd be saying who was behind the illegal pictures by now. Roy doesn't even know who he ought to hate.

Watch It On Weavers

* * *

Danny struggles to concentrate on the Digger Dogs, can't bring himself to look up the genesis of Sparrow-hooks either. Resilient code in there, he would have to brush up on his quantum computing. Improve upon what he only half-understood first time around. It's exhilarating to think about all the broad-brush stuff. Berry said what Weavers are showing will change how the world deals with AI. The law cannot hold. Exhilarating and scary. He doesn't care about the freaky women; they look pretty good naked which is a bonus. It's the robots that are running circles inside Danny's brain. AI could run the world if they're unleashed without proper controls. Run the world in the interest of whatever daft ideas they've been programmed to place on a pedestal. It looks like it's already happened. A good laugh watching the little people who don't even know they're being filmed. The question is: what kind of logic underpins the programme? AI need objectives, that's at the core of everything Danny and Berry have worked on. Digger Dogs must sift out impacted sand, all the other shit, know what's copper and what's not. What the little robot gnats in Connipia are hoping to find, he hasn't a clue. They could figure out how the girlies manufacture their unlikely dye. Make us some Connipian Blue.

He comes across a thread on Wires where a few geeks discuss the tech side of the daring intrusion. The filming of Connipians.

> ***Nothing to do with the people on the island. They can't programme their own televisions, not a hope with Sparrow-hooks.***

Danny has figured out this much for himself. Berry said something in that ballpark but Danny already knew. The remaining mining operations—potash and limestone—employ people who can wield picks or drive trucks. Not programmers. They have a couple of tourist hotels, weather and earthquake monitoring stations. Not a soul on the island who could do anything of this kind. Whoever set this up might be doing it from half a world away.

> ***Governor Boyson is connipulsive. He's arranged this.***
>
> ***Governor Boyson has the brains of a dormouse. He really hasn't.***
>
> ***Governor Boyson should stop it.***
>
> ***Governor Boyson wouldn't know where to start.***

Danny looks for other threads, no interest in politics. Governments are part of the problem; think they rule the roost inside their silly borders when the real life is going on across the airwaves. Outside their grasp. He agrees with whoever said Boyson couldn't stop it. With Sparrowhooks, it's pretty much the point. Programmed for a task and they will keep regrouping until they've ticked it off. If Boyson found a way to stop it, the devious devices would teach themselves the art of hypnosis and make him change his mind.

* * *

Justin and Tom walk down Hydebank, make their way to the canal towpath. They've smoked a bit of draw here a few times, it's not in the plan for today. First meet up since all the stay-at-home nonsense began. When Justin first heard there might be a pandemic, he wondered if everybody would start screaming, a few bodies lying out on the street. It's turned out pretty mild, a very poor horror movie. Tom keeps asking about Justin's gran, maybe everyone's thinking about Connipians now they're on the tele.

'Was it easy to do, back in the day? Do you think she could just board a plane and...'?

'A ship. No planes. No airport until twenty years ago. Only light planes, even now. It's tiny. Look it up, Tom. Everything about the place is on Nolly Knowledge.'

'...board a ship and rock up. "Take me to the Connipians." Is that how it worked back then?'

'I might ask Dad some more about it. I think she was a sort of scientist but not a very good one. You know, just made the tea and that.'

'Jesus, I can do that. I want to go there, see the Blue Houses. Meet the girls.'

'Tom, don't you think it's wrong? I know they look a bit sexy and everything...'

'Too right.'

'No! It's completely wrong. Spying on them when we said we wouldn't. And it must have been men with dirty minds like yours who made all those awful Mixed-Ups...'

'I'm not serious, Justin. Anyway, there's always abortion. Lots of different ways...'

'Not for Connipians; I don't think they do any of that. I feel dead sorry for them.'

'If your granny was a scientist, do you think she did experiments on them?'

'No...' His answer is a reflex, and Justin immediately worries that she had to. That his granny was initially horrible to the Connipians and then regretted it. Could explain the suicide.

'Lots of scientists did them. Wanted to find out how they can live off fruit, I expect. I'd have runny shits all day long if that was all I had to eat.'

'My gran killed herself, Tom. I think it was bound up with all that was happening down there. I don't know much about it but I expect she couldn't bear...'

'No, there's more to it than that, Justin. Not much has happened down there. Not in a million years. And all suicides are because of mental illness. At the bottom of it they are. The people who do it are to blame. Sort of. I mean, it's right to feel sorry for them, but they did it. What happens to Connipians hasn't anything to do with your granny here in Stockport, even if she'd been there. Not really.'

'She was living in London back then...'

'Same difference.'

'And my gran was actually Canadian but her and Granddad Winston lived in London.'

'Winston? Like in the war?'

'Winston's a black guy, Tom...'

'You can't have a black granddad, that's my thing not yours. Too pasty looking, you are.'

'No, I'm not related to him, my gran's second marriage or she wasn't married to dad's dad. Something like that.'

They walk beneath a bridge still following the canal side. There are four narrowboats moored here. None moving, none occupied. It's dark and even a little cold as they step into the shadow, a minor road crossing over their heads. A piece of tarpaulin seems to be stuck against the brickwork to the side. Might trip passers-by. Tom prods it with his right foot. The plastic sheeting grunts.

'Fucking hell!'

'Fucking hell, yourself.' The head of an old man pokes itself from the dirty blue plasticated fabric. Unshaven and unkempt, broad of face. Long straggly white hair, matted and dirty.

'Sorry,' says Tom taking two paces back. 'I thought it was just a blown-away bit of boat covering.'

'My bedding,' says the tramp. 'And it's not like I'm little-small.' He grimaces, scrunches up his dirty weatherworn face.

They both look upon the old man. Big black boots separating at the seams. Socks on show where the heels are coming away. A dishevelled old man and there's a hell of a lot of him. A big man, no guessing how old. Eighty in the face but he could be a lot younger. If he's spent a lifetime out in the elements, sleeping rough. A weathered face of uncertain age.

'You're homeless,' states Justin.

'Albert Einstein,' says the tramp.

339

God Help the Connipians

'Pleased to meet you, Albert.'

Tom punches Justin's arm. Not hard. The tramp laughs from beneath his tarpaulin.

'Sorry. It's not Albert, is it? But do you know, there's help for people like you? On account of the coronavirus. The council are putting homeless people into hotels or somewhere like that. Giving them meals while they're in there. Stay at home, that's the message. They want to look after you. You need to go in somewhere. Make sure you don't catch the disease.'

'I don't see any virus around here, sonny. Do you? Can't imagine the thing will just stop on account of checking into a hotel. As likely to be some virus there as under this bridge, I'd say. It isn't for me, lad. I'm not indoorsy, me. Can't be doing with it.'

It's not a horror movie but Justin is finding it a weird morning. The few people he saw on the street looked hostile, fearful even, as they waited in line outside the shop. Then this raggedy old man turns down free food, free lodging. The man has nothing, and he won't even try it. Happy with fuck all which is strange in its own right.

As they wander down the towpath, leaving Albert Einstein—or whatever his name is—to the comfort of his tarpaulin, Justin finds Tom to be unchanged by the pandemic. Talks about it as if it's a joke played on a stupid population. Justin is less sure; doesn't like him talking about the Connipians like they're sexy. Weavers is worse than the virus; shouldn't turn tiny girls into sex objects. Not that he hadn't thought of them that way himself throughout late-night Weavers. Regrets having watched it now. Regrets it but thinks about it quite a lot. The robots shouldn't be in the protected areas, and they certainly shouldn't be encouraging randy blokes to make their way out there. Even the Twelve Tribes would hate that, so whatever it is these Sparrow-hooks are playing at, Justin doesn't like it. Can't see the point either. Leaving them alone makes sense, supporter or detractor.

* * *

The widescreen is back on, the two brothers sitting and watching while their father is up in the kitchen behind them. Watching Weavers, the live feed. Seems like everyone is talking about the forests of Connipia. On Wires and at the supermarket where Justin picked up the milk. There's something about it in the newspaper, Roy read it but the boys didn't bother. Everything's on the web.

The camera focuses on two little Connipians as they crush the petals of blue flowers into a hollowed-out rock. One has a gourd of water, or possibly a clear juice. Small amounts poured on to the mush they are making.

Watch It On Weavers

The telephone rings and both boys look around. 'Sound down, please' says Roy, stepping down the four shallow steps from the kitchen-dining area where he prepares their evening meal. Roy scoops the telephone off the tiny cradle in which it spends its day. Throws a pair of conjoined oven-gloves over his shoulder where they come to rest, one dangling front, the other back. 'Hello again,' he says when he hears the voice. His half-sister, Edna, calling once more.

'Brother, brother,' she says, 'I've a-bad news, I'm sorry to say. It's old Dad, he's gotten the virus.'

'Gosh, that's awful, Edna. Is he very sick?'

'He says not, Roy, but you know the way he is.'

'Yeah. I guess so. Caught it? Where could that have happened. We're all staying at home, aren't we?'

'Talking to Ronnie at the paper shop, I could place a bet on it. He goes out to buy his News Explained come hell or high water. You know he always does that, don't you, Roy? He just gasses away with that man in the corner shop every day of the week. He should have stopped going, what with this coronavirus doing the rounds. It's just the way with old people, isn't it? Always doin' what they're always doin'. Poor old Dad. I don't believe you or me could have stopped him, not from gettin' his paper and not from catchin' this virus. A little telephone call couldn't do it. I told him to stay at home over and over and over.'

'Has he seen a doctor?'

'No one sees a doctor. You know he won't be doing with this See Your Face thingummy that everybody else is gettin' up to in these times. Doesn't have a computer or a hand-held whatsit, not Dad. I've not seen his face since it all started. I'll be phoning him every day. Get the doctor to him if he isn't fighting it off pretty quickly. That's what I'll do.'

'Edna,' asks Roy, 'do you have Weavers?'

'Everybody's got the Weavers but it's disgusting is what it is. I think we've all stopped watching it in this house. Maybe every house will stop now they've done this. It never was any good, all that Weavers. Plain nasty television, that's what this latest stunt is.'

'But everyone is interested, Sis. The writing they put on with the pictures is a total disgrace...'

'It is that. They're calling it the word of God on the Wires: saying it on my very own church thread. That's not the God I pray too, Roy. God doesn't talk dirty about defenceless little girls. After this is over, I've got to get me a new church.'

'Your church is connipulsive?'

'No one ever talked about it until now. Never heard a sermon about Connipians. Not a conversation. Not before this, and now I think they must be. Not me and Julie, just the rest of them. Don't want to help the poor Connipians because they were living this way before Eve. I don't think Jesus made those kinds of rules when he told us we should love thy neighbour. Not a bit of it.'

'Your church doesn't like them. Do you think it's because of Mum that you think the other way?'

'That they should leave them alone? Yes, I do. I hope I'd think it whatever Mum did or didn't say. I agree with her. Miss her every day, Roy. I really do. What about you? You don't think they should be showing all this, do you?'

'I'm with you, Edna. I can remember everything Mum ever said about them. I'd forgotten but it's been coming back. Seeing pictures of those people brought it all back to me.'

'Mum told me we should look after them before I knew who they were. I was born agreeing that we shouldn't even be on that island. And people like you more to the point, Roy. I don't mean it personal or anything but it's the men who have done all the harm. The Mixed-Ups. We've got the rest of the world; leave the little Connipians to their own lovely island, we really should.' Edna is laughing and crying at the memory of her mother, Roy can hear it. Picture it. 'She's still right and everyone else is still wrong. All of the people who go out there are wrong, wrong, wrong. Every miner and logger. And Mum said the anthropologists were no better. That surprises me even now but I don't doubt her. Our mum knew what she was talking about, what was best for Connipians. Always better off without us. That's the truth, Roy. Then and now.'

3.

After a week of illegal broadcasts from Connipia, half the country loving it and the other half hating it, the Prime Minister is to make a statement. His role in Connipia is obscure. A committee recommends who he should appoint as governor, and the New York Accords prescribe strict limits to what he or she can do. Or more simply, he: there has yet to be a female Governor of Connipia. And nor is the accord working, the protected areas are breached from time to time. The police on the island are more conversant with UK laws than those which the international body has set. Nothing's really done by the rules. Hard White and Pacific Stone get away with daylight robbery. Connipian wood finds its way onto the black market; Nolly Knowledge doesn't say it's sold via Weavers' dark sites, but Justin reckons it is. Reading loads these last few days, he's starting to see the bigger picture.

Even this announcement is preceded by a lot of guff about coronavirus. Justin is impatient, waiting for the part that interests him. Doesn't listen to politicians at the best of times, so their opinions about an illness—a virus that nobody can see—are sure to be pretty stupid. The Prime Minister and a scientist are standing side by side. Wittering on. Roy looks like he's listening. Worrying about his stepdad, that'll be why he pays so much attention.

Finally, the PM gets to the point. The one Justin has been waiting for.

> *There has been some...eh, em...some speculation about the Protectorate of Connipia. The Crown Dependency which we...that is...we...this country, Britain administers. Speculation that the forested lands have been invaded. Eh, it's not that bad. The...the...the speculation arises because pictures from there are being beamed across an independent streaming service.*

Justin thinks the Prime Minister doesn't seem terribly interested. Uncombed hair, stuttering and spluttering. Bleary-eyed Boris might have been watching the late-night fare himself, by the looks of him.

> *I have, today, spoken with Governor Boyson—whose jurisdiction begins and ends in the two towns and mining districts of the island, I might add, we don't go into the forests—and he assures me that nobody has breached the protected zone. They've checked that. No people have gone in. None of our lot. The problem is the...the... well it's robots: they're quite beyond our control. Tiny little robots that can fly, so the checkpoints and fences haven't helped. Which is disappointing, terribly disappointing, you might say, but there you have it. Technically the pictures being beamed are in breach of privacy laws established for the benefit of the...eh...the little...the Connipian ladies. The ladies and gentlemen. All of the Connipians, every gender they've got. Our primary concern at this time is to ensure this virus doesn't get into their zone. The protected areas. A bit worried it could be the end of them if we can't manage that.*

He glances across at one of the scientific advisers who share the room with him.

> *Can the virus jump to that species? Will the Connips catch it?*

The other man—white light reflecting off his shiny bald head—looks embarrassed. Flushed of face.

We don't know yet. Time will tell, Prime Minister.

Quite. Time will tell. We wouldn't wish it to take down those villages. The Blue House jobbies. We're trying our best to stick to the international agreements...that's what we're doing...we really are. So, as it stands, we can do no more than keep an eye on the situation. Can't stop the broadcasts, I'm sorry to say. Not initiated in this country and the network involved are properly licensed. And so long as it's only robots in the forest, the little...the Connipians can't come to any harm. We think the pictures coming back the lesser of two evils. That's it, best of a bad lot. Thank you. Now, can we go to questions?'

'They're doing nothing,' says Justin. His father glares at the widescreen.

In the last day or two, the younger son has asked Roy a lot about his late grandmother. He's even managed to stop watching the midnight broadcasts, so strongly does he feel these strange people should be left alone. It's got Justin back on regular porn.

'She was married twice and neither husband is my father,' Roy told Justin. Tried to draw a family tree but he's rubbish at that stuff. Three goes and he gave up. Briefly she was Ailsa Klassen, during her first marriage in Canada. Then later she was Ailsa Grant. Carried that name from the mid-seventies until her untimely death. Sometimes Donaldson: maiden name and she reverted to it between husbands. Roy's name was Donaldson at birth. Changed it when Winston adopted him.

'And she never went back to Canada?' asked Justin.

'No. When your gran left the island—after about four years, working with scientists or suchlike, volunteering to help young Mixed-Ups as well—she went to Australia before moving on to England. She joined a movement, Britain Leave, or something like that. All in favour of letting them be, writing to MPs to get them to agree that we pull out. Off the island, every last Sapiens. She said she often wished she'd never gone, except if she hadn't, she'd never have understood them. That's the thing: the Connipians were definitely better off when we'd not discovered it. Our ignorance was their bliss. I don't think I understood that until this livestream showed up the vile attitudes half of our lot have towards them.'

'But was she working with the scientists who did the awful things?'

'I don't think so, Justin. Not the awful stuff. Studying how they lived, not snatching them. You know she was in the group that took Steve Frame to meet them, don't you?'

'What!' Justin knew nothing of this. Critics called his first solo album, Blue is the Colour, the turning point in Frame's career. The start of his spiral into self-absorbed tosh. He probably lives well enough from the royalties from his earlier stuff. One-Eyed Temple still get airplay, but only a few diehards could possibly listen to the rubbish he's produced since the band split. Esoteric chants about the Connipians right to live the way they do. That they are better than us is the central message. Perhaps the best of those later tracks will get on the radio now it's in the news. Not by whoever's broadcasting on Weavers, obviously, and the songs were all pretty laboured. Justin only knows them because he likes One-Eyed Temple. He's never listened to any of his solo stuff twice.

'How long was she friends with Steve Frame?'

'I don't think it was like that,' says Roy. 'She just got on the assignment taking him into the forest. Because she knew about them, told Frame how to behave around Connipians. I don't think she and him were ever friends.'

* * *

The following evening, Edna phones again. An important update for Roy, for the family. Poor old Winston is in hospital. No visitors allowed, he's all on his own in there. Edna tells Roy that their dad is struggling away on a ventilator. Julie spoke to a nurse on the ward, got as much information as she could. Did it nurse to nurse. Told Edna they were doing all they could.

Justin knows his grandfather a bit, saw him fifteen months ago, and again the year before that. Gets a bit grumpy but he's funny with it. Both the boys—his northern grandsons, 'the whiteys' as he calls them—like him well enough. Know he means a lot to their dad.

When Roy comes off the phone, the pair talk about it, agree it's terrible news. Tough for the old man; ventilators sound horrible, and Justin's read that there aren't enough of them. Then he asks more questions about Roy's childhood. About his gran too. Slips in one or two about the timeline with Connipia. Danny has come down on hearing about his granddad. Doesn't say anything but listens in. It's his family too, must register with him one way or another.

* * *

Later that night, after Roy has gone to bed, Justin watches the widescreen. Tom told him earlier in the day that there hasn't been any Connipian sex on Weavers for the last couple of nights. Tom was

345

God Help the Connipians

disappointed and Justin pleased. This is no nature programme with its nasty subtitling, at least they've stopped the most invasive pictures. Parading girls naked who are sort of different and sort of not. Maybe the robots were monitoring the feedback. There has been a lot of outrage on Wires. Outrage and enthusiasm, both sides posting in capital letters.

Initially the pictures show only the Blue Houses, a circle of six, and others behind them, deeper in the picture. No Connipians, it might be late evening or early morning. That sort of half-light. Then the camera must move to a doorway, enter a house. Now, through the dim blue light, Justin sees a male lying in his cot. Could be the same one he saw a week ago.

This is a dead Connipian. If it is their natural state, it has not come soon enough.

'Pretty funny, eh?' Danny has come down, stands at the bottom of the stairs watching the flickering of the picture.

'Sick. Sick in a bad way,' says Justin. He looks daggers at his brother. Tells him what their dad told him earlier in the day: their own gran was there at the time of Steve Frame's fabled visit. Went with him into the forest, to the Blue Houses. Met the very people he's laughing at. Steve Frame thought they were worth stepping away from his rockstar gig for, only sang about Connipians once he'd met them.

'Justin, the little girls look great, but they've done nothing. These Sparrow-hooks are proper progress. Who cares about a few freaks who only lived so long because they happened to be on a distant island? Same thing as the dodo. Cute but useless. It can be a long wait for a decent predator if you're living in the middle of nowhere.'

'How can that be true? Every country on Earth banned the Sparrow-hooks, then we can't even police that. We destroy stuff and they don't.' He points at the screen where the only Connipian on show has run out of breathing life. Justin was thinking about the girls in the treetops, the way they climb up and work the skyfields. The picture of a feeble dead male seems to back up Danny's point more than his own.

'One way or another these robots could make a lot of smart people a very healthy payday. Just got to figure the how of it.'

'They'll destroy us! I can read, you know. That's why they were banned. If two equal forces follow military orders, increasing their destructive powers as they go, there will be no winner. They turn everything to shit. I know they're only playing with the Connipians. Hidden cameras and nasty commentary. Sparrow-hooks could do a million times worse than that; it scares me that they're even down there. Countries with nuclear weapons don't fight each other because it's unthinkable; robots will because the chaos caused makes no difference to them.'

'Yeah. But, Juicy, banning doesn't work so we have to figure out how to make the tech stay inside the lines. These are clever bots, the cleverest. They can read the airwaves. There has never been a robot versus robot war. Don't count the rubbish on television, it's not close to the Sparrow-hook's level. If there ever was, I think they might simultaneously back down. Realise they had to. Each facing an equal adversary. They're the most rationale of networks exactly because they access all the intel. Begin and end with the most penetrating logic. We're the emotional ones. Make mistakes based on how we're feeling. Back losers because we feel sorry for them.'

'We! What mistakes have the Connipians made? Why the hell have we even sent robots down there?'

'I haven't; you haven't. Following the orders of the Twelve Tribes, Only God's Children—someone like that—orders they were given long ago. Berry—my mate, he's a smarter programmer than me—he thinks they first inputted the instructions to an earlier version of the Sparrow-hooks. Probably bigger, certainly fewer of them. They had to calculate, work out how to multiply. Go small to evade detection. Build enough to make the operation a cinch. The instructions may pre-date the nanotech they rely on. Robots that learn will spot innovations and use it to fulfil the mission. Make connections we wouldn't think to. If the plan was to show the Connipians to the world, they waited until they could do hours and hours of genuinely covert filming. Make themselves as good as invisible to the girlies. Sparrow-hooks never do anything unless it's a guaranteed success.'

'How can they make more of themselves? Don't pretend Sparrow-hooks breed; I'm not that stupid.'

'Juicy, this AI is like totally brilliant. It will have read every thread on every web-page. The older-style Sparrow-hooks will have moved in on some newly decommissioned assembly plant. Adapt, produce, then get out of there. Genius stuff.'

'What do you mean? What's a decommissioned assembly plant?'

'They will have squatted in a closed-down factory. Could have been anywhere on Earth; could have used several different ones. I expect they spent a good while on R and D before making anything.'

'Rhythm and blues?'

'Research and development, div-head.'

'No matter how clever it is, the whole thing is rubbish. The message in the script, the disparaging nonsense written on the screen. I could write that. Wouldn't but I could. Why do they need all the technology when that's all their saying. They could have stayed away from the island

347

and just written that. Broadcast it without breaking the law.'

'No one would watch Weavers for a bit of anti-connip vitriol. It needs the pictures to grab attention. You're upset, Justin, but only because you've got a sentimental view of them. Little girls—they actually looked better in the old pictures, back when they wore wigs—but you get to see them half-clothed, starkers a few times. The pictures confirm that the words are right. Not the attention-grabbing ones so much, the subtler ones. They've been sick for thousands of years, Justin. They've never had healthy males, not since the last ice age or the one before that. And the freaky girls squeezing the baby juice out of them before they peg out for good, that was a pretty sick show. Pretty vampy girls if you think about it at all. I think the Sparrow-hooks have been programmed by religious nutters; it still proves Sapiens are better than Connipians. No need of a war to show we've more going for us than the freaks. They would have been gone years ago if we hadn't put a fence around the forest.'

On the screen four girls in blue wraps have lifted the dead male up out of his cot. They carry him away and the camera follows them. Out into the sunlight, must be morning on Connipia. They click quite incessantly and it doesn't sound like a funeral service. Just chatter, drumsticks on the metal rim. They enter a neighbouring Blue House, still carrying the body. 'Bloody hell,' says Justin. The cameras follow as the procession passes through a bamboo screen and down a gentle slope. Down, down. This is the first time a house has seemed other than a simple one storey. Deep into a basement, tiny lights at the sides of the walkway. Each looks quite intense but the overall lighting is still very dim. Not flames, Justin can't tell what source of light illuminates the way down.

'A Connipian crypt,' says Danny. 'This is new to me. There must be graves older than any others on Earth down there. Berry says the robots are going to let us learn all the early humanoid secrets. Everything that the girlies have been keeping to themselves.'

'He's not behind it, is he?'

'Justin! Me and him are really, really small fry. A million miles from ever pulling a stunt like this. Learning from it though. Our sights are on bigger mines than any in Connipia. Better shit than potash. And me and Berry don't want to break any laws. At least, not personally. If unstoppable robots break them and no-one could link us to it, then we'd be in the clear. You won't catch Berry or me standing in front of a judge.'

4.

Justin never got his promised furlough. Maybe down the line, for now the kitchen at The Bell Inn remains open. They cook meals for any who wish to collect them from the back door. And the landlady has sourced a couple of motor-scooters with thermal panniers; her son, Gregory, is one of the riders. Deliver us from evil.

Danny, and even Tom, laughed at Mrs Gantry's attempt to keep the place running. 'Relying on customers who can't use their own microwave.' Both said something in that ballpark. And it's true, Justin's not a chef. A one-day food hygiene course the extent of his training.

Roy is quietly pleased that his son has something to do. He finds his own unemployment a chore. Watching Weavers more than he ever thought he would, even down for the late, late show now and then. Saw one a week back that was very raunchy. A turn on, and not one he could enjoy. Felt his long-dead mum shouting at him from her faraway grave.

When Justin has left the house for The Bell, Danny working upstairs, Roy puts the screen back on. Flicks a couple of channels to check he isn't missing anything better, then settles for the livestream. Watching it on Weavers. It's night on the island, it shows only girls sleeping. Three in a single bed. Or a nest. Leaves not blankets. Blue leaves of many varieties. All dyed and preserved, joined together by thread or glue. No telling from this distance; nobody could quite fathom it back when we put their carefully crafted artefacts under our fanciest microscopes. One of the more interesting bits of written commentary tells Roy that their bedding might be hundreds of years old, so effectively do they preserve the leaves from which it is made. Then it criticises them for not figuring out blankets. Everything the robots write is daft. Never a kind word and what the Connipians have done is incredible. Leaves shouldn't even get that old, and yet they've managed it. They can do a hell of a lot that Sapiens have never figured. Two of the girls sleep with their heads together. Their bald pates show as a pair of breasts might, although their real ones are not on show this time. Wrapped in blue. The third girl is at their feet. Not so much sleeping as fidgeting. That's how it looks.

Below the picture, the depressing propaganda continues to scroll across the screen.

> ***Connipians have no written language of their own. Fifty and more years ago many of them learned to write in English and some in other languages. Since then, they have chosen not to utilise these higher skills. They don't do it because they don't value learning. Aptitude without a complementary attitude is of no value at all.***

Roy thinks about this. His mother spoke of using a sand tray and a finely pointed stick—a pencil without the lead—in order to converse with one or two Connipians. He thinks it's remarkable that they could.

Nothing primitive in learning to write without ever going to school. That's what she told him: they seldom wrote, and then did it as if they always had. Smarter than him or Justin, frankly.

> *Connipian girls seldom have more than a single child, although no law or rule determines they must not. Connipians are too anarchic to develop a proper structure to their society. They do not live in family groups, and share the raising of children. It is a recipe for homogeny and none rise up above the primitive lifestyle they have so long practiced. Climbing trees; eating fruit; sharing a handful of sickly men between hundreds of girls. Living this way before God set Adam forth in the world; they have forever been oblivious to the laws of Abraham. The spiritual plane remains far beyond the grasp of these creatures. They are not God's people. He didn't choose them, and if He created them, it was in error.*

Roy thinks the message along the bottom of the screen to be very odd. Robots sprouting Christian propaganda; doing it badly. A god who makes errors is hardly worth the worship. The spiritual plane stuff is utter rubbish, Roy doesn't think he's ever found one, and robots cannot possibly. Danny says the Sparrow-hooks are programmed with impeccable logic, so why would they even try religion. Adam and Eve is a fairy story, nothing more. The Connipians must be closer relatives to us than robots. Not that it has stopped us from falling in love with our smartphones and our tablets. We're the ones who have strayed, become aliens on our own planet. The Connipians have been true to themselves. They can write any rubbish on Weavers and those watching will still see a contented people. The robots—for all their technical wizardry—are proving themselves thick. Gadget-worshipping Danny sitting in the same boat.

As the camera roves around the room, Roy sees that the smallest of the three Connipians has now fallen asleep. She looks to lie across the feet of the other two. Face down. The blue of her tunic has risen up, bare thighs exposed right up to a bit of buttock. While the picture stays static a series of facts runs across the bottom of the screen.

> *We gave these animals refuge like we have afforded no other.*
>
> *If we had hunted them properly back when it was permitted, Connipians wouldn't even be here. Nobody to erect a fence around. We've all missed some*

opportunities, my friends.

The second one sends a shudder through Roy. He picks up the remote, contemplates changing channel. Could check the news: see what's happening in New York, Paris, all the places where the virus is causing havoc. While his eyes still linger on the feed from Connipia, the small girl goes into a spasm. Convulsions unlike anything he's ever seen on this feed. Before he knows what to think, both the other girls start shaking in the same way. Violent jerky motion. All are instantly awake, looks of the utmost distress rake across their faces.

Not sleeping so soundly now, says the feed. *Fun and games with the witless Connipians, that's the order of the day. Fun! Fun! Fun!*

As he grimaces at the sickening subtitles, Roy sees the girls have stopped shaking. They begin clicking together now. Each looking at the other, quite disoriented by what has happened. Unsure of themselves. The one which lay across the others rises up but she is unsteady on her feet. Falls back onto the other girls before extricating herself again. She seems to bow her head as she clicks to them and then they stand up as she did. One goes limp, falls straight back onto the bed of leaves; the other stands her ground. Sways a little.

'Danny!' shouts Roy. 'Danny, quickly!'

The door to his bedroom opens. 'What is it, Dad? I've work on.'

'Have you seen this? It's horrific.'

'What is it, Dad? What's happened?'

Danny comes down the stairs as Roy tries to explain, remember the exact words written on the screen. Danny takes the remote from him, a couple of buttons and he's tracked it backwards, starts to watch the brief episode which has upset his father.

'Terrible. They've got to go in and stop it now.'

'Not sure they can, Dad. The robots are really messing with them big time.'

'Why? What did they do to them?'

'Electric shocks, that's what it looked like to me. Sparrow-hooks can do pretty much anything they like.'

* * *

'I saw it,' says Justin. 'No punters so we had Weavers on the big screen. On the footie screen.'

'I thought you were supposed to be working.'

'Yeah, but there were four of us on shift. Couldn't all be in the tiny kitchen. Everyone has to keep two metres. We've a table set up next to

God Help the Connipians

the bar where Katie and me were doing all the prepping. It was awful what they did. I'd go out there and stop it. This virus is like an excuse to do nothing. Watching defenceless girls getting tortured. It's worse than awful. Katie and me both think that the Sparrow-hooks might've cooked up the virus.'

'I doubt that,' says Danny. 'You might be right about them spotting when no one would stop them though. Pretty unexpected twist, waiting until no one dares to help the girlies. Couldn't see how they knew it was coming, but that sort of AI has every trick up their sleeve. Might have been waiting for a soft-touch governor, and then they saw a better opening.'

'Can't you hack into them. Not actually you, someone in the know. Can't they reprogramme the fucking things?'

'Not if they're programmed to resist. It's not easy to hack into a bank, this level of AI must be way above that. You could ask them nicely, post reasoned arguments against their activity on Wires. You can bet they'll read it but I don't expect it'd work. If it looks counter to their objectives, they'll simply ignore it. Put you on the robot hitlist.'

'Horrible little connipulsive bots. What do you think they'll do next?'

Danny opens his palms, composes his face without a smile. 'I'm as clueless as you on this one, Juicy.'

* * *

Edna phones Roy, quarter past eleven at night. He'd already taken himself to bed, comes down to the landline when Justin calls him.

'It's Auntie Edna on the phone,' whispers his son. Then he goes to the screen and turns it off altogether. He thought his Auntie was crying. That was how her voice sounded when she asked to speak to his father.

Roy hears the terrible news: Winston Grant, his much-loved stepfather, has passed away. He drops the phone momentarily, puts his face in his hands. Pulls it back up by the chord and says, 'Sorry.' Sorry for dropping the phone or sorry for his grieving sister. Sorry for being only an occasional visitor to London and family in the last quarter of a century.

They talk and talk. Mostly about their dad. The man who has passed away. These are extraordinary times. No one was prepared for a pandemic, hadn't thought about it before they found themselves in the middle of one. That a deadly virus has come to live amongst them, and it has wrought these changes in how they live and when they die.

'Ah, Roy,' she says. 'At least I don't think he saw them. The pictures on Weavers. Never watched Weavers in his life, and he was put on the ventilator before it became big news. It would have upset him terribly. I'm glad he didn't have to see that.'

Watch It On Weavers

Roy cannot disagree. It feels like part of the pandemic—this simultaneous intrusion, broadcasts from Connipia—both coming into their lives in the same weeks.

'I'm sorry I wasn't there more. I loved him like he loved me, you know.' Never his real father, obvious at first glance, he always treated Roy as proper family, whatever story went before—no father named on Roy's birth certificate—continued to do so after Ailsa died. Mum. That can't have been easy for him. Not easy at all considering the way she left him. Them: husband and three. Odd that he and Dad grew apart, not estranged, just saw each other no more than once a year. Twice at best. Not even that the odd year. It began after Roy got married. Sky wasn't a racist; she talked with his stepfather plenty before the wedding. And at the wedding, Roy remembers that distinctly: the pair of them having a long talk. Or maybe she was a bit racist, just not in a way that made itself especially obvious. Didn't want to stay with his family; used to look down on where they lived. And Roy was brought up there. New Cross and Bermondsey. He could have got back in the habit, gone to see him more often after she up and left. Left him with the boys. There were a few visits, Winston was always good with Danny and Justin. Julie even brought him up to Romiley one time. Winston like a fish out of water: his only visit to the north, if you exclude driving trains up the East Coast mainline. He was a good dad in those early years but the bond might have been richer with his daughters. Roy appreciates all he did; thirty years have passed. Having a father is not the need it once was, and the only one he has ever known has passed away.

'I know,' says Edna.

While they are talking, Justin has gone up to Danny's room. He understood the gist of it before he went. When the call is over both boys come down. Roy tells his sons the sad news and they both nod their heads. Have already realised that it might be a big deal for him. They knew Winston, just not very well. Must be tricky for grandparents, when he was a kid, everything was different, and his formative years were spent on St Vincent, a world away. They associate him with Edna and Julie, their aunties. The grumpy old man whose daughters are so full of life. The laugh he never was. And never more shall be.

Roy tells them what Edna said. The little she knew about the few days their granddad spent in hospital. Beside herself with grief, she couldn't see her dad through his final days. Not a visit. She called herself a coward for following the rules. 'But she couldn't,' he told his boys. 'I don't want this thing taking my Edna with it on its rampage.'

Danny asks a question or two. Are they sure that it was the virus not just old age? He says the ventilator might have been worse than the virus.

God Help the Connipians

Roy disagrees. 'It's a tragedy first to last. This whole pandemic is a tragedy. Don't be having a go at the doctors, Danny. Not for trying their best. We're all going to miss him, and it won't do to be getting remorse or anger muddled up with our own feelings. Just missing him is bad enough.'

Justin doesn't say anything. Just looks at his dad. Roy's face has aged in a phone call. A sadness behind the eyes.

A few minutes later, Roy tells them he is going to phone Julie. 'Auntie Julie. Would you leave the room for a few minutes, please, boys. Let me have a private chat.'

The call is his first with his younger half-sister since this outbreak began. They too have grown a little apart although Roy has not even kept up with local friends in his eighteen months on disability money. Chronic back pain and he's a little ashamed of it. Only feels it now and then, but it's definitely still there. Can't imagine working, and he's not enjoying not. When he gets through, Julie speaks to him warmly, levelly. She is far more composed than Edna, he fears it's a veneer. She's been nursing covid patients in their final hours—Edna told him that—knows how to be professional. It can subtract nothing from the grief she feels, Roy is certain.

'We're going to miss him, Julie,' he says.

'Aye. Every time it rains, we'll be thinking of what he'd say. The moan, moan, moan.' There is a lightness, almost laughter, as she says it. No complaint on her part that this is how Winston was. And it's only how he has been these later years of retirement. His back might have been worse than Roy's.

'Did he used to talk about Mum?' he asks. Asks it out of the blue, he hadn't even noticed she was on his mind.

'I been thinking about Mummy a lot since they've been broadcasting these terrible things down in the Poplar place. In Connipia. She'd a-hated everything that's happening now. Gone on the barricades is what she would have done.'

'Do you remember Mum talking about all that? You were so young.'

'I remember. Loved her for defending the little women. I don't think our dad ever really understood that about her. Ever forgave...' As she breaks off speaking, Roy fears his sister is crying. He never intended to stir up these emotions. Isn't sure what he was seeking in the call. Just for her to know that she is in his thoughts. All this is so hard to communicate. He found himself picturing the girls on the screen. Their disorientation when they were electrocuted. Everything is unexpected in this life; so much we can never anticipate, never be truly prepared for.

* * *

Watch It On Weavers

Roy has turned in for the night, both boys are watching the widescreen. Sound on low, all they can hear is a bit of clicking. Not much of that, the Connipian girls sound frightened. The screen has already shown the three from earlier in the day, the girls the Sparrow-hooks gave electric shocks. They are all dead. Justin thought the explanation on the screen sickening.

> *Electricians might experience shocks like that two or three times a year. Or each week if they're not much good at their jobs. We are strong and these creatures are not. They received only a low voltage.*

'Can robots feel remorse?' he asks.

Danny snorts out a laugh. 'They feel nothing. Think clearer than we do. Feel nothing at all.'

'You don't seem bothered...'

'Long ago and far away. Miracle of geography that these guys are alive at all. Nothing against them but here we are. The twenty-first century. They've had a good run.'

'They're not a West End show, Danny.'

'They are, they really are. Look at us. Glued to it, aren't we? Like our grandparents once lapped up Jimmy Whist. God bless him.'

'Our gran must have hated him like I hate the bastard Sparrow-hooks. And the Twelve Tribes. If the shocks were so tiny, why did they die? It's not funny, Danny.'

'No. It's a tragedy. I'm not sure what the bots are trying to pull off down there. When they first did it, I thought it was just a trick. A bit nasty. My guess then was that they wanted to control the little girlies, be like the puppeteer. You know, the way electric fences pen in cattle. Kind of control them. I don't expect they figured this would happen, but they should have done. AI is supposed to be smart, it's like they didn't do their homework. I've been reading up about the girlies, just what's on Nolly Knowledge. Whenever Connipians have been forced to leave the island, it's killed them. Most of them. Can't last long away from what they know. Electricity has quite literally blown their minds. It must happen when zoos catch animals in the wild. Or when they used to do that. Everything is being stopped these days.'

'We bloody well should stop it but we can't. In Africa, I think it's only poachers now. Down there it's robots. Killing innocent people. Sort of people. You'd think the government must stop it now. Switch it over to the news, Danny.'

He takes his time. Rolls the remote around in his hand for a while first. Looking closely at the Connipians now on the screen. They seem to be preparing food again. Fruit. Sitting on the ground with a blue cloth—

leaf-made, most probably—laid out before them. They don't look to be enjoying their chores. Not any longer. Justin thinks the community down there must be grieving the deaths of the three girls. They won't be able to explain it. Can't see how they could; not if they don't even see the Sparrow-hooks. Death arriving like a thunderbolt. Eventually his brother flicks it to Wires News. Their dad calls this a whacky channel but both boys watch it. Currently it shows only a rerun of the day's briefing. Coronavirus and the state of British hospitals. The Chancellor going over the furlough scheme again. Money Justin would have preferred over chopping vegetables in an empty pub. Money for nothing would suit him, half the country's getting some.

Then they segue to a piece about America. The Presidential press conference, the idiot who their dad refers to as Donald-Where's-Your-Trousers. He sings it in a Scots accent whenever the man with candy-floss hair comes on the screen. No Roy to sing tonight. On screen an ageing medic stands aside as Trump rabbits on about a panacea which he thinks will stop the virus in its tracks. The doctor-chap doesn't seem to be endorsing his message: not nodding, not close to smiling at his words. Pretty much turning his nose up as the benefits of Chloroquine—the miracle that will stop the virus which has shut down the world—are expounded by the most powerful man on Earth, most powerful idiot. Along the bottom of the screen, the network has the last word.

> ***Weavers Wires strongly advises against the oral consumption of all fish tank cleaning products.***

Justin laughs. 'Who would actually do that!' he says, finger pointing at the bottom of the screen.

'It's mostly morons who watch this channel, Juicy. They don't want to take any chances.'

Eventually, while pictures move across makeshift hospitals in New York and Northern Spain, the ticker spells out a few factoids about the situation in Connipia.

> ***The British Government has tasked Governor Boyson with finding out all he can about the recent electrocution of three Connipians.***
>
> ***The protectorate authority is to offer help and protection to the Connipians through any channel they will accept.***
>
> ***The Government digital service is examining if they are able to disrupt the activities of the robot.***

'They've no chance,' says Danny.

'Why don't they call them Sparrow-hooks?' asks Justin. 'Everyone on Wires knows it.'

'No one wants to admit the breach of the international treaty, I guess. And they haven't caught any. Not caught any Sparrow-hooks, and they probably won't. Avoiding capture might even be their primary instruction. It would explain why they waited for a pandemic before they went in.'

'Mrs Gantry—landlady at The Bell—knows it's being done by Sparrow-hooks and she's as thick as pig-shit.'

As soon as the bulletin is over, Danny flips it back over to the Connipians. The girls are still scooping the flesh out of fruit gourdes, and then, as one, they rise up from the floor. Begin to move away. Quickly running, leaving the fruit task incomplete.

'What the hell is that?' says Justin. A triangular metal shape, twice the size of any Connipian, rolls over the spread-out cloth, makes bleeping noises as it goes. It has tentacles with which it picks up fruit, appears to throw some at the scattering girls.

> ***Sorry about the electric. A food fight never hurt anyone***
> reads the accompanying caption.

'I tell you,' says Danny, 'this technology is truly awesome. That must be hundreds of thousands of the tiny bots all grouped together. Maybe millions. Working in meticulously orchestrated union. Must scare the shit out of the little stone-age girlies. Funnier than the shocks, too. Amazing that they've figured the internet reaction. Toned it down to just chucking a bit of fruit.'

'Who sent those fuckers in!' shouts Justin, turning away from Danny, making sure to hide his tear-filled eyes.

5.

Next morning Roy and Danny eat breakfast together. Quite an early start, Danny will be working shortly. Roy feels a little annoyed, his son so upbeat when his grandfather has just passed away. And Danny is still excited about the stuff on Weavers, Roy thinks every second unforgiveable.

Justin sleeps in. Not required at The Bell until eleven o'clock.

'This coronavirus is a real tragedy,' says Roy. 'For me, Edna and Julie, obviously, and for thousands of others. It might be hundreds of thousands worldwide. People taken too soon because of a virus. Because of a stinking batch of bat soup in China, or whatever it was that set it off.'

'Yeah. Sorry about all that. I don't need to come to the funeral, do I?

God Help the Connipians

I'll be too many, I reckon.'

'Danny, you don't need to. I know you didn't know him well. He was a cracking father to me. Never knew my biological dad. Never knew so much as his name. It didn't worry me with a stepdad like mine. Looked after me great back when I was a lad, a schoolboy. I'm so sorry he's gone. Really wish we'd all gone down last Christmas when we easily could have. I'll regret it to my dying day.'

* * *

Danny's brain is firing on all cylinders. Watching the Sparrow-hooks last night did it. Not that you could see one jot of how they worked: he's clever, makes the connections. Harnessing cloud-strength into a tiny bot, working it in harmony with countless others. And it teaches itself everything it doesn't yet know, anything that will help with the fulfilment of a task. Burrows into knowledge to a depth humans can only dream about. Stronger than that probably.

He's been thinking about his dad, too. And the stuff Justin said about their dead granny. A few clicks on Weaver's Bran Tub can uncover a lot. Decides to put all that on the back-burner seeing as he's supposed to be working. Conatus have paid him handsomely for the past sixteen months and he's only given them a few strings of programming. Modifications to existing mining support software. The promise of more to come.

Berry, old chum, I've got a broad plan, he posts.

Pleased to hear. Hit me.

Gold.

Nice. If it's a heist you're planning, I'll sit out the bank and guns. Happy to tot up the takings at the end of the day.

Ho-ho. I need you to do the tech. Panning for gold.

Up the Yukon. No tech needed, just a sieve with fine meshing. Grow yourself a beard while you're at it. Bloody cold up there. Post me what you pan, Dan.

I'm serious, Berry. Hear me out. Where on Earth has no one ever panned for gold? Lots of untapped streams.

If you're thinking Connipia, you're wrong, Dan. They've been mining the shit out of it. Just potash and limestone down there. It'd be a right hole without the lovely little ladies.

I'm not thinking Connipia. About ten times colder.

F***ing freezing, in fact.

Whoa. Clever-clever. Pan Antarctica. No one's surveyed it properly as far as I know. Teeming with minerals, you can bet.

It was the Sparrow-hooks on Weavers last night made me see it. We've been trying to figure how Digger Dogs will outstrip mining with men, the problem is always control of the ground. We end up with a man at the top of the mine shaft controlling the Dog from a screen. More agile than regular miners but more expensive to set up, and we're going after mines of little value. Extracting the last of the coal or the copper.

I see it, pal. Use Sparrow-hooks. Fly them down there under the radar. Be the first. How do we fetch the gold back?

Sparrow-hooks could collectively meld themselves into a boat.

Ha! They could but that's where we'd get intercepted.

Berry, we're not doing God's work like the damned bots on Weavers. We're not going to let anyone know we're down there. If they don't know then they won't stop us. Bring it back by Sparrow-hooked submarine. We'll call it a day once we've made a gazillion bucks.

Berry sends him a smiley emoji with its tongue hanging out. This is a good idea. A big slice of developmental work needed: they don't actually understand Sparrow-hooks yet. And they'll need to lay down the principles for working with Digger Dogs while there at it. Keep the Conatus paycheques coming in. Panning in Antarctica is not for the fainthearted. Conatus wouldn't risk jailtime for its directors. This one's just Berry and Danny all the way. The idea is exciting. Robots grabbing gold from five million square miles of uncharted wilderness. Scarcely charted, he'll need to look it up.

Nice that Berry likes his plan.

* * *

Mrs Gantry has set Justin to washing up all of yesterday's returned trays and dishes. The new girl, Katie, is prepping food. She chops onions more deftly than he ever has. Worked in a proper hotel before coming to The Bell Inn. He's annoyed because he can't see the screen while he works. Chained to the kitchen sink. Katie and the chopping board, all the vegetables she has to peel and dice, are in the pub proper where the big screen shows Weavers. They're keeping a social distance, and that's a laugh. Two metres is an anti-social distance. He would much rather be in touching distance of Katie; hugging-and-kissing range would suit nicely. A shame Gantry's so strict on the rules. And Katie's not indicated if she'd be up for breaking them. They get along, it's not easy to read what it means. He doesn't know what she thinks about all the Weavers stuff either. Shrieked when the girls got electric shocks, he expects they're on the same side.

Gantry is on and off the phone every two minutes. Orders piling up. The ovens are on and they're making pizzas, selling them cheaper than the regular takeaways. The Friday special.

'She's only little,' says his employer, pointing at Katie through the doorway, 'but don't go throwing food at her.' Then she laughs out loud like she's told the best joke ever.

Justin bangs about in the basin. Scrubbing and scouring and not caring a damn. Knows better than to start talking about it all in here. He wonders what his gran would say. Hardly thought about her before this pandemic. It's a surprise, learning that she went to Connipia, that she was down there in the late-sixties. When all the colonies were wobbling. The Connipians never took up arms and that might have been their shortcoming. Or does it make them better. None of the violence that brought chaos into all the other places we clung onto until we no longer could. *We*, thinks Justin. He's British, always roots for England when the World Cup's on. His granny was actually Canadian, the other granny American and he's no idea who his granddad on his paternal side is. The Connipians wanted the British to leave, said it at the UN in nineteen fifty, didn't start shooting anybody about it. They asked politely and that seems to get you nowhere. Said it with a click, and exactly how reasonable they were got lost in translation. Justin's been reading all about it. How they asked the uninvited plunderers to give them a break.

'Did you see it last night? So bloody funny.'

Justin turns around and glares at Gantry. Can't think of a retort, not one that will put the old bat in her place.

'Really funny. The electric was better than the food fight. Little buggers don't know what's coming to them. Chucking food was funnier to watch, I suppose.'

'What's it to you, Mrs Gantry? Being nasty to them is horrible.'

'Sick people. Look at their bald heads. Not even properly bald. You can tell they should have hair, but it's fallen out. Congenital, it's called. From all that inbreeding. It was in the News Explained last Sunday. Not enough of a population to keep going on a tiny island; wouldn't have lasted this long if we hadn't protected them. And the newspaper said about people like you, Justin. You see the feeble men doing what they do with more girls than they can handle. Imagine that it's you. Imagine you could take their place. That's the only reason you're sympathetic. You'd think the same as me if they didn't put the dirty pictures on the telly.'

Justin stares at her. Nothing to say seeing as staff aren't allowed to swear.

'Ungodly lot they are. The sooner they're gone from the face of the Earth, the better. No hair and they paint everything blue. I'm for the robots.'

Justin turns and picks a stack of plates out of the dirty washing-up water, holds them aside and drops them onto the tiled kitchen floor. 'Fuck this job,' he says over the sound of crockery splintering across the room. Removes his white apron, drops and steps on it as he walks to the door. An employer who likes seeing little girls tormented. Killed. That's what the electric shocks did to them. It's not the job for him. No fucking way. If it stops her getting the pizzas out, he won't lose sleep over it. Those little Connipians deserve their independence, protection, leaving alone, and then people with Gantry's mindset have tormented them since we first discovered the island. They never fired a gun at a Brit, a million reasons why they might have. They're the real turners of the other cheek—we haven't a clue how it's done—then bullies like Gantry condemn them as unchristian. Ungodly, she said. And he really hasn't been looking on them with lust; did at first and then he stopped. Connipians are too little; men should definitely leave them alone. Stoney-faced, he walks across Romiley, doesn't think Katie was watching, listening. Might think he was complaining about the work when it was Gantry that did for him. Her attitude towards the Connipians. She was shouting at him as he left, it doesn't really matter what she said. Never listen to a gobshite. Tom said that and Justin agrees. Never wanted to be a washer up in the first place. It was local and a few mates used to come in the pub back in normal times, bar work was better than the kitchen. He'll go away when all the stay-at-home nonsense is over. He'd like to try Connipia, doesn't know how to go about it. London or Scotland would do. Find a job with more purpose. He could go and help Mixed-Ups like his gran did. Far more point to it than pot-washing.

* * *

Roy sits in the lounge, doesn't have the widescreen on. Looking into his phone, a puzzle book open on the coffee table in front of him. Justin doesn't mention walking out of work and his dad says nothing about how early he has arrived home. May not have registered it but Justin wasn't gone an hour.

God Help the Connipians

'Just texting Edna,' he says. 'The funeral won't be a proper one, more's the pity.'

Justin nods. 'I'm really sorry he's died, Dad. I only knew him a bit.'

'I know.'

'He was always nice to us.'

'He was that.'

Justin goes up to his room. Doesn't want to disturb his father's musings. Mulling over the family he left behind. His dad was brought up in London while Justin's only ever known Romiley, Stockport. He scarcely strayed out of the houses where his relatives live on the few times he's visited. Deptford, Lewisham. His dad must have left London when he was around the age Justin is now. He picks up his tablet, turns on Weavers. The screen of his hand-held is a joke. Cracked and shattered long ago. It's like a haze of silvery white through which he looks. Can still make it out. See the pictures, read the words. Back inside the Blue Houses, the girls seem to be getting ready for bed. One's curled up on a bed of leaves but the one standing is taking off her blue skirt. He thinks he should miss this, not look at her while she's naked. There was something in what Gantry said, if only on the narrow point of why Weavers keep showing it. Men can't help themselves from looking. He changes page—Nolly Knowledge—taps in **Mixed-Up**, wants to read about those other people. The product of men taking advantage of Connipian girls. The propaganda which accompanies the pictures on Weavers has been saying it's all false. Declared that no Connipian has ever been raped. The little women only too willing, say the lying robots. It alleges that Connipians are sirens walking around undressed to lure men into their trap. They want bigger babies than those their feeble men can give. It said God gives them the floppy-armed sort just to teach them a lesson. Justin has no time for the shit on Weavers, no time at all. Danny says artificial intelligence works on pure logic and then they write rubbish like that. Shit that doesn't make sense. Looking up to a cruel god. Robots made in the image of the moronic Sapiens.

He finds a lot of information on there about Charlestown. Stuff he never knew. An area of the town has been set aside for the Mixed-Ups; most of the help comes from Catholic charities. Then he reads that the law prohibits Mixed-Ups from entering Charlestown proper. Not allowed in town except for their own little enclave. They used to be given permits if they were doing interpreting work but that's all dried up. No one talks to anyone these days. This shocks Justin. They're disabled children. Adults actually; mostly adults because so few have come into the orphanages in the decade since contact has sunk to zero. The Connipians left to fend for themselves as they have long asked for.

While he reads about them, cookies float into the corner of his screen. Twelve Tribes and Only God's Children must be paying for them judging by the content. Drumming bigotry into the stuck-at-home masses. Then he clicks on one which catches his eye.

The Devil is not Tall says the tagline.

He reads the link, ignores the demands for donations, money to help secure the world from Satan's grasp.

> *We imagine our adversary to be very strong*, it says, *while a weak adversary may weaken us. Tempt us to mimic and adopt their ways. God gave man dominion over the animals, so why would we relinquish it? Never should we regard any beast of the Earth as our equals. That is not the way of a God-fearing people. Never must we shun His gift. It is our duty to rid the world of shiftless and inconsequential devils before our own species mimics them. Too many are defending the feckless ways of the immoral Connipian girls and women. The sickly men. Watch it on Weavers. Watch, learn and praise the Lord! This scourge should be banished from the Earth. We do His work.*

Justin clicks away. Back to the Mixed-Ups. He can't stand that connipulsive babble. He wonders why in hell Danny is so indifferent. Maybe Justin didn't really care before the pandemic, we've all learned a lot in these crazy days. How to avoid a virus which is mostly just washing your hands, lots about how other ways of life are probably as good as our own. Better. That's what Justin's figured from watching the Connipians. Watching it on Weavers. Do people really swallow all the crude commentary along the bottom. Gantry does, and Tom's mum. Are there lots like that. How can they hate people they don't even know. He thinks he should show Danny the last thread. It's only a cookie on Nolly Knowledge but it seems like a link. Could have been put up by the people behind the robots. Could have been put up by the robots, of course, they can do anything, apparently. Danny might know if the nutters in the Twelve Tribes and this Devil-Is-Not-Tall lot are one and the same. Ask him later, he's working right now.

He finds some writing by a Mixed-Up, someone who the page says died at the age of ninety on New Year's Eve, nineteen ninety-nine. Lived fully twenty years longer than any other known Mixed-Up. Forty years longer than most.

> *I am not concerned for the future of my kind*, she wrote,

God Help the Connipians

for we do not want one.

Tonkin, her name; Justin thinks he should have heard of her before now. It says she was at the New York conference. There are pages and pages by her on Nolly Knowledge. Link after link.

We Mixed-Ups are here only because men will not leave the Connipian women alone. They can overpower them all too easily, the girls are seldom more than a quarter of the weight of a grown Sapiens male. I have lived most of my life in Sapiens society, I can see that many cannot leave the female of their own species alone either, and that is not a fair fight either.

What is to be done? For the Connipians, separation seems right, but that will not be a true solution so long as Sapiens are on the island. A map-drawn boundary is not an ocean. Men have done much more than climb fences for what they are after. If Sapiens males are to remain on Connipia, I strongly recommend castration. If the Protection Authorities truly wish to prevent the rape of their wards, there is no alternative.

Connipian males are the more courteous by a long mark. They will do that which is required for procreation when the Connipian women ask it of them. They do not actively seek it out. There is much speculation about how they have become so physically limited but it is functional. They are not unhappy in their role, and the sexes in Connipia are not at war. Their society functions with a stability that puts half of the animal kingdom to shame. Impractical Christians querying the absence of marriage or monogamy within Connipian culture miss the point entirely. It might as well be asked of starfish. Sapiens attached marriage to their normative mating practice, those who think it started the other way round fail to understand how peer pressure works.

Meanwhile, in societies across all the world but Connipia, I have observed that there is no equilibrium. A growing women's movement is condemning men's overtly oppressive behaviour more and more forcibly, while the frustrations of those same males seem to multiply. Learning nothing, adapting little. Perhaps that is why they take advantage of the doll-like Connipians. They are easier to subjugate than their own. Shameless bastards, are they not?

> *I have enjoyed aspects of my life among Sapiens, enjoyed being an observer. My circumstances, nay, disability, seem to limit my role to exactly that, plus interpreting work which has afforded me a more independent life than most of my kind have ever managed. I feel like I have been watching the last days of an absurd people. The Sapiens and the Mixed-Ups, both. For my kind have no place on this Earth, no purchase within any society and we never will have. Can't even eat nicely, not that I consider myself at fault for this. Put here by the wrongdoings of a species that cannot contain itself.*
>
> *Only on Connipia do I see any hope for the longevity of a human species. Connipian life is calm, sure of itself, has none of the explosive qualities which shake the rest of the planet at the behest of creatures who have made up a god only to imagine they are it. The tiny humans are the ones worthy of this unlikely home in the stars. My good and late friend, Klapakipsy, a profoundly intelligent Connipian, saw no hope for her own people. Slipped from this life as something of a prophet, although that is not a Connipian trope. They repeat, they have little time for harbingers of unnecessary change.*
>
> *If we leave this Earth to the bats and toads it might be for the better. I wish it were the Connipians, while holding no delusions of influence beyond my incontinent pen.*

She's amazing, this woman; strange name, Tonkin. Floppy arms and she writes without bitterness. And how did she raise that incontinent pen to the paper. Can a Mixed-Up type on a computer keyboard? Justin's head swims at the thought of her.

* * *

Danny and Justin are watching it again. Late night. Their dad won't have it on any more. Says it's worse than awful. The robots are murderers. Can't forgive them for the three who died. When Danny suggested the food fight was funny—robots toning it down after the mishap with the electrocutions—Roy swore at him. And that isn't how their dad is with either of them on a normal day of the week. This stuff with the Connipians and losing his stepdad are getting him down. And Danny being a prick is in the mix.

God Help the Connipians

'You know what I've figured?' says Danny. The screen is a blaze of sunlight, the girls high up in the skyfields. On branches and lattices of broad leaves. Red and purple fruit amassed on plants rooted into the leaf bedding. The cameras might be smaller than moths, they can follow the little girls anywhere, show them doing anything.

'What,' says Justin, no longer expecting to be on a wavelength with his cleverer, less compassionate brother.

'Dad's age, he's fifty, right? His Connip-loving mum out in the deep forest...' Danny gestures the screen. '...with Steve Frame. Not a gig that an unknown Canadian girl can pick up that easily. The trip was sixty-nine. Nineteen sixty-nine. Do the maths, Juicy. Our Granddad is a rockstar. Shame it's not Ronson Johnson or Renzo. Frame is better than some bull-necked logger, I suppose. He's the daddy, got to be. And if Dario Renzo had gone to the forest, I expect his songs in the aftermath would have been just as crappy as Steve Frame's turned out. Not many good tunes coming from the stone age, are there?'

Justin looks at him, open mouthed. Never made the connection himself, but he searched out Frame on Nolly the night after their dad said she was down there with him. Read the lyrics of every track on Blue is the Colour. Most were airy fairy but one or two sounded a bit radical. 'What Are We Doing Here?' was a shaming song about British rule. They should play that one alongside the pictures on Weavers. 'Frame isn't so bad. Do you really think it's true?'

'Dad doesn't look much like him but I do. You do a little bit, Juicy. Got his looks. You and I are Steve Frame's grandkids. And Granny was probably paid shut-up money. That's why Dad's never been told.'

'Do you think he's figured it out.'

'Not got a very enquiring mind, has he, our dad? Not even interested in where Mum's fucked off to. Or who she's fucking now she's got there.'

'Shut up,' snaps Justin. Danny can be a right sociopath. It might even be what Conatus pay him for; it's got something to do with robots. Paid to come up with ways to fuck everything up. That's all robots do. 'It's not Dad's fault Mum ran off. It's her fault. She was...' Justin is red in the face. He seldom thinks about the mother he hasn't seen in eight years. Even memories are unreliable. The facts he knows are not endearing. '...like a Connipian man, having sex with whoever she liked.' He's said it now, but it sounds all wrong. The Mixed-Up on Nolly Knowledge said Connipian males are just fulfilling their destiny. The Sapiens are the ones who made up marriage and then they still jump fences to shag Connipians, and tonnes more go and do what Sky has done.

6.

Roy is to catch the early train to London, will spend only a short time in the capital. The spartan funeral. He'll be sitting in his own pew, might shed a tear or two, catch a word in the churchyard with Edna and Julie and then turn around. Come back up north to Romiley properly orphaned. Not a surprise at his age but it's the pandemic that's done it. A horrible way to go: alone on a ventilator. He spoke to Edna on the phone; her children won't be in attendance and nor will Julie's. Rules are rules. Just their partners and he doesn't have one. Not any longer, and not much of one back in the days when he did. He reckons Justin and Danny would have travelled down with him were it not for coronavirus. Everything about this funeral is depressing. Doesn't sound like it's going to be a fitting send-off for Winston Grant. Thirty years with British Rail, something to do with timetabling at the end. Worked his way up nicely. Decent pension. It is what it is. What Winston gets will be less than he deserves. It was that way with his wife as well, with Ailsa, and Roy thinks they loved each other. Hopes they did, his memories are a bit hazy. Winston never talked about the Connipians.

* * *

As soon as he has left the house, Justin switches on the widescreen. Danny is still supposed to be at work but he's on the same sofa, tablet in hand. Says he's on 'creative time' which sounds no more productive than what Justin's doing. And Danny has money tipping into the bank for it, lucky bastard.

It looks like sleepy time in the forest. The camera watches from inside one house and then another. It rests where a naked Connipian sleeps alone. This looks unusual to Justin. It would be boring if she was wearing clothes but she hasn't a stitch. Usually, they sleep in blue. Day clothes and night clothes about the same. Maybe they don't change their clothing very often. Connipians never look sweaty, not like the larger variety of humans. Her clothes could be in the washing machine. Justin grins at his own daft thought. Creative time. It isn't a laughing matter, he knows that. The naked one looks terrific but staring at her with his brother sat next to him feels wrong.

'O-ooh, very nice,' says Danny when the camera runs a close up across the whole of her body.

> ***Turns a man's head, doesn't it?*** appears on the bottom of the screen.

'What are they trying to do? says Justin.

'Max out on all the clicks. Classic Weavers.'

'But this lot aren't just selling ad space. They're conkers deep in all the connipulsive shit there's ever been. I told you about The Devil Is Not Tall group, I've worked out that they're behind it...'

'Yeah, must be from the same stable as the Twelve Tribes, that lot.'

'Then why try to turn the girls into a porn show? That must hack off their Christian backers.'

'You're onto something, bro. It's a ploy one way or another. Looking good, I'd say.'

The girl on screen has rolled onto her front, revealed her pale back, several wisps of hair on her head more evident from this view than when she faced the camera. Fair but long. Many strands. Her bottom is nicely rounded, the backs of her legs surprisingly fat.

Justin turns away. 'Maybe Dad's right.'

'Too hot to handle, Juicy.'

As Danny says it the opening of the Blue House suddenly lets in more light. It must be moonlight, the shade of the girl's back, her legs, turns from the light grey of the infra-red camera to the palest yellow. Then a string of flying ants enters the room and they all land upon the girl, cover her like locusts. She rises up and her deep distress is more than apparent. She begins to click but then a plethora of little flies enter her mouth, stifle the clicking until it stops altogether. The brothers watch as her white skin turns red. Blood seeping from every pore as if the invading ants have bitten her. All over her little body. Justin had felt a bit turned on and now he feels sickened that he liked looking. The Connipian girl cannot make a sound. Looks as though she's choking, blood pouring from her chin. From everywhere. As quickly as she arose, she slides back to the floor. And as they watch, the very shape of her changes. Turns from a human form to a brown dung heap. A pile. Justin knows they're nothing like ants. This is an attack of Sparrow-hooks; banned, prohibited, outlawed. It only means they have been taken out of the shop window. Everything is available round the back.

One slut less to worry about says the ticker.

'God, that was really sick,' says Danny.

Justin thinks it's the first time he has seen his brother look shocked, and this after five weeks of the vile stuff. The whole programme disgusts Justin. Every second. He snatches the remote from his brother. Blanks the screen. 'Fucking Weavers!' he shouts. Danny doesn't argue. Must see it how Justin sees it after this. He even thinks their dad got there first.

* * *

Justin is alone in the lounge when he turns on the late evening news.

Watch It On Weavers

Hopes there will finally be a government response to all that's happening down there on the island that this country still claims as its own. Sort-of claims, also call it a protectorate but that's a lie. Hasn't lifted a finger to help its rightful inhabitants in the eye of the storm. Once more the newsreader just bangs on about coronavirus. It's the headline story, same old tosh. Justin drums his fingers throughout the lengthy first segment. He feels sorry for his grandad: arguing about PPE and clapping the nurses won't make the virus go away. He pays it closer attention when the announcer moves onto the second story.

> ***And now our reporter in Charlestown with the shocking story of how a slew of robots have been into the area known as East Town and killed every Mixed-Up living there. These are people of mixed Connipian and Sapiens heritage, a pairing which unfortunately gives rise to their congenital deformity. Their lifeless arms. The robots' reasons for doing it are unclear. On the streaming channel which has recently been showing the Connipians—pictures which the BBC does not air and believe may breach international law—they have sought to deny that Mixed-Ups are the result of non-consensual relationships...***

At this point the newsreader—a man of his dad's age—stumbles on his words, coughs and apologises before reading the rest.

> ***...of rape. Ninety-eight of the poor creatures have died in this manner, all within minutes of each other. Our reporter talked to two nuns who could only stand and watch. And we must warn viewers that some may find the images and content of this report upsetting.***

Justin finds he is one of them. Turns off the set when the pictures show stains on floors that look nothing like dead people. Dead Mixed-Ups. Obscene that robots have turned a peaceful island into the wild west. The reporters are no better, calling people creatures. People like the one whose writing he read on Nolly Knowledge. Who knew more about Connipians and Sapiens than most people do about either. Worked out—after a careful weighing up of all the evidence—which were her better half.

He paces the lounge. Keeps picking up the remote and throwing it back down again. Shouts for Danny but he must have his headphones on. No one can stop them. Robots that can read everything on the internet will always keep one step ahead. He feels like breaking the

God Help the Connipians

television. It's not a robot, but it does seem to have a life of its own. Shows him things he never wanted to see or know. He's still pacing when the front door opens. His father has returned from London.

'You look like I feel,' says Roy, and there is sympathy in his tone of voice.

'It's the news, Dad.' Then he remembers himself. 'How was it?'

'It's all right, son, we've laid him to rest. Your granddad's at peace. What's upset you in the news?'

'I read an article by a Mixed-Up, re-read it and re-read it. She was dead clever.' His father listens as Justin talks about Tonkin, all that he has learnt. Then he adds the shocking postscript. Today, in a single hour, they've been wiped from the Earth. Every last Mixed-Up.

Roy hangs his head. 'How bloody awful,' he says. 'Rotten to the core. Those poor...' He can see his dad choking up. 'It was thoughtful of you, looking up what that lady wrote. Not just watching that awful channel. I've heard the name, Tonkin, can't remember much about her. Heard it from my mum, I think. Very brave of a Mixed-Up to say that they didn't belong. Each one only here because of a wrong done to a Connipian. And they can't have their own offspring, you know. It's the thing about one species breeding with another. It must have been an odd sort of life. And I'm with you, Justin. The government must do something about these robots now.'

'Danny thinks they can't, and I think even he's starting to side with the Connipians. You and I knew it was sick from the start, didn't we, Dad?'

'If someone can start them, they must be able to stop them. Or catch them and destroy them. Robots can't be cleverer than us, we wouldn't be so stupid as to make them that way. Surely?

'I think we are, Dad. The cleverest scientists made the atom bomb and the dumbest dictators are getting hold of them. It's what we do. Change the stuff that needs leaving alone.'

7.

Could be that a lot of adopted lads do it. Lads and lasses. Only after Winston Grant has been a few days in the ground—happening thirty years after his mother, God rest their souls—does Roy decide he has gone long enough without knowing. Hopes he can find out the name of his birth father. Or if that is beyond his grasp, learn as much as he can about his origin. Who loved Ailsa Donaldson after Conrad Klassen and before Winston Grant. If love it was.

He has a conversation about the matter with Justin. After the one about The Bell Inn, the father finally wising up to the fact that his son is working precisely no shifts. Hasn't done for more than a week. Roy wasn't cross, didn't blow a gasket like he might have done in the old days. There was a time when he seemed to harbour a lot of anger. Deserted by his wife, by Sky. Never truly angry with his sons, but without a better place to direct it. When Justin said the Gantry woman was connipulsive, that her views on what was being shown on Weavers sickened him, Roy said, 'You've done the right thing.' The country seems as split on this issue as it is on every other. Those who care and those who don't. Even the virus seems to have people for it and others against. Chasms are opening up, society looking like a warzone of angry words. It's all over Wires and the letters page of the Romiley Gazette. Immigrants; the mop-haired Prime Minister who has gone into the very same hospital that Winston Grant died in; girls in Blue Houses half a world away. We love them or we hate them, a fence between us and not a soul sitting on it.

'I've found myself needing to know. The birth certificate tells me nothing. A hospital in Sydney, but my mother had only been three months in Australia. New Zealand before that. I don't even know if I was conceived there. She was on Connipia before that so it was one or the other. A place far away. My dad was probably a New Zealander. I don't associate Connipia with love affairs. It doesn't sound the place for it.'

Justin wants to jump in, put his dad straight. Steve Frame is Roy's father; after Danny said it, he went and checked the dates. Looked in the mirror too, thinks his brother's right about the likeness. Not obvious but finding pictures of Frame when he was young isn't easy. Nothing before One-Eyed Temple. The dates of his visit to Connipia are public knowledge. It's all there on Nolly Knowledge, and it's in Frame's autobiography too. Justin pulled that up via the library-link. His dad still relies on newspapers and tele, can't find the obvious because he's never tried looking. Unless the entire tale of Ailsa Donaldson accompanying Frame into the Connipian forest is a tall story. She's not mentioned in the lyrics. His autobiography says he went to Sheldeep with a medical survey, accompanied by the governor's daughter and a "friend." Well, Ailsa Grant, née Donaldson, certainly wasn't the governor's daughter: Justin knows there has never been a Canadian governor of any UK colony. Learnt it when he was looking up the history of Connipia. A couple of dozen governors we've imposed. Brits, Brits, Brits. None were female and absolutely none were Connipian. Not appointed with the governance of a hominid-diverse island in mind, in Justin's view. His granny must have been the "friend," and it makes a lot of sense. If he'd gone with his bass guitarist, he'd have written the name; a secret lover is the one to keep quiet about. He's had a clean-cut image for a lifetime, recluse now but no scandal around Steve Frame beyond the mediocrity of his later work. Justin chooses not to say what he knows, doesn't tell his dad what the brothers have figured out.

Roy says he's going to begin his quest with a DNA test. He knows one parent was a Canadian of Scots descent, whatever comes back alongside that will set him on the trail towards discovering his father's identity. 'I want to learn who Roy Grant really is.' Then he laughs like it's a daft thing to say, and Justin doesn't think it is. 'Roy Donaldson, even. That's how I started in the world. Changed it to Grant when Grandad Winston adopted me. And Justin, if you and Danny do one too—the DNA check—we can see if they're saying the same thing. The accuracy of my test will be more reliable if you get the same reading from your unknown grandparent as I do from whoever my father was.'

'I'll ask Danny to do it,' says Justin. For a reason he cannot explain—even to himself—he wants his dad to find out about Steve Frame the slow way. Be his own detective. Wants to warn Danny off blabbing too soon.

* * *

When Justin goes upstairs and talks to Danny, his brother finds the whole thing very funny. Happy to play along. 'We'll find out what skeletons are hiding in Mum's closet while we're at it.'

Justin disagrees, tells him Roy's only trying to discover who is father is.

Danny explains how it works. Roy's DNA will show up his ancestral lineage, theirs will show Roy's and Sky's.

Justin says he knew that already.

The three of them agree to undertake this shared delve into the past, a family project. Roy will order the testing kits. They must each spit into an envelope, send them to a laboratory in Milton Keynes.

'Hey, bro,' says Danny, when it's just the two of them in the room once more, 'you've not been watching, have you?'

'No. It's all getting too much.'

'For me and all. They killed another about forty minutes back. Doing that to the girls the way they do is terrible. They should ban bloody Sparrow-hooks. They're evil.' As he says it, Danny thinks about Berry. Smarter than he is, and—following Danny's own suggestion—busily trying to work out how they could make Sparrow-hooks pan for gold in Antarctica. Both of them admitted they don't know where to start; computer games tell them as much as they know about this sort of AI. There's nothing about setting up real ones on the Dark Web, not as far as they could discover. How anybody from The Devil Is Not Tall ever got theirs off the ground, he has no idea. Might have set it off years ago, before the ban. Got the ball rolling, programmed a few to act in accordance with their given aims. The die was cast. Self-learning AI could have seen the ban coming, set up a web darker than the one normal geeks know about. The robots can scour on-line faster than we can put shit up there. Buy component parts through disparate channels that mask what's really going on. Replicate, replicate, replicate. AI will wipe your arse for life if you programme it that way. Does what you ask, doesn't question why it should be doing it. Capable of misinterpretation if the original instructions contain ambiguity. And whatever path they start down, no one is going to stop them.

* * *

The following evening, Justin says he is 'going out for a walk', the exercise which is permitted. In fact, he and Tom meet up in the precinct. They had texted and agreed to it a day ago. From there they walk out to Cherry Tree where a party is to take place. Facebook invite: they presume that the coronavirus police are pretty useless.

'First sign of a blue light, and we leave out the back and over the fence,' says Tom.

They each have a few tins. Four each—modest—think it unwise to get shit-faced. It'll be the first time they've broken lockdown beyond a stroll along the canal or kicking a football in Tom's back garden. Need their wits about them if there are problems. The house they go to belongs to Connor Rothwell. They were at school with him two years ago. He has a house, wife and kid now but the latter two are away for a few days. She's staying with her mother in Gee Cross. Wife and the little boy, plus her mum and dad, are in some kind of bubble whatever that means. Something to do with being allowed to break the rules. Good luck to them, lockdown with a nutter like Connor must be a nightmare.

The party is pretty noisy and Justin doesn't think it can last. He's just glad to be doing something normal for a short time. An hour will be enough. The sound system belts out John Tungsten singing In the Mood for Magic, and a few other oldies. If the neighbours aren't fans, they're sure to call it in. All the while a widescreen—same size as the one back in Underhill, Connor probably in as much debt as Roy—shows more of what everyone is talking about. Currently four girls are cutting up fruit, pressing it into the strange bags they make from stitching leaves together. The screen calls it ***the primitive jam of the Connipians***. Justin has been seeing this kind of put-down written about them for weeks. Expects the jam tastes good. A robot wouldn't know either way. They understand dick; just obeying orders which is the most moronic way to pass through life if you give it a moment's thought. Artificial stupidity, that's the truth about robots.

God Help the Connipians

Suddenly there is panic among the girls. Clicking like turkeys, horribly unnatural sounds to Justin's ear. He sees a strange six-legged beast. It looks like a plated dinosaur, but it isn't. A fuck-load of Sparrow-hooks magnetised together. Playing predator. Going to chomp its way through these four. He can see it all coming. Before he has time to suggest turning the set off—this is not party fare, it's like televising Auschwitz—most of the lads in the room are cheering.

'Rip 'em to shreds, lovely-ugly,' says a loud voice. A chant starts in the living room. 'Tear them up! Tear them up!'

Justin feels himself shaking. He went to school with most of these morons. They seem to think they're watching a horror movie. Laughing about machines killing the innocent. He walks out the front door, feels light-headed as he goes. Wonders if he should have thumped someone, cracked a jaw, but Connor's more the kind of lad to do that than he is. Justin never sought out Tom. The idiot might be laughing with them for all he's said on the topic. His mum's connipulsive and families have been sticking together through covid. The evening air is fresh, cold. Quite good to be outside. To know he's not in a room with that pseudo-religious garbage pouring out of the screen. A psychopathic religion, or maybe they all are. Walking back home, but there's no hurry. His dad will be upset. If he's heard about what's happening, he will. No doing anything about it from here. About the injustice being done on the far side of the world. He walks toward Marple Bridge. The wrong direction but he wants to be on his own for a while. After five minutes he puts his phone to his ear.

'Police please. Can I report a party? Terribly loud, might be a hundred people at it. Gotherage Lane. No, no name, please. Who? Me? A passing dog walker. I just heard it. Young people these days. Terrible. Must be spreading the virus something rotten. You've got to put a stop to it, officer.'

8.

On Wires there's speculation that the government will finally send a military force. Or they might ask Australia to do it. Much nearer and this is really urgent. Danny says they should but won't. He also says the Sparrow-hooks will beat the army. UK, Australia, any they care to send. The robots will have watched Star Wars and worked out the spec. Or they could conceal themselves in tiny nano-size hiding places for months and months while the protecting army spawn another generation of Mixed-Ups. He agrees with Roy and Justin about everything now. Sparrow-hooks are worse than Sapiens, and it's a closer call than we tend to let ourselves think. He admits his Digger Dogs are useless compared to the stuff down there. He has only an inkling about all the technology involved. Made a robot which ties a shoelace. He's not acting so superior today. Took his time coming around. Says the Australians won't go to Connipia because they're scared of catching the flu. Their father thinks the world needs ridding of both: coronavirus and Sparrow-hooks. And not of Connipians but they look likely to go first. Mixed-Ups already a thing of the past.

Roy sits in front of a game show—no more Weavers on the widescreen—as the credits roll, he turns it to the BBC. Danny and Justin are eating on the kitchen side, but they pick up their plates, move down from dining area to lounge to join him. Watch the news conference. See if whoever is standing in for the PM has the bottle to do what people on Wires say needs doing.

There is a continuity announcement, pictures from the inside of Downing Street on the screen and then the picture changes. It's like a curtain coming down. The Briefing Room erased from public view. The screen goes completely black and then bold letters appear:

THE DEVIL IS NOT TALL

'Are they in on it?' says Justin. 'The government behind it all.'
'Hijacked,' says Danny. 'Might be the bots, might be scammers.'
'What do you mean?' says Roy.
'Perfect time to hack the BBC. Every-one wants to know what the government's going to do about the girls in the forest, and find out if the virus has seen off the Prime Minister.'

Then the screen shows a peaceful-looking forest. Camera facing low, nothing but the trunks of trees and the forest floor. The width of the trees suggests the pictures come from Connipia. It certainly isn't inside number ten Downing Street. A girl walks across a small clearing. She wears blue but her clothing is not of Connipian fabric. A skirt suit, a white T-shirt beneath the blue top. A jacket. And she has a head of rich brown hair.

Hi fella's,' she says to the camera. Winks an eye. '***Some of these trees were standing when Jesus walked the Earth. Not that I cared for the guy***.

Then with her left hand the girl takes a hold of her own hair, pulls it down to the left. Off with the wig which she discards into the forest with a nonchalant toss. She is Connipian. One or two wisps of hair but basically bald. She twirls around as if for the camera and then the wig is back on her head. Odd to see it there when she threw it away a moment before. And it's a perfect fit, no adjustment needed.

God Help the Connipians

'How come she can talk?' asks Justin.
'CGI,' says Danny. 'None of them dress like that.'
'They did at the conference. Nineteen fifty.'
'Then, not now. It's CGI, for sure.'

> *For a million years we've been climbing the trees and eating fruit. Nothing but fruit.*

Now she tears off her skirt. For a second her legs alone fill the screen. Nothing beneath the skirt so it is more than legs but the camera doesn't linger. Shows her again from her top half only, she is tearing off the jacket, then the T-shirt. The camera wobbles so their view of the naked girl blurs with the drag of the pixels.

> *No idea how to make clothes like these*, she says.

Then she stoops to the ground, the camera steadies and she can be seen scooping leaves off the forest floor. They were not there before, no leaves beneath her feet before this shot. Justin gets it. Everything on screen is CGI, the lot of it. The leaves start sticking to her like feathers.

> *This, I can wear.*

In front of their eyes, the green leaves turn blue.
'Told you,' says Danny. 'I can do that.'
'You can't hack into the BBC,' says his dad.
'I wouldn't. Not for whoever is behind this crap.'
The leaf skirt looks more woven than it did a moment back. It's very short, her white legs more on show in this attire than in the western-style clothing the CGI girl first wore.

> *We can turn everything blue—clever little freaks that we are—and we certainly turn heads, wouldn't you say? Need to do that given the nature of Connipian males. Not an ounce of fight in a single one. They can't protect a girl, quite pathetic when you think about it. They just lie in bed day and night. We like your men better. You guys are the strong ones.*

The girl gives the camera a little pout. The picture scans downward showing her cleavage.

> *Pity is, our union only ever produced those awful floppy-armed stick-people. Worse table manners than a duck.*

The CGI Connipian laughs, a high-pitched cackle. *We dumped them in East Town for you to do with what you will. Freaks of nature, they had to go.*

Now she stares into the camera, suddenly unblinking. Again, her left

Watch It On Weavers

hand draws the wig from her head. Her stare seems demonic, the sound of clicking starts to rise up in the background although the girl on screen does not move her lips. It gets more intense, like a village of Connipians, a swelling excitement communicated through the clicked noise. Louder and louder until Roy begins to lower the volume with the hand control. Then it stops abruptly; the face on camera strains, she shouts, '*Got to go!*' Although the three in the room hear it only quietly, the pitch of their sound-surround just above zero. They can tell she shouted it as loud as she could, the sinews of her neck were straining as she did it, eyes screwed up into narrow slits. Then the girl splinters into a million little pieces. It's a cinematic effect. CGI can do anything, it's just the pulling apart of a picture. Nevertheless, Justin has his head in his hands. Pained from watching that bizarre message. The screen is—without pause— back in Downing Street. An official with little more hair than a Connipian is giving his assessment of the days coronavirus figures. Good news, he seems to imply, the Nightingale Hospital, which they built so quickly, is to be stood down. Not needed as inpatient numbers fall. It'll remain on standby in case there's another wave of sickness.

Sounds to Justin like it could all be over quite soon.

The camera focusses on the Prime Minister's stand-in. Justin didn't catch the name. A thickset bloke, looks like a rugby player. Dresses smarter than the actual PM ever manages.

> *'And we are definitely back on air?'* he queries. *'Right, right. We're going to get to the bottom of all that. On behalf of Her Majesty's Government, I am announcing today that for the protection of the Connipians, the Government will be transferring forty-five million pounds from our foreign aid budget to properly fence the protected areas. We cannot allow this to go on. The shocking scenes which Weavers has been broadcasting: none of us like it. They are saying many things about Connipians which are unproven and very possibly untrue proven. Whatever we think of them, our policy is to protect. Keep them as safe as we can. It's how it's been since nineteen fifty. Always will be. We shall put a stop to all this as quickly as we can. Any questions.'*

Roy presses the red button. Off. 'They've no ruddy chance,' he says. Pushes his head into his hands in imitation of Justin. The pair hold their dejected poses until Danny does the same.

9.

Just twenty-four hours later an announcement across all networks tells the world that the Connipians are dead. Every last one of them. Murdered by machines that cannot be brought to justice, and the victims lived outside of Sapiens law. For the best part of a million years, they did. And the best part was undoubtedly the time before any Sapiens turned up. That's the simplest truth. Some people watched the slaughter on Weavers; nobody in the house on Underhill did. All three are pro-Connipian, one a late convert. All on the losing side.

There is much hand-wringing and finger pointing across the news feeds. Wires and the rest of them. No government on Earth defends the technology. Danny has no idea whether it means mission over, or if the Sparrow-hooks will regroup. More carnage elsewhere on Earth. He can't think of another target, and nor did he see this coming. Not him, not anybody. They all thought it was sweet when the hidden people appeared on Weavers. Now it's a house in mourning. Losing Winston left a hollow feeling. This is devastation. Maybe every household feels it. Or more likely just fifty percent: ayes to the right, not contents on the left.

The following day, on the Weavers channel which showed it all from start to finish, a message appears saying that those who protected humanity from its greatest threat will now return to ploughshares. It does nothing to lift the mood in the living room but answers Danny's worst fears. In the bottom right of the screen the phrase from yesterday appears again, this time in far smaller letters.

THE DEVIL IS NOT TALL

Danny thinks the devil very small indeed—nano sized—as he goes up the stairs. Once there he brings up Wires and types in Berry's address.

Pull the project, Bez. I can't do it.

He looks at his screen. A green light on his Friends list tells him Berry is online. Must have seen the message in the corner of his screen. The man never leaves his desk, never sees sunlight. Danny is little better. No reply comes and Danny taps onto Nolly Knowledge, looks up the history of the Connipians. It seems to begin in sixteen ninety-five which might actually have been the end. Kinder if it were. Danny clicks away. A linked cookie takes his eye. An archaeologist has posted how interesting it will be to finally explore the protected zones.

> '*A civilisation that preceded our own, however stuck it became,*' he writes.

Watch It On Weavers

No Sapiens has ever laid eyes on where their dead lie buried, the bones of those who came before. Nor learned how they made their blue dye. This man can't wait to find out what is none of his business. Danny starts to think knowledge overrated. He brings Berry's profile up onto his screen. The man is actively on line—Wires open—he hasn't replied, hasn't acknowledged the request.

> ***Sparrow-hooks are evil***, types Danny. ***We should have nothing to do with them.***

He knows Berry will pick him up on the word. Evil doesn't mean anything; it's only ever been anyone's opinion. God is as non-existent as a robot's heart.

There is no reply to this either. Danny brings up his pages of theory about the Digger Dogs. Considers the limitations of the programme. They will collect and analyse geological data; sift the rocks they splinter. Draw out copper or coal but they haven't figured how they can recognise it before they start digging, much easier to analyse splintered fragments. They could go for gold if they got close to some worth hunting down. He is pretty clear about them; never planned them to be self-advancing beyond the narrowest of criteria. Not replicating themselves like the Sparrow-hooks have done. Agile and able to discern every element and compound, that was all. He and Berry had calculated a complex range of movements and a potential powerful force in the dogs' teeth and front paws. Not with fighting in mind, simply to prise ore from the rockface. Early miners used dynamite, and he and Berry wanted to be neater, less destructive. He wonders if even this technology could be abused. Shouldn't be so long as there's an off-switch. One kept in the hands of a sensible man. Are there any? It might be the problem: creating robots in our own image. A blind spot the size of a lifetime's blackout. How else have we been sleepwalking through history.

His mind is a puff of red mist as he scrolls through pages of theory, his calculations. They register nothing. What is it about all that's gone on in Connipia that's turned his world around? He has never worried about them, never gave the little women or their sickly menfolk a moment's thought before this intrusion. The bots were just being opportunistic of the virus, in his estimation, but even that's unclear. Nothing is certain. The operation might have long been planned to start this March. Coincidences do happen.

When the robots began showing the pictures, even when they electrocuted three girls, slung fruit at them, Danny was more interested in the technology than the welfare of the tiny Connipians. The local paper ran a story about a man on their estate who got community service for beating his dog with a stick, but Danny didn't give a shit. Human rights seem like a good thing but the beasts of the forests need to stake out their own territory. If lambs want protecting then they shouldn't have let themselves taste so damned good. He thinks it was one of the old comedians who said that; someone they never show nowadays. Danny remembers Roy quoting him when he and Juicy were still in school. They're all meat-eaters on Underhill. Only learnt a fortnight back that his granny was a veggie.

The machines have gotten out of control. As he thinks it, Danny knows it is a misrepresentation. They started out of control. How many times has he heard how warfare has prompted innovation. We save our best to achieve the worst.

> *What's eating you?* Berry replies, after fifteen minutes.
>
> *Some pangolin eaters let this virus out*, writes Danny, *you won't catch me doing the same with Sparrow-hooks. I hope the nutters at* **The Devil is Not Tall** *have really decommissioned their shit. We lost something today. You, me and the world lost something, we just don't know it.*
>
> *They did what they were programmed to. Doesn't matter whether you agree with it or not, ours would only pan for gold. Pan, and bring it to us to use for good or ill. Good in your case, I'm guessing. While I'm ok with cocaine and hookers.*

Danny types in a smiling emoji. Deletes it before sending. Berry's jokes are not that funny. It's a struggle to explain.

> *They might multiply until their panning melts all the ice down there. Sinks Miami and Bangkok. Maybe London if they work overtime.*
>
> *Give them a quota.*
>
> *Sparrow-hooks see through that kind of illogic. Less isn't more. It's only an art thing. More is more in the real world. You and me are both greedy bastards, it's why we thought of the project in the first place. And it's the bias we won't be able to help ourselves from programming into our bots. Our offspring.*
>
> *Someone's been reading up.*
>
> *I'm serious Berry. Pull the plug. We'll get these Dogs extracting copper from previously abandoned mines. It'll make more than enough money for me.*

Not agreeing with you, but it might be a good time to lie low.

No more dev. None at all, Berry. Don't make me report you over this. All governments will be re-ratifying the charter. Limiting AI.

Ha! I've gamed a bit, not managed to work out how the religious nuts got hold of the know-how. Nothing to report, Danny-boy. I'm clean.

We did quite a few background calculations.

Still recording it under Digger Dogs on the time allowance, weren't we?

Now Danny sends the smiley face. Quite funny that Conatus has paid them so well for planning a scheme they could never speak of up the chain of command. And that they made no progress beyond imagining how much gold might be down there in Antarctica. That was a formula based on the quantities of all the past goldrushes averaged out. The relative sizes of Yukon, Otago and the rest of them, as a percentage of the five million square miles of Antarctica. Multiplied out with optimism. GCSE maths at most. These two clever boys know their times tables.

10.

Danny has hooked his laptop up to the widescreen, enabled them to use it for See Your Face, or face-ache, as he calls this application. Auntie Edna and Auntie Julie are looking at them, or appear to be. Heads about four times their normal sizes were they truly in the room. They are in London, in their respective houses, each with a laptop perched on their own coffee tables.

'Thanks for this, it's so important,' says Roy. He seems a little breathless. Both sons are leaning back on the sofa, all three in a line although the father seems the most excited.

'And you said you got a message from Sky?' says Edna.

'Yes, but that's not why I'm calling. Not why I wanted this call.'

'Smile a while,' says Justin, grinning, quoting the tagline for See Your Face. Everyone who has sat through as much as one advertisement break since the start of lockdown has heard it.

'I think what I've to say is going to make you smile,' says Roy.

'And Sky? You're not getting back together, are you?' asks Edna.

'Shush,' says Julie. An ear-to-ear grin visible before she turns her head

God Help the Connipians

away from the camera. Neither Julie nor Edna liked her. Both of Sky's sons know that.

'No. It's a resounding no about that, Jules. Let me say...have you all got a cup of tea?'

The boys have coffee.

'We won't be needing something stronger?'

'No Edna. It's all good. But I've got big news, I'd like to think.'

'Well, we're all strapped in.' Edna must lean back on her lounge chair; they see her shoulders go back, and her head shrink a little smaller on the screen.

'I don't know why, might have done it long ago, but never got around to it. After Dad died...' Roy looks first at Julie then to Edna, unsure if they see the sad face he makes over the airwaves; hands together like a prayer. '...I got to thinking about the other dad. The one that's only mine, even if he never raised a finger. Not really looking to meet him, girls. He's not a part of my life. I just wondered who I was, how I began. Have you heard of this DNA testing?'

Aunt Julie laughs. 'Oh, we've got toothpaste and everything down here in London, Roy. I think Edna and I know what DNA testing is.'

'Sorry, I'm sure you understand it better than me. But you won't have known I was for doing it. Getting myself tested. You see, tracing back to find where your family history comes from can be revealing. The boys did it too, and that's where Sky comes into the picture.'

'You done it and all, boys?' says Edna. 'I hope our Roy is still your father.' She bursts into laughter and then instantly puts her face into her hands. Aunt Julie is shaking her head.

'Ooh, cheeky,' says Danny.

'Nothing like that,' says Roy. And after a pause he adds, corners of his mouth upturning, 'Bigger news.'

'Can I say?' asks Justin. 'Just about Mum.'

'Yes. You tell them that bit,' says Roy.

'Auntie Edna, Auntie Julie,' says Justin, 'Dad phoned up Mum last night to tell her that she's black. Me and Danny too, we're really cool with it. Mum was a bit shocked. Surprised at least.'

They can see Julie laughing. Justin really hasn't explained it: a white boy telling everyone he's black sounds a bit stupid.

Edna looks cross. 'I'm black, Justin. Not a big deal. It's what I've been my whole life. Normal is what I call it.'

'Yeah, but Mum was always such a snob...'

'And the DNA test says she's black,' Edna continues, 'but her skin looked pretty white to me when I last seen her. Who was it in your family? Do you know.'

'Dad thinks it's the American. There's a slave in there. In our genetic...'

'Slaves in a lot of family history, Justin. Probably more on this side of the Grants than on yours.'

'We know that's true, Edna,' says Roy. 'But Sky's mother—you might remember her from the wedding—she thought she came from a landed Georgian family. We think it was her grandfather who had an African mother...'

'Mum always said she was from money in Georgia. None left by the time her own mother came to England. Or "the old country" as Nanna Currie used to call it. And Mum never went to Georgia until after she left us...' Justin stops mid-sentence. He and Danny had thought it funny: they have the African gene that Roy doesn't. Talking about their mother upping sticks is heavier in the chest.

'Danny's going to follow it up on the ancestry websites,' says Roy. A hand on Justin's shoulder.

'Welcome to the club, boys,' says Edna, 'but it's not a funny thing in my mind. Not funny at all. Slave girls didn't just pop out their master's babies for fun, you must know that. Coercion. Rape. That's the general way of it. You got a bit of black and a bit of white rapist in you. I expect you'll be saying less to your friends about the last part.'

Justin looks back up at his auntie. Nods seriously at her assertion.

'He knows it, Edna,' says Roy. 'I've told him about that already.'

The five look at each other in silence for a few seconds before Edna cracks a smile. 'Pretty funny about Sky's DNA but that woman is seriously not welcome in the club. Not like you boys.'

Roy looks relieved that Edna has relaxed; Justin told it clumsily, there's no doubt about that. 'Let's move on to the big point,' he says, 'but before I say it, I've got to tell you how it all came about. These three DNA tests, we sent them to a company called Your Heritage. Danny found it; best review by price, he said. We had a kind of tiny dish with an airtight lid, only plastic, not flimsy or anything. All three of us had to take a cheek swab. Inside of the mouth, you know...' Roy gabbles on and on about the process, tries to explain how they can find DNA on anything, although his own understanding is imprecise. '...you see, the blurb said we would get a reply in four to six weeks, but really, Edna, Julie, exactly nine days after I sent them in—sent in all three—there was a phone call here in the house. A bloke called Dr Moro—I made him spell out his name because it sounded like tomorrow, but he told me it's Italian—rang us on the house phone. A really funny conversation. He wanted to understand our DNA samples, began by asking if he could come around and take further samples himself. Wanted to do it in person, and him a doctor. Do it in the backyard so we could keep the two metres except he wanted to step in and do the swabbing for himself. Our DNA was unusual; that's why he was so keen. This was nothing to do with Sky's side, you understand. That part was unexpected but not like this. My father side was the true oddity. It's all to do with my father. Quite astonishing really.'

Roy has been leaning into the laptop, his face must have filled the screens in the two London homes, quite large in the corner of their own widescreen. Now he leans back, hands behind his head. 'It was quite a shock, having a doctor so interested in where I came from. Dr Moro said on the phone, "We weren't sure it was possible, in fact, we were pretty sure it wasn't," you see...'

'You're going round the houses, Roy. Get to the point.'

'...the doctor even said, "just need to check your arms are working all right." Should have cottoned on when he said that, but I really didn't.' Roy has leant back on the sofa. The corner of the screen—or the entirety of the screens in London—has caught them smiling together, the father and his sons. 'You know that Mum, our Ailsa Donaldson as she was before getting together with Dad, God rest his soul, she spent a long while in Connipia. It seems I was conceived there. Connipian blood. Grandfather's...'

'A Connipian, Roy! That sounds a bit rum to me. Mum wouldn't be going into the Blue Houses, doing all that with one of those poorly men, little Connipian men. Surely not.'

'You didn't listen. My grandfather was Connipian, not my father.'

'What?' says Julie. 'How does it work, Roy. Grandfather Connipian, so you father was Connipian. Got to be.'

'Mixed-Up. He was a Mixed-Up, Julie. A big splash of Danish blood in me too. A Danish man who...well, you've already talked about it, Edna. How that came about.'

'It's not possible,' she replies. 'Mixed-Ups, I understood that they can't...don't...well it's not very nice but they called them human mules.'

'Dr Moro talked about that. Infertile was the word he used.' Roy has a bit of a smirk on his face. 'He said they've learnt something new from my case. That it might have only been the females with that problem. There were more of them than there were males, of course. Not as disproportionate as with the Connipians, but almost twice as many females. We learned all sorts from Dr Moro...'

'Oh, Roy,' interrupts Edna, 'boys, all the Connipians have been done in by those terrible robots. We've got to keep quiet about you. Some people in this world are after all the Connipian blood. We love you like we always love you, but you can't be blagging this everywhere. Not after all that's gone on.'

Julie is just watching. Looking at the faces on the screen before her.

Seeming to make eye contact one by one. 'Roy, I'm astonished just like you said it. Infertile is right, couldn't find the word in my surprise. It's hard to imagine Mum making love with one of them. Don't want to imagine it and I've got nothing against them. I really don't. Never did have. But they've no arms...are you really sure you have a Mixed-Up father, Roy.'

'Had, Julie. I'm as certain as I could be that he's not alive now. If he still was four weeks ago, I'll never know either way. Dr Moro was crystal clear about the connection. Not so much when he visited, took his swabs. I think he imagined our first samples were some sort of fake. Didn't think it after he analysed the ones he took personally. He gave us the result yesterday morning. Took time on the phone and promised to send us a written summary by post. Conclusive proof that at least one Mixed-Up conceived a child. I'm the proof. One quarter Connipian; the boys are half of that. And Dr Moro conceded that very little is known about Mixed-Up males. It was mostly the females who they knew to be infertile. Up until World War One they'd get forced into sex by men staying on the island for short-term work. Miners and loggers. No pregnancies ever recorded. Dr Moro had researched that. It was the source of the belief that they're infertile. The males have mostly only been intimate—had sex—with female Mixed-Ups. No documented cases of Sapiens women taking Mixed-Up lovers. Mum was a trail blazer. She really was.'

'We're the last of the Mohicans,' says Danny.

'A woman at church is a fan to this day,' says Julie, 'you know, fan of The Devil Is Not Tall. Their terrible cult of lies. You should keep quiet about...'

'I'm proud to be this staunchly on the other side,' says Roy. 'A Connipian, and I only wish there were more of us.'

* * *

Justin sends a text to Tom.

Really big news

Spill the beans

Teaching you a bit of patience

After typing it, Justin gets flooded with worry. His mother's another nutter in the Church of Rhubarb or whatever they call themselves. Tom laughed about everything Weavers showed, still laughing when it turned vile. They might be the kind of people who feel no hesitation in killing seven-eighths of a Sapiens for a little bit of Connipian. Murdered all the Mixed-Ups and they're fifty-fifty.

What's your news, pal?

God Help the Connipians

I'm mixed race, like you, Tom. Doesn't show up so much on me, but I am

11.

A day and a half later, the house is quiet: the dead of the night. Roy has been on a high since Dr Moro phoned him. Half a bottle of Glenfiddich in two days and he usually only has it Christmas week. He's come right down now. Seeing things in a very different light. Found the bottom.

Both boys are sleeping. Roy is looking through the understairs cupboard. Rooting around in it, bloody mess that it is. Finally, he finds what he always knew was in there. A box of rat poison. Looks for a date on the packet but there isn't one. Not as he can see. It's probably long past the use-by, the very stalest rat poison imaginable. What's the worst that can happen? If it kills him, he's already factored in the likelihood. In fact, it's the sum total of the plan. Do it before any other bastard can. Death by Sparrow-hook sounds a hundred times worse. Damn things might have hacked Dr Moro's DNA records. Unless they've been programmed to assume it can't happen. That's possible; however, optimism isn't flowing along Roy's veins tonight.

He takes the packet to the nearby dining table. Sits and reads the small print, reminding himself of how he should best use it. Nothing on the box says put it in your sons' coffee, and nor does he think of them as rats. Not Danny, not Justin. His eldest has come around, been very sensible since the horrors of the robot invasion became apparent. Never knew they were all Connipians. Not at the time. Roy, Danny, Justin: the last Connipians on Earth. That's the size of it. They're too good for this world, his sons, they're way too good. Justin was with the Connipians from the get-go. And that boy never had the pep talk with which Ailsa Donaldson put Roy on the right path. Instinctive, that was his younger son. And the other one came around. If Roy is too good for this world, he didn't recognise it until now. Will go out with them. Leave the connipulsive world to stew in its own juices. Connipians and Sapiens don't mix and he's got no chance of wiping out the other lot. Him and the boys don't belong in Romiley and their true habitat's been destroyed root and branch. Wouldn't have done so well down there either, not Roy. Can't be climbing trees with a bad back. Danny seems to know a bit too much about mining, taking the guts from the ground beneath our feet. He might be feeling pretty conflicted now he knows his true ancestry. Does it explain us or confuse us. Danny is always saying science never lies. Now they know their lineage goes back further than anyone else's. Anyone left alive. Progress, who needs it? Over in the blink of an eye.

Watch It On Weavers

That's what it looks like. Gobble up the iron or the bronze or the coal. Roy thinks that's what all this global warming is about: the error of our ways. Not his way, not now that he's a Connipian. There's a book on his bookshelf called The Age of Steam. And it wasn't an age at all, the briefest moment. We let off a bit of steam and that was that. His Connipian ancestors had the better ideas. Didn't think to enter the mad scramble to subjugate the world; understood instinctively that trying to make it what it isn't can't go well. Or maybe it wasn't instinct. They were clever, just not in ways that the greedy world has ever given them credit for. And Roy and the boys would make poor ambassadors for the lost Connipians. Can't click and never learnt how to make the fancy blue dye.

It's four o'clock in the morning. The best or the worst time to make this type of decision; Roy knows it must be one or the other. It is what it is. Deciding to do away with yourself, with your sons, four in the morning must be the time for it. A few days back, after the phone call from Your Heritage, from Dr Moro, before the bewildered doctor had been round and done the necessary—proved to himself that the first test was no mistake—Roy had shared it with them jubilantly. Danny said something funny. Justin was a bit obsessed about height, why the family weren't all a hell of a lot smaller, but even Mixed-Ups top four-six, fifty percent higher than their mothers. Boy or girl. The truly funny reaction was from Danny.

'A hell of a lot better than having Steve Frame for a granddad. I really thought your mum had bedded that old rocker.'

Roy had never thought of that. Perhaps he should have. She mentioned him a few times, that she'd gone into the forest with a popstar. He never put two and two together because he hadn't done the simple calculation that Danny did. Spotted how Frame's trip into the forest coincided with the time when he was conceived. Danny is smart, saw straight off what Roy has been missing lifelong. It simply happened to be irrelevant. Not the daddy. He wonders exactly what his mother did on Connipia, thought she'd told him everything and now knows she missed out the most important detail. His recall of Ailsa Grant, née Donaldson—lover of a Mixed-Up—is feeling a little less reliable. She said she'd got along with Steve Frame, that he wasn't as big-headed as she thought someone so famous would be. Nothing in the way she said it made it sound like he and she were terribly close. That might be why he'd never formed the idea that Frame could be his dad. And he isn't. Too improbable, although from his new vantage point—cognisant with a still more unlikely truth—he can't blame Danny for thinking it. Rockstars are mostly randy bastards. Men in general if he thinks about his Mixed-Up father, or more particularly the nameless Danish rapist

387

God Help the Connipians

who is his grandfather. The poor Connipians got three hundred years of that being done to them. It's only stopped because the bastards at The Devil Is Not Tall have gone and done worse. Enlisted fricking Sparrowhooks to do their dirty work. Ailsa Donaldson's purpose in going to Connipia is a bit of a mystery to Roy. She might have been a pro-Connipian crusader but that wasn't how she talked about it. More like a conversion. Most visitors are short term. Frame was there for five weeks. Take a look and turn around. Leave a Mixed-Up growing inside a Connipian in far too many cases. His mother wasn't like that, or rather, she brought the Mixed-Up away with her. Him—Roy—gestating inside her when she left. Maybe it was a proper relationship. Love between her and his father. Could be why she was so obsessed with Connipians. She saw everything from the Connipian viewpoint although, unlike the three in this house on Underhill, she wasn't one. None of that blue-eyed blood running in her veins; it's proximity may have quickened her pulse. It really must have, thinking over what she did while she was out there. That she alone knew her own son was pretty much one. It's been pretty lucky that his arms have worked like normal. Could have given the game away.

When Roy was a teenager, his two half-sisters still in primary school, he enjoyed watching football. Going to live matches with roaring crowds, loved the drama of it. His team were nominally the Hammers. They lived in New Cross but his dad—good old Winston Grant—wouldn't countenance a son supporting Millwall, the local team. Their supporters' reputation was fearsome. He remembers saving up money to get into The Den, he'd go to watch Millwall without his dad knowing it. The bus out to West Ham took too long, couldn't make an evening kick off and be back by bedtime. In those long-ago days, ignorant of a better way, he enjoyed the intensity of the rivalry those supporters ratcheted up with any other club in the land. Dirty chanting, hand gestures. Teenage Roy thought it very funny. Ten minutes to go, he would take himself out. He didn't hang around for the inevitable punching and bottle throwing that followed the final whistle. The brawling in the street: Millwall fans weren't all mouth. Fists and boots as well.

It's a dilemma. Fight or flight. He has worried since their video linkup that calling Edna and Julie was a mistake. Telling them what he has learnt about his own father; information he never sought while his stepdad lived. His sisters' reactions were nice enough; however, it's still the part of his life he cannot share with them. The thing he is and they aren't. His sisters are mixed race but look about as black as Winston did. He thinks they weren't so impressed that the boys are a little bit mixed race too, a bit black. They're more Connipian than they are West African.

Watch It On Weavers

About four times more if he's got his sums right. And what really troubles Roy is that Edna's church is a whacky one, Julie's too. They might even go to the same one, Roy isn't clear about it. He was never interested in God, nor was Winston. Not sure where his sisters caught the bug. And neither of them has a second for the Twelve Tribes, that couldn't be clearer. It simply sounds like their church has a few who are all in favour. If either sister blabs, the church's very own Millwall supporters would get after them. That's what has been playing out on Weavers these short weeks. Elimination. It must have been programmed into the Sparrow-hooks long before the broadcasting began. Ten years before, most probably. That's how Danny has explained it. The robots wouldn't show their hand until they'd worked out how it could be done without the possibility of failure. The pandemic was the window.

Roy looks at the box. The rat poison. This is the way to do the job for them, opt off a world that is not good enough for the likes of his sons. Let them have their progress, Sparrow-hooks and the people who made them can roll themselves in it all the way to hell. He loves his sons. And he will be killing them for love. Letting Sky know she is black in advance of ending it all was worth the phone call. Funny. Sky's probably connipulsive although she wasn't much interested in the test. Roy didn't tell her what it proved. A bit of Danish is as much as he let on. He was never going to brag about the Connipian stuff to Sky. Not got along with her since Justin was small, and she hasn't been back in the house since he started secondary school.

He hates the idea of some weird technology coming to finish off the Romiley Grants. He thought of asking Danny to hack into the damned things and programme them—the horrible Sparrow-hook robots that combine together in order to become monstrous—so as to stop them. He wondered if his son could suggest, in a computer programmers totally unstoppable way, that the flying robots attack Sapiens. Don't rest until the Earth is rid of the bastards. Less of a need because it's the road they're on anyway. The wars won't end so long as there's two Sapiens left to slug it out. Or just two robots. All made by fucking stupid Homo Sapiens, thinks Roy. He doesn't think of himself as one any longer. Three quarters isn't much. It's certainly not the best of him. Of course, they could lie low here on Underhill. It couldn't be more anonymous, a terraced house with an empty rabbit hutch out back. It's not like they have any fruit fields on the rooftop. Nothing to make the neighbours suspect. If Danny and Justin ever marry—not even marry, just start shagging, which men are apt to do—there could be more Connipians to follow. Not too obvious. Not small and perfect like the ones the world has lost. But their offspring will still be Connipian, will have got one over

God Help the Connipians

on the robots, on The Devil Is Not Tall. A torch held aloft.

Roy pushes the box of rat poison into the pedal bin in front of the kitchen units. He never had need of it. Doing nothing under the stairs for years; never been a rat in the house unless he counts Sky. High time he threw the damn stuff away and now he has. Must have been the whisky thinking when he first pulled it out of the cupboard.

He takes himself upstairs and looks into the open door of Justin's room. His son, deep under the duvet, just a bit of brown hair showing. He's not bald, not a suggestion of it, a lot more than a wisp of hair on him. Justin Grant, the son Roy won't be poisoning tonight, tomorrow. Ever. He steps as lightly as he can into the room, stoops to breathe on the mop of hair. Would like to kiss his forehead, doesn't want to wake him. Be found out sentimental. He lets him sleep, him and his brother in the next room. Roy closes his eyes for a moment, wants to be sure he is still there when he opens them. Justin. Justin and Danny. Justin, Danny, Roy: Connipians all.

Printed in Great Britain
by Amazon